Acknowledgements

A special thanks to my two sisters who contributed their unflagging support, and to a granddaughter who provided technical assistance.

Clare

A Hundred Miles to the City

by
Clare Samson

authorHOUSE®

AuthorHouse™
1663 Liberty Drive, Suite 200
Bloomington, IN 47403
www.authorhouse.com
Phone: 1-800-839-8640

This book is a work of fiction. People, places, events, and situations are the product of the author's imagination. Any resemblance to actual persons, living or dead, or historical events, is purely coincidental.

© 2007 Clare Samson. All rights reserved.

No part of this book may be reproduced, stored in a retrieval system, or transmitted by any means without the written permission of the author.

First published by AuthorHouse   10/18/2007

ISBN: 978-1-4343-1731-5 (sc)
ISBN: 978-1-4343-1732-2 (hc)

Library of Congress Control Number: 2007904480

Printed in the United States of America
Bloomington, Indiana

This book is printed on acid-free paper.

ONE

An uncommon quiet enveloped the farm. Even though hundreds of people, young and old, were gathered in the early morning hours for the estate auction, an eerie stillness shrouded the entire farm and the town to which it was attached by a narrow gravel road. Three figures in coveralls moved toward brick posts that marked the beginning of the farm's lane, shuffling through snow muddied in spots by the traffic of booted feet. The light flakes floated rather than fell, as if suspended in the milky air. The town couldn't be seen from the lane's gate, although the road was flat and the distance to the first house was a mere quarter mile. Parking for the day was to be accomplished along this short road and in the town. The streets had already begun to fill with pick-ups and trucks, most with Missouri plates, but some with Iowa or Kansas, as well.

The three figures moved with purpose, seeming to have more energy than the day warranted. In a way, the sale was a rating instrument by which the lives of the deceased might be measured, at least in the eyes of some. Farm sales always brought such people out, filling a need to assess their own accumulation of machines, tools--all the things needed to accomplish the task of growing things. But most of these folks, potential bidders and buyers, appeared to show concern and sympathy in their expressions.

Nods of recognition were passed as men and women in layers of winter garb walked through the gate toward the waiting crowd. Scores of prospective purchasers milled around lowboy hay carriers covered with rows of assorted tools, farm equipment and supplies. It would be some time yet before the auctioneer, a friend of many years of the deceased farmer, would switch on his microphone and greet the assemblage with announcements and friendly banter.

The snowfall was easing but a grayish mist hung in the air, wrapping the expectant group in a certain familiarity. This farm sale was one necessitated by the deaths of the owners, but over the last decade sales brought on by a struggling economy were held every weekend, winter and summer. Many in the present gathering shared the knowledge of recent hard times.

That so much property--so many tools, fence parts, machines, crates, cans, barrels, boxes of supplies--could be sorted and displayed in an organized manner was more than anyone had believed possible two months ago. Then it was December. PaPa had passed away on the first day of the month. His sudden, unexpected death in the night was a horrible shock. His family had little time to absorb their loss, with the demands of a fully operating cattle and hog business to attend to. If PaPa had been aware of his condition, he'd managed to keep it from those around him. Mercifully, friends and neighbors in the small community came to offer the family their services, equipment and expertise. Some came with possum-belly stock trucks to take animals to market. Some came to move tillage equipment back to the home place for the auction. The ensuing months had been cold and wet, but those who came to volunteer their assistance returned again and again to do whatever they could.

The three, who had walked into town to assist late arrivals in parking, returned to climb the short hill to the house, empty now of furnishings except for a few chairs and a table. Their steps were triumphant as they entered the warm space and sank down upon the folding chairs.

"What would the folks think if they were here to see this?" Coralea wondered aloud, though her own feelings were a hodgepodge of emotions she could hardly decipher.

Sherry drew off her gloves and sighed heavily. "I'm just glad this didn't happen when they would've had to go through it."

Barb poured coffee into three cups. "If I were prone to declaring miracles, I would say that was one!" she declared. "They nearly had to do battle to keep this place, but here we are."

"It must have been the combination of determination on her part and hope on his," Sherry speculated. She knew she and her sisters were of one mind when it came to assessing the attributes of their deceased parents.

"Mom was never one to give up, on anything," Coralea contributed, "and PaPa had a hard time even recognizing adversity." They all joined in a chuckle, indicating their approval of the man who'd been more than a father to them.

When the time arrived for the start of the sale the three came from the house, still clad in PaPa's coveralls plus layers of jeans and sweats, prepared to take up their places among those looking through the offerings. Each had specific things to "buy back"--things they wanted to keep but for which they would pay the going price. There would be two lines going, two men yelling out their sales cry at the same time: one on the hill behind the house where the household goods were assembled, the other down in the "park," toward the town.

Sherry, youngest of the trio, stood in the group at the foot of the hill. She looked down the row of old autos and trucks lined up along the lane, and on to where her '41 Chevy had been pulled across that roadway, from his side, in the grove, to her side, on the west. Granny had kept her side mowed with her little Ford tractor. PaPa was not to bring his machinery to her side--she feared if he parked it there it would remain forever, as it did on his side, eventually becoming a part of the grove itself. Sherry's nephew had cut saplings from around the old car so it could be moved from where it had sat--for over thirty years, it must have been. She remembered that PaPa bought the Chevy for her from her grandfather's estate so she could drive herself to basketball practice in the next town over. She hoped someone would buy it and restore it but didn't believe there was much chance of that happening.

Dave, Sherry's husband, had made countless trips up from Carroll, spending days at a time organizing the tools and machinery PaPa had spent his years procuring. Himself a collector of tools, Dave marveled at the older man's ability to amass antiquated equipment. An enormous array of hand tools was embedded in the dirt floor of the machine shed, covered by many years' accumulation of livestock and soil siftings. Many had been left in boxes, stuck away in corners where PaPa had never gotten around to sorting them. After weeks of cleaning and categorizing, Dave discovered sometimes as many as twenty or more of the very same tool. He lined them up in an orderly fashion, hoping other collectors would attend the sale.

The tallest of the three, Barbara, had a list of things to bid on for her children. Though each had been given items from the home of their grandparents, Barbara had learned of other, lesser objects they wished they could keep. In her way of being thoroughly fair, she wanted to secure these only if no one else in the family bid on them. As she dashed from place to place trying to keep up with the advance of each line, she mused on the spectacle of herself in the jumble of activity. She'd hardly been to an auction in her life. If PaPa were alive, this is where *he* would be, no matter whose sale it was--more interesting if he knew the owners, but not at all necessary. His habit had been to go to a sale every Saturday. She realized now he had probably gone for the camaraderie, though he inevitably returned to the farm with many bargains he'd won. Her mother had always said that whatever PaPa bought had a home for life. It would never leave the farm again.

Standing sentry for the place, the bare trees in back of the house nearly circled the furniture and personal effects set out on the lawn and driveway.

Among the feet of many strangers, Snowball, the farm cat, ran in and out, as if looking for something. The snow had ceased, but the air was still heavy with moisture.

Inside the house, a pot of stew simmered on the stove. Junior, the local storeowner, had sent it out for the family today, along with baked goods from his Hostess rack. Everyone knew it was a poor time for an auction, but the farm and house had been sold the previous day, February 12, and the young man who bought the place would soon want to move in and begin preparations for spring planting.

Too bad there hadn't been a son to keep the place going, or even a grandson inclined to farming, Coralea thought now as she looked around the empty living room. Having three girls was not every farmer's wish but she believed it had never bothered PaPa; most years he'd had a hired man to help out.

They all would have liked to keep the farm in the family, but that was not to be. Until the auction was complete and the estate settled, it was not clear whether there would be funds to pay off the debt incurred by the farm. Coralea's sisters had arranged the dispersal of assets so she could purchase a small portion of the acreage for herself--the piece referred to as the Penney Eighty. Each daughter knew her parents had made great sacrifices to hang onto the farm. Coralea considered now that the sacrifices hadn't all been tangible ones. She felt PaPa had been forced to deal with some shady characters. Moreover, he had done some things himself that were completely against his nature. That may have taken a higher toll from him than did the economic disasters. *How many here today would take such risks to retain the property they knew to be their very life's blood? Would I?*

Lengths of plastic sheeting had been drawn back from the display of household goods arrayed on the driveway. No high-power antique dealers would be present today, Coralea was certain. None of her mother's precious acquisitions had survived the horrible calamity that her parents endured a few years earlier. A few family heirlooms were saved and now dwelt in the homes of close kin. The highchair that had served PaPa's grandmother, mother, and down to his great-granddaughter had been spirited away to the Ruby house in Bedford. Coralea had claimed for herself the seed picture that PaPa's great grandmother had constructed with intricate artistry in the previous century. His grandmother's walnut dresser was now in the possession of a grandson's family. Little else remained of much value, certainly not enough to warrant the rental of an indoor facility for the dispersal.

The auctioneers for the day, Bob Catterson and his assistant, each wore broad, western hats, apparently standard headgear for their profession. They had chosen appearance over comfort, as everyone else was bundled in caps with earflaps, insulated coveralls and rubber boots. The money exchange part of the process would be handled by members of Bob's family, situated at a card table in the entrance to the basement garage. The big doors were raised to let people huddle inside for a respite from the cold air, and the sitting workers' feet were warmed by space heaters.

Other than this, only two objects remained in the cavernous basement--an old piano and a desk piled high with equipment manuals. The desk still sat at the bottom of the stairs where PaPa had left his work boots at the end of each day, and where a box could often be found with at least one baby pig being warmed by a drop light clamped to the stair railing. The mound of manuals was smaller now. Many had been placed on the seat of the appropriate piece of equipment, which stood in one of several rows down the length of the lane. Most of the machinery was old and worn. Few farmers in the area were able to purchase new equipment. In fact, much of it here had probably passed at least once through Bob's Madison sale lot, where area farmers shopped for something better than what they had--at least something that would do the job. PaPa may have been Bob's best customer at those Sunday afternoon sales, and the big pieces of machinery he hauled to Bedford on his flatbed truck were expected to serve him and any of his neighbors who needed help.

At noon the three daughters were seated at the remaining table. They had peeled out of their coveralls and now sat with bowls of stew before them. Darla, Bob's daughter, had relinquished her post in the basement to join them for a hot lunch.

"This must be a hard day for you," Darla offered.

"You can't imagine!" Barbara declared, then added, "You probably can imagine. I bet you've helped with lots of estate sales!"

Darla smiled, acknowledging the fact. "This one is different, though."

"How's that?" Coralea inquired, interested.

"You all seem to get along well. Usually the heirs are bickering about something. That can make our job pretty uncomfortable," Darla returned.

"I can see how that could happen," Barbara admitted.

Sherry smiled at their younger companion. "When we were little, our grandmother taught us to share by drawing straws," she contributed. "That's what we did here. When we got down to personal effects, such as photographs, writings and jewelry, we put them in three piles, then drew straws to see who got which pile."

"And you 'drew straws' how?" Darla pressed.

"When we lived with Grandma, she pulled a straw from her broom and broke it into three pieces. Then she hid them in her hand with just the ends poking out, so we never knew which one might be longest when we chose them. Grandma could be pretty tricky," Barbara answered with a friendly grin.

The picture wasn't too clear to Darla, but she went on to ask, "Did you all grow up on this farm?"

"Actually, Sherry lived here the longest, maybe a couple of years," Coralea replied, glancing at her sister for confirmation. "I was only here a couple of months. I've got to say, though, I've always felt my roots were here anyway-- maybe because the folks lived here for so long."

"It's strange, but I find myself wanting to come back, even though they're not here." Sherry's eyes glistened as she scanned the empty space surrounding the group. Her caramel eyes were the sole facial attribute she'd inherited from her mother. "It's so empty, and yet, it almost seems as if they're still here."

Noting the bare walls of the large space, Coralea glanced at the map of Kuwait her mother had a year earlier pinned up behind the new television she'd been so proud of. Saddam Hussein had invaded the country and Dona wanted to ascertain just where American troops were to be deployed. Nothing else remained on the paneled walls, most of the pictures having been doled out to family members prior to the sale. The empty space did seem comforting, somehow. Coralea remembered an article she'd read in the *Smithsonian* once, concerning microscopic particles floating in the air. Amazingly, tiny bits of sloughed skin remain suspended near the ceilings of rooms, sometimes for years--a macabre thought, she supposed, and decided not to mention it now.

"This place was precious to them. I guess that's why it's so dear to us. I think I'll always yearn to come back here," Coralea admitted.

Barbara sighed. "After this, I don't care if I never come back!" Her emphatic statement obviously took Darla by surprise, but the other two knew her feelings. They each had, at one time or another, suggested their folks leave the farm. That wasn't the outcome they desired, but being witness to the troubles their parents had encountered in recent years had been heart wrenching for the three. "I think Mom would have left the farm if PaPa had been willing, at least in the early '80s," she added.

Coralea shook her head. "No. She loved this place as much as he did. She'd have gone wherever he went, but she wouldn't have pushed him to leave here. She loved the old house still, even after it was gone."

"Her heart was here," Sherry agreed, though she wondered inwardly how her mother had managed to remain devoted to a life that held such challenges.

"How long has Dona been gone?" Darla asked, knowing the farmer had passed away only recently.

"Almost exactly a year," Barbara replied. She glanced at her sisters and shared a moment of sadness as their eyes met in remembrance. "We think our mother was a remarkable woman. But then, I guess we have good reason to be prejudiced! Did you know her?" she then asked.

"Well, yes, I knew them both, from auctions. And everyone in Madison knew Dona from her work at the Light Company," Darla assured her as she reached for a Twinkie to finish off her hasty meal.

"I think you could say Mom was a common woman who lived in uncommon times," Coralea philosophized.

The others nodded in assent.

"She convinced us we were very fortunate, though in many ways we certainly were not," Barbara added.

"What amazes me is that she returned to a life of housework and outhouses after she'd been in the city," Sherry stated. "We didn't know any different, but it must have been hard for her."

"If she'd known what awaited her, she might not have!" Barbara asserted.

Sharon raised her eyebrows and looked from one to the other of her siblings, wondering whether either really believed that.

"She did it for us," Coralea volunteered, adding an aside to Darla. "Our mother lived and worked in Kansas City for three years during the war."

"She really did miss the city. We probably never knew how much," Barbara conceded.

They each felt a special magic had left their lives when their mother died. Once beyond the stage in their growth when they'd craved their own unique "me-ness," each had happily acknowledged the gifts their mother's character bestowed upon them.

A kinship born of sharing the good times and the bad served to weave the little community together. On this day the children of the household, grandchildren and on down, felt the unexpressed but palpable concern of the people who populated the town and nearby farms. This atmosphere made the event less distressing for the three and their families, in whose lives the day's activities stood for the saddest of changes. From here each daughter had launched her own family more than thirty years earlier. Each grandchild had been welcomed to the family here. Each referred to the place as the home place. If he were going "home" for Sunday dinner, this was that home. Even the great grandchildren had spent many of their most joyous and carefree days and nights here--perhaps not the same house, but still, the home place.

When Granny and PaPa had moved here thirty-four years ago, it had been known as the Stingley place. Now it had taken on their name. How long would it remain so? What number of years would pass before their influence disappeared from the place that so long held their hearts, as well as their fortunes? Time and fate will eventually trump the devotion of lovers of the land.

One year ago the house had been full. It was about the same time, in February. Granny had suffered her second heart attack late at night on Wednesday and was brought to the hospital in St. Joseph with no signs of life. On Saturday extra cars were parked on the circular driveway behind the house, and people were going in and out of the sliding glass doors that led into the living room.

"Marshmallows! The marshmallows!" It was Sarah, pointing to the microwave oven from which Barbara had just pulled her reheated cup of coffee. "Remember the marshmallows!" Barbara didn't, of course. She looked with interest at the children, who were, as usual, underfoot in the kitchen.

"Granny decided to cook some marshmallows for the girls one day, and she put them in whole," explained Vikki, Coralea's daughter and mother of the two little girls.

"They blew up!" Hannah jumped into the conversation. She had been quiet all morning but now managed a big grin in recollection of the event. Sarah giggled. She remembered the utter mess that ensued and how Granny had laughed until there were tears in her eyes. Momma would have been upset, but Granny just let herself enjoy the fun. A sudden look of seriousness passed over Sarah's face and she hurried back to the little nest she and Hannah had created behind the wet bar. It had been their special place when they stayed with Granny. She'd let them use the TV trays, some Indian blankets and the corduroy pillows from the couch, and the little girls spent hour after hour being mommies and princesses and pouring an endless supply of make-believe tea. They now were satisfied to huddle down into their own private space. The adults didn't know they were really listening--for the sound of heavy footsteps coming up the basement stairs.

Outside, PaPa moved around in the pig lot, doing the things he had done every morning on this farm for the last thirty-odd years. He was grateful to have them to do. Those in the house meant to comfort him, but the sadness reflected in their eyes only made him feel worse. Some of the family had come to spend the night last evening and, while he was thankful not to be alone, he felt himself trying to do for them as she would have done. And he felt he had failed miserably.

The snow on the ground muffled the sounds of the farm. He heard only the constant slap of the metal feeders as the hogs found their own meals.

He methodically opened the taps on the water lines to replenish the stock tanks, then began filling five-gallon buckets with ground corn to carry to the farrowing houses. There was a commotion each time he threw back the upper door to one of the wooden sheds, but once he lowered the feed to the trough the old sow settled down and snuffled it up as her piglets scrambled about her. Usually he counted each litter as he fed the sow, but today he just moved on to the next chore.

A car entered the lane and he waved when he saw it was one of the grandsons with his family. They had come up from Shenandoah--most of the family lived fairly close. Vikki and her family had come down from Wisconsin the day before and today her brother Kelly, who lived in Seattle, would come up from Texas, where he'd been on vacation with his current girlfriend. He would bring her along. PaPa had met her years earlier, when the two had been high school sweethearts. He remembered liking her and was glad his grandson wouldn't have to make the trip alone. They would arrive in time to meet with the rest at the church.

The aging farmer let his mind wander as he made trip after trip across the frozen ground. He glanced across the field west to where railroad tracks once stretched out from Bedford. In the silence now he remembered the sound of the trains as they sped along on their way to Roseville and points south. It was a sound he still missed, even though a train hadn't run through Bedford in at least ten years, and the tracks had been removed for a good long time. Years ago when the train passed in the middle of the night it rattled the old house, the glass in the windows vibrating with the passing of as many as two hundred freight cars. Accustomed as he was to the sound, he had slept right through it unless he was outside checking on the livestock. Once he'd appreciated the appearance of the clamorous cars--they made him think of exotic, faraway places. But through the years his experiences had modified this romantic outlook and now he found he missed only their sound, and was glad the country was moving away from hauling freight by rail.

His last hired man had been killed at a crossing on his way to work one morning--a crossing he'd made nearly every day for several years. There was no unusual weather at the time and the track was straight and flat, so approaching trains could be seen from at least a mile away. PaPa had called the man's wife in Madison to tell her--it was probably the hardest thing he'd ever had to do.

PaPa had admired Roy. He considered him a good worker and a good person. Roy married a widow with three daughters and they had since had a little girl of their own. She wasn't old enough to be in school when the accident occurred. PaPa had a crushing feeling of being responsible, even though he knew he wasn't. The widow had been kind and understanding toward him, but still he had the feeling of not doing enough, or not doing the right thing.

He felt that way again now. He had known it was coming. They both knew. When Dona had suddenly become ill after having a very good, active day, he had asked her if she needed to go to the hospital, to which she'd replied, "Well, would you rather I die here or at the hospital?" Then the car wouldn't start right away and he thought maybe he should call an ambulance, but that would mean waiting twenty or thirty minutes for it to arrive, time he felt she might not have. So he'd gotten her into the car for the half-hour trip to St. Joseph. He wondered if things might have turned out differently if he'd made the other choice. He thought again of the widow and her girls and felt once more the pain of being alone.

Dona had handled their occasional conflicts with the railroad companies. Since the tracks ran through their farm, the rail line shared the responsibility for keeping up the fences along the right-of-way. As the railroad economy declined, fences were neglected so sometimes there were livestock on the tracks. It happened that a bull and a cow were hit at the same time, killing both, and the railroad refused to acknowledge any liability. PaPa would have let it go, even though it had been a costly loss--a prize bull plus a producing female. But Dona had made phone calls, written letters, threatened lawsuits and generally kept at them until the railroad company did, finally, reimburse them for the loss. He thought now of how she'd always stood up for herself when she felt she was right. There were lots of ways he was going to miss her and he was aware of many already.

"He's coming!" one of the girls cried, and they both rushed to the basement door, to be there when it opened. This was a ritual they had kept a few years back, when Granny and PaPa cared for them while their mother taught school in a nearby town. Then they were little, and he would grab them up and whisk them to the kitchen table, already set and ready for lunch. Now they were too big--six and eight years old--and they stood a little awkwardly, waiting for him to come in. He had a look of weariness about him, but his face didn't fail to light up when the children descended on him.

"Would you want some coffee or something before you clean up?" one of the women inquired.

His "I'd better be getting ready" took him toward his bedroom and he acknowledged those who had recently arrived as he went through the kitchen and living room.

A Hundred Miles to the City

"I guess we should move Mom's purse but I can't get myself to touch it. It looks so . . . well, like she just laid it there and will be back to pick it up anytime." Sherry referred to the pocketbook that sat on the bar beside the kitchen. They all looked at it but no one made any action toward moving it.

"I know it's got cigarettes in it and I'd just like to rip them to shreds!" This was from Barbara, who'd never hidden her feelings about the habit her mother hadn't given up, even after the warning her doctor issued following her heart attack five years earlier. Barbara had been angry and frustrated with her mother for not giving up the cigarettes, believing her health might improve if only she would.

By now all the family had arrived and gathered in small groups, waiting until time to go to the church. Outside the sliding doors a pile of cats warmed themselves against the hard glass. The roads had been cleared for the travelers, but it was a wintry day--very chilly, with a cold wind blowing.

Inside the house, the group waited for PaPa to emerge from the bedroom. The cluster of great grandchildren had taken their trappings and moved to the back bedroom where they would have more room to themselves. This was not an unusually large group for the house--most of the same family members had spent Christmas Eve here, when they had been served the traditional offerings of chili and vegetable soup. The holiday had always been a major event with Granny. Just yesterday one of the daughters had returned the many boxes of decorations to the storage cabinet in the basement. Granny had gotten them dismantled and boxed up but was unable to negotiate the stairs to put them away. This year she had again laid out Christmas ornaments on each available tabletop, plus hanging garlands and wreaths in windows. She chose to decorate her house on the inside, rather than the outside. Few passersby would see it, anyhow. So she strung lights meant for a tree across the fireplace, over the kitchen bar, and from window to window all over the large living area, so it seemed like those gathered were inside a Christmas tree.

When PaPa at last came out of the bedroom, he was wearing his light blue suit, a purchase Granny had insisted on at the occasion of a grandson's wedding a few years earlier. The suit had been worn to many weddings and graduations, but mostly it was the uniform he wore to funerals, where he was often called upon to serve as pallbearer. The people of the area knew he was always willing to help his neighbors in this way.

More than one in the gathering mentally noted that he was still, at 70 years of age, a handsome man. Strands of gray had overtaken his dark hair and wrinkles etched the sides of his eyes, but his youthful build reflected physically demanding work.

PaPa announced that he would bring the car around from the basement. He had always done this for Granny and continued in that way now. He had taken the car to Whitesville to wash it the day before, a thing he very seldom did. But now the old Mercury gleamed.

Hannah ran in when they began bundling up and announced that she wanted to go with PaPa--no surprise to anyone--so Vikki's family, PaPa's sister and Coralea, who now lived alone in Madison, all got into the big yellow sedan. Coralea felt herself hesitate, knowing that her mother had died in this car a few days back. She experienced a shock of reality that this was really happening and struggled to remain composed. To make more room in the front seat, PaPa reached down and moved aside the black boot-shaped ashtray that sat on the floorboard. Coralea wondered at his patience--the patience he showed now and the patience he had shown her mother throughout the years that had passed since she first had heart trouble.

It was but a short distance to town. The lane turned into a road which turned into a street that ran the distance through the town, six blocks in all. The street should have been named Church Street, as all the churches in the town sat on the macadam road that ran parallel to the railroad right-of-way. The first they passed was the Latter Day Saints Church, with a congregation drawn from most of the county. Then they passed the former Christian Church, now converted into the town community center. The building looked the same as before, except that the bell had been mounted on a platform near the entrance. Two of the daughters had been married here in December weddings, back when the structure was still used as a church.

The services would be in the Methodist Church, the only brick church in the town, on the next corner to the north. Coralea remembered that this had been Nora Martin's church. She had known Mrs. Martin as a child when she lived with her grandparents in the little house on the highway.

Mrs. Martin had lived at the top of the hill on the same road. Each day the lady walked down to town to the grocery store. The little girls looked with wonder at her pretty clothes and bright red hair, always topped with a fancy hat. Mrs. Martin always spoke to the children, who were rather in awe of her as their own grandmother wore plain sunbonnets and housedresses. Coralea remembered the many times Mrs. Martin had stopped at the girls' lemonade stand and bought a nickel's worth from each of them, even though she could never drink it all.

The group parked in the reserved space, then entered the side door leading to the church's basement. The Methodist ladies--many of them had been good friends of Dona's--would serve sandwiches and desserts, a light lunch so the mourners could visit before the one o'clock service. There had been no formal visitation at the funeral home, as all agreed Dona would have wanted none. In recent years she had stayed away from funerals as much as possible and PaPa had gone to represent the family.

The meeting area was filled with friends and relatives who greeted the group as they entered. Many were new to some of the family, so introductions were made and people began forming small groups of conversation between the tables and chairs.

A while later, PaPa said to Vikki, "I'd like to go see her now," so she and the little girls moved with him up the stairs to the sanctuary. Vikki and her mother had discussed having the children view their Granny's body in the coffin and had agreed that it would probably be best if they didn't. But now PaPa held Hannah's hand and they approached the casket. He held her up so she could see and neither she nor Sarah made any visible sign of being surprised or shaken. Vikki wondered whether he and Granny had discussed this sometime. She surmised that Granny had tried to prepare the girls. Vikki knew that once when Hannah had found her grandmother smoking she had begun to cry, and when Granny pulled the sobbing child close to embrace, Hannah had wailed, "I don't want you to die!" Granny had backed her up and said, as tears formed in her own eyes, "I'll always live in your heart." Vikki's own heart ached now with gratitude for the grandmother she had lost.

When the services commenced, the family members sat together in the pews nearest the altar railing. The warm hue of the wood in the old church made the chilly air less of a discomfort. On the casket, now closed, lay a blanket of red roses with words in gold spelling *Wife, Mother, Grandmother* and *Friend*.

Dona had not been a religious person in the usual sense of the word but had sought to live by the creed of the Golden Rule. Each of her family felt she had led a successful life and that, if there were a better place to be, she was surely there now. The minister chosen for the services was one who had retired but who still served the area and represented a generally Protestant doctrine. His sermon was simple, referring to an allegorical garden, probably inspired by Dona's choice of "In the Garden" as a song she wanted sung on the occasion.

"I come to the garden alone . . ." The familiar hymn brought Granny's voice to mind as Sherry sat beside Dave, her husband. The couple lived on a farm near Carroll, but this year had spent weekdays in a tiny house in Madison. Dave had recently retired from his work with the Internal Revenue Service and Sherry had taken a leave of absence from teaching so she could obtain her master's degree from the university. Her tears spilled as she imagined her mother's mellow, low-pitched voice singing the hymn. Dona had enjoyed singing to her girls when they were little and they had loved the soothing warmth of her voice. When the girls attended a country school, their mother was asked to perform at community meetings. She was proud of her talent and gladly worked on popular tunes to present to the small audiences.

After closing the final prayer, the minister sat, nodding as he did so to the pallbearers, grandsons of the couple, who were sitting in the front row. The ritual continued, with the boys bearing their special burden toward the back of the room. PaPa, along with Vikki's family, hurriedly followed. Some few moments later Barbara and her family left the pew.

As she moved up the aisle, Barbara glanced around at the many friends of her parents, as well as friends and co-workers of her own and of her sisters. She was surprised to see the man sitting in the back row near the door! She had called to tell him of her mother's death but didn't expect that he would come back to Bedford for her burial.

After Barbara donned her coat and went outside, she waited by the church steps and asked as the man and his wife approached, "Will you go to the cemetery with us?" She was not sure how she should address him. Conflicting emotions reminded her that she once knew him as Father, but what was he to her now?

The gravesite was at the top of the hill in the Anderson Cemetery. There had as yet been no other burials in this section of the graveyard. A green canvas canopy covered a small area around the casket, with two rows of chairs set to face away from the wind. The family took their places as the other mourners made a circle around the group. Later, when they had come here to plant flowers on Granny's grave, PaPa would tell Hannah, "I chose this spot because I figure from here I can someday rise up out of my grave and see our farm!" His place began a short distance to the south, where the gravel road curved at the top of another rise.

After a few words and a prayer from the minister, the family was invited to take roses from the arrangement in memory of their loved one. The daughters and most of the children each carefully pulled out a long-stemmed bloom.

"Will you go back to the house with us?" Barbara now asked the man and his wife. They both smiled to answer that they would. Though the air was still bitterly cold, many in the gathering remained at the cemetery for some time, getting reacquainted and visiting.

Back at the farmhouse, such exclamations as "My, how your children have grown!" "How long has it been?" and "What are you doing now?" could be heard among the adults, who chatted quietly in the living room.

The man who had entered with Barbara's family was introducing his wife, Lila, to Dona's sister. "Earlene, I'd like you to meet . . ."

"Not Earlene," Carrie replied. "I'm Carrie!" Embarrassed, he apologized for his mistake and she hastened to tell him that Earlene and her husband, Emmett, had both passed away a few years earlier. She realized that he probably still thought of her as she had appeared so many years ago, when to him she was Dona's little sister, not the mother and grandmother she now was. She also knew that practically all of the people gathered here were complete strangers to him and she sought to put him at ease by inquiring about his family and the place he now lived. Similar thoughts were on the minds of others of the group as they pointed out to him things that had either changed or remained the same since he had lived in the area many years ago.

Observing this activity, Coralea reflected on the man's manner. *He's still charming. No wonder he swept my mother off her feet--not once, but twice!* Her thoughts raced back in time to replay scenes long repressed.

It seems strange, he and PaPa being in the same place, thought Barbara. Several years earlier, when returning from a trip to Alaska, she and Don had stopped at the couple's home in South Dakota. The man had given up farm work to deal in antiques. It had been good to see him. She had introduced her husband and told the man of her family, awkwardly exchanging pleasantries while trying to bridge a gap formed of some twenty years.

When PaPa entered the house he immediately recognized the man and approached to where the couple sat, in order to greet him and be introduced to his wife. The two shook hands heartily. PaPa had known him many years before. They had, in fact, been friends. They had even worked together. Still, PaPa was somewhat surprised to see the man here--he hadn't been known to come to Missouri since his mother died in 1975, more than fifteen years earlier.

The woman by his side now said, simply, "He wanted to come."

Although their musings would forever remain unuttered, each daughter wondered what emotions her mother might be feeling if she were somehow still in touch with her earthly home--surely not mere forgiveness and understanding, as they had been accomplished long ago.

TWO

The town of Summerville lies on fertile bottomland in Bates County, a scant ten miles south of the Iowa line. Fifty years earlier the village of Reliance was pulled away from the banks of the Platte River by the Chicago Great Western Railroad as it worked its way south toward larger settlements. The town renamed itself and took up residence a half-mile to the west where the land came to a slight rise before rolling away to timbered hills and valleys. In the prosperous years around the turn of the century, several two-story brick buildings were built in the new town, including a hotel and an opera house. These buildings lined two sides of a square in the center of the town. A bandstand stood in the middle of the square, which had both parking places and hitching rails. The automobile hadn't completely shoved the horse and buggy into obsolescence in this part of the state, and on most days at least one team of horses stood hitched and waiting.

On certain summer evenings an all-male band played in the bandstand or at chautauquas in the area. Only two churches, one Methodist, the other Christian, were located in the town, both on Main Street. But lesser congregations of Baptists and other sects had rural churches, each with its accompanying cemetery. The townsfolk were fortunate to have two doctors and a drugstore to serve their needs. There was an I.O.O.F. in the town, as well as a Rebekah lodge and Ladies Aid Society.

A few years earlier, a brick schoolhouse had been erected on the north edge of town. It included a gymnasium, the only structure in the whole of Bates County where the young people could play basketball indoors. There was a gas station on each end of town, and, besides the livery, which now saw very little business, there was a modern garage. This new business had an oil pit with a hydraulic overhead lift. A general merchandise store offered groceries and hardware, as well as some dry goods, such as clothing and shoes.

But the busiest spots in town were the three saloons and the produce house. The saloons were fullest at night but were open most of the day and were frequented by older gentlemen who sat and played checkers by the hour and kept a steady stream of tobacco juice flowing into the brass spittoons at their feet. On pleasant days they sometimes sat on benches in the park, mulling over the current state of affairs and darkening the grass nearby with wet, brown stains.

Blacks' Produce House had a big corner doorway and large plate glass windows that looked out over the square. From there customers could visit and see what was going on in a large part of the town. On Saturdays the women of the community brought their produce to market, earning enough to buy staples for the next week's meals.

Cats of every size and color wandered around the store, brushing up against anyone who stood still for long. In the corner of the large room were saucers of milk to supplement the diet of these mousers, and the entire place had a cream-like smell, thick and sweet. A nearly-covered fly strip hung by the doorway, which had a tightly-fit screen door that sprang shut with a vengeance when someone entered and from which the cats had learned to keep their distance.

Twelve-year-old Dona stood with the baby perched on one hip as Retha smiled to acknowledge a smaller woman who had entered the store. The other lady was saying, "So this is the new Schmit baby. What is your little sister's name?"

"Carrie Edell," Dona answered as she gently jiggled the child.

"You must be a big help to your mother," the woman added.

Eeuw! Not entirely by choice, Dona thought. She'd heard that so often lately. Not that she didn't like her baby sister, she'd just rather follow her brothers around. Boys got to do things that were fun--like going fishing in Honey Creek and going with Dad when he took his rifle to the woods, hunting rabbits and squirrels.

She moved away quietly as the two women visited. She went to stand by the window and idly traced the *yremaerC* letters in front of her. She searched the park across the street, looking for someone she might know. Sometimes she would see an acquaintance, but not often. Then she saw a familiar face coming up the street toward her. It was Helen, a girl she had known when she went to Hope school.

"Can I take Carrie over to the park?" Dona asked her mother as she lifted the little bonnet up to cover the child's bare head. Her own head was covered only with dark curls, as she had finally convinced her mother that she no longer needed to wear sunbonnets. After receiving her mother's permission, she hurried outside to catch her friend before she passed by.

"Can you play?" she asked Helen.

"Just awhile, I guess. We have to be going pretty soon." The two girls crossed over to the corner of the park and sat down on an iron bench. Helen fussed over the baby a bit while Dona balanced her on her knee. She wanted to put her little sister down, as Carrie obviously wanted to be put down, but was afraid to for fear of what she might pick up out of the grass. And there were stray dogs that would come over and sniff around on her. *Eeuw!* So Dona attempted to amuse her little sister on her lap as she shared secrets with Helen. The two girls talked and laughed, catching each other up on events since they last met.

Soon Helen's sister came for her so Dona and Carrie were left alone. Some other kids in the park came to look them over but soon lost interest and resumed their play. Now and then a car went slowly by on the street, trailing a small stream of dust behind.

Dona picked up Carrie's little hands to play pat-a-cake. She was easy to amuse and was soon giggling and clapping. Dona thought that maybe it wasn't so bad being the big sister for a change. Although Carrie was messy and a real nuisance sometimes, Dona was glad *she* was not the baby anymore.

She thought back to a year ago, at Carrie's birth, when she had been taken to stay with a neighbor so she wouldn't witness the event. When her father came for her that night, he had asked, "Guess what we have?" She had guessed, "A new calf?" She knew the real answer, but also knew that she was not supposed to know so she had played the innocent. Her father wanted his children to be educated, but he also wanted them unaware of certain delicate facts of life. Thanks to Earlene, her oldest sister, Dona wasn't completely ignorant of the situation, as he had wished.

Now she looked around. She didn't see Miriam. She was probably at the drugstore, looking at magazines with her friends. The boys usually spent Saturday afternoon hanging around one of the filling stations. They would stay in town all afternoon until Dad returned at night to get them. Earlene had stayed home today--sewing or studying, Dona guessed. She would be coming into town tonight with Emmett, a boy from her class in school. They would probably go see a picture show at the opera house. Dona had been there a few times, though not lately, as there was no money for such luxuries now.

Dona looked up to see her mother waving from the steps of the produce house and remembered that she had been told she could pick out the sacks of chicken feed this time. Her mother would make her a dress for school from the colorful fabric of the sacks--something new of her own. Dona usually wore her sisters' hand-me-downs or those from her spoiled cousin, Emma Kathleen. She would appreciate having something to wear that would actually fit, for a change.

A Hundred Miles to the City

After finishing with their business in the produce house, Dona and her mother went on down the street to the drugstore, where Retha usually ordered medicine. Dona hoped there would be some candy for her. The large center aisle was crowded with shoppers large and small, and the busy cash register rang out over mingled voices. Miriam was there and surprised her sister by buying her a Coca-Cola at the soda fountain with a nickel she had earned ironing for a neighbor lady. Miriam was happy to be free of child-care duties for a while and chose this way of thanking her younger sister.

At four o'clock Sam Schmit gathered up his family at the corner of the square.

Dona handed Carrie up to Miriam, who sat in the back of the car, and scrambled up beside her.

"They're pretty," Miriam said.

In reply to Dona's quizzical look, she added, "The sacks. Would you like me to help you with your dress?"

Dona screwed up her face--she wasn't that confident in her sister's sewing ability. Earlene had become quite adept at fashioning skirts, blouses . . . even a coat once, probably better than their mother. But Miriam was younger, just fifteen. Dona wasn't sure. But, then again, her mother was always busy and probably wouldn't get to it until who-knows-when. And she knew her mother hadn't been very well since the birth of the baby. Maybe it would be best to have Miriam work on it.

"Will it be all right, Mom?" Miriam asked as she tapped Retha on the shoulder.

"Hop to it," was her mother's hasty reply.

"We can look in this *Vogue*," Miriam offered, as she held up a magazine that had been lying on the seat beside her. "Vera loaned it to me."

"I think, Miriam, that you'd better try the catalogue. Your sister's not exactly shaped like those ladies," Retha commented over her shoulder.

The Model A was less crowded on the way home, being lighter by two crates of eggs, half a can of cream, and two big boys. Sam was quiet, as usual, as the dusty car rattled its way out of town, beyond the western extent of the town's dwellings. They chugged along slowly, as Sam wasn't overly secure in handling the powerful machine. Dust swept in the front windshield, which had been rolled out to let cooling air into the vehicle.

They went west until they came to the Dowis place, then turned onto a dirt road and headed south to where their own decrepit barn could be seen atop a hill a mile farther. The dusty road was nearly level, the usual ruts beaten flat by the multitude of wheels that passed over it since the last good rain several weeks ago. They passed by the Brethren Church, where they occasionally attended services on Sundays, then crossed the culvert that spanned Honey Creek.

The house they soon arrived at was large but old and seriously in need of repair. The fence that once surrounded the house was missing in places, and chickens of various sizes scratched in the bare areas around the porches and on the path that led to the now-absent gate. The front screen door was patched and the whole house needed painting. It had a look of having been vacant for a good, long time, perhaps even found to be unfit for human habitation--which is exactly what Retha had surmised when she first saw the place. Then she remembered that beggars can't be choosers, and the family had moved in last March.

In reality, the Schmit family had faced a move almost annually for the last several years. When the Depression descended on the country, it hadn't been as much of a shock to them as it was to some because they had been having hard times already.

However, the hard times did get worse, so much so that in 1930 Sam had sold his farm animals and equipment and set out for Wyoming with the whole family, except for Earlene, who stayed behind with her Klodder grandparents so she could stay in school. Wyoming had been their destination, since one of Sam's sisters and her husband owned a ranch there. Sam had bought a tent so the family could camp out at night as they made the weeklong journey.

Their plans had mostly worked out, except that when they arrived they learned that there was no work to be had on the ranch and no provision for six more chairs under the table. So from there they went on, heading for the Cascades where huge logging outfits were operating. Sam heard of an opening for cooks in a lumber camp, so they pointed the car to the west and kept going.

At Yellowstone Lake, while Retha prepared to cook breakfast over a campfire, a brown bear loped into camp and made a move for the bacon she was cooking. Without uttering a word--doubtless she was too frightened to do so--Retha stepped over to the car and held the skillet into the window as far as she could reach, keeping the meat away from the bear but quite exposing herself!

Sam had been dismantling the tent and quickly came running, shouting and wildly waving his arms to scare the animal away. Startled, the bear turned and lumbered off into the woods, apparently not hungry enough to confront the noisy apparition that was Sam. While Retha sat trembling from the experience, the children couldn't help laughing at the sight she had made trying to save their breakfast. They already knew that their mother was a very determined woman.

A Hundred Miles to the City

Retha and Sam were hired as cooks at a lumber camp in Oregon where hundreds of men bunked in long, narrow sheds situated at the foot of the mountains. The pay was fairly good and the family all worked to help out.

It was a carefree time for the youngest of the family. During their stay there the children spent much of their time roaming the nearby hills, discovering plants and animals they'd never seen in Missouri. They received a lot of attention from the men in the camp, most of whom were at least temporarily separated from families of their own. But before long, Retha and Sam noticed some rough talk among the other workers, who made no attempt at being discreet in the company of youngsters. By the time fall neared, the Schmit parents had decided that the lumber camp was no place to raise children, so back to Missouri they went.

That was the fall they lived in a tent, the fall that Dona went to another new school, Hazel Dell. The oldest of the children, Grant, had quit school to help on the farm. Earlene would graduate from Summerville High this year, Miriam was a year behind her, and Hank was a freshman.

Earlene's finishing high school was to be a premiere event in the Schmit family. She would be the first to get a diploma, as Sam had completed only through the eighth grade at Elmo and Retha had gone through the sixth grade at Orrsburg, where a good portion of the students were Klodders--her own siblings and cousins.

Most of the time Dona felt living in the big tent was an adventure, like camping out in the woods. But to Retha, who had to cook over a campfire and wash dishes in a basin, it was misery itself. When it rained, almost everything got wet. Then the bedding would have to be spread on fences to dry. Luckily, before the weather turned really cold, Sam had found a place for them that an older couple had vacated to move into town. That had been their home until the next March, when they found this place and Sam once again put in crops, bought a few cows and chickens, and hoped for better times.

Sam carried the first of the bags of feed around to the back as the others climbed the steps at the front of the house. Dona shooed the nasty chickens off the porch as she carried in the few groceries her mother had bought. Miriam set Carrie down on the floor, whereupon Earlene jumped up from where she had been grooming her nails and picked her up again. She went to the kitchen to get a wet cloth to cool and clean the baby's face.

Earlene was dressed to go out. Everyone expected she and Emmett would be getting married soon. They had been friends a long time; he had begun courting her a few months before. Emmett worked at a filling station in

Summerville, and Earlene recently began working part-time at the switchboard in town. Everyone was pleased with the match, as Emmett was serious but fun and treated Earlene with genuine admiration and respect.

By the time their father had carried in the two sacks of feed, Dona and Miriam were on the back porch with scissors in hand, ready to dump the contents into the big wooden box that served as a storage bin. They were eager to get the sacks rinsed and ironed and hoped Earlene would be willing to help cut the pieces to fit Dona. She had learned to sew for herself without patterns. The flimsy tissue templates were hugely expensive, and, as her mother was fond of saying, "Necessity is the mother of invention--in these times, you cut corners wherever you can."

Sam did the few evening chores himself so the boys could have some time to themselves. They had worked hard all summer. If any farmers in the area needed extra hands for haying, not just the boys were hired on, but Sam as well. He'd rather not have to "hire out," but any cash they could earn was desperately needed.

Retha fed the baby and put her on a pad on the floor for a nap. Supper on Saturday was usually an informal affair, with everyone getting something for himself. They always had homemade bread on hand, and milk. Dona liked to mix the two and add sugar. Or, even better, to pour a little coffee and cream on soda crackers and sprinkle that with sugar. Anything, as long as it wasn't apples! Soon the new crop of fruit would be ready to pick. It seemed to her that this last year they'd practically lived on apples. They'd had them baked, fried, stewed, pickled, made into applesauce, apple butter, apple juice, apple pie, apple cake and so on and on. At the apple-a-day rate they shouldn't see the doctor around here for the rest of the century!

When Sam came in, Retha sat at the table with him, sharing the gossip she'd heard in town. He had gotten a plate and now poured a thick mass of sorghum molasses from a large can, enough to completely cover the bottom. As he listened, he used chunks of bread to sop up the deep brown syrup, his blue eyes twinkling as he enjoyed the sweet treat.

Sam's "farmer tan" made his face appear dark and deeply lined, and the lighter area at the top of his forehead had recently begun advancing on his hairline. The brown tint of his hair made the appearance of merry blue eyes somewhat of a surprise.

Sam moved to his rocking chair in the living room and reached for his pipe. He had never been a chewer of tobacco, but he did occasionally like to draw on a soothing pipe. Dona thought the smell pleasant. It was an aroma that gave her a sense of home and would remain a comfort to her throughout her life.

A Hundred Miles to the City

The floor of the room was bare, except for the scattered rugs that Retha had braided or crocheted from old rags. When Carrie awoke from her nap, she scooted across to where Sam sat with his pipe. He bent to pick her up, then talked to her in a quiet, man-to-baby manner. A game they often played together was "Cat."

He would say, "Grandpa lived at the top of the hill," and touch her forehead.

"Grandma lived at the bottom of the hill," and touch her chin.

"Grandpa had a cat that went down the hill to visit Grandma." He would trail a finger slowly down her face.

Then, "Grandma said, 'Scat!'" He would swipe four fingers up quickly, bumping her nose and ruffling her hair.

They went through that routine now. She clutched her hands together and shook with an open-mouthed laugh that showed four little teeth and a huge expanse of pink gums.

After a bit he hoisted her up and sat her on his shoulders. Carrie first put her hands in his thinning hair, then grabbed him by his ample nose. Sam responded with a hearty snort, whereupon she immediately threw up her arms, then clutched her own tiny nose. The others watched as the two galloped around the room.

Dona enjoyed seeing them having fun together. Her father was quite taken with this late arrival to his family, and she thought, without resentment, that he spent much more time with Carrie than he had with her. There had been four successive babies before her, so by the time of her arrival in the Schmit family both her parents were more than accustomed to the charms of toddlers. She suspected that after eleven years her father appreciated anew the joyous spontaneity of babyhood. Dona remembered the doll he had given her once. It was a beautiful big doll, the nicest gift she had ever gotten. It had been in the window of the hardware store in Summerville. She had secretly yearned for it but knew they could not afford a doll so precious. When Sam brought it home for her, she felt so special! She knew he had won it by signing up for a drawing, but she cherished it as her very own gift from him alone.

Anyhow, she was just glad he was here. Several of her acquaintances had no father at home. Some of the men of the community had gone off to find work to help sustain their families. Some had gone and never returned. Some had probably gone with the belief that they were easing the burden on their family by simply disappearing. At any rate, she considered herself lucky.

Dona thought of the "Happy Hooligans" at school. This was not their real name, and she didn't know how they came to be called that, unless it was a cruel joke taken from a cartoon or something. The family had three children, all younger than she. There had been no father in the house for a long time and there were rumors that the mother sometimes took in late-night callers to enable her to put food on the table. Some of the other mothers at the Hazel Dell School had formed a plan to send extra food for lunch with their own youngsters so it could be shared with the unfortunate children. When it was Dona's turn, Retha fried up some chicken--something that they did have--and sent it, along with strict instructions to Dona that she was not to just hand the food to them, but that she was to sit and eat with them. Retha wished her to be kind when making the offering. She knew the needy family were merely scraping nearer the bottom of the barrel than the Schmits happened to be at the time.

By the following Saturday, the girls had assembled Dona's calico dress on the old White treadle sewing machine and Miriam was now adding some lace for trim. Dona was glad she hadn't been asked to help with the stitching. Besides wanting her new dress to look store-bought, she found needlework distasteful. Her mother had tried to teach her to embroider, but her brother, Hank, had caught on quicker and had learned to crochet, as well. Dona admitted only to herself that she was a reluctant pupil and was soon accepted as being all thumbs when it came to needlework.

On this Saturday, Miriam stayed home to work on the dress, so Carrie was left in the care of the two older girls. Dona accompanied her mother to town to help with the produce and, maybe, go with Hank for a while. He sometimes allowed her to hang around, if he had no friends to chum with.

After doing business at the produce house and the general store, Retha and Dona went over to sit in the park. Dona would have liked to go looking for Hank but knew her mother wouldn't want to sit alone. Hank and Grant had taken off immediately when they first got to town. Grant was always eager to get away from the watchful and, he thought, critical eye of his father. And Hank, though usually very tolerant of her, was happy to be shedding his sister-shadow for the day.

About mid-afternoon, thunderheads began piling up in the west, blocking out the sun. It had been hot and humid all day, and now the air seemed to hang heavily. Overhead, lumpy clouds formed a bowl turned upside down over the little town.

The sounds of activity were loud to Retha, with a clarity that occurred only in an oppressive atmosphere. She assumed that Sam was unaware of the gradual but persistent change in the weather. He had a deep-seated fear of storms, having survived a devastating tornado when he was a boy. If they were at home, he would have had them all down in the cellar by now. Retha decided they'd better get in the car, where they frequently waited until Sam came out of the tavern. She looked out as the rain came down in large droplets, making splotches on the hood of the car. She hoped the rain would at least settle the dust and wash off some of the grit that covered everything.

She noticed Hank hurrying up the street. He made no move to cross to the park, seeming not to see her as he flew on to the tavern where he expected his father would be.

Hank hesitated as he opened the door. It was even darker inside and he knew he wasn't welcome here. But this was important--the excitement showed on his face as he searched the room for his father. He spied Sam sitting in a back booth with a couple of other men. As he approached, he caught the look of disapproval on his father's face.

"What is it?" Sam was apprehensive. He knew Hank wouldn't enter the bar unless it was something important.

"I got us a hog!"

"What?"

"I said, I got us a hog! I swapped my harmonica to Pete Jones for a hog!"

Hank saw his father stiffen and become flushed and knew then that he should have waited. He sensed a storm coming . . . bigger than the one outside.

At last Sam smiled and said, "Well, I guess you've just lost yourself a Jew's harp, boy. We don't need that pig." He could see that Hank looked confused and disappointed, so before he could say anything more to embarrass him, he got up and hurried his son out of the bar.

Retha saw them, standing face to face by the street in the rain, yelling and gesturing to each other. She saw Sam grab Hank by the arm and push him toward the car.

Hank threw himself into the backseat beside Dona. Anger and frustration showed on his face as he turned to stare out the window.

When Sam got in, wet from the rain, he gave Retha a penetrating look and demanded, "What do you suppose he did now?"

She sat quietly, looking at him. What could she say?

"He came in there and said, in front of everybody, 'I got us a hog.' Right in front of the whole damn place!"

He turned to Hank. "Did Grant put you up to it? Was this his idea?" he asked, accusingly.

"No," Hank replied, almost inaudibly.

"Son of a b_____, boy! I can't believe . . . "

"Sam!" Retha found her voice. She was not accustomed to him swearing in her presence. She was not surprised, however, that he blamed Grant. Ever since their older son had become an adolescent, Sam had let him know there was room for only one man in the house.

"Well, Jesus Christ!" he exploded. "What do you expect? He comes in and tells my friends we don't have enough to eat! How do you suppose that makes me feel?" He turned and threw the words back at Hank, "Have you ever gone hungry?"

This time Hank did not answer.

"Shit!"

By this time Dona was crying. She wasn't sure what for. Because her father's feelings were hurt? Because her brother's feelings were hurt? She wanted to put her arms around Hank but knew he'd push her away.

She could see her mother's jaw set.

There was complete silence in the car for several minutes.

Finally, Sam started the car and Retha asked, "What about Grant?"

"He can find his own way home!"

The rain was coming down hard now, and by the time they got by the Brethren Church the roadway was slick. The car swerved perilously from one side to the other, several times just missing landing in the ditch. No one spoke: the two in the front staring straight ahead; the two in the back looking at nothing out their separate windows as the landscape slid by.

After they entered the house, Hank sat down by the kitchen table and looked up at his father. He hoped that by now Sam had cooled off--maybe even realized what a boon that hog, butchered, would be to the family.

Sam just gave him a stern look of disapproval and said, "I guess you're too big for the razor strop now, but you won't be going into town on Saturday from now on! That goes for Grant, too!"

Hank seethed at having his good intentions crushed. Without a word to anyone he stomped upstairs and slammed the bedroom door. A lot of good it did to try and help out! His dad was too damn proud to reason with!

Miriam tried to comfort Dona. From what she could make of her sister's version of the events, she felt sorry for Hank. She knew how important the harmonica had been to him. He'd had it since he was twelve--had taken it out West, entertaining them all and playing for the lumberjacks, too. He'd learned to play on his own and could pick out about any tune on it. And, she admitted to herself, some pork would have tasted good!

"It's not the way you're thinking it is, Dad," she bravely said. "The Joneses can't afford to feed their hogs and nobody can buy them now."

Sam never even looked at her. He only said, "We aren't getting that hog!"

A Hundred Miles to the City

On Sunday morning Grant and Hank were sent to the Jones farm to drive the hog the two miles home. Sometime during the night Sam had listened to the voice of reason or, perhaps, the voice of reality lying beside him in the bed.

THREE

The summer sun had passed its peak and now the small clapboard house was bathed in the shade of an elm tree. It had been a lazy summer day for some on the farm.

The brown-haired woman in the doorway spoke. "Boys, don't forget to water . . . "

"It's his turn!" This from the larger of the two who knelt on the faded carpet in the middle of the room. The oval pattern of the carpet formed an ideal boundary for their game of marbles.

Both boys looked at their mother and shrugged perceptibly. What it had come down to lately was this: if there were a major disagreement or if a particular chore was left undone, both would be punished equally later on. Their mother knew this; they quickly recalled this, also. Passing through the kitchen, they each gave their mother a defeated look, then gave each other a shove as they went out, the door slamming behind them.

It seemed to Grace, their mother, that the two would never get along again. When they were young they had played together happily, pushing each other on the tire swing, giving each other rides in the wheelbarrow, even helping each other in little battles with the girls. But now they constantly annoyed each other, elbowing and tripping and throwing up challenges. They were like the little banty roosters in her chicken coop--always vying for cock-of-the-walk. Norman was a young man now and Junior was all knees and elbows and always outgrowing his overalls.

One after the other, the boys tumbled down the back steps and charged out through the gate and down the hill, leaving their apathy in the house along with their mother's concerns. It was a race, as usual, to the stock tank, and Junior, as usual, won it. He was bigger, already, though almost two years younger, than his brother, Norman, now fifteen.

A Hundred Miles to the City

"Ha! You're a real slowpoke! You couldn't keep up if I crawled!" shouted Junior as he reached up to engage the lever that would send the pump cylinder up and down to suck water from the well and into the reservoir.

Norm grinned. He felt good out in the pasture where the summer smells of growing things filled his nostrils. He was panting. He had given it a good effort this time.

The two workhorses sauntered over to taste the fresh water now pouring into the murky tank. The boys watched them and stroked their broad backs as they stood quietly, their tails flicking at the ever-present flies that pestered them.

The windmill clacked with the rhythm of the pump and now and then emitted a loud squeak as the vane turned and shifted the paddles into the wind. The day was warm, but not too hot, and the boys lounged on the ground for a short while. With his middle finger Norman flicked off a grasshopper that had landed on his leg.

"You had a head start," he stated, as if to excuse his loss in the earlier contest.

"I'm taller than you," Junior reminded him, which wasn't what Norman wanted to hear.

Before long the two were rolling on the soft ground, pummeling each other with playful, but telling, blows. When they grew tired of this pursuit, they lay back on the grass and watched a few thin clouds slide across the sky. Soon the cows would be coming in from the far side of the pasture and there'd again be milking to do. To the boys, life seemed to be a never-ending series of chores, and milking was not their favorite.

As one of the horses moved to return to his grazing, Junior grabbed hold of his tail, shouted "Yahoo!" and held on as the huge animal charged up the hill toward the house. The pair fairly flew across the uneven ground, the horse trying to outrun his tormenter and the boy yelping with excitement as his legs churned to keep up. Junior laughed aloud with the exhilaration of the effort, never hearing the muffled thud behind him down by the tank. His dark hair flapped in the breeze as the horse ran on. This was his best ride yet! The chickens that were scratching around in the bare path squawked, scattering as the hooves of the huge animal hit the ground.

The horse had pulled him almost to the gate! He let go, arms aching from the effort, and threw himself down on the ground to catch his breath. His gaze swung effortlessly down the hill to the windmill. A lump of clothes was lying on the ground by the tank. *No,* he realized, *that's Norm!*

Junior jumped up and tore down the hill, too scared to utter a plea for help from those in the house. His brother lay crumpled on the ground. *No blood,* he realized immediately as he quickly searched over Norman with his eyes. *He isn't breathing!* Junior felt panic and remorse as he picked his brother up from the ground and quickly struggled up the hill, holding Norman firmly around the waist, his head bouncing on his shoulder.

"Mother! Mother!" Junior cried as he reached the gate. He feared that Norman might be dead! Half of him wanted to help and half of him wanted to run away. He was as white as his unconscious brother, whom he now lowered gently to the ground.

Grace ran from the house, her mind taking in the reality of the scene before her. *Oh, God!* she thought.

"What has happened?" aloud now, urgently.

Junior looked at her helplessly, as his two sisters ran, screaming, from the house. They had sensed the horror of the moment as they caught the anxiety in their mother's usually calm voice.

"I don't know!" he answered, his chest suddenly tight.

Marly put her arms around her little sister as they knelt beside the still figure of their brother.

The child trembled as she looked imploringly at her mother and asked, "What's wrong with him?"

As the furtive hands of his mother stroked his face and squeezed his arms, Norman began to stir, then opened his eyes. The anxious group watched as he seemed to focus on their faces, utter a moan, and try to rise.

Again, "What happened?" from his mother.

"I thought you were dead!" from Junior.

"Old Blue kicked me," Norm finally replied, saying it as though he couldn't comprehend that it had happened. The boys had been warned before about trying the trick, and he wasn't eager to admit he had disobeyed his parents' orders. Earlier in the summer, he and Junior had discovered the fun they could have by hitching a ride behind a horse. Soon after their father noticed this activity, their fun had been cut short.

"The horse kicked you? That old horse has always been so patient, so gentle! Why ever would he go and kick you?"

"I did it first, Mother," Junior spoke up. "I grabbed Charlie's tail for a ride. I'm sorry! It's all my fault--I didn't listen to you and Dad." He looked so dejected she actually felt sorry for him, though she inwardly allowed that it probably was his fault.

As Grace studied her son lying on the ground before her, she couldn't decide whether to hug him or to smack him. Being the person she was, she did neither.

"Let's see if you can make it into the house," she said to her son as she and Junior pulled him upright. Norman winced in pain as he leaned on the two who were helping him up the steps.

"You'd better rest on the divan for a while," said his mother. "Your father will be home soon. I need to be finishing up with supper." She went back into the kitchen where he heard her opening and shutting cabinet doors.

Grace called to Patsy, her youngest, to run down to the cellar and bring up a quart of apples, and also a few potatoes from the bin. She asked Marly to peel the potatoes, while she mixed some biscuits for their evening meal. She liked to have it ready when Harvey got back to the house. He was over in the north field now, mowing hay, she supposed. She knew she would soon see him coming up the back lane on his tractor.

Grace dreaded telling Harvey about the afternoon's "accident." Not that she feared he would punish the boys, but rather because she didn't want to give him one more cause for worry. She knew that her husband had much on his mind since he lost the farm two years ago. It had changed him, as she knew was true of countless others in the country who had relied on banks that would ultimately fail.

Harvey blamed himself for whatever hardships they now had. He had wanted to purchase ten more acres to expand their small farm in Johnson County. To do that he had to borrow more on his land. The opportunity was there and the economy seemed stable. Then it was October, 1929, and everything in America changed.

Harvey's tractor was one of the few pieces of machinery he'd been able to keep after the foreclosure. He felt he had to keep it in order to start again, to make some kind of life for his family. He became a tenant farmer and settled on a place near Summerville, Missouri, just a few miles south of the Iowa line and only a few miles from where they had farmed by Junction. The land here was not as good, but he felt lucky to be on a farm where at least they could grow their own food. He'd heard of people in the cities in bread lines. At least he had a way of making a living, even if it wasn't the comfortable living he'd wanted for his family. In addition to the income from the farm, he served as substitute mail carrier for Rural Free Delivery west of Summerville. He was thankful that his wife was a frugal homemaker. She and Marly put up vegetables from their garden every year and they had a few fruit trees as well. He decided that times were bad but they could be worse.

Like both his sons, Harvey was darkly handsome, with penetrating eyes that appeared to harbor a secret, to anyone who didn't know him. His facial features were well defined, with no particular characteristic pronounced enough to be notable. He was of medium build, neither large nor small, and his muscular frame was typical for a man accustomed to hard physical labor. Patsy fell on him first when he reached the yard.

"Norman's been kicked by Old Blue! Come and see him in the front room, Daddy!"

Alarmed, he hurried to the house, but when he saw Grace, concerned but composed, he knew the boy must not be seriously injured. Norman was lying back on the divan, made comfortable, as much as possible, with the pile of pillows Patsy had gathered up.

"Let me take a look at you, son," Harvey said, as he knelt beside the divan. Norman unbuttoned his shirt to expose the scraped flesh on his chest, beginning to turn from red to purple in a circular area under his right nipple.

"Does it hurt very much?" his father asked.

"Mostly if I move, I guess," Norman answered. "I'm sorry. I was dumb to do it. I guess I scared Old Blue and he kicked out at me. I should've listened to you, Dad."

Norman went on to tell his father about how he had yanked Old Blue's tail and how the horse had thrown his foot back at him, knocking him unconscious beside the windmill.

"How did you get to the house?" Harvey asked.

"Junior carried me, I guess," was all he knew to answer.

His father looked startled. "That must be nearly a quarter of a mile! And he's hardly as big as you are!" It was not easy to picture this in his mind. Harvey gave his wife a reassuring smile as he mulled over the situation.

"Maybe it'd be a good idea to have Doc Farrell drive out to look at him tonight. He may be hurt on the inside. Doc's got a reliable car and the roads are in fair shape. Would you give him a ring, Grace?" Harvey saw the worried look on Norman's face and he reached out to tousle his son's hair before he rose and went out to clean up.

"What's for supper?" Harvey asked of Grace later, as he reentered the kitchen.

"Pork roast, mostly," she replied as she began setting the food on the table. "Marly, why don't you fill a plate for Norman to have his supper where he's at? It's probably best that he doesn't move around too much." She had called Doc and expected to see him here in an hour or so.

"Where's Junior?"

"He's still out milking. I suppose it'll take him quite awhile since he usually has help," Grace said.

"I'll go out and give him a hand, or two," Harvey said as he hurried out the back door.

After supper Patsy and her mother did up the dishes while Marly went to the rain barrel for water to wash her hair. The barrel was under the back corner of the house and she dipped the bucket down to draw out enough water for her purpose. Their previous house had had a cistern and water was pumped from it to the house so she hadn't had to go through all this to keep herself fresh. She was the only one who really seemed to mind, as the other children weren't as attuned to personal hygiene as she herself had become.

Marly had a beau now. Her folks didn't care much for him, but then, she figured, whose parents ever thought any boy was good enough for their daughter? He'd be by later to take her for a ride in his parents' Model T. She'd be grateful to get out of the house. Summer was boring, she thought, especially when you lived in the country. On most evenings she had to work in the garden with the other kids. On this evening it was decided that they'd take the night off and keep Norman company in the house.

"Can I have these shoes, Mother?" Marly pointed to a page in the Sears, Roebuck catalogue she had been leafing through. It seemed to Norman that all his sister ever did was mess with her hair and wish in the catalogue. There was a dry goods store in town, but she didn't like the shoes they carried there, thinking they were too plain. She'd be a senior at the high school in Summerville this fall and she was beginning to think of herself as an adult.

Patsy had been reading a book under the lamplight at the table. A little sprite of a girl, she jumped up and ran to the front window where she could see the doctor's car come to a stop in front of the house. Doc Farrell knew the family fairly well, as events such as today's occurred frequently in the family of four active children.

"How are you, Miss, and where is my patient?" he inquired as Patsy met him on the porch.

"I'm good and he's right in here." She led him into the front room where the rest waited.

After exchanging greetings with each of the family, the doctor opened his black bag and proceeded to examine Norman's injury. He felt around the damaged area and asked Norman a few probing questions before concluding that his injury was not serious. He had probably just lost consciousness when the wind was knocked out of him. At worst, he might have a broken rib, but Doc thought that unlikely.

Grace asked if he'd like some coffee before he went on to make another call. She seldom neglected to offer hospitality to anyone who arrived at her house.

Before the dust had settled behind the doctor's departing car, a Model T came up the road and turned into the lane in front of the house. A thickset young man made his way through the front gate and up to the porch. Again, Patsy was quick to get to the door and let the fellow in.

"Come in, Leonard," Grace called from her chair beside the lamp. Harvey was across the table from her, reading. He laid his paper down and spoke to Leonard, then said something about needing to sharpen a saw and left the room.

Leonard noticed Norman lying on the divan and moved to where he could talk to him.

"You're awfully quiet tonight," he offered, hoping to start a conversation.

"Norman had a little accident today," his mother volunteered. "I think he will be a bit quiet for several days. Let's hope so, anyway. Patsy, go see of Marly's about ready."

Norman then told Leonard the main points of the story concerning his accident, to which the older boy showed a small degree of interest. Norman was already getting tired of having to lie still and his soreness prevented him from enjoying anyone's company, so the two soon became quiet. Marly entered the room. Norman noticed how she was never present when Leonard came but seemed to "make an entrance" later. She was beginning to be a mystery to him, as were all girls, for that matter.

Marly had put waves in her short, brunette hair and was dressed in a skirt and blouse--light and airy, for the July weather. She hadn't much to say to anyone except "See you later," but her mother reminded her as she went out the door that she should be home by ten o'clock.

Grace jumped up from her seat and hurried to the door to call out after them, "Remember, the bridge is still out over by the Dowis place!"

After passing by the divan to stroke Norman's hair, she returned to her chair where she had been letting out the hem in Patsy' dress. It seemed to her she was always letting down or taking up the bottom of something. Marly could do her own sewing now, but the others were growing so fast Grace could hardly keep up with the necessary alterations to their clothing.

While this was going on in the house, Junior was outside taking care of the evening chores, without grumbling this time, which was noted by his mother, who thought, rightly, that he might be feeling a little guilty about his part in Norman's trouble. He had brought in buckets of water to the house and had taken the table scraps out to the pigs--he even shut up the chickens for the night, which was usually Patsy's job.

He was at a restless stage in his growth--always moving, or so it seemed to his parents. Tonight he chose to putter around in the yard. He spoke several times to his father, who sat on the back step sharpening a crosscut saw. The thought occurred to him that his father was always working on something. Harvey did take time to read the Summerville paper and occasionally the farm journal, but mostly he worked on stuff. Consequently, the equipment on the farm, though old, was in good condition, a fact that Junior failed to connect to his father's toil.

Seeing his father work hard, day in and day out, year after year, repeating the same tasks over and over, Junior often wondered, *What's it all for?* Already he was anxious to get away from the farm. This year he'd still be at Lone Star School--another year yet before he could go to town to high school with Norman. He and Patsy would soon be going to the country school that sat between their home and Summerville. Again he'd have to walk the two miles to school with just his little sister. How tedious it seemed to him!

On the top step of the back porch Harvey sat with the saw balanced across his knees. He considered this easy work--relaxing, actually. He could keep the rhythm of moving the stone over the metal and let his mind wander. He glanced down the road as Leonard's car disappeared around the far curve, unconsciously checking out its speed as he did so. It gave him a funny feeling--sad, somehow. Ever since she had gone to high school he had felt Marly change. Especially now, in Summerville. In Junction they had been near grandparents. Most activities involved family, and besides, he knew everyone in the community, as he had grown up there himself. Here he knew well only those within the Lone Star School District, and the other farm families on his mail route. He felt that Marly knew more people here than he did. She'd always been out-going and, since moving into high school, seemed to always be going off with someone to do something he had no part in.

The school in Summerville was nearly six miles away, and he usually took her in the old car, when he could keep it running and when the roads were passable. She was a stubborn girl, and always found some way to get there when he couldn't take her, even if she had to walk. She seldom had to walk all the way, as folks going to town were quick to give her a lift.

He sighed and stopped to check his work. The saw was sharp, all right, as far as he'd gotten, and he let his arm rest a few minutes before again picking up the whetstone.

A tire swing hung from a tree out by the back gate and he watched Junior as he dangled from it, drawing in the dirt with a stick. *Well, he's winding down, I guess*, Harvey thought. Amusedly, he thought also, *I don't know why I spend time worrying about the rest of them. He's the one that will take watching.* The boy was all arms and legs and couldn't seem to get them all going in the same direction at the same time. Harvey never knew where he might find Junior from one minute to the next. He was always moving on, starting something new before he accomplished anything. It would be a miracle if he were ever any real good on the farm. Harvey hadn't even trusted Norman on his tractor so picturing Junior there was a big stretch.

Dusk had begun to settle in when Harvey looked at the big elm and noticed a few chickens roosting in its lower branches. He walked out to Junior, who had come to a complete standstill in the swing.

"Want to help me get those chickens?" he asked, actually ordered. The two walked quietly to beneath the tree and slowly reached up under the birds that were hunkered down on a limb. Harvey nodded a signal and they each grabbed at the same time, snatching the sleeping birds before they could scramble away. They didn't do much squawking, even as they were carried by their feet, heads down, and tossed into the hen house. *It's like they knew it was coming,* Junior thought, then laughed at himself for having such an idea about chickens, as he figured they must be the dumbest animals on earth.

As they walked together back to the house, Junior reckoned to himself that his mother would have been quite upset if they had let a fox get three of her young Plymouth Rocks for his dinner. They were meant, instead, to be dinners of their own on some future Sundays.

By the time the two entered the house, the others had gone off to bed. The small house had only three bedrooms, so the girls shared a room, as did the boys. Norman was in bed and appeared to be asleep already so Junior quietly slid in beside him. Norman let out a low moan as he was disturbed and Junior was reminded of the day's frightening events and of his part in them.

The parents' bedroom was in the front of the house, having been a parlor before the Bowen family moved in with four children. As Harvey entered, Grace sat on the bed brushing her hair to the side where it bent around her neck and fell to rest on her breast. She wore a sleeveless white slip, airy but modest. He crossed the room and put his hand on her hair--so soft. He felt that there weren't enough soft things in the world anymore. He moved to the little rocker and sat watching her.

"I thought you'd be angry . . . *they* thought you'd be angry." She spoke in a low, quiet voice, the one she used when they were alone. The children often heard them in here at night, speaking so softly it seemed a language they couldn't understand. Neither of their parents talked much, it appeared to them, except in their room--a secret place reserved only for them.

"Well . . ." he said.

She looked at him. "Did *you* ever do something like that?"

"Well," he said again and grinned. "At least I stayed away from the hooves. Horses don't like that much. Yes, I guess I did try it a few times."

She gave him a knowing glance. No wonder he'd warned the boys. There's nothing like first-hand experience, and she figured Harvey had probably once been a lot like Junior was now--act first and think later, maybe.

The lacy curtains billowed into the room as a breeze swept from one window to the other. The couple had placed the iron bed between the corner windows to get all the cooling air the narrow openings would allow.

Grace laid her brush on the table beside the bed and Harvey rose and pushed the button to switch off the light. He felt soothed by this, and cooler. He'd never grown accustomed to the bright light that completely flooded the room. When he was a boy at home, they'd had kerosene lamps that warmed little circles of light around themselves. His body still obeyed the cycles of nature--rising and resting with the sunlight. The only light left in the room now came from outdoors, and he felt himself drawn to the comfort of their bed. A tiredness was with him that seemed almost constant. The bare floor was cool under his feet as he crossed the room to his side of the bed and sank down heavily.

The crickets outside sang so loudly that Grace felt she must shout to him, right beside her. "Can we go down to Junction on Sunday? I'll telephone the folks tomorrow and tell them about Norman. They'll want to see for themselves that he's okay."

"Sure. I need to get a can of gas for the tractor anyhow," he replied. They frequently traveled the eight miles south to visit her parents, who had retired from farming and moved into town a few years back.

"It'll give the kids a chance to be with some of their old friends a bit. Junior and that neighbor boy always hit it off, and Marly will want to run over and see Betty." She turned to face him. "I'm afraid Leonard is getting the feeling that you don't like him."

"Well, that would be about right."

"He's a nice boy . . . " she began.

"I don't know. He just seems so . . . common, I guess," Harvey said with a sigh.

Grace smiled to herself. She knew her daughter was not a raving beauty, but certainly her father saw her as one.

They lay quietly for a while, watching the shadows in the room as moonlight flowed through the fluttering curtains. How could he tell her that sometimes he felt as if his family were breaking apart--like he was losing control? She was so steady, trusting, confident.

"I'm worried about Marly," he said at last.

"And why?" she asked, knowing.

"I don't know. She seems different."

"She's never disappointed you."

"No."

"Remember when they had that box social at the school last spring?" Grace asked him.

"Yeah."

"Remember how so many boys bid on her box besides Leonard? And you were proud of her then. It was obvious."

"But this is different. Personal," he allowed.

"It's the way it's going to be," she answered flatly. "It's the way it should be."

He grunted and turned to face the night breeze. She put her hand gently on his shoulder.

Lit by the moonlight, the small room was a cocoon of quiet space around the bed. The patterned walls were soft and airy in their fresh dress of wallpaper. In an effort at making the house their own, the couple had hung new wallpaper. For their room, they had chosen a feathery figure that repeated across a pale background. Neither was experienced in the art of paperhanging, so the project had proven to be a test of will versus waste. Grace was reluctant to feel the squishy, lumpy paste on her hands. When the paper was wet, it either stuck tightly in the wrong position or slid off the wall where they wanted it to stay. Especially the ceilings had given them trouble.

Grace thought about this with amusement now. They had enlisted Marly's help, and though she tried, she was worse than her mother at handling the slick, gooey strips of paper. They had begun their work in this room, meaning to practice in an area that would see few guests who might evaluate their work. After cutting the first strip to the width of the ceiling, brushing on the paste, then "booking" it for a few minutes as recommended, Grace lifted the dripping piece to Harvey's waiting hands. He was balanced on a wooden plank stretched between two ladders, with Marly perched on the far one by the opposite wall.

He easily hoisted one end over his head and deftly aligned the edge to the wall before peeling back a layer to expose more of the wet surface. He slid his large hands carefully down the strip while he pushed it securely against the old, discolored paper. He worked his way quickly across the room, as his arms began to tire from holding the paper aloft. He was just about to reach Marly and hand her the end to fit into place when he noticed she was not making a move to help but was just sitting there with a broad grin on her face! At the same instant he felt the air stir behind him and looked around just as the long ribbon of sticky paper whapped him on the head and shoulders. It had loosened behind him, following him slowly across the room until finally the weight of the hanging mass pulled it all down.

A flash of anger quickly came and then passed as he saw the spectacle he had become. He was standing with his hair pasted down to his head, and a long train of white reached the floor beside him. Grace was trying hard to suppress an open laugh, and when she caught his eye he, too, burst out laughing. The three of them enjoyed the merriment for a few moments before both Grace and Harvey jumped to their feet and reached for the precious strip of wallpaper that now lay in a crumpled heap on the floor. They managed to save it to stick up again, with more success the second time.

Remembering this now, Grace experienced again the relief she had felt when she heard Harvey laugh, if only at himself. Moments like that didn't happen often these days, and she clung to them when she found herself beginning to doubt. Times were rough, but many of those she knew were having a much harder time of it than they were. She decided, once again, to count her blessings.

A short time later she heard Harvey snoring softly. She lay back on her pillow with her eyes closed. It seemed a long time that she lay that way, listening. Finally, she heard a car coming up the road and knew if she opened her eyes she would soon see a sweep of light burst through the front window as the beams from the car's headlamps pierced the darkness. A few minutes, then light steps on the porch. A moment or two, then the screen door being quietly closed. Little noises in the house, then giggles from the girls' room next to theirs.

Grace rolled to her side, threaded her arm around her husband's waist, and let the day slip away.

FOUR

It was a high crime day in Bedford, Missouri. Five outhouses had been toppled, and two goats and the superintendent's buggy were placed atop the new brick schoolhouse.

Lizabeth Ann Martin arose early the day after Halloween, eager to get to school. Nora was in the kitchen preparing breakfast for her family and her one lone boarder, the primary teacher at the town's school. Fresh autumn air mingled with the smell of eggs and bacon frying as Lizabeth came sweeping down the stairs and plopped onto one of the sturdy wooden chairs that were pulled up to the table.

"Just some bread and honey for me, Mom," she said as she reached for the bread, still in its wrapper.

"What's the hurry?" asked Nora, in a tone that made Lizabeth feel reproached. "You'll get there before Miss Pratt." She referred to her boarder, who prided herself on being prompt when arriving for her teaching assignment.

"I want to stop at Bobbie's--we have a project to finish." Lizabeth knew she was stretching the truth just a little, but not enough to worry her. "Bye. I'll be home by four for piano lessons!" A couple of younger kids would be coming in the evening for their sessions.

The fall day was brisk so she needed only the sweater she snatched from a hook as she dashed through the back porch. She hurried across the still-green grass and nearly sprinted down the hill toward the large, square house that was home to Rob and Mamie Brooks and their three daughters.

The sound of a car speeding down the hill behind her made Lizabeth hesitate before crossing to the Brooks' yard. She saw Rob leaving in his lumber truck, heading west to his sawmill. The giant jumble of machines sat just off the road about a half-mile out, where the land leveled approaching the Platte River. He nearly filled the cab of the huge truck, and she waved to him and wondered what he would think when he went past the school.

A Hundred Miles to the City

A flurry of colored leaves scattered before her as she kicked her way across the yard and up to the side door, where she called for Bobbie. Mamie came out, wiping her hands on a tea towel, and said to Lizabeth as she led her into the kitchen, "You look like the cat that ate the canary!" which caused Lizabeth to break into a broad grin.

"We've got to hurry on to school. Is Bobbie about ready?"

Lizabeth never knew what to expect at her friend's home. To her the place seemed in constant turmoil. Three big girls, the smallest towering over their diminutive mother, were always dashing in and out and either giggling or fussing at each other. They shared the same clothes and Lizabeth had decided that the first one up evidently had her pick of the wardrobe. She pressed her own skirt flat with her hands as she waited for her friend. She wished Bobbie would hurry--they might miss all the excitement!

"Okay, I'm with you!" Bobbie declared and waved goodbye to her mother as the two girls bounced happily out the door. Mamie had a feeling the two were privy to some secret and she had a suspicion as to what that secret was.

The girls walked side by side, hands laced together. The school was only a block and a half down the street and they expected at any time to hear shouts of surprise and amusement from the schoolyard. Their eyes sparkled with anticipation as they neared for a good view of the entrance.

Both girls stopped. They stared at the front of the school. Nothing was on top of the building! No one was in front of the building. Not one hint of anything out of the ordinary happening there at all!

Bobbie glanced at Lizabeth with a look of astonishment and disappointment. "What happened?" she wondered aloud.

Their desire to rush to school was immediately dashed and they slowed perceptibly as they approached the double doors that led into the wide hall. They stood for a few minutes in the dim entryway. The building was eerily quiet and they felt diminished by the seemingly massive space surrounding them. This was the designated waiting area for early arrivals but the two had never been here when it was actually empty. Mr. McDonald sat in his corner office, apparently engrossed in some paperwork on his desk. Earl Baker shuffled by, pushing his oily mop down the long hall.

They *were* early, an explanation for so little activity. *But,* Lizabeth puzzled to herself, *what could have become of the spectacle on the roof?*

Consumed by curiosity, they summoned the courage to move gingerly to the back of the building, where they still half expected to find a crowd gathered.

Quiet.

They saw no one, not even one of the teachers, as they passed along the hall and into the large girls' restroom. When school was in full swing, this is where the gossip would be flying. *But,* it occurred to Lizabeth, *Bobbie and I are the only girls who know about it!*

A bell sounded and was followed intermittently by the muted crunch of gravel as cars pulled into the parking lot alongside the building. One by one the teachers arrived.

The two girls lingered in the restroom until there were other students in the hall, then quietly slipped through the swinging door to join them. They were growing uneasy about the secret they sheltered. They didn't talk much but listened to those chatting beside them, hoping to learn whether anyone shared their guilty knowledge.

A hundred yards from the Platte River, Rob Brooks threw the switch that brought the massive wheel to life. Its dark metallic teeth spun white with a deafening whine that shut out any verbal interchange between the two men, Rob on one end of the hungry machine and George Gregg on the other. Rob fed in planks of hardwood and George caught them at the other end as they emerged, ripped into twin spans of pungent new wood.

Now and then the two men's eyes met and a smile passed between them. The secret they shared with only C.E. McDonald and Albert Cameron brought memories of escapades of earlier times.

Rob had been called out early in the morning by Albert, shortly after he was approached at the station by C.E. It was not C.E.'s way to get too excited about anything. He had dealt with spunky teenagers long enough to learn their perverse way of antagonizing their elders. So Rob took his truck, mustered out George at his place, and met the other two behind the school. For the second time, the long ladder was placed against the dark bricks and the four worked to undo the deed perpetrated earlier in the night.

Before the sun had climbed to the top of the ridge on the east edge of town, the goats were again frolicking in the Turner yard and C.E.'s buggy, with some of the dust knocked off, was settled back in its place in the shed. Before going in for the breakfast Mamie offered, Rob had laid the ladder beside his shed, again in its place by the alley.

It would be several years before the Brooks girls would learn that their father was one of the group that had pranked the pranksters.

Sophomore English class was taught by Mrs. Coleman, an ample lady who began each day with an informal chat with her students. She stood smiling before them.

"Did any of you participate in Halloween activities last night?" She pronounced it "hollow," as in "empty." She realized it was a leading question and expected she would hear some far-out tales.

"There was a party at the Coulters' last night," Bobbie volunteered.

"And how many of you went to that?"

Several affirming nods could be seen among the dozen students in the room.

"I took some kids trick-or-treating--my little sister and her friends," the Holliday girl chimed in.

Lizabeth and Bobbie were seated in the front row of desk-style chairs. They neither turned nor looked around but nervously concentrated on the tops of their desks. Lizabeth noticed JM scratched on hers and wondered if her brother had sat here and carved his initials into the well-marked wood.

The morning passed slowly for Lizabeth, who felt by now that she just had to talk to someone about the escapade of the night before. However, she knew she mustn't or she'd surely get into big trouble. Only once did she meet one of her cohorts in the hall and exchange a look of bewilderment with him as he passed.

At noon the students were free to go home for lunch, as many did, or they could stay and eat a cold lunch in Mrs. Walters' room, which doubled as a lunchroom. Lizabeth and her brother, Jimmie, were allowed to buy snacks at Earl Rickman' store, as many of the other kids did--either there or at the filling station across the street. The general store was just half a block over into town so those who went there got back to school with plenty of time left for a game on the baseball diamond or in the gymnasium. Consequently, many of the students chose that option.

The oldest Cline boy, now a junior, stopped by at the central office to visit with his mother, Abbie, who ran the switchboard during the day. The office was between the school and the store and Abbie often stepped out of the little one-room building to catch a student and put him on the line for a message from a parent. This happened today, as the group of children walked by, and Lizabeth knew the message surely concerned the pranks of the night before.

More cars than usual were angled into the allotted area for parking, which in Bedford was down the center of the main street. Many of those who had come to town today were in the store, and almost all of them were talking about the Halloween mischief.

Lizabeth caught snatches of conversation as she walked up to the long counter that held a display of packaged cupcakes.

Used to be hay bales burning in the street . . . a dozen outhouses rolled over . . . probably the youngest Turner kid . . . when I was young . . . a herd of goats and a haywagon . . . don't that beat all! . . . one of the Nelson's, I'll guarantee . . . how did they get them up there? . . . looked like somebody might have fallen into the two-holer . . . young hooligans!

On the east aisle of the store, Earl Rickman stood punching in prices on the chrome cash register. He was a rotund man with just a few strands of feathery hair swept across the domed pate of his head. He wore his customary white apron with his shirtsleeves rolled up, looking as if he belonged behind the meat counter instead. He ran the store, the largest business in town, entirely by himself, except for the occasional help of his niece, Hattie, who was as straight as he was round. Hattie's manner also differed from his, confirming Lizabeth's belief that fat people are jollier. She hoped he'd wait on her. He knew all his customers well and always had some personal and positive remark to offer each of them.

"How's Miss Martin?" he asked as she told him her order.

"Good. It sounds like there might have been some excitement in town last night!" She wondered what version of the events he had formed from the tumble of stories going around.

"Sounds like there were some doings at the school. Hard to say what-- everybody has a different take on it. Never as good as the old days, you can bet!"

Lizabeth took her pop and package of cupcakes and left the store. On some days she would cross the street to Richeys' Dry Goods store and browse awhile, but today she hurried past the old millinery shop, glancing inside the high window at the dark, now-empty interior. Her mother and grandmother both had countless creations they'd bought at the little shop before it closed during the Depression. Hard for Lizabeth to imagine now that fancy hats were ever produced there.

Well, if our prank were to be compared to other years, thought Lizabeth, *we did all right!* She remembered that last year a flock of ducks and geese had been relocated to another farmer's pond, and some impounded livestock were set free and herded into town--that and the usual spate of toilet tippings. She guessed her first Halloween out with the older kids had been pretty successful!

"Beth, wait!" It was Jimmie, crossing the street from the filling station.

Uh-oh! He knows, she thought.

"Hold on a minute! I forgot to tell Mom I'd be late from school. I have to stay for play practice. Would you tell her?"

"Sure. Did you hear about the stuff up on the school?" She wanted to know just what he knew.

"Albert said there were two goats and a buggy up there, and I guess he knows since he's always open by six!" The white stucco building with its two pumps sat at an angle to the corner, directly facing the front of the school grounds.

"Who does he think did it?" She had to ask it.

"He doesn't know . . . says they were just up there this morning." Jimmie wasn't surprised at his sister's eager interest. The whole town was talking about it.

"How did they get them down?"

"I think he knows, but he won't say--just grins when you ask him. I'll get it out of him later, I bet, if he knows." Jimmie worked weekends pumping gas at the Conoco station owned by Albert Cameron, and he felt they were pretty chummy by now.

The afternoon session at the school was quite the opposite of the morning's session. The hallway was noisy with laughter, playful kidding, and spirited accusations. It was difficult for the instructors to maintain order in their classrooms and all were obviously anxious for the day to be over. There would be conversations of great seriousness at some of the dinner tables in the town tonight.

The Martin household was one of these. After a pleasant, even quiet, meal with Miss Pratt, Nora confronted her children in the kitchen as they worked together clearing away the dishes.

"What is this I hear about the superintendent's buggy on the roof of our new school?"

Uh-oh! Lizabeth thought. Her mother had an uncanny knack of knowing what went on in the town and she felt a sudden spin of panic.

"Jimmie, I want to know if you had anything to do with the activities at the school last night!" Nora was doing her motherly job of questioning her son, even though she didn't believe for a moment that he might be responsible.

He gave her a direct smile and said nothing. He liked to tease his mother.

"Jimmie Martin, Junior! Tell me the truth right now! Did you?" she asked again, more forcefully this time.

He laughed and assured her that he did not.

Lizabeth, younger than he by two years, could have assured her mother that it was the gospel truth, of course--at least about the schoolhouse part. Her brother hadn't been a witness to those shenanigans, as she had. She felt like an instigator, in a way, knowing the boys probably went to such extreme measures to impress the girls who were present.

What Nora wondered, really, was not so much *who* did it, but *how* did they do it? The reaction that she showed to her children, though, was utter disapproval.

Lizabeth could have answered that one, too--long ladders, ropes, and several big, feisty boys.

Jimmie wondered why his mother didn't question Lizabeth, all the while knowing that she wouldn't. His sister was quite the little actress and wouldn't be suspected of being in any way culpable. Even if he had known that she was, he would never confess to it. He'd made it his personal mission to be her guardian a couple of years ago, after Father had abandoned the family completely.

His sister did have her charms, as he was aware. When he used to deliver the *St. Joseph Gazette* in Bedford he had hired Lizabeth, at a nickel each, to collect from his customers on Saturday mornings. If he found them home, they were likely to tell him to come back some other time, but when Lizabeth knocked on their door they always managed to find the money somewhere. She was too little and too cute to turn away.

"How's play practice coming along?" Nora inquired, changing the subject--to the great relief of Lizabeth.

"Fine," Jimmie replied. "We're using makeup and costumes tomorrow night. Just my good pants and a white shirt are all I need."

"Are you sure you know your lines? Why don't I run through it with you tonight?" she asked eagerly.

"It's okay, Mom. Lizabeth has been helping me, and besides, I left my play book at school."

Nora was clearly disappointed. She didn't even know what the play was about. And it was his senior play! She felt he could do it all right, as far as memorizing his lines. He seemed to enjoy studying, but she worried that he might get stage fright when the time came to perform before a gymnasium full of people. However, Jimmie seemed bent on doing this without her help, so she'd just have to hope he was adequately prepared.

Although slight in stature themselves, both children had already outgrown their mother. Neither had inherited Nora's auburn hair and redhead's complexion. Both were brunettes, with hazel eyes that hinted of humor lying just below the surface.

Nora knew she was blessed to have healthy offspring, both capable and willing to help out with family finances whenever they could. But, in the timeless pattern of doting mothers with growing teenagers, Nora could feel her children slipping away from her. It seemed to her that they were seldom home. Besides pumping gas at Albert's station, Jimmie often worked as a farm hand. In the summers he worked stripping bluegrass for Carl McGeorge, who owned their house as well as most of the bottomland in this part of the county. Lizabeth gave piano lessons, was in glee club and went to volleyball practice several evenings each week.

A Hundred Miles to the City

Resettling in Bedford had been easy for Nora. She had graduated from the old school herself in 1914--had spent her entire life near the town until she married Jimmie Martin.

They lived for a while in Madison and then in St. Joseph, where they'd had indoor plumbing. She had become accustomed to these amenities. Having to go back to carrying in well water and using outdoor facilities was quite an adjustment for her and for the children. She still had the comfort of her elegant furniture, though, and her determination to make a good home for her family.

Her parents, Jed and Merry Torrance, still lived in the farmhouse where she grew up and where Jimmie and Lizabeth were both brought into the world. The Torrances had lost most of the farm when the banks failed, and the land was now converted to producing bluegrass for Carl McGeorge. Jed had been a successful breeder of horses and mules and had hoped to hand the farm down in the family. Still, they had a comfortable living and helped Nora and her family as much as she'd allow.

Nora's income came mostly from her many piano students and her boarder, plus income from the chickens she kept. She enjoyed gardening and had one of the largest and most bountiful in town. Morning and evening, her broad-brimmed straw hat could be seen bobbing up and down as she hoed in the ample garden plot beside the house.

"How about reciting your lines for me, just to see if you're ready for an audience?" she insisted now.

"No, Mom," he replied firmly. "You'll have to wait for my great debut on Friday. My part's not really that important, anyhow."

Now in his seventeenth year, Jimmie had finally won the jeans versus overalls argument with his mother. He'd had a growth spurt at last and was no longer the smallest boy in his class. In his own personal assessment, Jimmie had passed from "puny" to the more creditable "wiry." He was tall enough now to be a starter on the school's basketball team, the Bears, a position that had recently given him cause for embarrassment. He was playing in an intramural game after school one evening. He'd quickly shoved his warm-ups down at the start of the contest and realized he'd forgotten to put on his shorts! Luckily, he had remembered the jock strap, but he was mortified and considered bolting for home. Instead he ran to the locker room and fetched the appropriate apparel, feeling a deep flush that he failed to shake the entire game. He thought he'd never have survived the dilemma if he'd done it at a night game in front of strangers--and worse, the whole town!

"Herbert's coming on Friday and bringing his girl friend and Aunt Sadie," Nora announced.

"Great!" Jimmie replied. He'd be glad to see Herbert. He was his oldest cousin and before they moved away had been like a big brother to him. Herbert was a twin, but his sister had died at three years of age with diphtheria, and Jimmie and Lizabeth never knew her.

"What time should we be down at the school?" Nora asked her son.

"If you want good seats near the front, about six-thirty, I guess." He didn't know if it would be good or bad to look out and see his family right in front. He was experiencing some nervousness at the prospect of being on the stage. Maybe he'd get a feel for it tomorrow night at rehearsal--he hoped so.

Lizabeth listened with one ear as she let her mind wander back to the pleasurable adventure of the night before.

Several kids from Bedford had gone out to Coulters', east of town, for a party. They'd bobbed for apples, consumed cider and candy, and played "kick the can." After the party some of them were returned to town in the back of Coulters' stock truck. They were singing and having a good time-- Lizabeth hadn't wanted the night to end. A large group had hung around in the schoolyard for a while, drifting around to the playground where they remained, swaying on the swings and lounging on the dry grass. A bright harvest moon hung over the town, flooding the yard with a warm glow.

Lizabeth didn't know who first came up with the idea. The youngsters sat gazing at the top of the school, which could be seen nearly as well as in daylight. Almost as one they knew there was an opportunity for fun right in front of them. The back of the building didn't look too tall. The other sides had a brick ridge atop the wall, perhaps for ornamentation or maybe to hide the gentle backward slope of the roof. Somehow, it seemed to beckon to them, as if calling for something to adorn the flat surface, so like a platform.

"How high do you suppose it is?" one boy queried.

"Ten, maybe twelve feet, I'd guess," said another.

"My dad has a really long ladder. It's out in back of the shed," volunteered Bobbie, as she smiled mischievously.

"Let's see what it looks like up there!" one of the boys urged.

So off they'd gone--a group of six boys, whispering loudly.

As they waited, the girls assessed the situation. The school faced the town, with a road and railroad tracks on one side, and no dwellings in back of the school before the first farmhouse a mile north. It was the farm home of Lizabeth's Torrance grandparents and she wondered fleetingly if they might be able to see the activities at the school. But she was sure they couldn't possibly, that far, at night. And besides, they would be in bed by now.

The boys soon came staggering across the schoolyard bearing the heavy wooden ladder. They anchored one end against the bricks of the schoolhouse and "walked" the ladder up to the building.

"Me first!" a large boy insisted, as he pushed his way to the front and mounted the ladder. Soon several were on the roof. The girls watched them silhouetted there, gesturing and talking excitedly.

They had evidently formulated a plan, for within an hour they had "borrowed" another ladder, coaxed two goats from the Turners' yard, and stealthily rolled Mr. McDonald's old buggy from its shed two blocks away. They also brought several lengths of rope, from which they fashioned a sling to hoist the goats onto the roof. The animals were raised aloft, bleating and pawing wildly at the air. Once set on their feet they scampered away to the far corners of the roof.

The topless buggy was not large but rather heavy. The boys attached ropes to the axles, then mounted the roof for the tremendous effort required to raise the clumsy object. It shuddered and lurched, wheels spinning dizzily in the moonlight, as the boys labored to haul it up the wall and over the edge of the roof. When they finally managed to get it set upright they rolled it over to the front of the building and positioned it on top of the main entrance. They then hurried to slither down the ladders and rush to the front of the school to admire their masterpiece.

"Hot diggity!" Charlie exclaimed. "Wait 'til old C.E. sees this!"

"Shhh! Don't let them catch us now!" whispered one of the others.

The group lingered awhile, praising their own efforts, then reluctantly began the task of returning the ladders to their appointed places and going home to await the excitement that the morning would surely bring.

Lizabeth realized she was smiling with these thoughts now and hurriedly turned away to stack the dishes up in the cabinet.

Dress rehearsal for the senior play was held on Thursday night. Mrs. Coleman was the class sponsor so her duties included directing the chosen script, a comedy as usual. It would be presented for the public the next night. She was both excited and apprehensive about the performance. It would be the first play enacted in the new school. The building had a real stage, with backdrops and red velvet curtains that slid noiselessly across the apron and could be manipulated between scenes. Mrs. Coleman knew a lot was expected of her on the upcoming premiere night, and she wasn't totally confident that either she or her actors would measure up to the anticipations of their audience.

The gymnasium was built onto the back of the school, like the leg of a T, with double doors on either side. Two tiers of built-in bleachers lined the walls of this large area, forming an auditorium of sorts. On this night the performers were to meet in Mrs. Coleman's room, in costume, to have make-up applied by some classmates.

"Your turn, Jimmie," Mrs. Coleman instructed, shortly after his arrival.

"You have to sit really still," Crystal told him as she draped a towel around his neck. He liked the feel of her hands on his face as she lightly rouged his cheeks. Then she worked on his eyes and he felt he would sneeze, but she managed to get some lines on his brows without poking him. Jimmie's high cheekbones were accentuated when he smiled, which, as now, was more of a shy grin than an open-mouthed smile. His prominent chin tended to overpower his lips and vie for dominance with the nose above. His eyes were bright beneath arched eyebrows, giving his face a slightly quizzical look. It was difficult for Jimmie to appear angry--an emotion he rarely experienced.

The lipstick was the hard part. Crystal kept telling him to tighten his lips but he didn't know how. She showed him and they began giggling and Mrs. Coleman had to give them her teacher look.

Jimmie couldn't believe how fluttery his stomach became when he was under the bright lights of the stage and facing the dark, cavernous gym! It looked different than at ball games.

His best buddy, Burl Dean Wardloe, had the most important role in the play. Burl Dean knew his lines perfectly and seemed to enjoy being on stage.

After several starts and stops the play progressed smoothly for a while. About five minutes into the second scene, Jimmie forgot his next line. He stood staring at Burl Dean and waiting for Crystal to prompt him from off stage.

"Preacher Brown's hog got loose . . ." came the words.

"Preacher Brown's hog . . ." Jimmie started to repeat, then broke into a smile as everyone started hooting and howling. No Preacher Brown in this script . . . nor hog.

Mrs. Coleman strode up to the stage and demanded to know what was so funny, but all Jimmie said was, "I forgot my lines."

"Okay, let's get serious, now. Back to Burl Dean's line at the top." She was ready to wring some necks if only she knew whose to grab.

After they'd finally struggled through the rehearsal, Jimmie went backstage to catch Crystal.

"Why'd you do that to me?" he demanded.

She smiled coyly and said, "Sorry. Just wanted to see what you'd do. Wasn't it fun?" He had a feeling she was part of a conspiracy to add a little levity to the evening. She was usually nice to him. He thought she even paid special attention to him sometimes. He guessed there was just no way to tell about girls.

On Friday, the evening meal at the Martin home was largely a waste of time and good food, as Nora was nearly as edgy as Jimmie at the prospect of his performance, and Lizabeth was too excited to eat. She was eager to meet Bobbie at the school and enjoy the excitement of another special occasion.

Nora was on the telephone talking with her mother when Jimmie paused on his way out the door. He told her he was leaving and nervously whispered, "The play's named after you, Mom." Lizabeth heard it, too, and gave him a surprised but approving glance.

Into the phone, Nora continued: "Will you and Dad come up to the house after the play? . . . Uh-huh . . . Of course he'll want to see Herbert, too, you know . . . Yes . . . We'll meet at the school . . . Bye now."

Nora thought about what her son had said, puzzling over it for a bit. Then she became engrossed in her preparations for entertaining her guests later. She had baked a batch of cookies that afternoon and now stirred together a simple fruit punch for her company. She arranged the table with the required serving utensils and set out glasses and small plates, then hurried to dress for the occasion.

It was almost six-thirty, and Aunt Sadie and her group were about to be late. Jimmie had taken the car on down to the school. He did most of the driving for the family now. Nora was spunky enough to learn to drive when she was first married but had happily turned that responsibility over to her son when he became of age. She hadn't needed to teach him to drive, as he'd had practice driving tractors.

Nora donned her hat and gloves, ready and waiting. She hardly left the house without a hat, no matter the occasion. She wore hats well, with her bright auburn hair and broad smile. A chaos of freckles danced across her face, but still she was a handsome woman.

Nora was just about to summon her daughter and step out the door to walk down the hill when she saw Herbert's car pull off the highway and into the drive. Before the group could alight from the car, she and Lizabeth rushed out to greet them.

"Well, my! You do look beautiful!" she said to Sadie, who awaited them in the back seat. Nora always paid a compliment when she greeted someone. She found Herbert's date "charming," and her nephew "dashing" and "debonair."

In the back of her mind Nora had worried that the Torrances might not come tonight. She hadn't seen them for over a year. Sadie had moved her son to St. Joseph to finish school after her husband had been found guilty of embezzling from the Bank of Bedford. The bank had gone broke in 1930, and Vincent had been loan officer when the funds were discovered missing. He had maintained his innocence, and no one in the family could believe him responsible. Most people in the town had a good understanding of the circumstances that caused him to be in such trouble, and several had appeared in court to plead on his behalf. However, despite their ardent support, he was found guilty under the law and sent off to the state penitentiary in Jefferson City to serve a term of ten years.

The trip to school was a simple matter of travelling a few blocks down the hill. By the time Nora and her guests arrived, the large parking area was full and people had begun leaving their cars on the grass. A large white globe glowed at each side of the double doors that gave access to the gymnasium.

As she stepped onto the wide sidewalk that skirted the side of the school, Nora noticed the Robertsons approaching. She felt a momentary stirring of animosity as she wondered whether they would speak to Sadie and Herbert. Calvin Robertson had been a schoolmate of Vincent's, and Nora was surprised when he failed to support her brother during his financial difficulty.

Nora put on her brightest face and spoke to the trio as they neared. They returned her greeting, but she thought them a little less than enthusiastic in their response. She wondered whether her brother would ever be able to atone for his "sins" in the eyes of some people. She was determined never to waver in her support of Vincent or his family.

Rows of folding chairs had been set to face the stage, and most were occupied, so the group had to sit near the back of the large room. As Nora read the program handed to her at the door, her eyes began to fill and she reached for her handkerchief. The name of the play was *The Best Mother*. Nora swallowed hard and blinked before she shared with Sadie the words her son had spoken to her before he left the house.

It no longer mattered to her how well he did or did not know his lines, or what some people might think of the Torrances. Nora's brown eyes glistened as the lights dimmed to herald the evening's production.

FIVE

By 1934 the town of Summerville had undergone visible changes. The hitching posts were removed from the square to accommodate more visitors to the annual fair, the livery stable was closed for a lack of equine patrons, and a skating rink had been built on the south side of the business district.

The passenger train that arrived daily from Des Moines often brought a long-absent male member back to the community. These men had a war-worn look to them, thin and haggard. Many had spent much of their time away riding the rails, not in the passenger cars, but lying on top of freight trains or clinging beneath the noisy behemoths. Hitchhiking was a safer means to a far-away destination, but the rails were much quicker, if less hospitable.

The local economy had improved some in the last year or two. President Roosevelt's social programs were beginning to be felt in America's heartland. Young men found work in the CCC camps and sent funds back to help their families at home. People still struggled to make ends meet, but the gloomy atmosphere that had hung over the community began to lift, replaced by confidence born of surviving in spite of great hardships.

The Schmit family was faced with problems related to the current economic climate. Earlene had graduated from high school and had married Emmett. They now lived in a tiny house in Summerville. As for Miriam, she was gone from home also, as she had left for California to find work where her friend was employed in Carmel. Vera's family had moved out West when they heard of opportunities for her father in construction.

On the day Miriam left, Dona felt the family begin to crumble. In a way, her older sisters had been buffers between her parents and between Sam and Grant. Despite the rigors of their circumstances, both older girls possessed a gentle dignity that inspired a peaceful atmosphere when they were present. Perhaps being nurtured in a more settled, affluent time in the lives of their parents had given them an inner security their younger siblings never knew. Whatever the reason, Dona sensed that their absence would cause the family to suffer in ways that vaguely frightened her.

Miriam was excited to be going. She had heard from Vera about the wonderful climate and beautiful beaches in California. Miriam had never seen the ocean. The chance for a new life opened before her. And, except for missing each of her family on a very intimate level, she was more than eager to leave the dreary circumstance that their lives had become.

Retha had given birth to a baby girl the year before. The child was born with a cleft palate and unable to suckle, so within a matter of days she had literally starved to death despite all attempts to nurture her. The child's birth and death caused great sadness in the whole family, and Retha went into a dark depression that would cloud her spirit for endless months.

As the train thundered into the depot, Dona stood on the platform with Miriam and her battered old suitcase. She hadn't much with which to start her new life. Dona had bought her a pretty handkerchief from the dime store in Rock Port and Retha had packed some sandwiches for her long trip. She carried these in a big purse, along with personal items and a supply of glamour magazines that were less than current.

Miriam waited nervously as the conductor alighted from the now-quiet train. He placed a portable step stool beneath the metal stair that gave access to the passenger compartment.

Miriam had felt the strife in the family grow with the years and in a way she would be glad to escape the tension she often knew at home. She gave Retha a hug and kiss and squeezed her younger sisters. She guiltily felt that her leaving was somehow a betrayal of them. She wanted to hug her father and the boys, too, but knew Sam would disapprove and so decided to just wave, which she did with as much cheer as she could muster and then hurried to board the train.

The whole Schmit family, including Earlene and Emmett, had come to see her off. Retha stood weeping, with her hands tightly clutching Carrie's little shoulders. The child stood in front of her and Retha clung to her to keep her from danger and also to give herself comfort. There would be no comforting words between Sam and Retha. Indeed, any stranger who happened to be passing through could read much of the family's history by their posture in the early morning gathering at the station. Sam and Retha stood separately, Retha holding onto Carrie, with Emmett and Earlene making a small group, Dona staying close to Hank, and Grant sitting by himself a distance away on some shipping crates.

With a deafening roar, the train came to life and slowly began rolling on the tracks, each successive car exploding into action as the couplings engaged with a clang. The family stood silently and waited until two loud blasts on the locomotive's air horn announced the presence of danger at the intersection. The train began to pick up speed, and as soon as the passenger car slid down the track on its way to Kansas City, Sam turned and headed for the nearest tavern, his frequent haven in times of despair.

For more than a year the Schmit family had lived in a small one-story house a mile west of Summerville. It sat nearly atop the blacktop highway, so for the first time in many years the likelihood of impassable roads was no longer a worry. The size of the house did present unique problems, however. The three tiny bedrooms, living room, and kitchen didn't allow room for the grown children to have space for themselves. That reality undoubtedly contributed to some of the problems within the family.

There had been fights, both verbal and physical, between Grant and his father for several years, which Retha had tried to mediate, making her feel bad for taking one's side against the other. Because Grant was more vulnerable and her son, she usually stood up for him in his altercations with Sam.

Grant had wanted to join a CCC camp, but his father wouldn't hear of it. Sam regarded the government-sponsored program to be a form of relief, and he was not about to accept that. The lad felt that his father thwarted him at every turn.

This spring Grant had gotten into a new kind of trouble concerning a young woman. Her father had come to Sam to complain that Grant had treated his daughter badly, disrespectfully, when they'd been out together. When Sam confronted Grant about the matter, he was sullen and resentful of any interference. He considered himself a man and would do as he pleased. So Sam immediately formed a new rule for Grant's behavior. He was not to see a girl from now on unless accompanied by someone else. He obviously could not be trusted alone with a woman.

It seemed to Retha that Sam put his feelings of pride before any concern for the well-being of his children. She began to deeply resent his attitude toward Grant and found it harder and harder to accept the treatment that she saw as cruel and abusive. Few kind words passed between them, and their strained relationship became a burden for the children of the family as well.

Retha joined the Dorcas Society, a local ladies' group formed to provide a network for sharing ideas to cope with the Depression. At the meetings the ladies suggested shortcuts to doing chores and gave hints for saving money in innovative ways. This bolstered the confidence of the women. Knowing they were not alone in their distress lightened their burdens.

Retha began to assert herself in the running of the household. She was less likely than before to just go along with anything Sam wished. She also joined a quilting group in Summerville, where the ladies met and sewed while discussing problems common to all. They caught up on the latest gossip and learned what was going on in other homes in the community.

The unfortunate result of this change in Retha's perception of herself was that it brought about a negative response in Sam. The stronger she became, the weaker and more inadequate he felt. Neither was conscious of this happening, but it was a widespread malady of men in the thirties. Many were able to work, yearned to work, but could find no opportunity for employment. This year the grasshoppers had come in swarms and stripped the leaves off the corn in the fields so the Schmits' only cash crop was Retha's chickens. She always ordered a couple of hundred baby chicks from the hatchery in the spring, raising them in the brooding house until they were big enough to scratch around for themselves, then letting them run in the chicken coop. In midsummer she and the girls would dress them and take them in to Summerville or Rock Port to sell. They had done well this year, except for those that had escaped the coop and been run over on the busy road in front of the house.

Retha was a hard worker and there was plenty of it for her to do, from sunup to sundown: raising a garden, canning, and sewing for her family. Sam often felt as if he were just another mouth to feed, as if he contributed nothing to the welfare of the family. It wasn't true. He kept firewood cut and split for the heating and cooking stoves, and he put meat on the table by hunting, trapping and fishing--his favorite pastime. Still, he felt that he was a failure in his role as breadwinner and couldn't express it or alleviate the situation in any way.

Retha suspected that some of the feelings of disappointment he suffered were due to some extent to the fact that her parents, also farmers, had been able to keep a good standard of living throughout the hard times. Unlike the Schmits, they owned their farm. It was located in the Orrsburg community, a short distance from Easton, and had been in the family for more than two generations. They had given Retha a large dowry when she married, as they had their other six daughters. Retha was the second in a family of twelve and had come to the marriage with an abundant knowledge of the rearing of children and skilled in the day to day tasks involved in running a household.

When the older children were young, Retha and Sam had been able to provide extras for the family, such as photographs of the babies at christening ceremonies. By the time Dona came along, these amenities had necessarily been pared back. At the time of Carrie's birth, such things were long-ago luxuries, and not a single picture of the child was taken until she went to school.

Surviving day to day became a difficult struggle that wore on the temperament of each of the family. There were some good times, as there are in all large families, but those times had become rare and precious. It seemed that Sam succumbed to a feeling of hopelessness that took control of all their lives. To Sam, life had become just one disappointment after another. He was adrift in a sea of melancholy, and his entire family was marooned there as well.

The wide-crowned trees over the park had been hung with powerful floodlights that illuminated the August night. The burning day had given way to the cool shadows of dusk by the time the Schmit family arrived in Summerville, and Dona rushed to meet her friends beside the bandstand.

The dress she wore was of gingham, checked black and white, with a broad, flat collar trimmed in white. It was the one dress her father had bought for her, when she graduated from Harmony School two years earlier. She had been given a solo to sing at the program, and he had taken her into Easton so they could together choose the dress--the first store-bought dress purchased for her. He hadn't attended the program the night she was promoted from the eighth grade. She guessed he'd heard her sing plenty of times at home when Retha accompanied her on the organ.

She felt good in the dress. Most of her things had been styled to fit her two older sisters, both of whom were slender-hipped and modestly flat, in the flapper style. Both Earlene and Miriam were petite and demure, their gentle dignity reflecting an inner confidence. Dona, however, was boisterous and energetic, displaying much less polish and composure. She was vibrant and spirited and unlike them in shape, as well as demeanor. She was decidedly full of form, having more curves than were required for her female role in life. With large brown eyes, an ample nose and a broad smile, Dona's features drew attention to her slightly full, oval face and gave her a dramatic, not dainty, appearance. Black curls swirled in disarray atop her head.

Dona's place in the family had become, since Carrie's birth, that of a middle-child's circumstance. After a long period of being indulged as the baby of the family, she felt herself transformed into an unappreciated, superfluous member of the household. She had begun to assert her independence and attempted to add color to her restricted existence by indulging in a rich fantasy life. Recently, however, she had given up her fantasy of being a boy and doing things with Hank. Her dreams now consisted of being in a secure home of her own and having vigorous, healthy babies, at least one of which would look just like Shirley Temple.

On this night her head was filled with the gaily lit, swirling rides of the traveling carnival set up in the town square. The usual sounds of the summer night were out-shouted by the staccato voices of excited revelers and the gay music that poured from the carousel turning near the center of the park. Other rides and small concession stands lined the streets surrounding the grassy square.

Dona and Helen, along with another friend, Bea, strolled slowly down the sidewalk that angled through the park. On one side were tables covered with jars of homemade jams and jellies, pies and cakes of various sorts, and huge vegetables, scrubbed and shining. Each display had a bright ribbon attached that announced the favor it had found in the eyes and on the palates of the judges.

On the other side, rows of handmade crocheted work, needlepoint, quilts, aprons and other domestic crafts testified to the home-making skills of the women of the community. Not *entirely* women. Retha had entered a set of embroidered pillowcases of Hank's, though he wouldn't allow her to put his name on them. He hadn't won a prize ribbon, but she was proud of his efforts just the same.

"Let's take a ride!" Bea exclaimed as the girls approached the merry-go-round. Its gaily-painted ponies reared and lunged, bobbing crazily in a fluid circle of color.

"I get the black one!" Dona shouted as each girl raced to catch an empty steed. She placed her foot on the metal bar and levered herself up to sit sideways on the hard wooden seat. Bea's long legs nearly reached the platform beneath her mount, and each girl grasped the shiny cylinder in front of her and held on tightly. A young man in dingy, stained overalls weaved his way through the now frozen beasts, collecting tokens from the eager riders. The girls flirted and posed for the boy's benefit, instinctively knowing that a smile from them would elicit an extra-long turn on the ride.

The bright lights surrounding the central mass of the carousel danced as the horses swung by. Circus-like music rang from the huge barrel organ, so loudly that the girls had to shout to be heard above the melodious, flowing notes. Dona threw her head back and let the night air flutter through her short curls. The soft skirt of her dress flapped gently against her ankles as the horse lunged again and again into the air, climbing a mountain of space. The ride was exhilarating! The girls laughed and shouted as they spotted acquaintances, and waved like children enjoying a great adventure.

The music, and the ride, went on and on until Helen began to feel ill. She was thinking that maybe they had overdone it with their friendly gestures when finally the whirling machine began to slow and the platform shuddered to a stop. One by one the dizzy riders stumbled off the boards of the narrow walkway, staggering drunkenly this way and that, nearly falling over one another. The trio clung together for balance, giggling foolishly.

After she had regained a sufficient measure of equilibrium, Dona strolled over to the young man who stood by the levers that governed the machine's action, waiting for a new crop of riders to claim the waiting animals.

"Where's the brass ring? Aren't you supposed to have a brass ring?" she boldly asked.

"What?"

"Carousels are supposed to have a brass ring you try to catch as you go around," she smartly informed him. "It's supposed to bring you luck!"

"Oh! Maybe you'll get lucky anyhow!" he suggested, as he gave her a lop-sided grin.

The girls snickered and elbowed each other as they walked away.

"You'd better look out!" Helen warned. "He may try to follow you home!"

Dona was hardly worried about such a possibility. Hank would always be there to oversee her safe passage back to the Schmit home. Dona had been warned not to associate with the "carny" people. They had a reputation for being reckless and even dangerous. Retha's admonishments were a little less than convincing, however, since her own brother had run away and joined the circus some years before.

"How're you doing, Toots?" Emmett spoke up as the three exuberant teenagers approached him and his wife where they stood holding hands. Earlene's other arm encircled a large floppy-eared dog that appeared to be stuffed with straw.

"See what we won!" she announced.

"How did you do it?" Bea inquired with interest.

Earlene gave her husband a conspiratorial smile.

"Very little skill and a whole lot of luck. Actually, you throw balls at milk bottles until the man gets weary and gives you a prize out of desperation!" she told them. "Are you girls having a good time?"

"Heaps! We've just begun! Have you run into the folks? They've brought Carrie." Until this year it had been Dona's job to take her younger sister around at the fair. Earlene was happy that Dona had the freedom of being out on her own for once. Earlene frequently asked her over to their house for overnights. She felt guilty for her own happiness with Emmett and would like to make life a little easier for her family if she could.

"See you later!" and the girls were off again, looking for more familiar faces as they wove their way through the crowd of people.

Smells of hot dogs and popcorn drifted through the evening air and mixed with the sweet aroma of petunias set in orderly beds along the park's wide sidewalk. The girls chattered and ducked around small groups engrossed in conversation and were themselves jostled as excited children dashed by.

Scattered between the rides and concession stands were small booths where vendors hawked gas-filled balloons and souvenir trinkets. Several tents had been erected to hide exotic temptations meant to lure nickels and dimes from their curious owners.

"Step right up! See the two-headed baby! She's real! She's a beauty! See her right before your eyes! She's here! One thin dime to see this marvelous glitch of nature! Step right up!" The animated barker called from the entrance to a garish, well-worn canvas tent.

Dona had no desire to go in. She gave her companions a disgusted look and turned to find a boy standing almost at her toe-tip. He was dark and smiling, but he wasn't talking. He just stood and waved a little paper thing he had on his finger. It was a Chinese puzzle toy made with a tube of woven paper that stretched to grasp your fingers when you tried to pull them apart--one of the variety of prizes offered at the games of chance on the midway.

Finally, he did say, "Hi!" and then turned away to rejoin his friends, who waited nearby.

In a moment she remembered where she had seen him before. He was the one from Arkoe School she had competed against in a ciphering match more than a year ago! She remembered her impression of him then--longhaired and clumsy. She watched the boys walk away and wondered why he'd come and gone so abruptly.

The next time she saw him, Dona was in the drugstore with Hank, having a soda and looking through a stack of old comic books. Lately she had begun staying in town with Hank on Saturday afternoons, just hanging around with friends. Often one of his buddies would invite her to a movie. It was just ten cents but it was more than she had, so she was glad to accept the offer. Hank was always there, too, so she guessed it really wouldn't be called a date.

She saw him come in, obviously with his brother, they looked so much alike. She found out after they left that the boys were named Bowen--June and Norman, June being the younger, taller one. Both were ruggedly handsome, with sharply chiseled features punctuated by dark hair and eyes. While Norman's countenance was open and friendly, June's heavy brow ridge gave him a reserved, moody look. His wide smile quickly revealed a gentle vulnerability that Dona found charmingly seductive. She hoped he would be in Summerville often.

A Hundred Miles to the City

Several months passed before she saw him again. This time he approached her and they spoke for a while. She learned that he was a junior at Arkoe High and would soon begin working weekends at the combination gas station and grocery store at Arkoe, a cluster of about half a dozen houses on Arkoe Ridge, near Junction. The Bowen family had moved to a farm in the vicinity a couple of years ago. Norman was out of school and working at the Merriman Lumber Yard in Summerville. His older sister, Marly, was married and just June and his younger sister were in school now. He seemed polite and interested, so she shared some things about herself and her family--only the more pleasant things, she acknowledged to herself. She hoped they would see each other again soon, and she told him so.

Next week he was there again, alone this time, and he asked her if she'd like to go to the show. It was a Shirley Temple film, so she was especially eager to go. He was polite and shy, with a deprecating humor that quickly put her at ease. She told him she had a good time and they agreed to meet again.

On the next Saturday night he asked if he could take her home. He had borrowed Norman's car for the night. She was happy with this arrangement, but she made Hank promise to go home at the same time so her parents wouldn't know she'd been out with a boy. Hank agreed, but let her know he was not willing to cover for her another time.

This meant she'd have to tell her family about June and hear the expected "too young for courting" lecture she knew would come from her father. She was fifteen and a sophomore in high school, but her folks were strict about dating rules and she wasn't eager to broach the subject with them.

Sam surprised her. She asked if a boy could come and pick her up to go to the movie and he didn't frown or preach to her, just asked who it was. He seemed pleased to know it was one of the Bowen boys. The family had a reputation for being serious, hard-working people, and Sam made no objection other than that she should be home by a specified time--*no excuses*!

By fall June had begun spending time at the Schmit home--joining them for Sunday dinner, playing checkers with Sam, helping with projects like woodcutting, even going along with the boys on hunting forays.

On an afternoon in early November, June persuaded Norman to take him to Summerville so he could attend a basketball game at the high school, where Dona would be playing. When word got back to the school board of the reason for his truancy, June was expelled from school for a week. It was that decision that caused him to announce that he intended to quit school, go to work full time, and buy a car. Grace and Harvey were upset and tried every argument they could conceive to get him to change his mind, but

June's interests had changed to other pursuits and there was no going back for him.

June had worked as a farmhand for a man named Mutt Hopkins and would work for him preparing the soil for spring planting and later putting in the crops. Mutt was pleased to have the broad-shouldered young man help him. June was reliable and capable and soon became a favorite of the entire Hopkins household.

Since the Brethren Church had closed its doors, the Schmit family now attended, infrequently, the Christian Church located on the main street of Summerville. The building was an imposing wood frame structure with a large steeple and beautiful stained-glass windows, obviously constructed when the parishioners enjoyed better economic times. The youth group was sponsoring a hayride, so Dona invited June to accompany her. She'd never been on a hayride, and her eyes sparkled with anticipation when he said he'd go.

On the appointed Sunday evening, June arrived to pick up Dona in his newly purchased, but decidedly used, Model T car.

"Want to go for a ride in a first-class jalopy?" he asked five-year-old Carrie when she appeared with Dona to look it over. The three piled in and they went for a spin down the black top road.

"Where did you get it?" Dona wanted to know.

"I'm working for it! Dad said he'd help me," June exclaimed. "Isn't it a beauty?"

He did have it polished and gleaming, she had to admit, though it seemed to do a lot of mysterious rattling.

"We'd better get on over to Summerville or we'll be left behind," she reminded him now.

"Home you go, little girl!" he announced to Carrie, who sat beside him on the seat, fingering the gadgets in front of her. The little girl's dainty features and wispy hair gave her a waifish look. She would like to go, too.

By the time they reached the church on Main Street, Hal Dowis was there with his horses and wagon, and several couples had already claimed their spots on the sweet-smelling hay that lay in mounds on the flat bed of the hayrack.

"Hi, Bea!" Dona called when she caught sight of her friend. They had played basketball together and were fast friends, although they formed a comical sight when seen together, as Dona was a petite 5' 1" and Bea measured nearly six feet tall.

"Don't push him off! He's too cute!" Bea yelled, which made June blush and wonder whether this was such a good idea after all.

The autumn air was chilly and fresh and smelled like decaying leaves. Hal had chosen a route on the blacktop to avoid the soft condition of the graveled side roads. The horses and the kids would have appreciated the more private atmosphere of one of the meandering dirt lanes, but there were too many chances of getting stuck in a mud hole this time of year, and Hal wasn't open to any complications he could possibly avoid. *Just please, God, let them all stay on the wagon until we've stopped*, he was thinking.

Other adults of the congregation had gone on ahead to the marker, where they'd made a bonfire and had hot dogs and drinks ready for the group. The "marker" was actually a post in the middle of the road that marked the boundary line between the state of Missouri and the state of Iowa. In some distant, earlier time there had been a fiery dispute over ownership of some trees that were favorite haunts for honeybees. Honey was a valuable resource as a sweetening agent in pioneer times, and so there had developed a major confrontation over which state actually encompassed the area. The resulting clashes were ever after known to as the "honey wars," although there were never any actual shots fired. The spot was two miles north of town. *Just about the right distance for some innocent spooning in the back of a hay wagon,* Hal surmised.

Spooning was a good description of the activities taking place in the cozy nests conveniently spaced for privacy on the swaying wagon bed. The clip-clop of the horses' hooves seemed to keep cadence for the night creatures that sang along the drainage ditches.

Dona felt secure and warm in June's embrace. She was accepted and needed in ways she had never felt before. They laughed and teased and cuddled and almost resented the interruption of the cookout to be offered at the bonfire.

A faint haze of color remained in the evening sky as the wagon arrived at the marker and Hal drew the big horses to a halt. A huge stack of split wood set on fire earlier was now burning steadily, a hot column of smoke and flames rising into the air and tiny particles of ash drifting down. The group speared hot dogs onto whittled sticks and roasted them over the coals at the edge of the blazing pile.

Someone had brought a ukulele, and the group sat on bales of hay and blankets spread on the soft ground, singing old favorites from school. "She'll be comin' around the mountain" rang out in the night air. With the encouragement of the elders present, they also harmonized on church favorites.

Their rendition of "Onward Christian Soldiers" reflected their enthusiasm and surely roused any nocturnal creatures inhabiting the area.

Dona was extravagantly happy as she sat with June beside the flickering firelight--all that was left of the blaze that had crackled and roared a short time ago. She was entranced by the tableau of the magical night. A sliver of moon hung over those in the group as they became subdued and talked quietly among themselves.

"This is about the time of night those big black snakes come out, isn't it?" Hal announced loudly to his wife, who sat close beside him. The couple moving quietly to the shadow of trees behind the hay wagon turned abruptly, and all in the group laughed as they sheepishly returned to the circle around the glowing embers. Hal decided it was time to head home while the evening still remained the innocent, Christian experience it was meant to be.

"All aboard, all who want a ride home!" he announced as he sprang upon the rack and gathered up the reins. Everyone wanted the choicest, most comfortable and most secluded spots in the hay, so they all scrambled on quickly and settled down with only a bit of shoving and jostling. Hal was surprised at how swiftly the group became quiet, after the boisterous singing, laughing and joking around the fire.

Nestled into a hollow in the hay, Dona and June resumed the intimate posture they had enjoyed earlier. They kissed tenderly but eagerly. She felt his strength. He felt her softness. Dona felt her destiny lay in the security of his insistent caress. She offered the acceptance he needed for the expression of his young manhood. The whisper of the wheels mingled with their soft murmurs of pleasure as the wagon rolled homeward through the dark countryside.

"Why don't we get married?" June asked, as the two lay entwined in an intimate embrace.

"What?" This hadn't occurred to Dona. Had June lost his senses? Her family still considered her a child. Could this really be happening?

"Let's get married." His voice was urgent.

"I don't know . . ." She was thinking of what her parents would say to this idea.

"Right away! You don't have to finish school. It doesn't make any difference."

She knew he was right about that. What everyone needed was work, not more education. Being in his arms like this was heaven--she thought she must have always wanted to be in just this place. Dona became happy, excited, scared, all at once! She was anxious to get away from that house, and June was so young and strong. She suddenly felt full of confidence and relief.

She could do what she wanted, for once. She felt a sense of freedom that she couldn't understand. She decided this is what she wanted and she would make her parents agree to it!

"Hal, do you have any water on board?" she heard someone call to the driver.

"What is it?" Hal was startled. He reacted with a quick flash of anger at the possibility that someone might have been smoking on the combustible mass.

"Something's smoldering back here. I think its June and Dona!"

Hal grinned with relief as he heard giggles and banter from the youngsters in back of him. June and Dona laughed as they brushed away the tangle of hay that the others had unceremoniously tossed at them.

Once again, Sam surprised his daughter. He guessed she could still finish high school since June was working and she had only one more year. Retha wept. It seemed to her that everyone was leaving. Dona had been a lively companion and help to her, even though she had been a challenge to raise. Dona frequently refused to assume the accepted female niche in life-- which Retha herself had begun to believe was simply to be content with the leftovers.

In the kitchen, Grace heard the agitated voices of Harvey and Junior in the front room. She was uneasy, as the relationship between father and son had grown tense since the boy quit school earlier in the year. She was disappointed herself but could certainly understand his desire to earn money for some of the things they hadn't been able to provide. Her own attentions had been focused on Marly and her problems recently. Their oldest daughter had married a couple of years ago and very soon after suffered the loss of a stillborn child. She was not happy in her marriage and looked to her mother for emotional support and guidance.

"You'd better come on in here for this, Grace," Harvey called to her.

She picked up a tea towel and hurried into the living room, drying her hands as she went. Junior sat quietly, with the hang-dog expression she was accustomed to seeing when he perceived he was in some kind of trouble. Harvey looked as upset as he had sounded.

Junior looked up at his mother, his dark eyes signaling his determination. "Dona and I intend to get married, Mom."

She was stunned. She hadn't expected this. "Where will you live? What will you live on?" she asked, knowing Harvey had probably asked the same questions already.

"For a while, with the Schmits. Sam has a plan to go out West in the summer when the crops are in. We would go and earn extra money to help us get started. Mutt won't be needing me for a while in the summer, anyhow--not until harvest time, and we'll be back by then." *He has a plan, at least,* she thought.

His father looked skeptical. "Don't you think you're both a little young for this decision?" Harvey asked, again.

"We need your permission, Dad," Junior pleaded.

"And you have Sam's okay on this, you're saying?" his father doubtfully inquired.

"He expects Dona to finish school. I don't know why she couldn't," Junior answered.

Grace felt her heart sink. This proposition must have been discussed at length in the Schmit home, and she could see her son was determined to carry out his plan. In her own mind she thought that perhaps any happiness a person could find right now might be worth the risk. Her mood brightened as she let in a slim shaft of acceptance.

"When would you be getting married?" she asked.

"Right away--as soon as we can. We don't want to wait any more." That statement from her son spoke volumes to her, and she allowed that maybe his decision was the best one for the circumstances.

Harvey spoke again, and Junior sensed that he had won his father over when he asked, "You won't be going out West to stay, you're sure of that?"

"I'll have work to do here when we get back, and Dona can go to school." He didn't see why it couldn't work out that way, having convinced himself, at least, of that likelihood.

Harvey sighed loudly. He gave Grace a look of resignation, and Junior knew the matter was settled. He felt elated and enormously relieved!

Plans for the wedding were simple. Dona and June would be married by the justice of the peace in Rock Port, the county seat. Norman and his girlfriend, Faye Brittain, would stand up for the couple at the ceremony, which would take place on a Saturday night in early December. Earlene offered to help Retha fashion a dress for Dona, and Junior would need a white shirt to top his one good pair of slacks. The bride and groom would return to Summerville to spend their honeymoon night at the local hotel, a custom favored by many newlyweds of the time. This night of privacy would be provided for by the Bowens, their contribution toward the occasion of their son's marriage.

A Hundred Miles to the City

At eight o'clock on Saturday night two carloads of young people were parked on the shoulders of the roadway at the "y" east of town, about a mile beyond the Platte River bridge. Bea and Helen occupied the back seat of the dark Chevrolet, with Bea's brother, Benny, at the wheel and Carl Short alongside him.

A few clouds drifted across the darkening sky as the group sat and watched the intersection that Dona and June would have to pass through on their ten-mile return from Rock Port.

"How long does it take to say 'I do'?" Carl asked.

Helen told him that her cousin had been married the summer before and that union had taken hours to complete. Of course, that had been in a church with a lot of extra rigamarole to go through.

"Surely, they'll be getting here soon! We shouldn't have any trouble spotting them, with all those cans we tied on their car!" Bea laughed. "They'll never get all those knots undone! Maybe that's what's taking them so long!"

"Hey! They won't bother with that tonight! It's onward to the hotel for them. I'm betting on that!" Benny declared.

The other driver left his car and came up to stand alongside Benny's window, where he leaned down and asked, "Are you sure you know where the wheelbarrow is?"

"It's right next door, behind the station. I checked to be sure this afternoon. D'you suppose June will hurry giving her a ride down the street?" Benny laughed at the thought of the spectacle the couple would make as they trundled along the two blocks of pavement required to satisfy their tormenters. The group planned on being the welcoming committee for a shivaree. They intended to intercede before the newlyweds could get safely inside their hotel room.

"I brought a box of Cornflakes for their bed!" Keith told the group before he went back to wait in his car, which held four more youngsters bent on showing the town a good time. The boys with Keith occasionally passed around a flask of liquor as they joked and reminisced about good times.

Few cars passed during the next hour. There was just enough light now to spot the silhouette of cars as they went by several yards in front of the waiting group.

"It's them! I'm sure of it!" Bea squealed.

Both drivers started up immediately and swung their autos onto the blacktop, heading in towards Summerville.

"Don't let them get too far ahead!" Bea urged now.

When the beams of their headlights illuminated the rear of June's car, bundles of tin cans could be seen crammed into the bumper, with one short string swinging wildly behind.

Now they were a caravan of three speeding toward the town, a real surge of traffic for that particular stretch of highway.

In the leading car, Faye smiled broadly. "I think they're following us!" she said to Norman as she leaned forward on her seat, straining to see behind them. "They must've been waiting. What will we do now?"

"Well, if I stop, they'll know for sure what's up," Norman responded.

"Take the bottom road," she urged. "Maybe we can shake them! If they follow, at least we'll know for sure they're out looking for Dona and June!"

Just before they entered the town, Norman turned sharply to the left and headed down the gravel road that led south beside the railroad tracks. The cars behind swung into line and were enveloped in swirls of billowing dust that filled the narrow roadway. Keith began to hang back, his vision decidedly hampered by the particles rolling around them.

"Don't let them get away!" one of the fellows in the backseat urged. "June deserves a razzing! Remember what they did to me?" Charlie remembered, if no one else did!

"What?" another kid wanted to know.

"Last summer they took me 'snipe hunting'!" Then they all remembered the hilarious prank that some of them, along with the Bowen boys, had pulled on Charlie. He was a newcomer to the community, having come from Chicago to live with his grandparents and to help out on their farm for his keep during the hard times.

Everyone in this part of the country knew the game was set up by luring the unsuspecting newcomer out into the woods and then leaving him "holding the bag" for snipes that were nonexistent. The patient boy, this time Charlie, had to find his way several miles back to town in the middle of the night. Those who heard of the adventure never failed to be greatly entertained by the plight of the hapless newcomer. Charlie felt a rush of embarrassment each time the word "snipe" reached his ears.

"We're really going to put them through it tonight! He deserves it!" Charlie exclaimed with eager anticipation.

"We'll have to catch them first," someone reminded him.

"That should be easy. He's leaving a pretty good trail," Keith sputtered in an exaggerated fit of coughing.

Faye looked at the fuel gauge. They had come several miles out into the country, turning down smaller and smaller roads. She pointed to the needle and gave Norman a half-worried look. She was a little concerned about getting home herself tonight. They had planned to leave June's car at the hotel and to walk on up to her house. June and Dona were actually spending the night in Rock Port where Norman had left his car for them. June's car at the hotel would convince any mischief-makers that the new couple was there. The hotel's proprietor wouldn't allow any non-paying guests upstairs. That had been their plan.

Now Norman laughed nervously as he realized they were perilously low on gas. If he'd been in his car, it never would have happened, but his brother rarely kept any extra fuel in the tank and now Norman foolishly began to feel that the laugh might turn out to be on him. Faye was a good sport--he appreciated that about her--but this might be pushing her forgiving nature a little too far, especially if she had to walk home from out here!

"I guess we'd better give up," he announced with a sheepish grin.

All three automobiles were soon stopped at the side of the road.

Norman squeezed Faye's hand and stepped out to face their pursuers, his customary lop-sided grin skewed rakishly. He walked back toward Benny's Chevy, now covered with a thick layer of dust.

When the two carloads of teenagers realized it was Norman and not June they'd chased around the back roads, they tumbled out of their cars and burst into shrieks of laughter intermingled with a few moans of disappointment. They had set their sights on a Summerville-style shivaree that was not going to happen, at least not on this night.

SIX

In just fifteen minutes they had left Missouri behind and were in Iowa heading west on Highway 2. Sam calculated that about three hours would be required for the first leg of their journey, and they should arrive at Omaha by noon or by two o'clock . . . or four o'clock, depending on the variety of car troubles they encountered. He had given the old car the once-over before starting out--had spent the last few days oiling and lubing and checking the inner tubes for any weak patches. But you never knew. They were carrying quite a load and pulling a small trailer besides. There were six in the car-- Retha, himself and Carrie, Grant, Dona, and June. Hank had gone with the Kansas wheat harvest earlier in June so no one was left at the farm. Retha and Dona had spent the last week dressing fryers for market and he had sold the two calves. Not much profit there, but some. Mutt Hopkins had offered to keep the two milk cows with his herd until the fall, when the Schmit family meant to return.

The farm was woefully quiet when they had arisen at six o'clock to get an early start on their journey. Carrie needed to take some familiar toys along for reassurance. She'd developed a confused mental picture of what life out West might be like. She'd heard her family speak of their earlier time there and knew they'd experienced both reward and disappointment in the adventure. Besides, she'd asked her father about his photograph of the logging camp. The panoramic scene included row upon row of mill workers posed upon some sort of bleachers. Their expressions were sober and earnest, and they were surrounded with a backdrop of large poles dangling on strings that seemed to hang down from the sky. When Carrie asked Sam how they did that, suspended the timbers in mid-air, he told her they were on skyhooks. She tried to picture ropes hanging down from the clouds. Her young mind couldn't conceive of a machine big enough to accomplish the feat, and so she remained perplexed about the marvelous mystery, and somewhat insecure as to what she might find in such a place.

Dona and June were both excited to be leaving and going for an adventure out West. Sam could see some of his own wanderlust in them. Retha wasn't eager to be out in the old tent again, but hopefully they could expect some kind of cabin to be provided for berry pickers when they reached their destination in Oregon. Grant hadn't much confidence about anything. To him this trip represented just one more thing to endure.

Sam was cautious when driving, and now, with the two-wheel trailer behind, June felt they crawled along. He hoped they wouldn't become a hazard when they got into some traffic. Sam had hinted that he'd like help driving on the trip out, so June hoped he'd soon be behind the wheel and they'd at last be getting somewhere.

They reached Sidney, Iowa, before they had to make their first stop--at an EAT-GAS filling station. June had been to Sidney once to a rodeo, but from here on everything would be new to him. Dona was eager to point out sights she'd first seen herself a few years ago, especially the mountains. Their commanding ruggedness had left a lasting impression on her.

The smell of the public restroom shocked Carrie. She would've preferred to have their two-holer here instead. The day was hot already, and the airless cubicle steamed with foul odors. She tried not to touch anything. Stinky and dingy, the yellowed linoleum was cracked and worn through in well-trampled spots. She wondered how long she could hold her breath.

The road across Iowa so far had been flat and straight, and the highway was in good condition, unlike the roads in their own corner of Missouri. They'd passed fields of corn that seemed to go on forever and were dark green and thriving, though the rain so far this summer had been scant and everyone feared the drought might last for another season.

"Can we stop and have dinner before we get to Omaha?" Dona asked from the back seat, where she sat wedged between June and Grant. She was quite uncomfortable, as she could move very little and was unable to shift her position at all.

"Let's wait until we find a campground. It should be about another hour or so. It will only get hotter this afternoon," Sam reminded her.

She was glad they planned to stay in Omaha for a while. She remembered the trip across Nebraska last time. It had been 112 degrees that day, and she wasn't sure she could endure that much heat while crammed into the car like this.

They arrived at Council Bluffs around noon but decided to go on over the bridge into Omaha before looking for a place to camp for a few days. The traffic wasn't too bad at mid-day, so Sam drove on through the downtown area by way of Dodge Street, figuring they could get a good start from the other side of the city when they were ready to continue their journey.

At last a camping facility was spotted that appeared to have vacancies, so Sam pulled in at the gate. A large man in bib overalls came out to meet them.

"How long do you expect to be staying?" was his greeting.

Sam told him, "Just a few days. We're on our way to Oregon, to the Willamette Valley--going out to help with the fruit harvest."

"A week's all we allow here," the man said gruffly.

"We don't plan to be here that long," Sam assured him.

"It's fifty cents a day. Pay up front." He wanted to make sure the terms were understood, even though a large sign on the gate stated the rate.

Sam reached for his wallet and handed the man a bill.

"Down that first lane to the left and under those trees yonder. The bathhouse is behind that fence. We have a snack shop here if you need basic items, like groceries and things," and he waved toward his place, which sported the sign, "Traveler's Roost, Welcome."

As they passed into the park, Grant made a comment concerning the quality of Nebraskan hospitality. It was obvious that the proprietor didn't enforce the one-week policy of the establishment, as several camping spots were occupied with lean-to structures and all sorts of household equipment were out on the grass. Lines had been strung between trees, and laundry hung limply from them. Camp stoves were set up and nearby tables and chairs were topped with supplies for living outdoors.

Retha took her parcel of food for the family over to a picnic table and began setting out fried chicken, deviled eggs, bread and butter. Sam unhitched the trailer while Dona and June laid the tent out on the ground and Grant went with a bucket and jug to get some water.

"June and I'll go to the stockyards and look for work this afternoon, if you think Grant can help you set up the tent. He's had plenty of experience by now," Sam suggested to Retha, referring to the many times his son had become disgusted with his treatment in their home and had gone out to live by himself in the tent. His anger usually lasted a few days, until he was sick of the hard ground, or the nights grew too bone chilling. When Hank left, Grant finally had a room of his own for the first time in his life. While Dona and June were at the Schmit home, Carrie was shuttled back to her old place on the sofa, her bed since leaving her bassinet.

After Sam and June went to seek out employment that might last for a few days, Dona and Grant set about erecting the ample tent. While it was large enough to accommodate the entire family, should the unlikely occurrence of a rainstorm materialize, the tent would be the sleeping quarters of Sam, Retha and Carrie. The others would sleep on old quilts and army blankets out in the open. Carrie was happy not to be sleeping outside *where animals could crawl all over you.*

When the tent was set up and sufficiently anchored, Grant went off to explore the rest of the campground, while Retha and Dona unpacked blankets and pillows. They arranged their belongings in the temporary shelter as conveniently as they were able. A couple of camp stools were unfolded and set in the shade of an elm tree that stood nearby. Retha sat on one and motioned for Dona to join her for a little rest and cooling-off period. It was nearly a hundred degrees and only a slight breeze stirred the mottled canopy overhead. Retha held a cardboard church fan she kept in her crochet basket, which she had set down beside her seat.

"Where will I sit?" Carrie demanded of her mother.

Dona smiled to herself at her mother's quick retort. "Just sit on your thumb and lean back on your elbow!" Her mother was always ready with just such a quip. Unlike Sam, who could spin a pretty good yarn, and often did so, Retha was more stingy with her words and frequently peppered her conversation with short, pithy sayings that made one stop and think on their meaning.

"I think I'll go and get cleaned up before the guys get back, Mom. Carrie, you can have my chair!" By then the little girl had found other distractions under the picnic table where she had found a shady nook of her own.

Dona remembered the kind of sanitation facilities such places usually provided--very nominal, as a rule, and seldom clean. She took along a few articles and walked up a small slope to the bathhouse. The outer door was missing, and she wasn't surprised to see that there were no doors or curtains on the shower stalls inside. She knew better than to expect anything approaching hot water. Thank goodness the place was empty so she could have some privacy. She undressed quickly, then stood under the running water, cool and soothing. The day was humid and her skin had become sticky with dust and perspiration. She thought she'd advise her mother to take a sponge bath in the tent, though. She wouldn't be at all comfortable in this big, open space, and they were all accustomed to bathing from a washbasin anyhow.

Dona returned to the campsite with her black curls damply clinging to her face and neck, but she felt refreshed.

"You come with me next time. You'd enjoy the showers," she told Carrie as she sat beside her at the picnic table.

"I don't want a bath in there. It smells bad. And there're bugs on the floor!" she answered.

"We'll see," Dona replied, with the standard response she used in disagreements with her little sister.

Under the wide crown of the elm, Retha sat with her needlework, her crochet hook working rapidly back and forth in her hands. A printed folder was in her lap. She periodically lifted it to check out instructions before going on with her project. Dona was always impressed with the beautiful creations her mother produced. In her hands, while she was working, the piece looked like a limp tangle of tiny thread. But when she was finished and had starched and shaped the article into rolling flutes of lace, a delicate design in perfect symmetry emerged. Many of the ladies in the Summerville community were accomplished at crocheting, but none had the patience and talent to turn out pieces that could rival Retha's. Dona felt temporary remorse that she hadn't tried harder to master the craft when her mother had encouraged her a few years back.

Dona regarded her mother with interest. When they were away from home Retha seemed to relax and enjoy her life. Dona didn't know why this should be so, but she sensed that some of the tension between her parents was left behind in Missouri. Perhaps here there were few aggravations and disappointments to remind them of their differences. Both seemed more accepting of the special demands of their own roles in the family. And, too, each more often acknowledged the other's contributions to their combined welfare. Dona felt strangely contented herself here--away from the cares, as well as the comforts, of home.

Dona noted her mother's hefty form as Retha sat working in the generous shade of the elm. She had been plump for as long as Dona could remember, though pictures of her as a girl showed a trim waist embedded in a buxom figure. All the Klodders tended to be portly, so Dona feared she was destined to display similar contours as she grew older. She had never been small and delicate, as Carrie now was. Even as a small child, she'd been round and firm, and of all her siblings, only Hank shared her substantial build. She figured that, since she had inherited the dark Klodder hair and eyes, she probably would have their shape, as well. She decided she would try to keep her girlish figure for as long as she could.

Later in the afternoon, Sam and June returned to the park with good news. The easy smile on Sam's face telegraphed their success before they stepped out of the car.

"What did you find?" Dona inquired as she hurried over to greet them.

"We were right to try the stockyards!" said June. "It's not a busy time for them, but they're cleaning the cattle pens, getting ready for the next rush."

"We'll be shoveling shit . . . again!" Sam laughed.

"I've had plenty of experience at that," June added. "That was my first job on our place. Dad always sent me out with the manure spreader. I guess he recognized my natural talent early on!" They all laughed, each having a mental picture of days spent cleaning out barns and hog sheds, evidence that the experience stays with one for a long time after the senses are bombarded with such smells.

An early morning haze enveloped the campground the next morning when Retha arose to heat coffee on a hastily built fire. The camping spots had grates built into concrete pilings on the ground, making cooking outdoors fairly convenient. The air was fresh and clean, and the men were invigorated by the promise of a profitable day of work ahead of them. After a breakfast of oatmeal and canned milk, the three set off with the lunch of cold meat sandwiches Retha had packed for them.

The day soon turned out to be another scorcher. Dona took Carrie for a long walk to pass some time. In the afternoon, the younger girl enticed two small children from an adjoining site to come and play with her beneath the wooden picnic table. The little girl, very near Carrie's age, was followed by a toddler, probably her brother, who wore only a dusty diaper and rings of sweat beads around his chubby neck.

By four o'clock the men had returned, as dirty as the children playing in the loose, dry soil. Tired and sweaty, they lost no time in getting to the cooling showers at the bathhouse. Before long, each found a shady spot on the ground to stretch out and rest. The relentless mid-day sun had sapped their strength, and they were happy to be laid off early.

On the next day a merciful breeze sent a spattering of clouds into Nebraska that cooled the air perceptibly, making their day much easier. Dona was glad when June suggested a movie for the evening. The long hours had been tedious for her, with nothing to do but wander around and entertain her younger sister.

After the couple left, with Grant along, Sam prepared his rod and reel and went to sit on the bank of the pond that lay down the hill beyond the elm tree. Retha and Carrie went along for a while, but the little girl found it hard to remain quiet enough to please Sam, so they soon returned to the tent. Wilson, the overall clad man who had met them when they arrived, joined Sam and sat companionably close so they could visit in hushed tones. He had become friendly once he was confident that the Schmits were working and could pay their bill. The two men commiserated on the trials of the times until the sun sank behind a stand of trees, the windbreak for a distant farm. No fish were caught this time, but Sam felt renewed, as he often did after spending hours lulled by gently rippling waves.

On the west side of the city, a few blocks of ancient brick buildings testified to the area's once having been a separate town. It had obviously been gobbled up by the spurt of growth occasioned by the arrival of the railroad. The movie house the group found in the neighborhood was old, but impressive to them, larger and more ornate than those back home. Dona was charmed by the picture shown and would remember it with appreciation for years. Grant enjoyed being with the couple. They treated him with respect, even seemed to enjoy his company. Since June had joined the family, Sam was more relaxed in his relationship with Grant, and the younger man was relieved and grateful for a new measure of acceptance.

After their third day at the cattle pens, the three were told that there was no more work. A large number of laborers had been employed to get the job done quickly, and now that it was accomplished scores of men were again without a source of income.

On the morning of their departure, Wilson came out and wished them well, and the Schmit family resumed their journey north and west, having earned enough money for a few more days of travel. The heat was back, and the highway shimmered as the car ate up the road that lay unswerving ahead. They rolled the windows down as far as they would go and hot wind rushed into their faces, drying the sweat as quickly as it poured from their skin. Retha couldn't bear her sunbonnet, and even Sam had peeled down to a skimpy undershirt, revealing naked, white shoulders. They stopped to get ice and rubbed it on their bare arms and faces, as the outside temperature again rose to over a hundred degrees.

The nights were bearable, so they decided to travel in the early morning hours as much as they could, and stop each afternoon to rest and sleep.

In a couple of days they reached the Rocky Mountains, where the splendor of the Grand Teton Range towered over adjoining foothills. June was struck with the immense grandeur of the sight. No photographs he'd seen had prepared him for the magnificent beauty of the vast, rugged peaks.

Progress through the mountains was slow but certainly more enjoyable, as the air was markedly cooler in the higher altitudes. The highway was narrow and winding, in some places threaded along the edge of a precipice, so Sam was more cautious than ever. The old car groaned with the heavy load it must pull over the passes. The scariest times for Dona were when they pitched down steep inclines and maneuvered endless switchbacks before reaching a level creek bed or valley. She felt as if her heart would pop out of her chest as the car swung around perilous curves.

Near Jackson, Wyoming, the family stopped at the ranch home of Aura Moon, Sam's sister. They planned to stay over to visit for a day or two before going on to Oregon. Aura's husband had heard that a nearby rancher needed a sheepherder and suggested that Grant might consider that. It would involve staying in an isolated cabin while the sheep fed on nearby foothills. He agreed to give it a try, so June volunteered to go with him for a while until he grew accustomed to the conditions. Then June would hitchhike on out to Oregon to rejoin the family.

The plan was acceptable to everyone, so the rest continued on across Idaho without June and Grant. In a way the trip was easier. They were more comfortable in the car without the big boys, but their luck seemed to have run out along with the two they left behind.

In a couple of hours they had a flat tire. Then about a hundred miles farther on, the fuel pump went out and they had to be pulled to a garage. The kind man who towed them ten miles to the gas station must have recognized their need, for he declined to take any pay for his generous help.

The man who ran the garage--obviously the only such place for miles-- was friendly but behind in his work. They would be forced to stay overnight until he could get to the task of replacing the pump. He offered to let them camp in back of the station and clean up in the restroom facilities. His wife even brought them a bucket of hot water from their house beside the station, so the Schmits felt they had been fortunate in having their troubles in that precise place.

Back on the road at last, the family continued on their trek to the West. Flat hills climbed to the horizon before them as the travelers journeyed on across southern Idaho, then into eastern Oregon where the hills stretched out to high, endless plains. The winds were dry and hot once more, and the scenery outside the car windows bleak and monotonous. The grass was dry and brittle above pale soil that meagerly covered the flat, rocky terrain. Few animals were seen along these expanses of roadway. Occasional cattle crossings were noted--there were no fences here, where it was obviously open range.

On the second day after leaving Jackson, the travelers reached the beginning of Oregon's pine forests. The dark green mantle of the hills refreshed their senses. The air smelled of damp woods, and shadowy dales in the magnificent hills offered coolness both real and fancied.

In another day, they reached the Willamette Valley and began searching for a location to begin the crucial quest for work. After stopping at one farm and having no luck, they went on to a larger outfit with the name "Nature's Best" on the gate. They were too late to get one of the few cabins provided for seasonal pickers, but there was a campground on down the road. They could start picking early the next day.

By now their money had run out. The fuel pump had taken a huge bite out of their budget and they were down to only a few rations of food.

The strawberries had been harvested once and this was the second picking, so filling the flats required searching beneath leafy vines that crawled along the ground. The newer fields had raised beds, where the workers didn't have to stoop too low. But most of the time the pickers must kneel or squat and feel around on the damp underside of the plants for the berries, smaller than those of the first picking.

All three adults joined in the task with Carrie tagging along, staying at the end of the rows with her doll and books. It was tedious for her but backbreaking for the adults, unaccustomed as they were to that particular kind of toil. By the end of the day, Dona had earned $1.50, having filled fifteen flats at ten cents each. She was bone-weary but felt good for having earned a little cash. The others had done nearly as well and were also glad when quitting time was announced.

Sam's feelings of satisfaction were dashed, however, when he learned they would not be paid at the end of the day, as they had assumed.

"What do you mean, no pay yet?" Sam challenged the man who stood at the truck receiving the crated berries.

"We pay by the week here," he said. "I'm sorry."

"Sorry!" Sam shot back. "We've come all the way from Missouri, and we're out of food and you're sorry?"

The man fidgeted and shifted his weight as he motioned for the next picker to approach.

"Did you hear what I said?" continued Sam, red in the face by now. "We've earned our pay for today. And we need it now."

"I'm sorry. I can't help you," was the man's reply.

"We're staying right here until we get paid!" said Sam, and he went over to join the others waiting by the car.

"What's the matter?" asked Retha, who'd heard nothing of the interchange between the two men but could see by Sam's expression that something was definitely wrong.

"He says they only pay on Friday. We can't wait until Friday. I told him we'd stay right here until they decide to pay us for the work we've done."

A Hundred Miles to the City

By now several of the other pickers were staring at them. Dona was embarrassed, but she felt worse for her father. She was aware of how hard it was for Sam to admit their plight to these people. She knew the same stubborn willfulness he now must be feeling. They had certainly earned their pay. Her back felt as if it were permanently molded into a stooped position.

The four climbed into the dusty car and assumed their waiting vigil.

In half an hour, all the flats had been counted and stacked upon the waiting trucks and the other pickers had gone off to their quarters for the night. The Schmits continued waiting. They were each beginning to feel discouraged and foolish when the foreman reappeared and walked over to them.

"This is just between us, okay?" he asked as he handed Sam the money the family had earned. "If you stay tomorrow, you'll be paid on Friday like everyone else." He did not smile nor make a friendly gesture, but Sam thought he saw a flicker of compassion in the man's eyes as he spoke.

The offerings of the campground they found were more meager than most they'd stopped at, but then, it was just two bits a day and that helped. They sent a letter to Aura, telling her where they were so June could find them when he got to the valley. They hoped they would hear something from him and Grant now that they were settled.

The Willamette Valley was nestled among high, green hills. The Schmits had noticed the lush appearance of the countryside when they first arrived. After the dry, parched appearance of the flatlands of eastern Oregon, this spot seemed to flourish like a well-tended garden. Because of the cost of gas and the fact that they had to fill up with oil each time they stopped for fuel, the family didn't take many sightseeing trips. But the farms nearby were beautiful, the yards edged with bowers of roses and other showy blooms. Retha would have liked to have such bounty in her own yard at home. Even in the heat of summer, people here rarely had to water their gardens.

The pickers were told on Friday that the fields would be finished by the middle of the next week, so there would be no more work here after that. The Schmits, along with most of the others, began looking for employment in harvesting a different crop. There were several growers raising hops in the area, so Sam asked around about possibilities for them there. He put their name in at a place with cabins, so they anticipated having a roof over their heads for a while.

On the day before they finished in the strawberry fields, Dona set her last flat of strawberries up on the platform and turned to spot June, leaning on their car and smiling widely. She gasped and gave her mother's arm a quick squeeze before running over to him. He grabbed her up in a big bear hug.

"I missed you so much!" she whispered into his neck.

He put her down and looked at her.

"You don't know how lonely I've been . . . " and he gave her another mighty squeeze.

She had missed him more than she'd thought she would and knew by the wetness of his eyes that he'd missed her as much. She had never in her life been so glad to see anyone!

When they got back to the campground, the group questioned June about his trip and also about Grant.

"He seems to be getting along great. I think he really likes the solitude of the place. It was driving me crazy, but he was as happy there as I've ever seen him," June said of Grant.

"What does he do all the time?" Retha asked.

"He reads a lot, and whittles. He was always coming back with a chunk of wood he'd found to whittle on," June told her. "There was sure not much to do there. Not even much to look at. Just hills and grass. And sometimes the sheep. He'd get on the horse every morning and ride out looking for them. He lost one last week, but that can't be unusual in a herd as big as that."

"You think he really does like it there, then?" Sam asked. He'd seldom known his son to be content with anything.

"Yeah," June assured him. "He wants to stay as long as he can. Of course, he may feel differently after a week or two completely alone. But I don't think so. He got pretty relaxed--quit shaving and everything. I think he'd make a good hermit."

"How was your trip out here?" Dona wanted to know. Actually, it had taken him only a little more time to make the distance hitching than it had taken them in the car.

"Folks were pretty good to stop. I got caught in the rain a couple of times--once in the mountains, and it was cold. Still, it was good to actually feel rain. I probably looked like a fool to most people, standing out there grinning and soaking wet."

Dona pictured him in her mind, his heavy hair clinging to his skin and his bright, even teeth showing in that fetching grin of his. She would've picked him up . . . in a wink!

"Mostly I got rides with loggers. They seemed to like company and were sure interesting to talk to. You probably noticed all the logging roads heading up into the hills, and a lot of clear-cut areas. I guess there's different opinions about the logging industry out here right now. It's been a boost to the area, I guess, but even the truckers think maybe it's going to hurt in the long run."

Carrie couldn't imagine anyone coming such a long way alone.

"Weren't you scared?" she asked.

"Well, no. Not really. You never knew what kind of people would pick you up, but it turned out they were all okay." He'd had one experience that made him uneasy but wasn't sure if he should mention it now. He didn't know how Sam might feel about it. He could be pretty opinionated--like, he had no trouble finding fault with the Jews. As with so many people hurt by the depression, Sam blamed the bankers, more specifically, the Jewish moneylenders, for some of his own misfortunes. And he sometimes said so, emphatically. *There's plenty of blame flying around, and some of it's bound to stick on some group, guilty or not*, June thought.

"I was picked up by a Negro one afternoon," June ventured to say. "He was driving a truck and took me a couple hundred miles."

"What was he like?" Carrie asked. She'd never met a black man. There were none in Summerville. The only black person she'd ever seen was the porter on the train.

"He was nice. He told me about his family, and we laughed and had a good time talking. When suppertime came, he stopped at a filling station outside a little town. He gave me some money and asked me if I'd go in and get him a sandwich at the café. I didn't know why he wouldn't go in, too, so I just asked him. He gave me a real funny look and said, 'You get so you know where you can go. I can't go in there.' Then I knew. I felt so bad. He'd given me a ride and been nice to me, and my own kind of people wouldn't let him come in because he was a Negro!"

"What did you do?" Dona asked.

"Just went in and got what he wanted, but I felt bad about it. I just didn't know what to say," June answered, and she could tell that he still felt bad about it now.

June helped with the picking on the last day in the strawberry fields. The next day they were at a place called, simply, Alton Farms, where they would pick hops for as long as the work lasted.

The work was easier there, at least for Dona. She was small and could move easily beneath the trellis-like wires mounted a few feet above the ground. The plants spread out over the fence-like webbing and the weight of the fruit pulled it down so it could be picked easily from beneath. She was quick at the work and nearly kept up with June. At the end of each day, she felt she'd made a real contribution; usually her efforts earned them at least three dollars. They picked through the week, including Sundays. They were told they wouldn't lose their jobs if they didn't work on Sunday, but they were all eager to make as much as they could before the work ran out.

The cabins were square, one-room structures with tin roofs. There was a crude icebox and a two-burner cooking unit, one bed with a stained mattress, and two cots with no mattresses at all. They rigged up a blanket in the middle of the room, to separate the sleeping areas, so they'd have some privacy. A wire already stretched across the room had likely been used for the same purpose many times before. There was an outhouse in back of each cabin and a small bathhouse at the end of the lane. Needless to say, they didn't spend a lot of time in the tiny, dark quarters.

The transient nature of their stay at the camp discouraged the family from getting acquainted with other pickers, who shared their lives on a nearly intimate level. Most people in the compound kept to themselves and were quiet and easy to live near. Probably they were too exhausted by the end of a hot day of picking to have any interest in socializing.

There was a river about a mile away so Sam, June and Dona spent much of their spare time fishing, managing to catch enough for a mess on several occasions.

It rained often, but in quick, gentle showers that came and went in the afternoons, quite unlike the booming thunderstorms so common in the Midwest. The pickers generally stayed out in the fields and continued with their work when the short bursts of rain occurred.

After a few weeks of picking from seven to five each day, every member of the family was weary of the monotony of the work and the dullness of the routine both day and night. Gradually the old miseries began creeping into their relationships. By the time the fields were finished near the end of August, all were ready to declare their venture over and return to Missouri.

June and Dona were eager for a place of their own, and June was ready to return to the farm work waiting at the Hopkins place. Retha hoped there would be something left of the small garden they'd planted in the spring--she felt certain there would be potatoes, at least. And she was ready to do some fall canning. They could always count on the fruit trees for a few quarts of apples and plums. They'd heard of the drought that again plagued the midsection of the nation and knew they'd need whatever supplies they could put up for the winter. They didn't expect much had changed for the better while they were gone. Having Hank out of school should help the family finances, though. Hopefully, he would find some kind of work for the winter.

The journey home seemed longer to Dona than the trip out. Hot, dry winds blew most of the time, nearly all vegetation had browned in the searing sun, and murky clouds of dust rolled off the fields along the highway. Crossing

Nebraska, they tied damp kerchiefs across their faces in an attempt to sift out the choking particles that swirled through the hazy air.

Grant was waiting at Aura's when they arrived, so the remainder of the trip was cramped, as before. Mercifully, they had no major problems with the mechanics of the car and pulled into Summerville just four days after leaving Oregon.

As soon as they heard of the family's return, Earlene and Emmett came to visit.

"We have news!" Emmett announced.

"Good news," his wife added. "We're expecting a baby in the spring!"

"Well, my goodness!" Retha was surprised. "Are you feeling all right?" she asked Earlene.

"Yes, mostly. I couldn't wait to tell you!" her happy daughter said.

"And we're buying the station!" Emmett added.

"Hap Hooker's?" June asked. Emmett had worked for Hap a couple of years now.

"Yep. Would you want to help me out on the weekends?" he asked June.

"Sure. As much as you need me! Maybe Dona and I can find a place in town."

As it turned out, the house the young couple found for their first home was on a small acreage just off the blacktop between Easton and Summerville. The little, square house had four rooms, with no gas or electricity but a good well just outside the back door. Their lane was connected to the highway by a dirt road that ran on by their place. The house sat on the side of a long hill with trees surrounding it on three sides. There were a couple of run-down outbuildings and a big garden spot but no barn or orchard. The place had a sad, abandoned look that hinted at years of neglect by previous caretakers, but it would be cheap to live there until they could afford something better. Dona hoped they could soon put up fresh wallpaper, at least.

Going to school was no longer important to Dona. She was happy to stay at home and fulfill her role as housewife. Besides, it would have been difficult to get to town in bad weather with the mud road, and on most days June needed the car to go to the Hopkins place. So she spent her days cleaning, washing, ironing and cooking. She soon realized there was a lot she didn't know about running a household and wished she had been more of a help to her mother when she was at home, especially in the kitchen.

In the early fall, Dona felt happy and secure in her home tucked away in the woods. The scant furnishings scattered throughout the small rooms had been left by their landlord's last hired hand, who had himself been a casualty of the depressed economy. When the Davises could no longer afford his help, he had left the area, riding the rails to the promise of better times in faraway places.

Dona spent her days alone, as June left every morning to work either at Mutt's or at the gas station in town. At first, she gloried in her independence. She traipsed the nearby meadows and woods, exploring the countryside as if it were her private domain. She took long walks among the hardwood trees, now adorned in russet and gold. She liked the damp, earthy smell of the rotting leaves on the forest floor and happily balanced herself on a fallen cottonwood that bridged the tiny creek at the bottom of the hill.

Sometimes she knocked on the door of their nearest neighbors, two elderly bachelors who lived a quiet life of seclusion in a house across the dirt road. The brothers were friendly but not comfortable socializing, so Dona spent most of her days alone, exploring the woods, reading, or listening to the radio. She didn't turn it on often, though, because the battery would run down and she and June liked to listen to their favorite shows in the evening.

Never having learned to drive, Dona depended wholly on June for trips to town or to visit the Schmits or the Bowens. She and June frequently went to his folks', as they now lived on the same blacktop road, three miles closer to Summerville. But when they went to town she seldom saw any of her old friends, unless she ran into them at a movie or at a rare dance at the Legion Hall.

After an extravagant fall, the winter wore on devoid of color and companionship. June was constantly busy with his two jobs, pumping gas on weekends in Summerville after his daily farming chores at Mutt's.

Following several weeks of this routine, June failed to come home at the expected hour one Saturday night. Dona's head filled with nagging doubts, about him, herself, their life together--all the circumstances of their relationship. It occurred to her that June had never mentioned his plans for the future--his hopes, his dreams. She really didn't know him, not on a soul-sharing level. She gradually realized they'd never discussed what they each wanted from life. They had just wanted to get married. And so they had. Her hopes and illusions for the future were suddenly threatened. She was vaguely aware of her own wretchedness as she sat in the unlit room waiting for his return--if he hadn't actually left her already!

By the time June arrived at the house, not all that late after all, she was in a state of dangerous disturbance. He stood at the door, squinting into the shadows, and caught a glimpse of his wife sitting stiffly on the couch. He ventured what he hoped would be a neutral remark.

"Why are you sitting in the dark, Honey?"

Whatever he said would have touched a nerve, and those innocent words were all it took. He intuitively knew she'd be less than cordial but hadn't expected the kick in the pants that met him.

She began a bitter tirade of angry accusations, throwing them at him as he entered the room. She continued, with a catalog of disappointments she didn't realize she felt. Hurtful words poured out before she could check them, and she immediately burst into tears of frustration and remorse.

June walked over to her and put his arms around her. She melted into his familiar embrace and sobbed as if her heart were broken. She was famished for his attention and reassurance.

He murmured softly, "I'm sorry. I stayed at the pool hall awhile. I didn't mean to hurt you."

She was confused by her own anger at such a trivial thing and embarrassed to have been mean and unappreciative of his hard work. A gnawing feeling of inadequacy crept into her as she breathed into the comfort of his encircling arms.

In a matter of days a wall telephone appeared in the front room of the little house. Dona hadn't realized how much it would mean to her to talk with her friends from school and with her mother. She commenced calling Retha almost daily, asking her advice on the many problems she encountered as she struggled to maintain a comfortable home for her husband. She began to realize how much she missed her old friends and began to regret not having finished high school. She missed the social aspect of her early life and yearned for the fading companionships she'd enjoyed.

The house was hard to heat in winter and the road was sometimes impassable. The couple often had to leave the car by the highway and walk out. On those occasions they would pull on rubber boots and slog their way through the sticky black mud. Sometimes they misjudged and got the car stuck, then had to wait for drying or freezing to occur so they could dig it out. Once the wheels got gummed up with mud and wouldn't turn at all.

June had bought a milk cow, which they kept in a small pasture behind the house. Dona hadn't wanted chickens--they were too messy. And, besides, there was no good place for them. The chicken coop wasn't tight, so foxes could get at them.

When June suggested she learn to milk the cow, Dona imagined herself a milkmaid, chasing Bossie around the back lot with a milk bucket each morning and evening. She wasn't on particularly friendly terms with the old cow and didn't fancy touching her in such an intimate way. But how could she refuse? Her husband went off to work every day of his life, and she sat in the house unskilled in needlework or any other house-wifely pursuit. She figured it was her duty and she would do the best she could.

As the rising sun lit the sky, Dona and June set out to corner the huge beast and acquaint her with a new morning routine. The milk stool was barely a foot high, made of two short pieces of 2 x 4 nailed together to form a T. Dona believed that perching on it would be a challenge in itself.

"You should pet her a little first to calm her," June told Dona. "She'll give her milk down easier if she's comfortable."

So Dona reached out to stroke the soft, brown side of the jersey. *Maybe this won't be so bad,* she thought.

"Always milk her on the right side," he warned. "Cows are trained that way and might kick if you go to the wrong side." Not something Dona wanted to hear.

He sat down to give her a demonstration of how the task should be accomplished. It looked easy. In response to his rhythmic tugging, the milk shot out in steady streams that rang against the metal pail, and soon the bottom was covered with foamy, white liquid.

"Just work from the top down," he said as he slowly showed her how to squeeze her fingers in succession on the warm teats of the generous animal. She practiced a few times with her fingers in the air--first finger down to the little finger, one at a time.

"And pull down with your hand at the same time," he added.

"Okay. I'm ready if she's ready," Dona announced.

She sat down carefully on the stool, too close to the cow, and nearly fell over backwards before regaining her balance and butting the cow with her head. The patient animal didn't seem to notice. Then she placed her hands on the front two teats and timidly tried to mimic the movements she'd practiced. Nothing came out. She tried a few more times, tugging in earnest as she squeezed her small fingers against the cow's soft skin. The mingled smell of manure and milk made her feel dizzy as she worked her fingers repeatedly up and down. A few trickles were all she could manage.

Finally old Bossie gave a swish of her tail and stepped forward, kicking over the bucket with the dab of milk in it and sending Dona over sideways, shrieking in dismay at her failure.

June laughed. He was disappointed, however, as he could see he wasn't going to be free of his milking duties any time soon. But he kindly said to her, "She's going dry now. Maybe when she's fresh with a new calf it'll be easier for you. I think I'd better finish if we're going to have any milk today!"

Dona was glad and sad and from then on definitely had a better appreciation of June's labors when he was out milking.

As the ground gradually warmed and ice-locked water meandered to the creek, Dona again went on forays into the surrounding woods. In May she searched out morel mushrooms down by the damp creek bed. The heavy odor of spring hung in the air as she wandered the woods, searching among the May apples and skunk cabbage that poked through the fallen debris of the tangled trees. Occasionally she stooped to pick violets and tucked them into her pocket for safekeeping. Under the forgotten fence of a distant pasture, the orange petals of marsh marigolds blended into the variegated greens of newly sprouting grasses.

Beside the house a row of lilac bushes bloomed in profusion, their sweet smell permeating the little house. A jar of lavender clusters was usually sitting in the middle of the oil-clothed table when June arrived home. Dona was intoxicated with their delicate aroma. The smell would linger in the memory of her senses for the rest of her life.

With the first shirtsleeve weather of spring, Dona and June were in the garden plot, laying parallel lines of hope across the moist, dark bed. Spring, the season of high hopes, brought a feeling of renewal to Dona. She knew the potential benefits of a bountiful garden and was determined to put a great effort into the undertaking. June helped her sow the seeds but after that was happy to let it be her project. He'd been working in gardens since he was old enough to hold a hoe, so from now on he was happy to do his assisting from across the fence in the form of advice, sought or otherwise.

Care of the yard was also relegated to Dona since she was home and liked so much to be out of doors. The part she mowed was a small area near the house, which she kept neatly trimmed. The remainder of the yard was colonized mainly by weeds and a few courageous flowers started by a hopeful tenant of long ago. A column of dandelions marched across the yard in the wet and warm days of late spring.

At last a whisper of green appeared, topping the valleys of earth so painstakingly formed across the wide garden. Dona went daily across the dew-wet grass to tend her fragile plants. An atmosphere of order prevailed in the neat garden and seemed to spill over into her life as well. She was enormously compensated by the thriving growth she had wrested from the earth. She could see the peas swelling in the pods and imagined her mother coming over with her huge pressure cooker, the two sitting in the shade shelling peas or snapping beans. Carrie would be old enough to take part this year. Dona hoped her little sister was becoming a better help to her mother than she herself had been.

By midsummer the couple had succeeded in making the little place their own. They would sit out on the step in the soft summer twilight and listen as the crickets and tree frogs took up their nightly clamor. Soon the surrounding shadowy trees faded into the dark, and flickering fireflies punctuated the depths with tiny beacons of light.

Before the year was out, Dona was expecting their first child, and Retha was also pregnant. The Schmits planned to move again, to the next in a long parade of homes in the community.

In March, Dona and June went to help with the move. They'd had to wait until the ground was frozen, so the day was miserably cold when they loaded up all the Schmits's belongings on two borrowed wagons and set out on the four-mile move. Dona was worried that the jostling of the rough wagon would be hard on Retha. Her mother hadn't been well all winter. She herself felt very well. She tended to think of herself as invincible, as is often the case with the younger generation.

Barbara June was born in May at the home of the elder Bowens. Because they lived on the highway and closer to town, Dona went there for the baby to be delivered. She stayed for a week so Mother Bowen, Grace, could help with the baby. One and a half years later Dona gave birth to her second daughter and Retha came for a few days to help out. Another year and a half after that, the third little girl arrived and no one came to help. Then, Dona realized, was when she really needed help.

SEVEN

The three little girls would later boast to their friends that they once lived in Iowa and their daddy worked right across the street in another state, as if this geographical coincidence made them special. Edgerton was the small town north of Summerville to which the younger Bowen family moved when Sharon was a few months old. The distance from their old home, an apartment above Emmett's station, to their new home was about five miles if it were bone dry or if the ground were solidly frozen, twice that far if they had to go around by way of gravel roads.

They first moved into a two-story frame house on the western edge of town. The house was on a hill, the land sloping gently away in either direction. The town itself was half the size of Summerville and sat nearly bank side of the Platte River. The city planners must have envisioned a larger populace than ever arrived, for the streets ran a distance of half a mile, with only three or four lots of each block ever built upon. A few large houses were scattered throughout the town, but most of the homes were simple one-story structures.

The main business in the town was where June now worked, Merriman's Lumber Yard. Mr. Merriman owned the gas station that sat beside this business and the lumberyard in Summerville, as well. There was a produce house, a grocery store, a restaurant and a post office, besides the school, in the town.

Both Dona and June were eager for the move to Edgerton. Since Mutt's boys were old enough to help on the farm, June no longer had a job at the Hopkins place. For that reason they had moved into Summerville. June was closer, then, to his work at the station. However, living upstairs in an apartment with two, then three little ones was difficult. Dona had thought she would enjoy living in town, since she would have more contact with her friends, but with the babies to care for, her time was largely consumed by childcare and household chores. She realized she did not know the meaning of "weary" until she was responsible for three little ones.

The town was well known for its taverns, and Dona resented the time her husband spent with his old friends. The circumstances of June's life had changed dramatically over the last few years. He'd become remote and withdrawn since the death of his father the year before.

Father Bowen took his own life at the age of forty-eight. Grace found him in the barn, where he'd hanged himself. He'd been in pain for months with headaches resulting, they thought, from bad teeth. He had been despondent periodically since losing the farm several years earlier. The entire family was shocked and grieved by the tragedy. Grace and Patsy went to Colorado to be with Harvey's mother, who had moved to Fort Morgan several years earlier. Grace felt the need to be with family and found work for herself in the city as domestic help in a private home. Marly left the area, too, remarrying and moving to Omaha with her husband, stepson and new baby.

June's brother, Norman, married Faye and the two lived in Summerville, where he worked for Mr. Merriman, and she worked in the local grocery store. They visited June's family frequently, often bringing something for the children. Norman liked to trade cars and often went to his brother's to show off a new model and to take everyone for a ride.

Winter set in early in 1940, with heavy snow blanketing most of the Midwest early in November. North of the Bowen house, the branches of tall cedar trees sagged under the accumulated weight of several inches of dense snow. The skeleton of a large elm broke through the river of whiteness that flowed across the front yard and down the hill to the back yards of the town.

A stiff row of power poles marched down the hill in frozen dignity, snow clinging to their gracefully drooping wires. The mesh fence that traced the neighbor's yard was a length of delicate lace decorating the crest of the snow. Dona had an urge to open the door and listen to the perfect silence of the winter morning.

The house was drafty and she noticed siftings of white on the west windowsills. She went to the rag bag and tore strips from an old skirt, which she punched into the cracks with a case knife from the kitchen. It wouldn't add anything to the décor but might keep the girls from catching so many colds.

June had gone off to work already, tromping down the road in four-buckle overshoes just tall enough to shield his pant legs from the wet snow. On most days he had dinner at the town's restaurant, just up the street from the lumberyard. Emmett's sister and her husband ran the eatery. Another of his sisters also lived in Edgerton, so June and Dona had relatives of a sort here. Other than that, they knew no one yet on a neighborly basis, but June was becoming acquainted with townspeople who came to the lumberyard for supplies.

Dona took the broom and swept the snow from the back step and the well platform. If she hurried, she could get started on her daily chore of washing diapers before the children awakened. She had finally gotten an old washing machine but used it only once a week, as it required water to be carried and heated. The kitchen stove was a wood-burning beast that must be coaxed to flame for each use. It helped to keep the kitchen warm but devoured a supply of finely chopped wood in no time at all.

The baby would wake up soon, so she hurried to get the fire going and the water on before the hungry child must be fed.

Crying from the other room. She rushed in to pick up Sharon before she disturbed her sisters, lifting her from her slatted bed in the parlor. The couple had closed off the upstairs part of the house and used it only for storage and to hang clothes on the cords June had strung across the rooms. There were always a few diapers Dona had pinned up inside where they wouldn't freeze. On some days they did, still.

The baby was eager for her mother's offering, and Dona crooned to her as she held her and snuggled into the big chair. Sharon was a compact little bundle, and Dona enjoyed holding her close, watching her with the soft brown eyes of an adoring mother. The three babies could try her patience sometimes, but Dona never tired of watching the miracle of their transformation into individual personalities with charms and frustrations uniquely their own.

Barbara came into the room and stood beside her mother's knee.

"The bed's wet again, Mama! Can't you make her stop?" If only she could. No matter how she bundled Coralea before putting her down, she often managed to wet through everything and dampen her sister as well. Barbara was a serious child and Dona already recognized signs of a meticulous nature in her firstborn.

"I'm sorry, honey. You'll just have to be patient until she gets big like you. Get me the brush, and I'll straighten up your hair for you." Dona pushed the girl's hair away from her face as she spoke. Dark, wavy tresses fell to Barbara's shoulders and drifted across her face. Luckily the girl's hair required only minimal care, as Dona's curls were natural and she'd never learned to make pin curls nor to braid, either.

Dona knew Coralea would soon come trundling through the door. Without Barbara's warmth, she would get cold and feel her wetness, apparently as surprised and upset by the condition of her bedding as anyone.

When Coralea came in crying, Dona laid the baby on a pallet on the floor near the oil heater, close enough to feel the security the warmth offered. No need to fuss with Coralea's hair; she had none. The little girl had been bald since birth, and her mother began to worry whether she would ever have hair. At least she was easy to clean up with a damp cloth. Now Dona would have to put the tub on the stove and heat more water to wash the sheets. She dreaded the task of wringing them out by hand, which was nearly impossible without making a mess on the kitchen floor. *Oh, well, she will grow out of it,* Dona thought. She hoped that Sharon would be a little more like Barbara in that respect.

When finished with the day's washing chores, Dona sat down on the living room sofa.
"Coralea, come on up here and lie down," she called as she spread a towel over the seat beside her.
The two-year old gleefully climbed up on the couch and stuck her toes toward her mother. She enjoyed this ritual, an activity only she and her mother shared. She smiled and put her chubby arms up and hugged herself over her head. Dona rubbed warm olive oil over her own hands, then slid them up and down the calves of the tiny legs. She nudged her daughter on the hip as a signal to roll over; a maneuver that caused the child to giggle as she flipped over and then buried her face in the soft towel.
Earlene had learned from her doctor in Summerville that there was a chance the girl's legs might be straightened if they were faithfully rubbed with oil and pressure applied on the malleable, growing bones. She had taken a picture into the doctor's office to show how her niece's toes turned in and her legs bowed out, mimicking the contours of a bow-legged cowboy. The doctor had offered the only advice he felt qualified to give but couldn't say for certain if it would really help to straighten the child's legs.
That's the outcome Dona now hoped for. Twice a day she massaged the crooked legs, pushing carefully and repeatedly against the outward bow of the long bone of each lower limb. Coralea didn't mind lying still for the time it took. She was getting all the attention from her mother, a treat that didn't occur often since the arrival of her baby sister. Dona told stories as she kneaded the little legs, with Barbara listening from her seat on a stool nearby.
Her mother's low, soothing voice and tender caress often lulled the relaxed child to dreamland and she might sleep for hours on the soft couch. Barbara was happy to have her asleep and out of the way, as she often spent much of her own playtime guarding her things from her sister. Coralea had a tendency to pull things apart to see what was on the inside.

June's work at the lumberyard involved stacking, loading, and delivering lengths of smoothly planed lumber brought in from the saw mill out by the river. He didn't mind the work and appreciated the time he spent out on the road talking to people in the community. He passed his free time at the station next door, where he often stopped after work to trade tales with Jack Fisher, who ran the station, and regulars who, like himself, enjoyed the friendly interchange. He occasionally helped out by pumping gas or patching tires if Jack were especially busy. It wasn't long before the older man recognized June's talent for mechanics and asked him if he'd like to come in on a paying basis on Saturdays, when there was often more business than could be handled by one.

In the winter months June spent little time at home in daylight hours. When there, he regularly needed to split wood for the cook stove. He often worked on the car. Though they didn't use it much, he liked to keep it running in case it was needed. He drove the lumber truck back and forth to work each day.

The couple spent much of their evening time together playing with the girls and getting them ready for bed. Dona and June both enjoyed Zane Grey novels but rarely found time to sit down with one.

Their mother read to the girls every night when they went to bed, repeating over and over their favorite nursery rhymes and singing familiar lullabies. Dona's voice was magically soothing, especially when she slowly told the singsong verse of the "Baby Ray" story that the children loved. The same rhyme was repeated with several animal names before the last verse:

"Up from the meadow in the deep, deep, deep,
Two little bunny rabbits creep, creep, creep,
Just to see if baby Ray is asleep, sleep, sleep."

The low tones of Dona's voice enhanced the melodic repetition of the familiar tale. There was no resisting the mesmerizing effect of those dreamlike words, and each child would fall into dreamland before she reached the last line.

Sitting on the front porch swing, Dona watched Sharon, now a year old, climb onto the worn boards of the low deck. Her short, blond curls made little ringlets on her damp forehead. She was the Shirley Temple Dona had wanted, with prominent, high cheekbones and a softly dimpled chin. The corners of her mouth curved up in an unbidden smile.

The summer heat penetrated the shade of the wide porch, and Dona felt it was too hot even to swing. This was her favorite spot in their new place. She and June often sat out here in the evenings and shared the events of the day as the girls played around them. Harvey and Grace had owned a porch swing, and Dona remembered swinging contentedly with her first newborn--such a long time ago, it seemed. The Bowens were both gone from her life now, and she missed their friendship and the accepting nature of their concern.

She rose to walk across the porch to rescue Sharon, who had tumbled into the soft dirt at the porch's edge. The big yellow cat lay sprawled beneath the window ledge. He moved only when the small child made unwelcome advances toward him. He had come with the place when they'd moved down the hill in the spring. Obviously a mature animal, he had left his playful kitten nature in the past and wanted only the nearness of humans, not intimate contact with them.

Barbara was on her new tricycle riding back and forth on the sidewalk that ran the length of the block. Past the church on the south was a small wooden bridge that spanned a drainage ditch. That was the limit to which the girls were allowed to wander, as the rail was too high to prevent them from falling into the dry ditch. Not far beyond the bridge was the road that ran into the business part of the town. The lumberyard was just across this road, and was joined at the north to the gas station.

The plain white church that dominated the block was called the Holiness Church. Dona was not familiar with that sect and wondered if it were a branch of Baptists. Her own ancestors were referred to as "Hard shell" Baptist, but she didn't know much about them either, except that her grandfather had helped build a church of that kind down in Missouri in Worth County.

Now Barbara allowed her sister to get on the back of the tricycle and was giving her a ride. Coralea stood behind her, clutching Barbara around the middle to keep her balance as Barbara pushed on the pedals and maneuvered the three-wheeler deftly along the level path. The children were barefoot, and Dona was tempted to slip out of her own hot shoes but knew her tender feet would feel the rocks and stubble that the girls ran across without flinching.

When June came down the alley with an armful of groceries, the two older girls ran to meet him, eager to see what goodies he might have brought them. He enjoyed watching their faces light up when he gave them a sucker or some other treat, as he almost always did. Dona once teased him by saying that he supplied them with cake but sometimes he forgot the bread.

He handed Dona the groceries and stopped at the pump to wash the day's perspiration from his face and arms. He took a long, cool drink from the tin cup that hung from the well and offered each of the girls a drink. Then he walked around the house and sat down on the front step, the girls at his heels.

"Did you want something?" he asked in **mock** seriousness.

Barbara laughed and said, "Please, Daddy!" and Coralea tugged at the bulging pocket of his overalls.

"Oh, is this what you wanted?" and he pulled out the pencil he'd used that day. "No? This?" and he pulled out a sweat-soiled handkerchief.

"O-o-oh! You wanted this!" and he finally produced two lollipops in different colors. "You'll have to wait for supper first, remember," he cautioned as he handed them over to the grimy, outstretched hands.

The two girls climbed up on the swing and held their candy patiently for a while, waiting for supper.

June had nearly succumbed to the drowsy serenity of the evening air when Dona came out carrying Sharon, who had awakened from her nap. She set the little girl down by June, who was lying on the cool surface of the porch. Sharon was soon crawling over him and he sat up and placed her on his knee.

"How would you like a ride?" he asked, as he crossed his legs and placed her straddling his left foot. Holding onto her arms, he began swinging his foot slowly up and down.

"Now this is Charlie. Giddyap, Charlie!"

Then he recrossed his legs and placed her on his right foot.

"And this is Old Blue. Giddyap, Old Blue!" He moved his foot wildly up and down, making her fine hair wave in the air. Her eyes grew large as her reaction hovered between terror and delight. She finally smiled uncertainly and he gave her a hug as he sat her down. He enjoyed the girls at playtime but knew he could never be content to stay at home with them day and night as Dona did.

One midwinter day, Dona looked out the front window to see a car stop in front of the house. She immediately recognized the Chevy Sam drove and went to meet him at the door.

"Well, come in!" she called. A blast of cold air rushed in as she held the door open for him. As he stepped inside, Barbara and Coralea ran in from where they'd been playing.

"Grampa!" each exclaimed as they rushed over to greet him.

"I'll just stand here on the rug. My boots are pretty wet. How're you all doing?" He gave the girls a friendly pat on the head. They were excited to see him. He liked to play with them and he often came with candy to share. Horehound was his favorite, but they each hoped he might have some lemon drops again. Horehound was not their favorite. But he reached into his coat pocket, brought out a bag, and handed them each a stick of the dark, molasses-sweet treat. They thanked him with guarded enthusiasm.

Dona expected Sam to drop by now and then, as he had set a line of traps over by the river and needed to check them periodically. He skinned the beaver he caught, and stretched and sold the pelts when the market was good. He considered himself extra fortunate if he caught a mink. Their furs sometimes brought as much as fifteen dollars apiece.

"How's Mom?" Dona asked, though she'd talked to her mother on the telephone just a few days before.

"She's fine, wants you to come down one of these days. I'm going to check my traps while the ground's still firm. I should be back in a couple of hours," he told her as he drew on his gloves.

She watched him go across the ice-crusted lawn. The snow lay without melting in the oblique winter sunshine. The flaps of his heavy woolen cap were pulled down over his ears, and his form appeared stocky in thick layers of protective clothing. She watched him take his rifle and a bag of something, probably bait, from his car and start across the road toward the river.

The crackle of his boots snapping brittle, half-buried twigs broke the soft white silence that blanketed the countryside. Sam relished the time he spent outdoors, even on bitterly cold days such as this. He noticed as a hawk slid smoothly over the tops of willows that traced the meandering course of the river. He hoped to steal the hawk's prey by shooting a rabbit or two, but it might be too cold for them to be out today.

He crossed several ditches where locked-up water would eventually seep riverward. He would cover a couple of miles as he checked the traps he had set.

To his surprise, he did happen upon some rabbits. The creatures had ventured out of their shelter, searching for nourishment in the harsh winter habitat. In a few minutes he had shot two and strung them together to hang from the old belt he'd fastened around himself.

He was greatly disappointed in his trapping endeavor, however, as only a few had been sprung, and those were now empty and had been dragged for some distance. He had to search for them, finally giving up without locating one of them. He hoped to find it when the snow was gone.

His step was slow and heavy by the time he returned to town. The little house where Dona and her family lived was fringed with icicles that sparkled in the afternoon sun. Smoke from the chimneys of the town rose skyward, straight white arrows piercing the blue mantle of day.

He went around to the back door and stepped into the porch, where he found a wash basin of chipped enamel to put the game in after it was cleaned.

"Can I go outside?" Barbara asked her mother, wanting to see her grandfather again. She knew he didn't often stay long when he was by himself.

"I guess. If you'll be sure to stay out of the way," her mother answered, then hurried to bundle her up and send her out the door.

By the time the child joined him, Sam had finished skinning one rabbit and had cut the feet off the second and tied him, hind legs up, to the fence post. Barbara watched him slit the skin down the soft belly and saw the steam curling from the still warm organs as the wet mass burst from the opening. Sam reached up into the cavity with his bloody fingers, stripping out the remaining entrails. He then slit the fur up the legs and proceeded to pull the hide down, turning the skin inside out, as her mother had often pulled the shirt over her own head, skinning a rabbit.

An instant wave of regret swept over Sam when he saw tears well up in Barbara's dark brown eyes.

"Does it hurt?" she barely murmured.

"No, he's dead. He doesn't feel anything" was all the comfort Sam could come up with.

She shuddered as she watched him cut off the head with an axe and drop the second carcass into the pan with the other sinewy body.

Before going into the back porch, he stopped at the pump to add ice-cold water to the pan. He offered one of the rabbits to Dona, which she gladly accepted for her family, and he soon left with the remaining meat wrapped in a paper bag, to become his own evening meal. Sam always tried to get home before six o'clock so he could listen to Gabriel Heater and the news. He was troubled by recent events in Europe, and followed world newscasts and commentary with increasing concern.

At the supper table that night, Barbara sat quietly, scooting her food around on her plate occasionally but taking hardly a bite.

"Aren't you hungry tonight, Babe?" her daddy asked.

"I just don't want that rabbit!" she blurted out.

"Grandpa got it just for us," her mother encouraged. "See. Coralea likes it." Her mother's testimonial didn't comfort her much. She'd seen some of the strange things her sister put in her mouth and knew her mother wouldn't care for some of them either. Barbara sat quietly, a frown darkening her face.

"You'll have to sit there until you can eat your supper," June told her firmly.

Dona couldn't understand her being so picky since she herself had been brought up eating wild game and had often sat down to a Sunday dinner of fried chicken shortly after seeing her mother wringing the neck of the doomed bird.

Barbara sat stubbornly for over an hour on the hard, straight chair. She didn't know how to tell her parents of her feelings. She had a whole new perception of the beloved lullaby her mother often sang to them about Baby Bunting and the rabbit skin. If Sam had been there, he'd have understood. And he'd have been sorry.

She nearly fell asleep and toppled from the chair before she was finally allowed to leave the table.

In the spring Dona and June were once again enlisted to help in moving the Schmit family, this time entirely away from the community surrounding Summerville. Dona wondered if maybe her parents were seeking a fresh start, wholly removed from the troubles of the past. After Retha's last pregnancy had resulted in a stillbirth, conflicts between Sam and Retha had escalated to the point where she had moved out of the home. Along with the boys and Carrie, she lived for a while in an upstairs apartment in Summerville, where she took in washing and ironing to help support her shrinking family. With encouragement from Earlene, Dona's parents had reconciled, though a strain on the thread of their relationship was still very much in evidence.

Following the Japanese attack on Pearl Harbor, Hank had enlisted in the army and was now away for basic training, leaving only Carrie and Grant at home. June had borrowed the Merriman Lumber truck to help in the move, which would be a distance of about forty miles to the south near Bedford, Missouri. They were moving southeast of town to a farm that was known as the Ellis place. Dona was impressed by the well-kept condition of the house and the carefully bordered flowerbeds arranged in the front yard.

She was happy to see her folks moving to a nice home, but Dona knew she would now see less of her family. She had learned to drive and had occasionally taken the girls over to see their grandparents for the entire day. She knew it would now be too far and too expensive to make such trips. June had encouraged Dona to get out on her own with the children. She felt he needed some time to himself, and she enjoyed the unhurried visits with her family.

Dona didn't know when her marriage had begun to fall apart. She'd felt for months that June was distant towards her and uninterested in their home or the little girls. When he was there, he was distracted and restless, and she realized he was spending more and more time at the station and the restaurant. They no longer shared any activities as a couple. She had willingly assumed complete responsibility for the children, knowing he worked hard and was still troubled by the tragedy in his own family. She had to admit to herself that maybe her family and friends had been right, that she and June had in truth married too young. He was only twenty-three and already had three children to support. Her own feelings indicated that the burden of such early parenthood was a tremendous challenge.

Dona felt that she had been an understanding wife. She wanted so badly to avoid the mistakes of her own parents and tried desperately to circumvent such discord in her own home. Maybe she had tried too hard. Maybe she hadn't made her feelings known when she should have. Maybe she hadn't been a good wife. She wasn't skilled in homemaking as her mother was, but she had been pleasant and supportive and was completely devoted to her children. She was alternately torn between hope and disillusionment. She would try to keep the doubts out of her mind.

On a Saturday afternoon in July, Dona and the girls walked up the hill to the grocery store in the business area of the town. Barbara and Coralea took turns on the trike and Dona pulled Sharon in the small red wagon. They walked beneath shade trees to avoid the hot sun, now a fierce burning ball in the western sky. There was a sidewalk for most of the way, so on some days the jaunt to the store was a pleasant outing. Today, however, the summer air hung over the town in stifling closeness, turning any movement into a huge effort. It was hot and humid inside the dark store, though several fans whirred overhead and both doors were propped open.

Dona decided to stop at the station on the way home. June had discouraged this lately, saying he was too busy to give any attention to the little girls and didn't want them getting in the way. But she thought of how the girls loved it when their daddy opened the big red Coca-Cola chest and brought out dripping bottles of soda for them to open on the metal device on the side. They fingered the heap of fluted metal bottle caps that accumulated in the catching box beneath the opener. June would get a bag of peanuts and drop a few in each bottle, making the girls squeal as fizzy bubbles tickled their noses. They enjoyed the salty taste of the refreshing liquid.

She didn't see June, but Jack was there, so she asked if her husband were around.

"No, he hasn't been here. I told him I wouldn't need him today," Jack said. "It's been so hot lately, I guess everyone's staying home!"

"Oh," Dona mumbled. "Maybe I misunderstood."

Jack saw how hot the girls were as they stared wistfully at the cooler.

He quickly pulled out a couple of bottles and passed them to Dona.

"Why don't you cool off?" he asked politely. She wondered if he were reading her mind.

"Thanks. I guess it's hotter than I thought. Do you mind if we bring the bottles back some other time?"

"Sure. See you later, girls," he replied. Dona had always liked Jack but was embarrassed now by the awkward turn of events.

As they slowly went down the hill, Dona's mind raced to countless possibilities. She was certain June had told her he was going to work today. Maybe she had misunderstood, she optimistically reasoned.

When June returned shortly after closing time at the station, he gave no indication that he had not been at work all day. She didn't know whether she would ask him or not. Maybe she'd rather not know. But she couldn't avoid confronting him with his deliberate deceit.

"We stopped at the station today. Jack said you weren't working." She felt as uneasy as he looked as he got up and hurried from her accusing gaze.

"Are you checking up on me now?" he angrily blurted out.

"It was hot. We stopped by on our way home. Where were you?" She felt sick and humiliated to have to ask, but she needed to know.

June said nothing as he stalked out the front door and walked quickly across the yard, then continued down the street toward some open fields. She sank down on the porch and buried her face in her hands.

A line of evening shadows crept across the front yard as June returned hours later. He sat quietly on the porch swing. Dona said nothing to him. She had nothing more to say.

Life in the little house was strained and uncomfortably polite for the next week. It was as if they each knew a storm was on the horizon but didn't know when or where it would hit. Dona spent the week fussing over the children, giving them lots of hugs and then crying privately when they were not close by.

The next Saturday June again left, as if to go to work, but this time he took the car. Dona knew when he stepped out the back door that he wasn't coming back. What would she do? Where would they go? What would become of her children? She had no money, no possibility of employment if she were able to work--she must take care of the girls. How would she manage? She felt overwhelmed, defeated.

Seeming to sense her distress, the children were attentive and thoughtful, and she felt her heart lighten as she gathered them around her. *Maybe things will look better in the morning,* she prayed, as she mechanically moved through the remainder of the day.

When June had not returned by morning, she knew she must make a hard decision. She would have to go to her folks'. She was determined not to be here if or when June decided to return. She put off making the call to Bedford. She didn't know what she would say.

Finally, around ten o'clock, she put in the call, trembling with anxiety as she listened to the series of rings repeated again and again. Her parents weren't home!

She would call Mr. Merriman. He'd always been good to them.

She had to do something, she thought, as the operator rang on his line.

"Mr. Merriman?" she uttered. "I don't know how to say this, but I'm afraid June has left me and I need to ask for your help . . ." She started to sob, despite her efforts not to.

He paused a bit before she heard him say, "I'm sorry. I've been worried about June. He's been preoccupied lately, and he didn't use to miss work so much."

"What do you mean?" she asked, already knowing what his answer would be.

"He's missed several days lately." He sensed her despair and immediately knew this information was a revelation to her. "Is there anything I can do to help?" he asked kindly.

"I guess we'll need a ride to my folks' place. I don't have a car and they live down by Bedford now," Dona sadly said.

"Of course I can take you. When do you want to leave?" he asked.

"Just as soon as you can go. I'd really appreciate it. I'd ask my folks to come for us, but they aren't home right now." She felt as if the whole world had deserted her.

"I'll be there in half an hour," he promised.

In later years, Coralea would remember the welcome sight of her grandparents' house as they turned onto the dirt road that went by the Ellis place. She also vividly recalled how happy she had been to find the sugar bowl on the table and to sit down to a big bowl of corn flakes. She was hungry! When discussing the experience many years later, Dona denied that the girls had ever gone hungry, but Coralea certainly remembered the feeling she'd had then. Probably in her desperate state of mind her mother had simply neglected to offer the little girls any breakfast.

EIGHT

Headlights jiggling on the distant gravel road signaled that her parents would soon arrive home. Dona went out to sit on the front steps, struggling to choose the right words to break the disappointing news to her family. She'd worried herself sick since Mr. Merriman brought her and her daughters down from Iowa. How could she ever repay him for his kindness? He had insisted she keep a twenty-dollar bill he quietly passed to her.

Dona had spent the long afternoon puzzling over the best way to approach the subject with her parents. What would they say? What if they couldn't, or wouldn't, take them in? She wondered what the girls must be thinking by now. They'd come to visit their grandparents and Grandma and Grandpa weren't even at home!

She wondered how Grant would feel with more people in the house. He'd had explosive episodes with just his immediate family around. Perhaps if she talked to him and made him understand their predicament, he would be patient with the little girls.

"It's Dona and the girls!" Carrie cried as she jumped from the car. Dona stood to acknowledge their homecoming as the girls ran across the soft grass of the yard. Carrie picked up Sharon and squeezed her tightly.

"How did you get here?" Sam asked, noticing that her car was not in sight.

Dona's face clouded as she replied, "Can I talk to you about that later, Dad?"

Sam caught the guarded edge in her voice and had a premonition of bad news from his daughter. He'd wait until she was ready--no need in rushing into an unpleasant subject.

There was an awkward pause in the conversation as Dona struggled with her emotions and her family waited anxiously for her to confide in them.

Retha spoke up. "Carrie, why don't you take the girls upstairs to your room to play? Show them the paper dolls you made yesterday."

After the little girls had followed Carrie up the narrow stairs to her room, the rest of the family sat at the kitchen table under the glow of a coal-oil lamp. Dona sensed the question hovering over the group.

"June has left us," she managed to say before breaking into tears.

"Now, are you sure of that?" her father asked.

"He's gone. He left yesterday morning. Things haven't been right. I didn't want to tell you, but he's been different for a long time." She didn't know how to say that she thought he'd found someone else. She didn't want to say it.

"What will you do?" Grant spoke up.

"I don't know," she replied. She felt completely lost and without any answers. She'd worried and worried about such a thing happening, and now that it had she was as far from a solution as she could get.

"You'll stay here with us," her mother firmly stated, "until you find a job and can take care of the girls. Don't you think June will help?"

"I don't know, Mom. He doesn't seem to care about any of us anymore." She sadly realized she was only speaking the truth. He certainly hadn't shown any concern for even the children lately. She couldn't stop her tears. She dropped her face into her hands and wept in muffled, racking sobs. Sam and Grant, uncomfortable witnessing her total collapse, left the room. Retha placed her hand on her daughter's heaving shoulder.

"Now, now. Maybe it will all work out," she offered kindly, but without inner conviction. She'd been aware of June's absence when Dona and the children had visited in recent months.

"I haven't told the girls. I guess I don't know how to tell them," Dona confided in her mother.

Retha sat quietly a moment before replying. "Why don't we just say you're going to visit us for a few days and see what happens?" Retha wanted to be supportive. She'd had similar problems of her own and knew too well of the heartache her daughter now faced.

"Thank you, Mom. I knew you'd understand. Do you think Dad will accept having us all around for a while?" Dona asked.

Retha was only outwardly confident when she said, "Of course he will."

The barren, uneven ground of the barnyard rushed by in a blur beneath Barbara's feet as she clung to the rope tied high above her.

"Don't let go!" Carrie called. If she did, Carrie would hit the ground abruptly herself.

Coralea watched from a stump nearby. She hoped it would soon be her turn.

The girls clinging to the ropes weren't equal in size but could still make the merry-go-round swing in a big arc. The two younger girls wore sunsuits

Retha had made from colorful feed sacks. Dust scuffed up during their play left a powdery film on their skin and clothes, sticking in the sweaty creases of their skin.

"My turn!" Coralea announced, and proceeded to take the rope from Barbara, who wasn't yet ready to sit out.

"Play fair!" Carrie warned. She exercised her auntly authority, though she was only seven years older than Barbara and thought of the girls more as playmates than as her charges. She was nearly a teenager now, petite and fair, like her oldest sisters.

Grant had made the contraption they were calling a merry-go-round. He fastened a crossbeam over the top of a pole left in the middle of the barnyard from some long-ago project. He hung a rope from each side so a good, fast ride could be had if one gave a running push and held his feet up high. Grant had been generous and thoughtful of the girls so far, to Dona's great relief.

A lazy breeze tickled the leaves overhead as Dona escorted her middle daughter to the little building out back. She had stacked up catalogues for a stepstool so the child could reach the seat of the two-holer. Her two-year-old could use the pot in the back porch, but Coralea was big enough to manage by herself here, at least with a little temporary assistance.

Dona smiled at her mother, who was working nearby in her garden, digging potatoes. Retha's face was shielded by the brim of her homemade bonnet. Despite the work she did, Retha had become quite plump with the passing years. One of the girls once said that she liked to hug her grandmother because she was so soft and you couldn't reach around her. Retha had laughed at that. She'd never been obsessed with her appearance.

This place is just what I always wished for the folks, Dona thought. The large house had wide porches and shade trees sheltered the broad lawn. A board walk led to the outhouse, with mounds of petunias spilling over from their beds between the walk and the garden. Early morning trips were pleasant, with the fresh scent of the flourishing flowers unlocked by the morning dew. Her mother's chickens were confined in a well-built chicken coop, not roaming over the yard leaving messes, as Dona remembered from other homes of her parents.

Coralea ran out to help her grandmother in the garden and was quickly cautioned to "please watch your step!"

This was the day Sam would take Dona to St. Joseph to the employment agency. She'd scoured all the towns nearby looking for work, with no success. Plenty of jobs for men, especially farm work. Already the rural areas were missing the young men who'd signed up to go to war, but female help was abundant.

June had asked for and gotten a divorce--he planned to remarry. He'd been down to visit the girls but hadn't much to offer in the way of support. Dona hadn't inquired about his life beyond common courtesy. She sensed he was experiencing some of the bleakness she had felt when he so completely disrupted her life. She knew she would never forget the love wasted and betrayed by him. It was obvious to her that he had no plans for an active part in his daughters' lives. There was no other option but for Dona to find work, and Sam had heard women were being hired to work in war plants.

Carrie went along. She and Sam would do some shopping in the city while Dona was at the employment center. Dona was eager to find work but scared, too. She knew it would mean a move away from the comfortable life she'd had lately under her parents' roof.

By the time Sam returned for her, Dona was waiting on a bench, a sheaf of papers in her hand. She was happy to tell him that they were not only hiring but also provided training for qualified entrants into the work field. Help was desperately needed in providing materials of war--not something Dona was eager to be a part of but at least a possibility of steady income. She was excited at the prospect, as she had never before worked for regular wages nor had money of her own.

It began to rain as they left St. Joseph. They would make the trip by way of back roads, through Roseville, cutting off a good three miles of the journey on 71 highway. By the time they'd gone through the town, rain was sheeting down, making it hard for Sam to see the road, even in daylight. About a mile from home near the Johnson County line, the sparsely graveled road turned liquid with mud. They approached a steep hill that pitched downward to a narrow bridge over a deep gully. By then Sam was nervous handling the careening car, so he made Dona and Carrie get out and walk down the hill to the far side of the bridge, fearing he might land them all in the ditch.

The girls took off their shoes and slogged slowly down the hill, sliding in the soft, oozy loam. They fought to keep from slipping off their feet and into the muck. Beneath them, water rushed down the steep slope in an intricate weave of tiny rivers. Mud squished up between their toes and sucked at their feet with each step. The slick boards of the bridge gave no more comfort than the heavy mud.

When they were safely across, Sam started the car forward, whipping the wheel left and right as the tires slid across the road, zigzagging alternately toward one drainage ditch or the other! The girls decided their father's fears for their safety were not so misplaced after all.

A grin appeared on Sam's face as he stopped the car near his bedraggled, dripping daughters. The girls laughed with relief as they climbed back into the car, water running from their hair and clothing and mud balled up on their feet. In a few more yards the car was mired in one of the inevitable mud holes of country roads and had to be abandoned. The three continued homeward, very wet and tired when their trek was completed. Sam and Grant would take the horses out after the mud dried and pull out the firmly anchored vehicle.

"Dad, I don't know if I can do it!" Dona began. "It will mean leaving the girls behind. The training lasts for two weeks and they expect us to be in St. Joseph for all that time."

They sat at the kitchen table relaxing after supper. Barbara helped Carrie with the dishes while the little girls ran about in the yard chasing after fluttering yellow butterflies.

"You won't know unless you try," he said. "Your mom will take good care of the girls." Dona was surprised by her father's supportive attitude. She thought he must have mellowed in the last few years. She hadn't expected the calm acceptance he'd shown her since their arrival into his home.

"I know that. But they'll miss me and I'll miss them! They've never been without me. Never." She would be lost without them, she was certain.

"They got along fine the other day when you were in St. Joe," Retha volunteered.

"But I was here at night. Maybe they won't sleep without me," she protested. "And if I do make it, the work may be in Kansas City." Just the thought of going to that big city alone made her stomach knot up.

"I'll tell you what," Sam declared. "If you'll go and give it a try for two weeks, I'll come and get you right away if you want to come home."

She knew she couldn't refuse. She had to have a job and here was an opportunity at last. The women coming in for the training session were to stay together at the YWCA. She'd be with a group, all new to the work like herself. That was some comfort. She didn't have any idea what kind of job assignment she might get. She'd had typing and shorthand in high school and assumed she might qualify for a bookkeeping job of some sort.

Saying good-bye to the girls was easier on them than on her. They had no perception of how long she might actually be gone. She worried that they might be too much for her mother. With Carrie now in school, Retha would be responsible for them full time, all day long, and Dona knew the three girls were still small enough to require a lot of attention.

"Now, don't you worry," Retha told her. "You can call and check on us every night if you need to. The girls can talk to you on the telephone. You'll be surprised at how grown-up they can be." Dona knew she was fortunate to have her mother's capable hands caring for her children.

On the morning she packed her suitcase and left with Sam, Dona kept checking the rear-view mirror to see the girls out in the yard, watching her go. They were gathered around Retha, standing very still and every now and then raising a hand in one more good-bye wave.

Outwardly the children accepted the change without complaint, but Retha recognized the sadness in their eyes and did her best to keep them occupied with little tasks and games. Sam taught them to play Chinese checkers and held Sharon on his lap as he sat in his rocker listening to the evening newscasts. Losing their father had been nothing like losing their mother. But they still had Grandma and Grandpa. After Dona left, Sharon spent a lot of time with Retha in the big wooden rocker. Retha never sang to her as Dona had, but the soft, fleshy cushion of her lap made the secure nest that Sharon's little body craved.

Even their grandfather acknowledged that the children needed to see their mother, so the first weekend, on Sunday, Retha packed a picnic lunch and all except Grant got in the car for a trip to St. Joseph. Grant was happy to stay home, where he would have some rare time to himself without the lively clamor caused by three small children.

Retha hoped it would ease the girls' homesickness if they could see where their mother was staying. The "Y" was big and Spartan in its furnishings. Dona shared a simple room with Jenny Thompson, a girl from Chillicothe. Dona liked her but found they had little in common, as Jenny was single and just out of high school. Dona felt herself a burden to the girl, with her constant talk of her daughters and how she longed to hold them.

In Krug Park, where Retha unpacked their ample lunch, roses bloomed profusely, still, in September, stair-stepping down the gently sloped hill. White trellises gilded a rock-edged pond at the bottom. A few ducks and swans floated serenely in the afternoon sun. The girls had never seen such a beautiful sight. They left their mother's side long enough to feed the pretty birds some bread from their sandwiches. Dona was aware of them clinging to her since her arrival, causing her both pleasure and sadness.

After lunch, they walked up a tier of concrete steps to a walkway edged with swinging gliders. They bunched up together and sat cozily facing each other on slatted benches that swung in tandem beneath the wooden canopy.

"Have you been helping Grandma?" Dona asked Barbara.

"I help her water the chickens and gather the eggs," she proudly replied.

"They are all lots of help," Retha claimed. "Even Sharon runs and gets me things, don't you?" Sharon looked up at her mother and smiled shyly.

"You're never naughty, are you?" their mother asked.

"Grandpa might have to spank Coralea," Barbara stated, causing Sam to grin. "She's always spilling her milk because she's not careful." It was obvious that she considered herself careful and wasn't at all reluctant to find fault with her pesky sister. Coralea was always tagging along and butting in when Barbara would like to play alone with Carrie.

Dad's razor strop, Dona thought. How many times had she herself been threatened with that wicked-looking strap of leather? He had never been known to actually wield it, but over the years Retha had employed the specter of it to good use as a powerful deterrent to bad behavior. Dona and her mother had swatted a little bottom with a swiftly administered palm when the need presented itself, but Sam's razor strop was reserved as the ultimate doom. The little girls had watched their grandfather flash his straight-edged razor back and forth over the slick, dark surface as it hung above the dry sink, and Coralea feared the day it might leave its hook beside the mirror and be used for a more sinister purpose.

"Better get away from those dogs!" Grant called.

Barbara looked over to where her uncle stood. He was working on a sagging hinge on the barn door.

"I'm only watching them," she said. It seemed to her that Grant was always bossy and disagreeable.

"Get on away, now. You don't know if they might be mean." He gave her a look that let her know he was serious.

He doesn't need to worry about me touching one of those ugly things, she thought. *Their lips look like liver and hang way down from their mouths!* Grandpa called them blue-tick hounds, but to her they looked sickly gray and were disgustingly skinny, not firm and stocky like Old Troub. She'd play with him if she wanted to play with a dog.

Sam had borrowed the two hounds from his hunting friend who lived near Rock Port. A foxhunt was coming up in about a week, over beyond Horton. He figured on going with his neighbor, Chance Holliday, who had hounds of his own.

"Are you wanting to go to the foxhunt Saturday?" Sam asked Retha one evening. She wasn't particularly interested in going. They'd have things for the women to do and there would be a box supper in the afternoon, but she wasn't well acquainted in the area so she wouldn't know many others there. Besides, she'd rather take care of the girls here at home, where they were easier to watch. All the yapping and commotion at such gatherings never had appealed to her.

"No, but I think Carrie would like to go. She's good friends with Reba Holliday and I don't think Verna would mind," she said. Verna was Chance's wife, whom Retha had seen in Bedford a few times. The Hollidays were the Schmits' closest neighbors. They had children near Carrie's age who went to Stingley School with her.

"You and Grant just go by yourselves. I'll fix up a supper for you to take." She knew the Hollidays would be glad to stop for Carrie, who'd enjoy spending the day with her friend.

The colors of autumn had begun to fade from the woods when the hunt was held in early November. Except for the fair at Summerville, Carrie had never seen so many people in one place. Dogs of all descriptions pulled at their leashes, eager to sniff each other. Their keepers greeted fellow hunters and listened for directions from the promoters of the event. Shrill, puppy-like yelps emanated from some of the excited animals, while others, perhaps more experienced, specially-bred dogs, sat quietly beside their masters. Celebrating its accidental liberation, an unleashed hound cavorted wildly among the tethered dogs, chased by a couple of shouting boys. The frenzied activity finally calmed as the gun-carrying men spread apart to form a living net that would sweep through the woods in search of prey.

Rows of cars and trucks lined the crest of the hill that separated the meeting area from the thick forest that spread to the western horizon. Two big tents were set up in the field near the highway. They would shelter the visiting families of the participants and serve as dining halls for the afternoon meal. Prizes were offered for successful hunters, and later in the day a turkey shoot would determine who took home the five birds that now gobbled confusedly in wooden crates.

Carrie had not been to such a meeting before and wasn't sure what went on, but she had confidence in her father's ability. Hadn't he told her many times of his spectacular luck one day when he was hunting squirrels and got three with one shot? They had been lined up on a tree branch, neat as could be, so he had fired once and that single bullet passed right through them all! She didn't remember when this happened, just his telling about it.

The temperature fell with the setting of the sun, and those who had competed in the day's events gathered their belongings and bade farewell to new and old acquaintances. Carrie went home with Reba and her family, sitting on the floor of the truck alongside the cages of the unsuccessful hunting dogs.

Only a straggle of animals were left tied to bumpers and staked out in the field when Sam and Grant herded the rangy, borrowed hounds into the back seat of their car and headed east.

Just a hint of color lingered in the sky as they pulled the car into the lane. A wooden crate was wedged into the open trunk. They had planned to release the creature into the chicken coop to surprise Retha when she went to tend her chickens in the morning. However, there was no smuggling the noisy fowl. Its frightened racket announced its own presence.

"Land sakes! What will I cook it in?" Retha asked when she spied the big bird. She was already mentally preparing a Thanksgiving feast for her family.

In November Dona moved to Kansas City with some girls from her training group. They took an apartment in a brick townhouse, one in a row of sand-colored buildings. She and Jenny were again roommates. Their room was the living room/kitchenette and their bed pulled down from a cabinet in the wall. When the Schmits came to visit, the little girls were fascinated with the Murphy bed but not quite sure if they trusted it not to spring up and shut them in.

Dona began to adjust to her altered role in life, herself childlike in her wonderment of the big city. She was able to take the train to Bedford for weekend visits, which she did at least once a month. Her daughters seemed to thrive under the care of their grandmother, and she felt some of the burden of responsibility lift from her shoulders.

The dream of again having his own farm was revived for Sam when he had an opportunity to own a place closer to town. Carrie would be going into high school in Bedford in the fall. It would be much more convenient if they lived on a better road, and the farm available was just two miles from town. Also, Barbara would be starting school then.

Only forty acres were included with the farm, but it had a house and a barn, and he could make the down payment now and hopefully pay off the rest if he had a few good years. He got a couple of draft horses on the cheap from Chance when the latter bought a tractor. Most farmers in the area were switching to machine power, so Sam found it easy to pick up the few pieces of horse-drawn equipment he needed for planting corn. On the Ellis place he'd used what was left on the farm when the Ellises moved into town. All of that would stay on the rented place.

Running out from Bedford to the east was a good gravel road, County Road H. About two miles out, beyond Clear Creek, a country lane led north from this, past a small abandoned house that sat just over the hill. The lane skirted that and went on to the north, tracing the edge of the woods that surrounded the creek.

The decrepit house had stood empty for a period, and no trace of paint could still be seen on its dark, gray boards. The square, two story structure had one porch, a large screened-in affair on the front corner that was obviously a fortress against marauding mosquitoes that bred in the damp woods nearby.

When she first entered the house, Retha was immediately aware of the musty, corncob smell of mice on the premises. This would require a real adjustment for them all. There was no water in the house, nor any telephone line to the place--which perhaps bothered her most of all. Being able to call her family had been a godsend to her in recent years and she didn't relish giving that up. The girls would no longer be able to hear their mother's reassuring voice on the phone. But having a place of his own was important to Sam, and they would be much closer to school.

The only livestock they brought to the place, besides the horses, were a couple of milk cows and Retha's setting hens. Sam figured he could get more cows once he and Grant fixed the nearly non-existent fences on the place. Half the forty acres were timbered, and Sam would put the remaining acres in corn.

When the ground warmed, Sam eagerly set about preparing the soil for their first crop. The girls liked to climb up on the wooden gate by the barn and watch as their grandfather broke the sod. He walked behind the plow, with the reins of the team's harness tied behind his back and strung beneath his arms. The sun beat down fiercely and caused trickles of perspiration to course down Sam's darkened face. The ground was rich and loamy, renewed from lying fallow for a number of years. He was confident they would have a good crop this year and it would not have to be shared.

Retha watched the girls from the screened-in porch. She was happy to see them run and play outside, as long as they stayed out of the barn. She needed to know what they were doing. She didn't want them pestering Grant. He'd been moodier since the move, reluctant to help around the place and spending more and more time by himself out in the barn or in the woods. He and Sam both fished the creek and caught a few mudcats, though they had to hike up the creek a distance to get to a waterhole.

Near Easter time, June came to visit the girls. He brought them each a papier-mache bunny and some colored candy eggs. They were bashful around him, unsure of their own feelings. He had enlisted in the army and would leave soon for basic training. He was also uneasy and didn't stay long. Dona was glad she hadn't been present for his visit. Just thinking of him still threw her into an emotional turmoil.

On an evening later that spring, Retha was sitting on a straight chair in the kitchen braiding Barbara's hair when she suddenly swooned and sagged to the floor. Sam rushed over to fan her and she roused shortly. Barbara cried and cried, thinking she was somehow at fault. The doctor in Bedford felt Retha had simply over-exerted herself and advised her to get more rest.

Following the scare with Retha's health, Carrie took over watching the girls after school each day so her mother could have an afternoon nap. Their favorite place to play outdoors was in the creek. It was just a few yards from the back of the house--near enough that the necessary outhouse was precariously close to the eroding bank of the stream. Carrie worried that a big rain would someday swell the creek and cause the weathered structure to fall into the raging water. At this time of year the creek was hardly running so the children were safe wading in its firm, pebbly bed.

"Let's make a dam, like the beavers do," Coralea suggested. She'd heard her grandpa complain about beavers damming up the creek. Maybe they could get some sticks and mud and stop the water from flowing away.

"We can make a swimming pool!" Carrie announced. That should keep everyone busy for a good, long time.

The girls busied themselves dragging branches of downed timber over to the creek. They worked for hours piling sticks and mud across the rippling waterway, eventually causing a puddle to back up the gently sloping creek bed. Almost as quickly as they stopped a leak in one point of their barricade, another gush of water spurted through somewhere else.

Raccoon tracks along the soft edge of the ditch inspired them to consider the likelihood of wild animals approaching and interfering with their plans for the creek. They conjured up self-scaring scenarios to entertain each other and cause Sharon to stick close to Carrie's side. They played in the cool water until Retha called them in to supper.

"Next time let's find some rocks. They're stronger and they won't wash away," Coralea suggested as they reluctantly left, their efforts drifting down the stream with the liberated water.

Word soon reached Miriam in California that Retha suffered from exhaustion because of her extra work with the children. Miriam thought she might be able to help with the care of the little girls--she and her husband had already considered moving back to Missouri. Lloyd had been raised by his own grandmother, who was now gone. He had no other ties to the region where they now lived. He found employment in Kansas City through the firm that he worked for in California, a floor tiling concern. His employment in Missouri would be with an affiliated company.

On the day the Wrights arrived in Missouri, Earlene and Emmett and their daughter came to the farm to welcome them. The Schmit family had a happy reunion, with all together except Hank, who'd recently shipped overseas to serve in the infantry in France.

Miriam and her husband had been to Missouri only once since their marriage, when they had only their older son, Tommy. He was close to Coralea's age and now had a brother, Tad, two years old. Lloyd was tall and slender with dark auburn hair that crowned his freckled face in thick waves. His hazel eyes were soft and friendly and the girls liked him instantly.

Dona came home for the weekend also. She was enormously touched by her sister's offer to help with the girls. As soon as Miriam and Lloyd were settled in their new home in the city, Dona and the girls would go and live with them. Dona counted the days until she could be with her children again, and could be the one to tuck them in at night. She wanted to sing the lullabies that soothed the little ones to sleep.

On a humid Friday night in June, Sam went to Bedford to pick up Dona at the train station. A crescent moon climbed up the eastern sky as they drove down the lane to the secluded farm. Dona was struck by the isolation she felt as they turned corner after corner on the old roadway. This must surely be the most out-of-the-way place her folks had ever inhabited. She couldn't picture herself returning to such a rustic existence. But she knew having a place of his own meant everything to her dad. In one more week, Dona and the girls would move to Kansas City to live with Miriam and her family in the comfortable bungalow they'd found. Dona marveled at the generosity of her sister and Lloyd. Daily care of five children would be a huge undertaking for the most expansive of women.

The sound of the approaching car brought all in the household to the door--except for Grant, who lounged languidly in an old rocker beside the front step. The girls scrambled around Dona, nearly toppling her from her feet. *My goodness*, she thought! *How they are growing!*

Retha smiled from the doorway. *Soon*, Dona thought. *Soon she can have some real rest. She's been so kind to us! Dad, too. He'd never desert his family*, she realized with a burst of affection. She felt such a stirring of gratitude for her parents she almost burst into tears.

"What's the matter, Dona?" Carrie asked her sister.

"Nothing . . . I'm happy! How have you been?" she asked with sincerity.

"Happy, too--that school is out!" Carrie replied with a smile.

Grant acknowledged Dona's presence with a nod, then retreated around the house. He had become more withdrawn lately and spoke few words to anyone. Dona could understand his feelings of sadness. This was a gloomy place, dark and rickety, and so remote--half a mile back in the woods on a questionable road. And he had made no friends in Bedford. Since he was out of school and the Schmits weren't regular church-goers, he had no opportunity for meeting people his age. And then, many young men of the community were absent, away in Europe fighting in a war that seemed to pervade their existence more with each passing day.

Dona and Sam had discussed Grant's situation on the way home from the depot. Sam was worried. Nothing he had tried would lift Grant out of his deep depression. Sam had long since realized that old animosities must be put aside for the sake of his troubled son.

"It's so hot tonight, Dona! Why don't you sleep down here where it's a little cooler?" Retha suggested to her daughter.

"Do you want to go up with Carrie for the night?" Dona asked the girls.

Sharon hugged her mamma's knee. "I want to sleep with you!" she cried.

"Okay. Barbara and Coralea can sleep upstairs on the spare bed and Sharon can sleep with me." Dona was exhausted after the week at work and the long train ride home. And she would have a busy day tomorrow packing the things the girls would take to Kansas City.

Carrie lit a small lamp and the girls followed her up the shadowy stairs. Barbara picked her way gingerly up the steps. Several mouse holes had been covered with tin can lids and one broken step was completely encased in screen wire. The little girls rarely went upstairs, partly because of the horrible stairs and partly because Grant's bed was in the first room, which led to the two back rooms.

A dusty clutter of fly remains dotted the bare floor. Several trunks and boxes of winter clothing and bedding were stacked along the wall. The stairway was open, with no protective railing on either side. From the top it looked to Coralea like a frightening chasm plunging to unimaginable depths. The girls stayed close to Carrie as they passed through the dark area into her small, orderly bedroom. She would put them to bed in the room adjoining hers as soon as she cleared off the single cot they would sleep on.

Coralea awakened in the morning with a powerful urge to relieve herself and knew she must hurry down the stairs without delay. She hesitated to go through Grant's room alone, but was propelled by the pressing urgency of the situation.

Grant had become hot in the night and left his bed to lie on the cool boards of the floor. With only a sheet wrapped across his shoulders and wadded beneath his head, he lay sprawled beside the open stairway. Coralea's first thought was of concern that he might roll into the fearsome pit of the stairwell. As she moved cautiously down the stairs she glanced over at Grant, his bare body illuminated by the light streaming in the window. She stared at him, surprised and shocked at seeing his nakedness so close beside her.

Retha heard the girl coming down the stairs and hurried over to see about her. When she was aware of the scene her son presented, she took Coralea's hand and pulled her away, saying, "Come on now. Don't look at him!" Grant awakened and felt his vulnerability. He uttered a string of profanities, and Coralea sensed she had done something very, very bad.

In a matter of moments, Grant was in his overalls and down the stairs, raving in a spate of words she didn't comprehend.

Dona was immediately alarmed!

Grant strode into the kitchen and picked up a butcher knife that lay on the counter. His eyes were wild with resentment and anger as he lurched into the room with the knife clutched dagger-like in his upraised hand!

Dona screamed and pulled Coralea behind her back.

Retha's face drained in fright as she tried to decide what to do.

"You must put the knife down, Grant. No one is trying to hurt you," she said, struggling to make her voice calm.

"That brat keeps staring at me!" he spit out venomously.

Dona stood stonily in front of him, too frightened to move or to speak.

A look of empathy crossed over Grant's face as he saw the terror in his sister's eyes. He dropped the knife to the floor and stumbled out the door, then sat down on the back step. His chin sank down on his chest in an attitude of resignation.

Retha realized that her son was completely out of control. Something would have to be done. She'd fought this reality in her mind for a long time and knew there was now no alternative. Grant would have to go to a hospital.

When Sam returned from doing his chores, he could tell from Grant's demeanor that a crisis was near. After talking with Retha, he offered to take Grant for a ride in the car to "cool off." Grant was compliant, willing to give over his troubles into someone else's hands.

Sam knew Grant would have to go to the State Hospital in St. Joseph but feared he might have another violent episode if he tried to take him there now. So he drove to the county seat in Albany to seek help from the officers there. Grant was silent all the way, with his head sagging forward, walled up in his own nightmare.

Sam sought out the county sheriff at the courthouse and then led him and his deputy to his unfortunate son, who still sat limply in the car. Sam had been through some hard times, but he knew this was the most difficult thing he'd ever had to do. He felt failure on a very personal level. Grant looked at him with bewilderment and betrayal as the two men took his arms and guided him toward their waiting automobile.

A mixture of hope and despair filled Sam as he faced the knowledge that he had just done either the best or the worst thing for his son. Tears coursed down his deeply tanned face as he returned to the farm and his confused and disappointed family.

NINE

On the occasions when Dona visited her family in Bedford, she took the train, departing from and arriving at Union Station. On her first trip she had been so fraught with insecurity she'd persuaded her roommates to accompany her on the trolley ride to the station. Now, many months later, she eagerly anticipated arriving at the cavernous structure, so full of busy travelers, each on his own unique trip to his own personal future. She loved to watch people stream through the gates of the big building and to imagine the exotic locations they might visit.

Her own trip on the "Bug" took two hours from the depot in Bedford, and she usually arrived just as the sun fell behind the city's magnificent skyline. She had memorized just which hill the train must top before the jagged outline of the high buildings loomed into view. Each time her heart skipped a beat as she caught sight of the bold structures shouldering the sky.

How her feelings for the place had changed since she first came to the city over a year ago! A wave of unexpected contentment came over her and she almost felt she had come home when she arrived in the bustling metropolis. How full of life it was! The city's boisterous gaiety had ensnared her already. Life here was exciting and simple, at once. There was so much to see and do, but one could stand back and observe, taking it all in while remaining separate, somehow. She appreciated the friendships she had made with the girls she roomed and worked with. Dona and Jenny were joined by Therese and Irma and the four were a tight group of confidantes, a family of sorts.

As the train pulled into the station, Dona thought of her folks back home and how sad they were because of Grant's situation. Her own feelings toward her unfortunate brother were confused and complicated. Only a week ago he had made a seesaw for the girls with an old plank and she remembered the time he had shown them how he could "walk" a barrel and had helped them to try it also. His actions had been so unpredictable. She wished there were some way to go back and relive the event that precipitated his commitment to the hospital. Maybe she could have done or said something to defuse the situation. She knew her folks had the same self-doubts, and she was as sorry for their sakes as much as for Grant's. Dona hoped her brother would be able to return home after the initial three months of mandatory testing and observation had passed. Not only were her parents missing Grant but their other son, too, as Hank had recently been sent overseas. "Somewhere in France" was the only location they had for him now.

In one more week the girls would be here, in Kansas City with her. She was eager to show them all the places she had discovered. And having Miriam here! Dona felt she was fortunate to have her family with her at last. Too late for spring fever, but that was the kind of boundless joy she now felt.

Dona smiled to herself as she opened the door to her unusually quiet apartment. She had never been here when everyone else was gone. She wondered where they were all off to. Her curiosity aroused, she stepped over to the bedroom door and rapped loudly, thinking that one of her friends might be home, just napping. When there was no answer, she tried the door, then slowly opened it.

"Surprise!" She was so startled she nearly fainted when a crowd of friends sprang from their seats, laughing and shouting.

"What's going on?" she managed.

Jenny grabbed Dona's hand and said, "It's a surprise party--your going-away party!"

Dona was completely awestruck. She'd never had a party in her honor before. This was a surprise!

"We're taking you out for a grand time tonight!" Joe said. He was Irma's current boyfriend. Johnny, Therese's beau, was here, too, and several others she had met at work or with friends, whom she didn't know quite as well.

"I'm going to take your place here, Dona," a girl named Jenny Green spoke up.

"I can see you're really going to miss me!" Dona chided her friends. "You've replaced me already!"

"Where do you want to go tonight?" Johnny asked. "You name it, we'll get us there."

"Anywhere?" Dona asked.

Joe answered, "We've got two cars. That should get us all there. What will it be?"

Dona had to think. They'd been to a lot of local diners, but walking distance from home and work was the perimeter of her experience. She had heard of a place called The Top Hat, so she mentioned that.

"You've got it!" Johnny replied with enthusiasm.

"Let's go. Time's a-wastin'," Jenny announced.

Dona was breathless from all the activity but unexpectedly content, too, in the midst of the animated young people around her. She would miss them all, she knew.

After they reached the place and enjoyed a hearty meal, Therese suggested they find a nightclub where they could dance. Johnny was a serviceman and would be sent overseas soon, so the couple sought as much intimacy as possible while physical closeness was an option. The city teemed with young men, but they were all here temporarily on their way to somewhere else. That "somewhere" was usually dictated by a branch of the service.

They stopped at a small joint just off Broadway, small by Kansas City standards but enormous to Dona. She'd never imagined such a place! There were people everywhere, sitting at tables, lounging by the bar, and standing in groups around the huge room. Many men were in uniform--undoubtedly some were out for a last fling before leaving for Europe to face the enemy. *You'd never guess the serious nature of their imminent mission*, Dona mused. Tonight they were all boldness and bravura, and she found them erotically attractive in their handsome uniforms. She was delighted when she was asked to dance by a smart-looking young man and doubly impressed when he proved to be a gentleman when they danced intimately.

At first the band played slow dance music. Dona recognized Guy Lombardo renditions she had heard. She knew there were jazz clubs in the city and wasn't surprised to hear the band break into a lively number that sent the crowd into toe-tapping appreciation. Soon the entertainers picked up the swing sound and dancers swarmed to the floor to twirl in spirited, torso twisting gyrations. Bobby socks and saddle shoes jabbed the air as youthful swingers kicked in exaggerated movements. Their convulsive dancing brought an amusing picture to Dona's mind--of herself kicking at nasty chickens that messed in her yard! She smiled, amazed at the energy flowing through the jubilant party.

She had to be coaxed to appear in the midst of the rollicking crowd but soon joined in the lively celebration, tossing her legs and arms to the insistent beat of the drums. She moved rhythmically, as horns blared and clarinets trilled. She was glad her skirt was loose and she could respond to the talking saxophone but feared she might also be abandoning her fine, Christian upbringing. Hair drawn back in two low tails, Dona flushed in exhilaration. Her buxom figure and tiny waist presented a winsome image among the spirited dancers. She felt emancipated as she moved with the partner of the moment. His hands clasped hers, pushing and pulling, in and out, left and then right, to the swinging sounds of "In the Mood." She felt surprisingly carefree in the veil of anonymity she enjoyed among so many strangers. A welcome sense of acceptance came over her as she relaxed in the intimate company.

Dim lights and smoky air combined to give the place an ethereal atmosphere. Dona felt as if she were floating--or maybe it was the alcohol. Her friends were generous and insistent in their hospitality. She was glad to have so many escorts. She was exhausted by the early morning hour when the group succumbed to the reality of the eminent workday. When they reached the apartment, she sank into bed and slipped seamlessly from trance to slumber for a few short hours of rest.

Northwest Missouri was blessed with a beautiful blue sky on the day the Schmits brought the girls down from Bedford and Lloyd drove across the city to pick up Dona and her few belongings. The girls were delighted to be going to the city to live with their mother and to have the added bonus of two cousins to play with every day. Sam and Retha were undoubtedly grateful for relief from the responsibility of the children, but Retha shed a few tears when she left the city without them.

Miriam and Lloyd's home was in the Avondale area of Gladstone. The names alone were melodic and magical to the children. The cottage they had bought was only a few years old, and construction materials were still stacked neatly in a corner of the basement. The pine wood gave the open space a fresh, woodsy smell and the children enjoyed playing there beside the forced-air furnace. It seemed to them like a huge octopus with fat, white arms that groped for the ceiling.

Lloyd helped the children make tiny wooden boats and constructed stilts that the older ones teetered around on. They liked to ride Tommy's scooter, so Lloyd made them another one, of wood, using old roller skates for wheels.

The car the Wrights brought back from California was too small to transport them all comfortably. The two-door coupe, with jump seats in the back, was large enough for their small family but not roomy enough for eight. So Lloyd soon traded for a large sedan.

Miriam and Lloyd were eager to explore the entertainments of the city, so weekends involved at least one adventure in the new car. Fairyland Park soon became their favorite attraction. To Dona, it was like the country fairs back home, except it was permanent and year-round. There were many more and larger rides, however, and also vastly more amusements for small children. There were miniature trains and cars and airplane swings in gay colors that rose and sank to lilting music. Many rides were outlined with twinkling bulbs that spun in a kaleidoscope of light. The children especially liked to watch the bumper cars crash and to hear the crackle of the whip-like tracer as it skimmed the metal ceiling, shooting sparks with each impact. Lloyd took Tommy on the bone-rattling ride while the others watched, laughing at their difficulties.

The day passed joyously. Everyone got to try a few rides and taste the fluffy sweetness of cotton candy before they called it a day and trudged to the parking lot. Each felt as if he'd truly been to a place of fairies.

After June entered the service, he learned he could get an allotment for the children, so he contacted Dona with the news. The checks for dependents would arrive monthly while he remained in the army. Dona was grateful for help in supporting the girls and was glad she could be more help with the Wrights' household expenses. June told her that he would soon be going overseas, he thought to France, about the same time Norman was being sent to England. He didn't talk much about himself but indicated that his marriage had not worked out and he was again single and ready to find new direction for his life. He seemed at loose ends, lacking real ties anywhere. She was frightened for him--partly because he was the girls' daddy and partly because she remembered the sweet boy with whom she had once fallen in love. Even though the war seemed like a distant turmoil, she had seen enough in newsreels to know the possibility of horrific danger. Dona hadn't told the girls of her divorce from their father, only that he was away fighting in the war. She thought that would be easier for them to understand and simpler for them to explain. Barbara would be going to school soon and would surely be faced with the question of where her daddy was.

Her own work in the war plant was a humbling experience for Dona. She had at first been treated with deference. Women were not expected, nor even allowed, to do the work that men did. When she was first hired, she was a "go-for," assisting the welders who actually worked on the airplanes. The company she worked for, Commonwealth, had taken over the American Royal building and converted it into an assembly line for constructing gliders for the war effort. Dona and Jenny Green worked on the construction floor with the men, while Irma, Therese, and Jenny T. held secretarial jobs in the office.

When demand for war materials was stepped up and male welders became harder to get, women were given the opportunity to become welders and hence to receive more pay. Dona and Jenny both took the training offered to aspiring welders. The testing trials were stringent, and they each failed to meet the requirements the first time they tried. Both practiced the skills they had been taught until they were adept enough to meet the high standards of performance set for certified welders. This happened while Dona and the girls were living in Kansas City, and her friends took her out to celebrate this milestone in her employment career.

When she first went to Kansas City to work, Dona imagined herself in fashionable clothes, working at a desk in an office somewhere. In reality, her uniform at the plant consisted of slacks and blouse, and she wore a bandana around her hair to shield against sparks from the welders' torches. Now, with her new classification, she would wear goggles and sometimes a helmet, as well.

The huge structure that housed the glider plant was outfitted with a gridwork of conveyors that moved the suspended metal framework of the gliders to workstations manned by welders and assistants. Several production lines were in operation, with a maze of catwalks connecting the workers to the network of equipment. Dona learned to balance herself as she leaned out at precarious angles to place metal seams at the necessary junctures. She received enormous satisfaction from her skillful performance at this work, and was soon accepted by her male counterparts as a worthy member of the team.

Since the children's move to Kansas City, Dona hadn't seen much of her old girl friends outside of work. Jenny G. had a car, but with gas rationing in force, pleasure driving was strongly discouraged. The group usually took the trolley to and from work, as did Dona. She lived some distance from her work site, so the ride each way was lengthy. Since the Wrights lived in a housing addition removed from the trolley line, she had a long walk home from her stop.

One evening an article appeared in the *Kansas City Star* concerning a woman who had been assaulted as she went home from work at a war plant.

"Dona, I'm afraid for you to be out walking alone at night," Miriam told her.

"We all have to take our turns on the night shift," Dona reminded her. Working the graveyard shift was hard on her in a lot of ways. She must sleep during the day, which was extremely difficult for her, and the noise of the children playing kept her awake, though they tried hard to be quiet.

"Doesn't anyone who works there live in this area that you could walk with?" Lloyd asked.

Dona thought about it. "I'm the only one who gets off at my stop. I guess there's no one. But it's pretty quiet out here. I'm really not scared."

"You never know what kind of person might notice you getting off alone and follow you," Miriam warned, the cords of sisterly love pulling on her worrying nature.

"I could always outrun the boogeyman!" Dona replied.

"I don't think it's funny!" Miriam admonished her. "You could be hurt badly, even worse!" Dona knew her sister imagined atrocities she'd rather not name. Miriam had lived on her own in California and wasn't ignorant of the brutal side of life.

The next day Lloyd brought home a small handgun.

"I know it's not a solution, but it will make your sister feel better," he told Dona.

"I wouldn't know how to use it!" she protested, as she hesitantly fingered the small but deadly weapon.

"I'll teach you," he replied. And he did, when they all went to an isolated place in the country the next evening. The little pistol was easy to handle but felt totally foreign in Dona's hands. She couldn't imagine actually pointing it at someone. She hated to carry the thing, feeling more danger with it than without it. But who knew? Maybe she would have to use it one day. She couldn't picture such a scenario, but if it would make her family happy, she would take it along when she worked at night.

In many ways, life with Miriam's family was easy for Dona and the girls. The children had never lived in a new, orderly house with modern conveniences such as an indoor toilet. The built-in bathtub was luxuriously roomy, unlike the galvanized washtub they had taken their turns in on Saturday nights. There was no water to be carried in, no slop to be carried out.

Dona and the girls were quartered in one long room upstairs, sharing a bed and a cot. An exhaust fan situated in the ceiling over the stairway pulled in a breeze through windows at either end of the house. The girls felt they were in their own little hideaway when they had their mother all to themselves up there under the eaves. And to Dona, the time was like the old days when they were babies and she told them stories as they lay awaiting sleep.

The boys slept in bunk beds in their bedroom on the main floor. Their room was hung with model airplanes Lloyd and Tommy had assembled from balsa wood kits. They had meticulously glued countless forms together to produce replicas of the planes used by the armed forces in the overseas campaign. Each was painted with insignia to identify its classification and origin.

Miriam was a marvelous cook, even hampered as her efforts were by the shortages that sometimes occurred. The household had rationing stamps for two families, since Dona was considered a head-of-household as well as Lloyd. Thus the group did not feel the imposed controls on food supplies as harshly as did some. When Dona worked the day shift, she often stopped by the market in Avondale to pick up the foodstuffs Miriam requested. Otherwise, Lloyd did the shopping since he drove to work and could easily manage the massive sacks of groceries that were required. The girls were delighted that Miriam always prepared a dessert for the evening meal. Dona thought it amusing that her sister allowed the children to have dessert only if they ate a good supper. She had never known her children to be anything but eager eaters, except for the rabbit that one time. There had never been a problem of too much food.

There was a sense of community in the neighborhood surrounding the Wrights' cottage, an area several blocks from a main thoroughfare. The hard-surfaced street stopped abruptly over the hill where a brushy wooded area fell away to a small creek, so little traffic passed by the place.

On many evenings, Dona sat in the yard watching the children play while her sister and her husband enjoyed rare time alone in their comfortable home. There were few large trees in the area, but two young fir trees in the front yard provided sheltered nooks for the youngsters to hide in.

Jody, a girl from down the street, often came to play with the children. Older than Barbara, she liked to be lieutenant of activities for the group. The girls had mixed feelings about her arrival on the scene. However, she was usually accompanied by a friendly dog that the children did enjoy. An assertive child, Jody often capitalized on her seniority by bossing the younger ones around. Sometimes she over-organized their games, and Dona had to suggest that maybe it was time for her to go home. Luckily, there was a small house with an elderly couple between the Wrights and the Garzees that served as a buffer between the two yards.

On some occasions, Jody marshaled her troops into orderly parades that marched up and down the street. Sometimes they were a band, making noises with whistles and sticks and waving flags. Sometimes they were a train, with tricycles and wagons tied together in a line. Tad, at two the youngest of the group, always got to ride in a wagon. There was sometimes verbal combat over who would be the engineer, but Jody usually managed to appoint herself to that exalted position.

When the moon appeared in the evening sky, the game might be changed to hide and seek or some kind of tag. Or the children might become distracted by flashing fireflies and commence to chasing the showy bugs. When they caught one, they sometimes ripped the glowing section off the poor insect and pushed it onto the back of a finger to be a diamond ring, a trick the neighbor girl had taught them, much to Dona's disgust.

After supper one evening, Dona suggested that she treat everyone to ice cream for the evening dessert. Her idea was met with enthusiasm by the children, who loved going out in the big car.

"Let's go to the ice cream parlor after we get the dishes done," Dona said as they finished the satisfying meal.

"Lloyd has been wanting to take the children down to the airport. This might be a good time for that, too," Miriam suggested. "What do you think, Lloyd?"

"Sure," he replied. "There's lots of daylight left, and we just might stay and see some planes come in at night."

"I think I'll stay home tonight and put Tad to bed early," Miriam told Dona as they worked in the kitchen washing the dishes. "I'm a little tired and just might turn in early, too."

The municipal airport had an observation deck so people could watch planes take off and land at the facility. The terminal was large but not too busy on the weekday evening. Newspaper and magazine vendors hawked their materials at small stands, and several booths that sold souvenirs of the city lined the side of the big room. The children took in all the sights of the huge place as they moved through to the end of the building, where an open deck faced out over the Missouri River.

A few planes were parked at the edge of the runway, some being serviced by crews in matching uniforms. Many of the planes had blue TWA letters emblazoned on the side.

"Some of them are little and only have one propeller," Coralea observed.

"Those are private planes, probably for two to six people. Some businessmen own them for short flights, like from here to Bedford," Lloyd told her.

"Can we go in one to see Grandma?" Coralea asked.

"I'm afraid not," Dona replied, laughing.

"How do they stay up?" Sharon asked, not able to imagine people in the air and not falling, as she knew she would.

"See those propellers on the front?" her mother said. "Each of those has a motor, something like a car engine, that gives it power to go through the air. The wings are shaped just right to help it stay up." She thought of the gliders she helped build that had no motors at all. She had seen demonstration films of gliders in action but still didn't understand the mechanics that made flight possible.

"Are these all American planes?" Tommy asked. Some of the models he and his dad had constructed were of British design.

"Probably most of these were made in this country," Lloyd answered. "In many ways the British are ahead of us in airplane development--some other countries, too. Do you think you might learn to fly one someday?"

Tommy was ready now, but the girls had doubts about the wisdom of the idea. Dona wasn't sure if she'd have the courage to go up in one herself.

When a plane appeared in the darkening sky, the children tracked it with their eyes until it dropped to the concrete with a soft whoosh, followed by a slap as the tires met the ground. They watched as the plane whirred down the runway. When one taxied to take off, they each held their breath as the wheels lifted from the surface and the graceful machine climbed over the trees. It followed the curve of the river, gaining altitude then leveling off high above the city. They thought it a miraculous sight and would have been content to watch for hours.

Night had fallen by the time the group left the airport. The tall buildings of the city loomed into the enveloping cover of darkness. The top of the Prudential Building glowed in gradually changing colors.

"How does it do that?" Coralea inquired, to which Dona quickly replied, "It's magic!"

"No. How, really?" she insisted.

"There are colored lights shining on the top that make the stone appear to be colored," Lloyd told her.

Dona liked her answer better.

They stopped at the Liberty Memorial, also awash in bright lights. They climbed the stair-stepped approach to stand beneath the towering edifice, staring up at the smooth surface that pierced the crystalline sky. The children were dwarfed by the vastness of the stone creation, their senses overwhelmed by the wonders of the city! They would remember such nights and such sights for a very long time.

In her last letter from Retha, Dona learned Grant had been home for a trial visit. Retha was upset by the outcome of the occasion. She'd hoped he might be changed, somehow improved in his emotional outlook. He instead seemed sad and morose, uncomfortable with his family. He had asked to be returned to the hospital--a stinging disappointment to his parents. He preferred the bars of the institution to living in his own home with them. Dona wondered if conformity to the hospital's routine gave Grant the security he lacked when free to make his own decisions. She feared her brother might have lost entirely the confidence to control his own life and sadly realized that she may have lost her brother forever.

On many summer evenings, an Indian blanket spread on the soft grass of the backyard became an island of intimacy for Dona and the girls. She liked to take the children to a private spot where they could relax in the stillness and share secrets. The wide backyard was surrounded by a chain-link fence that enclosed a small garden plot, a sandbox, and a martin house that sat atop a steel pole. The only tree, a mature elm, spread its branches over much of the house.

Purple martins descended in fluttering swoops, skimming mosquitoes from the evening air. A cool breeze scattered the cares of the day as Dona and the girls relaxed on their backs, looking up at a star-stippled sky.

"Can you find the Little Dipper?" Dona asked.

"There it is!" Coralea exclaimed.

"How about the Big Dipper?" her mother continued.

The girls were confused--too many competing dots of light.

"See," said Dona, pointing, "there is the cup part, up there, and there goes the handle across that way." It wasn't easy for her to pick out, either.

"What did you say the bright one is called?" Barbara asked.

"Venus," her mother answered. "It's also called the Morning Star."

"Why the Morning Star?" Coralea wanted to know.

"Hmmm. Well, maybe it's the last one you can still see in the morning when the sun comes up," she offered.

"Can we stay up and see?" Sharon wanted to know.

"You can try," Dona allowed, laughing to herself. She knew Sharon would be asleep within the hour and would have to be carried in and put to bed.

"What do you suppose Grandma and Grandpa are doing right now?" Barbara asked. She never asked about her daddy. She'd learned that mentioning him made her mother sad so she avoided that.

"I think Grandpa is listening to the news," suggested Coralea, "and Grandma's peeling potatoes."

"It's nighttime, silly," Barbara reminded her. "She's probably crocheting." Dona was amused at their simple interpretations of the life of their grandparents.

"Do you miss them?" she asked.

Three heads nodded.

"Maybe we can go and see them soon, before school starts. Barbara is going to be going off to first grade, you know, like Carrie always went every day. Will you miss her?"

Two heads nodded.

Dona gave Sharon a squeeze. Her little body was still soft with baby fat. Sharon's hair was fine and blonde, in ringlets around her face. Coralea's hair had finally come in brown, not dark like Barbara's, and straggled limply down to her shoulders unless someone found time to braid it for her.

"What did you do to help Miriam today?" Dona asked the girls.

"I picked up the toys in the basement," Coralea replied.

"I helped with the dishes and I set the table, too," Barbara said with pride.

"I played with Tad. She said that was a help, too," Sharon declared.

"You are very good girls and I'm proud of you," their mother told them. She really was, she realized, although she knew she couldn't take too much credit for their good behavior. It had mostly been the loving attention of their grandmother that had shaped them lately. She wondered when she would get to return to being a real mother.

"Will you draw on my back?" Barbara asked Dona. It was a game she and Coralea played in bed. They had always slept together; often all three girls were in the same bed.

Barbara turned her back to her mother, and Dona used her forefinger to slowly trace a picture on the smooth surface of skin beneath Barbara's shoulders.

"It's a house!" She recognized right away the straight lines of the peaked roof and the rectangle of a doorway.

Dona did Coralea next; everyone always got a fair turn. She drew a simple cat of two circles, ears, whiskers, and a long tail.

"Do it again!" Coralea pleaded.

Dona did, then gave her a clue, the next step in the game if it were necessary.

"There's a striped one that hangs around here sometimes," Dona stated.

"A cat!" Coralea confidently guessed.

"Do me now!" Sharon insisted. Her mother made a big round outline on her back.

"I know! It's a ball!" she said triumphantly.

Bored with this game, Coralea sat upright to face her mother. "Sing to us!"

"What shall I sing?"

"The Whiffinpoof song," Coralea suggested.

Dona mused that the girls often requested sad songs and wondered what inspired those choices. Did hearing heart-wrenching tales make them feel better about their own situation? Were they considering themselves fortunate in comparison? Maybe she should tell them "The Little Match Girl" again. But she couldn't bear to see the tears in their eyes that the poignant story always summoned. She began to sing.

"We are four little lambs, who have lost our way, baa, baa, baa. We are little black sheep who have gone astray, baa, baa, baa."

Her soft voice crooning the mellow notes seemed to lull the entire yard into listening stillness. She felt tears dampen her own eyes, perhaps because she knew she was genuinely needed. Or, maybe it was the realization that the girls truly adored being with her.

Sharon lay down on the blanket, snuggling up to her mother. "Sing me a story, Mama. One of yours," she begged, her drowsy state confusing her verbs.

Dona rummaged through her recollections for something that would satisfy them. They liked stories about themselves. Finally, she turned the "Happy Hooligans" of her own childhood into three little girls who grew up to be enormously fortunate, beautiful, and good.

Barbara laid her head on her mother's lap, and Dona combed her fingers through the long, silky hair.

The moon peeking through the leaves of the tree cast soft shadows across the yard. In the southwest, the faint glow from the lights of the city radiated in an arc over the horizon. At last Dona picked up the still form of her youngest child, and they made their way toward the beckoning light above the back door, Barbara and Coralea trailing the blanket along between them.

"Lloyd's been having stomach pains," Miriam said to Dona as they sat in the yard watching the children play. It was mid-August but the evening was pleasant, with a fresh breeze wafting across the newly mown lawn.

"You should make him go to the doctor," her sister suggested.

Miriam gave her a knowing look.

"You know how men are. He thinks it will get better if he waits. I think he's just trying to do too much."

Dona could understand her sister's concern. It was Lloyd's nature to be easy-going, but he was rarely idle, always puttering around with something after work or entertaining the kids.

"Maybe we could encourage him to relax more," Dona managed, thinking that was a pretty tall order in a household with five children six years old and younger. Her expression betrayed her thoughts and Miriam hurried to reply.

"Now, don't go to thinking you're the cause of it. People get sick, regardless. You know we don't mind having you and the girls with us." Dona thought how typical it was of Lloyd not to complain and considered, not for the first time, how lucky her sister was to have found such a man.

When he finally did consult a physician, Lloyd was told that he had an ulcer and should try to relax more and to avoid some of the stress in his life. The doctor recommended that Lloyd unwind with a beer each evening after work, so he tried that for a while.

Retha wrote with the news that Sam was looking for a place in Bedford where they could spend the winter. The drafty old house would be hard to heat, and if they could find a small house in town they wouldn't have the problem of getting Carrie to school each day. Dona immediately thought of the possibility of Barbara's starting school in Bedford. She decided to give some thought to moving the children back with her parents. Life would be easier for her mother in town and there was only Carrie at home now. She would do some figuring and see how much help she could offer toward getting a place.

In a couple of weeks, a suitable house in town had been located and Dona, the girls and the Wrights traveled to Bedford to look it over. Sam and Retha agreed to again care for the children, so Dona put money down on the house and would make monthly payments toward the purchase price. The little girls were happy to be rejoining their grandma and grandpa, and Barbara would be able to go to school with Carrie. The situation was working out well for all, it seemed. The Wright family would have their home to themselves, and Dona would return to living with her friends from work.

When Dona called to tell Jenny and the others about her latest arrangements, they were overjoyed to hear she would be with them again. They wanted to come and see the little girls once more before they returned to Bedford to live.

The four friends came and took Dona and all the children to a neighborhood theater to see *Song of the South*. The children were delighted with the whimsical story and sat with mouths and eyes wide with awe at the colorful animation of the beloved adventures of Br'er Rabbit and Br'er Bear.

During the last days of their stay in the city, they could often be seen, in twos or threes or even alone, swinging down the street in a pretend forest, stick and knapsack slung over their shoulders and singing at the top of their voices, "Zippity doo da! Zippity yay! My, oh my, what a wonderful day!"

TEN

    A large wooden sign stood at the corner of the main intersection of Bedford. It was embellished with red and blue stripes and sported a row of carved stars that trailed across the top molding. Rows of names, three on each line, advanced down the weathered surface and at the bottom in large letters "Baker, Wilson, Campbell American Legion Post 108" completed the pronouncement that the small community had already contributed heavily to one war in Europe. Now the lobby of the Post Office was adorned with a new, smaller bulletin board. It listed names of those currently in service, or, more poignantly, who were known to have made the supreme sacrifice their country demanded in the name of peace.

    Dona wondered why her parents had not placed a star in the window of their home, as was the custom throughout the country if a member of the household were serving in a branch of the armed forces. She guessed, correctly, that her mother resisted the reminder that the star on display might someday have to be changed from white to silver . . . to gold. She knew her mother would proudly display a star of gold if the horrifying reality should occur, but she struggled to keep this thought from surfacing in her mind.

    Returning to the small town on frequent weekends helped Dona escape the reality of wartime that existed for her in the city--in every uniformed young man she saw on the street and in every effort she made at work in the war plant. Stepping off the train in the dark of night--she often arrived on the 11:00 p.m. run--she would walk three blocks to the quiet little house and step into the simple security of life in the small town. She wondered whether she could keep her soul together without the comfort that the friendly atmosphere bestowed. Normally a solitary after-dark walk gave her the heebie-jeebies, but she had begun to associate her homecomings, however late, with the sense of fulfillment that was hers when she spent the weekend with the girls. On this night in early fall she was met at the door with the aroma of freshly baked bread--a smell that never failed to elicit a strong appreciation of home.

Dona awoke the next morning to the excited voices of the girls standing over her, and sleepily reached out from the sofa to give each one a hearty squeeze.

"Mom, there's the most tantalizing smell in here! Where are you hiding the bread?" A yeasty aroma permeated the house and gave her an appetite to which she was unaccustomed so early in the morning.

Retha came in from the kitchen, smiling.

"I hadn't intended to bake yesterday, but . . . " she began.

"Coralea lost the money for the bread!" Barbara volunteered, tossing an accusatory glance at her sister, who stood staring down at her chubby bare feet.

"That's all right now!" Retha sternly spoke up. "I shouldn't have sent her. She's pretty little to be going to the store by herself."

"I lost the dime," Coralea said sadly. "I looked and looked for it, but I couldn't ever find it." She had been jingling the two coins, a dime and a penny, in her hand as she walked the short distance to the store. When she realized she no longer heard a jingle the coin had disappeared into tall grass by the sidewalk. She had returned, crying so earnestly that Retha was incapable of being upset with her.

"Well, I just decided to do a little baking, since I hated to send her back, so we'll make do with home-made bread for a while and some chocolate cookies for later," Retha said. "We still have sugar stamps left over this month, anyhow. Come on into the kitchen for breakfast when you're ready. Dad has already gone out to the place to chore. He says that in a month or so the cows will be drying up and he won't need to make the trip out every day."

Make do with homemade bread! Dona thought to herself. *To Mom, sliced bread is a luxury, but to most of us it can't compare to her home-baked loaves.*

"Girls, I want to help your grandmother with a little housecleaning this morning. Then we'll go for a long walk this afternoon. How's that?" she suggested, as she maneuvered off the sofa and into the bedroom to get dressed. Carrie was still asleep in her small bed in the room that also held the bed shared by the younger children. She awakened as Dona and the girls entered to prepare themselves for the day.

"Guess what?" she asked her older sister. "I got to be Barbara's teacher yesterday!"

"It was fun!" Barbara exclaimed, as she sat down on Carrie's bed, demonstrating the new relationship she now shared with her aunt.

"How did you come to do that?" Dona asked.

"Mrs. Jones had to go home sick. She has allergies and she asked me if I'd take over her class for her! She was my teacher out at Lincoln School once, remember?"

Dona did remember. The young woman had been Mary Ethel Harper then, as yet unmarried. The folks had been living on the Ellis place. Later, the country school closed for a lack of pupils. Dona said now, "She must have thought a lot of you to ask you to do that."

"Carrie was a good teacher!" Barbara enthusiastically chimed in. "She read to us and helped us with our penmanship." She hoped Mrs. Jones would get sick often. Not too sick, of course, just enough to miss school so her aunt could be her own special teacher.

"Was Barbara a good student?" her mother asked Carrie.

"I only had to send her to the corner once!" Carrie teased, knowing no one could imagine Barbara misbehaving at school.

"I'm going to be a teacher someday," Barbara announced. She thought Mrs. Jones was the most elegant person she'd ever seen.

The little girls were charmed by their mother's presence during these visits. As her time in Kansas City lengthened, Dona had become an enchanting stranger in the eyes of her children, who sought to emulate her in little ways. They insisted on having their hair wrapped in a towel, turban style, after a shampoo the way she did hers. They must drink coffee, even though it was half milk, because she liked it. Sharon liked her eggs runny, like Grandpa, but other foods were chosen because her mother preferred them.

That afternoon Dona and the girls set off down the street for the walk she had promised earlier. Barbara had outgrown her tricycle and gladly handed it down to Coralea, who squeaked along on it now, trailing behind Sharon in the wagon Dona pulled over the smooth sidewalk. Except for a few places where tree roots heaved the concrete slabs into uneven ramps, the walks in the town were even and ample.

The group first walked to the store where Coralea had been headed the day before. They stopped at Herring's Grocery Store on the corner in the building that earlier housed one of the town's banks. An etched stone slab above the doorway would forever advertise the structure as the "FIRST BANK OF BEDFORD." Inside, the two proprietors, Jane Herring and Stella Walker, waited on customers, appearing as a Mutt and Jeff couple: Jane, tall, angular and brusque, and Stella, short and motherly. Two rows of glass apothecary jars with tin lids were placed in a low frame in front of the main counter, a successful sales strategy for tempting children with pennies to spend. Dona allowed each of the girls to choose candy from the generous selection of sweets arranged before them.

Across the street was Earl Rickman's grocery store, where Retha was right now shopping for the next week's meals. To the south of that large store a vacant lot contained a few board and block benches, with a movie screen toward the back. The town hadn't much to offer in the way of entertainment, but weekly films were free to the public.

Catty-corner to Herrings' Grocery was the produce house and feed store, run by Ben Coulter. Then there were a couple of smaller frame buildings, one occupied now by a café. Farther on down the street was a residence on the corner, a nicely kept home with several children, one of whom was in Barbara's first grade class. The family's dairy farm out on the main road produced the milk sold to many in the town, as well as to people in nearby communities. One had only to place an empty milk bottle on the front step, and it would be replaced in the early morning hours with a full one.

Down the street toward the south end of town were several more houses and one large structure Dona had heard was once a church.

"This is the church that went over the hill twice," she told the girls.

"What do you mean?" Coralea asked, not able to comprehend a building moving.

"You know where Old Bedford is, out where your friend Linda lives. That used to be the only town here. This old building was once a country church, but they moved it into town--Old Bedford. When the railroad tracks were laid down here, the town was moved, at least most of the town was, over the hill to the bottom here, where it would be close to the train. The church went over the hill again then," Dona related.

"But it's not a church now," Barbara observed.

"No. The people built a new church a few years later. It's the white one you go to now for Sunday school with Ana Ellis. I guess someone uses this building for storage, at least it looks like it," Dona surmised.

A small ditch formed the southern boundary of the town, then wended its way toward the Platte River a quarter mile west. Dona and the girls turned when they encountered the ditch, then walked to the gravel road that ran south out of town. The Stingley place was the only farm down that road. The stately, shuttered house sat prominently atop a knoll and could be seen through the trees a quarter mile from town. The Wisdom family who lived there now had two daughters, one of whom was in high school with Carrie. Maybe someday Dona and the girls would walk out there for a closer look at the pretty place.

They walked past the Christian Church, their church now that Retha had begun taking them to the primary class for Sunday School. The girls liked to sit on the little red chairs in a circle around Mrs. Ellis, as she talked to them about Jesus and the rewards of good behavior. Leaflets with pictures from

Bible stories were given to the children to take home, and the girls retold the tales to their grandmother. They'd inherited a bit of Dona's flair for drama.

The next house belonged to Stella Walker and her son, Johnny. He was slow, with a speech impediment that caused him to speak with grunts and gestures that sometimes scared the children in the community. It was accepted as fact that he was gentle, if hard to understand, and his erratic behavior was tolerated by most, though there were a few people who treated him shabbily. He helped at the store with menial chores and kept the large lawn around his own home freshly mown. His mother kept a vigilant watch on his whereabouts, to keep him out of trouble and to keep trouble away from him.

As they approached the alley where they would turn toward home, Dona stopped suddenly and knelt in the dust at the side of the road. She looked up at the girls, whose attention quickly centered on her.

"Did you hear that?" she exclaimed, eyes large with wonder.

"What was it?" Barbara quickly asked.

"Listen! I hear singing, very faintly. My, how beautiful!" And Dona began looking around in the grass beside the path. "It must be fairies!"

All three girls crouched around her . . . watching, waiting.

"Can you see them?" Coralea asked doubtfully.

"They're very, very small. You have to look closely. And you have to believe. There! I saw one scoot behind that blade of grass!" Dona motioned to indicate the spot as she spoke with great animation.

Barbara smiled tentatively and looked at her mother. "Where do they live?" she asked.

"Oh, fairies can live anywhere you believe they can," she answered. "Maybe we can make a special place for them here."

"Their houses must be awfully little," Coralea offered.

"I don't see any houses here," said Dona. "Shall we make one for them so maybe they'll stay?"

"Let's do!" Sharon eagerly agreed, expecting to see a winged creature at any moment.

"How big do you think we should make it?" Dona asked then.

Coralea held up her fingers, a few inches apart.

"I'll go see if I can find a little box that we can use. You stay here and watch and listen and I'll be right back." Dona hurried up the alley to their home, then returned shortly with a cardboard matchbox.

"Did you spot them yet?" she asked.

"No," Barbara replied, "but I think I heard them singing."

Dona smiled knowingly as she caught Barbara's eye.

"Let's put it right down here in the grass where they'll be protected," she suggested. "Do you suppose we should make them some beds?"

"How?" Coralea asked.

"Maybe we could use some tiny sticks and cover them with something soft," Dona offered.

Before long the girls were busy gathering materials and discussing the suitability of their choices. Entranced by the fairy world their mother had firmly planted in their imaginations, the little girls continued constructing dreamy scenarios for the creatures they knew to be just a tiny distance beyond their grasp. Dona left them to their play, figuring they would be engrossed in their new adventure for much of the afternoon. Indeed, by evening they had fashioned a home for fairies that they were sure would coax the timid beings into their sight very soon.

Rob Brooks noticed them working seriously by the alley and approached them to ask about their project. He carried his massive frame with the grace of a dancer.

"What are you so busy at, Little Missy?" he asked of Barbara.

"We're making a house for the fairies Mama saw," she assured him. Her bit of skepticism had disappeared as she was caught up in the delightful fantasy they had built. Rob sat down with them and listened as they recounted their activities of the afternoon.

Rob's own three girls were big now, and he missed the expressions of childish wonder they had so quickly outgrown. His oldest daughter was married, and the middle one was away at college. He definitely missed their presence. His youngest, Bobbie, was out of high school but still at home, working at Jacksons' Dry Goods store downtown. Bobbie had befriended Carrie when the Schmits moved into town. She was quite a bit older, but she'd invited Carrie to share in big-girl undertakings, such as styling hair and fixing fingernails, and she often asked her to go along to the outdoor movies on Saturday night. Sometimes they would take the little girls with them, if the movie were a Western, which it usually was.

Bobbie's friend, Lizabeth Ann Martin, had gone to Chillicothe to business school, then on to Madison to live and work, where she'd met Ivan Hoffman, from the Junction community. They had married and moved to St. Joseph before "Hoff" was drafted into the army. Like so many other war widows, Lizabeth worked and waited at home, hoping for her partner's safe return.

Rob had hung a porch swing from the branch of the big elm that grew in their backyard. He and Mamie spent many evenings sitting outside their back door, where the protected area around their porch connected to the Schmits' side yard. They encouraged the children to come over and use the comfortable swing. Rob had a nickname for each girl. Barbara was "Little Missy" and "Silly" and "Sally" were the younger two. The Brookses were good neighbors to the Schmits, with Mamie and Retha visiting each other often for little chats as the children played nearby.

"Comfortable" and "cozy" were Dona's descriptions of the little house her folks now shared with the girls. It was small but convenient. Sam no longer had to chop and carry wood as there was an oil burner to heat the house, and Retha had an electric range for cooking. They hadn't had electric lights, even, out on the farm. The prettiest feature of the house, Dona felt, was the hardwood floor of the living room. Two-inch oak strips were laid out in a parquet fashion, beginning with a small square in the middle and increasing to the edges of the room. It was like a work of art, and Retha kept it gleaming with frequent applications of wax.

That evening Dona prepared supper for the family. She actually enjoyed cooking now, as she and her friends had moved to a boarding house in Kansas City where they took their meals with the family of the house. Dona found she missed preparing meals for her own family, a development she had certainly not expected.

Sam came in empty-handed after spending the afternoon at the river. He guessed the leeches he kept in the cellar must not be the right bait for the season. He kept them in a pail in the damp, underground space, which caused the girls to be afraid to go down there for jars of canned goods. They imagined the slug-like creatures clinging to their skin and sucking their blood.

Dona studied her father as he sat by the radio listening to the day's news. He was beginning to gray at the temples, but other than that looked more youthful and rested than she had seen him in a long time. As they sat at the supper table, she asked Sam about the crops.

"Well, the corn has done well," he told her. "We might make a little on it this year." He usually tended to exaggerate a little, she knew, but not where income was concerned. "I'm thinking about making an offer on the Caddell place. Maybe putting some money down on it."

"Isn't that the old shack in front of your farm?" she asked.

"Yep. It's got good pasture and a good barn. I could keep more cattle. If you mess with five, you may as well mess with twenty," Sam said.

"How big is the place?" Retha wanted to know.

"Forty acres. That would make us eighty acres, about right for me to farm. Jacksons, on the east side, are ready to retire, so they're not interested in it, and Coulters, on the west, have more than they can handle already, with the produce house to run. I could probably get a pretty good deal on the place."

Dona knew owning the land would mean a lot to her father, who equated land ownership with personal worth.

"I hope it works out for you, Dad," she said sincerely.

Retha had mixed feelings about the place but kept them to herself. The home the Caddells left when they retired to town was more of a shack than a residence. But she did recall there being a good chicken house there, and a garage.

"Why don't we go out tomorrow and look at it?" Dona suggested.

Some time around midnight, Dona was abruptly awakened by the sound of a freight train rumbling like thunder along the nearby tracks. Vibrations rose from the ground and dissipated in the air around her. The nearness of a whistle blast often surprised her, but she'd never noticed how strongly the movement of the heavy freight cars could be felt in the town.

"No! No!" Hearing the frantic cry from the bedroom, Dona jumped to her feet and rushed to the adjacent room. Coralea was standing up in bed, wailing and backing up against the wall. By the dim moonlight that seeped into the room, Dona saw the other girls sleepily looking up at her. She reached over to awaken her panicky child as Retha hurried into the room, also.

"There, there, now. What is it?" Dona soothed as she held her trembling child. Coralea sobbed and clung to her mother, nightclothes damp with perspiration.

"She's been having nightmares about trains," Retha told her.

"Is that it?" she softly asked Coralea. The little girl nodded her head but didn't say anything. She still felt the terror of watching the huge engine leave the tracks and come pounding up the road toward her. She buried her head in her mother's shoulder to shut out the sight.

"I usually just rock her until she goes back to sleep," her grandmother said.

"Mom, I'm so sorry that she wakes you. You need your rest," Dona said with concern.

"Now, she'll soon get used to the train. They say once you get accustomed to the sound you can't sleep if you don't hear it!"

"I'll just put her here with me on the couch," Dona said. "You go on back to bed. She'll be fine here, won't you?" she asked Coralea, who again nodded her head.

Dona lay beside her frightened child and crooned a soothing lullaby. Her arm enveloped the soft, warm body, damp and musky from the sweat of agitation that poured from her. Sticky strands of hair clung to Dona's face as she cuddled the child comfortably against her. She had been unaware of missing the warmth of human touch but now realized with surprise that she was comforted as much as her daughter by their unplanned but satisfying closeness.

After climbing into the car Sam had parked, ready, in front of the house, Dona pulled Sharon onto her lap and made room for Carrie and Coralea beside her. They were a carload for the trip out to the country, but each was eager to look over the place Sam had expressed such interest in. Of course, they'd passed by the acreage many times in the past, on their way to the Schmits' farm. The road skirted the place on the way back to the old house. But they'd never inspected it--never looked at it with real interest before. Perhaps there were possibilities there they hadn't discovered.

The hill out of town loomed as the automobile climbed the incline that leveled off midway to the crest. Laboring in low gear, the car barely moved with the weight of its many passengers. A tractor swung out from a driveway at the brief plateau and Sam saluted the driver with a friendly wag of one finger. Dona glanced up to see a young man bouncing along on the high seat as the tractor put-put-putted down the hill past them.

"Who was that?" Dona inquired. The man was obviously young. Not many fellows of that age were around anymore.

"That's Jimmie Martin. He works at the filling station," Sam said.

"His mother's the lady you noticed this morning, walking by on her way to church," Retha added.

"With the red hair and the big hat?" Dona asked.

"Uh-huh. They live there, where he drove out. I hear he farms some of the bottomland—probably where he's headed now," Sam guessed aloud.

"You remember hearing Bobbie Brooks talk about Beth Martin?" Carrie asked. "She's his sister, but she's married now so just he and his mother live up here. I guess he supports her."

"She gives music lessons," Retha volunteered, which seemed to draw the conversation to a close.

The flat roadway gradually rose to another ridge, beyond which hills rolled away to a deep creek bed. To the north, a small timber was touched now with the first hint of fall color. Maple and linden trees scattered throughout the woods had begun to turn. Splashes of yellow met the sky, blue with scattered, wispy clouds. Sumac grew along the lane, adding a deep red border to the quilt of autumn hues stitched among the still-green fabric of oaks and hickories.

"That timber belongs to the place," Sam told them. "And the barn down there by the creek," he added as they reached a clearing at the foot of the rise.

Carrie spotted some milkweeds and remembered a project she'd heard about at school.

"Could I pick some milkweeds, Mom?" she asked.

"Whatever for?" Retha inquired.

"They're collecting them at school. It's for the war effort . . . I guess I really don't know how they might help," Carrie admitted.

Dona spoke up. "I think they use milkweed pods, the floss, for stuffing in life preservers--for floating in the water. You know, for safety on the ships."

"Well, we'd better go on back to the house and get you a gunnysack," Sam allowed. "We don't want that stuff getting all over the car."

"And I don't want that stuff in the house, either," said Retha. "You'll have to be careful with it!"

They turned beside the garage and drove along a pasture and down a small ravine before arriving at the farmstead Sam now tended from their home in Bedford. It looked more ramshackle than it had when they lived there, and the girls were happy to stay only briefly. Seeing the forlorn structure made Dona's heart sink and she fought to keep disturbing memories from surfacing--of that tragic time for Grant.

Sam went into the barn and re-emerged with a dusty but intact woven sack, which he shook out vigorously as he approached the car.

"This should hold as many as you'll find," he told them. "Be sure and keep them in the bag."

"Okay, Dad," Carrie assured him, as he turned the car around and headed back to the old shack.

When they got to the Caddell property, Retha noticed an apple tree near the middle of a small pasture. Its branches sagged with the weight of a bountiful season's fruit.

"I wonder if they'd mind if we picked some of those apples," she ventured. "They're just going to waste," an outcome she was not accustomed to allowing.

"I'll ask when I talk to them," Sam told her, as Dona sat remembering the sweet, heavy taste of her mother's delicious apple butter. There had been a time she would've liked to run from the sight of another apple. That seemed like such a long time ago, in another life, almost!

Carrie and the girls headed up the lane to harvest the milkweed pods they'd spied in the fence row, as Sam and the others approached what had once been a house. The windows and doors were intact, but the dark glass made it hard to see much inside. Scuffed linoleum covered the uneven floors and the whole house sank along with the contour of the hill.

"Would you look at this!" Retha exclaimed, peering into a long room at the back. "They've used this room as a brooding house!"

Dona looked in and had to agree that it certainly appeared and smelled as if chickens had been kept there.

"Well, it would've been handy," Sam allowed. "Those folks were getting old when they left the farm. They say it's been vacant for several years. I'm hoping they'll be happy to get rid of it."

The chicken house and coop were solid, as was the outhouse beyond them. A recently painted garage was obviously the newest structure on the place. It was nearly filled with old tires and rims, tools, boards, and cans of nuts, bolts, and nails--a lifetime's collection of mainly rusted hardware. The dirt floor was level and there were good shelves along the walls. Sam could see possibilities.

"What do you think?" he asked the two women. Dona knew he was seeking their approval but had already made up his mind about the place and would probably go ahead with his plan for acquiring it with or without their say-so.

"I can't see you living in that shack," she said with hesitation.

"We could work on that," he replied. "We wouldn't be moving out here anytime soon anyhow."

Retha smiled in agreement, sensing how much the scheme meant to her husband. She felt Sam had gotten a new lease on life since they had moved to the Bedford area. She wasn't about to dash his hopes now.

They walked down to the barn that was surrounded by dilapidated fences at the bottom of the hill, near the creek. Dragonflies darted over weeds that thrived along the edge of the creek. Huge grasshoppers leaped before the intruders as they neared the weathered structure. The barn still had a good roof and solid doors--an asset to the place, they all agreed.

"We'd better get on back," Dona suggested. "My train will be leaving in about an hour." Her expression betrayed her feeling of regret at ending the restful weekend she'd enjoyed with her family. She always dreaded the moment of departure when she'd give over her children to another, though her mother was the most tender, loving caretaker she could wish for.

They stopped to pick up the girls near the end of the lane. Carrie hurried to brush off Coralea. She'd been holding a dry pod and had punctured it with her fingers, hoping to feel the soft, silky down inside. It popped open and seeds with feathery tails were stuck to her hair and clothing. Sam opened his mouth to comment but reconsidered and only sighed in resignation.

"Could we have one for the fairy beds?" Barbara asked.

"We'll see," Dona told her. "You've gathered quite a lot, haven't you?" She thought of the little ball of aluminum she and her friends had amassed by peeling foil off the wrappers of chewing gum. It was hard to imagine such small contributions making a real difference in the war effort.

"Did you take your dime to school this week?" she asked Barbara. Dona gave the child dimes and Carrie quarters to take to school so they could buy stamps toward the purchase of a war bond. It would take a long time to buy one, but it made them feel like they were helping, at least.

"Uh-huh," Barbara replied.

"Did Mom tell you about the visitor she had the other day?" Carrie asked Dona as they were on their way home.

"Oh? Who was it?" Dona asked with interest.

"A tramp, I guess," Retha replied. "He just appeared at the back door one morning."

"Weren't you afraid to let him in?" Dona asked.

"I didn't. He just stood there until I asked him what he wanted. He said he would work for something to eat," she answered.

"So what did you do?" Dona couldn't imagine her mother being intimidated by anyone.

"Well, I just told him to sit down on the step for a while and I'd see what I could find."

"Grandma locked the door and made us stay inside," Sharon told her mother. "He was a dirty man, and raggedy."

"Now, he just needed a shave, that's all," Retha said. "I made him a sandwich and took it out with a glass of milk and some cookies."

"You should have given him some work to do," Sam said, thinking of how it would feel to ask for handouts.

"Well, I couldn't think of anything. He asked what he could do, but nothing needed to be done. Besides, I was anxious for him to leave," Retha admitted. Her generous nature didn't extend so far as to trust the stranger. She had even gone out to inspect the outside of the house after he had gone because she had heard that hoboes sometimes left a sign where they'd found an easy touch.

"Do you suppose he came in on the train?" Dona asked.

"I expect so. He was certainly a stranger to these parts. I didn't think there were many men riding the rails anymore," Retha said. She hoped it was the first and the last one she'd ever see at her door.

Caressed by the balmy air of the waning autumn day, Dona looked down the tracks to the north, where the "Bug" would soon come into view. The cinder shaft with its iron rails pierced the surrounding willows until the lines converged about a mile in the distance. The sleek commuter train stopped only if the flag were raised to signal a passenger's presence. Dona was nearly always the lone waiter at the Bedford Depot.

She'd said good-bye to her family at the house. It seemed to be easier there, where the children had the comfort of home to ease the separation. Dona had turned at the corner to wave one last time, and she held a familiar picture in her memory of Retha standing in the yard, her hand sheltering her eyes from the sun, the girls stair-stepped in front of her wide, flowered apron, watching and waving.

Dona knew the partings were difficult for them, too. She wondered if she could take them to the city with her, perhaps one at a time, for a visit. The Culvers, whose boarding house she shared, had two small children of their own, a boy Sharon's age and a little girl, a toddler. Dona decided to see if she could arrange this. A week wouldn't be too long. She would bring it up with Marge, maybe some week when she was on the night shift so she'd have days to entertain them. Barbara would probably have to wait until next summer, but she could start right away with Sharon. She and Ricky would make great playmates.

Dona felt cheered. Though she had grown to love Kansas City and her friends there, she was still torn when she boarded the train and left the town behind. Life here seemed to advance at a slower, safer pace

ELEVEN

May in Missouri. A million shades of green dressed the city in spring splendor. Every tree, bush, weed, blade of grass, even, seemed to have its own unique hue. For such a massive metropolis, Kansas City had an unexpected amount of greenery. Dona supposed this was due to the city's position astride the Missouri River. And she realized, also, that a good part of the city's beauty must be attributed to the skill of city planners and to the generosity of such men as William Rockhill Nelson and Richard Swope. Parks and boulevards laced the city together with a living mantle of green. Delicate wisps of new growth concealed the activity that had recently boosted the city's economy.

Dona and Sharon rode the streetcar down to the Alameda Plaza where they were to meet Miriam and Tad. The nearly empty car rattled along noisily as Sharon sat on her mother's lap where she could get a good view out of the window. A clanging bell sounded each time the car swung into a stop. Sharon's four-year-old curiosity caused her to observe the scenery inside the car as well as out. She noticed a cord trailing above the windows on either side of the compartment.

"What's that for?" she asked her mother.

"Watch. You'll see in a minute," Dona answered, knowing that likely someone would want off at a nearby destination.

Sharon sat waiting patiently on her mother's lap as an elderly lady reached up and pulled the cord, causing a jingle to be heard at the front of the car. The trolley suddenly began to slow.

"That's how you stop it!" Sharon said, excited.

"Well, not exactly," Dona informed her, then proceeded to explain the real workings of the apparatus.

Showing Sharon the city proved to be as much fun as Dona had expected. The child was in awe of everything about the place, just as she had been, and still was, she admitted to herself. The enormity of the city alone was enough to delight her, and the wealth of places to go and things to see were endless.

Dona was amazed at the abundance of goods in the big department stores and the obvious wealth of the people who shopped there. She was to join her sister at the Plaza to see the sights but certainly knew she would be making no purchases there!

Miriam would arrive by trolley, also, and would meet them by the fountain at Twelfth and Broadway. Dona anticipated seeing Sharon's expression as she first spied the beautiful statuary, its sparkling water lit by the midday sun.

Miriam and Tad were there when Dona and Sharon arrived, and it was obvious that the girl had eyes only for her cousin, whom she hadn't seen in several months.

"I see you're wearing your cowboy shirt," Miriam said, stooping to give Sharon a hug.

"She'd like to wear it all the time," Dona said of the blue shirt Sharon wore. Miriam had made a school dress for Barbara and had given the two smaller girls shirts she'd embroidered in a Western motif. She had obviously spent many hours hand-stitching the intricate designs. Dona thought the shirts were almost too pretty to be worn. Sharon and her sister spent countless hours "riding the range" and sitting beside imaginary campfires crooning "Home, home on the range . . . "

"Look at the big horses!" Sharon exclaimed as she checked out her surroundings. "And the dragons are spraying water!"

"Those are sea serpents," Tad corrected. He was younger by a year but liked to show his knowledge of "his" city. He was tall for his age and Sharon small for hers, so the two were nearly equal in size. His large brown eyes assessed his playmate as they stood awkwardly, getting reacquainted.

"How's everyone at Bedford?" Miriam asked her sister.

"Everyone's well now," Dona replied. "There were a lot of colds this winter--it seemed to take forever to find a week when I was on night-shift and Sharon was free of a cold, a sore throat, or something. You know how it is."

"How is she getting along with Ricky and Shelley?"

"Great. Marge thinks her two get along better when Ricky has Sharon to play with. He doesn't spend so much time bothering his sister!" Dona told her. "Marge's been good to watch Sharon when I'm gone or sleeping. I really appreciate her and Eddie. They've made us feel like we're a part of their family." Eddie worked in the same plant as Dona, doing identical work, but she knew his paycheck was substantially larger than hers. She guessed this was because men were usually the head of a household and women weren't. Whatever the reason, she felt extremely fortunate to have a well-paying job.

"I'm sure a couple of years ago they wouldn't have thought they'd have four women living with them!" Miriam said. Housing for workers now in the city was at a premium, and many homeowners in the area had converted their residences into apartments or boarding houses.

The group crossed over to walk beneath the canopies that sheltered the decorated storefronts. Graceful curves adorned the fronts of the Spanish style buildings, which were surfaced with cream-colored stucco. The area, busy day and night, drew an abundance of sightseers to the city. The two women exclaimed over the variety and opulence of the goods displayed in the tony shops.

"Wouldn't you like to have enough money to just go in and buy anything you wanted?" Dona asked dreamily.

"You know what Mom would say about that," Miriam returned. "'You may as well wish in one hand and spit in the other and see which one fills up fastest!'"

Dona laughed. "No harm in wishing! Let's go in and take the kids up in an elevator!"

The department store they entered boasted a pair of elevators, so they stepped into one. Sharon let out a gasp and grabbed the railing as the small cubicle reached the second floor and settled with a whoosh at the threshold. She screwed up her face with a worried look that could erupt into tears at any moment. When they were ready to go down, Dona decided to take the stairs rather than give the child another fright.

Miriam suggested they get ice cream and go over to the park beside the fountain. There were several benches, many already occupied by people chatting or just sitting in the restful shade.

Miriam and Dona found themselves a small seat by the fountain. The children sat on the grass nearby, watching the water gush from the mouths of the sea serpents.

"Have the folks heard from Hank lately?" Miriam asked her sister.

"They had a letter about a week ago," Dona replied. "I guess he's somewhere in France, but they don't know just where, as any reference made to his location was snipped out of the letter--for the sake of security, I suppose. Hank doesn't say much about what he's doing, mostly just writes about his buddies and how they spend their spare time."

"How can Mom write to him if she doesn't know where he is?" Miriam asked.

"She sends letters to him in care of the Government Post Office and they route them through, eventually. It takes at least two weeks," Dona told her. "The war has been on the folks' minds a lot lately. A boy from Bedford was killed in France--he was about my age, I guess. And then, June sent back some war relics he asked us to keep for him. That made the war more real to them, I'm afraid."

"War relics? What kind of relics?" Miriam puzzled.

Dona's face shadowed. "Mostly pocket watches and pipes, some of them fancy and old-looking. I think they've probably been taken off of dead German soldiers," she said with obvious disgust. "I don't think they're the kind of souvenirs I would want to keep," she added.

The two children had crept closer to the fountain and were on their knees searching for four-leaf clovers in the lush grass. Occasionally a gust of wind caught a swirl of mist from the fountain and swept it over the two, sending them scampering a few feet back. Their carefree frolicking attracted the gaze of others who were enjoying the small greenway, and the children soon became the center of attention.

"How does Barbara like school?" Miriam asked.

"I think she lives to go to school!" Dona answered, smiling, obviously pleased to be discussing her daughter's accomplishments. "She's learning to read. She has a few little books she can read already."

"Tommy likes kindergarten all right. They don't do much, though. I think his favorite part is the bus ride. He's always the first one out by the corner waiting for it." Miriam glanced at her watch as she said, "I'm afraid we'd better be going before long. He'll be getting home about 3:00. Are you still going out with Wolf?"

"Uh-huh. He's going to take us up to Bedford this weekend. I'm anxious for the folks, and the girls, to meet him. What have you and Lloyd been doing lately?" she asked her sister.

Miriam smiled coyly. "I was saving the news for Mom first, but you can tell her. I'm pregnant and the baby's due around Christmas. I guess you know we're wishing for a girl this time."

Dona laughed. "Well, you have been busy! Congratulations!" she offered. "I'm happy for you. Are the boys excited?"

"They don't know yet. I think they'll have a hard time waiting. It's hard enough for me!"

Dona could imagine the excitement in the Wright household when the boys were given the news. She envied her older sister in lots of ways, and having a stable home life was definitely at the top of the list.

A short time later Dona and Sharon were settled on the trolley, heading back to the Culvers' spacious brownstone. Dona was ready to retire for the day, so she could get a few hours' sleep before her shift at the plant. Sharon would nap with her for a while before the other girls arrived home from their shifts. So far the schedule had worked out well for everyone. Irma, especially, enjoyed entertaining the little girl.

Becoming involved with Wolf had widened Dona's circle of acquaintances. Like her, he wasn't from the city, but had an easy way about him that attracted others. That, and he was definitely good-looking. Dona had noticed him before he noticed her. They shared the same break room at the plant, although he worked in one of the offices. His job involved the procurement and distribution of materials. She had heard he was a college boy from Columbia and was surprised when he approached her to be introduced by a mutual friend. Her first thought was that he was so smooth he probably was the kind who lived up to, or down to, his name. He was known only as Wolf although he acknowledged Harold as his given name when she insisted he tell it. She had to agree that Harold didn't suit him.

He exuded confidence, which Dona admired. She had a feeling that his family hadn't suffered much during the depression, though she supposed it wouldn't be fair to consider him spoiled. Actually, he was very generous and they had gone out to many nice places. She enjoyed dating like the other girls, though she didn't feel it was exactly the same, somehow.

Dona found it hard to trust any man on an intimate level. Most of the friendships she made were transient, anyhow. But Wolf was going to be around for more than a few days. She felt she was becoming dependent on his attentions and wondered if the time they spent together might mean more to her than they did to him.

On Sunday, Wolf drove up in his Chevy coupe, car and man both polished and shining. Dona was impressed. She had been nervous, and excited too, about the trip to Bedford. Evidently Wolf wanted to make a positive impression, surely a good sign. She knew her mother's excellent cooking would charm him, but he hadn't expressed much interest in knowing her girls, so she was somewhat apprehensive.

"Well, you said you lived in a small town. I guess you meant it!" Wolf said with a grin as they crossed the bridge and approached the railroad tracks. The station boasted a large sign that proclaimed the identity of the town. Dona laughed, although she didn't see anything particularly amusing about the size of the place.

"It's the little, white house in the middle of the next block," Dona informed Wolf, as Sharon began to stir to get a better look at the familiar scenery. When the car stopped and the door was opened, Sharon hit the ground running to give her grandma a hug around the knees.

"My gracious!" Retha exclaimed. "I missed you, too!" The other girls stood beside their grandmother, looking at Dona with expressions that said, "You've changed, somehow." Or maybe it was the idea that their mother and little sister had arrived in the company of a man whose name said "big" and "bad" to them. Dona told herself that the girls' reaction probably had something to do with the fact that she was with someone other than their daddy, who, to them, was merely away at war. She inwardly acknowledged that she had only herself to blame for that misconception.

"Don't I get a hug?" she asked them. Barbara approached her, eyeing Wolf with a suspicious glance. Coralea stayed behind her grandmother.

"Come on in, now!" Retha said warmly as she held open the screen door. "Dad's still out at the place, but he'll be here any minute."

When they were all inside and introductions completed, including Carrie, who had emerged from the bedroom, Dona became aware of the closeness of the room, which suddenly seemed crowded with people. She'd never before realized the house was so small.

"Dona tells me you're a great cook," Wolf offered. "And she tells me she isn't," he added, with an admiring glance at Dona. "But I guess great cooks aren't what we really need right now." Dona knew he meant it as a compliment to her skill at work in the glider factory, but it sounded like a put-down instead. "What I mean is, your daughter's very good at what she does, too," he added, obviously trying to extricate himself from that diplomatic disaster.

Sitting across the table from Wolf, Dona was conscious of her friend's apparent discomfort. Carrie and the two older girls were eating at the coffee table in the front room. The kitchen was too small to accommodate any more chairs around the sturdy oak table. Wolf was charming, as always, but Dona sensed that he felt out of place with her family. It seemed to her that his cool blue eyes were taking in the clutter of the place, the pots and pans on the stove and on the counter. *This must seem very rustic to him*, she thought. Then she remembered the outhouse that sat modestly beyond the smokehouse, itself nearly connected to the back step. She hoped he'd not need to use it.

"So, you're from Columbia?" Sam was asking.

"Uh huh. My dad runs the Western Auto store there," Wolf answered. "I've been in Kansas City for several years, though. I don't think I'll ever go back there to live. There's not much to do there unless you're at the university. It's a pretty small town. Dona tells me you have a farm. My grandparents used to farm--until they moved into town a couple of years ago," he added.

"We'll run out there later and I'll show you the place," Sam offered.

"Why don't you go on and I'll do up the dishes while you're gone," Dona suggested to Wolf. "Then maybe we can take the girls to the schoolyard to play." The new school had a large playground with several pieces of equipment--swings, slides and seesaws--that the kids in town used for a neighborhood park.

"Mom, you go sit a spell and let Carrie and me clean up the kitchen." Dona hoped to spend some time with the children before she and Wolf had to head back to the city. Going by car cut the travel time down and was vastly more comfortable than the train, but they'd still need to be on their way by early evening.

Sam was eager to share his plans for the new place with the young man. He had purchased the extra acreage, with the old house, and had begun making major changes. So far, the going had been rather slow, as he was attempting to save some of the old boards to use in the new structure.

A flock of birds broke from the ground in the adjoining field as Sam's car topped the short hill leading to his new property. Dark, ambiguous woods formed a solid backdrop behind the site. To the west, tall cottonwoods stood serenely beyond the barn, where a creek formed the farm's boundary. A woodpecker's drill marked the cadence of the otherwise quiet afternoon, seeming to announce the men's arrival.

"I've decided to build a new house there on the foundation where the old place used to sit," Sam pointed out. The old shack had been moved several yards to the west and now sat several degrees from level on the gradually sloping hillside.

"How did you move it?" Wolf asked with genuine interest.

"Borrowed some tractors," Sam told him. "A friend and some neighbors came over and pulled it right off the foundation. As you can see, there wasn't much to lose by trying it."

Wolf noticed the draft horses and realized that Sam still farmed with old-fashioned horsepower. His own grandparents had used tractors ever since he could remember!

"I'm going to salvage as much lumber as I can from the old house to use in the new one," Sam informed him. "There's another old place back in the timber I'll tear down and use, also." Wolf didn't believe there could be much useable material in the weathered structure but didn't say so. He had to admit, though, that the setting was nice for a home, with woods front and back. The short lane that ran over the hill from the county road gave the location an aura of seclusion.

Sam spoke of his plans with animation, and Wolf allowed to himself that he admired the older man's optimism.

"Do they ever wear shoes?" Wolf asked, as the three girls ran ahead of him and Dona down the road toward the school.

Dona smiled. "Not too often, in the summertime. It's past the first of May. That's the rule in this family for going barefoot," she told him. She knew that Coralea, especially, was glad to be free of her everyday shoes. She had worn high-topped correctional shoes for two years now, even after her little sister had grown out of high tops. Dona had promised her she could have regular shoes for school in the fall. The specially constructed shoes had helped to straighten her legs, although Dona thought her ankles still sank in toward her insteps a little. But they were worlds better than they had been. She didn't mention this to Wolf but instead asked, "Didn't you ever go barefoot as a child?"

"I don't remember that I did, but I'm ready to try it if you are!" he said. He expected the lush grass to feel pleasantly soft beneath his feet. Soon their shoes were in a pile beneath one of the trees that formed the boundary of the schoolyard.

The girls were already on the play equipment, pumping up on the swings and running to climb the tallest slide. The bed of the slide sloped down precipitously a few feet, then leveled off briefly before plunging downward again to a small landing. Beneath the bottom of the slide the earth had been worn into a depression where countless feet--and seats, too, no doubt--had landed with an abrupt thud.

The children soon warmed to their audience, trying the big slide on their seats, their stomachs, their backsides. Dona gasped when she saw Coralea go down headfirst on her back, then flip over at the hump to finish feet-first on her stomach. Dona ran over to catch her and see if she were all right.

"You mustn't do that! You might fall off the side," Dona admonished her.

"She does it all the time," Barbara told her mother. "She's just a tomboy!" Which caused her mother to frown and for Coralea to look quite pleased with herself.

"They're growing up on you," Wolf observed. "They can probably do all kinds of things you don't know about."

Dona figured that was probably true and she didn't like it much. "I'm glad it won't always be this way," she said.

"I can't imagine you'd ever come back here to live," he told her quietly as they sat swaying on the chain-link swings. "What do people do here for entertainment, anyhow?"

"Well, I guess a lot of what we're doing right now. There are community meetings and people go to visit each other. There used to be a bowling alley above one of the stores downtown--duckpins, I guess they called it--but it's closed now. There's an outdoor picture show in the summer, on Friday and Saturday nights. If you're thinking of a nightspot, there's nothing like that here unless you count the tavern. Checkers and dominoes are the extent of the entertainment there." Only the men of the town spent any time in the local beer joint, she realized.

Metal pipes anchored the huge swings into the ground and were joined at one end to a set of bars stair-stepped at graduated levels. They appeared to be for exercise maneuvers, such as chin-ups. Wolf tried a few but found he was too tall to use the bars properly. The idea then came upon him to demonstrate a move he had often done as a child.

"Let me show you how to 'skin a cat,'" he said to the girls.

A dark look passed over Barbara's face. The two little girls rushed over to watch him closely as he grasped the metal bar over his head, pulled his knees up and through his arms, and dropped to the ground on his feet.

"Let me try!" Sharon eagerly pleaded.

"I'll help you, but let's have you use a shorter bar. If you should fall, this one's awfully high for you!" He helped her reach up, then guided her knees up and flipped her through with a twirl from his agile arms.

"Again!" He could see he'd started something as Coralea had found her own bar and was trying to turn herself through, which she finally did before yelling to her mother, "Watch me, Mom!"

Only Barbara timidly stood beside her mother, frowning.

"Why don't you try it?" Dona asked her. Barbara just shook her head, not realizing that it wasn't the awkward position she found distasteful but the words themselves that bothered her. She went off to swing by herself as Coralea boasted, "I can skin a cat!"

Dona glanced at the filling station as they walked by. She didn't see Jimmie, the fellow from up on the hill, and someone else was there. She wondered if maybe the attractive young man had moved away or had gone to fight in the war. There certainly didn't seem to be many young folks left in the town. She guessed maybe Wolf was right. There wasn't much to hold them here.

The house they now passed was occupied by a couple whose only son was overseas. Merry Torrance, an elderly widow, lived in a little square house across the ditch. It was the same all over town: mostly elderly folks. All over every town, probably, Dona realized--and not just here, in her country, but in many countries. Wolf was only still here because his job was important to the war effort. Sometimes it was a huge effort for her to remain positive about her country's involvement in the fighting in Europe. She wondered what it had to do with them here, anyhow. She felt a traitor for having these thoughts but sometimes couldn't help herself.

On the way back to the city, both Dona and Wolf were quiet. The visit had been restful but the day had also been charged with anticipations, discoveries, and disappointments. Dona had been eager to show off her children but disappointed in Wolf's lukewarm acceptance of them.

"I don't know how you do it," he said now. "You're too young for such responsibilities." What she heard him say, though, was "I'm too young for those responsibilities."

"Well, I guess I did have my family early, but that doesn't change the person I am, nor make them any less important to me!" she said petulantly.

"I admire your devotion," Wolf went on, "I just don't know if I'm ready for that."

Of course she understood. June had evidently not been ready for "that" either. She was heart-broken, but relieved, too. Now at least she knew in what direction their friendship was headed. From that day the two were friends only. They saw each other occasionally, as their realm of acquaintances overlapped and they were often included in group outings in the city. They discovered they had little in common to talk about anymore. Although Dona was physically in Kansas City, the focus of her life remained in the small town a hundred miles away.

Working the night shift at Commonwealth allowed Dona to see more of the city. She and Jenny usually had the same working hours. They often worked side by side at the plant, and Jenny had a car. The two frequently picked up Therese and Irma after their day shift and the foursome spent hours exploring the offerings of the busy city. Funds were a factor, so they usually went to a park or just strolled along the sidewalks, people watching and window-shopping.

Dona had come to realize that most of the people she met were in the same boat she was--youngsters from small towns who were probably here temporarily, also. More importantly, she knew that many were as backward in the ways of the city as she was. That knowledge and being a member of a tight group of friends gave her some measure of confidence.

The girls shared clothes, but only Therese was close to her size, as the other two were tall. The group spent some time in the big department stores, Jones's and Macy's. Dona bought a few things for herself, including a gray wool jacket and matching skirt with deep pleats in the front, in the style of the times. Saddle shoes and wedgies were the street shoes in vogue, but Dona preferred wedgies as they made her look taller. She had let her hair grow long in back so she could roll it up on a "rat"--a tubular form women rolled their hair around for extra body and smoothness. She sometimes used two small rats at the temples, which gave her face a heart-shaped look. Usually she just let the front fall loosely in soft curls. Everyone told her she was lucky to have naturally curly hair, but she found it wild and hard to manage.

Therese took her Brownie camera along on many occasions, and the girls posed at fountains and on the steps of the municipal buildings, anywhere the notion struck them.

One of their favorite places to visit was the Nelson Art Gallery. It was free and there was so much to see they went back again and again. The art treasures and historical artifacts contained in the magnificent building filled them with wonder.

Dona heard that the manicured lawns of the benefactor had been converted to victory gardens for the citizenry, but they must be located elsewhere, perhaps in the municipal parks far from the city's center. She knew Bedford had its own space for a community garden, although her folks didn't participate since they had their own farm. It was about a mile out of town, to the southeast, and was called the Penney Eighty. Located on a gentle slope surrounded by woods, the area hadn't been actively farmed for many years. Dona was told that the lady who volunteered the land was the daughter of one of the area's original settlers, Hiram Stingley. She understood that the woman, Eliza, had long ago been a teller at one of the banks that then existed in the small town. Both banks were gone now, having closed in the disastrous days of the Depression.

The four girls careened down the sidewalk, four abreast. When they were together they lost all shyness and acted as if they owned the city.

"Let's go into Jones's," Dona suggested. She didn't often buy anything for herself, but Coralea would soon be going to school with Barbara and would need some dresses. She wouldn't want to wear them, but she would have to. Dona remembered the woolen stockings her mother had made her wear when she was a child. Now the little girls were wearing them. Dona still recalled how uncomfortable they were, with a harness-like contraption that tied around the hips to hold them up.

They stopped first at Jones', but hit several more shops before deciding to find a diner and get their supper. They were downtown, where throngs of shoppers and workers swelled the traffic on the wide sidewalks.

Dona nearly stepped on a man before she saw him sitting on the sidewalk, leaning against the hard brick of a building. He had a tin cup in one hand and in the other a can of pencils. His gaze was fixed somewhere beyond the arc of people around him. Dona was startled to see that his legs were short, half as long as normal, and that his shoes, and his feet, were on backwards. She was shocked at the sight and felt the color drain from her face. Tears came into her eyes as she stumbled away, confused and upset by the cruel way fate had twisted the man. Her friends hadn't even seen him but were moving on up the street, as if the world were still the same. She remembered a poem she had read in a long-ago schoolbook. "I had no shoes, and I cried . . . until I met a man who had no feet." Her friends were perplexed at the sight of her tears when she caught up with them. She told them of the unfortunate man and learned that he was at that corner regularly. Even the beautiful city had its sad, heart-wrenching aspects. She hoped the man had someone who cared for him in a way other than with pity, such as now overwhelmed her.

TWELVE

In the fall of '44, Dona began her third year on the job in Kansas City. The war in Europe had raged on through the summer, but the tide was beginning to turn in the Allies' favor. There was speculation at the plant concerning the end of production--no war, no materials of war needed.

Dona harbored guilty feelings for dreading the war's eventual end. She knew she would be extremely relieved to have the horrors of the conflict over and to have her brother and others she cared for returning from overseas. At the same time, she knew what the homecoming of the servicemen would mean to her line of work, and probably to any other possibility of employment she might seek. The men who had sacrificed so much for the good of their country would of course be given back their old jobs. They should be offered whatever opportunities could be provided when they re-entered the work force. Certainly she didn't begrudge them that. Still, the future she faced was bleak.

She wondered what she would do when that reality occurred. The allotment checks would cease to arrive after June was discharged from the army--sometime next summer, according to his letters. He had been writing more frequently lately. His unit was pushed to the front, and he was threatened by the danger of combat. His letters reflected a sensitivity she didn't realize he possessed. She couldn't imagine what daily encounters with one's own mortality might do to a person. For his sake, and all the others, she prayed for a quick end to the conflict. She would just have to trust that she would find a way to provide for her family when that time came.

The house in the country that Sam planned was finally underway. He had salvaged lumber from the two old houses on the property and by now had the structure framed in, so it was obvious it would some day be a residence. That meant within the year he and Retha would move to their farm, leaving her with the house in town on which monthly payments would still be due.

She couldn't imagine how she would make a living in Bedford. As much as she loved the peaceful atmosphere of the tiny town, she wasn't sure she could ever live there again. She had become accustomed to the bustle of the city, and knew she would miss the excitement and energy that living there stirred in her.

A three-week recuperation period in the small town allowed Dona to become better acquainted with the townspeople. She underwent a hysterectomy in early September and was forced to take a month off from work to mend her body, and, she realized, her spirit. She hadn't had much sympathy with ladies who had female problems, but her own experience quickly gave her lessons in empathy and humility. Knowing that she would never have more babies wasn't particularly a disappointment to her. She had all the children she wanted already. But, knowing she could never become pregnant again touched her in a way she hadn't expected. Perhaps it was just the hormonal change her body underwent that made her feel so low. She found herself crying for no reason at all, except that a feeling of sadness had crept over her. Then she felt remorseful and berated herself for being such a complainer.

The problem had actually come upon her at an opportune time. Her latest suitor turned out, like Wolf, not to be the person she imagined him to be. She had often been told that if a thing seems too good to be true, it probably is. She was beginning to believe that might always be the case concerning the men in her life.

Now she was in Bedford, spending most of her days lying on the couch or sitting in the yard watching the children at play. Today was Sunday and the balmy day had warmed quickly.

She heard his tractor leave his place at the top of the hill and sputter down the steep incline to pass in front of her house. She looked up and waved as he gave her a one-finger salute from the level steering wheel. Dona noticed a lock of hair ruffling back from his forehead and saw the pale area at the top of his tanned face where his customary cap shielded him during long days of plowing, planting, tilling, reaping. His hawk-like nose gave him a commanding presence and was bracketed by ears that protruded from his head at a severe angle and gave his cap a substantial resting place. The sleeves of his work shirt flapped back on his arms, revealing a tan line across firm biceps, the mark earned by toiling out in the elements.

He had passed the house at least twice already this morning, accompanying his mother to the church around the corner. On most Sundays he spent the afternoon in the field, just as every other day. His grandfather, Jed Torrance, had passed away in 1942, and his grandmother sold the farm and moved to town. She now lived in the square clapboard house that sat catty-corner across the creek. According to Sam, Jimmie farmed on a cost-share basis much of the acreage his grandfather had once owned. Jed had been a successful breeder of mules, known throughout the area for his championship animals. But he had lost most of his property during the hard days of the Depression, so what was left at his demise was sold to support his widow, Merry.

Sam had carried the old rocker out to the front yard so Dona could sit comfortably in the afternoon air. As the sun bathed her in its healing warmth, she gratefully drank in the heady elixir of the balmy day.

Dona looked around when she heard the soft rustle of footsteps in the grass.

"Bertha! How are you today?" she said in greeting as she recognized her elderly neighbor.

"I'm fine. I came over to ask if you'd like to come to our house and see what Dee made for me." She referred to her husband, who was seldom seen out of the dwelling. He had to lean on a cane to walk, and his shuffling feet could barely maneuver the steps of the porch.

"Where are the little ones?" Bertha inquired.

"Oh, they're around playing in the shade, on the Brooks' swing. I think it's their favorite spot. They've got the area so scuffed up, I doubt the grass will ever grow there again," Dona replied, motioning to the side of the house.

"I'll go see if they'll come, too. I think they might like to see this," Bertha said as she crossed in front of the rocker. Dona hadn't seen the gray-haired lady often, as she usually stayed close to home, too, though she had been friendly when Dona had spoken with her. The little girls were instructed by their grandmother never to go into the McMurtrys' yard unless invited. She knew the nuisance children could be and didn't want them to disturb the elderly couple. Doc, as the townsfolk called him, was not in good health and was often crotchety. He had been a pharmacist but had given that up long ago due to ill health. The little girls were uneasy in his presence because of his sagging, droopy eye. His complexion was sallow and pasty from years spent as a virtual shut-in.

As they entered the neighbors' house, Dona noticed how dark the rooms were. The windows were layered with curtains so very little light seeped in. Dee sat in the front room beside a pedestal-shaped object that at first glance appeared to Dona to be made of little stones.

"What is it?" Sharon asked innocently.

"It's a plant stand," Bertha replied. "Dee made it for me with bottle caps!"

The tall, slender table was completely covered with row upon row of bottle caps.

"My goodness! How unusual!" Dona commented with interest. "Where did you get them all?"

"Albert brought them up from the station," Dee said in a shaky voice.

"Oh. I've seen him stop by with bags of something," Dona remarked. "You know, where we used to live, in Edgerton, someone had covered an entire corner post with bottle caps. It was right by the filling station. It wasn't neat like this, of course, but it became kind of a landmark. You remember it, don't you, girls?"

"I do," Barbara spoke up.

"I imagine the other girls were too young to remember," said Dona, smiling.

"How are you doing by now, Dona?" Dee asked, his words faltering but kind.

"I'm doing fine. I stopped in to see Dr. Barnett yesterday, and he said I should be able to go back to work in another week. I hate to think of leaving the girls, but I need to get back to the plant," she replied.

Sharon came out from behind her mama. She guessed maybe Dee was a nice man after all.

Bertha spoke to Coralea, "How do you like school? Do you like your teacher?"

"School's okay, but my teacher's prissy," the girl retorted.

Dona laughed. "They have Miss Pratt, the lady who boards with the Martins," she said, as if that explained her child's attitude.

"I like her, but she's not as nice as Mrs. Jones was. I wish she was back," Barbara volunteered.

Coralea had been in school only a few weeks. Retha had taken her to school on the first day, since Dona was in the hospital at the time. Dona felt she really didn't know much about their school or their teacher. She hoped when Sharon got ready for school she would be able to accompany her to that important event in her young life.

Retha had awakened from her nap when Dona and the girls came back across the yard. She opened the screen door and called to them, asking if they knew where Carrie was.

"She's riding her bike with Tina Cline," Dona told her mother. "Do you want Coralea to go get her, Mom?" Dona had bought the bicycle for her sister last Christmas to show her appreciation for Carrie's help with the children.

"I think it's time she came home. She's always running around with her friends, and it won't be long until Sam's home. Run along, Coralea, and stay on the sidewalks," Retha cautioned.

Soon Dona heard laughing and shouting from up the street and looked to see a boy coming down the road with Coralea perched on the handlebars of his bicycle. She was startled to see her daughter seated precariously on the metal bar, legs dangling on either side of the front wheel. She rushed to the street to stop them.

"What are you doing?" she demanded, as the boy shifted the pedals back and braked to a stop.

"Just giving her a lift home," he sheepishly replied. "She likes it."

"Don't you be doing that again, Coralea!" Dona scolded. "Don't you know you could get hurt?" The boy looked remorseful, and Dona felt bad for hurting his feelings.

Carrie rode up to the group.

"I'm sorry, Dona. I thought it would be okay," she said. "Charlie's really careful."

"Well, I think she'd better ride behind on the carrier next time," Dona warned. "That's just not safe. It's nice of you to bring her home, though," she added, hoping to ease his feelings of embarrassment.

Charlie Simpson lived a block up the road on the ditch side, and Dona knew Retha and May Simpson had become acquainted. The boy paid a lot of attention to Carrie lately, though he was a year or two older. Dona realized that her little sister was growing up and would probably have beaus calling before long--if Sam would allow it, that is. At fourteen, her sister was given a lot more freedom than she had been at that age. Carrie was pretty responsible, Dona conceded, realizing she was pleased that her younger sister might have some advantages she had missed.

Tina came pedaling down the road, flushed by exertion as the other two youngsters were. They had spent hours out wheeling around on the back streets of the town. Dona wasn't surprised to see Tina. She had only brothers at home and was always eager to spend time at the Schmits'. Her mother was usually at the central office downtown, handling the telephone communication of the area. The Cline family lived just a block away so the girls often visited back and forth.

"Why don't we take the girls down to the schoolyard to play?" Tina suggested.

"Can we, Dona?" from Carrie.

Dona sighed. She was happy to just rest in the yard and watch the girls play but guessed the outing would be good for them.

"If you go around by way of the sidewalks," she replied.

"I want to stay and read to you," Barbara declared.

"Okay," said Dona. "Don't stay too long now, Carrie," she warned. "It's not long until supper."

"Sure," the younger girl replied. So the three energetic youths laid their bicycles down in the yard, gathered the little girls, the trike and the wagon, and headed across the Brooks' yard, off on another adventure.

Dona didn't like for them to walk on the road. It was always busy, with traffic speeding down the big hill and people pulling in and out of the station down at the corner. She realized she spent a lot of time worrying about the girls. They were growing up, becoming independent, exploring new places, facing new dangers. *It's a good thing I can't see what they're doing all the time,* she mused. *I might never let them grow up.*

Barbara brought out a stack of books.

"Let's sit in the Brooks' swing," Dona suggested. The Brooks family was gone for the day--besides, they welcomed their neighbors over anytime. Barbara sat erect on the slatted seat, picture book carefully spread open on her lap. She was proud of her skill and appreciated the encouragement her mother was sure to offer. She read clearly and with animation. *She sounds just like me,* Dona thought. *I'm glad I read to her a lot when she was littler. Mom doesn't read to the children much. She hasn't time and she's happier crocheting when she has a spare moment.*

Nora Martin waved to them from beside the road before turning to walk across the culvert toward Merry's house. She wore a hat and gloves, obviously still dressed as she had been for morning church services. Nora thought Dona looked well and that Barbara was pretty there beside her, with dark hair cascading to her shoulders. Nora felt an affinity for the young woman, whom she had met a time or two. She sensed that Dona's situation was not so different from her own.

A short while earlier, Nora had stood at her own front door and watched as her son left on his tractor. She didn't like for him to work every day but was proud of his determination to be successful at farming. He hadn't much to start out with besides a strong, young back and a love for the country way of life. When Nora's father had passed away, Jimmie was given the many implements his grandfather had accumulated. This was a great help in getting started, even if he had no land to call his own.

Both he and Nora knew it would be a struggle, but there were few options. Nora still had her boarder, but she hadn't many piano students lately since Nora McMurtry had commenced giving lessons. The elderly lady had been a concert pianist and had played for huge audiences in the cities. There was no doubt she was a gifted, special teacher.

Nora was thankful that her son was still at home with her. She knew he had struggled with the decision of whether to join the fighting in Europe. She certainly did everything in her power to dissuade him. Her nephew,

Herbert, had entered the air force shortly after his father, her brother Vincent, was released from prison. Vincent had been incarcerated for ten years for embezzling from the Bank of Bedford. He and his wife soon found they could no longer live together happily and so now lived separately in different parts of the state.

Nora had two sisters with whom she was close--one lived in a neighboring community with her young family. But in most things, Nora depended entirely on her son. Besides being the breadwinner for the household, he served as her escort to many of the social events in town. It wasn't too much of a burden for him as a young man because few of his friends were still around. His best school friend, Burl Dean Wardloe, was reported missing in action last spring, lost somewhere in the Pacific. Jimmie was too busy for much of a social life, although he did attend ballgames at the high school on winter evenings. Nora admitted to herself that she was happy he had had no serious relationship with a girl. But she probably wasn't aware that she'd done everything she could to discourage such liaisons.

As she stood in the parlor pondering the course her life had taken, Nora had become conscious of wringing her hands--rough, calloused hands that did their share of the work around the place. She needed to get out of the house before she began to feel sorry for herself. Sunday afternoon was a good time to pay some calls. She stopped in to see her mother nearly every day--not to check up on her, as she was still quite spry, but Nora enjoyed Merry's company, and maybe she could help her mother with some little chore. She planned to do that before making other visits this afternoon.

As Nora stepped upon the front porch of Merry's small house, she called through the screened entry, "Yoo-hoo! Mother!"

Merry answered, and Nora heard her stirring in the front room of the house. It took her a bit to get to the door. She had begun to walk with more effort lately, and Nora observed that her mother's shoulders were more stooped than before, giving her a humped back look. Merry was neat and orderly in her appearance but had never been an attractive woman, with her round, flat face and hooked nose. The modest place of honor she held in the community hadn't been won by any outward asset but rather by virtue of being unafraid of hard work and of having a generous nature.

The two women soon sat comfortably at the kitchen table, drinking the tea Merry quickly brewed.

"Has Vincent heard from Herbert lately?" Nora asked the older woman.

"He only knows Herbert's still stationed in Britain," Merry answered. "They never corresponded much. It was always hard for Herbert, growing up with Vincent away like that. He never did quite know what to think. Vincent was always so close-mouthed about his troubles."

"Maybe if Sadie hadn't taken Herbert away to live in St. Joe, we could all have been closer," Nora suggested. "When they were kids, Jimmie looked up to him so. I wish they were better friends now."

"That's water under the bridge," Merry shrugged. "What do you have planned for this week, Nora? Have you picked all your vegetables yet?"

"Well, Mother, now that you asked, I'm wondering if you'd mind coming up and helping me put up some tomatoes. They're ripening all at once, as usual. We could can quarts for us and pints for you. I've got plenty of jars cleaned already. We could get an early start some morning--you can pick the day, except Wednesday. That's the Methodist Ladies' meeting day, you know."

They soon settled their plans for the upcoming project, and Nora bid her mother farewell and went on across town to visit an elderly friend.

Later that evening when Jimmie drove by the Schmit home, he glanced at the yard to see if he could spot her. She often sat out in the yard on a blanket, with the little girls lounging around her. He imagined her telling them stories or maybe singing to them, as they seemed to be listening, judging by their quiet postures. At other times, he'd noticed the children were quite lively. They appeared spellbound when they were with her on the blanket. He knew his mother was quite taken with the little girls. She often related some cute thing one of them said to her as she was walking by.

Following her return to work at the war plant, Dona slowly regained her former vitality. She was weak at first and tired easily on the job, so the girls at the apartment took over her household chores and coddled her in every way.

After her lengthy stay in Bedford, Dona made an effort to go home more often. She wanted a more active part in the lives of her children. Now that she was again on the night shift, she no longer arrived in Bedford in the middle of the night, but rather mid-day, so Retha and the girls often met her at the depot.

The children were full of stories about what they were doing at school. They presented her with simple gifts they had made from colored paper. Their main cause of excitement on her current arrival was news of the upcoming school carnival. Apparently the annual event involved the entire community and would provide funding for worthy school projects. They insisted she be present on that date so she could share in the fun with them. Dona intended to be there if she possibly could.

Later that evening, Dona and Sharon were at the store picking up some groceries. They had left Barbara and Coralea at the schoolyard where they could play with their friends. It would soon be dusk and was near closing time, so Earl Rickman was spreading excelsior on the floor, ready to sweep up the day's layer of grime from the wooden surface.

"How would you like a lollipop, little miss?" Earl asked Sharon.

She smiled shyly and thanked him, as she knew she should. She had come to expect such treats at the store, especially when she came alone with her grandmother. Dona teased her mother that the old bachelor must be sweet on her as he was always spoiling the little girls.

A jingle sounded as another customer hurried through the door. It was Jimmie Martin. Dona greeted him with a wide smile. She felt almost as if they were old friends, she'd seen him around Bedford so often lately.

Then she remembered something she'd heard earlier that day.

"I'm so sorry to hear about your cousin, Jimmie. I've been told he was killed while returning from Europe," she said softly.

He nodded.

"Were you close?" she asked.

"We were when we were kids," he answered after a moment. "When I was about her age," indicating Sharon, "he took me for rides in his goat cart. He was the oldest of the kids at M.T.'s and we all looked up to him."

"M.T.?" Dona asked.

"Mother Torrance. Mom always called Merry that when Beth and I were kids, and eventually it got shortened to M.T. Herbert was her first grandchild, so she's pretty upset."

Dona sensed that he experienced a deep sadness also as she listened to him speak of his past.

"Tell your mother how sorry I am, will you? She's always so friendly when she comes by the house." With that Dona turned to her purpose and then hurried from the store.

He seems so young and vulnerable, she thought as she led her daughter back to the schoolyard to gather the other two and return home.

The rain had finally stopped when the passenger train approached the Bedford station. It had been dreary and overcast for days. Dona looked for Retha and the girls, wondering if her mother had ventured out with them on this miserable day. She spotted Carrie standing beneath the long overhang of the building's eaves, an umbrella furled and leaning against the building she huddled beside. Her sister looked frail standing on thin legs, her sweater drawn tightly around her for warmth. She wore a scarf turban-style around her head, a cover for pin curls, Dona was certain. When Carrie saw her she waved excitedly.

Soon the hiss of air brakes could be heard as the "Bug" shuddered and settled to a stop. As usual, Dona was the only traveler to get off at Bedford. She hopped down from the train just as the sun popped from behind the scattering clouds.

"You've brought the sunshine with you!" Carrie declared as she picked her way around the puddles and approached the train. Dona took her cardboard suitcase from the conductor before he deftly pulled up the boarding steps and signaled for departure.

"Where is everyone? Is anything wrong?" Dona asked as the two made their way across the wet gravel toward the nearest sidewalk.

"Mom's busy with the girls. She's fixing them up for the big shindig tonight. They're so excited! Mom's got Sharon's hair up in rags and she was braiding Coralea's when I left. She thinks she's too big for long curls and she wouldn't sit still for pin curls, so Mom thought braids would be best. She wants to wear her overalls tonight. Mom said that would be up to you." Carrie explained all this in such a rush, Dona could see that her sister was also excited about the evening's events.

"I hope Mom's going to get some rest before the carnival tonight," Dona told her sister.

"She says she doesn't want to go," Carrie informed her.

Dona realized her mother probably looked forward to a quiet evening at home. She herself had mixed feelings about the upcoming activities. She didn't know many people in the town--no one on a good-friend basis, although she had met and liked several at earlier community meetings at the school and also when she had been shopping downtown. Then there was the family who delivered the milk. They had children the same ages as Dona's. Albert would probably be there with his wife and his son, who delivered the St. Joe newspaper. She guessed she actually did know a few people in the town and was eager to share in the spirit of fun and celebration the evening promised.

As happened at each of her homecomings, the girls descended on Dona with hugs and kisses and happy squeals. There was much excited talk about their plans for the evening and the challenges of their past few days at school. Retha excused herself and went to her bedroom for her customary nap. Dona had worked the night shift just a few hours earlier and was beginning to feel exhausted from traveling during her new bedtime hours. She suggested that Coralea and Sharon lie down with her for a while so they would be ready for a good time in the evening.

Sharon cheerfully snuggled down beside her on the bed the three girls usually slept in, like spoons. Coralea wasn't eager to rest, and Dona knew she would not be down for long. Dona wondered how Sharon could rest comfortably, with knots of rags tied up in her hair in preparation for long curls. Dona was never able to master the art of curling hair. She had watched as her mother sat with each of the children, smoothly turning the long strands of hair down around a strip of rag, then lacing the cloth back up the outside of the formed tube of hair and tying it at the top. Her own efforts resulted in knotted rags, tangled hair, and unhappy girls. Sharon slept close beside her, the air whuffling softly through her delicate lips, and Dona soon slipped into deep, restful sleep.

The full face of the moon hung over the right-angled town as Dona and the girls stepped out into the dusky twilight. The air was clean and crisp following the drenching rain, and the faint smell of drying leaves perfumed the night. It was now late October and the summer sounds of living creatures were beginning to hush from the borders of the drainage ditch that ran the short distance to the schoolhouse.

Coralea had succeeded in persuading her mother to let her wear pants instead of a dress, as she always must for school. Dona supposed she might as well, as Coralea never would be ladylike, regardless of her costume. Sharon's hair fell in long, soft ringlets around her head, with a few golden curls drawn up at the crown. Barbara did her own hair now, brushing it religiously until the dark waves shimmered with light. She had pulled it to one side of her forehead and clipped it back with a pair of plastic barrettes shaped like tiny pink flowers. Their mother was proud of the way her girls looked.

Her own choice of apparel for the night's outing was the gray wool suit she'd bought the year before. She felt it looked sophisticated. She hadn't dressed up much when she was in Bedford--she was usually at home with the children.

There would be a good crowd at the carnival tonight. Already the school's parking lot was full and more cars were parked across the culvert in the downtown area. Other families were walking from their homes to the site, just as Dona and the girls were.

The big double doors at the school's entrance were fixed open to let the evening air flow in. A few men stood near the entryway, talking in friendly tones and greeting those who approached. Dona spoke to Albert as the girls rushed in ahead of her.

"You'll have to tell me how this works," Dona said to a woman behind the reception table.

"I know, Mama," Barbara said helpfully. "You buy tickets here to play the games in the rooms. Our room has balloons and darts and a ring toss game in it."

A Hundred Miles to the City

"She's right," the woman answered, smiling. "Some things are a quarter and some a dime, so you may want to buy some of each. Then the concession stand, that's in the gym, handles its own money." Dona decided to buy just a few tickets now. They could always come back for more.

Carrie was to be in one of the high school rooms, helping with the cakewalk. She had come down earlier, bringing along the cake Retha made for the event.

"Come to our room first," Coralea urged as they wove their way around the table and into the throng. Dona hadn't imagined the school would be so full of people!

The primary room had been cleared, desks piled high against a far wall. A rope divider down the center of the room separated the two activities offered in the area. On one side a big board was propped up, with colorful balloons in uniform spaces. A line of youngsters waited their turns at the dart-throwing game. In the other part of the room a ring-toss game was set up and a shorter line of contestants eagerly waited to try their skill at that challenge. Everyone seemed to be having fun, though the place was filled with noise and people jostled each other in the active crowd. Dona and the girls decided to walk around and see what else was offered before getting into one of the slow-moving lines.

Another room had a grab bag and a fishing game, plus a little table near the doorway where one could guess the number of jellybeans in a jar. The girls all wanted to try the grab bag and ended up with little prizes. Then they guessed the jellybeans for a ten-cent ticket each. By now confetti was piling up on the floor. Every now and then a cloud of tiny paper dots would drift down around them, tossed by a spunky youngster as he scrambled by.

"Can I go with Verlene?" Coralea asked when her friend came up to show them the things she had won.

"For a while," her mother allowed. "I'll be at the Bingo table if you need me." She knew Bingo games were to be offered in one of the rooms, but they hadn't gotten to that one yet. Soon Barbara was off with some friends also, so Sharon and Dona were left to wander alone.

The halls were choked with children dashing in and out of game rooms. Streamers streaked through the air around them as Dona and Sharon made their way through the boisterous crowd.

They found the cakewalk set up in the next room. Several adults were standing on the numbered papers spaced evenly in a circle around the room. Carrie and Reba Holliday were seated at a desk where they took care of the tickets for the game. A few cakes were displayed on a low table at one side of the room. Dona asked Sharon if she'd like to take a cakewalk, and when there was an empty space she scooped up the little girl and joined in. When the music started the two moved from square to square. Sharon was disappointed when they didn't win a cake and pleaded with her mother to try one more time, asking if she could go by herself this time. Her little legs wouldn't make the stride between one number and the next, so she made quick running steps as the circle of people laughed in amusement. She was disappointed again but did enjoy all the attention.

Carrie said to Dona, "Reba and I will be done here at eight. Could we take Sharon around with us for a while?"

"If you want. You can meet me at the Bingo stand later. By the way, where is it?" Dona asked.

"Oh, it's in the gym by the food stand," Carrie replied. "We'll take you there in a few minutes." Dona would be glad for the chance to sit down awhile. She was beginning to feel very warm in the close crowd.

When they got to the gymnasium, Dona spotted Nora Martin's dark red hair and decided to sit down at an empty place near her. Nora greeted her and introduced her to the woman sitting between them.

"This is Caroline Black, Dona. I think her daughter, Lucy, is in Coralea's first grade class."

Uh-oh, thought Dona. She must be the one that Mom had some words with on the phone awhile back. Retha had told Dona about calling up the woman to complain about her dog. It seems the big German shepherd had blocked the girls' way one morning so they couldn't get into the school. At least they thought it had. They had gone home crying to their grandmother. Mrs. Black had claimed the dog just wanted to be friendly, but Retha told her it didn't matter what the reason was, the dog had kept the children from getting to school on time and she had better see that it was tied up from now on!

Dona smiled at Caroline, saying, "Yes, Coralea has mentioned Lucy, many times."

Uses her favorite adjective on her, she mused--"*prissy.*" The little girl wore shiny dresses, according to Coralea--*taffeta*, Dona imagined--and "you'd better not make her get them dirty!"

Dona played a few games of Bingo with no success, then won once, so she picked a pack of playing cards she would take home to Sam. He liked to play "Old Sol"--solitaire. He had taught the older girls to play and had them all playing Chinese checkers now.

"Mama, could I have money for some more tickets?" Coralea asked breathlessly as she rushed up, accompanied by a couple of other girls.

"You can have one more dollar, but this is the last," her mother warned her. "Be sure and check in with me again before long." And Coralea was away, sliding along on a carpet of confetti.

The crowd began to thin out. Many of the Bingo players had moved on to sit in small groups at the concession stand.

Dona noticed him when he came down the steps into the gym. He wore a white shirt with the sleeves rolled up to the elbows and a new pair if jeans. He looked fresh, with an obviously recent haircut. Lightly muscled and wiry, Jimmie moved like a man sure of his destination. She thought he looked older, somehow. He came and sat down beside Nora.

"I thought you might like a ride home, Mom," he said, when Nora looked surprised to see him. "How's your luck?" he asked her.

"I've won a couple of times," she told him, as she showed him the prizes she'd chosen.

"How are you doing?" he asked, turning to Dona.

"Well, not too good, but I've just gotten started," she assured him. "Do you play?"

"Why not?" he said, as he drew his chair up to the table.

She found him easy to talk to. He told her he had been out to see Sam's project and was impressed by the progress the older man had made. Sam had mentioned talking with Jimmie a few times. Dona felt the warmth of his body as he sat close to her. He smelled good, too, not like Dad and his pipe.

She heard a familiar giggle and looked up to see Sharon on the shoulders of one of Carrie's school friends. She was obviously having a good time riding on the big boy's shoulders. She held her little fist high over Dona's head, then spread her chubby fingers to release a shower of confetti down upon her mother. Dona threw her head back and laughed as she was enveloped in blotches of color.

"You little imp!" she cried. "You come right down from there! What has Carrie been putting you up to?" Whereupon Carrie tossed a package of confetti over all of them, and Reba sent streamers flying in all directions.

Nora laughed without reserve as she began plucking the tiny pieces from her hair.

"I'll get you back for this," Dona warned her sister as Carrie whirled away, leaving them shaking off the clinging bits of paper.

"I'm so thirsty!" Nora said. "Let's go get a cold drink. You come, too, Dona," she invited.

"How would you like some pop?" Jimmie asked as he leaned over toward Sharon.

"Yep," was her answer.

Later, when Dona had gathered her girls and was ready to walk home, she paused a bit at the door to say goodnight to Nora. Jimmie was sitting on his haunches on the front step talking with some men. Sharon walked out to where he was, took a good long look at him, then squatted down, mimicking his pose. She lost her balance and tumbled over, surprising herself and delighting everyone else. A scarlet flush bloomed out on Dona's face as she hurried to pick up and comfort her crying child.

"I think we've had a pretty big night," she said to Sharon's audience as she rescued the tired toddler and led the girls toward home.

Darkness had settled over the town, but the fragile glow of the streetlights lit their way to the little house up the street. Dona was deeply satisfied, feeling that tonight she had made new friends in Bedford.

THIRTEEN

Through the open end of the troop carrier, June could make out shadowy structures along the roadway. They must be passing through a village. There was little difference in the rumbling movement of the awkward vehicle as it lumbered over the rough streets of the town. If there had once been lights to illuminate the crossings, there were none now. The moon, however, was magnificently bright on this night, seeming to herald the importance of the coming day's events.

June was tired, clear through to his bruised core, and found it difficult to appreciate the raw exuberance of many of his outfit. He was mindful of the reality that history would be made on this day, but somehow the burden of the past months' struggles outweighed any glimmer of exhilaration he might have felt. He sat quietly and let his tired shoulders sway with the movement of the fully loaded truck. Like his fellow GIs, he was sharply outfitted and sat with his M-17 resting against his knee. The thought that had been running through his mind sporadically since they'd first entered France, nearly a month earlier, was: *This could be Missouri. This place looks just like home--it could be home!* The eerie sensation of this carnage happening on American soil crept through his entire being.

The part of France through which June's infantry division passed contained many small villages, and the countryside was dotted with farmhouses surrounded by row after row of hedge fences. Once, his outfit had fanned out to search the hedgerows for enemy stragglers that remained after the Allies won the area in their sweep across France. June and a couple of other foot soldiers happened across a woman and some children working in a field. June had been startled--their appearance was incongruous to the situation. He had posed the mental question, *What are you doing in the middle of the battlefield?* At the same time, their faces mirrored back the query, *What are you doing in the middle of our farm?*

The plain peasants spoke no English and displayed no fear of the men, but reacted with surprise at the soldiers tromping through the countryside. The GIs offered them candy and gum, which had been eagerly accepted in London, usually getting them anything they wanted. These workers didn't seem to know what the treats were and refused them, turning back to their labors as though no one else was nearby. The men continued on with their search, now and again looking back to see the woman and her family, still engrossed in their task.

Since that event June had thought often of the plain woman who toiled so diligently in the field. Her dark hair was pulled back beneath a scarf, her bronzed face showing the result of many days under the sun. She was cutting some kind of grain, and the children, a boy and a girl of elementary school age, bundled it together into neat stacks. Of course the woman had been doing the job that men should be doing--most likely she was the only one left to support her family. Only women, children, and old men remained in most of Europe to perform the daily tasks required to provide a living.

In those times of reverie, June often thought of his own children, his family. They had ceased being his family long ago, and still he had feelings of inadequacy when he thought of them. Perhaps seeing the desperate plight of the children of Europe caused him to be more sensitive of his own. He thought of the girls more often now. He missed them in ways he had not a few years earlier.

When June arrived in London--so long ago, it now seemed--he was acutely aware of being in foreign territory. He was overwhelmed by the enormity of the city and the splendor of the castles and cathedrals. But what impressed him the most was the utter devastation that had been dropped from the sky onto areas of the besieged city. By the time his unit arrived, the British were accustomed to scurrying into air-raid shelters. He knew that some of the people actually lived underground. How these people could go about their daily lives while under the constant threat of bombardment perplexed and amazed him. June had quickly developed an open admiration for the friendly Brits.

A succession of twin points of light jiggled behind the truck as the convoy crawled up the gently rolling hillside. A sputtering glow lit the faces of June's comrades as they slumped on parallel benches. Some tried to grab a bit more sleep while others talked in a subdued manner, holding cigarettes in carefully cupped hands to shelter the tips from the breeze stirred by the truck's advance.

Most of the guys here June knew by name, or a name of sorts, at least. Mostly the G.I.s were identified, among themselves, by nicknames. He had early on become Slick, as he flattened back his thick, dark hair, which had by now become fairly long. When wet, it lay plastered to the top of his head, swept back from his face.

A kid from Brooklyn, referred to as "Cityboy," spoke in a vernacular as hard for June to decipher as a foreign language. Pansy was a fellow who had once expressed distaste at getting his boots muddied. If no comic trait were obvious, the men would likely label a new man by his place of origin. June reckoned there must be at least a hundred guys in France now who were called Kansas.

Highlife. The name jumped into June's thoughts before he could stop it. The young soldier had been with the outfit until Normandy, when he'd stepped on a land mine and lost a leg. When June heard what happened to his buddy he had thought, *I'd rather not be going home at all than to be going home that way. Even when they aren't shooting at you or strafing you, they can still get you!* There was no safe time nor place here.

Hooch, another comrade, had been gone from the group when June returned after a two-week stay in the field hospital. Some of the veins in June's legs had been drained and the blood replaced with oil--too many long marches toting too-heavy packs. He hadn't wanted to hear what had happened to Hooch, but loose-lipped greenhorns couldn't help but jabber about the terrible realities of battle they never seemed to be able to escape--in foxhole, tent, burned out building, cave, or . . . June wanted to erase the memory from his mind. There was no way he could help his buddy now; it was best to forget him. Maybe knowing each other by trumped up nicknames helped the men avoid emotional attachments that would only hurt more when the inevitable happened.

The only thing June had found pleasurable about being in the army was the companionship of those in his platoon. He found it satisfying to be part of a unified group, working toward a common goal--actually helping each other instead of competing. In the service there was little class distinction. Everyone was needed--each person depended upon and valued as a part of the whole.

June's personal ambition was simply to not let his buddies down. He wanted to do his part--not fail his outfit when the going got rough. That worried him. He was scared, constantly! And he knew he hadn't yet been put to the test. His outfit had been on the mop-up detail, going in after the heavy fire had settled. He hadn't been forced to hold a dying buddy in his arms nor to look in a German's eyes and pull the trigger. Dead men he had seen, and plenty, but mostly the enemy after the medics had been through.

As his outfit pressed forward, June had done his share of liberating personal items from the lifeless bodies of slain Germans. He wasn't sure why he did it. Maybe it was his way of "capturing" the enemy. He hadn't known where he should send his collection--mostly pipes and pocket watches. His mother might not accept them. With both her sons in the infantry and her two daughters away from home, both married now, she didn't need to be reminded of the war.

Finally, he wrote to Dona and asked if she would keep the articles for him. They might be worth something someday. So he sent them to Bedford. One package contained forty items, including a sword, a bayonet and a couple of pocketknives. At first he didn't know what to say to Dona in his letters, but after corresponding a few times he began to grow easier with his messages. He appreciated having someone to write to. She kept him up on things that were happening in the States and always included news of the girls, sometimes sending photographs as well. For his part, June told her what he could of the activities of his outfit--mostly anecdotes of lighter moments which he expanded upon. Like many battle-worn men in the service, he tended to gloss over the serious business of combat and to elaborate on the day to day pitfalls of army life.

Shadowy effigies nearby became people as first light appeared. Beside the road, carts and horses, a few cars, and scores of peasants on foot had gathered to greet the Yanks. The caravan was nearing Paris and more and more people crowded the edge of the battered by-way. The convoy soon arrived at the outskirts of the city where onlookers waved small American flags as the GIs approached. June's mood brightened along with the landscape as he realized that the joyous greeting was directed at him and his comrades.

Dawn broke and a beautiful August day spread sunshine over the awakening land. The expressions of gratitude on the faces of the peasants gave June an immense feeling of satisfaction. After what they had been through, he didn't see how they could have a smile left in them. Since the Germans had walked around the Maginot Line four years earlier, these people had been exploited, and sometimes even beaten, by the occupying forces. Their homes had been burned, their animals slaughtered, and their women abused. June figured that if he were lucky he would someday be going home, wherever that was now. These people were already there. Their homes were absent. Their livelihoods ruined. Their families torn apart. But they were still hopeful, that was obvious, and June felt a certain kinship to them. The war had been hell for so many, but now maybe there was a chance of better times ahead for some of these unfortunate ones.

"Do you suppose we'll see the big guy?" the smaller fellow sitting beside June inquired with interest.

"You mean Bradley? Sure, we ought to parade right past him. All the other big shots, too. He'll probably give us a wave when he recognizes us!" An elbow landed in June's ribs as his face opened in an easy grin.

"Where do you suppose we'll be going next?" This from a large, burly fellow sitting across from June.

Simpson always had an answer for everything. "Don't you bet we'll be heading on over to take the Krauts in their own backyard?"

"You mean on into Germany?" little Jake, on June's left, broke in.

"This job's just started," Simpson barked. "You didn't think we were just going to fold our tents and mosey on home, did you?" he added.

June's gaze drifted back down the road to where they had been. He had a feeling, still, of wanting to turn around and head this whole thing back. They had been through some horrendous ordeals, but he had a gnawing feeling that there might be worse ahead. There were stories being thrown about of atrocities performed by the hated Nazis--worse things than he could have imagined in his most ghoulish nightmare! What if they were true? Even some of them. Again, he shut his mind to the thoughts that might drown his sensibilities if he should yield to them.

The staging area was in a broad field, far from the center of the city. June had never seen so much military might assembled in one spot. Thousands upon thousands of foot soldiers were moving into formation, while military hardware of every description sat by, ready to be placed into designated position.

June later shared with Dona, "I think the forces gathered in Paris were meant to impress the Frenchies with the strength of the Allies. Also, to let everyone know who is really in charge. There's a lot of worry among our brass about the allegiance of the Underground. So much damage has been done in the city by the French Resistance--I suppose to discourage the Gestapo. Whatever our reason for being here, I hope we stay awhile!"

As his division marched down the boulevard in the French capital, June noticed a beautiful cathedral, untouched by bombs or sabotage. He'd never seen anything so splendid! Sunlight lit the towering spires and set ablaze the colored glass of the windows. It looked as if the city was still standing, unlike bombed-out London, where buildings were reduced to rubble and the city's infrastructure completely destroyed. The Germans had taken care of their temporary quarters.

Again in a letter to Dona: "The march through the streets of Paris did wonders for our morale. Our unit was getting pretty discouraged. After weeks of hedgerow fighting, we might take a position, but then lose it again. Now maybe we're on the right track and can move ahead, though I don't know where we will be going next. I know where I would like to be going! Norm is in Italy now, according to Mom's last letter, but she hasn't heard anything for a while."

June hoped Norm was far away from his division. He'd heard of accidents of friendly fire and feared such a thing might happen. Nothing could be worse than that--shooting or being shot by your own brother! But Norm had been appointed a colonel's driver, so surely such a thing was extremely unlikely.

June didn't know when he had become such a worrier. He now worried about everything--*would the weather break tomorrow, would there be enough air cover in their next assault, would he still have his boots when winter came, would the Germans use their touted V1 and V2 buzz bombs?* He knew the GIs were kept in the dark as far as maneuvers were concerned, so there was no point in speculating about what his company's next move might be.

Following a short period of rest and recuperation in Paris, June's outfit was ordered to advance north toward Belgium. Their mission was to flush out pockets of German resistance as they made their way toward Germany and their ultimate goal--crossing the Rhine River and capturing the Ruhr district. The mines, factories, and smelters there were major providers of German strength.

June was disheartened to learn that his unit would again be engaged in hedgerow fighting. Earlier in the conflict, it had suffered horrible losses in the bloody combat that raged in the countryside. The dense growth aided the enemy, sheltering the Germans whose arms were more effective in close combat. Huge German Tiger and Panther tanks were able to break through the dense growth that stymied the Allies. The men of June's unit believed the German 88 the most effective artillery available. The powerful weapon could propel shells flat at ground level and could also bring down airplanes.

American ground troops had the M-1 Garand military rifle and the bazooka--June heard it was named for a hillbilly musical instrument. With good range, it required two men for operation, and was not effective in close fighting. The Sherman tanks of the Americans were fast and light but not equipped for such short-range encounters, and the tanks were vulnerable when climbing over the hedgerows. The Americans had 50mm machine guns mounted on the tanks, but the German tanks were nearly impenetrable.

In June's division, a maneuver often used was for a tank to penetrate a hedgerow and fire phosphorous into the opposing position. The white phosphorous fell on enemy machine-gun positions, eliminating them from battle. June had seen men die from this horrible weapon of war and was grateful that the enemy had a short supply of it. Resembling white snow, it burned through the clothing and skin of the helpless victim.

A Hundred Miles to the City

After the tank crew forged an opening, the infantry--June and his compatriots--were able to advance, supported by mortar fire and sometimes air cover. They attacked and gained a hedgerow, or lost one. The war in the fall of '44 was one of attrition, with replacements constantly called up. The fatigued soldiers fought on, hoping to break through the German Siegfried Line.

On their fourth day out from Paris, June's regiment awoke to mist that shrouded the area like a soggy comforter. So far the Germans they met had quickly surrendered to the Americans. A lack of replacements had weakened the German platoons, and the movement of armaments was at a standstill. The supplies that reached them were too little and too late. The Allied infantry captured demoralized and hungry men.

By ten o'clock the mist had turned to rain and the ground beneath the men's feet was slick and sloppy. The laborious advance across the fields began to show on the weary men. June slogged across a low field in close proximity to two other GIs of his group. Water flowed off their helmets in a steady stream. The fall rains had obviously set in a bit early.

"Wouldn't you like to be back in Paris right now?" Simpson, in the center of the trio, ventured as he labored to pull one foot and then the other from the mucky morass.

"Those French women were really something!" June volunteered. "They didn't miss a chance to celebrate their liberation!" He thought of his own sisters and wondered how they might act under similar circumstances. The unexpected presence of Marly and Patsy in his thoughts puzzled him. He couldn't picture either of them in such a situation!

Pansy, bringing up the rear, hurried to join the conversation. "There just weren't nearly enough girls to go around."

"I bet Slick over here had no trouble finding a soft shoulder to rest on," Simpson said as he nodded at June.

June grinned but made no comment. The evenings in Paris had been great, but mostly because of the comfort and safety he felt by being out of the battle zone. Anything beyond that was pure gravy.

June was aware of a faint "plop" behind him, then an enormous barrage of mud and debris blasted all three forward onto their faces in the mud! June feared he was mortally struck! He raised his head slowly and gathered his long limbs, turning slightly to check on his buddies. He resettled his helmet, careful to keep himself low to the ground.

"I'm hit, dammit!" Simpson cursed. He pushed himself up and June could see a rip in the sleeve of his shirt. A patch of red spread quickly, a thin line of blood seeping down his shirtsleeve and trickling out between his fingers. Tentatively, Simpson reached with the fingers of his left hand to grope the wounded area of his arm. He didn't exhibit much pain, but a gaping slash was torn across his fleshy upper arm.

"What about Pansy?" June blurted out as both men focused their attention on the smaller fellow. He was flat on his face, his arms flailing wildly and his fingers clawing the sodden earth. Simpson reached over and lifted Pansy's face from the mud. His eyes were wide open and he was gurgling through his mouth. He had been hit in the back with pieces of shrapnel from the potato masher--grenade--lobbed at them. With the mud spattered on his back, it was difficult to assess the damage to his torso. There were holes in his shirt across his back, near his spine. June feared he might be critically injured because his legs were not moving, though the rest of his body twitched violently.

"I can't move!" Pansy cried, choking on mud that oozed into his mouth as he gasped for breath. The men were afraid to move him. They knew they could harm him more if they attempted to turn him over.

The rain continued, inundating the ground around Pansy. June and Simpson hunkered down beside him and dug a depression beneath his face, forming a miniature gully to drain the water away from him. They didn't dare move out of their position. They had been spotted and would have to hold off their attackers until help came. There was not much hope of that happening soon, unless there were troops near enough to discern where the explosion had occurred. The three were partially protected by a hillock, so they would keep their heads down and fire an occasional warning shot until the medics arrived.

Within a matter of minutes the injured man became still.

"Do you suppose he's dead?" June asked with dread.

"He has a pulse yet--hasn't lost much blood. He's probably in shock," Simpson answered from beside the still figure of his buddy. "We'd better stay where we are. The supply line can't be far behind."

Occasional outbursts could be heard in the distance, but all was quiet in the depression where the three men lay half-buried in the mud. An hour went by while they maintained their position, fearing to draw more fire toward their gravely wounded comrade if they attempted to push forward.

At last the roar of motors could be heard as vehicles labored along the gravel road a short distance away. When the convoy could be identified as Allied support, June raised to a crouch and scuttled over to get their attention. He was soon back with a couple of litter bearers and a medic. After examining Pansy's back wounds, the corpsman strapped him to a board and turned him over onto the canvas litter. Pansy slowly opened his eyes and moaned.

"I've heard they're sending the wounded back to Paris," Simpson said as he leaned over his friend. "I guess you'll be giving those French dames one more shot at you, huh?" He hoped there might be some encouragement getting through to his pal, though he feared the days ahead for Pansy would likely be nightmarish.

"You'd better come on over to the truck and get that shoulder taken care of, private," the medic advised Simpson. "You've got a deep slash, but I'm afraid you'll still be able to hoist that rifle!"

By mid-December, the 28th Infantry had battered its way north. They had lost half of their members in the assault on the Siegfried Line and were sent to a period of rest and recuperation in a supposed "quiet zone". The Ardennes Forest was used by both the Allies and the Germans as a refuge in which to rest exhausted troops and to break in newcomers. June read in the *Stars and Stripes* of successes of the Allies, while he suspected German losses were inflated by Allied propaganda. The battle-weary soldiers waited uneasily for their call-up.

The picture-postcard look of the area contributed to the subdued frame of mind of many of the troops. Three large villages--Malmedy, St. Vith, and Bastogne--were located in the valley between hills darkened by fir trees.

According to information reaching the troops, the German army had lost more than a million men since the landing of the Allies in Normandy. Their fighting forces were strained by the long war and their resources were seriously depleted. Rain and mud made movement difficult for both armies, adding more challenge to the assembling of weapons of war.

The American line crumbled on the Schnee Eifel, a critical area for the German position. Sabotaged communications caused confusion in the Allied command, adding to the formidable task of the soldiers on the ground.

Amid this turmoil, GIs like June struggled to make sense of the carnage occurring around them. June by now had for himself only three singular purposes: number one, simply to survive; number two, to see home again; and number three, perhaps more immediate than the other two, to get warm. He had been so cold for so long! He wasn't sure he could bear the brutal iciness much longer. Finding relief became all-important to him--it over-rode all of his thoughts most of the time. Once, he discovered an abandoned tarp and sought shelter under it. He invited others to huddle beneath it, even though they'd been ordered not to muster into groups, as they would be more vulnerable. He sought to be a good soldier and had been warned that congregating would make the men easy targets. This worried him later, but at the time he thought only of the small comfort he had at last found.

Heavy fighting at St. Vith led to the evacuation of American troops. The men regrouped outside the town, some eventually becoming part of the SNAFU outfit that would battle to retain the area. The Germans took a valley to the south so the Fifth Panzer Army could advance and cut off the American 106th Division near Bastogne, where the roads were critical to the movement of artillery.

The men in June's division continued to fight the numbing cold as well as the enemy. The outfit floundered under constant attack, struggling to hold the line at Bastogne. On the eighteenth of December, GIs assembled in small groups at the edge of the village. They sat on fallen logs, stumps, or their haunches, opening C-rations or dragging on cigarettes--attempting to fortify themselves before the next assault.

An onslaught of enemy tanks burst from the woods! The Americans faltered, as the immense tanks roared into position. June and a nearby trooper dodged the first barrage of 88's but were caught in the open, vulnerable to enemy fire. Behind them, trees were topped and shredded by rapid sprays from the deadly 88s. The fog of artillery quickly shrouded the area as the German line advanced on the town. The critical roadway was lined with crippled crates that had been towed from their final encounter with superior armaments. The smell of spent artillery hung over the area like the stench of a burned-out building long after the fire is quenched.

June and his companions sought to advance in the standard method of foot soldiers--fire, move, throw yourself to the ground, get up and dash forward. The ground they fell upon was solid, with jagged particles of frozen mud that cut into their hands and knees. Heavy field packs added to the equation as the men staggered forward.

June was utterly exhausted as he threw himself continuously on. He moved in a stupor, as in a cloud. The air seemed warm but white vapor streamed from his nostrils. The soldiers were ordered to dig slit trenches for temporary shelter. Frozen earth yielded unwillingly as the men slashed with their trenching tools. June had nearly completed his effort when he felt a hot sting in his backside and fell atop his gear.

He was in a broad field, with daisies waving in a lazy breeze when he approached a slow-moving, meandering stream--so docile its banks were grass-covered. He might be near Summerville, strolling along beside Honey Creek . . . he must resist the urge to yank off his boots and plunge his aching feet into the cool, clear water . . . how far he had come from the sheltering shores of his boyhood!

He was in a broad field, crouching near a 105 mm gun, silently watching soldiers automatically loading and firing. He saw an explosion, then a flash over the heads of the American gunners. He yelled a warning not heard and saw snow that was not snow sift down on the soldiers. The men went up in flames before him, burning their image onto the battlefield and forever into his memory.

Such were the ramblings of June's semi-conscious mind as he lay in the aid station at Bastogne.

By December 21st Bastogne was surrounded by German troops. Allied infantry lacked power to challenge them, having been rationed to ten rounds of ammunition per gun per day. Supply planes couldn't fly because of dense fog that covered the area for days. The hospital unit was short of medical supplies and unable to treat the wounded. The German units that surrounded the town were too weak to advance, so the stalemate continued. By Christmas Eve the men holding the town were near to admitting defeat. Then the Luftwaffe bombarded the town with air strikes, killing many on the ground, including some in the medical compound. On December 25, June doubted that he would see another Christmas Day.

The battle for Bastogne continued. When the fog lifted, supplies were airdropped to the surrounded troops. Victories in nearby towns and at critical positions sealed the fate of Hitler's force on the Belgian front. The Allies finally succeeded in obstructing the advance of the German war machine!

Still, fighting around the town continued into the new year. The weather turned even more brutal, with snow piling up in waist-high drifts. Townspeople gave sheets and other white goods to the Allies to camouflage equipment. Often the wounded died of exposure before the medics could reach them. The once-peaceful forest was littered with bodies in uniforms of khaki and of gray. Burned-out buildings squatted among shattered trees, and spent artillery was scattered everywhere.

The battle raged on while June lay on a mattress on the floor of a church in the middle of Bastogne.

FOURTEEN

Evening newscasts brought the overseas conflict into homes across the country, even those most insulated by distance and purpose. The children, too, were informed of the progress of the destruction and carnage—they by newsreels that followed their favorite cartoons at the movie theater. Fighter planes dropping bombs, shells exploding tons of debris into smoky skies, tanks thundering over fences, buildings, *maybe people?* were presented by the big projector that declared on its double-barrel image, emblazoned across the huge screen: "the eyes and ears of the world are upon you." Dona feared the horrors depicted in the newsreels might now be happening to her brother or to June.

There were two air-raid drills in the fall. The Schmits had equipped their front windows with blackout shades, as called for by those in charge of the community's safety. The first drill happened when Dona was home, and she managed to make the exercise seem almost like a game to the children.

But in November, when the sirens wailed for the second time, Sam and Retha were startled and unprepared. They each had memories of the Great War, a lesson in savagery so brutal and assaulting that most of humanity thought it could never happen again. Sam knew, if he had stopped to reason it out, that the alarm was a drill, not an actual raid. His concept of a safe shelter was underground, so he herded the household out the back door and down into the damp, cold cellar--the cellar Dona refused to enter because of the leeches. The girls were terrified of the darkness and of the creatures they knew were waiting to cling on their skin and to suck their blood. They cried and complained so loudly that Sam eventually relented and let them creep back into the house, where they huddled close to Retha until a signal announced the ordeal over. After that disturbing experience, the girls, one and then another, had nightmares and awakened everyone in the house with their frightened cries.

June continued to send relics from the war back to the States. They arrived at the Schmit home, well wrapped in layers of newspaper and bundled together in misshapen packages of heavy, brown paper. There were usually a number of pocket watches and a few fancy pipes. Some pipes were long and curved and most were made of ceramics or ivory. One had the face of a man carved into the front of the long, white bowl. They were like no pipes Sam had ever seen and still smelled of stale tobacco and of the men who may have drawn their last breaths through them. Occasionally larger items were included, once a bayonet that was covered with oil. Retha suspected that made it easier to slip the cruel blade into the chest of an American soldier.

Hank was married now. His bride lived with her folks in Lenox, Iowa, where she waited and worried with her own family. Retha had hoped she might see all her children home this Christmas, there had been so much in the news about Allied advances in Europe. But so far, American GIs weren't coming home; they were still being sent. She'd be satisfied only when Hank crossed their threshold, and she could actually see and touch him. Retha worried about each of her children, though most of them had been gone from home for a long time.

Retha was pleased with the way Carrie had developed into a young woman. She was good help around the house, even though she spent much of her time on school activities or with her many friends. She had become a seamstress--Retha helped her construct her first quilt this fall. Now the girl was asking to take piano lessons. Her friend, Tina Cline, had been taught by Mrs. McMurtry--Nora, who lived a few blocks away. Carrie admired her friend's skill and hoped she might be able to learn also. The organ that Retha sometimes played was old, and some keys were out of tune or completely silent. The Clines offered to let Carrie practice on their piano and she was soon allowed to begin lessons with Miss Nora.

Barbara listened as Carrie practiced scales on the old organ. She watched, fascinated, as her aunt's nimble fingers scooted over the keys, tapping out melodies. When Barbara asked her mother if she could take lessons, too, Dona remembered that she had always wished she could play. The older Schmit girls had learned from Retha, but Dona had been too restless, or her mother had been too tired, so she never mastered even a simple melody.

On the day Barbara was to begin lessons, Dona went along to meet Miss Nora and to find out how she might help her daughter at home. The McMurtry house, Miss Nora's now that she was a widow, sat on a corner lot, its small front porch invitingly angled to face the bordering sidewalks. Inside, Miss Nora's piano and organ were in tiny, dimly lit rooms. Both were covered with photographs mounted in cardboard folders, portraits of the many students she'd taught over the years. All five of the Cline children were there, and Dona recognized other young people who came around to see Carrie. Miss Nora was over eighty, her fingers thin and delicate but still full of magic. She demonstrated some scales to show Dona what she expected Barbara to do before long.

Dona was surprised by how things sometimes fell into place. Barbara's piano teacher knew of a man who had a piano he no longer wanted. His wife, who had played it, had passed away, and he had no further use for it. Dona wondered if he were sad with it there reminding him of happier times. The player piano was extra heavy, so half the town was recruited to move it. By the next afternoon it had been muscled from Dan Simpson's parlor, across the street, up the alley, and into the Schmits' front room.

No one had yet mastered the playing of carols by the Sunday before Christmas when Retha prepared a holiday meal for her family, so the group gathered around and sang along to the music from a piano roll. To cause the paper tube to turn and air to seep through the holes that perforated it, someone had to sit before the keyboard and pump the pedals. That action worked bellows that forced air into a cylinder and set in motion gears that controlled the piano keys. Each of the children had great fun sitting, in turn, on the piano bench, pumping spiritedly away, and moving her hands across the ivories as if she personally produced the pleasing sounds.

Miriam and Lloyd came from Kansas City with their two boys and their new baby, a little girl at last. Earlene, Emmett and Lenore were down from Summerville, where they were living now in the remodeled filling station. Emmett had closed the garage and built rooms in across the back of the storage area--their bed now sat over what was once the oil pit. The small, but cozy, arrangement left little space for the station business, which now amounted to pumping gas and occasionally fixing tires or replacing windshield wipers. Early each morning Emmett performed his second job, throwing the Kansas City Star newspaper to rural customers who lived near the town. When the girls went with him they were amazed at how quickly their uncle could roll, band and toss the sizable papers over the top of the car as he drove steadily along.

The Schmit family exchanged modest gifts at Christmastime, but both Miriam's and Earlene's families also brought special things for the girls-- usually clothing they knew was needed. Lenore was a couple of years older than Barbara, so Earlene brought along some of her girl's out-grown dresses, to be handed down as each child grew into them. Dona and the girls were especially happy to get them because Earlene had done a beautiful job of sewing them herself. Dona appreciated her family's help in providing clothing for her children.

Excitement in the little house grew as Christmas morning approached. The tree stood decorated in a corner of the front room, with angel hair forming a silky halo around each colored light. The girls rose early, before dawn. In the middle of discovering the treasures left for them, they heard a rap on the front door. Dona sent Sharon to open it, and when the child pushed back the screen and peered out to see who was there, she saw a brand new teddy bear sitting on the step! As she reached out to grab it up, Dona exclaimed, "Look! It's Tucky! He's come back in a brand new suit!"

Sharon smiled and gave the bear a hug. She accepted without question that the bear had knocked on the door, but the other girls were puzzled about who had actually done the rapping. They never suspected their grandfather to be the one who'd provided the playful surprise!

Their mother's plan had been to replace the child's dirty teddy bear with this new one. The old brown bear was not washable and so had become quite filthy in the years Sharon had loved it. Its fur was matted and its stuffing settled down into lumps, so Dona had put it away in an attempt to replace it with a newer, better model. That worked, until Sharon was ready for her nap and couldn't sleep without her old teddy bear. So the battered but adored bear was found, and from then on Sharon had an "Old Tucky" and a "New Tucky."

For the children, the winter months were punctuated with shots to ward off whooping cough, daily doses of Vermifuge to prevent worms, and a diet heavily laced with raisins in an attempt to prevent boils. The town was down to one doctor, who was very busy treating everything from schoolyard injuries to lingering pneumonia. Retha spent her share of time with Dr. Barnett, if not for one of her own frequent ailments, then for one of the children's. By the time warmer weather became a possibility, all in the household were weary of long underwear and nightly Vicks rubs, and none more so than Retha.

Word was received shortly after Christmas that June had been struck down in battle in Belgium and was now in a hospital in France. He was to receive a Purple Heart for his injuries, which he later described in a letter to Dona as being "a long way from my heart." It was hard to tell with June. She knew he would make light of his troubles if he could.

Jimmie Martin enjoyed his free time in the winter months. He liked to read, and there were always things to be done around the house. However, the evenings were long. After spending most of the day in the house with Nora, he was eager to find other distractions to fill his later hours. It wasn't his way to spend time in the beer joint downtown. Jimmie, Sr., had run a bar in St. Joseph, and young Jimmie had observed some lax characters and knew he didn't want that kind of life for himself. Besides, the men who hung around Chance Holliday's tavern were older, seasoned veterans of the community, whose talk revolved around the war or glories of days long past.

Consequently, Jimmie often attended activities at the school, most particularly the basketball and volleyball games that pitted the local high school team, the Bears, against other schools in the county. A few short years earlier he had been one of those boys on the court, and he still appreciated athletic prowess and the dedication it required.

Jimmie remembered when he first began playing basketball. He was a freshman, and his cousin Herbert a senior, the tallest boy on the team. Herbert was a skillful ball handler, with a level of talent Jimmie admired. Back then they played their home games in the IOOF hall downtown. Albert once told Jimmie that when he was in high school the boys and girls both played basketball, and the practices and games were on a dirt court outdoors. Now the community had a new gymnasium with caged windows, and lights suspended from the ceiling in protective baskets. The hardwood floor was smooth as glass and gleamed with a golden waxed surface.

Now the girls played volleyball in competition, over a net stretched across the middle of the basketball court. Jimmie got to the school early enough to see part of the girls' game, which always preceded the boys' contest. The school gymnasium was the center of the town's social intercourse during the winter months, as practically everyone had a family member or close neighbor who was on one of the squads. Jimmie sat for a while by Mr. Stinnett and discussed the progress of the night's events. Harold Stinnett, now retired, had been coach at the school for many years and still attended most sporting events.

After the girls' volleyball game, Jimmie went up on the stage to visit with Albert for a while. Albert ran the clock for the game and was also responsible for sounding the buzzer to signal time periods for the contest. The score was kept on a large board that hung above the west door to the gym. Tin cards painted with numbers were mounted on loops, allowing them to be flipped down as VISITOR or HOME scored points. A high school boy performed this task with a long pole equipped with a hook.

Jimmie sat for a while at the scorer's table talking with Albert. A lock of hair persisted in tumbling from the low part in Jimmie's dark brown hair. Now and then he ran his hand through the wayward mass, training it back from his face.

A Hundred Miles to the City

He saw her sitting at the end of the bleachers with Carrie and two of the girls. She was dressed casually and had beside her a pile of wraps--coats and hats enough for half the crowd, it seemed. He saw Carrie take the two girls out of the gym. Time for popcorn, he guessed. Jimmie left the stage and went down to say hello to Dona.

"Short one tonight?" he asked her.

"Short one?" she asked back.

"Girls. Where is the other one?" he said with a smile.

"She's home with Mom. She has a cold. Carrie wanted to come to the game to see Tina play. She hopes to play next year, too," Dona said to him.

"It does look like fun. They're good, aren't they?"

He noticed the softness in her brown eyes and sat down for a bit.

They talked about the game, the players, the weather, her family, Nora, the war. He talked about his days playing ball. She talked about her children. He talked about the coming of spring. She talked about coming back to Bedford.

Carrie and Tina came back with the two little girls.

"Dona, do you want us to take the girls on home? They're tired and Tina wants to go home now, anyway," Carrie said.

"Well, I guess if they want to. I think I'll stay for a while longer. It's been years since I went to a basketball game," Dona replied, remembering the time, so long ago, when she'd played basketball at Summerville.

By the time all the coats, hats, and mittens were on, the game was underway. The two talked easily as they sat and watched the fast-moving action. Jimmie told her who each player was. She knew of some from conversations with Carrie. A couple of boys were sons of storekeepers in town, and some were country kids who had come to school in town as freshmen after graduating from one of the country schools. Jimmie knew which school each had gone to and who their parents were. She figured he must have lived here his whole life--hard for her to imagine, her own youth being spent with so much uprooting and moving on.

"I heard you had a run-in with Miss Pratt," Jimmie said mischievously.

"Well, I guess you might say so. How did you know?" Dona asked.

"She was complaining to Mom about the mother who came to school objecting about the way she taught reading. She didn't name you, but it was pretty easy for us to figure out who she was talking about," Jimmie answered.

"She's trying to teach reading without phonics," Dona asserted. "I can't imagine it. And that was right after she'd told the kids that the abbreviation for pound was pd., not lb. I don't know if I was really upset so much, I just wanted to see what the woman was like. I did go to talk with her. Mrs. Jones was so good last year, and Barbara learned so easily!"

"Did you get it all straightened out?" he asked.

"If you mean, did she agree to teach any differently, no. But I did find out that she means well--she just isn't as capable as other teachers I've known," Dona said with a look of resignation.

"So, is Coralea learning to read?" he asked.

Dona smiled. "Yes, but I think it's in spite of her teacher." A frown appeared as she added, "She's been having nightmares lately, but I don't think they have anything to do with school."

"Do you think maybe she's scared of something she's seen at the show?" Jimmie asked helpfully.

"Usually she says a train is trying to get her. She won't talk about it much, but she's frightened when she hears the train go through town. She's never been afraid to come and meet me and she's ridden on the train a few times and it was always a good experience. It seems to be scary for her only if she doesn't know just where the train is," Dona told him. "There doesn't seem to be much I can do to help her."

Jimmie sat silently thinking about something for a while, then spoke. "I think I kind of know how she feels. Something happened here in Bedford a few years back that really scared me. And I was older than she is."

"What was it?" Dona asked. She hadn't heard of anything like a train wreck in the town.

"When I was in the seventh grade, our school principal took the older boys out of school one day to see something down by the railroad track. It was a long way down the track, but you could see the place from the schoolyard. We all walked down the road, wondering what was up. He didn't say a thing to warn us, just that it was something we needed to see."

"What was it?" Dona asked again, though she doubted that she really wanted to hear his response.

"A man had been hit by a train. His feet were completely cut off and lay between the tracks, shoes still on the feet, like bloody boots! The rest of the man was a few feet on down beside the track. It made us all sick. I never felt so rotten in my life!" Jimmie nervously shifted his position, as if he wanted to flee from the disturbing image.

"Why did he do that?" Dona asked, wondering how a supposedly intelligent man could be so cruel.

"He said we should learn a lesson--that riding on freight trains could do that, and we shouldn't ever think of running away and hopping on a train like that man had. All I could think of was how it must have hurt and whether the man was alive after it happened!" Jimmie said, his face white with the memory.

"What did your family say when you told them?" Dona asked.

"Everyone in town was mad at him. They fired him from school. Some who knew him argued that maybe he did it for our own good. I couldn't understand that. That picture will stay in my mind forever!" Jimmie told her.

They sat quietly for a while, eyes on the game but not really seeing it.

"I had really loved trains. I used to run out to the pasture by M.T.'s house when I heard the train coming so I could wave to the man in the caboose as it went by. That was at about the same spot where they found the man. After that, trains looked completely different to me--powerful and dangerous, not wonderful and exciting. In a way, I guess Mr. McGee may have been right. We did learn a powerful lesson--that thrill and danger can have horrible consequences. Still, I hope that never happens to any other kids."

Dona saw that Jimmie was gripped again by the revulsion and shock of the experience. She wished she hadn't mentioned her child's problem. But then, she thought, sometimes it helps to get a thing out and talk about it. Jimmie probably hadn't spoken to anyone about the traumatizing event for years. She saw a seriousness in him she had not expected in one who seemed so innocent.

The game had reached the halfway point and Dona decided she should be going.

"Do you want me to drive you home?" Jimmie asked.

"Oh, no. That's not necessary. I'll enjoy the short walk. I've liked talking with you, though. Come by our place and visit with us sometime, why don't you?" she suggested, thinking how much she enjoyed his company, but not wanting to set tongues wagging in the town.

He said he would like to and she gathered her things and headed for home.

Dona stepped from the side door of the building and felt the crisp night air, refreshingly cool on her face. As she walked over the culvert beyond the school, she noticed the stillness of the night, as if the earth held its breath. Stars were splashed in an inky dome above, like snow in a globe--not floating to earth, but hanging, forever suspended in time and space.

Except for Sam, everyone in the household attended Sunday school the next day. The small Protestant congregation met at the town's middle house of worship a couple of blocks off the main road, down "church" street. The large, white building was a simple structure, with a belfry at the top. Three windows on either side of the church were not stained glass but were frosted, with arches at the top that lent a modest distinction to the otherwise ordinary appearance of the building.

The entrance was a simple large door that opened into a small vestibule, where the bell rope dangled on one side. Double doors swung open into the spacious sanctuary. Two rows of massive wooden pews marched toward the altar, which was centered on a raised area that stretched across the building. A piano was to the right of the altar and behind that, on the platform, was a circular arrangement of red primary chairs. The wooden chairs all faced a large seat that was occupied each Sunday by Ana Ellis.

Dona hoped her visit to Sunday school might allow her to meet some people of her own age in the community. Retha and the girls went regularly to the morning services, usually accompanied by Carrie. The congregation was divided into four groups for the religious lessons--the adult group that Retha sat with in the back of the area, the young people's group that Dona would join, the older children's group that included Carrie, and the primary group that occupied the little chairs around Mrs. Ellis.

Ana Ellis and her husband, Bert, had farmed at the Ellis home place until a few years earlier when they had retired and moved into Bedford. Then the Schmit family had moved onto the place as renters. As well as creating furniture for his own family, Bert now did carpentry work for others in the community. The couple was childless so Ana had turned her energies to civic interests. She was on the committee for most projects undertaken by the town leaders. Her needlework skills rivaled Retha's, and the two visited often, swapping patterns and neighborhood gossip over a cup of coffee or tea.

Most of the churchgoers were either much older or much younger than Dona. A few farm families brought their children in for services, so the young people's class might have six or eight members on a good day. Each of the groups had a volunteer leader who guided discussions with the help of a printed pamphlet, apparently produced at some central denominational headquarters. The primary class was given a small leaflet to take home as a study reminder of the day's lesson in Christian living.

Dona watched Mrs. Ellis as she spoke quietly to the children gathered around her. She was a large woman, with sharp features but a kindly manner. Boys and girls from two to eight years old sat at rapt attention as she spoke straight to each one. The children seemed to sense they were receiving very important information from her and sat without saying a word.

Greetings spread among the worshippers as the session came to a close and some moved toward the door. Retha would stay for the church sermon, but Dona and the girls would walk on home over the crusty snow that covered the street. An ample snowfall had occurred during the night and was now firmly packed by the traffic of Sunday worshipers.

"Someone at the door to see you, Dona," Sam called as she and Carrie worked to do up the dishes after dinner. She was surprised that Jimmie had responded to her invitation so soon.

"I'm busy in the kitchen right now," she said in embarrassment as she let him in the front door.

"I'll sit here and talk with Sam and Retha for a while, if that's okay," Jimmie told her. The little girls were busy in some other part of the house.

"It won't be long now until planting time," Sam began. Before long the two men were engrossed in talk of crops already harvested and crops yet to be planted. Retha sat quietly crocheting in her comfortable rocker. She had enjoyed a meal prepared without any assistance from her own hands.

Bobbie Brooks knocked on the back door. She was dragging a sled, and a pair of ice-skates were slung over her shoulder. She and Carrie planned to join other young people down at the old riverbed. Dona had bought Carrie some shoe skates and she was eager to try them out on ice for the first time. For weeks she'd wobbled around on them, waiting for a cold spell to freeze the ice thick enough so Sam would let her out of the yard with them.

"Dad checked out the ice this morning," Bobbie told Dona, who relayed the message to Sam in order to pave the way for Carrie's outing.

"Well, if it'll hold up Rob, I guess it'll be okay for the rest of you," Sam allowed, smiling.

"Why don't you bring the girls down?" Bobbie suggested. "If you want to, I'll leave the sled here so you can pull them down later."

Dona looked at Jimmie uncertainly. He indicated that he would like to go along, too--it had been a long time since he had been down to the area's prime skating spot. His classmates had scattered after graduation from high school. There weren't many opportunities for young people in Bedford, and then, many young men were overseas now.

"You girls go on and we'll be down later," Dona told her sister. It would take awhile to get the children bundled up.

"Sharon had better not go," Retha volunteered. "She's just getting over that bad cold." It was decided that the four-year-old would stay home and rest with her grandmother.

Barbara and Coralea took turns pulling each other on the sled, but Jimmie ended up towing them most of the way.

"You're a good horsey!" Barbara told him.

"Did you ever ride a horse?" Jimmie asked.

"Yes, we did," Barbara assured him.

"Only the ponies at Fairyland Park," Dona interjected.

"When I was a little older than Barbara we lived right over there," Jimmie said, pointing to the farm that lay down the road a ways. "My grandparents had horses and mules and we rode them all the time. We lived with M.T. sometimes, when Father was looking for work."

They had walked about a mile down the road that ran north beside the Bedford school property. Sounds of friendly horseplay could be heard from the site of the old riverbed, where the standing water was firmly locked in winter's grip. Some time in the distant past the Platte River had changed its course and left an oxbow impoundment some hundred yards east of its present, straighter bed. In summer the murky water yielded crawdads for the local fishermen, and in winter it afforded a reasonably safe place for youngsters to spend some of their pent-up energy.

The four had only to cross the railroad tracks and follow the beaten path to join the spirited group. For the briefest moment Jimmie experienced a shadow of discomfort as he remembered the long past but not yet forgotten accident of the hobo. The tragedy had occurred close to this very spot.

Dona was relieved to find several adults at the gathering--some she had already met. Junior Black was there with his daughter Lucy, and Albert and his son were there as well. Some older high school kids were there in couples, lingering around a bonfire that had been built in a sheltered area.

Carrie was gliding across the ice hesitantly--somewhat less smoothly than Dona had hoped. The girl's feet and ankles were tiny, and Dona could see that she was already tired. Dona was very careful in moving across the ice herself, as she still felt vulnerable from her earlier operation. Jimmie pushed the girls alternately across the ice on the sled, letting them zip along as far as they could coast on the slick surface.

After they'd been there for a while, Carrie removed her skates and began playing with the girls, too. They were having such fun Dona was glad when Carrie offered to bring them home with her later.

"Be sure and come home when it starts getting dark," Dona cautioned her younger sister before leaving.

Any discomfort they felt from the winter's cold was quickly forgotten as the couple began their trek into town. A cerulean sky stretched to the horizon. Not a riff of cloud disturbed the serenity of the endless blue mantle that blended nearly seamlessly to white, flat land. Only two houses could be seen to the west of the road, a mile beyond the steel truss of the river bridge. The hugeness of the sky shrunk the girders to an erector-set image carved into the massive stillness. The structures that were Rob Brooks' sawmill were draped in a curtain of snow that molded them to the contours of the land on which they sat. To the east lay the level expanse of the schoolyard, its layer of white disturbed only by the brick building that loomed over cartoon shapes mimicking merry-go-round, slides, and swings.

Voices from the skating party faded into the winter afternoon as Dona and Jimmie walked side by side toward the resting town. They walked companionably close but not touching. A red-tailed hawk flew down and lit on a snow-capped fence post, its hungry eye searching the furrowed field for any hapless creature that might have ventured from its burrow. It flapped away on silent wings, still hungry, still hunting.

Last year's ditch weeds sparkled with silvery drops of melting snow. Stubble from an earlier cornfield poked through the feathery blanket of white, like whiskers on a sleeping giant.

Dona untied the scarf from her head. Perhaps it was the exertion of the outing that warmed her. She welcomed the soothing air that wove its way through her dark curls.

One car had carefully passed around them since they started home, the driver pausing long enough to ask if they'd like a lift to town--to which both had quickly responded, "No. Thanks anyhow."

"Would you like to go to a show sometime?" Jimmie asked, pleasing Dona but not surprising her.

"Yes, I would," she replied, smiling, "but I can't be gone long. I come home to spend time with the girls and to give Mom a hand--she works so hard caring for them all week."

"There's a movie theater over in Whitesville. We could go there," he suggested. That town was just fifteen miles away, so the trip would be short.

"All right. I'll be back in Bedford in a couple of weeks. How would that be?" she asked.

And so their first date was settled upon. Dona had begun to think of Jimmie as a good friend and anticipated knowing him better. She thought of him as being much younger, though she knew from the year of his graduation that he must be only about a year younger than she was. Perhaps she felt so much older because of her experiences. She'd been married and had three children already, and as far as she'd heard, he had not even had a steady girl friend. She knew that the Schmits liked him, and she believed that Nora liked her also. It would be nice to go out with someone who already knew her family. Sometimes she'd felt as if she were masquerading as someone she wasn't when she had dated men in the city. It would be a relief being with someone who not only acknowledged the existence of her children but seemed to enjoy being with them too.

Shortly after Dona returned to the house, Carrie and the girls came in, faces flushed with exertion and excitement.

"There's a big crack in the ice!" Barbara told her mother. "It went all the way across!" She was obviously still concerned about it.

"There was a big 'boom'!" Carrie said as she dropped her skates beside the door and began to peel off her wraps. "Junior Black said it was still safe, that ice does that when the air warms up. But I thought we'd better come on home."

"He said that showed that the ice was really thick," Coralea added, finishing the afternoon's lesson, although she wasn't really convinced that she believed it.

Dona took all the wet mittens into the living room and laid them out on the tin mat that lay under the oil burner. She hoped the girls would lie down with her for a while. Her days and nights were still confused from working the night shift at Commonwealth. That would be over soon, she feared. Miriam had put in a word for her at Macy's, where she worked as a salesgirl. She told her sister that she would probably have to start in the stock room, which didn't bother Dona--she would be happy to have a job, however menial. She would be returning to the city tomorrow and expected soon to be faced with the challenge of beginning new employment there.

On their third date, Jimmie took Dona to St. Joseph. They would go to the Frog Hop, a night spot that featured live dance music. But first they would have supper at The Stag, the restaurant/bar Jimmie, Sr., managed. Dona was eager to meet the man. Jimmie had told her very little about his father, except that he'd left his family eight years earlier. She knew he had once been a farmer, or at least raised horses, because Jimmie had complained that he would just get a pony broken to ride good and his father would trade it off.

"Father's family lived down on the Empire Prairie, but only Grandma and Grandpa Van Heel are left there now," Jimmie told Dona as they drove toward the city.

"Where is the Empire Prairie?" Dona asked with interest, the name alone evoking fanciful speculation.

"On south of Culver City a ways . . . " he began. Seeing her puzzled look, he continued, "That's about six miles east of Bedford. We lived out there awhile and I went to Long Branch country school--when I was about eleven, I think. There's nothing there now except a church and a cemetery."

"So Nora's family are natives of Bedford, and your father's people came from the area around the Empire Prairie?" she asked.

"Pretty much--most of them anyhow. My granddad, that would be Grandma Van Heel's first husband, is buried at the Long Branch cemetery. And so are his parents. He was a pretty colorful character, I guess, although I don't really remember him. I do recall helping to stir the mash one time. He was a bootlegger, so I suppose we were at his still. When I was five or six, he died in Montana and his body was shipped home. I remember that because his corpse was around for a while, and they had the services at their house, which I guess was routine back then. Anyhow, I remember the smell . . . still." He laughed nervously, hoping the tale didn't disgust her too much.

Dona laughed. "I can't imagine you being descended from a bootlegger!" she said. "We had someone in our family who was hanged for a horse thief once. Well, I suppose once is all you can do that!" They both laughed at that.

They had taken Highway 169 to St. Joseph, and Dona remembered the time Sam took her to the city to look for work. So she told Jimmie about that experience.

"I was terrified. I didn't know how I was going to support the girls. I'd never worked before, really, and had few business skills. That day was very hard for me," she said. Sometimes she had that feeling again but didn't know how to tell him that. She wanted to appear confident, even though she often felt far from the successful, secure person she pretended to be.

"The ride home was wild!" she told him. "There was a rainstorm, a gullywasher, and the car slid all over the road. Carrie and I had to walk in the mud--we were covered with it! Then the car got stuck and we all had to walk home in the rain. It was the sloppiest mess you could ever imagine!"

"You're forgetting you're talking to a man who knows pig-lots," Jimmie reminded her.

"Well, maybe it wasn't that dirty," she allowed. "But you should've seen us. We were a sight! Mom hardly recognized us when we came tramping up the lane."

The forty-mile trip to the city seemed short to Dona. It was easy to talk to Jimmie, and he seemed genuinely interested in their conversation.

The Stag turned out to be small and dark, more tavern than restaurant. Jimmie, Sr., was, like his namesake, very easy to talk to. In looks, he appeared to Dona as an older, somewhat stockier version of Jimmie. He expansively treated them to a steak dinner, which Jimmie later assured Dona was not a frequent occurrence with his father. When they left, Jimmie, Sr., said he hoped to see more of her.

"Sometimes I stop to see him when I come down to the stockyards--" Jimmie told Dona when they were on their way "maybe two or three times a year. He seldom came around after the folks split up so we haven't been close, as you may have guessed." He realized she probably knew what that was like. The little girls' father was certainly never seen around Bedford.

The Frog Hop was located out on "the Belt." The popular name referred to the highway that ran along the eastern edge of the city. Most of the businesses that had sprung up along that busy thoroughfare had to do with automobiles. There were several gas stations, a few garages, a couple of car dealers and some motels. In addition to those, there were appliance stores and a recently opened restaurant. Most of the city's business was still being conducted in downtown St. Joseph in the vicinity of 6th Street and Frederick Avenue, with the industrial district lying farther to the south, close to the stockyards and the nearby Missouri River.

Jimmie guided the car through traffic that flowed steadily between the massive structures lining the streets of the downtown area. Most of the brick buildings were three or four stories high with impressive facades that testified to the importance of the work taking place within.

They passed the Kresge's store and Dona wondered aloud, "Maybe I should look for a job here. It would be closer to the girls." After VE Day was declared in April, her roommates at Marge's had been leaving one by one to begin their post-war lives. Soon Dona would have to look for another place to live, anyhow, since Marge and Eddie had only opened their home as temporary housing for those employed in the war effort.

"Aunt Sadie works in one of the dress shops here, but I'm not sure which one," Jimmie volunteered. "She lives by herself now over on Mitchell Avenue. We used to live in St. Joe when I was eight or so, down in the south end near Edison School."

"What did your father do then?" Dona inquired.

"More or less the same thing he's doing now . . . only at a different bar," Jimmie replied.

"Did you like living in St. Joe?" Dona asked, finding it difficult to imagine him in such a busy place.

"There wasn't much to do here. I spent a lot of time at the library. Maybe it would've been different if I'd grown up here. We lived in a big apartment building that wasn't very nice. I caught mice for the landlord for a penny apiece. I guess I was probably the town's youngest exterminator!" he said, laughing.

They passed the compound of buildings that made up the State Hospital, ominous structures of dark brick. *That's where Grant lives now,* Dona thought to herself. *No, not lives in--is incarcerated in,* she sadly admitted as she caught sight of steel bars on long, narrow windows. A depressing sense of responsibility shadowed her conscience as she thought of her brother. The Schmits visited Grant infrequently, as the trip was hard and it seemed to make little difference to him whether they were there or not. Dona had come up from Kansas City a couple of times with Miriam and Lloyd. Miriam was nearer in age to Grant and had been closer to him than her siblings were. Dona often wished that he might be brought home for a visit again but then thought of the awful burden for her mother if it didn't turn out well.

Jimmie turned at the Snow White restaurant and headed north on the belt. A neon sign flashed atop a roadside marquee announcing VACANCY at the Pony Express motel. Floodlights surrounding stations and car lots joined with streetlights to illuminate the way from one end of the belt to the other. Cars turning on and off of the busy highway only slightly impeded the rush of Saturday night revelers.

When they arrived at their destination, the parking lot was already nearly full. She hoped they'd be able to get in. The long building lacked decoration, other than the name painted in huge green letters above the doorway. The man sitting at the door looked them over as Jimmie paid the cover charge. They passed muster and he beckoned them on into the dimly lit room. Smoke swirled near the low ceiling, causing the scene to appear even more shadowy.

"It looks like all the booths are taken," Jimmie said, nodding toward the long row of padded seating that ran along the inside wall.

"Maybe there's a table," Dona suggested as they made their way beyond the bar, skirting the edge of the dance floor. They dodged dancing couples as they slowly found their way across the area.

It was obvious that they might have to stand for a while. However, after the next number the bandleader announced that the set was over and there would be a short intermission. Some in the audience gathered their things to leave, so Dona and Jimmie secured a small table near the corner.

Everyone appeared happy and relaxed to Dona. She felt at ease here with Jimmie. Looking around, she realized she didn't know another soul in the place, which for some reason made her feel even more relaxed. Maybe it was because she and her date were on neutral ground.

"Have you been here much before?" she asked Jimmie.

"Some. But it's been awhile. Burl Dean and I used to come down when we were just out of high school. Usually several people from Bedford and Horton would come down at the same time--just getting out and trying our wings, I suppose." He had a wistful look as he told her this. "People moved away or got married and settled down. Anyhow, eventually I knew very few people here, so I just stopped coming."

They sat for a while sipping the drinks they'd ordered. The band started up again and Dona wondered if they would dance. Maybe he would rather just sit and listen.

"Shall we dance?" Her unspoken thoughts were answered.

First, she was surprised at how soon he had decided to try it. Then she was surprised at the ease in which he took her in his arms and guided her onto the smooth wooden floor. He evidently hadn't forgotten the steps he must have learned well. The smell of his after-shave lotion soothed her senses, blotting out the cigarette odors that permeated the crowded atmosphere. She felt light in his arms and blissfully free of cares. If she had been tired, she now forgot that feeling completely.

"You're a good dancer," she complimented him.

"So are you," he said in return. "We should do this more often!" She felt the youthful hardness of his body as he led her over the dance floor. It was good to be held again. Her own body was saying thank you in so many ways. She felt as if her eyes must be shouting the message.

"Are you having fun?" he asked.

"Too much, I'm afraid. I'd almost forgotten how nice it feels to be held like this," she answered as she squeezed the hand that held hers. She felt the warmth emanating from his face as he placed his cheek against hers.

"I supposed you went out in the city a lot," he said to her after awhile.

"Yes, I guess in a way I have, but it wasn't the same, somehow," she said softly as they danced in an ever tighter pattern.

The band played several Glenn Miller tunes that pleased the crowd. The music was very danceable so Dona and Jimmie remained on the dance floor for a long time, embracing among the many couples who appreciated the swinging sounds of the instruments.

People began leaving in pairs and in groups.

"We had better be going, too," Dona suggested. "We're an hour from home, you know."

"One more dance? They'll probably stop playing soon anyhow," Jimmie observed.

On the way home they passed through Shenandoah. Nothing was stirring in the small town. Few cars were on the road this late. The blackness of the night and the hum of the motor lulled Dona into a dreamy state of awareness and she laid her head on Jimmie's shoulder. He put his arm around her and

A Hundred Miles to the City

held her gently. Dona was so deeply contented she felt as if she could melt right into him.

Bright lights abruptly startled her, and she raised her head quickly in response. They had pulled into Mid-way, a café and gas station that remained open all night to service the truck drivers on long hauls down 71 highway.

"I thought we'd better stop here," Jimmie announced. "I was getting sleepy. We'd better get some coffee."

The ground beneath her feet felt foreign, and Dona realized she also needed to be revived.

"Hi, Jimmie!" the waitress called as they stepped in the door of the small eating area. In the center of the room, the counter she stood behind was surrounded by a row of stools. There were a few booths, now empty, beneath the large front windows. Only two men occupied seats at the counter.

"Just some coffee, Dolly," Jimmie said as he and Dona settled into a booth.

"Do you know her?" Dona asked quietly.

"I usually stop by here if I'm on my way to the sale barn. Usually it's early in the morning--not this early, though."

"Why do you go so early?" she asked.

"Well, in the summer it's easier on the livestock because it's cooler. Besides, you have to get there in time to unload and register your animals for sale," he told her.

"How early do you go?" Dona asked with concern.

"Oh, sometimes four, maybe five, o'clock. The earlier you go, the less of a line you'll have to wait in to unload. There are usually quite a few trucks because producers who live close to the stockyards can deliver the day of the sale and won't have the cost of feed and pens for overnight," Jimmie explained. "It's not so bad. It's a different world out here in the early morning."

"I know. I had the night shift, remember," Dona laughed. "All I wanted to do was get home and get to bed!"

He reached over and took her hand. He looked at her intensely and Dona felt he was about to say something, but he picked up the check instead and said, "We'd better get on." She sensed a change in his line of thought. She saw it in his eyes. He was seeing a new crop coming through black soil in long, even rows. She wondered how many hours would pass before he'd be sitting on that tractor again.

She was very close to being right. He was seeing the winter wheat he would be cutting, golden grain flowing like quicksilver into his efficient combine.

Later that day Sharon awoke from her nap to exclaim, "Jimmie!" as she looked up and failed to recognize the dark-haired man who smiled down on her.

FIFTEEN

He came back into her life so easily, like fog rolling across the bottomland, capturing all forms in an irresistible embrace. Maybe it was the way he looked in his uniform--more handsome even than she remembered and more mature than she expected. In many ways he was a stranger to her. He was confident and calm, unlike she remembered him.

She hadn't expected him the day he appeared in Bedford, although she knew from his letters that he wished to see the girls, and she had certainly encouraged him in that intention. Still, she was taken off-guard when he arrived at the Schmit door, and she was completely embarrassed when Sharon failed to recognize her father. Of course, the child had been roused from sleep and had no idea she might see the man she knew only from pictures as her daddy, the soldier. It had been three years since the girls had seen him, four since he'd been their own.

June had arrived in the States just a few days earlier. He had no plans, he said. He just wanted to see everyone he had missed and wondered about. He wasn't willing to talk much about his overseas duty, other than to tell about the places and people he'd come to know and of his weeks in the army hospital--weeks that to him seemed endless.

When the glider factory shut down in the spring, Dona had taken a job at Macy's Department Store in downtown Kansas City. She and Jenny Green were the only two left at the Culvers', who had offered to let them stay as long as they needed a place in the city. But they would take no one else in.

Dona had been spending frequent weekends at home. She and Jimmie went out each time she was in Bedford, and she enjoyed more time with the girls, who constantly surprised her with their ever-expanding activities and interests. Now the oldest of the three spent long practice sessions at the piano, while the other two rode the range with Gene and Roy out in the yard.

Sam and Retha's place in the country was nearly completed, except for electricity, and they'd begun moving some of their things. On weekends when Dona was in town, they stayed at their new house, and Dona hired May Simpson to care for the children when she went out with Jimmie. Sometimes they would take the girls along, either to a movie or to the wrestling matches in St. Joseph.

Dona felt she was welcomed, finally, as a true resident of the town. She knew almost everyone by name and visited back and forth with her closest neighbors. As the townsfolk accepted her as one of their own, Nora Martin became more distant, less friendly, it seemed to Dona. She wondered if Nora felt threatened because of her relationship with Jimmie. There had been no talk of marriage between Dona and Jimmie that would cause Nora to resent her. Dona certainly couldn't see Jimmie abandoning his mother, but maybe that was a possibility in Nora's mind.

Later in the summer, Dona began receiving letters from June. He wanted to see her again. From the intimacy of the letters, she knew what he meant. She felt she was being courted by mail. He tenderly addressed his letters to Amapola Dona, a term he'd heard in a current tune, meaning "pretty little poppy." She was flattered, but ambivalent in her feelings toward him. He wrote beautiful letters, touching accounts of his dreams, his plans, his regrets. She knew she would see him again, and began to anticipate their eventual meeting.

Dona had knots in her stomach on the day she was to meet June alone for the first time since the end of their marriage. She was confused about her own feelings and unable to understand the feelings he claimed he had for her. She wondered what they would say to each other. Would they revisit old hurts or pretend they had never happened? Would she deny the feelings of betrayal she'd harbored for so long? How could they bridge the gap that four years apart created? She wished she had said no to his pleas.

The man she met and talked with was not the boy she had known. The familiar mannerisms were still there, but this was a different person, a person she no longer knew. There was no doubt he was changed. Being in a war, seeing all he must have seen--it was no surprise that he was aged beyond his years.

In his letters he'd called her "darling" and "sweetheart", terms he'd never before used with her. She had been "honey" to him then. He told her of the times he had wished he had her and the girls to come home to, times when he lay in a foxhole and hoped for a future. He asked her to forgive him for being "a real heel." He had been too young to settle down and he thought maybe she'd been too young, too. She found herself remembering the shared experiences that brought her such satisfaction when they were first together. The times of pain and disappointment seemed insignificant compared to the rewards of their earlier union. Feeling an unexpected tenderness and warmth toward June, Dona realized that he had been gone from her life but not from her heart.

June offered her a cigarette. She had noticed he had taken up smoking. She wondered if that was why he seemed more mature, more at ease with himself. She had tried a few cigarettes with her friends but hadn't become accustomed to the habit, as he obviously had. She saw the firm way he held the cigarette between his lips, the smoke sliding sensuously from his mouth as he continued to speak.

He asked her about Coralea's legs. He said he thought maybe all those hours she spent massaging the crooked legs had helped. She began to cry, realizing he had noticed her efforts and still remembered that time in their lives. He asked her why she was crying. She knew she could never make him understand, but felt as if she might regain a part of her past that had been lost. After they divorced, those earlier years were gone from her. Along with losing him, she had lost all the experiences they had shared, the good as well as the bad. She wept because she knew he wanted to remember them, too.

Dona and June decided it would be a good idea for him to spend a weekend in Bedford with the girls--to see how his reappearance in their lives might affect them. When that time came, Dona was again nervous. She didn't want to expose them to unnecessary hurt, but she had to give their relationship a chance. As it turned out, they welcomed him back as if he had only gone off to war, as they had been encouraged to believe. To Sam and Retha, his homecoming simply meant that he had returned to shoulder the responsibilities he earlier shunned.

In December, 1945, June and Dona were married for the second time. They went home to the house in Bedford. The first night they were reunited as a family June blew up some "balloons" for the girls to play with. Dona was embarrassed because she recognized what the long, opaque tubes really were. The girls noticed they were extra large and not colorful, as balloons usually were, but they enjoyed the buoyant toys nonetheless.

June just laughed and assured her, "I won't be needing them again!"

By the next summer June had repainted the little house, fashioned shutters for the windows, and rebuilt the front porch. He captured the town as he had recaptured her heart. He was welcomed to the community as a hero returning from battle, even though he denied having anything to do with the outcome of the war. He was chosen as mayor of Bedford that year, a post no one sought but one that was accepted as an honored position in the town.

June had ordered a new truck with his separation pay from the army, but it was slow in arriving, so he bought Rob Brooks' old lumber truck and began hauling items for people in the community. By the time his truck was delivered, he had built a reputation as a dependable, hard worker. He hired out to transport grain and livestock for farmers and was kept busy most of the summer hauling bluegrass for Carl McGeorge. At the time of the fall harvest, Jimmie hired June to help get the crops in, and the two men continued to work together for the next couple of years.

The slow pace of life in the small town was a welcome change for Dona. She at last had time and opportunity to attend to the needs of her family and took great satisfaction in doing so. She still made mistakes in the kitchen and still disliked needlework, but she threw herself into being a wife and mother and taking part in community activities. Sharon started school in the fall, so Dona's days were free for pursuing her own interests. She joined a bridge club made up of young women, some of whom lived in town and some from nearby farms. On many days she went with June in the truck, if the run were short so she could be home by the time school was out. Or, if the day was pleasant and June wouldn't be home until late, she sometimes walked out to visit Retha at the farm.

One day June brought a puppy home with him. The girls loved the furry ball of black and white that they named Tootsie. They fussed over him and carried him around until Dona was afraid the puppy might become sick. He quickly became a beloved pet and followed the girls wherever they went.

On fall evenings when the air was cool and the companionship of playmates beckoned, the girls took the dog and went to the schoolyard to play. They often played work-up, a game of softball managed with just a few players. The children who came to the ball field were of different sizes and ages, but in that game everyone had a turn at each position, so it was a favorite pastime.

Sharon was six years old now, had entered school, and never hesitated to try anything that the rest of the children undertook. Short for her age, she was also the youngest of the group.

The ball field at the back corner of the schoolyard was outfitted with a backstop, and base markers were imbedded in the ground. Area baseball players used the site for town team games, so it was always well-maintained.

Usually the first one to hit upon playing ball would shout "Pitcher!" followed immediately by "Catcher!" from someone else, then "Batter!"

"Batter!" "Batter!" This was often accompanied by a debate about who claimed what, when. Then, eventually, those who were left with no assignment chose the remaining positions, starting always with first base and continuing on around as long as there were children available. No one knew who'd made up the variation of the game of baseball--it had just been passed down from earlier generations of kids seeking fun and exercise.

As practically always happened, the older, louder kids got to be up first, so the game was well under way before Sharon worked up to the batting box. She had played before so she knew to wait her turn but was careless--or so overly-anxious to finally get her chance to swing the bat--that she stood too close to the batter, whose wild swing whirled around in a big arc and clipped the side of her head. The scalp wound immediately began to run with blood and Sharon immediately began to scream.

The boy who had swung the bat stammered, "I'm sorry! I'm sorry!" and turned white as a sheet. He stared at her for a moment, shocked at what he'd done. Then he grabbed her hand and pulled her toward the front of the schoolyard. Barbara hurried along, supporting her sister and ordering Coralea to "Go get Mama!"

Coralea took off running up the street and the rest hurried across the road to Dr. Barnett's office.

"Sharon's been hit with a bat!" Coralea excitedly yelled at her mother as she ran into the house. "She's bleeding really bad!"

"Where is she?" Dona asked in alarm.

"I think she's at Doc Barnett's," Coralea answered, breathlessly. By now she was crying, too, thinking about the blood spilling from her sister's head.

Dona ran down the street, with Coralea behind her trying to keep up. She saw the group of children on Doc's porch but couldn't see her daughter. When they got closer, she saw Sharon on the porch step, with old Dr. Barnett bending over her, pressing a thick bundle of gauze against her head. Her light hair was darkened with blood and Dona fought the impulse to scream.

"I'm sorry! I . . . I hit her!" Donnie Cline stammered as Dona rushed up. She could see he was about to cry, too. She was relieved that Sharon was sitting up and alert and seemed to have good color, though she appeared frightened.

"Will she be all right?" Dona asked of Doc, working over her daughter.

"It's not too deep--scalp wounds bleed a lot. I'll tape it up, and if she's careful she won't even have to have stitches," he answered in a concerned tone.

"How did you know to come here?" Dona asked Barbara.

"Donnie comes here all the time," she replied. "He gets nosebleeds at school." She remembered the many times she'd seen her classmate clutch his face and tear down the sidewalk, blood streaming down his elbow.

"Usually about once or twice a week I can count on someone getting hurt over there," Dr. Barnett was saying. "Sometimes I even see them coming."

"What will we do when you leave?" Dona asked. She'd heard that the doctor had retired and was planning to leave the community. His age had begun to hamper his ability to practice medicine.

"You'll get along," he answered, to reassure her. "Maybe someone else will come to town. I've made lots of calls. Let's wait and see."

The children began to drift back to the schoolyard, but Donnie lingered with Dona and the girls. She suspected he felt worse than her daughter did.

"I'm sure Sharon will be more careful from now on," Dona said as she smiled at Donnie, hoping he got the message that she didn't hold him accountable for the accident. Sharon nodded in agreement and managed a hesitant smile also, as she leaned against her mother for comfort. It would be awhile before she'd be eager to play softball again.

Most of Missouri's rainfall comes in the spring. In the fall of 1946 it came in the fall, and it came in one sudden, devastating downpour. It started in the morning and continued through the afternoon. By five o'clock, drainage ditches were filled with run-off from the rain-soaked soil. Because Bedford lay at the base of a bluff bordering the Platte River bottom, the water was not only massive in volume but extremely fast-moving as well. Luckily, it occurred during the weekend when the children were home from school, because the schoolyard quickly became isolated by muddy water surging toward the Platte River.

The yard at the Bowen house became a lake with islands of grass emerging. Across the road, turbulent water rushed wildly along. It gurgled just beneath the culvert supporting the street that tied one side of town to the other.

All of the family gathered at the front window, watching the water's advance and wondering if and when it would stop. The rain had ceased already, but the water continued to rise.

They saw Merry Torrance come down the hill from Nora's and guessed she must have been visiting her daughter and decided, since the rain was over, that it was time to go home. During the two blocks of her approach, the height of the churning water rose to the level of the side street and began to rush over the top of the culvert. Merry's house was beyond the raging water.

The little lady wore short galoshes over her shoes and clutched an unopened umbrella in her hand. She neared the inundated street that passed to the other side of town.

Dona saw Merry hesitate, then begin wading into the edge of the unleashed stream! She shouted to June, "Please stop her! Don't let her go in there!"

By the time June reached Merry, the water was over her galoshes, but when he spoke to her she turned and gave him a look that said, very plainly, "You'd better not touch me!"

Dona rushed out and the two of them stood helplessly as Merry continued on into the murky, swift-flowing water. She walked slowly but steadily on. The water was up to her knees and wetting her skirts but she moved on toward her house. Dona and June watched wordlessly, each fearing she might be swept away at any moment!

Merry kept walking forward, on out of the water, never turning to look back--up to her house and into her door.

"Can you believe she did that?" Dona asked June.

He grinned in relief. Then he said, "She must be too ornery to die."

They attempted to check on Sam and Retha, but the phone lines were down. Abbie, at the central office, told them Clear Creek was out and the road was closed where it passed over the creek beside the Schmit place.

When they finally made it out to the farm the next day, Sam showed them how far the water had come up on the barn. Clear Creek marked the western edge of his land, and the old barn sat very close to its banks. Sam had worried about a calf that was in a stall when the water rose, but it evidently managed to stay afloat long enough.

The river was out on the fertile bottomland, nearly surrounding Bedford. Crops still in the fields would likely be lost. The bridge was damaged by floating debris and must be repaired before heavy vehicles could be allowed on it.

Several changes occurred in the town in the years immediately following World War II. The most notable and least appreciated of these was Dr. Barnett's retirement and eventual move from the community. He'd been kind and generous in his ministrations to the sick for nearly thirty years. Though he tried, as did others, to solicit a new physician for the area, he failed to coax even one prospective practitioner to come and look the place over. There had never been a true doctor's office in the town--those who tended the suffering in the small community had always worked in, and out of, their own homes.

Now the people of Bedford had to go to Horton for medical attention, and that was four miles to the west. Beyond that, those ailing or injured would have to travel nowhere short of Whitesville or Madison for their medical needs.

Dr. Hancock was known for his work on giantism. He'd gained national recognition for his study of human growth anomalies. He had once been host to a man who was eight feet tall, and had in his office an entire skeleton of a man of similarly impressive height. His home in Horton was dark and Gothic, so many of the children feared to go there, due to the presence of the skeleton and the gruff appearance of the doctor himself. Older, more worldly youngsters were eager to visit the doctor, partly to satisfy their developing curiosity and partly to claim certain bragging rights. Whatever the case, the people of Bedford couldn't accept Dr. Hancock as their own doctor and from then on generally chose to make the long trip to a larger town, if their condition permitted.

The outdoor movie, once located on the empty lot near the general store, was moved across the street to an abandoned space lying between Chance Holliday's tavern and the corner post office. Dr. Liston, a dentist, came from Maitland to run the twice-weekly show. He enclosed the area with a tall, wooden fence, and bleachers were installed in the back so the place, though not indoors, was certainly more private than before.

Doc Liston charged patrons of his shows a quarter, fifteen cents for those under twelve. Popcorn was sold in brown paper sacks for 10 cents a bag. The movies, run from a projection booth at the top of an adjoining shed, were most often Westerns, or classics that had been released some time earlier. From the street, a narrow alley led back to the ticket booth where either Doc or his wife sat. This passageway helped discourage dogs from following their masters in and pestering the crowd. Moviegoers trickled in a few at a time until there were often as many as fifty or sixty folks in attendance.

The Bowen family spent many summer evenings at the popular little theater. It was a meeting place where young and old could mingle with their peers, getting better acquainted or catching up on the gossip of the week. Those nights were special for Dona. She welcomed the chance to share in the fantasy lives of those on the screen. Places she'd never see were there for her and her family to enjoy, and characters too bold and too beautiful to be real colored the everyday life she now knew.

Leaving the movie, the crowd shuffled out along the straight corridor toward the dimly lit street. Dona dreamily ushered her family along to the music of records Doc played for the exiting of the theater--usually tunes such as "New Moon Over my Shoulder," or "Candy Kisses."

Much of Dona's communication with others of the community occurred in response to activities of the children. In one circumstance, she found it necessary to apologize to Wilma Cameron, Albert's wife. Their son, David, was the town's current paperboy and usually a responsible ten-year-old. When he came home from his route one day with his clothes drenched, his father landed on him with all fours, in a barrage of verbal humiliation and the threat of a good spanking. When Dona heard about it later, she felt compelled to make things right for the boy. Her girls had been in their front yard on the hot summer evening, having a water fight out of tubs they had left warming in the sun all day. It was Dona's suggestion that they toss a little water on David to cool him down, so he shouldn't be blamed for joining in the fun. He was getting wet anyhow. The kids all had a great time until the water was gone and David realized he should get on home.

Wilma responded to her explanation as Dona had expected a concerned mother would. That was the beginning of Dona's lasting friendship with Wilma C.

Sometimes after they had been to Sunday school Dona and the girls stopped to see Mary Lamb, the petite lady who lived in a tidy bungalow across the street from the Christian Church. Mary was usually listening to a ballgame on the radio when they arrived. She enjoyed the children, as she was over eighty and didn't get out often, even to go downtown.

Stella Walker and her son, Johnny, lived in the next little house, and Dona and the girls often met them as they were coming home from their church. The girls were no longer afraid of Johnny, who walked in jerky movements, with his arms drawn up at his sides and his head cocked at an odd angle. He tried to speak to them, but the sounds came out in spits and grunts, so he couldn't be understood, but his friendly smile conveyed messages that his voice could not.

Dona often ran into Nora Martin after church, or when she was downtown. She'd become friendly again--more than friendly, it seemed to Dona. She gushed over the girls, calling them precious and lovely, and paying them exaggerated compliments. She bragged a lot on Harvey. She called June "Harvey." She said he was the best worker she'd ever seen and "wasn't he just the most handsome man?"

When June got his stock truck, he had the side of the cab lettered with his name and address. He decided to use Harvey, as most of the townspeople knew him by that name. Dona wondered if he might have been teased about his name in the army. She supposed that he was of a rather mature age to be known as "Junior," or even a form of it. But he would always be June to her.

Al Wilson, another Junior, had recently bought Earl Rickman's grocery store. After graduating from high school, Al had worked for Earl a couple of years. Now Earl was ready to retire so Junior took over the thriving business. Calvin Robertson, who owned a small store across the street, had retired and closed his store. So now the town had only one other grocer, Jane Herring, whose store was located on the corner of the block. Stella Walker still worked for her.

In addition to the customers who lived within the town itself, the small business community served a good-sized farming area. Although improved roads and better automobiles drew more and more trade away from local merchants, many country people still depended on the convenient stores for their necessary purchases. Their trips to town were infrequent, perhaps occurring just once each month.

All the family went for rides in the big truck, their only auto. If they went to the farm to visit Sam and Retha, the girls rode in the back, surrounded by the high stock rack. They must stand at the front and keep their hands firmly around one of the boards. Both Dona and June were amused one night at the movie when they heard Coralea arguing with another little girl. The other child's father was a trucker, also. They heard Coralea proclaim, in an adamant voice, "My daddy has more scoopshovels than your daddy!" That particular claim to fame struck them both as very humorous.

One Sunday afternoon June took all three girls to the river bridge to fish. They first dug in the yard for fishworms and found a few more in damp places under rocks. June tried to teach them to bait their own hooks, but the worms were too wiggley, or too nasty, for them to handle. They spent an hour sitting as quietly as they could on the bank, while June encouraged each one to hold her pole still and keep her eye on the bobber.

Finally Barbara got a bite that they managed to land, so they took their day's catch and went home to present it to their mother for frying. June cleaned the half-pound fish and Dona cooked it, as if it were, indeed, a prize haul.

Little curly-haired Tootsie had been a member of the family more than a year when he met a sorrowful end on the highway in front of the house. The dog had a habit of chasing cars, those going slow enough to present a reasonable challenge. He had been scolded over and over and swatted with a rolled-up newspaper, to no avail. The dog just would chase cars. He had given them several scares already.

June was always careful when he pulled away from the yard in his truck. On the morning of the accident, the girls had gone to school by the time June was ready to leave on a job. The dog followed him out, as usual.

After backing the truck from its place in the yard, June shifted and eased forward toward the big hill. He heard a yelp and felt a thud! A car that had passed by screeched to a halt as June stopped the truck and jumped out to see what damage had been done. He shivered when he saw the mangled heap of fur lying behind his rear wheels. Dona ran out of the house with a stricken look on her face.

"You've run over Tootsie!" she cried, tears ready to spill.

The driver of the car, Jake Waters, rushed up to see if he could help, and quickly realized the little dog was beyond help.

"I'm afraid I scared him beneath your wheels," Jake said in apology. The look on his face revealed that he truly thought it was his fault.

"It was bound to happen," June told him. "It's not your fault, Jake. We tried to keep him from chasing cars. He just wouldn't learn."

The dog was badly broken but still alive and whimpering in pain.

"I'll have to shoot him!" June stated dejectedly.

She knew he was right. The dog was suffering horribly. June went into the house and returned with his rifle. He picked up the limp body of the poor animal and put him gently into the back of the truck. This was one of the "daddy's jobs" that he could very well do without.

That day at noon when Dona tearfully told the girls that they had lost their pet, she tried to make them feel better by saying they would get another dog. That did not comfort them. They wanted Tootsie. No other dog would do. And she felt the same way. It would be some time before the family would acquire a new pet.

The little house had a good-sized yard around it, flat except for the mound formed by the cellar a few yards from the back door. Usually Dona or June did the mowing with a rotary mower that clipped the grass off short and even. The girls were getting big enough now to help with this chore.

One evening Coralea pushed the mower across the back yard. It was heavy so she lunged to get it to move. The mower sprang forward, skipping over the slick grass, and she fell down hard onto her knees. A sharp pain raced up her leg and she jumped up clutching her knee, then ran toward the house. By the time she reached the door, her lower leg was covered in blood.

Dona gasped when she saw the blood running down Coralea's bare leg.

"My goodness! What have you done to yourself?" she demanded, as she wound a kitchen towel tightly around Coralea's leg.

"I just fell down," Coralea said, wondering herself just how she had gotten into this predicament. "I was just trying to mow the backyard!"

The flow of blood abated after a bit and Dona inspected the wound, a deep one-inch gash beneath the kneecap on Coralea's right leg. It would have to be stitched. June was working up at the Martins', so Dona knew she must run up and get him.

She hurried up the hill to Jimmie's house and knocked loudly on the screen door. As she did so, she glanced into the screened porch and saw him sitting in a tub, bathing beside the back door. Blooming out in a scarlet flush, she blurted, "I'm looking for June. Is he around?"

"He's still out in the field on the tractor. Is something wrong?" Jimmie asked from his vulnerable seat in the little tub.

"Coralea's cut herself badly and I need to get her to a doctor right away!" Dona anxiously replied.

"If you'll wait out in the car, I'll be right out," Jimmie said.

She was embarrassed but knew it was all she could do.

On the way to Horton, Dona broke down and started sobbing. Now that the crisis was more or less over, she fell apart.

"Don't cry, Mama," Coralea said from the seat beside her. "I'll be all right."

She was so concerned about her mother's condition she forgot to be afraid of Dr. Hancock, whose touch didn't hurt at all.

Only a few houses in Bedford could be said to be impressive. Since the town only came into existence in the late 1800s with the arrival of the railroad, there were no buildings of any great age, although some houses and businesses had been moved from the site of old Bedford. Those structures would likely be placed in the dilapidated classification. Perhaps half a dozen homes in the community were of two stories--most of the residences had been built around 1900-1920 and were modest, one-story dwellings.

The Gregg house stood high atop a hill to the north, not actually within the boundary of the town. It boasted a large barn and a two-car garage that sat apart from the house. George Gregg, Sr., had made his money in the lumber business when the town was growing.

Up the hill to the east, three large houses faced south, each having broad front lawns and long, level driveways. The middle house was of stone, with a large set of stone steps leading to a massive porch that gave the front of the house a look of superiority. The house on up the hill was inhabited by the Martins and had an acreage with a small barn.

At the foot of the hill two more large homes graced the intersection a block south. One was the home of Bill Cline and his family. Several large trees shaded the lawn, and a spacious porch ran around two sides of the building.

The other was perhaps the most impressive home in the town. Its two stories were decorated with ornate gingerbread work. It, too, had a large porch and was further adorned by picture windows with leaded glass panels. The house was sparkling white and appeared to be the retirement home of country people who'd moved into town and now spent long hours applying their cultivating skills to their yard. Immaculate flowerbeds flanked the formal porches and bordered the wide walks. In truth, Cecil Black had never been a true farmer. He had been a gentleman farmer, renting out land for others to work for a share of the profits.

Cecil, Jr., lived across the street, on the other side of the Cline house, with his wife and only child, Lucy. The girl was in Coralea's class in school, but the two seldom played together. Mrs. Black, Caroline, came from the city, and appeared to insulate her child from the influence of other children in the town. The two girls had been thrown together in one endeavor, through no wish of their own. Coralea had sung in a musical number with Lucy at a community meeting arranged by her teacher. They had performed "Singin' in the Rain," replete with umbrellas and taps on their shoes. Dona was just as surprised as anyone at her daughter's appearance in the unlikely role. Of her three children, Coralea was certainly not the vocalist.

Dona wasn't sure whether she disliked Caroline Black for any particular reason or just because she seemed aloof. She and Caroline were members of the same bridge club and so had conversed from time to time, but Dona knew she would never accept Caroline as a personal friend and suspected the feeling was mutual. For one thing, Caroline's vocabulary was expansive, making her appear more educated than others in the group.

The women were near the same age and most had children in school. When they got together at the home of the hostess, they invariably had a good time and Dona looked forward to the twice-monthly parties. She sometimes came home with the top prize but enjoyed the get-togethers even when she wound up with the "booby" prize, a gag gift for the player with the lowest score at the end of the afternoon.

When it was her turn to host the game, Dona bought special tally cards and fussed over the right prizes to offer. Welcoming the group to her house was a special treat for her. She felt she was at last a true member of the community when the women sat down to enjoy the afternoon at her tables.

"Bill's playing at the New Dell this weekend," Edith announced. "Why don't you all come down?" She was the middle Brooks girl, who'd married a local boy a few years back.

"He plays the steel guitar, doesn't he?" Dona asked.

"Yes, and he's good, too. You really should come and hear him. The band plays all kinds of music--country, bluegrass, big band. You name it, they'll play it," she added.

Dona was in the backyard getting in the clothes when she heard June pull into the driveway. She loved the smell of the sun-freshened towels and brought each one to her face for a good whiff before dropping it onto the heaping basket. She was singing to herself when he stepped around the corner of the house.

"You're in a good mood tonight!" June observed. "You must have brought home the grand prize today, huh?"

"Not exactly, but I'm not the booby, either," she laughingly told him. "I used to win nearly all the time when I played with the girls in K.C. These gals are really good! They must've been playing a long time."

"Where are the girls?" June asked.

"Sharon's over at the Brooks' and the other two are around the block riding the bike," Dona answered. Barbara and Coralea took turns riding the bicycle they had inherited from Carrie, who'd decided she was too old now to ride a bike.

June sat on the porch step and lit a cigarette. Dona wondered if she should ask him now and be disappointed right away or hope for a while longer that he'd agree to go to the Dell. He never had cared much for dancing and didn't know any of the group very well, so she figured he probably wouldn't want to go.

"Bill Lynch is going to play with a band in Shenandoah this weekend," Dona began. "Edith thought it'd be fun if a bunch of us went down to hear him Saturday."

"Who's 'us'?" June asked.

"Oh, just the ladies in the bridge club and their husbands," she replied hopefully.

He hadn't said "no" right away.

June smiled at the thought as he said, "We'd look kind of funny driving up in our stock truck!"

Dona quickly answered, "They wanted us to go together, in one or two cars. Gail and Ross have a big car and she said they'd drive a bunch. And Junior Black would probably drive, too." She could see he was giving the idea some consideration.

He was thinking she probably missed the good times she had in the city when she was on her own.

"We haven't been anywhere lately, have we?" he said. "I guess if you really want to, but don't expect me to dance."

Of course she'd agree to that. At least for now. Maybe she could get him to change his mind after she got him there.

"Oh, good! I'm sure Mom will watch the girls. Can I tell them we'll go, then?" Dona asked.

"Sure, now what's for supper?" he said as he followed her into the house.

"Hop in!" Gail called to Dona and June when she and Ross pulled up in their big Mercury.

"How're you doing?" Ross asked as the couple settled themselves in the back seat.

"Great!" Dona replied, smiling at June in satisfaction. "Do you suppose there'll be a big crowd tonight?"

"I suppose so," Gail answered. "We haven't been there in ages. I imagine there've been a few changes in the place."

"They're pretty much all the same, if you ask me," Ross volunteered. "I hear that Bill's band is pretty good, though. He always played the piano, but I never knew he played the guitar. I wonder when he picked that up."

"Edith says he learned in the army. I guess they wanted entertainment for the troops, so he volunteered and picked it up from some of the guys," Dona said.

"That's a heck of a lot more useful than the stuff I learned!" June stated.

"And what was that?" Gail asked.

"Oh, things like how to clean a latrine and how to pull K.P. duty, mostly. And how to get taken at every kind of poker." June said dryly. "Can you get some music on that machine, Ross? We need to get in the mood."

"I can get Del Rio, Texas, if I'm pointed in the right direction, and I do believe I am!" he said as he twisted the dial in search of the country station.

"Who else is going from Bedford?" June asked.

"Junior Black is supposed to pick up J.B. and Jackey, and Joe and Kathleen, too, I think," Gail told him. "We'll make a nice little show of support for our local boy."

The New Dell was on Highway 71 at the south edge of Shenandoah, the narrow building joined at one side to a motel. A popular nightspot, it was the only place nearer than St. Joseph that held dances on a regular basis.

When the door swung back, Dona heard a smooth rendition of "Stars over Texas" emanate from the large room. The dance floor was crowded and the murmur of voices mingled with the sounds of the hidden musicians.

"There they are, in the back!" Ross announced, as he took Gail's hand and led the group around the edge of the large dance area. They caught sight of the members of the band, decked out in casual western fashion.

"Well, look who's finally here!" Junior Black called, as he and Caroline whirled by in a quick spin. The music was loud and lively and most couples were out on the dance floor enjoying the beat.

"Edith saved us a table!" Jackey said as they approached the group seated around a small table near the bandstand. "We've got you some chairs, too," she added, motioning beside her.

"How's it going?" June asked loudly of J.B., who sat stiffly alongside his wife. The nearness of the band made conversation difficult at the crowded table.

After they had waited several minutes, June took drink requests from the group and headed to the bar to see if he could hurry along the service.

"My, you really have to watch out for your derriere out there!" Caroline announced when she and Junior returned to the table.

"You'll just have to learn to pull it in a little!" Junior said as he gave her behind a friendly pat. Everyone laughed.

Dona noticed the smooth way Junior danced Caroline out onto the dance floor. They made a striking couple. *You'd never take them for country people*, she thought. In fact, if there were any classy people in the place tonight, they were surely the Blacks. Caroline was always a sharp dresser. Tonight her jersey dress clung to her well-endowed figure in all the right places. Dona knew Caroline wasn't the prettiest of the group, but she had a certain magnetism, and she seemed to ooze confidence. Caroline's light brunette hair fell in trained waves around her face. Dona's own dark curls went wherever they would. Dona caught herself assessing the other women in the group and realized how childish she was being. She came to have a good time, and she made up her mind to do just that.

"Don't you dance?" Caroline asked June.

"Not if I can help it. I've never been inclined to fancy footwork," he answered, grinning.

They all agreed that Bill was quite good on the steel guitar. They clapped and hooted when he picked out a solo part in "Turkey in the Straw." Edith smiled with pride as the group showed their appreciation for her husband's talent.

When the band paused for a break, Bill came over to the table. They congratulated him on his musical ability and offered to buy him a drink.

"Thanks, but I play better sober," he assured them. Those in the large group were able to visit during the relative quiet between sets. Dona was having a good time and thought that June was, too, although he still hadn't stepped out on the dance floor.

When Bill got up to rejoin his fellow musicians, he patted J.B. on the back saying, "Drink up, folks! The more you drink, the better I'll sound!" They raised their glasses in a sloppy salute as he settled down behind his instrument. The twangy sound of his electric guitar slid the musicians into their next number and couples quickly made their way back to the dance floor.

For much of the night, Dona and June sat alone at the table. Even J.B. finally got enough liquor in him to brave the quick pace of the music. Dona and June relaxed at the table, watching the graceful flow of dancers gliding across the floor. Caroline and her husband passed very close to where the two sat. The meld of their two bodies looked like one figure moving rhythmically to the western music. Dona was aware of June's eyes on Caroline. She wondered if he were just watching, or watching and wanting. She was disgusted with herself for thinking that. June had been a loving husband since they reunited--she thought she'd ceased doubting him.

Later in the evening Caroline reached across the table and put her hand on June's wrist. She turned his arm slightly to see the dial of his watch. She was laughing and saying something Dona couldn't hear. June reacted to her touch with a look of embarrassment. An innocent exchange, Dona knew, but she felt her chest tighten in an involuntary reaction.

The band was into a rocking rendition of "The Wabash Cannonball" when Ross announced that he was ready to go home.

"I'm afraid my flame flickered early tonight," he said.

Dona and June were both enjoying their evening out, so Dona suggested they stay just awhile longer, until the set was over, at least.

"Why don't you stay and go home with us?" Jackey asked. "We can just sit a little more cozy in the car, can't we, Junior?"

"Sure. There's always room for a couple more, as long as you sit skinny," he replied.

"Not much chance of that," June quipped, giving Dona an ornery glance.

They stayed until the musicians had played their last tune. By that time the band sounded like Bob Wills and the Texas Troubadours to most of the group. J.B. had asked Dona to dance once, out of kindness, she was sure. Dona and June had tried one dance, but he was acting so silly by then that they both agreed the best place for them was on the sidelines.

Out in the parking lot, Dona accepted Junior's invitation to sit in the front seat, so June climbed in beside her. By then the back seat was full, with two couples packed tightly together.

"You can sit on my lap!" June offered when he saw that Caroline had no place to ride.

Giving him a teasing look, she replied, "Just as long as you don't get any ideas, now!" and climbed into the front seat, also. Junior turned the key and took the Chevy out of the lot and on the way home. Dona brooded in silence all the way back to Bedford.

When they arrived in town and the Bowens were delivered to their door, Dona rushed into the house in tears. In a wave of pent-up emotion, she threw herself across the bed and sobbed uncontrollably. June followed her in. He was taken aback by her outburst.

"What in the hell is the matter?" he exploded. She didn't answer.

"You're the one who wanted to stay!" he said gruffly as he sat down on the bed and began to undress. She got up and stomped out into the living room.

He felt the emptiness of his bed and remembered the emptiness of his life on the long nights when he had wished he had her back. He got up and moved unclad into the next room. Her soft sobs broke the night stillness. The dim light entering the room from the street lamp revealed Dona curled on the sofa, with one throw pillow covering her head and the other clutched tightly in her arms.

"Is this about Caroline?" he asked as he sat down beside her feet, which were still encased in shoes and stockings.

"What do you think?" she quietly murmured. She lacked the strength to argue about it, even.

"I'm sorry if that bothered you, but it's not like you to act this way," he said gently, hoping he would hit upon the right thing to say.

"It made me sick the way she was flirting with you. And I could see that you were just eating it up!" she charged.

"Did it ever occur to you that maybe she's jealous of you and that's the reason she acts like she does?" he asked.

"Jealous of me? Why would she be jealous of me?" Dona asked, puzzled.

"Well, she's the one who's treated like an outsider here. She has no family close, and Junior said she had a hard time making friends here. According to him, she has some really low times. Didn't you know that?" June said in explanation. "People treat her differently because she talks the way she does and also because she has epilepsy. You knew that, didn't you?"

Dona had heard that and guessed maybe it did make people uneasy around her. Caroline had never had a seizure that Dona knew of and so she hadn't thought much about her illness.

"According to Junior, she's not even supposed to drive a car," June said, "although I think she does sometimes anyhow."

Dona thought this over. It was hard to imagine what it would be like to deal with that kind of an illness without the support of your family close by. She had to concede that she felt sorry for Caroline in some ways. She'd heard that Caroline couldn't have other children. That must be hard for both her and her husband. Caroline had the education that Dona envied; she'd been a college girl when she met Junior, but the experience failed to benefit her in her present situation.

Although she never came to consider Caroline a good friend, Dona did come to have a more compassionate perception of the woman she once resented in such a personal way. As is often the case, familiarity bred not contempt, but understanding. She also came to realize later that Junior Black was more than just the favored son of one of the town's prominent families.

SIXTEEN

Across the country, the nation's economy boomed with a housing surge as thousands of men reentered the workforce, seeking the American dream of owning their own "little nest somewhere in the West." Quick, low-cost homes were built in sub-divisions for the growing middle class. In colleges and universities, GIs took advantage of the GI Bill to secure an education. Those who had lived through the Depression tried to forget it, and the rest found it hard to believe the stories of those who had.

Times were not so good in rural areas. Small farmers found it difficult to compete with big landowners who used efficient, new machinery. Many opted to sell out to larger concerns rather than take on the debt that new, expensive equipment required. Sam was nearing retirement age so his options weren't abundant. His solution to the situation was to seek work elsewhere, and his first choice of region was Minnesota, where the fishing was good and the weather tolerable.

Carrie had married Frank Moffitt, her high school sweetheart. She dropped out of school in her junior year to begin life as a farmwife in a nearby community. Frank had completed a tour of duty in the navy, and the little girls thought him quite a handsome fellow in his white uniform and cute sailor hat.

After Carrie left home, the Schmits were free to pick up and go wherever Sam's job search would take them. He shortly found work as a flagman for a federal highway project in Minnesota, so he and Retha spent the summer in Granite Falls, with her cooking at the restaurant of the motel that was their temporary living quarters, and Sam alternately flagging and fishing. It was a good life for both of them.

Back in Bedford, the girls continued in school, all three now in the same intermediate room. Lily Thomson, from Madison, was their teacher. She was a stern, serious schoolmistress, but the girls found her to be fair and liked her in spite of her unyielding disposition.

Several families by the name of Wilson lived in the community--some related, some not. One such family lived in the south part of the town, two blocks from the Bowens. There were several children in the family. Mr. Wilson had a good job with the county road crew, but Mrs. Wilson had been ill for a time, so conditions in the home were less than the best. Dona had had no occasion to visit with the family, so she knew nothing about them. Her girls stayed on their own block, so the two families had not become acquainted.

There were no screens on the large windows of the school. The girls' room was on the east side, in a straight line south of the ball diamond out back. Inside the building, one had to negotiate halls before emerging to the outside. The favorite game at recess was kickball, and the most sought after positions of the game were on the kicking team that was up first.

It happened one day that several of the girls' friends decided to boost Sharon out of the window, so she could run out and claim first ups for them. When their teacher led the group out in an orderly fashion, those at the end of the line scurried to the open window and sent Sharon on her mission to stake their claim on the ball field. She did and it worked. The problem was, Carl Wilson tattled to the teacher about the escapade, and Mrs. Thomson turned her fury toward Sharon and her cohorts. In the twinkling of an eye, she relieved the group of recess privileges for an entire month and sent them to see the principal.

An angry assortment of children faced Carl at the school door at the end of the day. He lost no time assessing the situation and took off running down toward the railroad tracks. The other children went in pursuit of the scoundrel and chased him all the way home, shouting and throwing insults. Carl's mother probably wondered what had gotten her child home from school so quickly, but he never told her.

When word of her children's naughtiness reached Dona, she sat them down and lectured them on appropriate behavior. Then she called on Mrs. Thomson at the school, thanked her for her guidance, and offered her support at home. The girls heeded the lesson in proper conduct and tolerance and truly regretted their hasty decision to retaliate. After considering the adventure from their schoolmate's point of view, they had to concede that they were definitely in the wrong, and they faced the boy with a tardy apology. Before long, the girls had become good friends with the Wilson children and began playing over at their house.

Eventually each of the girls was declared old enough to visit around the town on her own. Going downtown was all right, too, as long as they stayed away from traffic and didn't loiter inside the stores, making nuisances of themselves. Sometimes they would be sent on an errand for their mother.

In the small town everyone knew everyone else, so there was never concern about their well-being when they were left to their own pursuits. There were always people standing on the corners talking or perhaps whiling away the time on a bench outside one of the businesses. Men often congregated at the big door of Bill Lynch's garage. There were usually a couple of guys working there, plus a few waiting--in addition to some others who were just there to catch up on the news of the day.

One afternoon after school, Coralea and Sharon walked home the long way around--that is, through the downtown area. It was more interesting than the path beside the highway toward their home. June was at the garage chatting with a group of fellows. They saw him and hit upon an opportunity--they were very near Jane Herring's enticing candy counter.

"Can we have a nickel, Daddy?" Sharon asked when he noticed them.

"Sorry. Not today, girls," he said quickly. He flushed when he saw the look of disappointment on their faces. He was usually a soft touch.

Jimmie stood close by. He reached into his pocket and brought out two dimes.

"Here, girls, the treat's on me today," he said as he dropped the coins into their hands.

They thanked him and happily hurried down the street to Herring's store.

That night when Dona tucked the girls into bed she told them they must never ask their daddy for money like that again. She tried to make them understand that he didn't always have money with him and that it embarrassed him not to be able to give them any. They understood, but it made them sad because they hadn't meant to hurt their father's feelings.

The issue of money came up occasionally in the Bowen household. The income from June's trucking wasn't enough for a comfortable living for the family, even with the extra cash he made working as a farm hand. The girls were told that if they wanted extras, like fireworks for the 4th of July, they would have to earn the money themselves.

One endeavor they were successful with was picking and stemming gooseberries. During the berry season, early June, they went out to their grandparents' farm and picked from the wild bushes scattered in the timber. Dona helped and the children peddled the berries to people in town at fifteen cents a pint or a quarter for a quart, twice that if they were stemmed. When the fireworks stands opened for business, they had capital to purchase enough rockets, fountains, sparklers and firecrackers to cover the top of the card table. Then they made plans for the spectacular celebration they would have when the big day arrived.

Another money-raising scheme they tried was selling seeds for spring gardens. Their mother's encouragement kept the girls focused on their sales strategies. The girls could depend upon a few customers to buy whatever they were selling. The elderly people of the town were especially generous in their support. The girls could count on making a sale at the Wisdom place south of town. They loved to go there because the house appeared regal to them. Perched on a high hill behind a picket fence, the stately house overlooked the town, the river, and a vast area of bottomland that stretched away to the south. The front door that opened to them had an elegant entry hall, with an open stairway on one side and a fancy parlor on the other. Elmer Wisdom and his wife were both friendly and eagerly listened to the girls' simple sales pitch before deciding they needed whatever wares were offered that day.

During the period since her remarriage, Dona had gradually taken up smoking. Most of those in her bridge group smoked, and by now June was nearly a chain smoker. With Dona, it wasn't a steady habit--she often lit a cigarette to help her relax at the end of the day. Sometimes in the evening she sat visiting with June over coffee and cigarettes.

He rolled his own now, in an attempt to cut down on the cost. He bought little bags of tobacco and packages of thin cigarette papers. He held the ends of a little paper carefully between his left thumb and middle finger, pressing with his forefinger to form a trough. With his right hand he slowly shook out a small amount of tobacco into the paper, then delicately ran his tongue along the upper side of the tube. He gently turned the wet edge over the opposite side, carefully smoothing the long, white cylinder into nearly perfect roundness. He was so adept at this trick that the resulting cigarettes were as uniform as those in a pack of Pall Mall's.

By the spring of 1947 June was ready to try a new endeavor. He had been doing farm work for others and decided he might as well be working for himself. So, when Chase Richey announced he was retiring and moving into town, June approached him to make a deal. He was sure Dona would agree to it because the Richeys' 120 acres lay right alongside the Schmit farm. After some negotiating, the two men decided that a fair arrangement would be to exchange the property in town for two years' rent on the farm, plus outright ownership of the farm equipment and livestock on the place.

Dona's first reaction to the scheme was one of disappointment, as she loved the little house she had come to feel was their very own. And she enjoyed living in town. But, she could see that June was restless, and they certainly had a hard time making ends meet the way they were going. She would be close to Sam and Retha, near enough that the girls could walk over the hill to visit their grandparents.

The house was older, but a little larger, than the one they left in Bedford. Dona supposed it would be called a one-and-a-half-story house, with a large bedroom in the upper area. The walls angled up toward the ceiling, following the shape of the roof, and gave the room a feeling of security and seclusion. June placed a large chest at the edge of the stairwell to prevent sleepwalkers from taking a tumble. The strong smell of old wallpaper hung over the place.

Downstairs, Dona and June's bedroom, the kitchen, and the living room were the only other rooms in the house, but there was a porch at the front and another screened-in area at the back. A smokehouse was right outside the back door, with the necessary out-house to the side of that.

A small chicken house sat nearby on the east of the house, and a large, old barn and several corncribs were on the north. The open-front machine shed west of the lane held the farming implements left with the place. It was obvious that Chase hadn't made any recent investments in machinery--an old tractor, a plow, a disc, some corn-planting equipment, a manure spreader--enough, June hoped, to get him started, at least. The buildings were arranged on a gentle southward slope that ended on the front at H Highway.

The girls had anticipated the move because they'd be nearer to their grandparents, and they would have all those animals to enjoy. They especially liked the sheep. Sam had never kept sheep, so this was their first experience holding the cuddly little lambs and watching them as they sprinted around the pasture, sometimes jumping straight up and spinning in the air. June cautioned them against chasing the sheep because the animals' delicate leg bones might snap if they panicked and fell. He knew they needed to keep coyotes away from the farm, so he brought home a black and white collie-mix dog.

There were a few milk cows with calves and two workhorses. The children were not to ride the horses, though they seemed gentle. On one day, when their parents were busy elsewhere, the girls couldn't resist the temptation to fulfill their horse-riding ambitions. They had been cowboys astride the big tractor tires many times--it would be really grand to be on a horse that actually moved! Barbara didn't care much about the horse, but she would help the other two.

The animals were huge draft horses. The girls weren't big enough to put a halter over the head of one, so it would have to be a reinless, bareback stunt. Sharon would have the honor of being first--perhaps because she was always eager to be first at something, more likely because the other two had given some consideration to how far they might fall if they were to slide off. Sharon climbed to the top of the wooden gate and Barbara and Coralea used bits of hay to coax the horse near enough so she could climb onto its broad back. She bravely hung onto the mane. Luckily the horse wasn't in the mood to run or Sharon would have gone flying. The other two girls took turns holding hay in front of the horse's nose to inspire it to move forward.

Sharon and the horse had made a trip across the barn lot before June spotted what they were doing and came on the run to rescue her. All three girls benefited from some harsh words from their father, but Barbara and Coralea were also scolded for putting their little sister in harm's way. Sharon was glad they did. She was the only one who got to ride the horse on that day, or on any day after that.

Following the move to the Richey place, June sold his truck and bought a car. They would need to take the children to school now, at least when the weather was bad. Star of the West School, which the girls would attend, was a mile northeast. The fence separating the Richey place from the Schmit farm also marked the boundary of the Bedford School District, so now the girls would go to a one-room country school.

When Dona took her daughters to enroll and to meet their teacher, she was surprised at the size of some of the children in the room. Grades one through eight were taught in the school, and there appeared to be around twenty-five students. The girls were understandably hesitant to begin in the new school.

Right away there were problems of adjustment. They had to take their lunch here, instead of walking home for dinner as they had in town. The majority of the students, plus the teacher, were Catholic and so said a prayer and made the sign of the cross at lunchtime. This was foreign to the girls, who told their mother they felt like outsiders.

There were many disruptions in the school day because of the behavior of some of the older students, especially one boy, who was fifteen years old. Bigger than the teacher, he was allowed to get away with bullying the smaller children. Dona advised the girls to stand up for themselves, which they did and promptly managed to get into several fights. Coralea and Sharon were challenged repeatedly, but Barbara managed to stay above the fray. She had figured out there were other ways to win a war besides fighting. Dona thought that surely things would improve as the children became better acquainted.

While waiting for planting time, June decided to make some improvements on the place. His first plan was to remove a hedgerow at the front of the property. The former owner had begun the task but hadn't gotten very far, so

June set to work on the project. He soon learned that the undertaking was an ambitious one. He spent days attacking the gnarled old trees with saw and ax. After getting the brush cut and cleared away, no small task, he tackled the job of removing the stumps. The roots were imbedded into the soil so deeply they couldn't be pulled out with the tractor. His ax bounced, rather than sliced, as he took mighty swings at the orange tentacles.

Dona could see him from the house. He seemed to be waging war with the obstinate wood, and he was definitely losing. He would spend days fighting the tangled growth before pulling out a single stump. It appeared to be a personal thing, him against the hedgerow. He seemed to hate the thing. She wished he would just let it go and put the new fence around it!

Things did improve for the girls at Star of the West. They soon gained the respect of their schoolmates and were welcomed in games of Andy-Andy-over and kick-the-can during recess. The girls were good at ciphering matches and spelling bees, especially Barbara, so they gained a measure of acceptance and were quickly chosen on teams for competitions.

For their part, the girls began to see their classmates as playmates, not enemies--particularly the ones they walked home with. If the roads were dry, they walked the short way home from school with three of their schoolmates, and if the day was nice they often took the long way around on the blacktop in the company of five others. Many confidences were shared on those trips home at the end of the day.

A genuine appreciation for the efforts of the teacher resulted from observing her at work each day. The young woman lived with the family closest to the school, a quarter-mile across a pasture, and she walked to school every day. She was also the janitor of the school. She started the fire in the morning and cleaned the floor in the evening. She usually doled out such jobs as carrying in water and coal and cleaning the erasers, but still she was there before anyone else got there in the morning and remained long after everyone else had gone home. It was obvious that she tried to handle the big kids, even though they were actually taller, and mightier, than she.

Besides guiding eight learning levels in their daily lessons, the instructor also had to plan and execute programs for the holidays and community meetings, which involved the parents. Anyone connected with the school could see the teacher had a daunting task before her, and the girls soon accepted the hard-working woman as friend rather than foe.

Twice each year a community meeting was held at the school. A performance of some kind was offered by the students, with additional entertainment provided by members of the community. The girls told their teacher that their mother could sing, so she was asked to perform. Dona picked "Buttons and Bows" to sing for the group. The girls were proud to share their mother as an entertainer, and she enjoyed the experience also, as she hadn't sung for a group since she was in high school in Summerville.

Dona missed her friends in Bedford. On most days she saw no one but her own family. She still longed for the companionship of the girls in Kansas City with whom she had roomed and worked. She corresponded with them occasionally but never got to the city for a visit. She hadn't even seen Miriam and her family recently. The threat of infantile paralysis kept many away from the city. Miriam's children were no longer allowed to use the public pools for fear of the disease, which more likely threatened the young but was known to strike adults as well. The dreaded affliction had begun to dampen some of the post-war exuberance experienced by many.

The Bowen family sometimes traveled to Summerville, where June's brother and his wife lived. Norman now dealt in new and used cars and Faye worked in the local bank. They had no children to share their tidy home, but the girls were entertained by a huge orange cat that prowled on massive paws throughout the comfortable house.

The trip up to Summerville was a welcome outing to the girls. Besides the Bowens, they could expect to see Earlene and Emmett and their daughter, Lenore. Lenore was rather spindly. She had always been a delicate child, so her parents constantly encouraged her to eat more to fortify herself. When the girls visited, their cousin took them to the drugstore a couple of doors up the block from the filling station where the family lived. The four girls sat in a row on the high stools of the soda fountain. They watched as the clerk mixed their treats in large metal containers, bigger than any of their glasses at home, then clamped them onto a noisy machine that whipped the ice cream into a delicious chocolate froth. He poured half the thick, creamy liquid into fancy serving glasses as they eagerly watched, mouths watering, knowing there was a second helping awaiting them. They thought Lenore must be the most spoiled child in the world to get to do this every single day!

Another part of the trip that struck the children's fancy was going through the small town of Glenwood, which was on the Platte River bottom about halfway between Bedford and Summerville. On one of their trips, they had seen a huge ball of string, nearly as high as the man standing beside it. The ball was in the open door of a garage just off the main street of town. They heard later that it was claimed to be the biggest ball of string in the world, so on ensuing trips through the town they would look to see if they could again catch a glimpse of the wonderful marvel. Their grandmother saved string but they couldn't imagine anyone ever collecting that much!

A short walk across the pasture to the west brought the girls to the door of their grandparents' house. Sam and Retha were often gone in the summer, on their seasonal term of employment. But for the rest of the year all of the Bowens appreciated the nearness of the Schmits. Retha came over to help Dona with the canning. June helped with the big garden the Schmits had put in behind the chicken coop. He remembered the orderly, abundant gardens he had seen in Europe and knew they would be glad to have their own vegetables for the table next winter. Sam came over in late fall to help June shuck the year's corn crop. It was all done by hand, using a hook attached around the wrist on a leather strap. Horses were used to pull the high-sided wagon down the dry rows of corn. The animals were accustomed to this chore and didn't need anyone to drive them, just an occasional cluck to start them out and a "Whoa!" to stop them.

Except for the pitcher pump in the kitchen, the Richey place had no plumbing--but there was electricity, thanks to the Rural Electrification Association. The girls often spent the long winter evenings up in their cozy bedroom. Dona and June would miss them for hours at a time. Barbara liked to read and was usually occupied with that pursuit, while Coralea and Sharon played on their side of the room with their paper dolls. Whenever they got a new book of the two-dimensional models, the two girls spent hours cutting out dolls and paper outfits. After they finished meticulously cutting out the cardboard shapes of the dolls and the thinner accessories, they folded back the tabs and tried each fashion on the proper figure.

The girls endowed their paper characters with every imaginable talent. There was no feat they could not perform, no riches they did not possess. If the star of the moment were to walk into a make-believe room, its mistress would tilt the cardboard cut out back on its stand and advance it across the floor in inch-long steps. If riding in a car, the subject would zoom across the floor to the accompaniment of a mouth motor, and if it were traveling to a far-off destination, it would fly through the air, its paper clothes flapping from paper holds on cardboard shoulders.

One evening when they were thusly occupied upstairs, the girls heard the phone ring in the kitchen below. Shortly they heard a soft moan from their mother, followed by a pitiful wail that sounded like, "Oh, no!"

"What's the matter, Mama?" Barbara asked when she reached the bottom step.

Dona didn't answer--she just stood there, crying. June came in from the front room when he heard the girls running down the stairs.

"What is it, Dona?" he asked with concern.

"Tad's been killed," she said weakly. "He was hit by a car! What have we done to deserve this?" Barbara was stunned by the terrible news and by the statement her mother had hastily uttered in her grief. Was there some way they might have been responsible for the tragedy? For a long time afterwards she was puzzled by this possibility.

It was difficult for the girls to grasp the idea that their little cousin was gone. Except for animals, they'd had no exposure to the finality of death. The sadness in the house touched them with a depth of feeling they hadn't before known. The two boys in the Wright family had been close playmates of the girls, even though they had seldom seen them in the last couple of years.

The Bowens' car wasn't dependable for a long trip, so Dona called Hank and asked if she, June and Coralea could ride down with him and Beulah to Kansas City for the funeral. Miriam had called to ask if Coralea could come to help Tommy cope with the loss of his brother. Dona was glad of any help she could provide for her sister's family. She knew that the loss of a child had to be the hardest circumstance a parent could ever face.

Dona didn't find the situation too difficult for Coralea. She was there, but her presence wasn't much comfort to the grieving older brother nor to his three-year-old sister, who went from room to room asking, "Where's Tad-e? Where's Tad-e?"

Dona believed her child had accepted the fact of death. She'd seen her cousin lying peacefully in the coffin and had asked no questions about the experience. Several months later, when the family was shopping in Madison, they were in the Woolworth's Dime Store when Coralea tugged at her mother's sleeve.

"Look! It's Tad!" she announced, pointing at the back of a boy disappearing around the counter.

"No, Coralea. Tad is gone," Dona replied, speaking kindly but firmly to her. The girl would not be satisfied unless her mother would follow around the counter and look. She was dismayed when Dona steadfastly refused and only repeated what she had said before. For a while Coralea still believed that she had really seen her deceased cousin. Dona could see that wishful thinking had outweighed her daughter's grasp of reality.

Regardless of the current state of family finances, Dona convinced her children that they were in the midst of good times. Compared to her childhood during the bleak Depression days, the times might have been said to be "fat."

Dona sent the girls to school each day with their lunches packed in oval, tin pails, with lids to keep everything fresh. Some of the students had only brown paper bags that were assaulted by the weather on the slow trek to school. The Bowen girls often brought grape juice to school in pint jars. On one day an older boy persuaded Barbara to trade with him because he remembered the grape wine he'd had at a sledding party at the Bowens'.

A fifty-year record snow had fallen, nearly covering the fence posts and turning the countryside into a school kid's dream. Dona and June invited a few families over for an evening of outdoor fun for the youngsters. Hot chocolate and marshmallows were offered to the children when they took a break from sledding and sliding, with June's homemade wine being provided for the adults. Some of the older boys of the group managed to spirit away a jug of the wine and thoroughly enjoyed the added warmth they felt as they cavorted in the chilly moonlit air. After that introduction, the boys regarded all purple drinks as the same special elixir, so they coveted the girls' lunches. Dona thought she was being very careful in selecting the unfermented bottles of grape juice, but sometimes she wasn't really sure.

So Barbara traded, lunch for lunch. In later years Barbara remembered the coarse, dry sandwiches her classmate brought to school. At the time she had felt sorry that he had thick-sliced homemade bread, spread only with jelly and peanut butter. Years later she realized what a treat the bread was, its tantalizing aroma and yeasty flavor unattainable by store-bought bread.

Except for Norman, who still lived in Summerville, June saw very little of his family. His mother had moved to Fort Morgan, Colorado, to be near Patsy and her husband. Marly now lived in Omaha and had been down to Bedford only once in the three years since June's return from the service. Marly's own family consisted of a stepson and a son and daughter of her own with her second husband. The girl, her youngest child, had recently come down with scarlet fever, and it was thought that keeping her quiet and relaxed would aid in her recovery. Marly asked if their older son could spend a couple of weeks with the Bowens. He'd never lived on a farm and would probably enjoy getting out of the city and away from the constraints of a sick house.

Becoming acquainted with a twelve-year-old boy cousin was an education for the girls. It was also a challenge for Dona and June to keep peace in the family while he was with them. Rick delighted in teasing the girls, who took many of his pranks too seriously and complained to their mother about his behavior. Dona wanted to help out her sister-in-law if she could, and besides, she felt compassion for the boy's stepson position in his family.

The first aggravation that the girls endured at the hands of their cousin occurred when Dona sent them to pick mulberries for a pie. They had spent an hour diligently plucking ripe berries from a tree out in the pasture. Rick told Barbara he would help her get more berries from the top of the tree if she would pass her pail up to him. He climbed onto a low branch and she trustingly gave him her ample pickings, whereupon he sat smugly on his perch and proceeded to eat every berry. She yelled at him and cried, to no avail. He came down, grinning broadly, when the berries were gone.

After she had listened to the girls' tale of woe, Dona decided the best thing to do was to laugh, which infuriated her girls but made her an ally of her exiled visitor.

Sharon had often wondered what it would be like to smoke cigarettes. She thought the habit was attractive and, from observing her parents, thought the experience must be pleasurable, also.

"Hey, why don't we give it a try?" Rick suggested, as he showed her the cigar he had picked up from the end table. June didn't care for cigars but had been given one by a friend, on the occasion of his baby's birth.

"Mama will get mad," Sharon warned, knowing Dona's attitude concerning her children and smoking.

"She doesn't need to know," he assured her. "We can hide somewhere, like in the outhouse. They'd never look for us in there." Sharon wasn't sure of that, but she was immensely curious, so she went with her cousin into the little toilet.

"You first," she told him.

After a few tries he managed to get the cigar lit. He took a couple of puffs, then handed the cigar over to her. She sucked on it briefly, then sputtered a bit. The two took turns, passing it back and forth. Sharon coughed, hating the foul taste in her mouth, but didn't want to admit she was disappointed.

Dona walked by and heard the commotion in the outhouse. When the smell of cigar registered in her senses, she guessed what was happening.

"Come right out of there!" she demanded as she banged loudly on the wooden door.

Rick tossed the cigar down the hole, but the lingering smoke was a dead give-away to their activities. Dona gave them a good talking to and sent them to their beds to think it over. *I had no idea when I said okay to that kid staying here that my girls would soon be smoking old Stogies out behind the barn*, Dona thought.

"I think maybe we should let them smoke a little more," June proposed when he heard of the experimentation of the afternoon. He lit a cigarette for each of them and told them to go at it. He was entirely right in thinking that a little more intensive puffing might teach them a lesson. Soon they were both feeling sick and wishing they'd never seen a cigar or cigarette. Dona suspected that the experience would deter Sharon from smoking for the rest of her life.

Usually Dona took the girls to school in the car. By afternoon the day would warm up so they could walk home. Besides, quite often June had the car off somewhere else by the end of the day. Lately, he was spending more time in town and less time farming.

Dona noticed that her middle child had become quiet and withdrawn. She was concerned when Coralea was sick one day and couldn't go to school. She had no fever but complained of a stomachache, so she was kept home. Dona observed no signs of physical illness the rest of the day, so she told Coralea that she'd better go back to school tomorrow.

When Dona and the girls arrived at the schoolhouse the next morning, Coralea began to cry, moaning and clutching her stomach, so her mother decided she could stay home another day.

"Why don't you want to go to school?" Dona asked Coralea after they returned to the house. "You've always liked to go. Is something bothering you about school?"

"No, school's okay," Coralea replied.

"Is someone picking on you at school?" Dona continued quizzing her.

Coralea sat quietly brooding, then shook her head.

"What is it, then?" Dona asked in exasperation.

The girl didn't answer but lay on the couch curled up in a ball, refusing to communicate any further.

"You *will* go to school this morning," June told Coralea the next day. So she got in the car with the other girls. The closer they got to the school, the quieter she became. When the other two got out, Coralea threw herself on the floor of the car and refused to go.

"What am I going to do with you?" Dona demanded, as she gave Coralea a look of total dismay. "If you won't tell me what's wrong, how can I help?"

"I think I'd better go to school and talk with Mrs. Arms," Dona said to June later. "Maybe she has an idea of what's bothering Coralea."

That afternoon Dona showed up at the school and had her girls wait while she talked with their teacher. Mrs. Arms, the current instructor, was a motherly little woman whom Dona had met on several occasions. She tried to be helpful but was unable to think of a reason for Coralea's negative feelings about attending school.

Coralea knew what was bothering her. She just didn't want to talk about it or perhaps didn't know how to tell about her predicament. The older boy, the one who was known as a bully, had grabbed her a couple of times and tried to tickle her. He had caught her in the area at the back of the classroom where the water bucket was kept. The small space was opposite the entry and coatroom and was used as the library for the school, with a high case of books separating the area from the remainder of the classroom. His tickling of her crotch made her uncomfortable. She hated for him to touch her but was too embarrassed to do anything except avoid him as much as she could. She stopped going to the back of the room for drinks.

Soon after that, when she was coming back from the outhouse, he met her on the steps of the building and said, as she quickly skirted her way past him, "I'm going to f--- you!" She didn't have any idea what he meant. She'd never heard the word, and if she had, wouldn't have known what he intended to do to her. She just knew that he meant to hurt her, so she was petrified. Mrs. Arms kept a watchful eye on him all the time, but she wouldn't be with them on the way home.

The next day Coralea was sick--and the next day, and the day after that.

On Monday morning, Dona offered to go into the school with Coralea if that would make her feel better. She'd had her talk with Mrs. Arms and was convinced that there was nothing going on at school to harm her child. Coralea decided that she could do it on her own. She was still worried about the big boy, but after that he left her alone. Possibly he suspected that someone else had found out about his sneaky activities.

Several years later Coralea learned the meaning of the word that had both scared and puzzled her. She wondered then how many other little girls he had threatened, probably all those he felt he could safely intimidate.

"Mrs. Arms wants me to play for the next community meeting," Barbara announced as she and her sisters walked in the door one evening.

"Of course you can do that," Dona assured her. "What does she want you to play?"

"She doesn't care," answered Barbara. "She just said I should choose whatever I'd be comfortable with."

Dona thought a minute about her daughter's options. The pieces in the red book Mrs. McMurtry used for lessons were mostly waltzes, sonatas, or Stephen Foster melodies.

"Why don't you play some of your sheet music?" Dona suggested.

"Lili Marlene?" Barbara asked.

"That, or one of the others," Dona answered. She had given each of the girls a song printed on a folder the last Christmas she was in the city. She had hoped that some day each girl would be able to play her own piece. Barbara still took piano lessons from Miss Nora each Saturday morning, but the other girls hadn't yet shown an interest in learning to play. Barbara easily mastered her song and the other two as well.

"That's my favorite," Barbara stated. Dona was glad she picked her own tune because it reminded her of a movie she had once seen that starred Marlene Dietrich.

While each of the girls had friends whom she enjoyed in the rural school, close attachments were not formed during this time, nor did Dona and June strike up an easy acquaintance with any other farm family of the Star of the West area. Others were solidly entrenched in the community, many having been born and reared on the very land they now occupied.

Dona found herself thinking more and more about her years in the city. She still missed the four girls who had become her bosom buddies. While the Bowens lived at the Richey place, Irma and her husband came to see them one time, to show off their two small children. The boy and girl both had Irma's bright, bouncy curls. Dona appreciated the effort her friend had made to visit but also sensed an uncomfortable strain in the interchange. The huge gap in the ages of the children precluded any meaningful camaraderie among them, though the girls sought to entertain the toddlers as much as they could.

Shortly after Dona and June moved to the farm, the bridge club in Bedford broke up. Edith and Bill had gone out West and J.B. and Jackey moved to Maryville, so the group had already lost members before Dona began missing meetings. Many times the car wouldn't run, or June would need it, so Dona had to phone her regrets to the hostess of the day. Eventually the remaining few players stopped setting up meeting dates at all.

Several sheep were lost during the severe winter months of '48-'49. Some of the lambs died as the result of freezing temperatures at the time they were born. June didn't know enough about sheep to foresee when the ewes would drop their lambs and to keep them in the shelter of the barn. It was discouraging for him when he attempted, but failed, to help in their struggle for life. A few more sheep were lost to coyotes, despite the ferocious barking of Tippie, the would-be sheep dog.

June's attempt at farming proved increasingly unsuccessful. His old equipment was constantly breaking down. The tractor was out of commission more often than it was usable, and he had to rely more and more on the horses to do the work that must be done to make the place productive. June had never been in charge of maintaining farm equipment--he had used the machinery of others who had the skills necessary for keeping implements in good working order.

One afternoon June stormed into the house and grabbed his rifle from the back of the closet.

"What are you doing?" Dona asked in bewilderment.

He didn't answer her, just walked purposefully out to the barn lot and shot the white horse in the side.

Dona paled as she witnessed this. She couldn't believe he would do that! He had always been gentle with the animals--more patient, certainly, than she would have been at times. When he saw blood trickle from the side of the startled animal, June dropped the rifle and rushed to grab the head of the beast and stroke his wet muzzle. Dona could see that his action had hurt June worse than it had the horse. It took a few days for the small wound to heal over on the horse, but Dona and June were both disturbed by the swift severity of his reaction to a brief spell of stubbornness in the dumb animal.

To Dona, the harsh weeks of winter seemed to wear on and on. The girls were growing up, with interests of their own, and needing her less and less. As their worlds widened, she felt hers shrinking. She taught them to dance on the hardwood floors of the small living room, remembering the gay times in Kansas City when she'd enjoyed the stimulating nightlife with her carefree friends.

She missed the companionship with June that had fulfilled her when he first returned from the service. He seemed more remote as the days passed. He spent many hours away from home, working for another farmer when he got the chance or just killing time in town. She knew he was worried about finances, as she was. The two years' rent period was up and Mr. Richey wanted more money than they could afford to pay.

Even having Retha close didn't protect Dona from the feelings of isolation and neglect that began to overwhelm her. Although she attempted to put on a happy face for the girls, a deep sadness crept over her that was difficult to hide.

Early in the spring Dona was faced with a devastating situation that threatened to shatter the little confidence she had in her second marriage to June. He was gone from home all day and failed to come home at night and all the next day. She feared the worst--accident, abandonment, suicide, even. His father had become depressed and had made that fateful choice.

The girls had fears similar to their mother's. She didn't know what to tell them to reassure them. How could she, when she so badly needed reassurance herself?

When June drove up the lane and managed to face her, the story he told her was one he thought she would accept--that he had been arrested for drunk driving and had to spend the night in jail. She knew she had to believe him if there were to be anything left between them. And so she did.

SEVENTEEN

Pete Adams' place was an unlikely spot for a bright new beginning. The old bachelor had kept the yard and the outside of the place looking neat, but on the inside the house was a mess the likes of which neither Dona nor June had ever before seen or could imagine. It was obvious that for the length of time Pete lived on the place, he had never done any interior maintenance nor thrown anything away. Dona guessed that the wallpaper must be at least twenty years old--dark, discolored, and peeling in places. Water stains sagged down the wall beneath the flue covers. Window shades were shredded or missing. The linoleum in the large kitchen was scuffed, with holes worn clear through in a much-treaded path from door to sink to table.

Worse, even, than the general run-down condition of the structure was the trash that the hoarder had accumulated over the years. The floor of the parlor was completely covered with old newspapers, magazines, and discarded catalogues. The mountain of paper refuse had been thrown into a stack that nearly reached the ceiling in the center of the room. Dona was relieved that there was no garbage among the sprawling mess. A major mouse problem would have put the task completely beyond her.

No electricity existed in the house, or running water, which was strange since there was a claw foot tub in the room obviously designed to be a bathroom. The tub had a drain, but no water was piped in. Dona wondered whether the long, narrow space had once contained a dry sink and perhaps a commode of some sort.

The kitchen had built-in cabinets and a sink with a pitcher pump. Both Dona and June could see possibilities in the place and hoped they could restore it to a semblance of its former respectability. Though a horrible housekeeper, Pete Adams was a generous man. Rent for the place would be low, and he would supply all the materials the Bowens needed to bring the long-neglected dwelling back to a livable condition.

It took Dona and June a month to clean the trash from the place and another to strip away the old wallpaper in the main part of the house. They'd leave the small bedrooms until later, after they had moved in. The girls helped scrape the walls and carried out buckets full of musty gobs of wallpaper to be burned in a big pile.

After a couple of months of intensive work on the house, June had to begin preparing the fields for planting, so Dona and the girls were left with a good part of the restoration work. Dona painted the woodwork herself and hired Verna Holliday, Chance's wife, to help her with the papering. Verna was the area's professional paperhanger and so that phase of the project proceeded smoothly. By the time the family moved, in April, the house looked, and smelled, like a new place.

The barn stood a short distance to the west of the house. Pete hadn't been actively engaged in farming for quite a few years, but the fences on the place appeared to be hog-tight, so June decided he would switch from sheep to pigs. Those animals would surely be hardier and less labor-intensive. He sold the two horses and all the sheep except one, the pet, Corabelle, a twin the girls had raised on a bottle and couldn't bear to give up, knowing that "sold" also meant butchered.

June drove the remaining livestock down H Highway the half-mile to their new home. The lane they reached was notched into a bank alongside the blacktop road and ran a hundred yards south to the house. An orchard of pear and apple trees paralleled the lane and stopped short at the yard. A wire fence encircled the yard, with a row of lilac bushes near the back of the area and a cluster of roses beside the front porch.

Barbara's room would be in the parlor, a single section of the house that stretched north. This large room had porches front and back. There was no heat in the room, so it would be usable only part of the year. The lone heat source for the structure was an oil-burner that sat in the living room. The piano would go in Barbara's room, where she could practice without disturbing the rest of the family. She was developing into a young lady and would appreciate some privacy.

For a small weekly allowance the girls were now expected to help with the chores. Barbara would help her mother in the house, and the younger two would carry slop to the pigs and milk the two fresh cows each evening. After a few lessons in technique, Coralea and Sharon mastered the art of milking, but they were constantly challenged with getting the cows to hold still for them. June expected them to take a bucket and a stool and to milk the cows wherever they happened to be--in the pasture or in the barn lot. Cowkickers for the back legs would have helped, but the girls weren't aggressive enough to shackle the substantial Jersey milkers, so they ended up milking a little, then getting up and following the cow until she decided to stop again, yelling, "Whoa, bossy!" all the while. Needless to say, a lot of milk failed to make it to the house.

The lamb, Corabelle, had gotten quite large by the time of the move. She was allowed in the yard and was beginning to be something of a nuisance. Corabelle had a habit of crowding up against a person and nudging with her nose. The animal was the lone one of her kind now, so her human keepers were the only companions she had. The mistake that finally determined her fate happened when Dona and June had asked the Schmits and their friends, the Hollidays, over for a fish fry and a few beers. Somehow the frisky lamb believed the back porch was her domain and she butted Retha off the side. That was the end of the lamb's pampered position in the family. The next day June announced that he would sell the animal, regardless of the girls' sentiments. He brought home a new softball bat and glove to assuage their grievances and to help them accept the decision.

Chance, Sam's hunting buddy, had given up farming since his accident a couple of years earlier. Very late one night he was on his tractor, on the way home from his tavern. It was freezing cold and slick, causing the machine to overturn and pin him underneath for the remainder of the night. By the time he was found the next morning, the hand caught under the weight of the tractor had to be amputated. Some claimed it was a good thing he had a lot of alcohol in him or he would have frozen to death. Dona doubted that his inebriated condition had any positive influence on the mishap.

Again in the Bedford school district, the girls were glad to be back with their old friends. Also, they enjoyed playing in the big gymnasium during noon hour. The exhilarating play was unsupervised and gave the students a chance to get to know others not in their class. Barbara and Coralea were both in the intermediate room, which included fifth through eighth grades, while Sharon was in the primary group.

It became necessary, once again, for Dona to intervene at school on behalf of her children. The family dog, Tippie, followed the girls to school one May morning. The dog had suffered an injury to his head--they assumed he had been hit by a car. A large gash in the dog's skull had begun to heal over, but a drool oozed from his muzzle. He showed no other signs of injury or illness, so they let him continue with his country dog's privilege of freedom to roam.

"What is the matter with your dog?" Miss Parks asked. She stood at the entrance to the school as the children responded to the morning bell.

"We don't know for sure," Coralea answered, unconcerned.

"He's foaming at the mouth!" the teacher asserted. "We can't have him here at school!"

"I'm sorry he followed us," Barbara began. "He doesn't usually . . ."

"You'll have to take him home!" she stated firmly. "He may be a mad dog. We can't have him at school."

She was definite in her directions, so Barbara left school and walked all the way back home again, a distance of nearly two miles. Dona couldn't believe her eyes when she saw Barbara and the dog coming in the gate.

"What's the matter?" Dona asked.

"The teacher says Tippie may be a mad dog," Barbara said in dismay, worried that she was in trouble, as well as her pet.

"She thought you were with a dangerous dog and she made you walk home with him?" Dona asked, voicing her disapproval.

"I didn't know what else to do!" Barbara answered, confusion clouding her face as she reconsidered her options.

"I'm going in right now and give that teacher a good piece of my mind!" Dona stormed. Which she proceeded to do immediately.

After she had talked to those in charge at the school, Dona began to calm down a little. She had to admit that the animal might be perceived as a danger to the students. The incident caused her to gain a reputation as something of a rabble-rouser, but the girls were impressed that she stood up for them so vocally. Henceforth, the dog was kept in the yard until his battered body had healed.

Only one girl from the group at the Culvers' in Kansas City was still unmarried. Jenny Green lived in Independence now and was secretary to a law firm there. She and Dona corresponded by mail occasionally, but Dona hadn't seen her in a few years.

"How about if I ask Jenny Green up for a couple of days?" she asked June, as the two sat on the edge of the porch enjoying the evening air.

"Okay with me," he replied, "But there's not much here to entertain her."

"Jenny's not the kind who needs to be entertained," Dona assured him. "Besides, I want to show off our place!" She was proud of her accomplishments and knew Jenny would be impressed. "I could have some of the girls over for bridge. Jenny loves to play."

Later in the summer Jenny drove up from Kansas City. She couldn't believe how the girls had grown up and told them so several times. The girls enjoyed her almost as much as their mother did. She was interesting to talk to and as fun loving as Dona had described her. Dona appreciated Jenny's unaffected ways, and envied her easy self-assurance. Jenny had adjusted well to her post-war life in the city.

"You have everything you always wanted right here, don't you, Dona?" Jenny asked her friend as the two sat sipping coffee at the kitchen table. Rays of morning sunshine slanted through the window, throwing bright angles of light onto the new linoleum.

"Well, yes, I guess maybe I do," Dona said hesitantly. "I have to admit, though, I do miss some of the fun we had in the city. I guess no one's ever completely satisfied, are they?" She chose not to mention the emptiness that gnawed at her in subtle and fleeting episodes.

"You've got your girls with you and the home you always wanted. I should be so lucky," Jenny cheerfully assured her.

Dona smiled. "Want to go swimming today? We have our own pool, you know."

"Pond, I'll bet!" said Jenny. "I'm game! I can just wear my shorts and a top, can't I?"

"Clothing's optional," Dona allowed, arching her eyebrows at the thought, "but we'd prefer that you did!"

The whole family spent the hot afternoon splashing around in the cool water of the stock pond. The bottom was muddy, with holes where the hooves of the cattle had sunk into the muck. Sometimes a frog plopped into the water near the opposite bank, sending out circles that spread across the surface and met the choppy disturbance surrounding the humans. June had brought an airplane inner tube home from St. Joseph earlier in the summer, and they all took turns floating on it.

Dona spread an old comforter down on the ground in a grassy area. She and her friend sat on it and watched the others play in the water. June attempted to teach the girls to dog paddle. Tippie was in and out of the water doing the real thing and then shaking himself off, spraying water on everything in range. Dona was glad her friend had come. She had missed seeing Jenny. She had been closer to her than to the other girls in the city. They had worked side-by-side for more than two years. *My friend is right,* Dona thought. *I am contented--most of the time, at least.* Sometimes she wondered whether she had the capacity to be truly satisfied.

The younger girls gave up their room so Jenny could have some privacy while she was with them. The second morning when she awoke she told the girls of her startling experience in their bedroom.

"I woke up and saw some light fixtures on the wall. I was eager to see them this morning in daylight because they were so pretty. Then, when I awoke this morning, they weren't there!" she told them.

"We don't have electricity, you know," Dona reminded her friend.

"Well, yes, I remembered it then," Jenny continued. "But I swear they were there last night!"

"You're spooking us. Better not get these girls to thinking there's something strange about this house!" Dona warned when she noticed the girls were caught up in the playful invention. "You know what fantasies kids can concoct." They shared a laugh at that because they both knew Dona was the one with the over-active imagination.

The women enjoyed their game of bridge that afternoon. There was only one table, as most of Dona's bridge group had left the area, but the ones who were present had a good time and bragged profusely on Dona's results with the place. She hated for them to leave—she had enjoyed the day so completely. She was even sadder later on that evening when Jenny packed her things into her car and headed back to the city.

The other two girls were envious of Barbara's having her own room. She had a small bed all to herself, plus an abundance of space in which to keep her private things. Her room was fresh and breezy, and she could practice the piano uninterrupted or read a book in solitude if she wished. Except for an occasional game of jacks, she no longer played with her younger sisters. She was so much better at jacks that there was no real contest in that pursuit. The littler girls were still at the "pick-up" stage of the game, but she was able to go right on through "eggs-in-a-basket" and "around-the-world". Her only challenge was when they went to Carrie's and her aunt played with her. Carrie was pregnant with her first baby now but was still able to do most of her chores as a farmer's wife. She and Frank rarely made it down to Bedford to visit with the Schmits or Bowens. They had begun their married life with a determination to succeed on their own farm and were sparing no effort to make that dream a reality.

Hog prices had been up for a while, so June's plan for marketing pigs did bring the family some needed income. However, he was quite mistaken in his assumption that the animals would take little care. The fences were good, but the pigs were downright clever in searching out weak spots and affecting an escape from the pigpen. June spent a good part of each day rounding up the vagabonds. And when he wasn't around, it was up to the rest of the family to guard the security of the farm. It became commonplace to have at least one pig in the yard.

Tippie was ever vigilant in his watch over the meandering animals, but his animated barking and nipping was likely to send the dumb creatures squealing off in a direction they didn't need to go. If one of the girls saw a pig heading down the lane toward the road, she scurried down through the orchard to head him off before he could reach the blacktop. Each of the family began to wonder whether the enterprise was really worth it.

Thinking how much the girls liked horses, June agreed to let a friend from town pasture his riding horse at their place for the summer.

"There's a surprise for you out in the lot," June announced to the girls one afternoon. It didn't take them long to tear out the door and run past the barn to take a look.

"I hope we're not sorry about this," Dona said when she saw the size of the horse. She could still picture tiny Sharon up on the back of the huge draft horse out on the Richey place.

"This one's used to being ridden. John says we can ride him as much as we like. He's supposed to be very gentle," June assured her. "Who wants to be first?" he asked as he turned his attention to the children.

Barbara didn't. Coralea hesitated. So June picked up Sharon and put her on the back of the big horse. Dona thought she looked awfully small up there. June led the horse around for a while, making sure he was comfortable with his rider, then he handed the reins up to Sharon. Dona held her breath. The horse walked a little ways down the path, then turned and plodded back.

"Are you ready to try?" June asked Coralea.

"Sure," she replied enthusiastically.

The sleek animal was as tall as the draft horses, but far less bulky. He was all black except for a diamond-shaped patch of white on the front of his head and white "boots" on his front legs.

Coralea rode the animal up and down the path a couple of times, then tried to turn him where there was a little gully. The horse turned, but stumbled, lowering his forelegs just enough to cause Coralea to tumble off over his head.

Dona turned white before Coralea had time to jump up and dust herself off.

"No more of that! Not without a saddle to hang onto!" Dona emphatically announced.

"She should get right back on," June insisted. "She may always be afraid of horses if she doesn't do it now." So back up she went. But he kept hold of the reins. "Easter" was only ridden by June from then on, except for a few times when he led the horse around the barn lot with one of the younger girls on his back. Barbara didn't care to ride him.

Sometime in the former century the Horton Picnic had begun as a weeklong chautauqua. By 1949, it was transformed into a three-day event that closely resembled a county fair. The celebration was definitely the premiere event of the year for the farmers and town folk of the area. The citizens of

Bedford and Horton flocked to the festivities in droves, leaving their cares at home and forgotten.

Tents, trailers and carnival rides were pulled into the fifteen-acre fairgrounds that bordered Horton on the west--on a strip of land that was itself bordered by the banks of the 102 River. A large parking area began at Rt. H, just beside the river bridge, and covered half the allotted acreage.

Rides were set up in a circular arrangement, with the midway running down the center. To the north end and close to the town was a stage faced by makeshift bleachers stepped down the gently sloping hillside. The whole conglomeration was encircled by the trucks that had brought in the fair's attractions, as well as the vans and trailers that were the living quarters of the carney workers.

Not all of the show's workers were outsiders. The largest food stand was run by a local family, and had been for several years. Many of the townspeople did their part to support the event by helping direct traffic in and out of the big parking lot.

"There's Effie Stamps. She's here every year." Dona noted as June drove their '37 Chevy down the sloping entry into the parking area. The elderly lady was stooped and looked as if she should be using a cane. The grass was already beaten down in a pattern of rows. Effie waved her flashlight, directing them to park in the prescribed manner.

"This is probably her big day of the year," June reckoned. Dona realized that it certainly was one of her family's favorite days, as well. The girls had been saving for weeks so they would have money to spend.

The lights that flooded the fairgrounds illuminated much of the surrounding area, so they had no trouble making their way over the rough contours of the grass-matted parking area. The tall Ferris wheel loomed over them already, even though it stood at the far end of the midway. Bright lights and exuberant voices welcomed them into the gay festivities. Dona knew the girls would shortly find friends of their own to accompany them.

"You can find me at the Bingo stand," she announced before they had a chance to go far. Within a few minutes each of the girls had found a friend and wandered off in pursuit of anticipated thrills.

Dona and June strolled together down the midway once, stopping along the way to talk with people they knew. The usual pitchmen hawked their wares and sold games of chance to gullible youngsters. Dona talked June into riding on the swings with her, even though he didn't care much for the whirling movement of the carnival rides.

She swung her feet gaily as the music started and the chair-like seat slid out over the bank of the river. She delighted in gliding out into the dark space and away from the closeness and noise of the crowd. The speeding machine flung the swings into an ever-higher arc above the dark water. She smelled the corn coming into tassel in the field just across the narrow expanse of water. She was enveloped in solitude strangely soothing, even as it was exhilarating. She felt she could drift away, up among the stars. The ride began to slow and the swings gradually dropped to dangle, gently swaying, from the delicate chains that tied them to the circle of steel above.

June staggered off with a peaked expression on his face. Dona recognized at once the sure sign that he hadn't enjoyed the ride as she had.

"I think I'd better find a place on dry land and sit down awhile," he told her. "I'll meet you later at the Bingo tent."

She nodded in agreement as he disappeared into the blackness between two huge trailers.

Both Coralea and Sharon had been by to ask for money, and Dona had won an Indian blanket by the time June found his way to the Bingo game.

"Its about time for the show. If we hurry we can find a place to sit!" Dona suggested when he made his appearance. "I told the girls we'd meet them there."

The area in front of the stage was packed and the show had already begun when they found space on a bench near the top of the hill. The emcee, a local storekeeper, was announcing the name of a woman who had attended the fair every year since its inception more than fifty years earlier. She stood up to wave modestly from the front of the audience.

When the girls found Dona and June, they sat down on the ground near their feet. One of the acts on the evening's agenda was a female contortionist. She managed to twist her limbs into all sorts of improbable positions. She bent her body backward to touch her head with her heels. A little dog aided her in her act. She curled her body backwards into a ball and the tiny animal walked down her middle while she rolled along the stage. The dog trotted between her legs as she tumbled over in an inside-out somersault.

"I wouldn't mind being that little dog!" June announced, loud enough to be heard by those sitting nearby. The girls heard some of them snicker and Dona "shush" him in embarrassment. They weren't sure they understood his comment but could see that their mother disapproved.

The variety show was the culminating event of the fair. The Horton Picnic closed for another year. Weary revelers straggled back to their cars and the slow process of emptying the parking lot began to the flashlight orchestration of the volunteers. Each of the Bowens was tired and ready for bed, but much too excited to sleep for a long while.

That fall, the Bedford School District began a bus route to pick up children who lived on farms. Several country schools had closed because of low enrollments, so more students would be coming to town from outlying communities. The girls would be picked up and delivered to their own lane. This would be a real boon to each of the Bowens, as the girls wouldn't have to walk to school anymore, nor would Dona or June find it necessary to get the car out on bad days to take them into town. There was one disadvantage, however. The girls could no longer stay in town after school to stop at Junior's store or to chat with their friends for a bit.

The family began spending much of each Saturday in town. All three girls now took piano lessons from Miss Nora. She returned ten cents to each of them for a lesson well mastered, although Dona thought the woman must simply enjoy being generous, for she had heard the younger two practicing. The girls would take their change down to Junior's for a Hostess cupcake treat. Another stop they usually made was at Richey's Dry Goods Store. Mr. Richey kept boxes of old comic books that had been traded 2 for 1 for new ones. That arrangement kept everyone coming into his store and buying new comics, also.

The winter of '49-'50 brutalized the Midwest with icy temperatures. Howling winds blew for days at a time. It was impossible to keep the house warm enough to be comfortable, even with the bedrooms shut off from the rest of the house.

On laundry day, Dona found it difficult to dry the clothes. She strung lines across the kitchen where she could hang the lighter things. She found that if she laid the jeans and overalls outdoors, over the fence, they would nearly freeze dry if she left them out for a few days. After she brought them in, stiff as boards, and thawed them on the backs of chairs, they became limp and only slightly damp. Their sudsy smell permeated the house but cooled it considerably at the same time.

June went down to the pond several times each day to chop holes in the ice so the livestock could drink. He was glad he no longer had the sheep. They would have been decimated by the savage conditions that assaulted man and beast. Even the birds and woodland creatures were holed up out of sight and sound. Sam's beaver boards, usually covered by now with pelts stretched to dry into ironing-board shapes, hung empty on the side of his garage. Winter had been cruelly long and hard before February ever arrived.

Overnight a ten-inch snow fell, silently blanketing several counties in Northwest Missouri. Near dawn, granular droplets of sleet pelted the western windowpanes with a soft whisper, like salt tumbling in a shaker. Obviously, there would be no school that day.

The relentless frozen rain continued until a layer of crystals covered everything in an inch-thick armor of ice. Light filtering through the moist air revealed an absolute whiteness covering every horizontal surface. The northwest side of everything perpendicular was painted with a thick overlay of white. Bare branches of trees stretched white-gloved fingers into the moist atmosphere of the winter morning. The wire fence was a net of milky white surrounding the yard, capturing everything enclosed in an eerie stillness.

June buckled his overshoes to the top before leaving the porch to check on the livestock. He expected to sink down into the deep snow. Instead, his substantial weight remained atop the icy crust and only repeated stomping with his massive feet broke through the fused surface of ice. He found pigs and cows huddled together in the tight barn, where he expected they would be. The chickens were safe in the hen house, where they had already been shut in for several weeks. The pump was frozen up. He would have to carry water from inside the house--one more concession to the endless demands of the savage season.

After this onslaught of ice, the next day dawned bright and clear. Many schools would again be in session. Bedford would not. School officials deemed it too risky to endanger the children, and the new bus, on the ice-covered roads. Bright sunshine brought warmer temperatures and the combination of those two factors melted the uppermost crystals of ice covering the deep snow. By afternoon a thin veneer of moisture slickened the surface that the storm had spread like frosting over the countryside.

Later, Dona heard of how some youngsters had labored to get home from school that day. The children always walked across pastures to get to their one-room school. In the afternoon sun, they had become trapped in swales and couldn't purchase a foothold on the glassy surface. They kept sliding back down the inclines, unable to surmount the small hills that loomed between them and their home. Only the early dusk and rapidly falling temperatures aided them in their struggles and allowed them to continue on, exhausted, to their warm house. On the next day the children arrived at school with bottle caps tacked beneath the heels of their shoes.

On the second day following the storm, Dona and the girls got out the sled and bundled up for some welcome fresh air. The day was cool and crisp--and so still Dona believed she might hear the tinkling of a tiny bell miles away. The surface of the snow had refrozen to a solid sheet of ice. The girls had fun sliding on the smooth surface of the yard. They giggled as they watched their dog stepping lively, his toenails clicking in an effort to pierce the surface and gain elusive footing.

Barbara and Sharon sat together on the sled, with the older girl holding the rope and bracing her feet against the wooden crossbar that would guide the runners. Dona gave them a small push before her feet slipped from beneath her and she fell onto her hands.

The sled and its eager riders picked up speed as they passed through the pasture gate and on toward the pond, a hundred yards down a westward slope. The sled disappeared over the ridge as Dona realized that Barbara had no control over the direction she and her sister flew. Dona thought of the pond at the same time she remembered it would now be frozen over. Then, before she could scramble down to catch sight of the children, she remembered that June had been cutting holes in the ice for the cows. Her heart leaped into her throat as she struggled to maintain her footing on the frozen surface.

Sitting on the sled near the opposite side of the pond, Barbara and Sharon smiled broadly at the thrilling ride they'd had over the icy snow. They were astonished that they had slid so far and waved excitedly at their mother, who mentally measured their distance from the jagged heap of ice rimming the hole that June had repeatedly opened. They weren't so close as to be in danger but near enough to provoke grim images in her mind. Dona decided the girls could go ahead with their fun as long as she was there to guard the hazardous spot.

Winter came early and stayed late that year. By the time the crocuses were up, everyone in the family was extremely grateful for that welcome sign of spring.

In the summer, Rick was again invited to spend a couple of weeks with the Bowens. June assured Dona that his nephew wouldn't be any trouble. *He's nothing but trouble*, thought Dona. The girls soon discovered their cousin had matured since they had seen him two years earlier. For one thing, his voice had changed, and he was about a foot taller.

The girls thought Rick was cute and appreciated his company when they went to the movies in town. They took him with them to the Horton Picnic, where he fit well into the role of big brother, a sibling that each of the girls had wished for more than a few times as she was growing up. They actually resented the times when Rick went with June to perform a task around the farm, which he did quite often. June enjoyed having male company for a change, and Rick was fairly strong and able to help with the chores.

Rick slept on the floor of the front room. He claimed it was cooler there, as the night breezes flowed in through the screen door. He had been at the Bowens' about a week when a strange thing happened.

A scream from the bedroom shared by the younger girls awakened Dona and June. They rushed into their daughters' room, moonlight from the open window illuminating the scene.

"What's the matter?" Dona asked, worried.

"Something was under the bed!" Sharon cried, huddling against her sister.

"I saw it go out the door!" Coralea added, obviously distraught, as she nodded toward the doorway.

"Well, what was it?" June asked, ready to get to the bottom of the matter.

"I don't know," Sharon told him. "I felt something furry when I put my hand down behind the bed!"

"Maybe it was Tippie," June suggested.

A look of horror still registered on Sharon's face. "It didn't feel like Tippie!" she insisted.

"Tippie's not in the house," Dona observed.

"When it went out the door it looked like a curtain or something," Coralea attempted to explain.

They thought of Rick. Maybe it was he, with a sheet covering himself.

Coralea again described how the apparition had "sort of floated through the doorway" right after Sharon screamed.

June lit the lamp in the front room. Rick was still asleep in front of the screen door. The door was locked with a hook latch that would certainly keep the dog from entering the house. They awakened Rick.

"Do you ever walk in your sleep?" Dona asked him.

"I don't think so. Why?" He was truly confused as to what was going on and why everyone was up in the middle of the night. They explained to him what had happened, but he was unable to shed any light on the spooky event.

Rick forever denied having anything to do with scaring the girls that night. And none of the others thought it likely that he had, either. The experience became the basis for their subsequent belief that perhaps Pete Adams' house was haunted.

Just a short distance south of the house, the family's garden was enclosed in a fence. The girls were encouraged to help their mother work in the garden that summer. Their efforts were rewarded with a bumper crop of vegetables. They'd already helped Dona pick, snap, and can the green beans. Rainfall was ample during the setting-on of the blossoms, and the summer heat hadn't threatened the growth of their major crop.

A Hundred Miles to the City

This year Dona had tackled the job of canning without Retha's help--except for the loan of her big pressure cooker. The heavy metal pot was the size of a small wash tub, large enough to hold nine quart jars or twelve pints. The girls helped with the process until it was time to flip up the clamps that circled the side and to secure the massive lid in place. A steam cock at the top regulated the pressure, and a soft lead valve would blow if the pressure became dangerously high. Dona had heard of explosions that had done gruesome damage, so the girls were not allowed in the kitchen once the pressure in the cooker started the steam cock to jiggling.

Dona listened to the rattle of the metal weight bouncing on the cooker to gauge whether the pressure was built up just right. She must time the intervals of jiggling per minute to make sure the pressure inside the contraption was doing its job of sucking the air out of the glass jars. Dona needed to concentrate so she banished her helpers to the outdoors to complete other phases of the task. She despised the loud racket made by the contraption and found it hard to relax until the thing was cleaned and set aside, to be returned later to the Schmit household.

In the girls' estimation, the most rewarding aspect of the season's efforts was the abundance of fruit on the melon vines. Nearly half of the garden was covered with vines of various shades of green. Their broad leaves completely hid the dark earth below. If one looked carefully, she could see the lighter hue of half-grown muskmelons scattered among the sheltering leaves. To one side were leaves of a darker color that were thrust aside in places by the green stripes of watermelons; they held the promise of juicy red treats at some not-too-distant time. The girls had been out thumping them already, although they'd been told that it might be weeks yet before any would be ripe.

"Mama! The cows are in the garden!" Coralea shouted as Dona and the girls returned from a trip into town.

"Good grief! I hope they haven't wrecked the whole thing!" Dona cried as she charged toward the animals that now stood placidly munching beside the fence they had walked over.

"Shoo! Get out of here!" Dona yelled as she picked up clods and pelted them. "Those are Jake Waters' cows," she stated darkly as she turned to survey the damage.

"They've trampled our watermelons!" Sharon wailed. Red splashes of color could be seen among the shredded green mass that had borne their precious produce.

"Those damn cows!" Dona cursed.

The girls looked at her. They had never heard their mother swear before. June had let Jake bring his cows over to pasture at the Bowens' farm for the remainder of the summer. Jake constantly struggled to provide for his large family of seven children. They lived in Old Town and he could no longer afford to rent a pasture for his animals. June had felt sorry for him and knew his own herd would never consume the growth the grasses had achieved during the mild season.

"I guess your garden must have looked really good to them," June allowed, when they complained to him of the disaster. "We'll just have to buy a few melons. We could never have eaten that many anyhow."

The girls were dismayed that he didn't show more sympathy for their labors--efforts that were now wasted. And they weren't too fond of Jake Waters, anyhow, because they still blamed him for the death of their pet, Tootsie, years before.

Earlier in the summer, June had a calf butchered at the processing plant in Horton. He sold half and the family kept the remaining packages of meat in a rented locker. Occasionally either Dona or June went to Horton to pick up a couple of the frozen packages. One day when Dona was there to get some ground beef she noticed that there wasn't as much meat left as she thought there should be. She talked to the proprietor to see if someone could have mistakenly gotten into the wrong compartment.

"You know we keep the keys and only give them to authorized persons when they're requested," the worker assured Dona.

"Yes, I guess that's right. I just was sure we had more meat left!" Dona explained. She was puzzled, but could see there was no sense in arguing with the man. That evening she told June about the problem.

"I'm certain we should have more meat left," Dona told him with concern. "We can't have eaten that much so soon!"

"I gave some of it to Jake Waters," June confessed.

"Well, why did you do that?" she asked.

"They needed it. I guess I felt sorry for them," June replied.

"Do you really think they need it more than we do?" Dona angrily challenged.

June sat quietly for a bit. She could tell he was becoming upset with her. "Would you rather I'd have let them go hungry?" he demanded of her.

"They're not the only ones who might be hungry before long!" she fired back at him. Dona realized, much later, that Jake had probably again received blame for trouble he had no part in. The missing meat most likely went to another needy home.

The girls heard them arguing. They were getting used to heated confrontations between their parents.

Just a small corner of the living room separated the doors to the two small bedrooms. Raised voices easily carried from one room to the next. Frequently the children could hear anxious tones and muffled sobbing coming from their parents' bed.

"We wouldn't be having so much trouble if I'd gone on the wheat harvest," June was saying. "If you hadn't pitched such a fit, I'd have gone."

"What would we have done while you were gone?" she asked of him. "I can't run this farm by myself!"

"The girls could have helped you. They do a lot of the work around here anyhow."

"They can't lift those big bales or carry water to the pigs!" she curtly reminded him.

"You could've gotten some help," he insisted.

"Dad was gone, too, you know," she reminded him.

"You could have gotten some help in town."

She didn't ask him if he had anyone specific in mind. "I don't like to go begging for help," she told him.

"Look, we've been over this before. It doesn't help. What's done is done." He attempted to drop the subject, but invariably they found another argument to pursue.

"Mama! Ma-ma!" Coralea cried out.

"What is it?" Dona called from her bed.

"My stomach hurts!" Coralea wailed.

Dona got up and went into the girls' room. She sat down on the edge of the bed and ran her cool hand over Coralea's forehead.

"You do feel hot. Shall I get you a drink of water?"

"Uh-huh."

Dona stayed and patted her daughter's tummy for a bit, trying to soothe her. When Coralea was quieted Dona went back to her bed.

The next night the same thing happened. But this time when Dona returned to her own bed the argument between her and June resumed. Coralea began wailing again and wanted to come sleep in their bed.

This routine went on for several nights before Dona was certain that Coralea's complaints were definitely tied to the heated discussions she and June were having in their bedroom. Coralea had found her own method of keeping peace in the house. This conclusion caused both Dona and June remorse and each felt individually responsible for the turmoil in the household. They determined to keep their differences more private if they could.

Dr. Liston would be closing his outdoor theater in another couple of weeks. It was mid-October and the evenings were becoming too chilly for sitting outside. Dona and the girls had gone into the movie, while June would spend his time at the tavern next door, which he often preferred to do.

A short while into the movie Dona became cold and decided to go out to the car and get the blanket they kept there. She told the girls of her plan and that she would be right back.

When she got to where the car had been, it was no longer there, and she couldn't spot it as she glanced up and down the street. She would go into Verna's Joint and ask June where he'd put the car. The tavern was dark and smoky but she saw right away that her husband was not there.

"Have you seen June?" she asked Chance, who sat with a small group of men.

"He left just a bit ago," Chance told Dona. "Is there something you need?"

"No. I just wanted a blanket from the car," she told him as she turned to leave.

She decided to wait for June. She stood just inside the narrow entry to the movie where she could see anyone who might be coming down the street. She smoked a couple of cigarettes as she waited impatiently, wondering where he could be. An empty feeling crept into the pit of her stomach as she tried to keep herself calm. After half an hour, she decided she'd better go back into the movie or the girls would be worried.

"I couldn't find the blanket" was all she said about her absence.

June sat in the car waiting for them. It was parked where they'd left it before the movie.

"How was the show?" June cheerily asked the girls.

They gave him a rundown of the high points on the way home. Dona said nothing. The pale light of the waning moon revealed only the outlines of the farm's features. The house was completely dark and uninviting.

"We'll be in in a minute," Dona told the girls as they tumbled out of the car. She sat stonily in the front seat. June got out to follow the children into the house. Dona caught up with him at the gate.

"Where were you tonight?" she demanded.

"You know where I was. At Verna's," June stated.

"You weren't at Verna's. Where were you?"

The girls heard a scream. As they ran from the house, they saw their mother grabbing the fence to pull herself up from the ground.

"Get out! Leave me alone!" she shouted at his back as he stormed through the gate. Dona sank down and dropped her head to her knees and cried. The girls knelt beside her quietly. She felt utterly frustrated and alone.

"Mama, are you all right?" Sharon asked, even though they all could see that she was far from all right.

"Yes. Don't worry. I'm okay. Just my feelings are hurt. I'm sorry for you to see that," she said with concern.

"What happened?" Barbara wanted to know.

"It's okay. We were angry," Dona lied.

"Where's Daddy going?" Coralea asked.

Dona thought about him for a minute. He was still important to the girls, at least. She had to let them know that their world hadn't completely come to an end, as it seemed. They all got into the car and headed down the lane.

He had walked on east another mile when they stopped and he got into the car.

EIGHTEEN

"No, Earlene! I won't hear of it! If you want to help me, that's certainly not the way to do it!" The color that had drained from Dona's face moments before rushed back to darken her countenance as her eyes flashed in determination and disgust. Dona stood to face her sister, who, though taller, appeared to lose stature as she was abruptly confronted.

"But, Dona, you can't expect Mother to take the girls again . . . "

"I wouldn't ask her. She would if I did, I know it. But no, I'll find a way myself. I worked before--I can again! I won't let the girls be separated! Do you realize how that would hurt them, on top of everything else?"

Emmett sat on the edge of his chair, looking vastly uncomfortable. Dona's reaction had startled him completely.

"Don't you think it would be best to have them in comfortable homes? There's no way you can work and be home for them, too," he ventured uncertainly. Dona realized the couple's appearance had been planned with more than sisterly love in mind. Suddenly the visit that at first seemed an expression of genuine concern had turned into a plot with an ulterior purpose.

"It was Hank's idea," Earlene continued, as if the subject were still open to discussion. "You know how attached he and Beulah are to Sharon."

Of course Dona knew that. Her brother and his wife had lost two stillborn babies, and would never have children of their own. She was sympathetic to their situation, but expecting her to give up her children—she had had all the losses she could handle already!

The four girls, who'd gone into Barbara's room to inspect the box of hand-me-downs Lenore brought with her, now crowded into the doorway. Voices raised in discord had captured their attention. Even Lenore, who had arrived with the gaiety of a well-kept secret, expressed an attitude of surprise and dismay.

Dona forced herself into a degree of composure as she saw the anxious expressions on the faces of her children.

"I know you mean well. I am grateful to you for the offer. But we'll find a way, somehow. Things are different than they were before. You wouldn't believe what kind of help the girls are now." She managed a tentative smile as she nodded their way.

Hearing those words and observing the stances of the adults, the three girls sensed what was going on. Tears came to their eyes as they recognized the stress their mother attempted to hide.

"I'm sorry, Dona. We didn't mean to upset you," Emmett said in his kind way. "Maybe we'd better go on home now. But we are serious. We wouldn't have come if we weren't. We just want what's best for everyone. You know that, don't you?"

Dona felt too shaky to stand but rose to see her sister's family to the door while the girls stood quietly, waiting to learn what had transpired between their elders.

"Mama, what is it?" Barbara asked when she thought her mother could answer without breaking down.

"It's okay, girls. Their intentions were good. I know that. But I want you to know I'd never consider, even for a moment, giving any one of you up to anyone! Come here . . . I need you around me now." Bursting into a shower of tears, she threw her arms around them and hugged them to her tightly. She could only wonder why her sister would think she'd consider such a proposal.

"You're squeezing us, Mama!" Sharon said as she squirmed free.

Maintaining her daily routine was nearly impossible for Dona while her life was in such turmoil. She was in the kitchen starting supper when the phone rang. The jangling of the bell ripped into her consciousness. It was Retha, and the sound of her mother's voice filled Dona with relief, which she neither expected nor completely understood.

"Carrie called," Retha reported. "She thinks the baby will come soon. They're on their way to the hospital in Madison right now."

My goodness! Dona thought. *I've been so wrapped up in my troubles I forgot all about Carrie's condition.*

"Is everything okay?" she asked anxiously.

"I think so. She sounded really chipper on the phone," was the reply. Both women had worried about Carrie's first pregnancy because she'd been sick early on and she was a tiny thing, besides.

"Dona?" Retha continued. "Why don't you come home for a while?"

Home? Dona let out a long, slow breath. No one could understand how much that word meant to her right now. She began crying softly.

"Oh, Mom!" she managed between sobs. She wondered if Earlene's family had stopped by there, and if they had, what kind of exchange had occurred. Dona knew her mother to be very stubborn and thought it unlikely she would yield to advice from her eldest daughter.

"You mean, all of us?" she asked cautiously.

"Well, of course, all of you. Can you come right away? Dad can be over to get you in two shakes of a lamb's tail!" Dona felt her heart lighten. She hungered for reassurance and acceptance.

She hesitated.

"Mom, don't you want to go . . . " she began.

"Mrs. Moffitt will be going up to help Carrie for a week or two," Retha volunteered, anticipating her query. "Carrie's room here is empty, and there's the cot in the living room. Dona, you've no business being over there without a car or anything."

"Thanks, Mom." Dona hung the receiver up by the wall and sank onto a nearby chair. *I think we'll gather up a few things and go the way we are. I can come back later for more of our stuff,* she thought, glad to be making a positive move. She was so grateful for the support of her folks!

A few days later, Dona was alone at the Schmit place. Retha and Sam had gone into town and the girls were in school. The insistent ringing of the telephone startled Dona, and it was several seconds before she remembered that the two-long, two-short pattern was her folks' ring.

"Hello?" She thought maybe Retha was calling from the central office in Bedford.

"Dona?" a female voice asked.

"Jenny?"

"Yes! How are you?" her friend asked.

"I have been better. How did you know where to find me?" Dona asked.

"Miriam called me. She told me about your problems. I'm sorry, Dona, and I want to know if there's some way I can help."

Dona sighed.

"Jenny, I wish there were. There's just nothing that can be done. I feel so defeated--and worthless, I guess. Sometimes I feel like sitting down and quitting! I know that's not an option, but that's the way I feel!"

"That doesn't sound like you. You've always had so much spunk!" her friend exclaimed, hoping to raise her spirits.

"Oh, Jenny! I handled it all wrong! It has been so hard on the girls, and I know it's partly my fault!" Dona said emphatically.

"When I was there last year, I thought everything was going so well," Jenny ventured.

"We were trying. We both wanted it to work. To be honest, I wasn't happy at Pete's place. It never seemed like home, no matter what we did to it. It didn't seem like ours and I knew it never would. It was just so lonely there--I can't explain it, but I felt so awfully alone!"

"Maybe you were, in a way," Jenny offered.

"Yes, I guess I really was . . . for a long time." Dona heard a click on the wire and realized someone was listening in on the party line.

"How are the girls taking this change in their lives?" Jenny asked, changing the course of the conversation.

"Well, I guess as well as can be expected--not much talking about it, but some nightmares. They are just sad, as you'd expect. Telling them was the hardest part. I can still see them sitting in a row on Barbara's bed, so quiet, and obviously dreading the words they expected to hear. I tried to explain how we'd remarried mostly for their sake, but I'm afraid that wasn't at all comforting. I could almost see them thinking 'but you don't think we're worth it any more?' Jenny, I never felt so low. I don't want to blame June and have them hate him--I know it isn't all his fault. I've always wished I were back in the city. I was never satisfied there on the farm." Dona sobbed as she added, "I shouldn't be complaining, but it hasn't been easy lately."

Dona continued by telling Jenny of the visit by her sister, who had wanted to adopt Barbara as a playmate for Lenore, just two years older, and the possibility of Hank and Beulah taking Sharon to raise.

"What about Coralea?" Jenny asked.

"I guess we never got that far. I'm afraid I was rude, but I was so upset with them! I can't imagine why they would think I'd give up my girls! I'm still angry!"

"Can I come to see you?" Jenny asked, wanting to help.

"Better wait awhile, Jenny. I need to get my life together first. I've been looking for a job. I went to Whitesville yesterday--it's just fifteen miles away. But no luck there. Tomorrow I'll try in Madison. There're lots more businesses there. Maybe I can find secretarial work. I can still type and take shorthand. So far the girls have been able to stay in the same school--that's important to them. I've told June I have to have the car and he's agreed to that. He knows I have to work."

"What about June?" Jenny inquired.

"He's back on the farm. As far as I know he intends to stay on there, but I don't expect he'll be much help financially . . . he hasn't been so far," Dona regretfully added.

"Miriam tells me she and Lloyd have another son now and that Carrie just had a new baby," Jenny ventured.

"Uh huh. We went to see her for the first time last night. They live just a few miles north of here, up by Atchison. The baby's a cute little blue-eyed bundle named Linda Edell, the middle name after Carrie. Frank insisted."

"You'll call me soon and let me know how things are going?" Jenny asked.

"Yes, and I appreciate your call. I mean, I really, truly appreciate your calling! You don't know what it means to me to have someone who cares." Of all her old friends, Dona thought that Jenny knew her best.

"What does she do in there?" Sharon wanted to know. "What *is* a 'sponge' bath anyhow? Doesn't she get too cold with all her clothes off?"

Retha smiled. Barbara was thirteen now and becoming more particular with personal hygiene. All the girls took turns in the galvanized tub on Saturday nights. After they had carried in buckets of water and heated them on the cook stove, they placed the round washtub behind the pot-bellied stove that stood in the dining area of the simple house. They drew straws for who got to bathe first, when the water was hot and clean. Sam went outside and occupied himself with some little chore in the garage while Dona and the girls bathed.

On every other evening, Barbara took a basin of hot water into the cold bedroom and warned the others to stay out. There were no doors on the bedrooms as yet, only heavy curtains, but that barrier kept heat from the big wood stove confined to the living area of the house.

"She doesn't take *all* her clothes off," Retha told Sharon.

"Then how does she take a bath?" asked the inquisitive girl.

"Well, the way you do it is," Retha began, "you undo your blouse and wash down as far as possible. Then, you put that back on and take down your pants and wash up as far as possible . . . and then, you wash 'possible'," and she laughed as the child gave her a puzzled look. Retha obviously enjoyed the playful probing as much as her inquisitive charge.

Dona was surprised at how her family fit easily into her parents' home. She knew her folks had to make concessions. Sam no longer dressed behind the wood stove in the front room but peeled quickly from one set of long underwear and hopped into the next in the cold bedroom.

A Hundred Miles to the City

The house was a simple rectangular structure with two bedrooms on one side, each opening directly off the living-dining area. That large space was partitioned only by the presence of a room-size carpet on the front part and linoleum on the back half, which contained the table and the heating stove. Behind the dining area, a doorway led to the small kitchen, which opened on the side to a narrow washroom. That space contained cabinets and the dry sink where Sam shaved each morning. So far, the back porch was non-existent. Once they had moved into their new home, the Schmits had made little progress on the finish work. But, still, Dona was amazed that her dad could actually build a house. Sam's own father had been a carpenter, and Sam had grown up learning to work with wood and the attendant tools.

It was into late October now, and the nights were becoming cool. The house was heated with wood and the fire went out each night so the air was quite cold by morning. Sometimes there was a skin of ice on the water bucket in the washroom. When they went to bed, the Schmits, and Dona and Barbara, who shared Carrie's room, each took one of Retha's irons with them. They had been heated on the stove and wrapped in dishcloths, ready to be placed beside chilly feet under the heavy comforters. This arrangement helped make the cold rooms more bearable. Coralea and Sharon shared the cot in the living room, so they were cozy and warm for most of the night.

Dona never heard her mother complain about getting up early every morning. By six o'clock, Retha had stoked up the embers in the big wood stove and built a fire in the cook stove. By the time everyone else was up, the house was warm and the stove was ready for cooking breakfast.

One of the girls' chores was to fill the wood box on the front porch. Each day Sam split logs out by the timber. The girls stacked the sticks on their arms and deposited them into the wooden container beside the door. They filled a coal hod with cobs left from feeding corn to the chickens, another of their frequent tasks.

Retha seldom ventured from the house during cold weather, as the girls took over the care of her poultry--that is, with the exception of occasionally killing a bird for a delicious meal of fried chicken. That Retha accomplished for herself by wringing the neck of the doomed creature until the head was severed. The body flailed away in the yard, spraying red over the grass. Then she tied its legs to the clothesline so the blood could continue draining. The girls were nauseated by the smell when Retha dipped the chicken in a bucket of scalding water and hurriedly plucked out the large feathers. She then singed the remaining, down-like hairs with a flaming newspaper held beneath the carcass like a torch.

It was a gruesome, fascinating sight to watch, but the girls managed to put the process out of their minds when they sat down to the resulting dinner, which was sure to include mashed potatoes and Grandma's thick milk gravy. Dona was envious of the delicious food her mother prepared with her meager equipment. Many of Retha's meals were accompanied by cornbread she had made in an iron skillet and cut into pie-shaped servings or else dough that she fried on top of the stove in finger-shaped biscuits.

The Schmits didn't often have dessert, but there was always a compote of Retha's preserves on the table or else a comb of honey Sam had robbed from his bees. In the proper season, he donned his helmet-like hat with the netting on it, took his smoker, and gently removed the racks of honeycomb from the bee boxes that sat out in the far pasture. The girls liked to cut off chunks of the golden honey-filled comb and pop them into their mouths to savor, sucking out the sweet nectar and chewing on the waxy residue like gum--until it became too crumbly and they had to spit it out.

The jar of Retha's butter churn had broken during one of the family's many moves, so now she made butter by simply shaking salted cream in a jar until it formed a soft mass. This she separated from the translucent whey, which she poured off and saved for another purpose. She pressed the butter into a mold, then turned it out into a dish and set it on the table, to be enjoyed whenever anyone became hungry.

In November, Dona began working at the Light & Power Company in Madison. She liked her job right away and quickly became acquainted with her coworkers. An older lady took her under her wing, giving her advice and encouragement as she learned the routines of the office. At first Dona worked in the billing department. She enjoyed the coming and going as the townspeople stopped in to pay their utility bills. Her broad smile and friendly manner drew the attention of her employers, and she was soon moved to the front desk where she would wait on customers.

The half-hour trip to and from work was the only drawback for Dona, especially if the weather were bad. When the days began getting shorter, she left before sunrise and returned home in the dark. She had a scare once when the car's headlights failed while she was on the highway, but for the most part she had no trouble getting to work.

One of the requirements for employment in the office was that the ladies wear nylons to work. Dona did that at first but soon realized she couldn't afford that luxury out of her modest earnings, so she began covering her legs with leg make-up. She enlisted Barbara's help in drawing a line down the back of each calf with eyeliner to enhance the appearance of hose. That deception worked for a while until her immediate supervisor noticed and informed her that she must adhere to the rules of the workplace. She gathered her courage and spoke to the office manager, pleading with him to make an exception.

Being aware of her financial situation, he agreed to this adjustment of the rules. Dona understood that the shortcoming would not be mentioned again and appreciated the allowance made for her. Later that same man brought cast-off clothing from his own daughter to share with her girls. The well-appointed young lady's hand-me-downs went a long way toward their school wardrobe for several years to come.

At the center of the circle drive in front of the Schmit house stood a stately elm tree. Dona parked her car beside it, on the grass, so it wouldn't be in her father's way when he came home. She spent much of her time sitting alone in her car, often enjoying a cigarette. It was a place of privacy and solitude, which she sometimes needed. Occasionally one or more of the girls would join her, and they'd talk and laugh as they used to on the blanket in the Wrights' back yard.

They often discussed the day's events or aired their individual grievances, but sometimes their conversation would turn on more elusive matters, such as the reason for some occurrence or the nature of things in general. One night Barbara brought up the subject currently puzzling her. Someone at school had expressed a belief in reincarnation and Barbara asked her mother what it meant. Dona had never had discussions with the girls about religion. They'd gone to Retha's church and accepted the doctrine of that Christian faith as far as they understood it.

"Reincarnation means coming back to life, after you've died, as something else--or maybe, some other person. Some people believe that when you die that's just one phase of your being and that your soul goes on into another phase, or another being." Dona tried to make it simple, although she knew the concept was difficult for a child to grasp.

"You mean I might have been someone else once?" Sharon asked.

"Well, yes, I guess that is what some people believe. They think people have different incarnations at different times, like someone alive today might have been someone else a long time ago. Or, maybe, if someone died now, they might come back as a new baby and live again. That's hard to understand, isn't it?"

"Do you believe in reincarnation?" Barbara asked.

"Well, I don't know for sure that it's not true. Many wise people believe it might be so. If it is, do you know what I'd like to come back as?" Dona asked, feeling their curiosity grow.

"What?" from Coralea, eagerly.

"A butterfly. They're so beautiful and so free. Wouldn't it be wonderful to fly like a butterfly?" Dona thought this a pleasant conjecture and smiled as she thought of her girls exploring such subjects. She must stop thinking of them as little children.

"You know, we'll need to look for a place in Madison in the spring," Dona told them, and saw their faces fall visibly. "We can't stay here with the folks forever. It's not fair to them."

"I don't want to move," Coralea stubbornly stated.

"I know you don't want to leave Grandma and Grandpa, but I need to be in Madison for my work. A lot of my paycheck goes to keeping the car running. And, I need to be there so I can do my share of working on Saturday mornings like everyone else," Dona told her.

"I don't want to go to that school. It's too big!" Coralea said emphatically.

Dona knew Barbara and Sharon felt the same way but didn't want to cause more trouble so they said nothing. The year at Bedford School had been a good one for them, even though they had had the divorce to deal with. The Black Oak School had closed last year, and there were some new students going into town now. Several were interesting boys, and the teenage girls were beginning to notice them.

At school, the presence of the children of their father's new lady friend made the girls somewhat uncomfortable. Alta had three children, all younger than Sharon. June had returned to the farm to live, and the woman now lived there with him. They'd invited the girls over for a weekend so the youngsters could become acquainted. It wasn't a happy experience for anyone, as the girls resented the new person in their mother's place and weren't inclined to be friendly with her children, either. The only complaint that they carried home to Dona, though, was that Sharon had to clean up her own mess after she was sick from eating too many strawberries. That was the only time an effort was made to meld the two families.

Not long after that incident, Alta's aunt and uncle sued for custody of her children, charging her with being an unfit mother. Eventually, she and June were married, so she lost her children only temporarily. Dona felt a strange mixture of hatred and pity for the woman, whose relationship with June had begun a couple of years earlier. She'd asked him to take her to Illinois to find her husband, who had deserted her and the children. The man never returned to Bedford, as far as Dona knew, not even to prevent his children from going into foster homes.

Before moving to Madison, Dona and the girls would have to find a furnished apartment. Dona had taken from Pete's place only the piano and the desk Sam had made for her from an old radio console. They never used the player part of the piano any more. It was so loud Dona feared it would disturb the Schmit household. The girls practiced their piano lessons and Retha occasionally played hymns on the piano. Her old organ had finally been dismantled.

One Sunday afternoon Dona thought they all might enjoy some lively music, so she went to get the box of piano rolls. She was surprised to find the box nearly empty.

"What has happened to the music rolls?" she cried.

"I burnt them," Retha told her. "You never used them and I was out of kindling."

"But, Mom, I wanted to save them. Some day we would have enjoyed them again!" Dona wailed.

"Well, it's done, anyhow," Retha stated matter-of-factly, and Dona could see that her mother was not going to apologize. She had a feeling that Retha disliked the loud music more than she admitted.

Sam's car sat in the middle of Main Street, angled beside a few others in front of the large grocery store. In the brisk air of the February afternoon, Retha approached with a paper sack filled with the groceries she had just purchased at Junior's. She set the sack on the floorboard and climbed up to settle on the cold seat of the automobile. School would soon be dismissed and the girls would come chattering down the street. Shortly the children who lived in town scattered down the street in small groups, hurrying to get in from the cold of the winter day. Eventually Retha spotted the three approaching, carrying their lunch pails and a book or two each.

"What kept you?" Retha asked as they neared.

"They were having ball practice in the gym," Barbara answered. "Can we go back, since Grandpa isn't here yet?"

"Now, you know your grandpa expects you to be here when he's ready," Retha reminded them as they reluctantly climbed into the back seat. "He won't be long."

The look on Barbara's face indicated that she had her doubts about that.

"What did you get today, Grandma?" Sharon asked.

"Nothing special for you. Just some bread and sugar and some canned goods," Retha informed her, wishing she'd been able to put a treat for them on her bill at the store. Junior was generous to a fault with credit, but she'd rather not abuse his good will.

They sat quietly for a while, waiting.

"What did you say is going on at the school?" Retha asked, looking for a way to pass the time.

"They're having basketball practice and Barbara wanted to watch. She thinks Willie is cute!" Coralea declared.

Barbara shot her a challenging glance and retorted hotly, "You're the one who wanted to stay!"

The girls quibbled some before that line of discourse died down. They waited awhile longer. Occasionally shoppers left the store and waved to them before getting into their car and leaving town. A couple of people stopped to exchange pleasantries with Retha before continuing on their way. Eventually theirs was the only car left on that end of the street.

"When's Grandpa going to come?" Sharon asked anxiously, already knowing what her grandmother's answer would be.

"When he's ready."

They were becoming quite cold, as the sun had disappeared, draining away any idea of warmth it suggested.

At last Sam came up the street from Verna's Tavern, where he had spent the last hours having a few beers and playing dominoes with the bar's regulars. He didn't appear to be in any hurry. The girls sensed their grandmother's aggravation but knew she would say nothing in front of them.

The engine clattered to life and Sam turned the stiff wheels to take them to the highway and up the big hill toward home. The girls settled back in the seat, glad to be on their way at last.

As the car reached the small plateau halfway up the hill, the outside tire fell off the blacktop. A ridge of snow grabbed the tread, causing the vehicle to careen into a shallow ditch beside the roadway. Everyone gasped in shock at the unexpected direction they were suddenly headed. They were then surprised by the gentle, gradual stopping of forward motion as the wheels plowed into the deep accumulation of snow.

Startled by the wayward lurch of his automobile, Sam sat in stunned silence for a few moments. The girls in the back looked at each other in amused anticipation of what might happen next. Their grandfather's personal dignity was definitely threatened by the unfortunate turn of events, and they knew better than to open their mouths just then.

Sam levered his door open, stepped out, and assessed the situation from all angles. "Maybe we can push it out," he stated optimistically. Just then he heard the sound of a tractor starting up. He looked across the road to the Martin house, which sat on the north side of the highway. Jimmie had evidently noticed their plight and was coming to help.

A few words passed in greeting between the two as Jimmie attached his log chain to the front bumper of the car. The younger man sprang back upon his tractor and pulled the chain taut with the powerful machine. The car shuddered and moved forward, plowing through the thick snow as it was eased back upon the roadway and up the hill. After their rescuer stopped to disengage one vehicle from the other, the children gave big waves of thank you as Jimmie remounted his tractor and turned down the hill toward his home.

"You were lucky help was nearby," Dona said later when the girls told her of the evening's mishap.

"I guess we were lucky it was only a little ditch," Sam volunteered. "Jimmie said Nora saw us go off the road from her front window, where she sits to read."

Dona sensed that her father was embarrassed by the episode and felt perhaps she should be angry with him for putting her family in danger--driving them home after he had spent time in the tavern. But, she knew he and Retha probably wouldn't have been out in the weather at all if the girls hadn't been waiting for a ride home from school.

Shortly after supper that same evening, Dona sat working a crossword puzzle while the girls finished up the supper dishes in the kitchen. She rested comfortably with her feet up, letting her mind wander. She took account of her folks sitting on the other end of the long room, Sam on one side of the small table and Retha in her rocker on the other side, near the wood stove. Retha was working on a quilt block, evidently concentrating on keeping her stitches even. Her heavy hair was up in a bun, as always. Dona couldn't remember ever seeing it otherwise. Very few strands of gray could be detected in the ebony mass.

On his side of the table, Sam sat in his comfortable rocking chair in front of the radio. The paper he had been reading lay folded on the table. The pipe he usually clenched between his teeth had slipped out of his mouth and tumbled to his lap. Sam had been listening to Gabriel Heater and the news, as he did every evening. The news was over long ago and a comedy show had come on. Dona could hear sporadic laughter as she sat across the room.

They seem happier lately, she thought. *Maybe it's because there are others here with them. I would think they'd be ready for some peace and quiet in their lives now.*

Sam's hair had grayed and was thinning. Deep lines etched his face, still deeply tanned from last summer's work in the hot sun. He appeared to be tired but content, and Dona was enormously grateful to see her father enjoying at least a small degree of comfort.

Thanks to the Rural Electrification Association, most homes in the county now had electricity. Sam had the house wired, so they did have electric lights, but, other than the radio and Retha's washing machine, there were no appliances yet--not even a refrigerator. In warm weather they kept the perishables down in the cellar with the jars of fruits and vegetables and the bins of potatoes. Dona would like for her mother to have more modern conveniences, but if Retha wanted them she didn't say so.

Now Sam's head was tilted back against the rocker, and he snored softly. Dona knew that in the next few minutes his chin would drop and his false upper teeth would fall down, clacking and waking him up.

She guessed it was time she made her last trip of the day, outside to the privy. That was the part of farm life she detested the most--having to go to an outdoor toilet. And this one was a good distance away, through the chicken coop on the other side of the hen house. She bundled herself up and took the flashlight from beside the door. No use putting it off. It would only get colder.

Sometimes when Dona came home from work, she found the girls playing pitch with their grandfather. Or maybe Chinese checkers. They played on a wooden board Hank had made for him. Hank had drilled holes in triangular patterns to hold the colored marbles in place until they were moved, or "jumped," across the star-shaped game. Sometimes the girls would win at that, but not often--never at checkers. Sam had spent too many years competing. He couldn't allow them to beat him in an honestly fought contest.

Now and then Coralea and Sharon were on the floor, poring over a magazine that offered a contest of some kind. They imagined they'd win whatever wonderful prize was offered, and Dona always managed to get the box tops, stamps, or whatever else they needed to send with their hopeful entry to the company that sponsored the thinly-veiled advertising gimmick.

As soon as they had made their effort and sent it in, they turned their attention to the Montgomery Ward's or Sears, Roebuck and Company catalog, leafing through page after page of fancy clothes and alluring toys. They chose how many children they each would someday have and what they would buy for them, including furniture for their houses. This amused Dona, but saddened her, also, as she knew their dreams to be remote from their reality. On the other hand, she thought perhaps dreams were what nearly everyone relied upon. She couldn't deny that she always had.

Stanley and Marge Benson visited at the Schmit home a few times during the winter. They lived on a farm a half-mile away. Usually, Retha and Marge occupied themselves with sewing projects while Sam and Stanley discussed events of a political nature. Stanley was short and round, with less hair than Sam, and wore striped overalls wherever he went. He and Sam got in some heated arguments, as each man was opinionated and the two held diverse views on most topics.

On one occasion they'd gotten into a debate concerning religion. Sam's family were hard shell Baptists and he had always lived in communities of like-minded people. Here there were many Catholic families who farmed in the area. In fact, they were the predominant group to the north and east of Bedford. A thriving convent and monastery were just a few miles away, and the landowners of the area were obviously successful. Perhaps Sam was jealous of their cohesion. He argued that they seemed to care only about one another and weren't interested in contributing to anything except their own welfare.

Coralea lay on the cot, listening. Many of her friends at Star of the West School had been Catholics, and several of the new kids at Bedford School now were, also.

"I don't think you're being fair, Grandpa. Lots of the people I know are Catholics, and they're nice!" she spoke up.

Sam gave her a surprised look. It quickly became a frown, and he said, "This is none of your business, Coralea, and you need to sit up on that bed!"

She was confused and hurt by his attitude and complained to her mother about it later.

"He didn't intend to be mean to you," Dona assured her. "He's just of a different generation. He doesn't think a child should presume to enter a serious discussion between adults. And you shouldn't have. It wasn't your affair."

"But why was he so angry?" Coralea asked.

"I remember when I was about your age he told us it wasn't proper for girls to be lying around in a prone position when strangers were around. That may seem odd to you, but that's how he feels. It won't hurt you to do as he wishes."

"But he was mean! I don't think he likes me!" Coralea pouted.

"Now, wait a minute! You know that's not true. Maybe he never says he does, but you can see it in his eyes, can't you?" Dona suggested to her.

Dona thought about her words for a minute and realized they were true. Her father never made any gesture of appreciation, yet she always knew he cared for them. She guessed the fact of his being there was proof enough.

Sam carried the flat cardboard box into the house, tilting it sideways so its large width would slip through the doorway.

"My goodness! I didn't expect them so soon!" Retha exclaimed as she saw what he carried. "Wait. Let me put some newspapers down." She hurried to cover a spot beside the bedroom curtain. She didn't want her carpet soiled.

"Ben waved me down to tell me they'd come in," Sam told Retha. They had been delivered to the produce house earlier that day. Sam knew Retha was eager to get started with her spring project.

She knelt and gently pulled off the lid of the box, which was perforated with holes on the sides. She quickly scanned the moving mass of downy softness confined in the partitioned box. She was happy to spot no dead birds, although she was concerned that a few appeared sluggish in their movements. With a gentle motion of her hand, she scooted some over to the side as she counted to make certain there were twenty-five in each of the four compartments. They were all there, and she was pleased to see that there were a few black ones. She thought they were a little hardier.

"It's a good batch! Maybe we won't lose any this time," she declared confidently.

"I bought some oatmeal, too. I didn't know whether you had enough to start them out on," said Sam as he headed back to the door.

"Would you bring in the waterers, too? They're in the garage--on the far side, under the shelves. I'll need all four for a while." She hoped Sam had gotten a large box of oatmeal, as she could expect to find a premium inside-- probably Royal Ruby glassware. She nearly had a set of the red, faceted glasses already.

When the girls returned from school, Sharon was first through the door and still had her hand on the knob when she heard strange noises. Her face lit with surprise when she spotted the box on the floor, now bathed in the light of the brood lamp Retha had placed beside it. Sharon fell to her knees and leaned atop the open box.

"Your chicks came!" she exclaimed.

"Careful, now!" her grandmother warned. "They're fragile, you know."

"Can I hold one?" Sharon asked eagerly.

"Better not," was Retha's reply. "If they're handled too much, they'll get sick and die."

Sam sat close by, watching the scene.

"You hover around them like you were the mother hen!" he teased Retha.

Coralea reached in to stroke a bird on its soft, yellow back. "Some of them are sleeping," she observed.

"They're not used to the bright light," Retha remarked. "They're just a few days old, you know." She saw that the girls could hardly keep from touching the interesting creatures. "You can each pick up one, very carefully. Don't clutch it. I've seen little children squeeze them too hard." She decided they might as well get the urge out of their systems, while she was watching.

A Hundred Miles to the City

The chick Sharon picked up squirmed and tickled her, causing her to drop it. She squealed with dismay as it landed on the floor. Retha quickly snatched it up, looked it over, and replaced it in the box.

"It's okay. He's a tough one," she assured Sharon. "Don't you want to hold one, Barbara?" she asked then.

Barbara gave it some thought but said, "No. I don't think so. They are cute, though, aren't they?"

"Are you going to keep them in the house, Grandma?" Coralea asked as she put the chick she'd been holding down among the noisy brood.

"For a few days--until they're a little bigger. Then I'll take them out to the chicken house and put a light up there to keep them warm."

"Will they go to sleep at night?" Sharon asked, beginning to notice the racket they were making.

"I guess we better hope they will" was all Retha volunteered.

Retha's chicks were precious to her. She usually kept a few hens for layers, but since she and Sam had gone to Minnesota in the summers she hadn't been able to do that. She had bought only a few in the fall to supply the family's needs. Now Sam was down to one milk cow, which gave only enough milk for the family. So she had been without any cream or egg money for quite awhile. This new batch of pullets would give her a little income when they were ready for dressing, in a few months' time. She decided not to mention that part of the process to the girls just now.

Nearly every day, Dona found herself conducting an inner debate on the advantages and disadvantages of moving her family to Madison. Since she had first mentioned the possibility to the girls, she had felt their attitude progress from disappointment to resentment. She knew that for her own sake, she should make the move. She hungered for independence, while at the same time she realized how much she relied on the emotional support she received from her parents. Of course the girls appreciated being in a secure home. She didn't want them to lose that, but she was determined not to be a burden on her folks. Before long her dad would want to go to Minnesota to reclaim his summer job with the highway department. Retha assured Dona that she really didn't want to go this year--she'd prefer to stay at the farm and tend her garden and raise her chickens. She was ready to settle down in one place. Still, Dona thought that if she and the girls weren't there, Retha might change her mind and accompany Sam north. Surely that would be best for the two of them.

Once she had made up her mind about the course of their future, Dona had to convince the girls that the move would be a positive one. Despite the inconveniences of their Spartan existence at the Schmit place, the girls were quietly contented, obviously thriving in the familiarity of their temporary home. Dona could certainly understand their not wanting to relocate to a larger place--a town full of strangers. The people of Bedford had always been good to them. For the most part, the girls had no real recollection of life in the city, as she had. She wondered if maybe she were being selfish by insisting on this change in their lives. Sometimes she was sure that once the split was made the girls would appreciate the chance at a new beginning, as she knew she did.

So far the girls hadn't relayed to her any slight they received because they were from a broken home, but Dona was fearful that someday they would be faced with such a situation. She'd rather have them in a more impersonal place, where the details of their pasts weren't so intimately known.

After a trip to Madison where they looked for housing, the girls became resigned to their situation, except for Coralea. Her stubborn nature surfaced full-force, and she refused to speak to anyone in the family for nearly a week. She spent most of that time lying on the cot, refusing to do anything she wasn't obligated to do. Dona was torn between comforting her with concessions or being firm in her own resolve to do what she believed to be best for all of them.

It was well into March before Dona found a suitable apartment in Madison, one that she could afford. The upper floor of a small house on Third Street, it was across the street from the high school. The grade school where Sharon would go was a block over, and the walk to her own work at the office would be only three blocks in the opposite direction. The place was furnished, so they wouldn't have to buy anything. The four rooms were tiny and dark, but the younger girls would no longer have to sleep in the living room, as they could share a cot in the small dining room. Dona couldn't expect much privacy, as the owners, an older couple who lived downstairs, would share the one bathroom in the house. It was located at the top of the stairs, in the middle of the apartment. She supposed that would at least be better than going outside.

On what was to be one of the girls' last days at the Bedford school, Dona arose to find a thick fog had settled in. The trip to Madison would be slow and treacherous.

"I'd better start early," she announced to Retha, who was preparing for the day in the still-chilly kitchen.

"Better get up, girls," she said as she gently shook the shoulders of the girls on the cot.

"What's the matter?" Coralea asked when she realized how early it was.

"You'll have to get ready in a hurry," Dona told them firmly. "We've got to get started early. You can hardly see out there, and I need to get to work on time."

"But it's so cold in here!" Coralea complained.

"I'm sorry, but we've got to get started early," Dona reluctantly repeated.

"You go on ahead, Dona. I'll take them in to school pretty soon," Sam volunteered from the bedroom.

"Are you sure?" she asked, hoping he would say "yes."

"Go on . . . and be careful!" Sam warned. He wasn't comfortable with her driving back and forth every day.

An hour later the girls were ready for school and getting bundled up against the frigid winter air.

"Hurry up, Grandpa!" Barbara said as she drew on her boots. "We don't want to be late for school!"

"Hold on, now. It's early yet," Sam cautioned as he threw a big piece of wood into the stove.

By the time he finally got everything together and they all went out to the car, the girls were exasperated with him.

He knew with the first grind of the starter that the cold car was not going to run.

"Can't you do something, Grandpa?" Sharon pleaded, after he had tried several times, unsuccessfully, to get the engine to turn over.

"It's not going to start. I'm sorry."

"Isn't there anything you can do?" Barbara begged.

"Well, I can put a trouble light on it and warm it up--then maybe it'll start. But that'll take awhile. You'd better go back in the house," Sam told them.

"We'll be late!" all three protested.

"You don't have to go to school today," their grandfather suggested.

"We'll walk!" Barbara announced.

"No. You just go back in the house and wait," Sam instructed them.

The girls got out of the car, but rather than return to the house they headed up the lane in a determined row. Sam watched them go, shaking his head and wondering where they could have inherited such willfullness.

The fog had lifted, but a net of moisture filled the air, making the stiff breeze of early morning bite into their exposed skin. At the end of the lane, they turned west into the wind and realized how much they needed the wool scarves they each wore. By the time they reached the lane to Pete Adams' place, Sharon was complaining of cold fingers. Her coat had no pockets so Barbara told her to pull her mittened hands up into her sleeves. After one more hill, they'd walked a mile and were aware of the poor decision they'd made when they defied their grandfather. Now it was too late to turn back. By this time of morning everyone who was going to school or to work was already there, and not one car passed the girls as they hurried on toward school, the older two repeatedly stopping to wait for Sharon, who was quite a bit smaller than her sisters.

They came to the ridge marking the last expanse they must cross before they reached the hill down into Bedford. The imposing valley was a half-mile wide and the wind, blowing straight at them, stung their faces like needles. Sharon began to cry. There was nothing to do but go on. No use to turn back now--it was much too far.

The girls began to feel they would never reach their destination, but at last they did and tumbled gratefully into the double doorway of the school building, greatly relieved to be in where the air no longer burned. They clumsily pulled off their scarves and mittens and tried to remove their boots but found they couldn't get their frozen fingers to complete the necessary maneuvers. Their numb fingers and toes began to ache and throb with pain as they regained feeling.

When they entered their classroom, all the students and their teacher stared at them in disbelief before recognizing their predicament.

"Surely you didn't walk . . . " Mrs. McJimsey began, rushing toward them.

Barbara nodded. She was worried about Sharon, whose fingers were white and stiff and who was now crying in earnest.

"Come with me. Let's run some warm water on those hands," their teacher said, as she herded Sharon along the hall. They were followed closely by the other two, whose main discomfort now was concern for their little sister.

When the warm water hit Sharon's skin, she screamed as if in agony. Her worried teacher didn't know what else to do for her. *Maybe I should have tried cool water first,* she thought. Even the gentlest touch to Sharon's hands caused her to wince in pain.

Mrs. McJimsey decided that the best thing to do was to call the Schmit household and see if they could come and take Sharon home, where she would be more comfortable. The other two girls insisted on staying, and she figured they had earned the right to make that decision for themselves.

Sam finally got the car started and he and Retha went to the school for Sharon, who was by now only too happy to spend the day at home.

Dona heard all about it when she got home from work.

"Why didn't you make them stay home?" she demanded of her father.

He gave her a withering look.

"He told us not to go, Mama," Barbara admitted.

"Well, why didn't you listen to him?" Dona asked in resignation. She had that old feeling of helplessness again. At least when they were in Madison she wouldn't be so far away from them all the time. Maybe then she wouldn't have this out-of-control feeling.

Dot McJimsey called the Schmit home later that evening.

"I was concerned about Sharon," her teacher said. "Is she going to be all right?"

"Yes. She's okay. She'll be back in school tomorrow. Thanks for doing what you could to help," Dona said sincerely, although she wasn't convinced that warm water was the best way to treat Sharon's frozen fingers.

"Have you thought about letting the girls finish out the year in Bedford?" Mrs. McJimsey asked. After the events of the day, she was aware of how much it meant to them to be in school there.

"What do you mean? We've already taken an apartment in Madison and we'll be moving this weekend," Dona reminded her.

"Lily Thomson drives down from Madison every day. Couldn't the girls come with her until school is out? I'm pretty sure she'd be willing to do that. Shall I ask her?" Mrs. McJimsey suggested.

This new idea floored Dona for a minute. *Might there be a chance it could be worked out?* She knew that nothing would make the girls happier!

"I guess I never thought of that possibility," Dona told her. "Would that be okay with the school? I mean, we won't be living in the district then."

"I'll ask, if you want me to," the teacher helpfully offered.

"If there are no objections with them, I'll call Mrs. Thomson and ask her myself," Dona said. She remembered the girls' teacher as the one who had disciplined Coralea and Sharon for the " jumping out of the window" stunt earlier. The girls thought her to be strict, as she tolerated very little nonsense, but they also regarded her with respect.

By the weekend, plans had been laid that would allow the older girls to continue on at Bedford until the end of the school term. Sharon would begin school at the elementary school in Madison. Dona felt better having her youngest in town with her.

Mrs. Thomson lived four miles south of Madison, so each morning Dona took the girls out to her place before she left for school. Then she picked them up each evening after she got off work. Now, instead of being on the road herself each day, the girls would have to be. But it was spring--the roads should be good. And the solution certainly made the move to Madison a happier occasion than it might otherwise have been.

The girls grew to know their former teacher as a real person. Mrs. Thomson was an imposing lady with a firm, but friendly, smile. Her own children were just getting on the bus that would take them north to their school in Madison when she set out down the road south with the Bowen girls, going their chosen way.

Both of the girls would always remember the special kindness offered them by their grade school teacher. Years later, when each young woman settled into her own career choice, Dona was certain that this early experience had helped to guide the direction each had taken. And she knew that the burden of her own responsibility for her children had often been alleviated by their desire to please their perceptive teachers at school.

NINETEEN

Weaning her children, as well as herself, from the Bedford community was more difficult than Dona had anticipated. For the girls, the town and its inhabitants were the only constant in their young lives. The comfort and independence gained by the move to Madison hardly compensated for removing them from the nurturing presence of their grandparents. Throughout the spring of 1951, Dona had misgivings concerning her decision to move the family to the larger town. She quickly found that it was a lonely life, for herself as well as for the girls. After spending each day at work and at school, they spent their evenings alone in the small upstairs rooms. They seldom used the yard, as it didn't seem at all like theirs. They must use the front door of the house to enter or leave their apartment. The open stairway had no hall but was part of the Nielsens' living room. They felt like intruders each time they entered or left their living quarters.

The Nielsens were friendly enough, but the elderly gentleman seemed gruff to the girls. Dona thought perhaps four females living upstairs was just too much for his reserved nature.

While she was glad the older girls could complete the school year in Bedford, Dona knew that in a few months they would be completely estranged from any friends they had known. Then they would be faced with a summer spent in the small rooms by themselves while she was at work.

Adding to her disappointment with her new situation was Dona's certainty that her folks were unhappy with her decision to move away from Bedford.

"Why is Dad angry with me?" Dona asked her mother when she and the girls had driven down for a visit.

"He's not angry," Retha assured her. "I think he's just bothered by your having to apply for welfare."

"But, there was no other way!" Dona protested.

"I know that. It's just that he's always been against any kind of government handout. He thinks families should take care of their own." Retha admitted to herself that it was a quality about her husband that she both admired and regretted.

After giving that some thought, Dona replied, "Yes, Mom, I see what you mean. After all those years trying to keep his family off welfare, this is probably a big disappointment to him. But it's my decision--he shouldn't feel like it reflects on him!"

"Maybe it just reminds him too much of the hard times during the Depression, Dona. You were too young to know what those struggling years took from him," Retha told her daughter.

Dona certainly didn't celebrate the idea of welfare, herself. Although June had offered virtually no assistance in raising his daughters, when he left the area completely she'd applied for and was granted aid for dependent children. She was dismayed, but not surprised, at June's failure to provide funds or other help toward the support of his children. Dona was sure they would be faced with additional expenses once the girls were in the city school. They would have to live as frugally as possible and hope that Providence *would* provide.

The scream of a siren startled Dona as she lay beside Barbara on their bed, easing into slumber. An ambulance raced by on the way to the hospital, located on down Third Street. She had found it hard to get used to the nightly activity on the busy street. The front of the house was intermittently lit by the sweep of headlights as cars came down the hill that curved in front of the Edison School building. Even though her bedroom was on the back of the house, Dona's fitful sleep was frequently interrupted.

Tonight the first ambulance was followed swiftly by others and by police cars as well. The younger girls, who slept at the front of the house, awoke to the alarming noise of traffic streaming by.

"What do you think has happened?" Barbara asked her mother when they gathered to look out the narrow window beside the girls' bed.

"It sounded like an explosion earlier," Dona remembered. She hadn't given it much thought at the time. She'd assumed it was back-fire from a nearby car.

"There must be lots of people hurt!" Sharon said with concern. At least four ambulances went by. Then, several minutes later, a steady procession of vehicles appeared from the west, quickly passing by on the softly lit street.

The next day at the office Dona heard the awful news of an explosion on the west side of town, near the college. A gasoline storage tank had blown up, propelling flames and debris into the rear of the girls' dorm a half-block away. There was one fatality and many other girls suffered burns, one critically.

For weeks afterward Dona would lie awake at night, listening. She couldn't force from her mind thoughts of the suffering those young women were going through, and she realized how little difference there was in their ages and that of her own girls. No determination had been made of the cause of the blast, but many opinions were offered on the inherent danger of such storage in close proximity to housing facilities. An abandoned railroad track ran through the area, and the property was used as a warehouse district for several area businesses. Eventually it was determined that such tanks should be placed underground for the safety of the public. As noted by many in the town, Dona included, a tragedy was required to spur action toward costly, but sensible, solutions.

When her hands first began to itch, Dona thought it was probably the strong detergent she was using. She found herself scratching at her hands when she sat down for a few minutes. So far just the palms were blotchy. She would have to ask the girls to take over clothes-washing chores for a while. They could manage that with just a little overseeing from her. They'd been helping with the laundry for years now anyhow. The family was allowed to use the Nielsens' wringer washing machine that was down in the basement. There was a walkout entrance to the backyard where the clothesline stood, and the Bowens always spent Saturday morning taking care of that chore. It had been a cold assignment so far, but soon the weather would be warming up.

After switching laundry powders for a couple of weeks, Dona could see that her first assessment of the problem was not correct. Her hands were breaking out in sores, especially on her palms and between her fingers. Now she began to worry that it might be caused by something at work. She was probably allergic to something she handled every day. She had no other negative reaction to the substance, just the problem with her hands. She guessed she'd better stop and see Dr. Watson. Retha had doctored with him for most of her life, and his office was just up the street.

"What is your problem today, young lady?" the elderly man asked when she entered his small cubicle.

"My hands are breaking out in blisters," she replied, holding them out for inspection.

"I'd say you're allergic to something. Have you changed anything that you normally do or begun eating some food that you hadn't before?" he questioned.

"I can't think of anything. I've changed laundry soap, thinking that might be it, but it didn't help. As far as I know nothing's different at work.

I've been doing the same job for several months now, and this only started a few weeks ago!"

"And no new foods?" Dr. Watson probed.

"No. We eat a lot of bread and lunchmeat and canned soup. I can't think of anything new or unusual I might've eaten," she assured him. "What can I do?" She hoped he would have a solution for her. She was worried that the condition would get worse and she wouldn't be able to do her work, and could even lose her job!

He frowned.

Not too much assurance, she thought.

"I can give you a topical ointment, but I'm not confident that it will help. You probably have something in your system that's poison to your body. You may need to see a specialist."

Oh, no, Dona thought. *Not another expense!*

"Can I just try the salve, at least?" she asked then. "Maybe it will work."

"Of course, but if there's no improvement in a week, I want to see you back here so we can get you in to see an allergist in St. Joe," he said firmly.

Dona thanked him and left with her prescription. This was one more expense she hadn't figured on.

By the end of the week, she realized Dr. Watson's diagnosis was correct. She was worse, not better. The itchy blisters had turned to running sores that needed to be covered. Whatever she was allergic to seemed to be building up inside her. She knew she would have to go to someone who could determine exactly what was causing the painful reaction.

Dr. Watson called in an appointment for her and Dona drove to St. Joseph. Handling the car was not easy, with her sore and bandaged hands. The young doctor who saw her ran some patch tests on her back and asked questions concerning her lifestyle and daily activities. Then he told her he didn't know what was bothering her, for he found no allergic reactions to the commonly suspected substances he had tested for. She was greatly disappointed, as she had hoped for some sort of magical elixir that would mend her mottled, swollen hands.

Dr. Watson's next suggestion was no more appealing to Dona than the first had been. He proposed that she might have a nervous condition and should take medication to ease her reaction to the stresses of her life. Dona admitted her problem might be caused by excessively worrying about her emotional and financial responsibilities. She knew she had been smoking a lot recently, trying to soothe herself. She had even had to ask the girls for help in lighting up a cigarette a few times. That had been difficult for her.

She preached to them against ever taking up the habit, but she felt she needed her cigarettes to calm her nerves. *Do as I say, not as I do,* she ruefully berated herself.

Dona began to feel like a bona fide invalid. Barbara became adept at changing Dona's bandages, and each of the girls assumed more of the household chores. The older girls did the washing and ironing, and Sharon did her part by keeping the apartment tidy and dust-free. Dona's supervisor suggested that she take a week's sick leave to help her recover from her physical setback. He was kind but adamant in his request, so she figured she should do her part to relax and help herself recuperate. He assured her that she was a valuable employee they didn't want to lose, which went a long way toward easing her mind.

A few days after beginning her prescribed drug treatment, the sores on Dona's hands began to dry up, and the swelling that had made her feel clumsy began to subside. When the girls were home from school they treated her like a queen, doing everything they could to make her comfortable and to keep her mind occupied. Dona was touched by their sympathetic concern as they administered to her. As she became aware of their strength she grew confident that she would recover quickly. The feelings of anxiety and dread slid away like silver ashes tumbling from the tip of her cigarette.

By the summer, Dona's hands had healed completely and she was back at work full time at the light company. The long days of summer she had anticipated with trepidation turned out to be restful, not worrisome. Her daughters were capable enough, even eager, to manage the household. They shopped for food at Dan's neighborhood store, just a block west of the high school. They easily carried the sacks of supplies from the small in-home grocery store.

Between their apartment and Dr. Watson's office was a junk car lot that Dona heard was once a swimming pool. Parts of the pool's edge peeked through the jumble of horse weeds left from several summers' unmanaged growth. Cars, trucks, all manner of metal castaways were piled in the area, to weather and rust indefinitely. Some years before, a child had drowned in the poorly supervised pool, and the people of the town hadn't yet gained the confidence or desire to replace the facility.

As far as Dona could see, there were virtually no activities, at least no free ones, available to school-age children during the summer months--except for the public library, which the girls visited frequently. It was free, if it weren't for the over-due fines someone in the family often incurred. Dona knew it wasn't because Coralea read more than the other two, but she constantly lost track of when her books were due.

When Dona mentioned the dearth of opportunities for children, someone at the office told her about the Red Cross swimming lessons. There was only a nominal fee, a dollar each. A bus would take the youngsters from a meeting place on the courthouse square to the Lake of Three Moons, up in Iowa. It was a half-hour trip each way and open to any child beyond the fourth grade, so all her girls could participate.

"We'll go up to Penney's and get you each a new swimsuit," Dona told the girls that evening. "You'll meet some Madison kids--then you won't have to start to school this fall knowing no one."

"But we already know how to swim!" Sharon declared.

"That's all right," her mother assured her. "They'll teach you how to do different strokes. And it'll be at a pretty lake with a sand beach, not like the muddy pond we used to swim in!"

Coralea wasn't too interested in making new friends, but Barbara and Sharon were enthusiastic, so Dona decided they would all sign up so they could look out for one another. They would go each day for two weeks, if the weather permitted.

On the first day of their lessons, Dona took an hour off from work so she could see them settled onto the bus and ready for their new adventure. She found it required some cheerleading to get them into the mood for a positive experience.

After a couple of days at the lake, the girls revealed their enjoyment of the trips by chatting happily about their day when Dona got home from work. They gave her an account of new acquaintances they had made on the bus and tales of accomplishments they had mastered. They each liked their instructors and only complained on mornings when the sky was overcast.

Dona was glad she'd encouraged them to join in the swimming lessons. The girls made no fast friends but had at least gotten the idea that city kids were not all that different from themselves--except for one girl Coralea's age, whom Sharon reported to be "so rich, she has a bathroom of her very own!"

The mention of a trip to South Missouri brought a smile to Dona's face.

"Jenny, I can't be running off on a vacation! We want you to come and spend the week with us," she said with a trace of regret in her voice.

"Now, don't say 'no' right off the bat," Jenny pleaded with her friend. "I've been wanting to do this for years, and you know I'll need a companion--I'd never do it alone. Please. There won't be much expense for you. I'll take my car and we'll stay together in motels I would've gotten anyhow. A little change of scenery would do you a world of good!"

"But, that wouldn't be fair to the girls. They've been waiting for me to get some time off so we could do something together. We wouldn't be going anywhere, except to Bedford, but Mom is counting on us coming down," Dona emphatically stated.

"Wait a minute, Dona! It's not like you'd be gone that long, just a few days. And I'll bet your mom wouldn't mind having the girls visit her for a while. Didn't you say that she'd be alone at Bedford this summer?"

Realistically, Dona knew Retha would welcome the girls' company. She seemed to appreciate the few weekends they had stayed with her since school was out. The trips to the farm had been good for all of them. After the small apartment, there seemed such freedom in the country, and it was almost like camping out, having to pump well water and everything. Shade from the big elm kept the house cool, unlike the stuffy apartment in town.

"Mom wanted us to come down and help her clean the pullets for market sometime," Dona said. "I was counting on doing that during my time off, too."

"I can't say that I'd be much help there," Jenny confessed. "But, how long could that take, anyhow? You surely have nine days, counting weekends."

Gradually, Dona began to consider the possibility of a few days of sightseeing with Jenny. She guessed she would enjoy the time to herself and the temporary suspension of some of her responsibilities. Maybe the idea wasn't so far-fetched after all.

"Let me think about it, Jenny. I do appreciate the offer, and I know we'd have a great time together. We'll just have to see. I'll talk to Mom and feel her out about it. If she's not real keen on the idea, I'd rather just forget about it. You understand, don't you?"

"'Course I do. You'll really think about it, though? I've got some interesting places picked out that I'd like to see. Let me know soon, and say 'Hi' to the girls." Jenny closed the conversation cheerfully, hoping Dona would find a way to take her up on her spur-of-the-moment proposition.

As soon as she broached the subject with her mother, Dona knew her decision was made. Retha was obviously pleased at the prospect of having the girls with her for a few days.

"Carrie's just a few miles away--we can call on her if we need anything. Maybe she'll bring the baby down and the girls can play with her," Retha suggested. Dona knew the girls would enjoy that. The child had such a pleasing disposition, they would probably fuss over who got to hold her.

"Can we get the chickens done first, Mom? So we'll have that out of the way?" Dona asked.

"Okay," Retha replied. "Do you really think the girls can help?"

"They can try," Dona assured her, feeling confident that the older girls would have no trouble learning to dress a chicken. She had found they could accomplish many chores she had thought them too young for.

"Yechh!" Barbara said as she watched her grandmother draw her huge butcher knife across the belly of the first bird. Retha stuck her fingers into the split carcass and pulled until the cavity popped open, spilling blood and entrails into the dishpan of cool water.

"This is the easiest part," Retha told her.

"It's got to be the stinkiest part!" Barbara retorted.

"Now you have to find the heart, liver and gizzard and cut them out before you throw the rest of the innards away," Retha stated. "See? And be sure you empty everything from the cavity so the meat will be clean." Retha's hands moved so swiftly it was hard for the girls to follow her motions. Dona supposed her mother's dexterity with her crochet hook gave her agility and precision for accomplishing many tasks.

Before they got the hang of it, Dona had to lead each of the older girls through their first solo attempt, and she was sure that Sharon shouldn't try it at all.

"You can pump the water for us," Dona told the youngest girl. "That's probably the hardest work of all." They were sitting in a circle by the front step, a busy work detail three generations deep. Dona watched as Barbara and Coralea gingerly fished around in the gory masses floating in the pans before them. She figured it would be quite awhile before they would want to eat any fried chicken.

Dona had finally learned to kill a chicken herself, out of necessity, and not the way Retha did it, by wringing their necks. She instead used a narrow board, which she placed on the neck of the struggling bird. Then she placed her feet on the ends of the board, standing with her weight holding the plank in place. She pulled up swiftly and firmly on the legs of the chicken, trapping its head and causing the board to sever the neck of the creature. She knew she must do it resolutely because she didn't want a suffering animal on her conscience. It wasn't an easy task for her to accomplish, but she took over that chore so Retha could apply her nimble fingers to the deliberate motions of cutting the carcasses into pieces. Quite an operation was going before long, with Retha and the older girls doing the dressing and Dona and Sharon taking care of the rest of the process.

By the end of the day they were all quite tired, but there were twenty-six fryers packaged, ready to take into town to the produce house.

"I don't think we're going to make our goal of seventy in two days," Dona lamented to her mother.

"Don't worry. A few of them will just have a short reprieve, that's all!" Retha said, and her freckled face broke out in a reassuring grin.

When Dona met Jenny in Kansas City a couple of days later, she was satisfied that she wouldn't be greatly missed at home. The girls had set a tub out in the yard, preparing for some water fun of their own. They had assured her they could walk to town for anything they might need while she was gone. Some time on the farm with Grandma was all the vacation they desired, especially when Dona promised them that next year they would spend her week off going somewhere together.

Jenny had made out an itinerary and marked a Missouri map with the route she hoped to follow.

"We'll go to Jefferson City first. You're sure you're willing to just ride along, Dona? If there's somewhere you want to go, we can change our plans, you know," Jenny suggested.

"Sounds good to me. I've seen the capitol buildings of Iowa and Nebraska, but I've never been to our own," Dona replied.

"I told you I applied for a job with the Foreign Service. They've accepted me and I'm expecting to be sent overseas in a few weeks. I think I should become more knowledgeable about my own government before I spend time in other countries."

"I could never do that, Jenny," Dona told her friend as they continued down the busy highway.

"You mean because of the girls?" Jenny asked.

"Well, that, too. But, no, I was thinking that I couldn't just leave my family and everyone I know and go to another country by myself. It would be wonderful to see other places, but I wouldn't want to be so far from home." Dona believed she would feel more like a person in exile than an adventuress.

"There's no one to keep me here, though," Jenny said matter-of-factly.

Dona smiled.

"Maybe I'll meet a handsome prince or a rich duke or a duke's third cousin, twice removed!" Jenny said, laughing.

As the two women talked on through the afternoon, Dona felt herself relaxing in the company of her old friend.

They reached the state capital around three o'clock, at the peak of the summer heat, but huge elm trees made the air seem cool, and inviting. Obviously a very old town, Jefferson City had all the charm and stability Dona had expected it would. Inside, the capitol building was constructed of marble and rich, walnut wood, making it stately and enduring, cool and warm, all at the same time. At the center, an open dome rose above a spacious rotunda. Elegant stairways led to the second story, where murals graced the surface of the curved walls that lined the balcony. The pictures were very large. They made Dona feel as if she were in them herself as she walked by, watching the perspective change along with her progression.

"What a beautiful place!" Jenny exclaimed, more than once.

Dona certainly agreed.

"You know what my old friend, Jimmie, would say about this place?" Dona asked.

"What?" Jenny wondered.

"That it would hold a lot of hay!" Dona laughed.

"Do you ever see him? Jimmie?" Jenny inquired.

"No . . . well, yes, I did see him at the Horton Picnic last month. He was with a girl," Dona told her.

"Did you know the girl?" Jenny further pried.

"Not really. Her name is Amabelle Catterson. Her folks bought the Torrance place north of Bedford--the house where Jimmie was born, actually."

"Is he still as handsome as ever?" her friend asked then.

"Yes, I guess so. He hasn't changed much in the last few years--just looks more mature, I think," Dona admitted, and caught a teasing glance from her friend.

"Don't even think it, Jenny. He's still a farmer!"

"And he's still there!" Jenny reminded her.

"I don't need any changes right now," Dona announced. "I want things to stay the same for a while, a long while!" She realized she really meant that. She felt as if she were beginning to regain some control over her life.

From Jefferson City they traveled south to Bagnell Dam, intending to stay for a day at Osage Beach on the Lake of the Ozarks. Dona was impressed by the size of the huge concrete structure that held back the great expanse of water.

"How long has this been here?" Dona wondered aloud.

"Let's stop at the tourist center and find out about it," Jenny suggested. The small office they located offered a pictorial display of the history and construction of the dam. They were surprised at the beauty of the area, even before the lake had been formed. Before the project was begun, deep valleys and heavily forested hills stretched for scores of miles, with little trace of human habitation. Now, what had once been a little hamlet was the town of Osage Beach--a popular resort attraction that swarmed with fun-seekers.

A Hundred Miles to the City

A line of shops, with swimwear and curios mainly, lined the street opposite the sandy beach where Dona and Jenny spread their blanket. They intended to catch some rays of afternoon sun. Paddleboats with noisy children churned across the lake's surface outside the line of floating buoys that marked the area for swimming. Dona couldn't help but reflect on how much the girls would have loved it here. Besides the beach, other entertainment was offered along the main strip through town--things like bumper cars, fun houses, and miniature golf. However, she enjoyed just lying in the soothing sunshine.

From Osage Beach the pair drove on to Elephant Rock State Park. Boulders the size of . . . well, elephants, and much larger, too, were strewn over several acres--some piled against each other, some partially emerging from the rugged terrain. Dona thought of thunder when she first saw them. They looked like someone had "upset the potato wagon," as her mother used to say to her when she was a child and a thunderstorm raged outside. Dona and Jenny perched for pictures on the big rocks, as they once posed, pin-up style, back in Kansas City.

The confusion of formations in Johnson's Shut-ins, where they were the next day, caught and swirled the water that cascaded through the fantastic area. According to the pamphlet describing the place, the phenomenon was created by lava that had flowed more than a billion years ago. People came to wade and cavort in the rills and pools, as the clear water coursed down the sloping waterway. Dona guessed there must be a hundred people in there now, but it was such a large area it didn't seem at all crowded. They were tempted, but Jenny and Dona decided not to join in the fun, as they wished to reach Camdenton before nightfall.

Dona had no idea what to expect when she and Jenny stopped for a tour of Bridal Cave the next day. Her only exposure to the concept of an underground cavern was through reading Tom Sawyer and learning of Becky Thatcher's unfortunate adventure. She supposed it would be a dark hole in the ground filled with bats, perhaps, or inhabited by other slimy creatures akin to Sam's collection of leeches down in the cellar.
She was astounded when they passed through the first narrow, damp tunnel, and stepped into a large room-like opening. Its glistening walls tumbled down in multi-colored ripples of rock. Slick, wet mounds reached toward the ceiling, high above in the dimly lit chamber. She saw other formations that dripped like icicles onto groping columns rising from below. Electric light bulbs placed behind the masses cast forbidding shadows that

faded into absolute blackness. An occasional "plop" could be heard, but otherwise, only the voice of their guide interrupted the eerie silence.

Dona wanted to tell the girls about the exciting world that lay beneath ground that looked so ordinary in the world above. According to the guide, the cave was more than a mile long, and countless others in the area hadn't even been explored. She couldn't imagine the kind of person it would take to first set foot in such a place!

Not far from Camdenton was HaHa Tonka Castle. This was the last "X" on Jenny's map. It wasn't a castle, really, but more a "ruins." They made a twisting trip down a wooded vale, then up the side of a bluff overlooking the Ozark River. The road was rugged and narrow, and each time they turned and climbed higher up the steep incline Dona feared they might meet a car coming down. About half way to the summit was a parking area with just a few cars angled into graveled parking spaces.

Not the tiniest wisp of vegetation stirred as Dona and Jenny followed the well-trodden path through the trees and up to the clearing. Dona hoped to find a breeze at the summit. The heat was stifling. Both women wore light cotton blouses and Jenny sported fashionable shorts, but Dona wore dark pedal pushers, as abbreviated a costume as she ever donned. It wasn't an easy climb up for either of them.

"Remember the time we all went to the top of the Liberty Memorial?" Dona asked Jenny, as they stopped momentarily to catch their breath.

"Uh-huh! And Irma and Joe were lost for a couple of hours," Jenny reminded her, smiling at the recollection.

"I don't think 'lost' is really the right word, Jenny. 'Separated,' maybe . . . and just from us, definitely not from each other!" Dona remarked.

"Those were sweet and carefree times, weren't they?"

"I guess they were, in a way. I really loved the city, but I don't think I realized how much until I left it," Dona told her, wistfully.

"I'm sure we all have times we'd like to go back to," Jenny assured her.

"You know, I don't feel that way so much anymore. I think for a long time I missed the people, the activity, the excitement. There was always something important happening in the city. My life on the farm was so quiet, it seemed far away from real life. It's hard to explain, but I felt like I was in limbo for a while," Dona expressed to her friend.

"Have you ever considered moving back to Kansas City?" Jenny asked.

Dona gave that possibility some thought.

"I don't really want to live there again--I just miss it! I guess I really like small towns best. Places where you know everyone."

"How do the girls like living in Madison by now?" Jenny inquired.

"They're getting used to it. Now that they know their way around, it doesn't seem so frightening to them. Barbara has had a couple of baby-sitting jobs already!" Dona told her.

"Whew!" Jenny panted. "It's really hot today!" Her short hair was damp with perspiration and she pushed it back from her face. Dona's friend couldn't be called a classic beauty, but her well-defined, angular features gave her an orderly appearance.

Several imposing structures, of sandstone, could be spied through the thinning trees. Originally erected at the turn of the century, the main building had burned in 1920, then shortly after its reconstruction, had burned again. Perhaps realizing its prime location for lightning strikes, the wealthy industrialist who had built the country retreat gave up. Everything wooden had burned or rotted away so that all that remained now was the craggy skeleton of the once magnificent estate.

Dona and Jenny continued up the uneven footpath, past the stone water tower and the barn-like garage, to the edge of the bluff, where massive walls loomed against a streakless summer sky. Large porticos on the front and side of the structure were originally planned to deliver guests into posh opulence, but the era of entertainment at the remote location was short-lived.

The two joined a handful of other sightseers moving in and out of the massive doorways of the castle. Dona leaned against the stone balustrade that enclosed the southern balcony. Weather and countless hands had worn the rough stone down to a polished surface. Now it radiated heat, as every surface seemed to do in the midday sun.

Dona gazed over the imposing wall and across the meandering Ozark River below to tree-covered ridges in the distance. The basin must be several miles across, for as far as she could see hills and valleys rose and fell in an undulating carpet of green. *Surely*, Dona thought, *there must be houses down there, and roads.* She'd never seen such a vast, pristine spot in the state of Missouri.

She turned to walk across the stone balcony and looked into a narrow opening, once a window, she was certain. The main part of the structure was completely empty--an enormous gaping expanse the size of a gymnasium, but seemingly even more vast due to the absence of a roof. At each end, a massive wall of stone sliced the sky above as it rose to hold the now-missing rafters. Any evidence of the floor of the ballroom was now gone. Partitions in the basement outlined spaces once used for cooking and utilities. On the side adjacent to the large balcony were a few smaller room-size areas that she learned had been powder rooms.

Dona envisioned the fancy people who had attended the celebrations in the sumptuous party-room she rebuilt in her mind. She saw lithe ladies in flapper dresses lounging in gilded chairs, with cigarette holders limply held in tapered, manicured fingers.

"I tried to teach the girls to do the Charleston," she announced, " . . . when we lived at the Richey place."

"They were pretty young then," Jenny remarked. "How did it go?"

Dona remembered enthusiastic arms and legs flying all over the place and herself going into a fit of laughter and tears at the sight.

"Let's just say they were good sports about it," she generously stated, knowing she could never adequately describe the scene that had thrown her into such an amused state.

"This is a unique place, but I'm really feeling the heat, Dona. Shall we go on back now?" Jenny suggested. She would have been enormously grateful if there were a drinking fountain on the place. It was thirty years too late to expect any such amenity.

The final leg of the trip was just a few hours. They would go to Jenny's air-conditioned apartment, and Dona would spend a comfortable night before returning to Bedford the next day.

"I'm glad I have a couple of days left with the girls before I have to go back to work," Dona announced as they rode along in the steamy car.

"You're so dark, they probably won't recognize you!" Jenny teased. A week in the summer sun had tanned both women, whose time was usually spent working indoors.

"Well, I'll sure recognize them!" Dona said emphatically. "But I'm glad you talked me into this, Jenny. I feel renewed--like I could tackle the world!"

"I hope it doesn't need tackling!" Jenny laughed.

"You should have seen me last spring," Dona told her friend, "when I had the trouble with my hands. I was a real basket case. I feel like all that's behind me now, though."

"Great!" Jenny replied. "You do seem more like your old self." Dona wasn't sure if that was good news but was happy to be feeling more or less whole again.

"Thank you so much" spoken to Jenny seemed woefully inadequate to Dona as she prepared to return to her own home. How could she ever repay her friend for the thoughtful and generous companion she had been? The gift of Jenny's friendship was beyond any reciprocation Dona could imagine. The city had charmed her, but its most rewarding aspect had been the companionship of the people she knew there.

A Hundred Miles to the City

Later, as she revisited highlights of her trip with Retha and the girls, Dona recognized an unexpected result of her short vacation. She hadn't imagined that a change of scenery might bring about a change in herself as well. She now saw herself as more secure and independent. She had felt that all they had was hope. She knew now that hope itself was a powerful force. Perhaps she just needed a good pep talk from her friend. At any rate, her confidence was given a substantial boost and she welcomed the challenges ahead with fresh enthusiasm.

The girls seemed to have grown up overnight. Already she had made note of changes, especially with Barbara and Coralea. Both were taller than she was now and showed contours expressing their teenage maturity. Dona regarded her daughters in a new perspective, beyond the physical aspects of this plateau in their development. She sensed her children passing from dependents to companions. She began to see intriguing possibilities in their futures. Looking at her situation in this new light, Dona realized her own circumstances were more to be envied than pitied. She determined to take positive steps toward securing better opportunities for her family.

The first change she made was in renting an apartment on the south side of town. For years, residents who lived on the north side of First Street were referred to as "North Enders," with the assumption being that the designation somehow made those people inferior--a silly notion, she knew, but one that was pervasive in the town. The new apartment was in a large, older house on South Main. It would be noisier than where they were, and it was small, in an upstairs location, also. At least they would have a private stairway, and when the lower unit became available they could move down.

School started smoothly for each of the girls. After the first day's apprehension passed, all reported liking their classes and their teachers. Both Barbara and Coralea went from a classroom with four levels of students to a class where the students moved from room to room, according to the subject matter. Sharon went to the grade school and her group had only two teachers. Dona felt the girls adjusted well to their new routine.

They also joined the First Christian Church in Madison. Dona chose that congregation because Retha had started the girls there in Bedford. All four attended church services together after the girls had gone to the Sunday school sessions. The girls were baptized into the faith in the baptismal font beside the beautiful sanctuary.

Standing on the small platform, June appeared as an apparition before her. Dona had answered a rap at the door, assuming it was their landlord delivering a message. She took a step back when she recognized June.

"Hello, Dona," he ventured.

"What are you doing here?" she asked uncertainly.

"I guess I just wanted to see you and the girls."

A flood of emotions swept over her. June sounded the same, but he looked so much older! Maybe it was the pale evening light. The small streak of white, for many years barely noticeable, had broadened to punctuate his coal black hair, still swept back from his forehead.

Her hesitation surprised him.

"I should have called . . . " he began.

"You couldn't. We have no phone," she told him.

By then Sharon had joined her at the door.

"Come in," Dona offered as she unlocked the screen door.

Words of greeting and a few polite questions passed between father and daughters. It was obvious to Dona that the girls were uncomfortable with this sudden intrusion back into their lives. They hardly looked directly at June and seemed nervous and uncharacteristically shy. Each girl related to him with a mixture of eagerness and awkwardness, perhaps unsure of her own emotional stance. Dona saw that he was either unable or unwilling to communicate with them in any meaningful way.

She offered to make some coffee.

He would like to stay for a while.

She found a package of cookies.

"Still the little homemaker, I see," he laughed as she brought out the sandwich cookies she'd hurriedly unwrapped.

Dona smiled.

"How is Mother Bowen?" she asked, in an attempt to get a conversation going.

"I haven't heard from her lately. You know how I am about writing," he replied.

She smiled again, remembering the intense letters he'd written to her while he was in Europe.

"Norm and Faye went out to Colorado this summer," Dona remarked. "They said she was thinking of returning to Missouri."

"I see you still have the German stuff," he said when she offered him the silver ashtray.

"All of it," Dona assured him. "Would you like it back?" she offered.

"No!" he said, emphatically. She could see that he wanted to distance himself from recollections of his war experiences.

The evening wore on and the girls drifted away to do their homework. They were aware that the attention their father demonstrated was for their mother's benefit, not their own.

June and Dona sat on the sofa.

He told her a few things about his troubles during the past year, knowing that his problems would draw more sympathy from her than the passionate interest he demonstrated, though his roguish ways had always charmed her.

She felt the nearness of his body. It had been a long time since she'd experienced a hunger for intimacy with anyone. She was almost willing to reciprocate his advances. Still, her thoughts were encumbered by the memory of betrayals as definite as the animal desires so urgently compelling her now.

It became apparent to Dona that June was waiting for the girls to go to bed. At the same time, she had the feeling that they were hoping he would leave. She began to see things through their eyes. They were old enough now to know what was going on, and she was painfully aware of the fears registered on their faces as they said goodnight to him. They had been hurt enough by the years of misplaced devotion she had squandered on him.

As she sat alone with June, Dona found herself resenting the assumptions he must have made about her feelings for him. She asked him to leave.

"Are you sure this is what you really want?" he asked her sincerely.

Her "Yes" was nearly inaudible, but firm.

She didn't rise to follow him to the door. She didn't want to watch him leave again. She did listen as his footsteps fell steadily on the stairs, never hesitating for an instant. She ground out her cigarette with finality in the silver ashtray. Now would be a good time to throw away those love letters. They were in a shoebox, tied with a blue ribbon and stuffed under her bed. But she knew she wouldn't. Besides the girls, they were all that remained of the sweet, gentle boy she had loved.

TWENTY

Madison--population in the '50s, around 8,000.

The Johnson County Courthouse dominated the downtown area, which was bisected by U.S. Highway 71, the main north-south artery through America's heartland. The concrete roadway stretched from Louisiana to Minnesota, carrying traffic through the center of the town and lending a commercial atmosphere to the otherwise rural aspect of the area. Trucks rumbled through day and night at all times of the year, but many more during harvest season. Three sale barns on the outskirts of town were testimonials to the importance of agriculture to the community.

A stranger arriving in the area would see a right-angled town with an abundance of churches and gas stations, as there appeared to be one or the other on nearly every corner. But, on a hill on the west side of town, the Teachers' College, once the State Normal School, spread across a quarter-mile section of land. Its red brick structures were ruled over by an Administration Building that looked out over a campus adorned with avenues of powerfully built, wide-crowned elm trees. Country and college--a strange mixture, but obviously a viable combination, as the area thrived.

Railroads had once run through both sides of the town, and a now-deserted depot still stood between the campus and the residential area next to it. The rail line's only purpose for being still in evidence was a decrepit creamery that now relied on milk trucks to serve its declining clientele.

The functioning train station was on Depot Street, located a mile east down a gentle slope from the courthouse square. A couple of rail lines ran through, with freight trains regularly hauling coal, grain or other cargo to points mainly north and south. A flat mile on farther east a bridge spanned the 102 River. Dona heard that the river received its strange name for its miles of length. It joined with the Platte River at Agency, after which both spilled into the current of the muddy Missouri.

By the time they had lived in Madison a year, Dona knew she had chosen the right place for her family. It was liberating to her not to be known as "so and so's daughter", or "so and so's wife," but merely as " the lady who works at the light company." She wasn't the only single mother in town and didn't feel judged on past mistakes or family history.

Financial worries were nothing new to Dona. She couldn't remember a time when she wasn't concerned with her economic situation. Her employment with the light company allowed her to relax somewhat in that regard, and her income was supplemented with a small monthly check from ADC--Aid to Dependent Children. When an opportunity for overtime work at the office became available, she took it, hoping to ease the financial strain. Many evenings she stayed late at the light company, typing address labels onto tin stamps--engravings that would be used by companies for mailing lists.

Still, there was absolutely no money for extras in her budget. Each time the cost of a pack of cigarettes went up she considered the advisability of giving up smoking, knowing she probably wouldn't. It was the only luxury she allowed herself and she felt justified in that one small indulgence. Once in a while one of the girls would complain about the unnecessary expense, usually when told they couldn't afford something she thought she just had to have. But for the most part the girls were aware of their mother's needs. Each evening when she returned from work, Dona sat in the living room awhile, enjoying a smoke and reading the newspaper. She needed the quiet time to unwind after her busy day at work.

Providing clothing for the girls took up a good part of Dona's budget. The school had a dress code--skirts only for the female students. No jeans or slacks were allowed. Besides Lenore's hand-me-downs, the family was given discarded clothing by one of Dona's co-workers and by her boss's daughter, a recent graduate of Madison High School. Dona and the girls were glad to get these treasures. All the items were of good quality and still stylish. Since she and the girls were of short stature, they rolled down the waistband on the skirts to make them fit. Dona lacked the sewing ability to tackle re-hemming the tailored clothing. With just a few nice skirts they all shared, except for Sharon, who was too small, the girls could add blouses and sweaters and be well dressed.

The family hadn't the funds to buy school clothes in the fall, but once a year they went shopping in St. Joseph for an Easter outfit apiece. Their selections would be their Sunday best clothes for the summer and also their back-to-school costumes in the fall.

When they made the trip to St. Joseph, near Easter time, Dona and the girls went from store to store comparing styles and prices. They spent hours trying on and fussing over the new-smelling garments they might eventually choose. Most of the time their search for bargains was conducted in small, inexpensive dress shops, including Lerner's and The Vogue, or else in the United Department Store. They never went into Townsend and Wall's nor Einbender's. Both were much too exclusive and Dona understood that you had to dicker over prices to get a good buy in the latter store.

The long day of shopping was interrupted with the treat of lunch at the Kresge soda fountain. It was a day they all looked forward to each year and one that Dona had to scrimp and save in order to finance. When the girls got older, reasonably priced Easter hats were added to the day's wish list.

Though they regularly attended the Christian Church, on Easter Sunday Dona and her family rose early to go to sunrise services offered by the pastor of the Methodist congregation. The popular preacher gave his stirring homily at the local drive-in movie theater. Window-mounted speakers delivered his words of praise and comfort to row after row of cars filled with worshippers of all religious persuasions. Notwithstanding the stuffed horse that adorned the bunkhouse, for one morning each year the Trail Ride Drive-in was transformed from a theater into a temple.

As she saw it, Dona's biggest challenge lay in guiding her three teenage daughters--or corralling, controlling, cajoling, or inspiring them, whichever adjective applied to the fleeting moments of their many moods.

Entertainment could be had by simply sitting on the porch swing watching the world go by, as it all surely would if one remained there long enough. The large Goad house sat atop an embankment close to Highway 71, near enough to feel the change in vibration as drivers of big rigs shifted gears. A steep grade approached the business part of town on a hill to the north. Dona was surprised she didn't feel a blast of wind from the air brakes of the massive machines, if they ever actually slowed down.

The Goads were generous with their yard, so besides that pastime the family played croquet on the flat side lawn. Often a few neighborhood kids would be there leaning on mallets and taking their turns whacking the wooden balls toward the nearest street or ditch. Dona was patient with the youngsters' childish pranks, and her house soon became a popular meeting place for the girls' friends.

At first concerned about leaving the girls home unsupervised during her summer working hours, Dona soon realized they were very good at policing, as well as entertaining, each other. The younger two complained that Barbara began projects she insisted they help out with, such as cleaning closets or organizing drawers. Dona found they got a lot of work done if she offered an outing or treat of some kind for the successful completion of the household task, washing and waxing the hardwood floors being one that usually required some extra encouragement. There was no mystery to this arrangement and all accepted it as their way of life at the time. Dona was content to make the decisions for her family by using such methods of friendly persuasion.

The rule for daytime visitors at the house was that all guests had to remain in the yard or on the porch. Nothing less than an emergency would warrant an exception. Calls to the light company for arbitration were to be made only if someone's well-being were in danger or if the house were on fire. Generally, Dona was able to depend upon the girls' acceptance of their responsibilities, and she never had any complaints from their landlord concerning their behavior.

Following World War II, the student body at the college increased significantly with an influx of servicemen attending on the G.I. Bill. Across the tracks from the Administration Building new housing was opened which was dubbed "Vet's Village" and was solely for the occupation of former soldiers and their families. The structures were metal quonset huts that had been relocated from a former POW camp in Clarinda, Iowa. Besides these older students, an additional group of sailors attended a special summer school offering. Dona let her girls know they had no business talking to any of these fellows if they happened across them uptown.

Dona continued making weekly trips to Bedford to visit her folks and to allow the girls to continue their piano lessons with Mrs. McMurtry. Coralea had dropped out, but Barbara and Sharon still practiced faithfully and both were able to play hymns and simple sheet music.

"Do you want to drive?" Dona asked Barbara. "We'll go by way of Glenwood if you do."

"Sure," Barbara eagerly responded. She'd taken driver's training in school and all she needed was a little more confidence in herself when she was behind the wheel.

"The road's straight and flat for several miles," her mother assured her.

Highway 136 went from Madison to Glenwood, then made a ninety degree turn south toward a spattering of residences arranged next to a large Catholic Church and convent. Gargantuan barns and spacious, well-kept grounds were part of the convent property, and Dona understood that the community was self-sustaining, with productive farmland, orchards and a dairy included in the operation.

The purpose of the community was obviously to sustain the inhabitants of the abbey that dominated broad hills to the south. A huge red brick monastery was at the center of the compound of buildings. It was surrounded with several lesser but also massive buildings, where the students who attended the seminary were educated and housed. Often black-robed priests strolled the grounds, with other young men in evidence out jogging or riding bicycles for exercise. The girls had once been in the gymnasium for an inoculation program for students of area schools. This was in response to a smallpox scare a few years earlier, while the girls were enrolled in the nearby Star of the West School. Dona would like to go there herself and see the inside of the church. She'd heard it was magnificent and that it was known throughout the world.

Dona didn't expect much traffic on the road at this time of day. Farmers were already wherever they were headed on their tractors this morning--had probably been at work for hours. Dona had become aware of the cycles of farming since she'd been on the road so much the past few years. In the spring, she'd encounter tractors with cultivators as early as the fields had dried sufficiently. Then the stubble strewn across the countryside would be magically remodeled into a corduroy mantle of soft, black loam. As the scene shifted to summer, a startling emergence of green quickly overlaid the fields in a patchwork of varying hues and textures. The rich bottom land beside the highway had been laid down by the Platte River eons ago and now held the wealth of the county, waiting to be coaxed into production by the efforts of its current stewards. It seemed that simple to Dona as they drove along beside the hump of the railroad right-of-way that paralleled the highway.

In summer, Dona would be on the lookout for tractors pulling lowboys of hay, stacked so high they swayed perilously with each dip in the roadbed. Slow-moving combines would crowd their way along the highway in the fall, causing other traffic to slow and honk. During the autumn months, trucks heavy with corn and soybeans were headed for the elevators and drying bins. That was her favorite time of the year, when she was often outside enjoying the spectacle of Missouri's hardwood forests.

Dona realized that she hadn't been tuned into the process when she had spent all those years on the farm. Maybe she had more time now to reflect on the positive aspects of rural life since she was no longer involved in the day-to-day struggle.

Barbara had no trouble steering the big Pontiac down the smooth blacktop road. Only a couple of curves broke the comfortable monotony of twelve miles of flat, straight highway leading into Bedford. Barbara's gear shifting wasn't too smooth, but on that roadway there were only two stops before they reached their destination and Dona took over the driving. Barbara was very cautious, so Dona's nerves weren't too strained during such trial periods.

After the girls had finished their music lessons, they usually went downtown to Verna's Joint for ice cream cones. Verna's was the town tavern, but she also had a case filled with deep cylinders of ice cream in tempting flavors. The youngsters thought her offering was the best ice cream, at the best bargain, of anywhere in the world. They could get an overflowing double dipper cone for ten cents--just the amount refunded from their lessons. What a treat!

Occasionally Barbara and Coralea supplemented their small weekly allowance with money from babysitting jobs. They liked to stop in at Groves Drug Store after school and have chocolate cokes with the crowd there. Dona encouraged this as long as they didn't stay late or spend too much. The soda fountain was just a block north of the Light Company where she worked. The youngsters who hung out there were cliquish and the girls were at first uncomfortable around the affluent kids of the town. Many students rode the bus home to the country, while some stopped at one of several places uptown to socialize before walking on home. Dona remembered how she had felt left out of activities in Summerville because she'd been a farm kid, and wanted it to be different for her daughters. Retha had told her children that they were not poor, but Dona never really believed it. She would like to convince her girls that they were, truly, as good as anyone else going to the school.

Most of the girls' babysitting jobs were with an eight-year-old boy whose parents ran the Candlelight Inn, a combination tavern and gas station north of the Goad house on South Main. The couple lived a few blocks to the west so the girls could walk over and they were brought home after midnight, the bar's closing time.

When Barbara was fifteen and Coralea thirteen, they took on a regular cleaning job for a local lawyer. He shared an office with a young attorney who was just beginning his law practice. The men were nice to work for and allowed the girls to be flexible in their hours, sometimes hiring them to do extra typing, also.

Besides this weekly job, the girls cleaned house on Saturdays for Barbara's English teacher, wife of the lawyer. They had a lesson in compassion when they began at her house. Mrs. Ebling was a particular lady who seemed haughty and aloof at school. But, seeing her at home in an informal setting and in her everyday clothes, the girls quickly recognized the generous nature of the enigmatic woman. In one upstairs bedroom was a large baby bed. An emaciated old man lay there in a diaper, with a catheter attached to the side of the bed. He was Mr. Ebling's father, himself once a noted judge from the Rock Port area. The Eblings had cared for him in their home since he first became helpless. Their depth of personal dedication made a lasting impression on the girls and gave them a refreshing example of devotion within a family.

Due to its location in America's farm belt, Madison offered opportunities for employment in the summer to kids who weren't afraid of hard work. Dona wasn't sure that description fit her girls, but she did encourage them to sign on for detasseling corn in July. One had to be fourteen to qualify for the work, so Sharon would have to stay home by herself while the other two were gone all day. But Dona would be home for lunch and could check in on her then.

Both Cargill and DeKalb seed companies had planted large fields in the Weston area, so workers from Madison would be transported forty miles, with travel time included in the $1.00 per hour pay scale. This was vastly more than they could make babysitting, so Barbara and Coralea were eager to give it a try, although they had no idea what the job entailed.

The crew met at the courthouse early in the morning to climb into the back of a stock truck for the trip. The girls recognized a few other workers from Madison, besides Coralea's friend, Patty, who'd signed up with them.

When Dona got home from work their first day on the job, Sharon had started supper and Barbara and Coralea were stretched out on the bed and sofa, respectively, sunburned and obviously worn out.

"Well, how was it?" Dona asked, though quite aware of their state of exhaustion.

"Grueling!"

"Hot!"

"Miserable!"

"Grimy!"

Their answers came in a barrage of complaints.

"Does this mean you don't want to go back?" she asked then.

"No. It just means we're tired and can't move!" Barbara assured her from the other room.

"You should have seen them when they got home!" Sharon chimed in.

"We were a mess!" Barbara stated. "I've never been so filthy! We walked home down Market Street so no one would see us."

"Can you come and get us tomorrow, Mom?" Coralea asked.

"Well, I've got to work, you know . . . " Dona began.

"But we won't be getting home 'til five o'clock. They let us off early today because it was the first day."

"They could see we weren't going to last," Barbara told her mother.

"Some of them said they weren't going back tomorrow," Coralea said. "They thought the work was too hard."

"But you think you can do it?" Dona asked skeptically as her daughter's form lay, sprawled and drained, before her.

"I feel pretty good now that I'm home--and cleaned up," she announced. "Nibs on the first bath tomorrow!" she hastened to add.

"I think you'd better find some straw hats to wear tomorrow," Dona suggested. "You both look burned already."

Boys and girls rode together in the truck that took them to the fields, but once there the crews were separated and given assignments by their foremen. Most quickly became accustomed to the motions required to pull the tassels from the tops of the corn stalks. They soon found that it helped to be tall, with long arms.

On most days, when the weather was dry and hot, pollen from the maturing tassels rained down onto their hair and stuck to the perspiration on their faces and arms. If the preceding night had brought showers to the area, the ground between the rows was slippery or sticky, forcing them to take more time maneuvering down the long rows. Besides the hindrance underfoot, each time a worker reached up to pull down a stalk so she could remove the tassel, an accumulation of water spilled out of the valleys where the leaves emerged, wetting her thoroughly. The hat idea hadn't worked out, as the stiff tentacles of the corn leaves easily swiped them off.

Each day when they arrived home the girls calculated how much money they'd made so far. Barbara planned to spend her earnings on clothes, and Coralea wanted to make enough money to buy a secondhand cornet. She'd joined the band the year before, playing on a rental instrument. On Sunday they got time-and-a-half for overtime pay. When the fields were ready, the tassels must be removed promptly to avoid unwanted pollination, so it was critical that the workers were both speedy and thorough.

"The foreman comes behind you and checks your row," Barbara told her mother. "If you miss too many you get fired--some people have been already."

"You don't want to see the foreman coming out of your row with a bunch of tassels in her hand!" Coralea declared.

"How have you been doing?" Dona asked.

"She found a couple on mine the other day. I don't know how I missed them!" Coralea told her mother.

"You wouldn't believe how long the rows are sometimes, Mom!" Barbara interjected.

"You get real hot in there and you feel like you'll never get to the end of the row! And you're praying that if you do, there'll be a bucket of water waiting for you!" Coralea said emphatically.

The fields they worked were clean, that is, free of weeds and orderly. Most were on flat bottom ground in Atchison County near the Missouri, Nodaway, or Nishna Botna rivers. The pattern to be maintained was two rows left with tassels, then six detasseled. This somehow allowed the correct degree of fertilization for the seed corn. By the time the detasseling crews were brought in, the corn stalks soared five to seven feet tall and the ears had developed silks, still soft and damp. A strong odor permeated the atmosphere near the fields--a thick, musty smell that hung in the air and filled the lungs. The girls would be startled, years later, by the mixed feelings that scent abruptly called to mind.

Between each field was a grassy beltway where the truck driver waited with cans of cold water. When the workers emerged at these blessed oases, they had a few minutes to sit and rest. The first ones out had a good break before all the workers were through with the rows. Sometimes they would be asked to go back in and "dig out" one of their comrades, who was still back in the jungle of green

On crisp mornings, when there was a gentle breeze, the work could be almost pleasant. Then the softly swaying masses of corn seemed to whisper. But on most days the sun beat down mercilessly, the air in the long rows was stifling, and the whisper turned to a hiss. One worker had fainted in her row. The girls decided not to tell their mother about this incident right away. She was such a worrier.

Jeans and long sleeved shirts must be worn to protect against slicing cuts from sharp leaf edges. Usually the girls wore halter tops so they could peel off their shirts if the heat was so oppressive it outweighed the cutting danger. Both girls developed blisters on their shoulders from long days spent under the scorching sun.

As they became acquainted with the other workers, the girls began to enjoy the trips up and back. There was constant chatter and occasionally someone told a joke or an amusing story. Before the truck made it back to Madison, the group usually started up the "Hundred Bottles of Beer" song, so their entrance into town wasn't exactly discreet. However, Dona was there to meet the girls and spare them the humiliation of being seen bedraggled and sweaty by anyone else they knew.

In the two weeks they worked, each girl made over eighty dollars. Assuming that the work was half as laborious as they'd described it to her, Dona was proud of them for sticking it out.

Dona was pleased that Coralea wanted to spend her money on an instrument. She had been in the band for a while and her mother realized her motivation was mostly that her friend was in the band and that going on band trips was fun. Coralea rarely practiced, but Dona had to admit to herself that she couldn't complain about that. She was disappointed, though, that the new horn didn't sound any better than the old one had.

"Guess what, girls?" Dona asked one evening as she came in the door. She usually walked home and was tired and ready to sink into her easy chair for some time to herself. Not waiting for an answer, she continued, "We may get to go to Minnesota this summer!"

"How?" Barbara asked with interest, wondering what miracle might have provided the wherewithal for such an extravagance.

"I'm going to be hostess for the 'Dream Kitchen!'" Dona exclaimed. "You remember--the fancy room under the Light Company. They've asked me to help with it. That means overtime, maybe a couple of evenings a week."

"But, where will Grandma be?" Sharon asked, remembering Retha didn't always go north with her husband.

"She told me she intends to go up with Dad this year," Dona informed the girls.

"When will we go?" Coralea asked.

"Whenever I get my week's vacation," Dona replied, " . . . in July or August, I imagine. Won't that be fun? Grandpa can take you fishing in a lake. There are lakes so big there you can't see across them!"

"Can we go when detasseling is over?" Coralea asked. She anticipated earning some money for herself again.

"I imagine we can arrange that," Dona allowed.

"Can we stay at a motel?" Sharon asked.

"We'll just stay with Mom and Dad, wherever they are," Dona replied. She knew her folks would be tickled to have visitors from Missouri, especially them.

After more excited inquiries from the girls, she knew she'd have no trouble getting them interested in the trip.

Working at the Light Company was already a rewarding experience for Dona. She spoke with many Madison residents at least once a month when they came in to pay their utility bills and she had become quite comfortable talking with the customers. The girls were surprised when people they met in their transactions in town always knew their mother. Dona Bowen was the pleasant woman who always smiled her greeting at the Light Company.

For a nominal fee, civic organizations could use the company's facilities for meetings or entertaining. Individuals also rented the Dream Kitchen for special occasions, such as wedding anniversaries or family re-unions. To Dona, being hostess of the Dream Kitchen soon became the most rewarding aspect of her job with the power company. She wore her nicest clothes for the job, as she had more personal interactions with the public.

On nights when she was called to serve, she left home early so she'd have time to admire the spotless white stoves and refrigerators before anyone else arrived. The custodian kept the place meticulous, but Dona still polished the chrome knobs and handles, running her hands over the smooth, gleaming surfaces and wishing she had them to use in her own kitchen. Both gas and electric models were hooked up for use by the public, so prospective buyers could compare features of both types of appliances. The modern conveniences of the Dream Kitchen included all manner of labor-saving devices, inducing visitors to check out the offerings on the sales floor upstairs.

Dona couldn't conceive of having such wonderful appointments to actually use, but she did enjoy fantasizing about the possibility. She saw herself demonstrating the latest models of each apparatus, as she had once seen in a commercial on the television at Miriam's. She envisioned herself pulling a casserole from the oven as she stood, smartly clad in a frilly apron and smiling in the security of a happy, affluent home.

Sometimes reality broke into such reverie as she thought of her experiences in her own kitchen. The girls had started referring to her casseroles as Mess # 13, or Mess # 206, etc. Her concoctions were usually based on tuna, Spam or lunchmeat, with extenders of some kind. Whatever leftovers were available she tossed in also. Actually, some of the experiments turned out quite well, and her family bragged about them, asking to have them again. But the same dish never happened twice. She liked to think that was because she was so creative.

Dona decided to ask her family over for dinner on Easter Sunday that spring. Everyone came except for Grant, who was in an institution, and Earlene and Emmett, who had recently moved to Oregon.

The three-room apartment was full of family that day--more people than she had ever cooked for. It seemed strange to Dona not to go to Sam and Retha's for the occasion. The Schmits had been hosts to family get-togethers for as long as Dona could remember. But she was happy to be taking over some of the work for her mother.

By the time August rolled around that year, Barbara was working at the new Dairy Queen, built next door to the Goad house. Sharon had taken over Barbara's part of the cleaning job uptown, and both she and Coralea had toiled for two weeks in the cornfields. Sharon joined the high school band, so she wanted to buy a trombone. Dona thought the girls looked sharp in their crisp green and white band uniforms, and both girls were benefiting socially from their involvement with the music group.

As the time for their journey approached, Dona had second thoughts about making the trip north. Her car was old, the tires weren't good, and she didn't know the road. But, she'd promised the girls this vacation three years ago, and now that they were helping with their own expenses, she felt she had to make good on her word. Highway 71 led to Granite Falls, Minnesota, where Sam and Retha were staying. Maybe she was thinking too much of those previous trips out West with her parents when they were truly balanced on the edge of economic doom. Barbara had her license now, so maybe she could help with the driving if Dona got tired.

Luckily, the week of the trip started out pleasant and mild, so the big Pontiac was comfortable with the windows rolled down. As they neared the Iowa state line, they passed large cornfields lying just beyond the right-of-way.

"Phew! Smell that corn!" Sharon complained.

"It does have a sweet, sickening odor, doesn't it?" Dona commiserated.

"I'd sure know that smell anywhere," Coralea added to the conversation.

"Did your crew do that field?" their mother asked.

"I don't know," replied Coralea. "They all look alike to me. I didn't pay much attention to where we were going. When the truck stopped, we just fell out and went to work!"

An even grid of dark and light stripes ran for a distance to a line of trees that marked the meandering path of the Nodaway River. Rows of frothy tassels dominated the spaces between dark ribbons of green marching in uniform bands across the flat earth. Before each stripe stood a DeKalb seed corn sign in the shape of a voluptuous ear of corn--a pretty splash of color that punctuated the end of the planting.

Her perception of the girls' efforts changed considerably when Dona saw firsthand the size of the undertaking. The length of the rows and the density of the plants made the task of removing every single tassel look daunting. She wasn't sure she could have done it herself. Considering the utter exhaustion of the girls when they had finished a day pulling tassels, Dona understood why they failed to see the beauty of the orderly display. She thought it looked immensely rich and productive, unlike the small plots in her corner of Missouri, which were often on slopes and irregular in shape, following the contours of hills and valleys.

Just beyond Clarinda, a sudden wobble in the back of the car alerted Dona to tire trouble.

"Uh-oh! I'm afraid we have a flat!" she announced as she gradually slowed and pulled to the side of the road. She wished now she'd swallowed her pride and asked Hank to check the tires before they started out.

Dona had had plenty of experience changing tires, but soon another motorist noticed the four females in their plight and pulled over to lend a hand.

"This spare doesn't look too dependable," he remarked as he lifted it into place. "You'd better get your tire fixed right away and replace it."

They went on to a gas station to have the tire checked, only to hear it was ruined beyond repair and they'd need to buy a replacement. That would take a sizable chunk out of their travel money. Dona reluctantly gave some consideration to turning back. This was not a good way to begin their adventure. But, she hated to disappoint everyone, especially her folks, who had let her know how much they looked forward to the visit. She bought the most reasonable tire that looked like it might hold up and made up her mind to forge ahead, with the hope that their bad luck was behind them.

The girls took turns sitting beside Dona in the front seat. The wide, deep seats gave them room to stretch out, and they'd brought pillows along to make the hours on the road more comfortable. Dona had wondered about entertaining them on the long trip, but the girls were full of observations about the countryside. She realized they'd seldom been out of the state of Missouri.

For a while, Sharon napped beside her mother in the front seat. Her hair lay in soft blonde folds beside her face. She had given up the pigtails she'd worn for years and now her hair was cut short like Coralea's. Sharon's hair had darkened as she matured and was now the color of ripe wheat, not as dark as Coralea's yet, and lighter, still, than her oldest sister's. Barbara managed to inherit some of Dona's natural curl, so she never pinned her hair up in curls as the other two did. Dona had become proficient at helping the girls braid their hair, but putting in pin curls was beyond her.

Dona began to sing to keep herself awake. They had been on the road several hours--about an hour behind where she'd planned to be by now because of the flat. She could see they wouldn't make the trip up in one day, as she had hoped. They would have to stop at a motel. That would make the girls happy. The highway was straight and flat, but she'd rather not ask Barbara to drive. She wasn't that experienced, and it would be a lot of responsibility for her.

They sang some of the old songs Dona taught them when they were little, then continued on with a few songs from high school chorus that they sang in rounds. Dona especially liked "White Coral Bells" the way the girls sang in their clear, high voices. At home they often sang in the kitchen as they shared in doing the dishes after supper. Somehow the work got finished quicker when they harmonized. It was definitely finished with less squabbling between the sometimes-contentious siblings.

By evening they reached Spencer, apparently comparable to Madison in size. It was situated on an ox-bow lake formed by the Little Sioux River. The motel where they stopped was on a curve across the road from this lake, the largest body of water the girls had ever seen.

Early the next day they came to Lake Okoboji, which was vastly larger. On the other side of the water was an enticing carnival the girls would've liked to stop for, but one day of their vacation was already gone and the Schmits expected them soon. Dona wasn't prepared for that kind of extra spending, anyhow.

"There are plenty of lakes to see in Minnesota," she assured the girls.

" 'The land of 10,000 lakes' is what it says on the state's license plates," Barbara contributed. "I wonder how many of them Grandpa has tried out."

"I'm sure he'll show us a few," laughed Dona.

The first thing they noticed about the Granite Falls area was the abundance of rocky outcroppings. As they traveled into northern Minnesota, the level land gave way to wide elevations that broke through the thin soil in gray, angular masses. The vegetation was scraggly and not so vividly green as in Iowa. In spite of all the lakes, the land seemed drier, and poorer. It was pretty, in a way, Dona thought, and not like anywhere she had been. She was glad they'd continued on with their journey.

Retha enthusiastically greeted them at the door of their place, a renovated motel room. Sam was at work on the highway crew, so Retha ushered them in and made room for their things in a corner of the place. Dona could see that it was going to be a cozy few days. There was a bed, a couch, a small table with chairs and a tabletop gas cooking unit, all very compactly fitted into one room. There was just that area and a tiny bathroom, but they wouldn't be spending much time inside, anyhow.

Dona thought she'd never seen her mother look so rested. Retha's tanned face had lost the anxious, drawn look she'd displayed for some time. She had evidently spent some time sitting beside Sam on the bank, relaxing with him as he fished.

"Dad's taking a couple of days off while you're here," Retha told Dona. "He's too tired to do much in the evenings when he's worked all day in the hot sun."

"He doesn't need to entertain us, Mom. We're just glad to be here with you," Dona assured her mother.

"Oh, he's been waiting for you to get here! You're our only guests, besides the Hollidays, who were here one weekend. Girls, you've grown even more!" She wanted to give them each a hug but figured they thought themselves too old for that.

The first place Sam took them the next day was to a huge lake where he often went to fish.

"My goodness! It has whitecaps!" Dona exclaimed as they strolled along the shore. She was surprised at the coolness of the air blowing off the foamy surface.

"It's not usually this choppy," he told her. "It's pretty windy today--not much good for fishing."

"What kind of fish do you catch up here?" Dona asked.

"Walleye and northern pike, mostly, and carp. No catfish in the lakes, but you might get some at the river. I'm thinking we might go fishing there tomorrow." The girls thought that was a great idea and informed him that they would try their best to be quiet for him.

Sam used stinky bait he made himself out of Limburger cheese. The girls thought it was disgusting, even worse than worms, but they were happy to take a pole and watch for the bobber to disappear. There was a lot of excitement in the group when they caught a "keeper."

"There's a carnival here on the ice in the winter," Sam told them.

"On the ice?" Barbara asked, incredulously.

"Yep! Ferris wheel, merry-go-round--all of it."

"How do they do that?" Sharon wanted to know. As far as she could see, such a thing was beyond the realm of possibility.

"The ice gets so thick, you could drive a semi out on it," Sam explained. Dona noticed his blue eyes still had the twinkle she had always admired. "The ice is sometimes as much as two feet deep on the river here. It makes a clear, smooth place for the carnival. We've never been here during the winter, but I've seen pictures of the winter carnival. It really does happen!" Dona could see the girls trying to make up their minds whether to believe him or not. She did, anyhow.

On their last day in Minnesota, Dona sat with her mother at the table, talking.

"Hank thinks we should sell the farm and move up to Lenox near him and Beulah," Retha announced.

Dona looked at her mother in surprise. She hoped her parents weren't seriously thinking of making such a move. A sea of sadness engulfed her as she gave the possibility some thought.

"We sold the back forty to Benny Coulter last year. You knew that," Retha went on to say.

"But, Mom. That place is home to you. You've surely been there longer than anywhere else you ever lived!" she blurted, feeling a sudden tightness in her throat.

"We could sell the place, buy a house in Lenox and live on Sam's Social Security. We'd be near Hank then . . . "

Why did Dona feel as if her brother were taking them away from her? She couldn't begin to explain the feelings her face betrayed.

"There's no one left in Bedford for us anymore," Retha was saying. "Stanley and Marge have moved into town and the Coulters turned their farm over to Benny awhile back. We haven't any neighbors now."

It hadn't occurred to her before, but Dona imagined now how lonely it must have been for her mother out on the farm the last few years. Of course, it would be better for them to be close to Hank. Still, she couldn't shake the feeling of loss she was experiencing.

"We won't go right away. Dad wants to work on the highway one more season, if he's able. Hank says it'll make a lot of difference in his Social Security," Retha said reassuringly, aware of the anguish Dona felt.

"I'm surprised he's agreed to take those checks," Dona stated.

"Well, we really have no choice, I guess. It's not an easy decision for him. You know that."

Dona couldn't conceive of her folks agreeing to leave their home. Hank must have scared them into the decision. No. She didn't believe that. Her brother was compassionate, and she knew his devotion to his parents to be as true as her own. Dona dreaded telling the girls of their grandparents' plans. She knew the move would mean they'd be seeing them less often. Lenox was a lot farther away, up in Iowa--beyond Edgerton, where she and June had lived with their babies.

As she tried to project an attitude of approval, Dona wrestled with her confusing emotions. She didn't know why she sensed such impending loss. It was as if her last ties to Bedford were being broken. She reminded herself that not all of her days there had been happy ones, but that didn't assuage her misgivings. It seemed to her that she and the town shared a history she might soon lose. Strangely, she felt as if she could soon lose a large part of herself.

TWENTY-ONE

Dona soon came to terms with Sam and Retha's decision to move to Lenox. She realized her folks had spent a good portion of their lives being there for her and the girls. They certainly deserved restful retirement years while they were still in good health.

The girls, Dona realized, had grown away from close attachments to their grandparents. While Sam and Retha were not openly critical of the teenagers, Dona sensed a subtle resentment of their boldness and an unspoken disapproval of their attire. She didn't consider shorts and halters too risqué—she would wear them herself if she thought they looked good on her. But her folks were of a different generation, and Sam was, after all, a hard-shell Baptist, though he'd never practiced his faith to the extent of attending church, at least not in the years that she could recall. Her folks had been very strict with her--less strict by the time Carrie came along. But they never fully accepted the casual modern dress or behavior. She knew the girls considered their grandparents old-fashioned, and fervently hoped they didn't lose sight of the fact that the generous couple had lovingly nurtured them through some very rough years.

As a result of her new job, Barbara could buy her own clothes and no longer depended on hand-me-downs. She spent most of her earnings on dresses she ordered from the Lana LoBelle catalog. Her trim figure easily fit into standard, ready-to-wear sizes. She wasn't eager to share her nice things with her sisters, which disappointed them, but Dona thought that was reasonable--she had earned them for herself.

Both Barbara and Coralea now had boy friends whom they dated regularly. These occasions often involved school functions or evenings at the movie theater. In the summer, the Trail Ride Drive-in Theater was the frequent destination of many of the town's young people. Sometimes the girls went on double dates--just the sisters and their beaus. Dona was no longer responsible for taking the girls everywhere they needed or wanted to go, for their friends took them to school, as well.

Dona didn't miss having her own social life until the girls started going out. She had had few dates in the years since moving to Madison. She had occasionally gone out with a fellow from Shenandoah. She once stayed out until the early hours with this salesman, whom the girls didn't care for, and they had been awake worrying about her. When she attempted to explain that as an adult the rules were different for her than for them, the girls protested that the same rules they had should apply to her as well, as she had the added responsibility of three others depending on her. She had to acknowledge that her circumstances could and should make a difference in her expected behavior. She vowed to remind herself that she was a role model and did not want to jeopardize the respect she had earned from her family. In many ways, she felt she was maturing along with her girls.

Dona's new relationship was not serious, and she began to realize she didn't care much for the man even as a friend, allowing to herself that his traveling salesman occupation did nothing to enhance his personal appeal. She suspected that being the head of a household had given her a feeling of freedom she'd grown more than comfortable with.

The girls had grown up so fast--Dona felt unprepared for the independence they demonstrated. She could hardly believe that when school reopened she'd have three daughters in high school! It seemed to her that a new issue surfaced on a daily basis. How late should they be allowed to stay out on dates? Could one of them go on an overnight trip with a friend's family? Could they babysit overnight? A lot of serious decisions had to be made, and she wanted to get it right and also to be fair.

One summer, Dona and the girls spent her two week vacation at the Schmit farm by Bedford. They considered it a relaxing get-away, even without Retha present, as she was in Minnesota with Sam. Dona's family made a trip to Lenox, Iowa, to visit Hank and Beulah. They had located in that town to be near Beulah's father, who was alone now. Hank and his wife had moved to a newer house and were eager to show it off. Short trips to visit friends and relatives were major sources of pleasure for the group during the years they lived on South Main Street. Gas was fairly inexpensive and the excursions they went on were usually within a thirty-mile radius of Madison.

In the Schmits' absence, the lawn had grown unmolested, so their house was surrounded by a wild scramble of grass. This made their stay seem even more like camping out when Dona and the girls took over the place. No animals remained, except the cows that grazed in the pasture Sam had rented out for the season.

One pleasant day they decided it would be fun to cook out, so they made preparations for a campfire back in the woods—far enough that they couldn't see the house. To get to the "back 40" they must avoid the pasture with the cows because of the menacing bull in with them.

The biggest elm tree Dona had ever seen stood beside the gate that led back to the long-deserted homestead. Beneath it, two massive corner posts marked the entrance to nowhere, it appeared. The long-abandoned roadway they followed was so overgrown it was hard to recognize. Coralea knew her way back to the old place, though. She had no trouble leading them. She was Dona's woods-walker. When Barbara would be reading or primping and Sharon would be daydreaming or helping her mother with something, Coralea would be out roaming the countryside, discovering nooks and crannies along the creek and listening for the voices of the forest creatures. Dona, too, loved the country sounds, especially the lonesome, cooing calls of the mourning doves, and she considered the nightly racket of the crickets and cicadas to be a special kind of bedtime song.

Abruptly, the path through the woods ended where a pond had been bulldozed into place. There was no trace of the old clapboard structure that years before had been cannibalized for Sam's house project. The old barn was still there, the doors gaping black holes with rusty pieces of farm equipment lurking in the recesses.

Dona's stomach began to knot as she remembered the gloom of the place where her brother lived before he was put into an institution. As the girls recalled their experiences on the place, Dona happily realized they remembered only the pleasant parts of their stay there while in the care of their grandparents.

Hot dogs, marshmallows and lemonade, their usual picnic staples, were prepared and enjoyed by Dona, her girls, and a friend of Barbara's from the Bedford community. Getting out in the woods for such relaxing hours was a treat for all of them, but especially for Dona, who loved to don old, comfortable clothing and chat with her daughters and their friends. She also appreciated the low-cost aspect of such adventures.

When the phone rang at the farm that evening, Dona and Sharon were the only ones there. It was Friday and the two older girls had gone to the Horton Picnic with their beaus. Most of the calls they got in Bedford were for the girls. Barbara's boyfriend, Don, was especially chatty. Everyone knew the Schmits were gone for the summer, so Dona wondered who would be on the line when she took the receiver down from the old wall phone.

"Jimmie?" she repeated after he identified himself. She was surprised, in a way, to hear from him.

"Mom saw the girls in town yesterday, and they said you were down for a few days . . . " he began.

"Oh. They did tell me they ran into Nora at Earl Rickman's store--I mean, Al Wilson's store, now. I guess it'll take me awhile to get used to that change." She felt her conversation meander aimlessly.

"Mom was as giddy as a schoolgirl when she got home. She said they were having too much fun--reminded her of herself and her girlfriends when they were young and hanging around in Bedford."

"I hope they weren't causing problems," Dona worried.

"Oh, no! I didn't mean that. Mom enjoyed talking with them. I think she got a kick out of remembering the old days when she was a girl. She still has pictures of sleepovers she had with her friends. I imagine my mother was as ornery as any kid that ever lived in Bedford," he said as he laughed, a little nervously.

Dona found that hard to imagine, Nora a teenager, but she'd never gotten to know Jimmie's mother very well. She wondered why he had called, though she had to admit to herself that she had hoped, perhaps even planned, that he would.

"Why don't you come out?" she suggested. "Just Sharon and I are home this evening."

While he was on his way, Dona dashed around tidying up the place, while her mind rushed around remembering times past. She and Jimmie hadn't had a very serious friendship. He was younger than she--not by much, but she had always felt much older. She often suspected that's why he was attracted to her--she appeared worldly and self-assured. At least she had attempted to. There were times through the years when she had speculated on what a life with him might be like and wondered whether he had had similar flights of fancy.

Their reunion was as uncomplicated as it could possibly be. She greeted him warmly as a dear old friend, as in reality he was, though she knew at one time they had been more than friends. They talked of the community--which of her acquaintances were still around and such. Ross and Gail had moved away. Junior and Caroline Black still lived in the same house in Bedford. Edith and Bill Lynch were out in Washington state.

Dona wanted to ask Jimmie about Amabelle but assumed she was no longer a part of his life. Probably Mrs. Martin didn't like her. Amabelle was Catholic, and besides that, her family now lived on the farm Nora's father, Jed Torrance, had lost a few years earlier. And Dona sensed that no woman would ever be good enough, in Nora's mind at least, for her son.

"How is Merry?" Dona asked. "Does she still live in the little house by the ditch?"

"She's still there," Jimmie assured her.

"I remember the time she waded the floodwater to get back to her place. She's pretty spunky!" Dona declared.

"I come from a long line of spunky people," he told her.

"Well, that could be good . . . or otherwise!" she suggested.

"Bertha McMurtry died this spring. She was your neighbor, you remember."

"I'm sorry to hear that. I guess Dee's been gone for several years," Dona recalled.

"Calvin decided to close his store, so now we have just two grocery stores in town. There hasn't been a new house built in Bedford for twenty years, I bet. Not unless you count the houses Rob Brooks built across the creek for two of his daughters. He made them by splitting and moving the depot. Trains don't stop in Bedford anymore. And I've heard that Chase Richey is closing his dry-goods store. The town is shrinking, Dona!"

"Where's everyone going?" she asked.

"Somewhere else, I guess," he replied with a shrug. "Everyone was upset when they consolidated the schools last year, but the classes had gotten down to where there were fewer than ten kids in each grade, so they just about had to. They couldn't afford to hire enough teachers for the high school subjects."

"At least there's still a grade school," Dona volunteered.

"It's hard on a town to lose its high school. It seems like all the activity leaves along with the kids. I guess I shouldn't talk, though."

"What do you mean?" *Surely Jimmie isn't planning to leave, too.*

"We moved out to the McBain place this spring. Didn't you know?"

"Where is that?" she asked with renewed interest.

"Well, if you went straight north of where we're sitting for a mile you'd be in our front yard. We live in the next section."

"Section?" she asked.

"Square mile. Most of the country is marked off in mile sections. You may not have noticed, but there's generally a road of some kind at the end of every section. For instance, if you take the road over by Stanley Benson's place north for a mile, then turn back west and take that section road a half mile, you're at our place," he told her.

"That's Joey Davis's house!" Sharon chimed in. "We used to walk to school with him to Star of the West. Only he got to ride a pony, usually. We didn't think that was fair, because we had to go twice as far as he did. And we felt sorry for the horse because it had to stand in the pony shed all day waiting for school to be over."

"The Davises lived there for a few years, but it's been known as the McBain place for a long time. Do you know the house, Dona?" he asked.

"Is it a two-story stucco with a big front porch?" she ventured.
"That's the one."
"Why did you move?" she asked, finding it hard to imagine him and Nora living anywhere but in the house on the hill in Bedford.
"More acres, and easier to get to," was his answer. "Besides, the house is more modern, if you know what I mean."
She knew. Sam had finally gotten the electricity hooked up, but plumbing on the place was nonexistent.
"How does Nora like it there?" she asked.
"She says she does. She's taken up driving again since she can't just walk down to town any more. She has a good garden spot, and she's always messing around in the yard. Come and see it. She'd like to see you."
Dona wasn't too sure about that, but maybe she would go anyhow. She knew there was a side to Jimmie's mother she had never known. She thought of the quip June had repeated to her once, back when he was working for Jimmie. Nora had put on layers of cold-weather garb to do the chores and had remarked, "I can't die now. The undertaker would never get to me!"
Dona thoroughly enjoyed Jimmie's lengthy stay.

Next morning, the first topic of conversation was opened by Sharon.
"Guess who was here last night?" she asked her sisters.
"And guess who has a date to the Horton Picnic tonight?" Dona added.
They had no trouble guessing.
"You can drive over to Horton tonight," she told Barbara. The Saturday night program included special culminating events they didn't want to miss. "You can find us at the Bingo tent if you need anything." She looked forward to not having to follow the girls around but was a little reticent at the thought of starting gossip. Then she realized that probably few people cared about her personal life!

Some weeks later, Dona would decide that her family had quite a lot of spunk, also. The girls wanted to walk to their grandmother's, a twenty-mile trek. One last hurrah before school began.
"But you've never walked more than a couple of miles!" she protested.
"We'd have all day," Sharon urged.
"All you'd have to do is come down and get us," Coralea added.
"I can't come until after work, you know. And what if one of you got sick--too hot or something? It is August, remember," Dona warned.
"We'll be walking right by Carrie's place. She could help us," Barbara suggested, as she gave her mother a reassuring look.

"You're planning on going the country way? That helps some. There's no way I'd let you walk down Highway 71."

"Please, Mom. School's starting soon, and who knows when we'll get another chance!" Coralea begged.

"Just how many of you plan to make this journey?" Dona asked, beginning to see possibilities in the adventure.

"Oh, maybe seven or eight," Coralea proposed. "We should ask Lone to go, too, since she and Patty are such good friends."

"Lone?" Dona asked.

"Leona Brown, Mom. You know her!"

"Oh! Of course," Dona acknowledged with an amused smile. Lately the girls had taken on shorthand forms of their names. Barbara was almost always "Barb" to everyone but her mother, and Coralea was "Corky" or "Cork" to not just her family anymore, but to everyone who knew her. June had commenced calling his youngest daughter "Sherry" long ago and it had stuck.

"I suppose you and Patty hatched this up," Dona guessed.

"Uh-huh," Coralea responded, "and Lana wants to go, too."

"She's pretty young. Do you think she can do it?" Dona asked, remembering Patty's little sister.

"Lana's got more energy than any of us!" Barbara assured her.

"I suppose I could bring picnic stuff down and you could have a campfire at the farm," Dona offered, warming to the girls' enthusiasm.

"Oh! Thanks, thanks, thanks!" Sharon squealed.

"On one condition . . . " Dona continued. "I take you out to Beason Corner and you start from there. I'd rather you didn't walk along Highway 40. It's too busy."

A sack of snacks, a bag of sandwiches, and a small jug of ice water were taken along in the car, which was jam-packed with eager girls. Getting a ride for the short stretch of highway east of Madison cut four miles off the undertaking, but the group still faced a sizeable challenge.

"Stay to the side of the road," Dona cautioned. "Stop and rest now and then--it's going to be hot! And call me when you get there. Good luck!" She was impressed with their youthful vitality as they began their journey but wondered how long it would last. The girls' ages ranged from ten to seventeen--she hoped no one would have trouble keeping up the pace.

Dew still lingered on the roadside grasses, birds chirped noisily, and spirits soared as the crew of seven girls bounded down the beckoning roadway. Dona almost wished she could join them, but not quite. Actually, she couldn't remember ever having that kind of energy. Not that the day off from work

A Hundred Miles to the City

wouldn't be appealing, but she couldn't fathom walking that distance willingly, especially on a day that promised to be more than comfortably warm.

By the time they had walked three miles to the lane that went up to Carrie and Frank's house, the girls were already tired enough to decide not to add another half-mile to their outing. They would like to see Carrie's young family, but the long hill was sufficient to deter a visit.

They'd been on the road three hours and had consumed their snacks and drained their jug of water when they reached Route H, the state road east to Bedford.

"It's probably four more miles!" Barb announced. "Can we make it?"

Everyone answered "yes," with varying degrees of conviction.

After walking two miles farther, they trudged, sweating, into Bedford. Hot and exhausted, they had shed their outer shirts. They decided to rest in the schoolyard for a while. The intimidating hill out of town looked as if it went straight up, the blacktop shimmering with waves of heat.

By two o'clock they were on the last leg of their journey--still determined but markedly slower than when they began. Once atop the massive bluff, the girls gratefully looked down to a long stretch of level roadway. Just past Old Town, a stock truck pulled up alongside them. It was Jimmie Martin.

"Want a ride?" he asked, seemingly not surprised to see them there.

The girls gave each other questioning looks, then decided to take him up on the offer--all except Sharon.

"I'm going to finish walking!" she said firmly.

"Aw, come on!" Barbara urged.

"Nope! Go on. It's not much farther. I'll see you there." Her mind was made up, so they argued no more and off she went up the road.

The remaining girls climbed into the back of the truck and sat down to rest, leaning heavily against the rack. They thought Jimmie was a real godsend . . . until he drove on past the Schmit farm! Another mile out, he stopped the truck, jumped out and grinned up at them.

"Now you'll all be walking the same!" he declared.

When they protested, all he said was, "Well, you got to rest and cool off, didn't you?"

Jimmie must have calculated about right. As the grumbling girls approached the Schmit lane from the east, Sharon was just coming up the hill from the west. She could hardly believe her cohorts weren't already there, resting and waiting for her to drag in. She didn't hide her pleasure when she learned the truth. There were some animated complaints, but they all concluded that the trick hadn't done them any harm.

When Dona arrived a few hours later, the girls had regained their energy and happily told her of the surprising end of their daylong adventure. It was obvious to them that their mother had asked her friend to check up on them, and he'd taken it upon himself to add a little mischief to their fun.

It was as if she had moved into a new phase of her life when Dona began seeing Jimmie again. Events of the past years took on a different perception for her, as long repressed emotions teased her memory. She sensed herself relinquishing a struggle she thought she had long since surmounted. Her past became mixed with her present, stirring confusing loyalties that sometimes haunted her.

Dona hadn't heard from the girls' father for years. Neither had Norman nor Mother Bowen. A year earlier Dona received a confusing letter from a woman who claimed to be June's wife, and she included a picture of a baby boy as testament to the relationship. Upset, Dona showed the photo to her children, saying that she supposed the child was their little brother. Years later they would learn that was not true, but at the time the information was taken for fact. No address was given, only an Ada, Oklahoma, postmark. Dona was surprised that she still had an emotional reaction to news of her former husband.

Life in the apartment on South Main changed as the girls became young women finding their own niche in the adult world. Some days Dona felt extremely proud of her efforts as a single mother, and at other times she was certain her good intentions were futile and her children would go as they would, despite her concerned guidance.

It was obvious to Dona that the girls were pleased with her renewed friendship with Jimmie Martin. She supposed they welcomed him as a positive diversion in her life--she would no longer be so involved in their activities. Although they seemed not to mind her interest in their affairs, she sometimes felt she might be mothering them too much. She knew there was a thin line between soothing and smothering and wondered how often she'd stepped over it.

Jimmie and Dona had such a good time at the Horton Picnic they had gone on the next weekend to the Junction Picnic and then to the Midland Bluegrass Festival later in the fall. Dona was charmed with Jimmie's youthful enthusiasm. He obviously enjoyed the gaiety and commotion at these events and she began to feel childlike herself--lighthearted and carefree, as when she'd thrilled to the fairs in Summerville at that long-ago time!

When they were on these happy nights out, Dona was amazed at how many of the people in the adjoining communities knew Jimmie personally--and how many he casually informed her were relatives of his. *He must be related to about everyone in the county,* she thought.

At the Bluegrass Festival he decided to try his luck at the baseball toss. Players were to pitch baseballs at a pyramid of milk bottles a short distance away, in an attempt at knocking them over. Jimmie found the goal harder to achieve than he had expected. Dona pointed out a teddy bear she fancied that hung in an array of stuffed animals meant to lure prospective gamblers to the game. She watched as Jimmie tried again and again, with no success, to topple the stubborn bottles. After he had made countless twenty-five cent attempts, a crowd began to gather. Dona could see that Jimmie enjoyed the attention and his determination to win the bear was only getting stronger. He began to perspire but still grinned broadly. A lock of hair fell across his damp forehead.

The carny worker saw that he had a stayer, so he pulled the bear down and set it on the counter.

"What will you name it?" he asked.

"Whickerbill!" Jimmie replied. Dona wondered where that came from.

"Hey! One more good hit and it's yours!" the toothless fellow prodded.

It was an hour before they walked away with their prize.

"This must be a very expensive bear," Dona ventured.

"About twenty dollars' worth," Jimmie admitted, tapping his slim billfold. The look of satisfaction on his face told her he thought it was worth it, but all she could think was *That was money enough to pay half our month's rent!*

The girls were impressed with the "Whickerbill" story their mother related and she cautioned them that the toy was too precious to handle recklessly. They could hardly imagine such an extravagance. They weren't used to anyone spending money so easily.

Sometimes the girls were included on the outings Jimmie and Dona planned. He liked to take them to things he had enjoyed. One Friday night the girls went along to the wrestling matches in St. Joseph. The contests were held in the City Auditorium, easily the largest building they had been in. The place was dark and smoky and not too clean. The seats they settled into were near the top of the arena where smoke accumulated, making the atmosphere warm and hazy.

Early in their friendship, Dona realized that she and Jimmie would rarely get to any event on time. He obviously didn't consider he'd put in a full day's work unless it had at least begun to get dark. Tonight, with St. Joseph an hour down the road, they had missed a good half of the evening's entertainment.

No matter, though, as several lesser matches were held as warm-ups for the feature encounters of the night.

Two well-known wrestlers were on the bill the evening they attended--Gentleman George and Handsome Harry Rice. These two muscled he-men didn't square off against each other, however, because they were both good guys and so were matched against fellows of the villainous sort. Gentleman George's blonde hair fell in ringlets to his shoulders, handy for the bad guy to tug on. Harry Rice was a local young man who was equally showy. Neither won his bout but only because his adversary had used unfair tactics, and, of course, there would be a grudge match coming up to even the score.

From their perch on high, the girls quietly observed the antics of the scoundrel selected to test the fortitude and sense of fair play of each current wrestling hero. As the rogue approached the ring, ardent shouts arose from the adjacent row of spectators. Arms rose in the air in mock challenges as the crowd enthusiastically entered into the spirit of the contest. Dona wouldn't have been surprised to see over-zealous fans pitch something at the flamboyant villain, who, for his part, strutted with arrogance and occasionally threw menacing looks at the aroused audience.

The response of the crowd to the exaggerated antics of the showmen was both unbelievable and amusing to the girls. Jimmie could see they were a little too sophisticated to appreciate that type of entertainment.

In the spring, Sam and Retha sold their remaining acreage to a young farm couple from the Star of the West community. The Schmits would stay on the place until fall, when the new owners had gotten their crops in and were ready to relocate. This would be Sam's last year on the road crew in Minnesota, and Retha opted to stay on the farm for one last summer. Dona sensed that her mother had ambivalent feelings about the proposed move to Lenox. Sam was seventy-five years old now, a fitting age to be moving into town and closer to family, but Dona's heart ached when she thought of her own ties to the Bedford area being broken. She recalled the years she'd spent on the Richey place just over the hill, when the girls could run over to see their grandparents anytime. It was so comforting having them close. She knew that time was over and recoiled at the reason--her folks were getting old. *Everyone faces this*, she thought. *Why is it so hard for me?*

This summer she and the girls would mow the yard at the farm so it wouldn't get in a wild state like last year. Dona noticed the lack of flowers around her mother's house. Only an old rose bush grew at the corner of the garage, another sign that her mother was slowing down. Retha once delighted in her flower gardens. Dona remembered the hollyhock dancing girls her mother had shown her, and then her daughters, how to make. Now she tended only the African violets she kept in the house. She still had a knack with those, treating them with the same tender care she'd given her family through the years.

Dona began spending more time in Bedford, with her mother and with Jimmie, as he worked his fields or tended his livestock. Mrs. Martin was friendly enough but still cool toward her. She seemed to begrudge the new interest that took her son's time and energy away from her own companionship. Dona understood her feelings but at the same time resented her efforts at curtailing Jimmie's social life.

Sometimes the girls accompanied Dona on her trips to Bedford. Jimmie invited each of them to drive the tractor around the field, under his guidance, of course. Dona was apprehensive because she still remembered the near-mishap that occurred when June once let Coralea steer his big tractor. She knew how dangerous farm equipment could be and wondered whether Jimmie realized how fragile her children were. Consequently, she kept a close, motherly eye on each new undertaking that involved heavy machinery or large animals.

Dona and the girls visited Nora and Jimmie at his house and were introduced to the many cats and kittens on the place and Nora's dog, Suzie. She was a border collie, friendly and gentle. Nora had named all the cats, too.

"She's named the milk cows, too," Jimmie informed them.

"Well, they can't all be 'Bossie'!" Nora interjected.

"But, 'Mary' and 'Josephine'?" he chided.

"They all look alike to me. How *do* you tell them apart?" Dona queried.

"By their personalities, of course," he told her with a grin.

"How's that?" Dona asked further.

"Well, one's a kicker, one's a high-jumper, one's easy going, and so on. They're nothing alike when you get to know them."

"Just how well do you get to know them?" she asked, laughing. "I think I like 'Mary' and 'Josephine' better."

"They all do their thing . . . " he assured her, "hopefully for a good many years." She'd rather not ask what happened when they were put out to pasture!

When one of the girls came up with the idea of camping overnight in the woods, Dona's reaction to the suggestion surprised them all.

"It sounds like fun!" was her quick response. "We won't have a place to do that much longer. I can take you down this weekend and I'll stay at the house with Mom. Unless I'm invited, too," she teased.

"You wouldn't want to go," Sharon assured her. "We hope to have quite a few girls."

"We've got to fit in the car," Dona warned.

Barbara considered this for a minute. "I can get Don to take some of us down," she volunteered. Her boyfriend never complained when asked to convey her and her sisters around.

"Where will you get a tent? I don't know anyone who has one," her mother asked.

"Wardloes have a little one," Coralea stated. "I've seen them sleep out in their backyard in it."

Soon the girls were off to plan the details of their trip. Dona hoped their Girl Scout experiences would give them a realistic idea of the things they would need for an outdoor, overnight stay.

When she mentioned the planned excursion to Jimmie, he suggested they use his truck tarp for a tent. It would probably cover them all and it was certainly strong enough. He might even hose it off for them first.

Unwavering sunshine graced the day when the crew arrived in Bedford. The eight girls spent the afternoon on a spirited walking tour through the town, traversing nearly every street as they merrily chattered and poked fun at each other. They spent a good hour hanging out at the schoolyard--trying the playground equipment, looking for 4-leaf clovers, and discussing their plans for the rest of the day.

By the time Dona gathered them up and they got back to the farm, it was nearly seven o'clock and the day had begun to cool. A few scattered clouds appeared in the sky, but as yet nothing menacing. It took the girls two trips to haul their gear back to the pond, where they would set up their tents and build a campfire.

"I don't want to be a wet blanket, but what if it rains?" their grandmother asked as they said good-bye at the house.

"It can't!" they replied, almost as one.

Dona and Retha watched the girls take off toward the woods, their arms laden with blankets, pillows, food and flashlights. They smiled at each other in the knowing way of experience, each recalling bittersweet memories of past nights in the outdoors. Dona was certain that her days spent in the makeshift lodgings were much more carefree than her mother's had been.

"Well, are they going to get wet?" Dona asked as the girls disappeared around a corner. The women looked at each other and nodded simultaneously.

A Hundred Miles to the City

There was no doubt in their minds what the outcome of the night's adventure would be.

Shortly after midnight Dona awoke as a thunderclap boomed ominously close to the house. A storm had materialized and the girls' camping experience would likely come to a swift, disappointing end. She wasn't surprised to find Retha already moving about, closing windows.

"They're probably on their way already," Retha guessed. She didn't expect the girls to tarry when the rain began to fall.

An hour later, she and Dona still waited in the house while rain pelted the roof and poured from the gutters in steady, rushing streams.

"They've probably gone to the old barn," Retha guessed.

"No, Mom. They pushed that down after they built the pond back there."

"Oh! That's right. I'd forgotten. I guess in my mind the place is still the same as it used to be, old house and all." A sad expression clouded Retha's features for a brief moment. Then she brightened as she added, "I can't believe they were so excited about sleeping out under that pig tarp!"

"Me, either. I guess it makes a lot of difference if you're sleeping in a tent because you want to or because you have to." Dona gave some thought to the fact that neither she nor Retha had mentioned to the girls that the Schmit family had once lived in a tent.

"That, and knowing that you have a house to go back to if you want," Retha concurred.

Shouts, squeals, giggles, and a few mild expletives emanated from the group as they hurried along the slippery trail back to the Schmit home. They saw the lights on at the house as they rounded the lane through the corner posts and dashed the rest of the way through unrelenting rain.

Dona and Retha stood at the door, ready to relieve them of the tangled mass of soggy bedclothes they tried to hold up out of the mud. Already, newspapers were spread in the corner of the big room, awaiting the bedraggled, dripping adventurers.

"How did you know we were coming?" Sharon asked.

"You were making enough noise to wake the dead!" Dona assured her.

Dona helped the girls make a pile of their things and then brought in wet towels so they could wipe their muddy feet. More dry towels sopped up the wetness in their hair. Retha found some old shirts of Sam's to offer the girls for nightclothes. She was enjoying the boisterous interruption as much as anyone.

"What time is it?" Lana wanted to know.

Retha nodded toward her softly ticking alarm clock.

"Two o'clock! I haven't even been to sleep yet!" Lana moaned.

"How about some old quilts on the floor for the rest of the night?" Retha offered. She certainly didn't have enough beds to go around.

"Just lean me against the wall!" Patty declared dramatically.

The next morning brought sluggish awakenings. No one was eager to return to the pond for the rest of the gear, but they finally accomplished that chore, with the exception of the big tarp, which they spread out in the sun to dry.

The weekend was a disaster as far as their plans went, but each of the girls talked enthusiastically about the escapade for years to come. To some degree, at least, their mettle had been tested by the elements and they considered themselves triumphant.

Both Dona and her mother joyfully marveled at the youthful exuberance of their guests. Retha's face beamed and she welcomed them back when they prepared to leave. Dona sensed her mother had enjoyed the adventure shared with a new generation, even though the circumstances of the camping experience were vastly different from her own. Dona expected her mother was missing her grandchildren already, even before her move to Iowa.

A curious sensation swept over Dona, and she was unexpectedly mindful of her own eventual loss. Her parental responsibilities had been such over-riding factors in her life for so long, she hadn't considered how she would feel when they came to an end. There certainly had been times when she'd wished for more personal, private space, but now that the reality loomed, she dreaded the bleakness she imagined.

Their mother's enthusiastic and unabashed support served the girls in good stead as each one found a place for her own modest talents in high school. Barbara earned a spot in "Who's Who in Missouri High Schools" and ranked in the top six of her graduating class. Coralea, a junior, spent most of her time as a disciple of her English teacher, working in both journalism and publications, as well as being an active, though admittedly untalented, member of the band. Finally, in her freshman year, Sharon had begun to mature physically. She was voted princess of her class for the yearbook, and was also busy with band activities. Dona knew each considered the school year to have been a successful and satisfying one.

During the preceding year, the girls had welcomed Jimmie's active role in their lives. He remembered their birthdays and gave them thoughtful gifts at Christmastime. When the planting season was finished in the spring, his visits became even more frequent. His presence at the events in their lives was appreciated by the girls as well as by their mother, who began to rely on his pleasant companionship and willing support.

A Hundred Miles to the City

Jimmie accompanied Dona to Barbara's high school graduation ceremonies. She was grateful to have an escort—and a handsome one at that. Coralea and Sharon both sat with the band, ready to play the opening number for the evening's program.

The large auditorium was packed, as usual at such events. Jimmie was late, also as usual, but they had reserved seats near the front, so it didn't matter this time. Rows of folding seats rose in tiers toward the back of the vast space. A classic mural of Roman figures marched along the upper reaches of the plastered walls. High overhead, the ceiling appeared almost cathedral-like, with tin panels deeply embossed in geometric patterns. Red stage curtains with long braids of golden fringe added to the elegant atmosphere of the setting.

Moved by the occasion and by her own place in the serious ceremony, tears came to Dona's eyes.

"What's the matter?" Jimmie quietly asked.

"I don't know . . . just thinking too much, I guess," she replied, blinking back the welling tears and attempting a smile. She was happy and very proud. Barbara would get a scholarship that would allow her to go on to college, just what Dona wanted for her. But she wasn't ready for her daughter to leave the nest, or "fly the coop", as Retha would put it.

"I never graduated from high school," she confided in her friend. She remembered Jimmie telling her that his was the first class to graduate from the new school in Bedford. She had only told him that she had gone to Summerville High School.

"Do you wish you had?" he asked now.

"Well, I guess, in a way, but you can't change part of your history without changing it all, I suppose. By the time I was Barbara's age I'd been married two years and had a baby. It seemed so right at the time, but it seems impossible now, doesn't it?"

"You didn't miss out on much by not graduating, did you?" he asked.

"I guess not, but I wish I had a diploma. When I was growing up, the people I admired most were my teachers. I thought they were very wise and they were always so kind to me!"

"Doesn't Barbara want to become a teacher?" He remembered them discussing that before.

"Uh-huh. I think that's because she's had instructors she admires, too. I guess Don's going on to college, also, but I'm not sure what he plans to take."

"Do you think they're serious?" Jimmie asked.

She felt certain they were.

"If you mean, do I think they'll get married, I suppose I do, but they're not even engaged. They've been going steady for a couple of years. Don's been nice to all the family--he's fun to have around." Dona knew she couldn't have chosen better for her oldest daughter but was still surprised to hear herself say it when she added, "I hope they do."

The rest of the family was on the front porch when Don brought Barbara home from graduation ceremonies. The night was warm and they still felt the closeness of the crowded auditorium. *Don and Barbara make a very handsome couple*, Dona observed to herself. Don was tall and slender with dark hair that stood in a short crewcut. Both young people twirled their tassels in the air as they approached--his green, hers white.

"We get to keep these!" Barbara announced.

"Hey! How about going for a ride in your convertible?" Don suggested to Jimmie.

"With the top down!" Sharon piped up.

Jimmie drove a blue Ford convertible just a few years old. He seldom put the top down, however.

"I guess we don't need to be afraid of rain tonight," he allowed. "Sure. Where do you want to go?"

"Let's buzz Jack's," Coralea suggested. She had been learning to drive and she could see herself behind the wheel of that car. Don had stepped in to guide her driving lessons when Dona's patience, and nerves, wore thin.

"Sure," was Jimmie's reply, so they all piled in and waited patiently while he undid snaps and cranked back the canvas covering. It was quite a process, after which he secured the folded top under another flap of cloth.

"Did you like the speaker tonight?" Dona asked her oldest daughter. The local pastor, who gave the address, had pointed out the challenges that lay ahead for the graduates. He had stressed the importance of establishing a framework for meeting their desired goals in life.

"Everyone keeps asking what we're going to do now that we're out of school," Barbara stated. "We're just going to go on . . . more school!" And she looked over at Don, who nodded.

"I thought maybe you had other plans," Jimmie teased.

"Speaking of plans," Barbara fired back, "we're wondering what kind of plans you have!" She gave her mother a wink and everyone watched Jimmie's neck get red as he fished for the right thing to say.

"Well, I'm thinking I could get married," he stated.

"Are you thinking of marrying my mother?" Barbara asked, somewhat surprised by the speed at which the conversation was moving.

"I'm thinking so," Jimmie stated as he gave Dona's knee a gentle squeeze.

"Would that be all right with all of you?" Dona asked, as if she had just then imagined such a proposition.

The girls ever after claimed that *they* had chosen Jimmie as their stepfather.

TWENTY-TWO

They were married in Hernando, Mississippi, by a justice of the peace. He wore his one suit and she wore her best dress. He was thirty-five and she was thirty-six, and they were both hopeful that the new life they were beginning would bring them contentment.

The honeymoon trip was short. They called home after they were married to tell their family they were, indeed, wed. The girls had been both excited and apprehensive about the event, since Jimmie and Dona had made no arrangements before setting out on Friday evening. Dona gave some thought to how the girls would accept the fact that she would spend the night with Jimmie before they were married. At the same time, she knew they were pleased to have him in their lives and probably wouldn't make anything of that small indiscretion. Since her girls believed the union was of their own manufacture, pleasing them was a foregone conclusion.

Not so with Nora. The news couldn't have been a surprise to her, but her reaction still brought uneasy feelings to her new daughter-in-law. Jimmie had broached the subject several times, in his way of teasing talk with his mother, so Nora knew, before the day that he flat-out announced that he and Dona planned to marry, that her life was about to change dramatically.

On the night Jimmie brought Dona home for a discussion of their related futures, Nora had made up her mind to accept the inevitable.

"I'm so glad Jimmie has finally found someone like you," she gushed when they met in her living room, testing the waters in preparation for some weighty decisions concerning her future, as well as theirs.

Dona sat on the overstuffed sofa, not as comfortably as she had on several previous occasions. In recent months she and Nora had become friendly, almost relaxed, in each other's company. Sometimes she fancied Nora even welcomed the interest she showed in Jimmie.

"I hope you don't feel like I want to take your son away from you," she ventured, hating the crass way that sounded, but knowing it accurately expressed her feelings.

"Oh, no. And the girls are so precious!" Nora hurriedly replied. "We've watched them grow up, you know." She tried to smile, but the effort was movingly ineffective.

"Mom, we need to make some plans," Jimmie quickly spoke up.

"Well, what should I do?" Nora pleaded. In spite of herself, she was near tears already. "I don't think we can all live in this house together!"

Dona looked at Jimmie expectantly--they had already discussed this privately.

"We could get you a place in town to stay," he ventured. "You'd be close to M.T."

"What would I do?" she blurted, tears flowing freely now.

"You wouldn't have to do anything," Dona volunteered. As she spoke, Dona saw Nora grip the arms of her chair, struggling to keep her composure. Could it be that Nora thought of this as her home and that her son just happened to be living with her still? Of course. Why would she think differently? Nora had always worked on the farm, often doing things a man should have done. Dona's own tears welled up.

"What would I live on? You're young. You've always taken care of yourself. You don't know what it's like to depend on someone. You probably expect to just move in and be the 'lady of the manor!'" Nora challenged as her face flushed in anger.

"I certainly don't intend to quit my job," Dona assured her.

"Well, I don't see how you can be away all day and help run a farm, too! She doesn't expect you to do it all yourself, does she?" This last she addressed straight to Jimmie, who was a little more than perplexed at the direction the discussion was headed.

"Mom, we'll make it work somehow. Other people do--we can."

"But you're taking on a ready-made family. You don't know what you're getting into!"

Nora's last statement completely destroyed Dona's intention to keep the exchange from escalating into a full-fledged feud. She hastily got up and moved to the front door, which she let bang with an interjection behind her.

By the time Jimmie had gathered his varied emotions into some sort of resolve and followed her out, Dona had lit a cigarette and was sitting on the wide porch railing taking in deep breaths of night air. Nora's dog, Suzie, had joined her and crowded in close to her feet. *Such fleeting allegiance,* Dona thought wryly as she regarded the animal.

In a reassuring gesture, Jimmie put his arm around Dona and gave her a squeeze, saying, "She's always talking about living back in town."

"But not without you!" she assured him back.

Stepping into Nora's life proved difficult for Dona on several levels. Rejoining the Bedford community, even though Sam and Retha had moved away, seemed almost like going home to her; but returning to farm life was a bittersweet blessing. Her early years as a child of the rural community had been chaotic at best--impoverished even, during the Depression era. And although she felt fortunate with her family as far as mutual consideration and caring went, she couldn't deny that their years on the farm were times of struggle and frequent disappointment. And those with June were times of loneliness and hardship as well.

With an extra hour added to her work shift each day for travel time, she certainly had less opportunity for leisure or relaxation. It didn't take long for her to realize that there was little room in Jimmie's daily schedule for either of those commodities. His workday began before sunrise and ended after sunset, if then.

Nora had been right in her concern for the chores of the household. Sharon soon took over the morning and evening milking operation, and Coralea looked after the chickens and prepared the noon meal when Dona was at work. Barbara accompanied her mother to Madison each day to go to her own job as clerk for an insurance agency. No one found much time for Nora's garden, although she sometimes drove out to weed and water and gather produce. She always picked extra for the family in the house and encouraged them to help themselves. She was never one to waste garden goodies.

Nora had found a place for herself in town--the upper floor of a large house just two doors down the hill from where she and her children had lived. Jimmie bought her a used car so she could get around, and she seemed to be adjusting well to her new placement.

The first year on the McBain place proved to be a true testing ground for Jimmie and his new family. The house itself seemed to balk at the burden of three extra women. First the plumbing system stopped working, at least quit working efficiently. Sometimes the cistern pump would quit, and buckets of water would have to be lugged up the stairs to flush the stool. Luckily, there was a pump near the back door of the house so this adjustment could be made. Then the drains would back up, and Dona would arrive home to find Jimmie working with a "snake" to open up the conduit that reached somewhere beyond the front driveway. The rented auger was a monster that defied human efforts at subjugation. But, eventually, with just a few "Son of a b___"es uttered, Jimmie eventually won out and coiled the slimy thing back into its case.

Then, the water they were using from the cistern developed a strange taste and odor. On inspection by Jimmie, a critter--it must have been a mole since there were obviously some in the yard--was discovered floating on the surface of the dark water.

"We'll have to scrub it out," Jimmie announced to the rest, after he had given them the stomach-turning news. "I'll pump it out and let it dry for a few days . . . then we'll see what you're made of," he added with a suggestive smile.

Cleaning out the cistern was their first real undertaking as a family unit. Privately, Jimmie didn't expect much help, and Dona wasn't at all confident that it could be done, but the girls were determined to meet the challenge.

A long ladder, a droplight, bleach and scrubbing brushes were gathered for the undertaking. It was a pleasant Saturday morning in the early fall. Everyone took their shoes off in preparation of descending the big ladder.

"It doesn't smell as bad as I expected," Dona volunteered.

"It doesn't smell good!" Barbara shot back.

Jimmie draped the light over the edge of the opening, then lowered the ladder into the massive concrete structure. His voice sounded hollow as he climbed down, encouraging his followers into the damp cavern. Sharon and Coralea went right down, with Barbara and Dona watching from above.

"We'll need a stepstool to reach up to the waterline," Jimmie called to Dona as she lowered a five gallon bucket of clean water from the well. Barbara went to get it and another bucket of water. She was happy to be on the fetch-and-carry detail.

The large utility brushes were clumsy to handle, but stiff and effective in brushing off discolored particles that clung to the concrete walls. Soon, enough water had dripped off elbows to thoroughly soak every worker and gather in a large puddle on the uneven floor.

Dona decided to take Sharon's place after she'd been scrubbing for a while. Once down the ladder, she realized that she was in a huge concrete jar buried in the ground. The walls were fairly smooth but were stained above the water line with rings of black and green--probably some kind of growth she'd rather not name. Cobwebs clung to the dry upper shoulders of the structure, like sheets of gauze--powdery with years of accumulated dust. She decided those needed to be swept down if the job were to be complete.

"It's cool down here," she reflected aloud. "I guess the earth pretty much insulates it, doesn't it?"

"Well, so far it hasn't frozen, but I'm not about to say 'never,'" Jimmie allowed with chagrin.

The scrubbing went on for most of the afternoon. The ones above dropped down rags, and those in the cistern sopped up the acrid water and put the dripping cloths into buckets to be hauled back up with ropes. Later they would burn the mass of material they now scattered on the grass nearby.

Dona found herself wondering how it would feel to be down in such a place when it contained water and was sealed with its heavy wooden lid. Coralea wondered how the thing could have been constructed in the first place. Jimmie wondered how much longer it was going to take them to complete the task--he had other chores waiting for him.

By the end of the undertaking, Dona sensed that her girls had passed an important test of sorts. The girls felt as if they had truly contributed something to the upkeep of their new home, and Jimmie understood that his new female charges were not afraid of getting their hands dirty.

Finally, the fall rains came and the large storage area once more filled with ground-purified water. For a few days Dona boiled the water the family would drink or use for cooking, but after that they gradually resumed using the cistern water for all their needs.

After living with him for a while, Dona knew why Jimmie was so physically fit--his energy was boundless. His working days began at sunrise and seldom ended by sunset. And every day was a working day.

Jimmie's youthful enthusiasm constantly amazed Dona. She had never thought of herself as a lazy person, but she wondered at the energy with which he began each day. He wasn't just ready to get out of bed each morning, but eager to perform the work he had set for himself. To him, each day presented fresh possibilities--it seemed as if he were born anew with each sunrise and welcomed the hours ahead as precious opportunities for completing his tasks.

When her own daily job was completed--including travel time, which proved relaxing to her--he was still going strong, and she'd have her housework finished long before he came in for the night. His energy seemed to run into her, and she found herself with more vitality than she'd had in years. She knew this was not because her life had become simpler. It hadn't. Her girls were now in three separate schools. Her work site was twenty-five miles away, and she had a bigger home and larger family to care for.

One evening when Jimmie was working late, Dona went to the field to encourage him to quit and come in for the night. When he saw her car approach, he stopped his tractor and hurried over to meet her. She immediately thought, *Oh, no! He's afraid something's wrong at the house! I shouldn't have come.* However, when he stepped close, she knew by his playful grin that he had no such misgivings.

There was a farm pond nearby, and she soon found herself splashing, childlike, in it, her nude body tingling with the coolness of the water. It was a relaxing, joyful romp--completely unexpected and totally exhilarating. In the water, the couple seemed blissfully alone and hidden, even though the lingering light of dusk shone on their shoulders as their arms entwined in a gentle embrace.

"I can't believe you've never gone skinny-dipping before!" Jimmie teasingly whispered in her ear.

"I guess I went from child to mama pretty quickly, but I feel almost like a teenager now," she admitted. "It's fun!" It was true that she felt like a young newlywed in lots of ways. Sometimes she wished that she and Jimmie could have a child, but she didn't tell him this. He seemed satisfied with the family he had accepted, and she didn't want him yearning for something that could not be. She was both happy and sad in this knowledge.

If Dona had thought her life on the farm would be quieter, or less complicated, she soon had to rethink that idea. Each day began early and noisily. The sounds of highway traffic passing by her previous home in Madison were no match for the clamor of the hooved and clawed creatures on the farm. Squawking, mooing, crowing, bawling, braying, barking--the world awakened with a blast at her new home in the country. On the days she didn't have to get up and go to work, there was still no staying in bed beyond sunup--it seemed an unwritten rule of agrarian existence she must have forgotten.

Quiet on the farm? Dona thought that laughable. The constant clatter of activity and the coming of spring compounded each facet of her life. With the spring thaw there were bad roads to challenge her. Baby animals were being born, keeping her husband on the run both day and night. While most births were accomplished unattended, Jimmie knew that the best outcomes required his timely intervention. If the little squealers weren't amassed before her in nursing position a cantankerous old sow was likely to roll over on her own newborn. A calf left out in bitter temperatures might suffer frostbite on its delicate ears.

During her first year back in the country, Dona was frequently surprised by the sensual stimulation of her surroundings. The earthy aroma of burgeoning growth overwhelmed her at times, reminding her of the cycle of life in constant repetition on the farm.

There were ongoing flaps in the front yard, when amorous roosters leapt upon hens and pinned them to the ground. Occasionally Jimmie had to shut Suzie in the corncrib until her season in heat was accomplished. But the most shocking display of carnal ambition that Dona witnessed was the behavior of the little white pony, Daniel. One mare, a pretty palomino, shared the pasture with the gentle little horse. He was usually very docile and allowed himself to be petted and haltered by the girls, and Sherry rode him now and then.

The mare was just a few yards away from the kitchen window, where Dona was inside, washing the dishes. The pony approached and stood beside the mare for a short time. Dona saw the mare flick her tail and noticed a brownish liquid exuding beneath it. The pony, also, noticed and began licking the area. The larger horse stood for this for a while, then whinnied--urgently, Dona thought. The pony moved around to the front of the mare and their muzzles touched, as if in a kiss. It looked to Dona as if he were seeking her permission. He got in position and mounted her. She stood patiently for a while. Every sinew in his body seemed to struggle to achieve his goal, but his legs were too short.

After holding the receptive stance for a time, the mare appeared to become restless, and kicked at the pony, causing him to retreat a few yards. The mare shook her mane and moved away, leaving the pony with his head down in the grass. Dona watched him, wondering if he were suffering from the rejection and saw a liquid ejaculate from his still distended organ. While she was almost spellbound at the time, she wished later that she had been able to give the ardent creature a boost somehow.

It occurred to Dona that, in all her years of rural experience, she'd never had such an intimate glimpse of animal behavior. She admitted to herself that her daughters were probably getting a basic sex education course also. When she told Jimmie of what she had seen, he just laughed and said, "Where there's a will, there's a way!" But he must have been wrong, as there was not an ensuing pregnancy in the mare.

If Dona had one regret for marrying Jimmie, it was that she was now very busy--which didn't make sense to her at all, with the two older girls living in Madison and herself with a life partner. Her day's activities lasted until the lights went out at night. Not that she was tired by all the demands on her. She felt great--fulfilled, needed, productive. She just wished for more time to enjoy those feelings.

Barbara and Coralea were spending the school year in a rooming house for college girls, which now the older one truly was. With her obstinate concern for self-preservation, Coralea had convinced her mother that she desperately needed to finish high school in Madison and that she also needed to be present for all the activities seniors are involved in. So she was allowed to join five other girls, all freshmen at Madison State Teachers College, as long as she adhered to the rules of the housemother/landlord. The girls shared a kitchen and the Martins supplied their daughters with provisions from their meat locker.

On most Fridays, the girls returned to the farm with Dona after work. Sunday was the only day the family spent any leisure time together, and that was usually without Jimmie, as his barnyard duties were unaffected by the "seventh day of rest" doctrine. Jimmie owned a television set, so Dona and the girls enjoyed their first real exposure to the somewhat new medium. Saturday night they often watched *My Hit Parade* with regulars Snookie Lanson and Rosemary Clooney--a particular favorite of the girls, who were eager to keep up with the latest trends in popular music. Then Don picked the two girls up on Sunday afternoon, suitcases packed with clean clothes from Saturday's wash day.

When Nora moved to her own place in town, she had insisted on taking very few items with her. The place was already furnished and also fairly small--besides she'd rather not break up the furnishings of the house. Dona thought perhaps Nora imagined herself moving back before long. At any rate, the place remained much as Nora had left it, with the addition of the foldout couch the younger girls had always slept on, which was placed in the dining room. Nora had left M.T.'s piano in the living room, so Dona had made a gift of their player piano to the Christian Church in Madison, happy to no longer be responsible for arranging the move of the heavy instrument from place to place.

On a sunny morning in late fall, Dona sat in the big chair in the living room. The girls were off to Sunday school, and Dona had already put on the roast--homegrown, of course--that would be their dinner. The summer stimulation of animals on the farm had begun to subside and the place was unusually quiet. The long living room, which stretched across the entire front of the house, was orderly, as always. The family did most of their living in the dining room, where a couple of rockers added to the comfortable capacity of the old sofa. An oil furnace just below that room now poured a voluptuous stream of hot air through the wide grate. Above that airway, on the second floor, a smaller grate was open in the floor of the bathroom. When everything was working right, as it now was, it was a convenient setup. French doors led into the front room, where Dona sat musing.

She was surprised that she felt so at home in the house--surrounded as she was by Nora's furniture. The house had a unique smell, as all houses do, and it was decidedly of farm. There was a shower in the basement where Jimmie washed off the day's accumulation of dust, sweat and animal essences, but, somehow, the barnyard smell crept in and gave the place a warm, musty quality. Dona thought perhaps it was that homey smell from her youth that subconsciously pleased her.

Seldom did Dona have such time to herself. She decided to do a little exploring. She'd hardly seen the attic, though they had moved some boxes of clothing up there where they'd be out of the way. As in most houses of this age, there was definitely a shortage of closet space.

The attic ran from front to back of the house and had a wooden floor, though the rafters remained uncovered. Dressers, trunks, items of various descriptions were lined up in an orderly fashion against the slope of the eaves. Dona's gaze fell on the handmade walnut cradle that Jimmie had told her was originally made for his grandmother and that her children, Nora and her siblings, and both he and Lizabeth had occupied as infants. The high chair was there, too--obviously very old; not fancy but plain and sturdy, as Dona imagined the people themselves to have been. She wondered how it felt to Jimmie to have his past right here above him. So close. He had never had to let it go. Hard for her to imagine. She seemed to have nothing tangible left of her past, except for the desk Sam had made for her from a radio console. She treasured that.

Through the window high over the front porch, Dona looked down to the driveway and the dirt road connecting the McBain place to the rest of the world. That road was now a dark mass of deep ruts that the girls would soon be sliding their way home over--she hoped. She could only surmise that they had actually made it into Bedford, as the muddy road topped a rise before it joined a gravel road to the east. They hadn't come walking back for help, which would have had to come by way of a pull from Jimmie's tractor.

Dona hadn't felt that the girls really had to go, since the road was in such bad shape after last night's drizzle. However, they each had their duties in the tiny congregation. Barbara and Sharon took their turns in playing hymns for the service, and Coralea kept attendance records. Actually, Dona thought the girls accepted the hazardous road as a challenge. She'd watched them start out earlier, Coralea behind the wheel. The driveway had some gravel, so they got a running start, making the turn onto the road just slowly enough to stay out of the ditch, then keeping up forward momentum until they'd topped the little hill and slid out of her sight. She knew now that she didn't want to be watching when they made the homeward swoop, so she hurried down to her preparations in the kitchen.

Sam and Retha drove down from Lenox when Coralea graduated from high school in the spring. Nora joined the family for the trip to Madison to attend the ceremony. The thawing relationship between Dona and her mother-in-law suffered a setback when Nora commented that it was too bad Sam didn't have a better hat to wear for the occasion.

That summer Coralea and Sharon each spent a week with their grandparents at the small home they had purchased in Lenox. They enjoyed the time spent with the older couple, but both girls complained later that they were frightened by Sam's erratic driving. They both noticed that Sam had begun to "take his half out of the middle of the road," which made topping the hills rather unnerving.

Coralea planned to attend college in Madison, along with Barbara, and Sharon was ready for her junior year at South Johnson--the consolidation of Bedford and Horton school districts. So far Sharon had ridden the bus to Horton, the site of the high school, but next year she wanted to go out for basketball, so transportation would be a problem. Jimmie and Dona decided it would be too expensive to again keep two girls in Madison, so in the fall the older girls would be commuters to their college classes.

Part of the land that Jimmie rented for row crops was on the bottomland just west of Bedford, so he made frequent trips on his tractor through town, often pulling cultivation equipment. He visited his mother often, sometimes stopping when he noticed her car at M.T.'s. His grandmother didn't leave her house much any more, so Nora spent a good deal of her time at Merry's--helping her as much as the independent lady would allow.

"Anyone home?" Jimmie called through the screen door as he stepped up on the tiny porch. Merry still lived in the little house across the ditch that ran alongside Rt. H, the main road through Bedford.

"Jimmie!" both women answered at once. He had known for a long time that he was the main worldly concern of each of them. This realization was both a blessing and a burden, but he knew that the affection he returned bound him to them both.

After they'd exchanged the customary pleasantries concerning weather and wellbeing, Merry asked Jimmie how things were going with all his new women.

"We're getting along fine," he replied. Then he thought a minute about some of the changes having four females in the house had incurred.

"Well, it's pretty hectic sometimes--seems like someone always has to go somewhere. I can't keep enough gas in my car!" He thought about some of the other female-related activities he was too embarrassed to mention. "It seems like Sherry and Corky spend half their time with their hair up in pin curls. I'd forgotten how Lizabeth used to run around with a kerchief tied around her head."

"Just be thankful you don't have to do that to be pretty," Nora chided her son. She'd gone to a hairdresser herself for years and had her auburn hair color replenished on a regular basis. She never mentioned it to anyone, but her mother and son certainly knew she persisted in that personal vanity. Over the course of the last few years her wavy hair had gotten progressively lighter and redder.

"Didn't I see old 'Pekora' in town the other day? You must've decided to fix her up," Nora suggested to Jimmie.

His face flushed and he hesitated before answering.

"Yes and no," he returned, a sheepish grin creeping across his averted face. "The old truck has been out for a ride, but it was sort of unauthorized."

"What do you mean?" asked Merry, who wasn't at all sure she was acquainted with Pekora.

"Well, the girls were pretty antsy out on the farm the other day and asked me about the old truck Mom used to drive around the place. I said, 'Sure it works--it just doesn't have brakes.' I guess they didn't see that as a significant problem, so they asked if they could drive it to town. I've done it myself. I just take the back way, to avoid the hill. So I told them it was all right with me. Just Corky and Sherry--Barb was at work."

"Did they have any trouble?" Nora asked, amusement as well as concern showing in her brown eyes.

"No, they didn't, but we did!" Jimmie stated, remembering his wife's reaction when she heard what he'd allowed her daughters to do. "Dona was really mad when they told her about it--madder at me than at them! I just figured they could handle it." Nora could see that her son was going to have a hard time ever saying "no" to the girls' requests.

The two girls had gotten the truck running and out on the road in no time. On the route to town, there was just one intersection where they would not have been able to stop for something coming from the other direction. Aside from that, the trip was fairly flat, and they had just coasted to a stop when they arrived at their destination. They admitted later that it was a little scary. After that, Pekora never left the barn lot, and the girls decided to avoid the wrath of their mother by walking to town if they had to go.

"How is your garden?' Jimmie asked Nora, knowing she took great delight in her vegetable patch and was always eager to discuss its progress. By now the growing season was well under way.

"Lots of lettuce, radishes, carrots and onions. Need some?" Nora offered.

"Tomorrow when we have hay hands we would sure appreciate some," he replied.

"Do you want me to come and cook?" she offered. Cooking for one, or just herself and Merry, didn't give her much of an opportunity to prepare elaborate meals, as she once had.

"Oh, no! Corky and Sherry are expecting to fix dinner for us. I think they have it all planned. There'll just be three more hands this time. I think they can handle it," he ventured, admitting only to himself that his confidence might be misplaced.

When the meal was served to the four hungry men gathered at the Martins' kitchen table, words of praise for the efforts of the cooks flowed freely--not so much as acknowledgement of a tasty meal but for encouragement for the novice cooks whose efforts were appreciated. Jimmie told Nora later of the cherry pie Sherry had been so proud of, until she realized she should have checked that the can of cherries she used were of the pitted variety. On another occasion, one of the girls used a tablespoon of coffee grounds in a recipe, supposing they would dissolve during cooking.

The Bowens and Martins had been a family for little more than a year when an incident occurred that would secure for Jimmie a lifetime of admiration and devotion from his three new daughters. It was one of those times that happen quietly, almost secretly, in one's life, that conspire to describe the true outline of the individual. And nature itself set the stage for the little-noted, but dramatic, event.

Since school had started in the fall, Dona took the two older girls to Madison with her each day--Barbara to college classes and to her work at the insurance office, and Coralea to her freshman activities and her new part-time employment as student help in the campus business office. The girls usually drove the car on, so they could get to the various places they needed to be. Then they picked up their mother at the end of the day.

Most of the work turned in by college students required the use of a typewriter. An old Royal machine that Lizabeth had used at business school in Chillicothe was brought down from the attic and put to use. It sat on Nora's library table that dominated one end of the front room. The big room was often chilly in the winter months, but it was a quiet place where a person could concentrate on the task at hand. Each of the girls had taken a typing course in high school and was able to thump out her assignments with a fair degree of accuracy--until the old machine became painfully sluggish and made the task nearly impossible.

"Can't we rent one from the typewriter exchange?" Barbara asked her mother. "We could all help pay for it."

"I suppose we could," Dona allowed. "How much do you suppose they'd want for one for a few months?"

"I can go tomorrow and see," Barbara volunteered. She knew of other students who took advantage of that option and expected it wouldn't be too costly. The place let you apply the rent money on the future purchase price, if you decided to buy it.

When they planned to pick up the typewriter, the store was closed for Thanksgiving the next day, so they were unable to get it.

"I'll pick it up on Friday," Dona assured them. "You'll still have time over break to get your papers typed." The girls were clearly disappointed since they'd planned to use every day of the holiday to get their essays completed.

The fall was particularly wet in 1956, so the roads in the area had progressively deteriorated until even the graveled by-ways were hazardous. Then it rained all day on Thanksgiving, so Dona found it necessary to take her car out to Rt. H, just to be certain she could make it to work on Friday. Jimmie would take her out on the tractor, and, if it were necessary, pick her up there in the evening. This arrangement didn't have to be made too often since the roads froze up in colder weather and were again passable.

"I don't think we can manage a typewriter on this thing," Dona announced to Jimmie as they carefully made their way out to the highway the next morning. Big clumps of mud sprayed up behind them as the big tires of the tractor squished in the deeply rutted roadway.

"Go ahead and get it. Maybe the sun will come out and dry things up a bit today," Jimmie said in his optimistic way. She gave him a doubtful look, but he continued, "If not, I'll rig up a basket of some kind."

It was nearly six o'clock that evening when Dona made it to the corner where Jimmie was to wait for her. He was there all right, but the tractor was nowhere in sight, and rain was falling in a steady stream. Wet and muddy, he carefully got into the car after she had pulled to the side of the blacktop.

"What happened?" she quickly inquired, looking him over with concern.

"Well, the tractor's in the ditch on the hill by the Benson place," he told her, exasperation showing on his face. "I'm afraid we're going to have to walk home from here."

"Did it tip over?" Dona asked anxiously, scrutinizing him for signs of harm.

"The front wheels balled up so I couldn't turn them. I just drove right off the road--no control at all! There's no getting it out, I'm afraid."

Dona thought of the bridge that spanned a usually dry ravine between their place and the Benson's. She thanked whatever divine intervention there might have been that he was not at that point when the accident occurred.

Back at the house, the girls had prepared supper and were waiting for Dona and Jimmie to appear. A rare fall thunderstorm had set in, and the evening darkened early. Flashes of lightning could be seen in the distance, and thunder grumbled in low vibrations, muffled by the increasing rainfall. Now and then one of the girls went to a front window and glanced out to see if their parents were coming.

Jimmie and Dona chose to sit it out in the car until the rain subsided. She turned the car on to warm them up a bit, as she was beginning to shiver and he was drenching wet.

"Better check the flashlight that's under the seat. I'm afraid we're going to need it," he said, realizing there were no other options if it didn't work. By the time the rain slackened, it was quite dark outside.

Jimmie opened the back door of the car and lifted out the typewriter.

"Surely you don't intend to carry that all the way back to the house!" Dona exclaimed.

He groaned a little as he took a few steps but smiled to indicate that was precisely what he planned to do. She brought the flashlight and plodded along beside him. The sparse gravel gave them some traction as she played the beam of light on the ground before them.

By now the girls at the house were finding it hard to concentrate on anything but the safety of their elders. One after the other, they passed into the front room and gazed anxiously to the east. It was now impossible to see anything beyond the arc of illumination surrounding the pole light in the yard. The front porch light was on also, but its feeble glow was swallowed by the lowering night.

Suzie, the black and white border collie, had come from her place of shelter and was sitting on her haunches, her muzzle pointed to the east and her ears at attention. She sat expectantly on a knoll by the end of the driveway, unmoving but alert.

Dona and Jimmie came to the Benson place, abandoned for several years now.

"Maybe we can go in and rest a bit," Dona suggested. She hadn't much to carry, but the sticky mud made their progress extremely tedious.

"I'm sure it's locked," Jimmie cautioned her. "Let's just sit down here for a bit." He indicated an old piece of machinery that had been brought to the lane and marooned there. Little could be made out beyond the dimming rays afforded by the flashlight Dona held. She turned it off to save the batteries.

"I'm not sure I could do this if you weren't here," she told him.

He found enough energy to chuckle. He was so accustomed to doing his chores after dark that he could almost sense where objects were. True, there were usually animal sounds around to guide him, but he'd never thought of the dark as being much of a handicap.

As time continued to slip by, the girls in the house became even more unnerved. They completely abandoned the kitchen and spent more and more time gazing out the windows. The rain had ceased, but the thunder and lightning were getting closer.

The house itself seemed to have lost its animation when Jimmie left on his tractor--it was as if it were held in a state of suspension along with the girls. As their anxiety increased, each girl had her private fear, but no one wished to give it a face by speaking it out loud. Their eyes never met as they paced and peered, keeping vigil in the lengthening minutes.

At last Jimmie and Dona came to the crossroad that marked the end of the section. Only another half-mile to go, but the batteries of the flashlight were giving out, so the rest of the way would be even slower, as their steps would have to be measured more carefully in the darkness.

"They should have been back a long time ago . . . " Sharon hesitantly stated.

"Maybe Mom had car trouble coming home," Coralea suggested.

"She'd have called us," Barbara allowed. Then everyone was quiet once more. The spectre of the tractor in a ditch, on top of their mother and Jimmie, had entered each girl's mind. Stories about Chance Holliday's long-ago accident and frequent warnings from Dona about the dangers connected with farm machinery had made lasting impressions on the three. They each had a sense of dread concerning the situation that lurked there in the inky darkness. The house became cold and impersonal to them. The circle of light beneath the security lamp, before a beacon for homecoming, had changed to an island of isolation.

Suddenly, Suzie shot from her spot like a puppet jerked across a stage. She made no sound as she bounded into the night, disappearing down the rain-darkened road.

Sharon leaned over the back of the sofa with her head pressed against the windowpane. Flashes of lightening fluttered across the eastern sky, illuminating two figures on the crest of a rise far down the road.

"It's them!" she shouted. "I saw them! They're coming!"

As if a mysterious switch had been flipped, the place came swiftly back to life. The cold glow of the porch light became a protective cocoon as the girls waited and watched. Barbara stood rigidly in the "mother hen" attitude she often assumed when she was alone with her sisters.

Just as it appeared the storm might abate, a fresh series of lightning bolts flashed jaggedly across the sky. A clap of thunder rattled the very foundation of the house, plunging the girls huddled on the porch into a new set of worries. Occasionally streaks of lightning ripped to the earth, illuminating the landscape as in noonday light. In those instances, the girls checked the progress of the two returning. They were advancing piteously slowly--their position on the long flat space changing but little in reference to the few scattered trees that loomed along the fence rows. Utter blackness returned in a split second, shrouding their steps and returning them to the uncertainty of the unknown.

Barbara didn't know if she could stand the constant switching from elation to deflation as the storm repeatedly assaulted the travelers. Lightning crackled in the charged atmosphere, as if some angry deity were taking stabs at those on the road! She preferred them spirited back into impersonal darkness.

Finally, the three who were gathered on the front porch saw human forms take shape. Suzie danced out in front of the two as they emerged from the murky gloom that edged the driveway.

"What's he got?" Coralea wondered aloud.

"It's the typewriter!" Sharon exclaimed. Her entire body reflected an expression of complete surprise.

The three girls tore down the steps as one, rushing to meet the bedraggled travelers. Barbara took the typewriter from her new stepfather with not a word of objection from him.

"How did you manage to do this?" she happily questioned him.

"Well, I guess you needed it," were the simple words he spoke.

To the rest, those words were etched in gold, and engraved on their very future.

TWENTY-THREE

While the resolve to marry may have been Dona and Jimmie's most meaningful decision as individuals, their decision to buy the Stingley farm was surely their most momentous as a couple. Although Jimmie had sacrificed much of his youth to gain his place as a successful farmer, he did not own any of the land he cultivated. Dona knew that possession of the land itself was vital to anyone who sought to call himself a true farmer.

They had been married less than two years when an opportunity arose to purchase the place. It had belonged to a Stingley daughter but rented out to a succession of tenants, some who strived to keep up the place and some who did not. The most recent renter had been of the latter variety, and the buildings and grounds had deteriorated to a startling degree since the Wisdom family had occupied the home when Dona's girls were peddling garden seeds and gooseberries.

Still, she remembered it as the elegant place it had once been, seeing possibilities that even Jimmie viewed with skepticism. For him the condition of the house was secondary to the state of the barns and outbuildings that rambled across the property. He saw the size of the barn, not its condition, just as he measured the value of the land in the possibilities of production he foresaw.

In preparation for the move, the family had packed their belongings into boxes, so by the first of the year Jimmie could take possession of the farm and settle in to begin the first year's planting. They were to take over in January, but the current tenant still, in February, had not secured a new place for his family. The Martins agreed to bide their time until the first of March, when the change of stewardship would be critical.

During that time of upheaval in their lives, Dona and her family received word that Sam had passed away. He and Retha had gone to Easton to stay overnight at his brother's. They had nearly completed the twenty-five mile journey when Sam stopped to fill the car with gas and realized he had left his billfold back in Lenox. So they made the trip back for it and arrived late at their destination and not in the best frame of mind. Sam died peacefully in his sleep, but Retha felt that the tiring journey, plus a heavy, late evening meal, had put her husband in his grave.

When the family went to Rock Port to view Sam's remains, his lifeless form lay in a bed in the funeral home, his burial not yet arranged. To the girls viewing their beloved grandfather in bed, Sam's death was a disturbing reality. Dona sensed that her mother faced a difficult adjustment, even though the life she and Sam shared for more than fifty years had certainly been plagued by insecurity and tumult. There was no doubt in Dona's mind that her parents had enjoyed many of life's most quietly rewarding blessings as man and wife. She was comforted to know her mother would continue to live in the couple's house just a few blocks from Hank and his wife.

Remembering what it meant to Sam to have his own place, Dona now felt the hopeful anticipation that had buoyed his spirits. She had once accused her husband of being an eternal optimist, but regarding the old house, she saw not the dilapidated reality, but a masquerading castle whose possibilities stretched to a fairytale horizon. The structure was large and imposing on its mound of earth, but the once-white facade had grayed with age. Its narrow, wooden boards were discolored in places, the paint cracked and peeling from the ravages of countless seasons of wind and weather.

Even the brutality of the harsh winter failed to dampen Dona's spirits when the family finally brought their household belongings to their new home. It would take Jimmie several more weeks to accomplish transferring the animals and farm equipment to his newly acquired property.

Their new residence presented certain challenges to the family. The place had been modernized years earlier, but the water system had been in disrepair for some time and it would again be necessary to use the "little house out back." Jimmie would put that matter at the top of his list of pressing projects to attend to.

The big house and its helpmates--smokehouse, springhouse and cellar-- were gathered atop a small hill and encircled by a white picket fence, similarly neglected but sound. A few large cedar trees stood in the yard and gave the whole compound the appearance of looming over the surrounding countryside. The approaching lane curved around to the back of the hill, making the front entrance nearly inaccessible, although a set of crumbling concrete steps led a short distance up the hill to the north gate. On the west, the hill rose abruptly from the flat bottomland, holding the house aloft, as a ship setting out to sea, or more fittingly in Dona's perception, drifting into a safe harbor.

It was possible to see Bedford from the house, though huge elms would seclude the place during the summer months. Dona was happy to note that the road into town was flat, straight, and heavily graveled. She could expect no more slogging in mud when she came home from work.

There was a basement under half the house, which Dona soon found to be infested with mice. Anything stored there had to be brought up by someone else. There were plenty of cats on the place, but evidently not enough. Her employment at the utility company made it affordable for Dona to purchase appliances for the old kitchen. Before many months passed, the bathroom and kitchen had been fitted with new or used equipment, and a wall furnace installed to supplement the warmth put out by the huge fireplace in the living room.

The little nuances that set the home apart were precious to Dona, as tiny jewels form a fine tiara. The transoms above the doors were badges of nobility, not windows that rattled and constantly needed to be dusted for cobwebs. In summer, the windows and doors were opened so the softest breeze swept across the hill, washing away the closeness of the humid air. If some of the rooms had to be closed for the winter, it was not a hardship of space but a boon to coziness that made those frigid times special, also. There were eight outside doors to the house, which were never locked. They were the means to letting the world in, not to keeping it out.

The house was drafty, with noises frequently discernable in the perimeter of the structure. These didn't startle Dona for she chose to romanticize them, feeling the phantom pops and creaks were part of the signature of the place.

There were four large rooms upstairs, so each daughter claimed one for her own, and the rest of the family's odds and ends were placed in the extra room at the north, which Dona pronounced to be the toy room.

The room Barbara chose for herself was the largest--an airy space with windows on three sides, an outside door to an upper balcony over the back porch and an enclosed stairway down to the kitchen. Separating her room from Coralea's was a curious backward lock, which Dona later learned was installed to keep the kitchen girl in her quarters back when the place was more of an estate than a farm home.

Coralea's room was smaller, but had a closet, while Sharon's room, next to it, was large and furnished with a wardrobe so massive that previous owners must have deemed it too heavy to move. This room, too, opened onto a balcony, and like the first described, its railings were now missing. To the front of the house was the remaining room that ran alongside the large hall and open stairway. The extra room on the bottom floor, the parlor, now became a library with Nora's oak table and several wooden bookshelves.

The house had definitely lost its splendor years before the Martins moved in, but Dona envisioned a resurrection under her guidance and was eager to learn all she could about the place. When she and Jimmie read the deed over carefully, they discovered that a piece of land now annexed to the farm had originally belonged to a distant ancestor of Jimmie's, Moses Hawk. He had been one of the earliest settlers of the region, along with Hiram Stingley and his brother.

In May, Coralea married her beau, Cliff Simpson, who was in the army at Ft. Sill, Oklahoma, and Barbara and Don planned their own ceremony for December. Sharon would soon be a senior, on the threshold of leaving, too. For a short time Jimmie and Dona discussed the possibility of adoption but, realistically aware they were both nearly forty years old, accepted the fact that such an undertaking would not be wise.

Dona began to direct her maternal instincts toward the home she and Jimmie shared. Before their first summer in the new house passed, Dona had laid a brick sidewalk to the back fence and constructed a fishpond with rocks the family gleaned from the Penney Eighty. That parcel of land lay directly east of the home place and Jimmie planned to put it under cultivation soon.

Jimmie took on a hired hand--a fellow from town, Rafe Overman--to help on his expanded acreage. He also increased his herds of both cattle and hogs and became increasingly immersed in his farming operation. Jimmie fixed lunch for himself and Rafe, usually sausage and eggs, or they would eat in a little restaurant that had opened in Bedford. Rafe wasn't overly ambitious, but he could drive the tractor down the long, bottomland acreage, freeing Jimmie from many hours of fieldwork--hours better spent on more challenging projects.

Dona heard the door slam in the back porch. Jimmie often came to the house mid-morning to check in, on days when she was home from work. But this morning he had been gone only an hour or so.

"That damn Rafe!" he announced abruptly as he stepped to the fridge for a drink.

"What's he done now?" Dona obligingly asked.

"He's going to be getting a surprise soon, probably tonight!" Jimmie replied, a sly grin creeping across his face.

"Maybe I should rephrase that. What have you done now?" she asked. He was obviously enjoying some part of the situation caused by his hired hand.

"I saw him taking gas from one of my tanks! He filled his gas can and set it around in back of the shed. He probably means to pick it up after work this evening when I'm not around."

"And?"

"And I poured the gas back and filled his can with water!" Jimmie admitted, half sheepishly.

"You didn't! That'll cause a real mess for him," Dona complained.

"Well, he deserves it. I already pay him more than he's worth, and he knows it!" Jimmie assured her as he walked back out the door.

Dona had to admit that the man would take advantage of Jimmie if he could, even though he outwardly seemed honest and accommodating. Just a few weeks earlier he'd been caught confiscating oil from the farm.

Jimmie had complained to Claude Davis, who did most of his mechanic work, that the overhaul on the tractor he'd done earlier must not have worked because it still used oil. Rafe had taken several cans with him to the field each morning. He claimed it was needed to keep the tractor running.

Claude laughed when he heard this and told Jimmie, "Trade tractors with him one day and see what you think!"

Jimmie did and he thought just like Claude. The tractor wasn't the problem. Dona knew that Jimmie hadn't exactly confronted Rafe, but the underhanded dealing had stopped when Jimmie informed Rafe that he was sure he would make it through the day without extra oil. Maybe gentle hints just didn't work with Rafe. Dona could see that her husband was enjoying the present scenario. Rafe might be a weasel, but Jimmie was just as ornery!

Mrs. Martin took a job at the cap factory in Whitesville and moved to a different house in Bedford, situated between Merry's home and the school. She visited Dona and Jimmie often, usually in the evening, and insisted on walking out from town, saying she enjoyed the fresh air and needed the exercise. Her daughter, Lizabeth, hadn't been back to see Nora for a few years, although Jimmie had taken his new family to Davidson, Texas, to be introduced to her and Hoff at their lake home. Beth held a secretarial job, he managed a miniature golf course, and they had a little poodle they adored but no children.

The girls' cousin, Lenore, was to be married in June of 1957. Earlene asked Retha to come out to Oregon for the ceremony. She had wished for both her folks to be present--they hadn't been out for a visit since she and Emmett had settled in Martinsville a few years earlier. Now it was too late for that, but maybe someone could accompany Retha on the train. Dona felt she was too indispensable to the farm at the present time, and Barbara had her work, also, so it was agreed that Sharon would make the trip. It would be a challenge for the two of them, as Sharon, just sixteen, had never traveled on her own before and Retha had relied on Sam to take care of such arrangements. Dona worried the entire time they were gone. Her concern was for the most part unfounded, except when Sharon and her grandmother got off the train in Salt Lake City for an ice cream cone and nearly missed making it back on time.

When the two returned to Missouri, they brought photos and tales of the beautiful occasion and of Earlene's abundant rose gardens. Dona was envious of their experience and wished she could visit her elder sister, but knew there wasn't much chance of Jimmie leaving his work on the farm.

Shortly after Dona arrived home one evening, she spied Jimmie approaching briskly across the yard. It was unlike him to come to the house at that time of day--he never wanted supper before seven or eight o'clock. Worried, she met him before he reached the back porch. His expression gave her no reason to think anything was amiss, so she greeted him with her usual broad smile. She sensed he was eager to share his news, but a little wary, too.

"How would you like to go for a ride?" he asked.

She was tired, but he didn't often ask for her help with anything, so she said, "Sure!"

"A long ride. A very long ride, out to Oregon." He looked expectantly at her. She didn't know what to say. Confusion clouded her face.

"Oregon, the state?" she asked hesitantly.

"Uh-huh. In the truck," he quickly replied, feeling she might be overjoyed too soon if she didn't know the particulars of the proposition. That really confused Dona. She guessed there must be some farm-related reason for such an odyssey, but couldn't fathom what it might be. She was about to fault him for keeping her in suspense when he continued, "Carl McGeorge wants some blue grass headers hauled out there. It's a chance to make some money, and I thought you might like to go. We could go on over to Martinsville after we unload the machinery."

"How could you get away?" she asked. "For that matter, how could *I* get away?"

"You've got vacation time coming. Couldn't you use that?" he ventured. Dona almost laughed at that. It would be some vacation, she thought. But, then, it would be more of a trip than she expected they would be taking. Jimmie wasn't one to travel much and to be away for any length of time was impossible for him.

"How could you leave the farm?" she questioned, knowing he must have some way in mind, or he wouldn't have considered the undertaking. "I don't think Rafe can handle it by himself."

"I could get Jim Ed to come over every day to see if everything's working and do the evening chores. I'm sure he'd be willing."

Of course he would, Dona realized. She knew that no matter how busy he was, Jimmie always found time to go where help was needed and figured it was probably the same with others, including his neighbor.

"We can make the trip in August. By then, I'll have things caught up around here and the crops will be put by until harvest. What do you say? Shall I tell him 'yes'?"

Dona thought seriously about it for a while. She knew Jimmie had never been through the Rocky Mountains, as she had, and she remembered the perilous passes that had terrified her in a car. She wasn't eager to make the trip in the truck. Still, it was money they could use, and she was anxious to see her sister's family again. So "yes" was the message Jimmie sent by phone to Carl McGeorge that night.

As planned, one Friday night in August the beast roared into the lane and shuddered to a stop at the bottom of the hill. The creature was more of a behemoth than Dona envisioned when she had wondered how Jimmie could position five of the contraptions onto the stock truck. She had seen such equipment in the fields on the bottomland west of town. It was several years back and the bluegrass seed industry had since migrated from the prairies of the Midwest to the high plains of the Northwest.

Four of the headers standing on end and one lying across the top was the solution she'd been unable to decipher. Her unspoken reservations about the wisdom of their upcoming adventure sprang to the surface when she saw the mass of machinery that would truly be dangling above their heads as they journeyed westward.

They set out at 4 a.m. the next day. On another Saturday Jimmie might have been taking off at that hour with a load of hogs for the St. Joseph stockyards. Dona had made such trips with him, when they'd go to the Hoof and Horn for breakfast after checking in at the holding pens. This morning seemed not so different as they set out, with a large bundle of their personal belongings stashed snugly at Dona's feet.

"Just 2,000 miles to go!" Jimmie playfully announced as they bumped across the cattle guard and he steered toward the lights of the sleeping town.

Riding with Jimmie in the cab of the truck, Dona was surprised at the comfort she felt. The trepidation she experienced earlier had vanished. The space was roomy and she sat up high where she could see fields and forests as they passed in an unbroken diorama before her. She knew her unexpected ease wasn't due to the improved condition of the roadways but to her confidence in

A Hundred Miles to the City

her husband behind the wheel. She'd thought the truck with its cumbersome load would be hard to handle, but instead, the weighty combination of machine and machinery gave a feeling of substance and stability. It seemed to cling to the surface of the road as they flew along.

Jimmie sat with his billed cap securely on his head, the breeze through the open windows ruffling his collar and cooling the sweat on his neck. His muscled arms lay easily on the steering wheel, hands relaxed but ready. Dona thought how this must seem like a real holiday to him compared to the work he usually did each day.

They had come through Nebraska and entered Wyoming before their first night's stop. During the long day their conversation was centered on the condition of the countryside and the quality of the crops growing upon it. The season's heat had taken its toll, and brittle dry patches had developed along the edges of some fields. In a few flat areas, irrigation devices sprayed glittering plumes of water over endless rows of soybeans. Jimmie's comment was "What a waste of water!"--thinking, most likely, of the time it took him to pump water from his deep well to fill the stock tanks. And he had to compound that with the time it took him to keep the pump operating.

On the second day out, they neared the Continental Divide. The flat lands fell away as the truck labored into higher and higher elevations. Fields gave way to craggy outcroppings and then to rounded foothills, eroded in striated patterns that told of millennia of wind and water abrasion. The green growth that formerly dominated the landscape turned into muted gray that softened the rugged terrain and cooled the atmosphere. No longer did an occasional pheasant strut across the road in front of them, and the prairie dogs were left behind when they entered into the high country.

"It isn't good for much, is it?" Jimmie commented as he surveyed the broad expanse of featureless, undulating prairie.

"My brother used to tend sheep somewhere in this area," Dona flatly stated. A faraway look crossed her face as she focused on a distant drama that she didn't want to pull into the present. "I wish he still did," she added sadly. Her correspondence with her brother consisted of one visit a year, when she brought him a carton of cigarettes, and maybe a watch, if he needed a new one.

Jimmie remembered the story of her oldest brother and regretted his statement.

The form of an abandoned cabin could be seen tucked into the side of a broad hill, not yet a part of the ground it sat upon. Dona envisioned Grant there, whittling or reading, and happy, as she was almost certain he now was not. Before she knew it, words about her brother came spilling out, and she felt a strange relief as memories gave form to feelings she had forgotten. She found herself telling Jimmie of the many hardships her family had faced in the harsh years of the Depression.

"I guess Grant was one of the reasons my parents separated. And Earlene was the one who talked Mom into going back to Dad." Dona knew that she herself had been upset by that decision. It seemed to her that her father never treated her mother the same after that. Retha suffered not by any outward affront but by the subtle hurt that a lack of appreciation engendered. Dona couldn't count the number of times she'd wanted to throttle her father for intentionally omitting Retha's birthday or Christmas. She'd asked him once if he couldn't get her mother a pair of nylons, or something--anything. But, stubbornly, he refused. Talking to Jimmie about these things soothed the turmoil that had crept into her consciousness. Maybe it was her way of putting Sam to rest.

"We didn't have it so bad," he admitted. "But I think the hard times had a lot to do with Father leaving." It seemed strange to Jimmie to hear himself say that aloud.

"Weren't your family farmers, too?" she asked, knowing the Torrances, Nora's family, had lived on the home place for many years.

"Yes and no. My grandparents were. Father wasn't. I don't think he ever felt at home in Bedford, either," Jimmie told her.

"Where was he from?" Dona asked.

"Over by Culver City--you know, in the vicinity of the pasture where I keep the cows, south of Route H. We lived over there when I was in the grades. I went to Long Branch School for a couple of years," he told her. Dona knew where that was. Her girls' school, Star of the West, had gone there for softball games in the spring and fall.

She remembered Jimmie's mentioning once that his grandfather had been a bootlegger. "I wonder how Nora and your father ever got together. She's so religious," Dona ventured, then grinned. "Well, I imagine he was handsome and charming and she was pretty and spunky," she said, answering her own question. She had met Jimmie, Sr., and felt that Jimmie definitely resembled him.

"What did your father do then?" she asked.

"Different things. Some trucking. Some farming. But mostly running bars. It was a pretty good occupation during the Depression. People always found money to buy drinks," he said wryly. "Those years were hard for Mom, but she tried to make the best of things."

"I'm surprised Nora never remarried," Dona stated. "She was young enough and she's certainly not shy around men."

"I think she always expected Father to come back, even after he'd remarried--at least until Robby came along. She always seemed to be . . . kind of, waiting," he said by way of explanation. Thinking back on her own experience, Dona didn't discount that possibility.

He went on to tell her of his own tribulations as his mother struggled to raise him and Lizabeth alone. Dona felt as if she were gaining a part of his past. Somehow, he managed to mix in a sense of humor, a trait Nora had mysteriously developed and passed on to her children--and one that could not be attributed to most in the dour Torrance clan.

"Did you say Retha is planning an auction?" Jimmie asked.

"Uh-huh. Hank talked her into moving to a smaller place there in Lenox," Dona replied.

"Maybe we could buy Sam's old car for Sherry," Jimmie suggested. "She could drive it to ball practice." He was thinking of her complaints when he arrived late to take her to Horton.

"Well, Mom won't use it, of course," Dona agreed. Her mother had never learned to drive and now relied on her family for trips to the doctor or any visiting she wanted to do.

As their journey took them closer to the rugged mountains, Dona's apprehension resurfaced. She remembered the steep grades and treacherous switchbacks that dominated mountain traveling. She had been driving on some stretches, when the highway was straight and flat, to give Jimmie a break. She knew it would be up to him now to handle the truck and its huge load. Her nerves wouldn't allow her to attempt maneuvering the massive machine through the mountains.

A marked improvement in the roadway put her mind somewhat at ease. They both remarked on how the new highway had been cut right out of the side of the mountain and wondered how such a feat could have been accomplished. In many places, the roadway traced the flow of a stream, but in other places it sliced right into canyon walls.

Unlike in the earlier days, when Sam's car had to hug the inside of the curves, this surface was wide, with shoulders on both sides for emergency stopping. Now and again, a drive-out allowed travelers to stop their cars to enjoy the spectacular vistas and to take photographs. Around every curve of the road, a new and more gorgeous sight appeared, with rock formations, jagged and ominous but breathtakingly beautiful. Trees held tenaciously to cracks in the seemingly solid façade, causing the pair to marvel that plants could survive in such an environment.

In some places the rock walls were perpendicular but in others looked as if they had buckled and folded into themselves. On a distant range--the Tetons,

Dona determined on her map--snow still appeared on the highest peaks and reached down into the crevices, like icy fingers clutching the earth below.

Just before reaching Pendleton, the couple came to a section of road construction. Huge yellow earthmovers rumbled beside them, each enormous tire on the vehicles larger than the whole of Jimmie's truck. Caterpillars labored on the edge of the mountain, seeming to defy gravity in their effort at rearranging the rugged landscape. An orderly progression of boreholes could be seen on the exposed face of the rock, blasted away to yield to progress. Dona wondered how long the rock had existed before it was brutally shattered and reshaped to meet the demands of modern traffic. She noticed women working as flagmen, the job her father used to do in Minnesota. They appeared hard and weatherworn and she suspected they must possess a special toughness to survive among the construction crews. She had learned by experience that men often resented females taking over jobs that were formerly their domain.

On the relentless incline down Soldier Pass, Jimmie put the engine into low gear. He wanted to avoid using the brakes too much. Midsummer sunlight scorched the roadway, contributing to the real danger of burning out the brakes on the steep grade. Dona saw a line of cars forming behind them and knew they would soon be leading a caravan down the endless slope. She silently apologized to their fellow travelers as the weighty machine crawled carefully down the long side of the mountain. She thought that the truck and its load were probably less of a hazard than Sam had been. At the same time, she found it amazing that her father, with his conservative ways, had possessed courage enough to bring his family out here, with no real promise of better times or employment.

As the procession continued to hunker down the steep slope, she thought of their cargo--their reason for making the hazardous trip.

"Why did Carl McGeorge stop growing bluegrass?" she asked curiously.

"I suppose the market shifted to the West Coast," Jimmie offered. "Or, maybe the soil or the climate of Oregon turned out to be better suited to growing it. That happens. Maybe it couldn't be produced as cheaply in our area as it could out here, and he couldn't compete."

"Didn't that mess up a lot of farmers?" she asked. "I thought they used to call northwest Missouri 'The Bluegrass Capital of the World.'"

"They did. Whether it really was or not, I don't know," Jimmie grinned. "And Carl called himself 'The King of Bluegrass!'"

"That's quite a come-down--his going out of business!"

"It probably didn't hurt Carl much. He was ready to retire, but a lot of growers had to switch crops. That's a big expense," Jimmie remarked. Her pensive look led him to add, "That's the way of the world, Dona. Times change. Now we plant more soybeans, and so far there's a good market. Grandpa Torrance used to raise horses and mules, before he sold out to Earl. Everyone began buying tractors and there was no need for the animals anymore."

"Is that why he lost his farm?" Dona asked, though she knew the subject was something of a sore spot with the Torrance family.

"Well, it came at the same time as the Depression, which didn't help."

"I thought the farmers who owned their land were the lucky ones then. At least they could grow the food they needed," Dona stated.

"But they still had to pay taxes on that land. It has to be productive to pay for itself," he told her. "It can't just set there idle."

She'd never thought of that. It had been Dona's belief that if you were a landowner you had it made. Her family had always been renters and didn't even own the crops. She knew Jimmie had been eager to have his own place, but she was beginning to see that there were many facets to land ownership she didn't fully understand.

After Dona and Jimmie delivered their cargo to eastern Washington, they continued on to Portland on Route 84. The scenic roadway ran alongside the Columbia River and was truly the most awesome locale that either of them had ever visited. They passed The Dalles that Earlene had often written about and concurred with her generous assessment of the area's beauty.

They arrived at Martinsville late and exhausted by the glut of traffic they had encountered near Portland, but tremendously happy to see their hosts.

During their stay they were introduced to the new son-in-law, with whom the Harts were obviously quite pleased. Emmett insisted on driving them to Mount Hood and up to the beautiful chalet where local enthusiasts went to ski. It was below the summit and free of snow at the time, but Earlene told them that during the winter snowdrifts often reached the eaves of the structure.

Emmett was currently employed driving a logging truck, so he entertained them with stories of his experiences in the mountains. He described one incident in detail. The truck's steering went out, and he was only able to bring the rig to a halt at the very edge of a sheer drop off, front tires dangling over the side. Dona recalled the escape ramps for runaway trucks Jimmie had pointed out earlier. She was already concerned about the need for such structures; now besides worrying about their own brakes failing, she would fear being run over by one of the big eighteen-wheelers. Still, she remembered that Emmett enjoyed telling a good story, so maybe he exaggerated the danger a little bit. She hoped.

They stayed with Earlene's over two nights, then rose early to begin on the long road back to Missouri. They arrived back home just a little over a week after they started out.

"Those damn pigs!" Dona groaned in exasperation as the truck passed into the lane. Their bulky forms could be seen in the periphery of the security light. "They're rooting up the park!" Some had escaped the barnlot to find better pickings in the grassy area at the foot of the hill. This wasn't the first time the monsters had ravaged the area. She'd driven them back in and complained to Jimmie before, plus, she hated the pig smell of the nearby lot. He'd only laughed and reminded her--"That's the smell of money!" She was relieved to learn they hadn't penetrated the yard. Other than that disgusting discovery, Jimmie found all in order on the farm, with plenty of work awaiting him at sunrise.

There was never a period in Jimmie's life when he'd been around babies--human babies, that is. So when the first grandchild, a girl, came home, Dona wondered how he would respond. Maybe he would be uncomfortable holding her, or afraid of her, or maybe, even, indifferent towards her. None of these happened. He delighted in holding the baby, seeming at ease with her the moment he saw her. Dona thought maybe his vast experience in animal husbandry allowed him to feel comfortable with the little one. Both grandparents delighted in having the babies around, as first Coralea, then Barbara gave birth to a baby girl to add to their growing family.

In 1958 Sherry graduated from high school and started college, living in the dorm at Madison. She soon found that sharing bathroom facilities with fifty other girls was not her cup of tea, so she returned home for a while, then took a room off campus. She graduated three years later, moved to Chillicothe, and began her teaching career in high school English. She enjoyed her first assignment in the large school but was occasionally mistaken for a student. Indeed, she was barely twenty-one at the time. She met her future husband, from Iowa, and they set the date for December.

By the time Sherry and Dave March were to be married, there were four grandchildren in the clan, as a boy had been added to each young family.

The wedding would take place at the Christian Church in Bedford, as Barbara's had a few years earlier. The oldest granddaughter would be the flower girl, and Sherry's college roommate was chosen as maid-of-honor. Dave's buddies from Iowa would come down to be his attendants.

A Hundred Miles to the City

The wedding ceremony went off without a hitch, with the exception of the flower girl's forgetting to toss the rose petals before the bride, which only endeared her to the watching company.

After the newlyweds were waved off in front of the church, Nora, Barbara and Coralea hurried back to get the kitchen in readiness for the following event. The reception dinner would be served in the same room, so Dona wanted the cabinets clear and tidy.

Up until this time, the girls had referred to Nora as "Mrs. Martin." They had spent time with her at family gatherings but hadn't really gotten to know her well. Each thought Nora overly solicitous. Dona supposed Nora wanted to be pleasant but didn't know how to treat the three granddaughters who were flung upon her as full-grown teenagers.

The girls were panting from their hurry-up transformation from wedding guests to kitchen help, but Nora arrived at the door full of smiles and eager to begin her assignment. She stepped into the back porch and stamped off the bit of snow that clung to her shoes. A generous amount of the white stuff had fallen during the previous night.

"My goodness! It looks like you've gotten everything done!" Nora exclaimed as she assessed the two long tables. They were accompanied by an assortment of straight-backed chairs, drawn up into position.

"Mom wants us to get the dishes done and everything cleaned off and put away," Barbara said to Nora as she motioned to the sink, where pots and pans were stacked in disarray. "The food's ready to be set out, but we need to get this cooking mess cleaned up before everyone gets here." She began organizing the utensils in left to right fashion, as she always did when she washed the dishes.

Coralea and Barbara had slipped into their tennis shoes, both for speed and comfort, but Nora bustled around in her customary two-inch heels.

"Good heavens! What all are we having?" Nora asked as she mentally counted the containers used for cooking.

"Plenty!" was Coralea's answer.

Nora had brought relish trays out the day before. Dona knew that she would spend a lot of time artistically arranging vegetables and dips. Nora put a lot of store in presentation.

The three stood together by the sink, preparing for their task. The light that spilled from the window cast a circle of comfort on winter-bare bushes just beyond the panes. Fluffy chickadees could be seen hunkering between the brittle branches. Abrupt blackness framed the little scene in a tableau worthy of John J. Audubon.

"It's homey here, isn't it?" Coralea observed.

"'Home is where, when you go there, they have to take you in . . .'" Nora recited. Neither girl had ever heard Nora quote anyone. When they looked expectantly at her, she continued. "Some smart person somewhere came up with that--maybe Robert Frost?"

"Not exactly a happy thought, but comforting, I guess," Coralea stated, amused. Neither she nor Barbara had lived there for as much as a year's time, but both felt as if it were their coming-home place.

"Honey, let me do that. You'll get all mussed," Nora offered to Barbara, who had run water in the sink and was preparing an extra basin for rinsing. Nora, ever prepared, had brought an apron, which covered most of her tailored dress. Barbara felt herself being pushed aside at the sink and decided to let Nora take over.

"You wash. We'll dry and put away," Coralea suggested.

"I'm afraid I'm a little out of practice. I don't have many dishes to do anymore," Nora announced. She swished and scrubbed, pushing pots and pans around hurriedly. Their guests would be coming anytime and she was determined to be prepared. Dona came in and began setting out dishes from the refrigerator.

Now and then the three at the sink jostled each other in their hurry to put the place in order. They'd been at their task for quite a while before Nora decided to kick off her shoes. Standing beside her, Barbara felt herself abruptly towering over her grandmother. She hadn't realized Nora was so short. And Nora didn't realize she was falling off her shoes and into the girls' hearts at the same time.

"This is almost as much fun as Jimmie and Lizabeth and I used to have!" Nora announced.

Both girls looked at her.

"What? You didn't know Jimmie could do dishes?"

Barbara laughed aloud at the caricature in her mind of Jimmie at the sink with dishwater dripping from his elbows. In the years since his marriage to her mother, Barbara had certainly never seen him in that maidenlike pose!

"He was more interested in hanging around the kitchen than in working, though. He and his sister would aggravate each other by putting pans to soak instead of scrubbing them." She smiled and freckles played around the laugh lines in her face.

"On his night, Jimmie would put sudsy water in a stubborn pan and set it back so Lizabeth would have to do it on her night. Then she'd do the same to him. One time they'd stuck so many pots and pans away "soaking" that I ran out of anything to cook in!"

"What did you do?" Barbara asked with interest, finding it hard to believe her stepfather had ever taken part in washing dishes.

"I said, 'I'm calling them all back in,'" Nora replied, chuckling. "They were stuck everywhere, some on shelves out in the porch!"

Nora continued telling the girls tales of Jimmie's boyhood, including the time Dona had caught him bathing in the washtub in the back porch. The girls hadn't heard about that.

The girls were greatly amused by Nora's descriptions of the embarrassing moments Jimmie suffered as he was growing up. And Nora was delighted to share them with her interested listeners.

"I have pictures. Come to my house sometime and I'll show you. He really was a darling boy!" Nora assured them.

Now and then Barbara left the group to check on Stewart, her six-month old, who was sleeping in the cozy bedroom behind the fireplace. The three toddlers were up in the toy room, exploring among the leftovers from the girls' own childhood.

Voices were heard as visitors approached the back door. Nora immediately filled the sticky pan she was scrubbing with soapy water and stuck it in the drawer beneath the oven. The girls laughed with her as they scrambled to get the counter dried and towels hung up. A month later Dona discovered the pan under the oven and wondered how and why it came to be there. Thereafter, Nora received many ribbings for shirking her pot scrubbing duties. The incident was mentioned whenever some of the family shared time at the sink.

When the guests began arriving, most hurriedly entered at the back door, allowing only a small whiff of December air to slide in with them. Jimmie had bladed off a large area so friends and relatives could park safely, away from deep snow and the precipitous bank of the hillside. Now he brought in a couple of logs for the fireplace, then took off his coat and began to mingle with the assembled group. It wouldn't be long before he would get into his coveralls and go out to do the most necessary of his evening chores.

Nora assisted with greeting and taking coats. She was acquainted with a few, some of Sharon's high school friends, with whom she chatted happily. Dona noticed that Nora didn't retire to the edges of the gathering but mixed easily with the young people. They seemed pleased to visit with her, and Dona realized that Nora's presence was truly an asset in making everyone feel comfortable. More important, however, was Dona's discovery that Nora sincerely wished to play an active role in the affairs of the household.

When Sharon introduced Nora to the Marches as her grandmother, Nora gushed, "Aren't you just darlings to come all the way down from Iowa. Your David and Sharon make the sweetest couple!" Usually this kind of speech from Nora caused Sharon to assume a look of patience and forbearance. Now as the two exchanged a knowing glance, Dona noticed a smile of acceptance on her daughter's face.

The girls had enjoyed working with their new grandmother that day, and for some reason, from then on she was known affectionately to them not as Mrs. Martin, but as Nora. The diminutive woman would never be the substantial figure that grandmother Retha was to the girls, but she did become a meaningful presence in the lives of each in Jimmie's adopted family.

TWENTY-FOUR

The golden years. That term is often used to describe a time of reward and relaxation. Had Dona later assessed the periods of her life, she might have said the '60s and early '70s were hers, and she was certain Jimmie's, also. She would remember those days as sunny, the seasons mild, the years profitable. They weren't always. The rains sometimes didn't come when needed, and the crops weren't quite as good as Jimmie had optimistically envisioned. But, as a child of the Depression, with those times as a benchmark, she was easily satisfied. And the times were truly good for most during those years.

Her children were gone from home--married with children of their own, healthy and thriving. They were scattered in other counties, but not too far for easy visiting. Sharon had quit teaching to raise her family. She and her husband, an Internal Revenue Service agent, were buying a farm near Carroll, a few miles south of Chillicothe. Don and Cliff, husbands of the other girls, both coached and taught industrial arts in small schools and Coralea was working on her degree. The young families seldom missed gathering at the farm for holidays. Those were the best times for Dona, for many other relatives joined them, also. The role of host for family get-togethers had passed from Retha to Dona.

The big house was roomy enough for the whole clan when they assembled for Christmas. At that time, Jimmie would throw a gigantic log on the fire-- the yule log, Dona would say--and the house was toasty-warm, with the scents of pine and hickory wafting throughout. Once, all the girls and their families spent Christmas Eve there, so the tree, situated in the bay window in the front room, was surrounded with gifts, wrapped and unwrapped, stretching to the middle of the spacious room. That Christmas Jimmie brought Charlie into the back porch and set all five of the children up on his back at once. The docile pony, happy to be in out of the cold, patiently stood and allowed a torrent of pats and giggles to engulf him. Dona worried for her floor but was used to having an occasional animal there, nestled into a big box with a heat lamp clipped on the side. She marveled at her husband's incredible care and patience in handling the vulnerable creatures. He treated each one as if it were the only animal on the place and its survival paramount. So far, none of the little strugglers had made it on into the house.

Before they had lived on the place five years, Dona succeeded in getting the entire house renovated. Her first project was to paper every room and refinish the woodwork in the main rooms. She had help from the girls and their spouses, but did most of the work herself. She was most proud of the walnut mantel that she stripped herself, then oiled and rubbed until the wood appeared soft and glowing.

Everyone pitched in to repaint the outside of the house, even Jimmie. The green shutters were removed, repaired and repainted. Barbara had brushed paint onto the picket fence during the summer she had lived on the place--it was still crisp and white. A statue of a colored boy in valet garments stood holding a hitching ring beside the front entrance. A huge swing hung from the oak tree at the foot of the hill. Dona had asked the light and power men to hang the nylon rope when they came with their cherry picker to replace a security light. The sprawling conveyance could be drawn back to the old steps and swung out in a magnificent arc. Not just the children of the family, but Dona as well, soared over the park, toes pointing to the sky.

A new machine shed now occupied the area to the east of the lane. Dona would learn later that the original Stingley house had stood there. The foundation of an earlier barn was still intact nearby, and a row of hickory trees remained, marking the edge of a previous roadbed.

The barn that now served the farm dominated the hillside to the east of the house. Once an amazing structure, the unpainted board and batten exterior reflected years of weathering and disregard. At the front, the barn was a two-story building, the floor level with the path that forked off from the lane. The cavernous haymow was in good repair, but the rotting floor of the barn was no longer deemed strong enough to support the tractor or loaded wagons. This observation prompted Jimmie to have the new machine shed built.

Dona enjoyed being outside, so she happily assumed the job of lawn mowing. Jimmie bought a special mower from a golf course and attached it to his little Ford tractor so she could mow the park as well as the yard. The front wheels of the tractor were wide-set so she didn't fear mowing on the hillside. Each year she reclaimed more of the grassy area beside the lane, so eventually the house began to look much as it had in its prime. Dona enjoyed driving the tractor so much that she mowed the right-of-way toward Bedford and on into town as well.

Dona went back to school, taking classes in Madison to prepare for her GED exam. She had always wanted a diploma, but the main impetus was to qualify for courses in figuring income taxes. Keeping records for the farm had grown into a formidable task, made even more daunting by having to haul everything off to a tax accountant each quarter.

After gaining her diploma and attending sessions on tax laws and practices, Dona took over maintaining the books for Jimmie's farming operation. He was surprised at her expertise in performing the myriad calculations necessary for completing the complicated forms. She occasionally went for a refresher course to catch up on the transformations farm returns inevitably underwent.

Her main obstacle to keeping orderly and complete records was Jimmie's difficulty in saving farm-related receipts. She wanted to list everything that could honestly be included in the "farming expenses" column. The figures she worked with amazed her. So much money coming in and going out! At least on paper.

Still at her job with the light company in Madison, Dona now drove a light blue Ford Fairlane. It ripped through Bedford early each morning and sped equally fast toward home each evening. She made her time on the road as short as possible. Jimmie teased her about being a blue blur to people along the way. Still, when she was on an errand for him, he appreciated her expediency. Each evening when Dona pulled into the lane, Tippie, the farm dog that succeeded Nora's Suzie, waited by the gate. He must have known the sound of her car, for he was always there to greet her. He never left the lane to go toward town, always staying in the yard, waiting by the house if she were home. The hackles on the dog's neck stiffened when a pig approached the picket fence, and he charged toward it, barking an emphatic warning. The cats could rub against Tippie's legs and eat from his pan, but pigs would not be tolerated!

Saturday was sale day, obviously an unwritten rule that Dona finally accepted. At first, she was a little put out at Jimmie's insistence on attending auctions so regularly, as he rarely took time off to do anything else. Sundays were no longer days for visiting. If she were to visit relatives, she'd have to do it alone, or they would have to come to her.

Accompanying Jimmie to farm auctions started Dona on a quest of her own--that, and the antique furniture Jimmie had inherited from his family. Merry Torrance passed away in 1968, leaving him a beautiful oak dresser and some smaller articles. Dona thought they fit nicely into the old house and began to look for other period pieces. Soon she was going to her own auctions while he went to his. She had no particular object in mind when she went to an estate sale, but often managed to bring home a piece or two that she fancied and that she believed to be good buys.

One of the men from the light company was also an auctioneer and called many of the estate auctions in the area. He, and soon others in the trade, began expecting her to show up at sales and to enter the bidding wars that contributed to successful auctions. Knowing she couldn't compete with the moneyed collectors, she enjoyed finding treasures that escaped their attention or ambition. She brought home a fainting couch for the big bedroom upstairs, a wicker teacart for the back porch, cinnabar vases that she placed in the transom above the kitchen doorway, and a beautiful walnut bed for her own bedroom.

Jimmie encouraged her in these pursuits. His own purchases usually amounted to more than hers, both money-wise and size-wise, and often weren't any more useful to the farm. He wasn't likely to pass up a bargain, needed or not. Sometimes he'd bid on items just to keep the sale moving along. Occasionally Jimmie and Dona went to the same auctions, which could also be viewed as social events, as most of those present were acquaintances of the owners.

On these occasions Dona began renewing friendships from the past. Ross Gates and his wife Gail were still in the community, as were Caroline and Junior Black. They still lived in Bedford and he farmed much of the bottomland that had belonged to his late father, Cecil Black, Sr.

Besides those earlier acquaintances, Dona became familiar with others in the area. The congregation of the Christian Church had disbanded due to shrinking attendance and the building was converted into a community center. Jimmie served on the board, so Dona contributed much of her time to activities that supported the townspeople's interests.

Through her association with the town board and the starting up of the community center, Dona became better acquainted with Amabelle Johnson. The two had spoken at an earlier time, when Amabelle came out to return Jimmie's senior picture. He'd given it to her earlier, when they were dating.

Amabelle had called ahead to tell Dona she was coming. *To prepare me, or to warn me--what in the world will we have to say to each other?* Dona wondered. At any rate, it gave Dona time enough to make up her mind not to like her. But the moment Amabelle came walking across the yard, Dona felt her defenses crumble. Dressed in a simple skirt and blouse, Amabelle carried herself as if she were entirely unconcerned with how she looked or what kind of impression she was making.

Dona invited her into the house for lemonade. It was early evening and the soft breeze had been no match for the summer temperatures. Amabelle's light brown hair lay in gentle waves brushed back from her face in an attempt at comfort. Her friendly manner assured Dona that the visit was meant to be one of pleasure for them both.

"We've been packing--getting ready to move to Bedford," Amabelle announced. "I came across this picture and figured you might want it for yourself." The gray cardboard folder she offered Dona held a youthful picture of Jimmie, handsomely attired in a dark suit.

"Thanks. I do. Jimmie told me you and Norb were moving onto your folks' place. I see that they've had a new house built, across the road," Dona ventured.

"Dad's ready to retire, but he doesn't want to leave the farm. It's been home to him and Mother for so long, I don't think they'll ever leave entirely. Norb and I are going to build onto the old house and do some remodeling. You'll have to come out and see it when we're done," Amabelle suggested.

Dona remembered that the farm had once been the Torrance home place, where Nora grew up and where she and her family once lived when Jimmie was young. She was sure it held many memories for her husband.

"Where have you been living?" she inquired, by way of making conversation.

"Over at Atchison--by Norb's folks, where he's been since getting out of the service," Amabelle replied.

They continued chatting amiably in the airy kitchen.

"We've applied for an adoption," Amabelle announced abruptly. "We're going to be getting a little girl in just a few days!"

Dona was surprised when Amabelle shared such personal news with her. But then, observing the pleasure expressed by her visitor, she realized it was news that just had to be shared. News too good not to share!

"Well, I'm happy for you!" Dona said, and meant. "You're going to be really busy for a while!"

"I hope I can handle it," Amabelle worried. "I've waited a long time to become a mother. I'm not sure I'm qualified."

Dona had to laugh at that notion. She could testify that motherhood happened to the unprepared as well as to the experienced.

"It's a good thing that's not necessary, or we might be an extinct species!" she mirthfully contributed. The sound of her own laughter added to her ease as Dona relaxed in the company of the other woman.

After Amabelle left, Dona considered her interesting guest. Slender and graceful, Amabelle appeared to be exactly what Dona was not, and she hadn't wanted to like her. But she had to admit that Amabelle was charming and very easy to like.

Eventually Amabelle and Norbert adopted two children, the second a boy. He would some day take over the farming operation begun by Bill Catterson, Amabelle's father, after the Torrances moved from the place.

The acquisition of the church building for a community center brought the people from the area together as they had not been since the consolidation of the schools a few years earlier. Folks from surrounding farms, as well as the townspeople, turned out to help in the conversion of the substantial old structure. Once the building was repainted and the church bell removed from the belfry, people began bringing in artifacts they wished to share permanently--mostly old photographs and articles from the town's earlier newspapers. The last had ceased publication in 1938, so the community's events were now recorded only on the *Madison Daily Forum's* society page.

The local American Legion post had disbanded also, so many of their records were turned over to the new facility. The big wooden sign that listed veterans of armed conflicts was placed against the back wall of the former sanctuary, along with a glass case where smaller objects could be displayed.

The community incurred some debt in procuring the structure, making it necessary to rely on volunteer support for supplies as well as labor to get the organization up and running. The group decided that fundraisers would be needed, so bake sales, raffles and card parties were held after the church pews were sold and removed.

Surprising Dona, Jimmie suspended his farming duties to attend the monthly meetings, though he rarely made it on time. When he arrived on this day, cars were parked randomly where the gravel widened in front of the center. He entered through the small vestibule at the back of the sanctuary. Only two long tables and a few folding chairs occupied the large space, contributions from the now defunct legion. Standing to one side on the bare wooden floor were two sturdy flagpoles, draped with the American and Missouri flags. Three tall windows on each side of the large room were open to let fresh air flow through. Inverted v-shaped cornices and frosted panes gave the place a church-like atmosphere.

The group had chosen Junior Black to be their spokesperson, and he was speaking when Jimmie drew up a chair and joined the small gathering.

"We need a better way to raise money," Junior was saying.

"What we need first is to get some water into this place," Kenneth Livingston interjected. "We can't expect folks to go tottering to the outhouse when they come to card parties, especially at night. One of our not-so-young people might fall and break something."

"We 'not-so-young' folks appreciate the concern," Gladys Robertson chimed in. So far she hadn't been an active member of the group, but she never failed to let her opinion be known. Her husband's grocery store had closed a few years back, and the couple at last found some extra time on their hands. Gladys was organist for Methodist Church services, a position she'd held for at least thirty years. At seventy she was the senior member of the group.

"Where would we put a restroom?" Junior queried.

"We could partition off a corner of the altar area," Kenneth suggested. "There's room up there that generally isn't used." Raised two steps above the congregation seating, the altar spanned the entire width of the room and occupied a full one-fourth of the building. Not long ago Ana Ellis had led the primary section in Bible study there.

"If we're going to bring food in here, we need a refrigerator, and a kitchen sink of some kind," Wilma contributed.

"You know," Eddie Jones spoke up, "We're going to have some other decisions to make if we bring a water line in. We'll have to close down in the winter, or the pipes will freeze. There's no way we could heat this place all winter." Eddie was the man to go to for the key to open the building, since he lived just a few steps away. The janitor at the grade school, he and his wife lived in the only new house in Bedford.

"Maybe we could run some auxiliary heat in the restroom and go with heat tapes as a precaution," Kenneth suggested.

"As cold as it gets, I don't think that would do it," Eddie insisted. He anticipated some added responsibilities. He was the town's general maintenance man--the one likely to be summoned for emergency repair work, such as a furnace that didn't work or a pipe that had burst.

Junior looked for suggestions from others in the group before saying, "Why don't we just go with modernizing the place with a restroom for now? We could leave the outhouses where they are for backup. How do you all feel about that?"

"How're we going to pay for this?" Kenneth asked. "We've used up most of the initial donations for start-up. It'll be quite an expense."

"Couldn't we do most of the work ourselves?" Eddie suggested. "Jack Flint could handle the electrical part."

"Sure. We could assign him that, since he's not here to defend himself," Junior laughed.

Eddie slid his chair back from the table and worked a toothpick in his mouth for a bit.

Clare Samson

"Maybe we should go with what we have until we get the funds to move on this proposal," he suggested. He sat with his arms stoically folded across the breast of his customary striped coveralls.

"We need a fund-raiser that will generate a bit more money than a bake sale," LaRue Coulter commented.

Several ideas were bounced about before Gladys suggested a publication of the history of the town.

"We have a lot of good material in photos and news clippings. We could compile what we have, interview the elderly in the community . . . do some research at the courthouse, perhaps."

"That would be interesting to those of us who've grown up here, but I'm afraid we wouldn't have a very large market for selling books," Jimmie said uncertainly.

"Maybe we could include a larger area, like the county," LaRue returned, "--put in interesting stories about the past that are being lost as our older generations pass away. Don't you enjoy hearing tales about people in the area? Like, for instance, about Dr. Hancock and his studies on giants."

"It's going to take awhile to get something started," LaRue worried. "I'm sure we have several in the community who'd help with such a project, but to get a book written and published--that would take at least a year."

"Dona would probably work on it," Jimmie volunteered. She was interested in the history of the region, and she had become acquainted with many of the elderly who would know about the area's past.

Tiny Wilma Cameron shifted her position and raised her hand slightly, preparing to speak.

"Why don't we get up a committee to pursue this 'history book' idea--look into cost of publication and so on to see if we can expect to generate enough interest to make it pay off?"

"We could put out a call for help on this in Junior's paper," Jimmie suggested.

Before the group called it a day, they had produced a short plea which would later appear in Junior Wilson's paper as: "Interested in perservering our hisstory? Join us at teyh comunity center one June 20h, by Junior Black, for the bord."

Wilson's store mailed a mimeographed missive to area homes each week, free of charge. Junior did his own typing, and ran the copies himself, and since he was a religious man, always included a bible verse--in somewhat altered form, also--along with the current prices of certain commodities. His readers were happy to receive this communication, as much for the humor as for the news. They were certain the service was unique to their neighborhood.

A Hundred Miles to the City

At first Dona had reservations about the project. Already Mary Lamb was gone, and Nora McMurtry. They'd had first-person knowledge of much of the area's past. And W.B. Thompson had passed away just last year. He was editor of the last newspaper in Bedford. It seemed to Dona that the past was passing quickly, along with Mother Torrance, who left many family pictures with Nora, but not much in the way of local history.

There was much to pique Dona's interest in the history of the community. She would like to find out more about the old house and the Stingley family that had built it nearly one hundred years ago. And there was the matter of the gravestones down on Bid's place, one of the parcels of land Jimmie had acquired. Bid Browning now worked for her husband, but he wasn't in good health and had sold his farm with the stipulation that he could continue on the place for the remainder of his life. A couple of tombstones, very old and devoid now of markings, lay against a fence at the bottom of the bluff. Bid knew nothing of the origin of the stones nor did anyone else Jimmie had questioned. Dona wondered how far back they might date.

Her husband's interest in the land was quite different from hers, Dona knew. When he spoke of a certain farm, especially one he might be able to buy, his eyes danced with anticipation. It was almost as if he were procuring Paradise when he acquired first the Looker place, then Bid's place, and then the Anderson place. She'd heard people say that they settled on a place and put down roots there, but she could see that, with Jimmie, it was quite the opposite. The land seemed to send up tendrils into him, tying him tenderly but securely to his future and his past. She knew that most farmers truly loved the land, but her husband had a devotion to dirt that she'd never be able to understand. She felt connected to the Summerville community, but the itinerant nature of her time there must have robbed her of such an attachment. Expecting Jimmie to live anywhere else than where he was would be like passing a life sentence upon him.

Many changes had occurred in Bedford in the fairly brief time since Dona had first come to the community in 1942. There was no longer a doctor in town, no dry goods store, no produce house nor movie place--nor tavern, even. She guessed the population was at least one hundred fewer than it had been twenty years ago. The railroad that had caused such an astonishing transformation was said to be in fatal decline. Already many tracks were being ripped up in parts of the Midwest.

Several community members came to the advertised meeting, including Dona. In addition to the board members: Amabelle Johnson, Caroline Black, Chloe Simpson and Meredith Long. The Longs had been neighbors to the Martins when they'd lived on the McBain place. Dona liked the younger woman. She had four daughters and a son, all in school now. The youngest of the girls had been named for Nora, which Dona felt was quite a compliment to her mother-in-law.

Dona doubted she would enjoy working with Caroline but had to admit she'd likely be a capable contributor. Junior's late mother was Marva Black, one of Hiram Stingley's five daughters. Caroline would be a good resource for the family's history. Along with Moses Hawk and Peter Johnson, both ancestors of Jimmie's, the Stingley brothers were among the settlers of the region.

The group agreed that several old-timers of the area should be interviewed, if they were willing. Dona would contact Woodrow Nelson. She was eager to get started and promptly made an appointment to speak with him.

Her first interview was quite rewarding. Dona took along a tape recorder to preserve Mr. Nelson's memories. He had been a schoolteacher and had spent his early years in one of the area's country schools, which happened to be the Stingley School. Now gone, the building was situated a mile south of Old Bedford, on a corner of William Stingley's farm. Woodrow described the one-room structure and recounted activities and practices he'd experienced while teaching there. He had also taught at the wood frame school that was erected in new Bedford--the two-story building that stood upon the hill. Jimmie had gone there until the new brick school was built down the hill, just before his senior year.

Mr. Nelson shared some maps of the Washington Township area. Dona was most interested in a drawing that showed Indian trails, river fording points and other area landmarks, including Black Oak Grove, where the first white settlers located. One symbol on the map was a series of wavy lines that indicated a buffalo wallow. Judging by the places she could identify on the rudimentary map, which didn't show the location of new Bedford, she thought perhaps the wallow might be located on the Stingley place. The direction given indicated that it was southwest of a huge cottonwood tree, another landmark indicated on the illustration.

If she interpreted the line drawings correctly, the spot must be southeast of the Martins' house. Mound's Ford was marked plainly, and the house had been called the Mound Manse for a time. That amused Dona, for the house was certainly--or had been, at least-- elegant, but far from what she envisioned a mansion to be. The old riverbed was about halfway between the hill and the Platte River. Its course wandered across the field and in places was deep and contained stagnant water. If the river had straightened recently, that old waterway may have been the site of Mound's Ford. She would look into that possibility and see if she could find the buffalo wallow, which she thought might be on Jimmie's land. Maybe she could talk him into traipsing around the countryside with her to search for it.

Retha's family persuaded her to move to Bedford. Across the street from the community center, the house Retha settled into was old but sat on a large corner lot, with a spacious lawn. Dona and Jimmie took care of the yard work, and Retha tended the flowers that bloomed by the back step. Hank and Beulah had moved to Pumpkin Center on Highway 71, so they visited regularly. Hank now drove a tank truck for Skelgas, delivering bottled gas to rural customers. He spent much of his spare time painting in oils, mostly scenes from his memory of the Oregon coast. Dona was pleased when he shared some of his work with her.

One day Retha was at Dona and Jimmie's when the oldest grandchild quizzed Dona about family history. Vikki was a third-grader and members of her class were to construct their family tree for a unit in social studies.
"Mom can help you with that better than I can," Dona told the girl, who was ready with pencil and paper to document her ancestry. Retha smiled in her mischievous way.
"What would you like to know? You've already gotten names and birth dates from the family Bible, haven't you?" The children addressed her as Grandma Schmit.
Retha, Vikki and Coralea sat at the massive oak table that dominated the kitchen. Dona was nearby on the sofa bed she'd brought down from the apartment in Madison. She was aware of something different about her mother but couldn't quite put her finger on it. Retha's hair was thinning but still black, with just a few gray hairs visible--not nearly as many as she had in her own dark curls. Retha's freckles were paler, and her skin had begun to sag loosely around her face. But it was none of those things. Dona had grown accustomed to those gradual changes in her mother's appearance.
She finally identified the unfamiliar aspect. It was the apron. Retha was not wearing one. She didn't look right without it. Dona reflected that it was a strange way to define her mother but realized the apron was a big part of her being. How different their lives were, hers and Retha's. She'd hardly ever seen her mother without an apron. Retha seldom went out. Usually her family had come to her and she was generally in the kitchen while they were there. Dona was glad to see her mother arrive at a place in her life where she didn't need to wait on other people--and where her home was modern and comfortable.
"I remember being told that one of our relatives was hanged for a horse thief," Retha said with a sly grin. "I don't suppose that's the kind of history you want, though."

Dona gave her mother a questioning look. She'd learned that before but had never heard Retha acknowledge it.

"Well, that's not the kind of information people talk about. You just didn't mention those things in the family," Retha continued, knowing she would probably never have spoken of it herself unless she had been asked directly, which she was. After all, it was a part of their past and might be lost forever, if not mentioned now.

"Why don't you tell her about the Millison girl?" Dona asked her mother. That was a subject that had been hushed up in their family, but she had learned it from somewhere.

"Well, she would've been a cousin to your grandpa . . . no, great grandpa," Retha began. It was clearly not a story she was comfortable relating. "She got herself in a family way and her sister took her in. She lived with her sister and her husband until her time came. Then when the babies were born--they were twins--the couple claimed them as their own children, and I guess everyone believed they were."

"It looks like people who knew them would have noticed," Coralea stated skeptically.

"The sister went around for months with a pillow stuffed in her dress, and the Millison girl stayed in the house where no one would see her. Only the doctor who delivered them knew for sure whose babies they were." Retha believed that the charade had been successful, but Dona had heard the story as gossip in school, so perhaps the doctor hadn't been very discreet.

Those stories satisfied Vikki's curiosity and definitely added a little color to her perception of her ancestry. Dona wondered how many more titillating tales her mother had squirreled away in her memory. She wished she'd had this kind of talk with Retha a long time ago. But, her mother had always been very tight-lipped about family affairs--*tight lipped and tolerant,* Dona gratefully acknowledged.

Another Saturday, another sale day. Dona hadn't gone. The weather was nasty, and she saw nothing listed in the sale bill that caught her attention. Jimmie had been gone all day, as usual--he wouldn't want to miss anything, so he often went early and stayed late. She knew he especially enjoyed the homemade pies that were offered at the lunch wagon—she would have to work on that skill herself someday.

When he came into the back porch it was early yet, just after four o'clock.

"I bought you something at the sale today!" he announced.

"Well, where is it?" Dona queried. He looked empty-handed to her.

"Out in the pick-up. I didn't know if you'd want me to bring it into the back porch."

"Well, what is it?" *Not an animal,* she hoped. He read her thoughts and laughed.

"It's a welding outfit. Maybe you could save me from having to take everything in to Galen." His statement was more of a plea. Dona's expression rapidly went from surprised to pleased to dismayed--surprised he had considered it, pleased that he thought maybe she could do it, and dismayed knowing she probably couldn't.

"It's been a long time since I tried to weld anything . . ." she began.

"It would save us some money if you could, and a lot of time. Galen can't always get to things right away, you know," Jimmie encouraged.

"It's probably not like what we used at the war plant," Dona objected.

"Maybe. There are manuals," he assured her, smiling confidently. He was a firm believer in reading instructions.

"Well, bring it on in here and let's take a look at it," she finally agreed, not wanting to disappoint him.

In a couple of trips, with Tippie at his heels, Jimmie brought in all the paraphernalia included in the transaction. Dona immediately knew this would be a challenge! Still, she had mastered it once, maybe it would all come back to her. She'd never have guessed she would again be using the skill she had learned in the war plant in Kansas City. It had been over twenty years since she'd held a sparklighter in her hand or worn goggles.

In the weeks and months ahead, Dona attempted to do some welding, on old pieces from the shed or little objects from the house. Sometimes she could get the weld just right, but just as often her efforts didn't work out and the break ended up in worse shape than when she began.

She didn't mind trying to mend the broken pieces. Handling the tools brought back pleasant memories of the days she'd spent in Kansas City. The friendships she'd made then were now just parts of her past. Except for Jenny Green, she corresponded infrequently with the girls who had once been such close allies. Jenny worked overseas for the State Department, so they hadn't seen each other for several years.

While she made some progress, her painstaking efforts showed meager results. Regulating the gases to provide a neutral flame was challenge enough. Then, maintaining the proper distance and angle from her work surface required a steady hand and a lot of patience. Too much acetylene and the metal boiled, producing a surface that was pitted, and hence a weak weld. Too much oxygen and sparks flew and white foam formed on the surface--a weak weld, also. Too fast or too slow and the bead was uneven, or floated, or failed to penetrate properly. Many variables came into play that made the task formidable, and a time or two Dona considered admitting defeat. However, if she could help cut the time Jimmie spent trying to mend broken equipment, her efforts would be worthwhile. And, he had such confidence in her abilities, she didn't want to disappoint him.

Her first attempt on an actual piece of farm machinery was a T-fillet joint where she had to make several passes to lay on a series of beads. When she finally finished, she was somewhat disappointed in the outcome.

"It's a mess!" she said, frowning.

"It doesn't need to be pretty," Jimmie encouraged. "Let's see if it holds."

It did, and she got another job--not that she was looking for one.

"Why don't you learn to do this?" Dona asked Jimmie one day as he aided her in aligning and holding a juncture. A piece of the corn picker had broken off, and the problem was in a part that couldn't easily be disassembled so she was in the machine shed, lying on the ground. She smelled mice in the place and knew that pigs occasionally wandered through. If she couldn't get it mended, Jimmie would have to take the entire machine in to the garage in town, and it would be out of commission for *who-knows-how-long.*

"They have welding classes in adult education in Madison," she informed him. It had been many years since he'd been in school, but Jimmie liked to keep up on farming innovations by attending meetings and lectures sponsored by the Co-op or MFA. He agreed to the course and she signed him up.

"Joe Vetters is in the class," Jimmie told Dona after the first night's session.

"I used to play bridge with his wife," Dona volunteered.

"She was a Wisdom and once lived in this house. That was probably before you moved to Bedford, though," he added. Dona remembered admiring the stately old place back when Elmer Wisdom had lived here.

By the time the course was complete, Jimmie and Joe had struck up a friendship, and Joe asked the couple over to play cards. Jimmie didn't play bridge but knew how much Dona enjoyed the game, so he determined to give it a try.

When Dona heard of the invitation, she was more than eager to spend an evening out. They sometimes played pitch at the community center, but other than that, she and Jimmie had made no time for mutual friendships. Besides, Dona would like to have Kathleen over sometime and show her what she had done with the house.

The Vetterses were not close neighbors, although their farm would be connected to the Martins' at one point if not for the Platte River. The bottomland that stretched southward from the house's hill was bordered on the south by the meandering waterway. To get to Joe and Kathleen's, though, one had to go through Bedford, west on Route H a mile, then south again.

Blonde and petite, Kathleen didn't fit into Dona's perception of a farm wife. She couldn't picture the dainty woman out grubbing around in the garden, or, more improbably, milking a cow! Joe was tall and slender. Their daughter Ann most resembled him. She had played basketball with Sherry and had also been in her wedding.

"Ann's married now and living in Horton?" Dona asked.

"Uh-huh. Rick's still with us, though he's not here much of the time. He's helping Joe right now, but he's looking for something else."

"Just because you have a son doesn't mean he's going to want to farm," Joe said with a sigh. "And I don't want him to, if he doesn't really want it. It's too hard if it's not what you want to be doing!"

He got no argument with that.

Kathleen had spent only a short period of her life in the Stingley house, but it had been the home of her parents for many years. She was impressed with the many improvements Jimmie and Dona had made to the outside of the place, and assured them that she was eager to see the inside, also. Dona would be more than pleased to show off the place, the focus of her energies for the last several years.

Picking up the game of bridge again after so many years was not difficult for Dona. And they were all patient with Jimmie.

"Couldn't I just be the dummy for every hand?" he pleaded.

"Not so fast!" Kathleen retaliated. "We wouldn't want to put that much stress on you."

"We used to see you at ballgames sometimes," Joe said. "They were fun, weren't they?"

"Well, yes. The ones we actually got to," Dona said, shooting a sideways glance at her husband, who only ignored the intended barb. "In reality, it was probably as much my fault as his that we missed so many. They were usually on Friday nights, and by then I was tired and didn't want to go out again," Dona confessed.

"It seemed like I was always in the middle of something, or there were cows or pigs out that had to be rounded up," Jimmie admitted. He would like to have gone to more of Sherry's basketball games, but there was always something pressing to be done on the farm.

"I wish now we'd have taken more time," Dona declared. "Is Ann still playing softball?"

"Uh-huh, with the town team from Horton and a traveling team from Madison. She lives for it. But we don't go much. It's not the same, somehow," Kathleen allowed.

"Someday there'll be grandkids you can go watch," Dona assured her, realizing it wouldn't be long before her own might be playing ball somewhere.

The evening went quickly, and before long they were saying good night and promising to do it again soon. That didn't happen--the "soon" part. But the four did continue to meet at one or the other's house off and on for the remainder of their lives.

Now and then the Martins received a call from a neighbor informing them that their cows, or pigs, were out. It was not unusual. Many farmers in the vicinity had bad fences. In fact, there was enough of a problem in the area that lawsuits were sometimes threatened. It seemed to Jimmie that his livestock were determined to go visiting just when he was busiest. However, no matter what he was doing, he would stop, get into his pick-up and go out to hunt down the culprits and see them back into the proper perimeter. He wouldn't want strays in his fields any more than his neighbors did, nor did he want to be the cause of an accident if a driver came upon an animal in the roadway.

Over the previous decade, Jimmie had bought other small farms close to the home place when the former owner retired, moved away, or passed away. The fences on these places had already arrived at their limit of service. And then, fence building was a low-priority activity for Jimmie. He was much more likely to patch up the old than to erect a new, sturdier barricade for his livestock. Sometimes, coming home, Dona would meet an old sow headed into town. If a cow should make it into the park, it had some respect for the cattle guard, but pigs weren't so discriminating. Coralea's husband, Cliff, a bricklayer, had erected two sturdy posts alongside the entry to the lane. These were topped with a pair of wrought iron lanterns Jimmie bought at a foundry in St. Joseph. Usually Dona thought they added a bit of class to the place, but when she saw a parade of pigs passing through those portals she had to laugh--and then stop the car and head them off.

When Dona went down the hill to tell Jimmie of the latest such phone call, he was in the machine shed working on the combine. It was a mild fall evening, and he'd been making good progress in the bean field until the breakdown.

"The cows are out on Buholt again," Dona relayed. He looked tired and she hated to give him that news, but there was nothing else to be done. He pulled himself from under the big machine and wiped his hands on a grease rag lying nearby.

"I'll probably be late for supper," he informed her as he walked resignedly toward the pick-up. He had better just go by himself. Bid was busy with the chores and he might not finish by dark the way it was. Jimmie knew there was no chance now of getting back into the field today.

He drove up the "racetrack" road toward the Penney Eighty. He would need to open the gate so the cattle could get back in. He mentally noted places where they might have breached the fence, and decided on some he would be sure to check out.

The gravel road that turned south saw quite a bit of traffic--there were several farms on down that way. About a mile past the corner he spotted his Angus cows working their way through a bean field, tromping down brittle vines and scattering ripened soybeans into the dirt. He drove beyond a bit, then drew the truck to the edge of the gravel and rushed into the field yelling "Yaw! Yaw!" loudly to get them moving. He would have to herd the animals on the road for a ways, not something he liked to do, but he hoped few cars would be on the road this time of day.

Light and sinewy, Jimmie bounded across the rows easily, talking to the cattle, persuading them to head in the right direction. He sometimes had trouble keeping them in a compact group, but this time they followed each other in a docile line out to the road, kicking up a summer's worth of dust as their hooves scuffed along the shoulder. Spurts of gravel skidded beneath clomping feet as they gained the roadway. Occasionally one of the animals stopped to nibble on an alluring clump of grass by the wayside, causing Jimmie to plant a hand firmly on its flank.

Sumac along the fence row had just begun to fire up the season and tops of a few maple trees glowed with an early touch of yellow. Jimmie didn't mind this type of outing. At least he had a chance to stretch and move around a little. If not for losing the time in the field, he would enjoy it.

As the procession neared the entrance to the pasture, Jimmie swung out and drove them smoothly through the gate. The cows picked up their pace and trotted off to join the rest of the herd, udders swinging wildly as they lumbered down the gently sloping hillside.

Now he had to walk back for the pick-up. He would cut across the Penney Eighty to save a little time. And he wanted to check some places along the fence. Now and then a rivulet washed out soil from beneath a fence so that a cow could pass under it.

Jimmie walked south along the crest of the hill before cutting left into the timber. He skirted the edge of a small pond nearly overtaken with cattails.

Deeper into the woods he noticed the variety of trees growing randomly together. He recalled a unit on forestry he had had in agriculture class in high school. He had illustrated his notebook with the different kinds of trees native to the area. He identified some now as he made his way over fallen branches. There were lots of oaks--white oak, burr oak, black oak. Hickory, honey locust, some maple, a few sycamore. The shagbark hickory stood out--it was easy to spot, with its shredded overcoat. There were several walnut trees of good size. He could sell these, if he had to.

Three ponds were aligned in a row down a gully. The land surrounding the first two sloped gently toward the water, but the third pond was deep in the ravine, with sides so canted he had fenced it off with strands of barbed wire, fearing his cattle might tumble in.

As he walked along, the gully's incline increased so he had to watch his footing. Choosing his way with his head bent to the earth, Jimmie abruptly noticed a huge tree trunk three or four times larger than anything else around. He looked up and saw that it was a cottonwood tree. That was a surprise to him, as cottonwoods were generally found in low places near streams or rivers. This one was halfway up the side of the hill.

He stepped back to get a better look at the top. The enormous tree rose high into the canopy but was sheared off, with the top third of its growth missing. A black scar ran down one side of the tree, indicating a prior lightning strike. A large limb lay on the ground atop small trees it had crushed in its swift descent. Broken as it was, the tree stood as tall as the others that clung to the hillside. The ridge of trees could be seen from the house upon the hill, and Jimmie wondered why he hadn't noticed this one before. He puzzled about the location of the tree, speculating that perhaps it had been here so long that the gully had eroded for decades, leaving the cottonwood high and dry. It had surely been buffeted by endless storms. He imagined the sight it must have been with its full crown. The tree still lived. Oval leaves of silvery-green spun in the breeze overhead, adding a faint "whoosh" to the muted woodland atmosphere.

For some reason, Jimmie thought of his Uncle Vincent, maybe because the older man had paid the Martins a visit a few evenings earlier. He had certainly weathered some storms. His very life was a lesson in fortitude. Like the tree, he endured. Despite the ravages of time and fate, he persisted--did what he needed to do. Lasted. Maybe it was the Hawk willfulness, the same that had allowed his mother, Merry, to live well into her nineties.

Jimmie couldn't picture his uncle in bib overalls, but he wondered what kind of man Vincent might have been if Jed Torrance hadn't lost his land in the Depression, and if he had remained on the farm. Would he have derived strength from the land, as Jimmie knew he did?

A Hundred Miles to the City

Vincent Torrance was little changed from the man he had been thirty years ago, when he was taken off to prison. He had lost both his children. His former wife lived in another city. He had no one in Bethany where he now lived. But he went on, always in a tailored suit and tie--forever the immaculate gentleman he'd always been. He continued to make his living by his mind, not as a bank teller now, but as an insurance adjuster. Jimmie had been saddened by his uncle's circumstances. But there could be no pity for a man who maintained his dignity throughout the hardships Vincent had weathered.

TWENTY-FIVE

It happened every spring. Not exactly like clockwork, but usually in February, like now. Jimmie left the house to do his morning chores. Before he got across the yard he felt it. Something had changed. It wasn't something he could see--still snow on the ground and the earth frozen beneath it. The sounds were the same as all the days before--a few winter birds up early, groans and grunts from the lot where the livestock were sparring, an occasional thud as one of the beasts jockeyed for position, the clanging of metal against metal as hogs poked their snouts into big round feeders.

So much the same, and yet the world was entirely transformed. A quickening was underway, as if life itself prepared for a rebirth this very morning. Maybe it was something he sensed, the way animals seem to know a storm is brewing. He tried to explain it to Dona once, but words couldn't convey the rapture that filled him with the possibility, the promise of that special time.

She didn't need to be told. Dona was keenly aware of the difference in her husband. He was always optimistic, but at these times his spirit was boundless, as if he were itching to get at something, knowing it would turn out well.

She thought it might be that very quality that kept farmers going. So much of their future rested upon the whims of nature, some inborn knowledge must assure them the fates will ultimately be with them. Perhaps it was this kinship with the soil that caused those like Jimmie to feel as timeless as the land beneath their feet. Both Jimmie and Dona knew winter was not yet over. Spring was still a long way off, but as of now the brutal season had lost its grip. In a few more days, summer birds would be returning and the tread of a foot on the frozen earth would sink in just a little, ice crystals giving way to liquid in the rich, black earth.

Jimmie knew this metamorphosis to be both a blessing and a curse. The moisture in the soil would be a boon to spring crops, but between now and then much mud would have to be endured by him and his animals. Often the lot was so muddy the cattle languished in the deep mire. He felt the extra burden of slogging through the soft places, and the tractor had even become stuck in bottomless ruts a time or two.

Still, the spring season was ever one of hope and expectation for Jimmie. It was certainly not a time of rest, as the young on the farm were ready to be born, and their arrival rarely coincided with pleasant weather or personal convenience. He would get up in the middle of the night to go out to a farrowing shed, with no complaints about the dark, the cold, or the discomfort. He had only relief in the piglets saved, though sometimes he uttered a few choice words when an ungrateful sow assaulted him.

Sometimes Dona felt that satisfaction for Jimmie came in the struggle itself. He was boyishly happy if he saved all eleven or twelve in a litter. Or, if he succeeded in some simple pursuit, like finding the right set of the throttle on the tractor. It could then idle for hours in freezing temperatures, while he went from bin to barn and back countless times in completing his daily chores. It seemed to Dona that the more the farm took from Jimmie the more he gave to it, and cheerfully, as if it were that much dearer to him.

She guessed he was a true farmer--one who'd never take an afternoon or evening off to sit in a bar nor go from place to place, always looking for something better. But her father had had six children to provide for, plus that was during the Depression . . . *for God's sake--how could I make such a comparison*? The older she became, the more respect Dona had for the man her father had been.

To Dona, life on the farm was filled with contradictions. Basically, a farmer put everything he had into breeding and raising livestock; all his resources went into the nurturing of life. Then, on down the road, so to speak, the end result was death in a slaughterhouse. It was difficult for Dona to reconcile the gentle, compassionate person Jimmie was to the callous outcome of his pursuits. He owned guns, though he'd never in his life used them for hunting. Killing dogs or cats was impossible for him. If not for the rigors of nature, the farm would be overrun with pets. Even wild things like skunks or opossums felt only the sting of a BB if they ventured near the chickens. His solution to coyote attacks was to keep the hens shut up in a grain bin. He did threaten once to "walk him around the post" when an owl snatched a tiny kitten.

There were times when he was forced to use his rifle. Charlie, the pony, had foundered and his hooves grew so long and curled they crippled him. Jimmie had trimmed them repeatedly, but the condition only worsened so the horse had to be put down. That was a very difficult duty for Jimmie.

On spring mornings as Dona backed the car off the hill, the sun seemed to rest on Hogback Ridge. The line of trees that crowned the crest of the bluff was named for the scruffy wooded area on the eastern horizon. On clear days, bright rays startled her early-eyed gaze, but when moisture hung in the air, the misty orb merely squinted at her.

Dona found the daily trip harder to make as the years went by. Not that she didn't enjoy her work at the light company. She still worked at the front desk where customers came to pay their bills and she was acquainted with nearly every family in Madison because of this. But, during her twenty years there many of her early co-workers had been replaced. Dona was now the old-timer there. She and Jimmie discussed the possibility of her quitting her job--early retirement would allow her to help on the farm.

A call came into the office from Junior Black. Bid had become ill, so now Junior was helping Jimmie with the spring planting. Immediately she thought the worst. Dona spent much of her time worrying about accidents that might happen.

"What is it?" Dona asked in a quaking voice.

"Jimmie's in the hospital! Don't worry--I think he'll be all right. I brought him down to Sister's Hospital. I think you'd better come." Junior spoke hurriedly to ease her anxiety.

"What happened?" she demanded, suddenly weak and breathless.

"I'm not sure. He was out cold when I found him, but he came around and asked me to bring him to St. Jo. He didn't want an ambulance. I couldn't understand him very well," Junior told her.

"He hasn't had a stroke . . ." Dona began, wondering why Jimmie couldn't speak clearly. She was haunted by visions of her husband pinned under a tractor, mangled in the power-take-off, or mauled by a horde of pigs. She pictured him being struck by every casualty ever known to happen to a luckless farmer.

"His face is smashed, Dona. It's hard for him to talk. They have him in emergency right now. You need to come." He repeated.

Why am I hanging on the phone? Dona knew what she should do but couldn't grasp what was happening. She felt faint. The air around her was thick, and she swam through it automatically, quickly telling her boss she must go and leaving before his offer to go along could sink in.

The trip to St. Joseph took forever. She was afraid to go into the hospital and at the same time couldn't enter quickly enough. Junior was there waiting, a look of assurance thinly covering the concern on his features and in his awkward stance.

"He's stabilized. They're waiting for you to sign some papers so they can take him into surgery," Junior hurriedly told Dona.

"Can't I see him first?" she asked the nurse who was preparing to pass her some papers.

"I'll ask the doctor," she answered, then disappeared into an adjacent room.

"How did you happen to find him?" Dona then inquired of Junior.

"We were supposed to meet at the machine shed this morning so he could get me started for the day," Junior began. "When he didn't show up, I went looking for him."

"Where did you find him?"

"He was lying in front of one of the pig sheds. I don't know how long he'd been there--maybe an hour. I'd waited a long time. It's a good thing there wasn't much bleeding!"

Dona thought that it was a good thing Junior hadn't decided he had a day off and gone home when Jimmie failed to show up. But she knew he wouldn't have done that. She was aware of a special connection between those of the rural community. They looked out for their own, and Junior, even though he was not a true farmer, shared that watchful concern. She most certainly would call him a friend.

"What do you think happened?" Dona still wanted to know.

"The only thing I can figure is that maybe the wind caught the door and it smashed into him. It's awfully windy today!" Junior reckoned.

"I know. It nearly blew me off the road this morning!" Dona told him. It was odd that she hadn't noticed it on the way down to St. Joseph.

The doctor came out to speak with Dona.

"Your husband's hurt pretty badly, but I think we can repair most of the damage. He's lucky his eye wasn't involved in the trauma," the doctor told her. "You can go in and see him, but he's heavily sedated, and he can't speak because of his injuries."

She should have anticipated the prospect, but was shocked by the needles and tubes that ran into Jimmie from so many machines. The condition of his face distressed her. Already swollen and discolored, his left cheek was ripped, with a long gash crossing under his eye and running toward his ear. Jimmie tried to speak but gave up and waved weakly in recognition--to reassure her, she knew. She felt her tears well up. He looked so battered and helpless!

The doctor took a few minutes to describe the extent of the injury and explain the surgery he would perform.

"His cheekbone is shattered," the doctor was saying. "We'll have to wire it together and maybe put in a steel plate. We won't know until we get in there. His vital signs are good, and he hasn't lost much blood, so he should do all right."

Jimmie had never been admitted into a hospital, and Dona found it hard to accept that he was there now, flat on his back and totally vulnerable.

"Will he recover?" she asked anxiously, meaning *will he ever be the same as he was?*

"He should do fine," the surgeon assured her. "He seems to be in good physical shape."

When Dona reentered the waiting area, Junior was still there. She explained to him as well as she could her husband's condition and prognosis.

"Tell him not to worry about the chores, Dona," Junior told her.

"I hadn't even thought of that," she admitted, frowning slightly.

"Word's around by now, I'm sure," Junior stated. "There's probably help out there already. I'm not much of a stockman myself, but I know enough to get by."

"He'll probably want to hire someone for a while," Dona guessed, but she was glad not to have to face that determination right now. She encouraged Junior to go on home. She would be there during the surgery, then she would make some decisions later.

It took awhile to prepare the patient for the procedure; then the surgery itself was hours longer. Dona waited nervously while Jimmie was in the recovery room, even though she'd been assured that the operation went smoothly. A Sister at the hospital told her of a house up the street where relatives could get a reasonable room. Dona called and made arrangements to spend the night there. When Jimmie was in the intensive care unit and sleeping soundly, Dona headed for Bedford to gather her things for the overnight stay. *I'd probably better bring enough for several days*, she realized.

As she parked beside the picket fence, Tippie came to the gate to greet her. *He didn't meet me at the lane--he must not have heard me drive in,* Dona mused. The brisk wind hit her as she stepped from the car. The security light lit the yard, but the house was eerily dark. The wind moaned as it swept over the hill. Something on the other side of the barn was loose and intermittently punctuated the groaning sound with a hollow "whack!"

The cats were missing by the back door. *They must be holed up in the barn to escape the piercing wind.* Dona stepped into the porch, then turned on the light as she entered the house. She had the uneasy feeling of being a visitor. Her own house felt foreign to her. She turned on the bathroom and kitchen lights, which made the spaces beyond seem that much blacker. She flipped the switch to the ceiling fixture in the living room and heard a faint snap as the bulb burned out.

The door to the front of the house was still closed. She was glad--the front seemed so far away from the safety zone of the kitchen. She had never felt like this in her own home. She wished now she hadn't been so graphic when she'd entertained the children with her "Little Willie" ghost stories. Sounds she'd never noticed before rattled just beyond her range of vision, on the other side of a wall or a door.

The house seemed to move in the wind. It always vibrated when a train rumbled by a quarter mile to the west, but this was a humming movement, subtle but palpable. The furnace was on, but the house seemed unusually cool, and unfriendly. She couldn't imagine why she felt this way--like a stranger in her own home! She quickly got together the things she needed and was headed for the door when she spotted the note on the table. It was from Jim Ed. "The chores are done. I'll come until you tell me I'm not needed."

The place seemed suddenly warmer, but she hurried away still, leaving the kitchen light on behind her. She couldn't stand to see the place look so deserted.

The next day Jimmie was confused and aching, but he did manage to convey to Dona, with grunts and scribbles on a pad, that Junior's guess had been correct. The pig sheds had doors, or hatches, on the roof, so the sows could be fed and watered with little disturbance. He had been leaning in to pour a bucket of water into the sow's pan when a blast of air caught the flap and sent it crashing into his face. His memory of it was sketchy, but he thought that's what must have happened. Dona pictured the scene with horror. Thank goodness it was Junior Black, and not a less-responsible hireling who was to meet Jimmie that morning!

That evening Junior came to the hospital to check on Jimmie and to tell him that his neighbors had come and prepared much of the bottomland for spring planting. Dona could imagine the relief that must be to her husband.

There had been a big crew for the day. They had all brought their tractors and equipment. Jimmie hoped they had at least used the gas in his barrel, but they probably hadn't. No corners were cut when helping out an ailing or injured friend. An unspoken agreement existed in the farming community when it was "payback" time. Even though the ones who pitched in to help often weren't the ones you had helped, eventually the circle came around.

After another day in the hospital, Jimmie returned to the farm with the promise to remain immobile for at least a week. He did stay in the house the next day, but beyond that he couldn't sit idle while others did his work. Dona went back to her work place, knowing full well that his vow to be mindful of the healing process would be breached. She would just have to believe he would do no more than he could take.

Jimmie's voice had a strange, hollow sound for quite some time, but finally a faint scar across his cheek was the only obvious remnant of the accident.

Her work on the historical publication served as an introduction to many members of the community for Dona. Besides interviewing long-standing natives of the area, she was asked to contribute her and her husband's personal histories for the book. Of course, Jimmie knew whom he was related to in the area, and also the connection, but it fell to Dona to assimilate the information for his family's story and to write it in an appealing fashion. She would get help from Nora in starting on the Torrances and go back from there. Jimmie was a descendant of Moses Richey, an early settler of the Platte Purchase part of the state. In fact, the man was buried in the Stingley cemetery that was on Jimmie's land, part now of the Penney Eighty. Dona found this history to be fascinating on a personal level and truly enjoyed the hours she spent sleuthing through old record books, abstracts, and census reports. She decided to quit working in Madison and devote more time to her own interests, which at the time involved pursuing information for the White Cloud Township book.

One of Dona's goals for the fund-raising edition was to determine the types of buildings that had stood on the lots in Old Bedford, as well as to ascertain the names of their occupants during the town's heyday. Her search took her to the abstracts at the county courthouse, where she looked for deeds of sale in the voluminous compilations in storage there. She used this resource, along with census records from the genealogy room at the library, to identify the structures and their inhabitants.

This was endlessly time-consuming, but enormously fascinating as well. The village that now contained only a handful of houses had once been as large as new Bedford. In fact, many of the same buildings had been moved over the hill to their new locations in the 1880s when the railroad tracks were laid. One aspect Dona found interesting was the frequency in which the town's central lots had changed ownership, in some cases yearly. A site might have been a livery, a blacksmith, a grocery store, a seamstress shop; an endless variety of services were offered consecutively.

Other fruitful sources were the files from earlier newspapers, which were available on microfilm at the college library. There were no pictures, as that technology was not available for the meager capital of small town printing shops of the time. However, articles and advertisements colorfully written made up for the lack of photography. And illustrations did exist. They were simply in a line-drawing format.

A Hundred Miles to the City

Through the years Bedford had had three different newspapers. The heritage group borrowed pieces from each one, but mainly from the *Bedford Monitor*. One of the entries from it read, simply, "Go to McDANIELS' PLACE – Best 15 cent Meals in the City – Meals at All Hours – Lodging 25 cents." Another notice in the advertising section read "Uncle G.T. Staples came in Saturday and ordered the MONITOR sent to his son, W.J. Staples, in Madison. Come all ye and do likewise."

In one edition was a short piece condemning the evils of drinking--this was before Prohibition--that ended; "How long must we put up with this?" Then, in the same paper, the ad--"An exchange tells of a fellow who every time he gets on a spree insists on paying a year's subscription to his town paper. He has already paid for the paper to January 1, 1926. An effort will be made at the next press to ascertain what brand of whiskey the man is drinking in order that it may more generally be placed on the market." Dona got a chuckle out of that one and decided it must be included in their book.

Much of the material the group chose to print referred to commodities and the unit cost of the items. An amazing list of proprietors ran stores in the town during the first part of the century, so the writers included names of businesses and their owners as often as possible. Neighboring communities were featured in the society section, with an account given of who rode the train seven miles to visit an aunt in Atchison or who spent the day shopping in Madison. It was hard for Dona to imagine a trip to Madison being a noteworthy event.

For pictures to include in the publication, the group appealed to community members. There was a good response, with scenes depicting the town as it once was and events in the lives of long-ago townspeople. One such photo showed twenty or more Model T cars parked diagonally in the middle of Main Street, as cars were still parked until just a few years back. Another was of Lloyd Masters in his WWI soldier's uniform, standing in front of the school that sat upon the hill. A picture of Dan Simpson, Wilma's father, featured the man's first automobile, purchased in Bedford for $729.

Many photographs of Jimmie's family were saved by Merry and Nora. Dona spent several enjoyable hours going through albums and boxes of old photographs with Jimmie's mother. Nora had quit working just a few years earlier. She had continued driving to work at the hospital in Madison until she was into her seventies. Now she spent her time visiting, writing in her diary, and tending to her cat, "Jillie."

Dona was closer to Nora now, as each had leisure time to socialize. Once last winter, the two women had hauled out the girls' old sled and had taken a ride down the steep hill in front of the house. Jimmie thought they'd both taken leave of their senses when he caught sight of them careening down the snowy embankment! They laughed like children! Dona wished her own mother could still enjoy the pleasures of life as Nora did.

Judging by the poses in the Torrance pictures, Dona could see that Nora was always fun loving. Just as Sherry had usually been the one to take the reins if there were mischief involved in her own family, Nora was the one giving her sisters and the pet dog a ride in the pony cart. In one charming photograph, she was one of four rosy-cheeked girls attired in frilly nightdresses and lacy nightcaps. Their smiles told of merry-making ahead as they prepared for a turn-of-the-century sleepover. There was a formally posed picture of Nora's father, Jed Torrance, in front of the family home, showing one of his championship mules.

Dona was impressed by the number of photographs of the family. She could remember only one picture of herself as a child, taken by a relative when Sam and Retha had gone to welcome a new baby. The aunt had sent them the picture of the infant in the arms of eight-year-old Dona, who wondered if her curly hair always looked as wild as it appeared in that likeness.

A distant cousin of Jimmie's sent him a document of the Torrance-Lower genealogy, which made Dona's task decidedly easier. She would be able to spend more of her time learning about the Stingleys and the history of the old house.

When Dona asked for Jimmie's help in finding the buffalo wallow, he didn't respond with much enthusiasm.

"How would we know it if we found it? There are plenty of low places the pigs wallow in. I can show you some of those!" he kidded her.

"It might be on your land . . ." she suggested, suspecting that might whet his interest.

"What makes you think that?" he asked, a bit more seriously.

"I have a map," she volunteered. Of course she had it nearby, in case the quest should get beyond the talking stage. "Woodrow Nelson gave me this. He didn't remember where he had gotten it, but some places are marked that might help us locate the spot."

The hand-drawn map was faded but legible. Landmarks were numbered and also represented by symbols noted in the simple key at the bottom of the yellowed paper. Wavy lines denoted the location of the buffalo wallow. The closest other landmark was designated by an X and identified as "big cottonwood tree."

Jimmie looked at the map for a moment, then glanced up at Dona.

"I think I know where that tree is!" he exclaimed. She was surprised at his sudden change of heart.

"You do?" she asked.

"Over in the timber on the Penney eighty. I nearly ran into it one day when I was getting in some cows! It's topped off, but it has been huge. Doesn't it look like that's about where it would be?" He indicated the spot on the map. "Mound's Ford must have been just down the hill from here. And here's Clear Creek over here. We know where that is."

"It looks like it would be quite a ways south of Old Bedford. Can we go look? It's too wet for you to do anything today anyhow." She knew he had most of his acreage planted, except for one part of the bottom that he referred to as "that soggy son of a b___!"

"I'll tell you what," he said. "Let's take some sacks, and if we can't find it we can at least look for mushrooms!" They usually found time in the spring to spend an hour or two searching for edible morels. The elusive treasures were hard to recognize in the leafy clutter of the forest floor.

"If you can find the tree again, we can start there and go southwest. It's hard to tell how far, but maybe we can judge by the distance to the river." Dona knew they couldn't even depend on the location of the Platte, since it had been known to leave its banks to form a new course.

"Bedford's not even on this map!" Jimmie announced with surprise. "Here's Black Oak Grove, north of town, and Mill's Ford. It looks like hundreds of acres are just marked SWAMP, some of the best bottomland in the county! I wonder when it was drained, and who did it." If the map were accurate, everything between Bedford and the Platte River had once been worthless--hard for him to imagine, although that might account for his parcel of "soggy SOB."

They parked the car by the gravel road, then cut into the timber on foot. Jimmie had no trouble finding the tree again. From there the pair walked purposefully south and west. Their path followed the ravine where three ponds had been formed. At the lower end, beneath the last and deepest reservoir, they found a depression that was, definitely, soft. It was at the edge of a field Jimmie generally planted in soybeans, lying just before the land rose toward the wooded bluffs.

"Well . . . it could be," Jimmie ventured, not wanting Dona to jump to an unverifiable conclusion.

"It's big enough, don't you think?" she asked. "Wouldn't that be something, to have a piece of history right here?"

He laughed. There was no denying the possibility. He guessed their claim would be as reasonable as anyone's. Subsequently, she made it a point to show some of the grandchildren the location, just in case it really had been a buffalo wallow.

Later, they went in search of another spot shown on the map. It was purported to be a groove in the earth at the crest of the bluff, made by countless wagon wheels passing on their way west. They found a place on Hogback Ridge that satisfied the description. To the amazement of them both, the location they believed to be correct was on the Anderson place, an eighty-acre parcel of land Jimmie had acquired just a year earlier!

It became evident to Dona that Jimmie's past was inexplicably entwined with that of the area she'd been charged with documenting. The names of Torrance and Hawk appeared in every issue of the by-gone newspapers. Generally, the occurrence mentioned was a social event, or perhaps some endeavor undertaken on behalf of the citizens of the town. Several of Jimmie's ancestors had been shopkeepers, so their names often appeared in pleas for some business or trade.

As she scrolled down page after page on the microfilm reader, now and then Dona came across a startling news item. She had heard of Jake Waddell because she read of his conviction for the murder of a woman in Albany. That monstrous event had come to her attention when she lived in Madison.

Perhaps the fate of the Herring family was preordained when Jake was let out of prison in 1924. The young couple lived on a farm near Bedford with their two small children. One night the father sat in on a game of poker at another man's house. Jake Waddell was present and lost badly to young Herring late that night. By morning, the Herrings had been murdered to avenge the bitterness that seethed in Jake's unsettled mind.

After satisfying the due process of law, Jake Waddell was hanged on the courthouse lawn in Madison. Detailed accounts of the courtroom proceedings appeared in all the local publications, including *The Bedford Monitor*. The only person Dona ever knew of in Bedford by the name of Herring was Jane, proprietor of a grocery store during the 1930s and 1940s. She learned from Jimmie that the Herring family so ruthlessly murdered were distant cousins of the Torrances.

The committee concluded that most communities had similar tragedies in their foregoing existence and decided to include the dismaying tale in their book, as it was, indeed, a part of the area's past. All agreed that events that told of people's progress weren't necessarily positive, and that the bad should be included along with the good if their work was to be a realistic chronicle of their township's earlier years.

Reading the accounts written by other contributors inspired Dona to put forth her best effort in recording the people and events she researched.

A Hundred Miles to the City

Her co-authors were obviously talented writers who knew how to attract and maintain the interest of their readers.

After a year in the creative process, there was a big push to get the book published before the nation's Bicentennial celebration. At last, the final manuscript was delivered to Wright Printing in Madison, with hopes that it would ultimately be accepted as an accurate portrayal of history, and become a moneymaker for the organization as well.

The community center had been repainted in preparation for the event, and red, white and blue bunting was draped beneath the belfry to adorn the front entrance. Cars and pickups lined both sides of the street, and a crowd had gathered in front of the podium that stood on a lowboy trailer. Inside, refreshments awaited the completion of the program.

The flag had been ceremoniously raised by the simple man who lived up the street with his aging mother. Dona had to win this concession from some of the group. They had wanted the honor to go to someone more "suitable," but she argued that Johnny had raised the flag for every special occasion since the building became the town's social center.

The mayor led the group in the Pledge of Allegiance as those gathered solemnly cast their eyes toward the flag. The high school band, in maroon and black uniforms, played "The Star Spangled Banner." A public address system borrowed from the school allowed the speakers to be heard above the slight movements of the crowd, grown-ups hushing children and the occasional barking dog.

The day was mercifully cool for July 4th, even though the sun's rays were unimpeded by clouds or any other shade. After local leaders were introduced, a speaker from the State Bicentennial Committee made a presentation to the group. The current leader of the town board said a few words to dedicate the placement of the old church bell. It had been refurbished and was mounted on a concrete platform, with a bronze plaque that listed highlights of the town's history. It would be used to call the community together for future affairs at the meeting hall.

The town leaders were so pleased with the day's program and with their fund-raising efforts that they determined to henceforth have an annual celebration. Perhaps they could have a township fair of some sort. The book the community had collaborated on, entitled *Platte Purchase*, was well received at the gathering. Demand for the book was brisk for quite a while after the Bicentennial event and sold out in just a few years.

Shared experiences such as this are the threads of connectedness that knit a community together. Often they are happy, uplifting events that fill the communal heart with satisfaction and joy. But, on other occasions, sadness and hurt overwhelm individual souls and poison the faith of all. In a town the size of Bedford, no person suffers but that they all feel the pain.

The railroad that had brought the populace together and served it well over many decades was going into swift decline. Trains no longer ran on a dependable schedule, and none stopped at the site of the now-absent depot. When a locomotive appeared, it was followed by at least one more engine and scores of--sometimes up to two hundred--railcars, often carrying enormous hoppers of coal to feed a hungry power plant to the south.

The fall rains had set in. School was again underway and the young people of the area were spending much of their time on activities based at the consolidated school in Horton, four miles to the west.

No light had ever been installed at the crossing, just the conventional X-shaped railroad sign. In days gone by, travelers routinely stopped and looked down the tracks. They expected a train might be approaching. A blast on a mighty air horn always sounded an additional alert. But within a lifetime, the presence of a train at the crossing had gone from practically always to hardly ever.

Albert Cameron's filling station occupied one corner of the intersection a block into town. It sat catty-corner facing the elementary school, the perimeter of which paralleled the iron rails. The Baxter family lived in Old Town. They had four children--all of school age and involved in after-school activities. Dot McJimsey, the schoolteacher, and her husband lived south and west about a mile. Gail and Ross Gates had built a new house recently. It was west on H highway, between the two towns.

At 6:27 one fateful evening, four teenagers were riding together, their destination a meeting at the high school to plan an upcoming school event.

At 6:30 two beautiful bodies were being swept along in the burgeoning drainage ditch that emptied into the Platte River. Two mangled but equally beautiful children were crushed inside wreckage borne a mile down the tracks by a massive murdering machine.

One family lost its only child. One family lost the daughter they'd waited so long to have. Two families suffered the torture of excruciating injury and miraculous survival. No one in town escaped the tragedy. Everyone felt it. For years.

Attempting to explain the unexplainable was futile. Maybe the rain was so loud and unrelenting that the speeding bully could be neither seen nor heard. Some of the townspeople admitted that the fates had managed one kindness on that day--on account of the storm Albert did not see the accident that took his daughter's life.

TWENTY-SIX

Surely Jimmie's first choice of land ownership would have been the Bill Catterson farm. Dona had always known that. She could tell by the way he talked about the place. After all, it had been the safe haven of his youth--the place his family had returned to whenever one of Father's pursuits went sour. The Maple Leaf Farm, so named because of its nearness to the like-named spur of the early railroad, was almost entirely bottomland--level, productive, and easy to get to.

The conglomeration of parcels that Jimmie now owned included acres of every sort: woodland, hillside, marginal pastureland, and some flat bottomland. Much was difficult to reach for cultivation. Some of the tillable sections were three or four miles away, over dirt and gravel roads--and then on, over hills and across fields with no road at all. He had acquired the last twenty acres of Eldon Wardloe's former dairy farm, on H highway, to finish the 640 acres he was determined to own. His goal was a square mile of land. Shown on a range map, nothing could look less like a square mile than the six separate holdings that Jimmie, and the bank, now possessed.

Since quitting her job in Madison, Dona had gotten to know much of that territory fairly well. She often took Jimmie a fresh jug of water or a cooler of lemonade when he spent a long afternoon planting or cultivating. Sometimes, she'd pack a picnic lunch and they'd eat on a blanket spread on the ground alongside the field. Her senses feasted on the wonderful aroma of newly mown hay drying in the sun. After the voracious baling machine did its work, gigantic bundles dotted the field like miniature haystacks rolled up by an agrarian giant. She thought of the little bales that Sherry used to handle when she was still with them. The wiry girl would hoist them up to the bed of the lowboy, nearly as easily as the lads Jimmie hired in the summertime. He paid her as he paid them, and she'd finish her summer with a suntan envied by her "townie" friends.

Nearly every young man in the community worked for Jimmie at some time. Once, when Coralea came to visit, she was surprised to see the fellow who had "touched" her when she'd gone to school at Star of the West. He seemed bashful, even polite, and she wondered if he remembered the disturbing incident as clearly as she still did. She was glad that the passage of time had made her less fearful, and him more self-controlled.

Now a young man worked for Jimmie as a full-time hired hand. Dale Livingston had recently married and was starting up a farm of his own nearby, so he supplemented his income by hiring out.

Many of Dona's frequent trips to outlying farms involved driving one of the tractors, often to pull Jimmie on another one or on some piece of equipment that had broken down. The bane of his existence as a farmer was the quality of the machinery he had to work with. It seemed that everything was used, way past the point of being worn out. In spite of his efforts at keeping working parts greased and sharpened, almost daily something would snap and require Dona to run to Madison or St. Joseph for a part, and him to spend valuable time making the repairs he could handle himself. With Galen no longer in business, breakdowns he couldn't deal with had to make the expensive journey to Whitesville, fifteen miles away.

Some of Jimmie's equipment was fairly new. He had purchased a dual-wheeled tractor with a cab, bringing about his first experience with farming in relative comfort. The huge tractor was necessary to pull the sixteen-row drill and cultivator. Loans for this kind of outlay were easy to obtain. Banks were eager to participate in the boom that increased productivity and expanding markets fueled in U.S. agriculture. A mini-industrial revolution occurred in America's heartland in the 1950s and 60s. As Sam had been involved in the earlier wave of mechanization, Jimmie and his colleagues were caught up in the push for larger farms and bigger equipment. This was expected to result in efficiency and to bring down the basic cost of production.

Sam had chosen to stop farming rather than make the tremendous changes necessary to compete in the new farm economy of his day. Jimmie was young and eager to adapt and expand. He was a voracious reader and easily kept up on the current innovations in farming by subscribing to available farm journals and stockmen's publications. He seldom missed the morning or noon market reports on the radio, as they dictated many of his daily activities. When the market was up, off he would go with a load of pigs to the St. Joseph stockyards, often with Dona by his side.

Of the smaller holdings that Jimmie had bought as he expanded his farming interests, Bid's place was the one to which Dona was drawn. The ancient house, vacant now and open to the elements, sat back off the gravel road upon a small rise. Tulips still greeted the spring each year and a large lilac bush fragrantly followed. Bid had brought her some starts from the bush a few years back. They now bloomed at their new location beside the brick posts marking the lane to the big house. Two mulberry trees in back of the old place were loaded with fruit in their season. Dona had transplanted yellow and purple iris from that yard to her own, lining a section of the picket fence with them. So far the pigs hadn't invaded the area with their marauding snouts.

The main improvement Jimmie had made on Bid's place was a large pond for the cattle. He had asked the conservation department to stock it with bass. Dona liked to bring her rod and reel there to go fishing on Sundays, sometimes bringing one or two grandchildren along, at which times Jimmie often joined them.

A few catfish had been put into the pond by Coralea's family, who had it's own way of catching fish. Sometimes Dona joined them for a wiener roast on the riverbank. The path that went over the hill beyond the abandoned Browning house led to a bean field and then on to the Platte River. It was an excellent fishing spot if catfish were wanted, and one didn't mind working for them. The family of four hauled tents, sleeping bags, coolers, lines and bait through timber, down a bank, and onto a sand bar to set up camp for an overnight stay.

Dona preferred they go there, rather than to the Black River Bridge, south of Bedford. It had been a favorite community swimming and fishing hole for years. Not that the water was so deep--she knew they were all swimmers and the children were old enough to look after themselves. But, to get to the other side of the river and the sand bar, one had to cross a railroad trestle--the kind that was long with substantial gaps between the ties. It gave Dona the heeby-jeebies and she'd just as soon not think of her grandchildren in that perilous position.

When the Simpsons came down to fish, they usually brought their catch up to the house to clean the next morning. Sometimes they'd have twenty or more catfish they had caught on trot-lines set out across the river. They would take them out behind the house and clean them on the bank, heaving heads, fins, tails and innards out for the cats to enjoy. Jimmie and Dona were always glad to get a mess or two of the tasty fish to fry. She had to admit, the family met with a lot more success on their outings than she did. Still, Dona preferred to fish as Sam always had--sitting on the bank soaking up the sun.

"How about going to a basketball game this weekend?" Dona asked her husband at the breakfast table. It was March, and local teams were finishing up their basketball season.

"Where?" Jimmie asked, hedging a little because he was pretty sure he knew the answer to that already.

"In Kirksville," Dona returned, smiling. "If they win tonight, Cliff's team and Sherry's team will both be playing."

"It's a long way over there just to see a ball game."

"Kelly won't be able to go unless we do. He wants to stay in Madison for his own game Thursday night," Dona continued, still hoping to persuade Jimmie.

"Well, tough titty!" Jimmie stated, grinning with the earthy saying he knew would get a rise from his wife.

"You know Corky always goes with Cliff and the girls. She'd feel bad if Kelly couldn't go. He follows the Glenwood teams, too, you know."

A state-wide basketball tournament for girls had been instated in 1972, and the Cardinals--the Lady Cardinals, that is--from the Glenwood/Elmo consolidated school had been successful in capturing a first, second and third place in the four years since its inception. Sherry was teaching in Carroll now and helping with that school's basketball program. Dona knew she and her family planned to travel to Kirksville if their team made the cut.

"If they should both make the finals, they'll play each other!" Dona enthused.

"I suppose you'd want to stay for another game then," Jimmie said with an exaggerated groan.

"I suppose I would!" she assured him.

Eventually, Dona managed to convince Jimmie that they really needed to make the trip so their grandson could attend the post-season games. Dona and Jimmie took a motel room Friday night, for Northeast Johnson and Carroll won their semi-final games and ended up facing each other for the first place trophy on Saturday. Jimmie was willing to stay over, since the final contest for the 1A class was scheduled for the morning, and he could get home to do his chores later in the day.

Once again, Northeast Johnson took the tourney, after a hard-fought, close contest. Excitement ran high during the morning, sweeping Dona's emotions along with the fervor of the crowd. It had been years since she'd attended a basketball game, and the energy level of the audience, as well as the participants, was remarkable to her. She could certainly contrast it to the game she and Jimmie had first sat side by side to watch in the gymnasium at Bedford so many years ago.

Early in their marriage the couple took one special vacation alone. After they had been wed for seven years, they drove to New York City for a sightseeing tour. That was longer than Dona had been married to June, and the couple decided to celebrate. Their weeklong odyssey took them to many well-known landmarks, including the Empire State Building, the Statue of Liberty, and Times Square.

They most enjoyed the evening they spent at a concert by the Supremes, a female vocal trio. The romantic, glittery performance completely charmed them both. Knowing how they'd stretched their budget to make the trip, Dona wouldn't have spent the money on the high-priced tickets for the event, but Jimmie insisted. Perhaps he remembered that Dona had displayed an early talent for singing and wanted to make this an especially memorable time for her.

Neither had attended a live concert of such caliber--with stars they had actually seen on television! The sound system was fantastic, the costumes stunning. The gorgeous women put on a spirited show that mesmerized the entire crowd. The performance was certainly the highlight of the Martins' New York anniversary trip. Henceforth, their celebrations would be held at home, fondly reliving the exciting journey and their memorable evening with the Supremes. Dona would never hear them mentioned or see them on television without commenting about the way they appeared in person.

The jangling telephone awakened Jimmie and Dona. He climbed out of bed and hurriedly crossed the few steps into the kitchen where it hung on the wall.

"Hello."

"Will you accept charges for a call from Denver, Colorado? Lizabeth Hoffman calling," a woman's voice asked.

At first Jimmie was confused, as he knew no one in Denver. Then Beth's name. But what would she be doing in Denver?

Dona noticed Jimmie's hesitation before he said "Yes." She wondered who would be calling this time of night. It was very late--that usually meant bad news.

"Beth?" she heard Jimmie say, then louder, "Lizabeth? What is it, Beth?" urgent now.

"What? Oh, no! What happened?" His voice had dropped to a whisper.

"What can I do to help?" she heard him ask after a bit.

"Yes . . . I will. No . . . I won't. Don't worry. We'll come down."

A long silence. Then, "Call us tomorrow and let us know. I'm sorry, Beth. I wish there was something I could do."

Another long silence.

"I guess we'll wait for your call, then. Bye."

"Hoff's dead!" Jimmie said as he sat down on the edge of the bed, his shoulders drooping in a despondent attitude.

"How did it happen? Is Lizabeth all right?" Dona asked. Her first thoughts were of a traffic accident.

"He had a heart attack! They were on a trip in Colorado. She's in Denver."

"You should go," Dona said, thinking Jimmie should fly out to help his sister. Lizabeth must be devastated, with no one around to help her. But Jimmie couldn't fly--he would become airsick.

"She called from the hospital. She said the staff there have taken her under their wing, and she'll make arrangements to have Hoff's body shipped back to Texas tomorrow. She asked me to tell Mom in the morning," Jimmie told Dona.

"This is going to be hard on your mother," Dona worried. "She was really fond of Hoff." Dona didn't know him very well, since the couple had made few visits to Bedford. She realized that she and Jimmie hadn't made many trips to Texas themselves.

Nora took the news better than they thought she might--stoically, as if she weren't surprised by the next loss in her life. She was eager to go to Texas to be with her daughter, so the three made hasty arrangements and were on the road early the next morning.

When they arrived at the Hoffman home, they were surprised at the abundance of support offered by Beth's friends and co-workers. Jimmie's sister obviously enjoyed a wide society of fellowship at the lakeside community of Davidson.

Their stay was brief but personal, and Dona felt she came to know Lizabeth much more intimately than before. The woman was at once business-like and personable--putting everyone at ease, though most were strangers to each other. Over the years Lizabeth had picked up a slight Southern drawl that gave her voice a charming, mellow quality.

With not so many freckles and a brunette's complexion, save for her mother's saucy red hair Lizabeth might be a younger version of Nora. Dona hadn't noticed the resemblance until closely observing the two women together. Lizabeth had that same quality of finding the humor in a situation and making the most of it. Dona wished she could spend more time with her.

Nora hinted that she hoped her daughter might consider a return to her hometown but soon realized there wasn't much chance of that wish becoming a reality. Lizabeth's life was still centered in her adopted community, even though her husband was gone.

When the short visit ended, none of the three felt their leaving to be an act of abandonment. The fabric of Lizabeth's life was patched but permanent, not the shattered remnant they had each feared to find when they set out upon the journey.

Thinking of Lizabeth, not alone but certainly away from her own kin, Dona considered how Jimmie must have felt when his only sibling left home. She herself had always been closest to her brother Hank, but when he left home there were still others. She'd never been alone in that particular way. Granted, there had been times she'd wished she were. *No, not in reality.* She contemplated the idea of having no family around, and the thought deeply depressed her.

It must have been sad for Nora when she realized she'd not likely have any grandchildren of her own, Dona thought. She had once presumed her mother-in-law had used up her maternal passions on her two children but knew now that she was mistaken. It seemed that Beth shared with Nora the same simple philosophy for living--she would start from where she was and make the best of whatever her circumstances were. No "what-ifs" or "what-might-bes." No guilt nor recrimination. Dona realized she could learn a lot from the two.

Both Jimmie and Dona enjoyed the times they spent with each of their eight grandchildren. At first there were birthday parties to go to. Then, when the youngsters came of school age, programs to attend. Dona was there at Vikki's first piano recital. She and Jimmie went to summer ball games at least once for each child--T-ball, then softball and baseball. Kelly and Stewart were both active in high school sports; Kelly mostly basketball, and Stu mostly football. Shelley, Barbara's youngest, was a pom-pom girl for the Shenandoah Savages and also marched with their award-winning band.

Sherry's children lived farther away, so visits with them were less frequent, but the Martins kept up with their activities, nonetheless. J. had become interested in music and could play several instruments in high school but eventually settled on the guitar and played in a local rock band. Valerie was the distance runner for her high school track team in Hale. Tami competed in the "brain bowl" when she, the youngest, got into high school.

Barbara's oldest child, Debbie, liked to write and did a piece that touched Dona's heart. Her essay, entitled "The Enchanted Forest," told of sharing her grandmother's fantasies in the woods the two explored that lay west of the house, just beyond the railroad tracks. Dona's spellbinding tales of wonderlands and the fairies that inhabited them had ignited the girl's imagination when she was just a toddler.

Often Jimmie was too busy to accompany Dona to events that were important, or at least interesting, to her. She didn't hesitate to get into the big

Mercury and make the trip by herself. Many times Nora would go along, and sometimes her friend, Ruby Masters. Ruby and her husband had returned to Bedford after his retirement. He had been a traveling salesman, and so the couple had made their temporary home in several Midwest cities. There were no children, and now that Lloyd had passed away Ruby was alone. She and Nora had been close friends in high school--Ruby was one of the girls pictured in the charming photo Dona had seen at Nora's of an early-in-the-century pajama party.

Dona enjoyed driving and often volunteered to take the town's elderly ladies on outings. She found the women to be friendly, fun, and helpful. She finally began to take a real interest in cooking and was soon swapping recipes and trying out complicated dishes on her husband. She even learned to make a decent pie crust, which pleased all in her family.

In the mid-seventies, certain climatic conditions contributed to a crisis in the local farm economy. First, there was a year of very wet weather--too much rain in the spring and the men couldn't get their crops in. The fields that did get planted washed out and had to be replanted. In the summer, overabundant moisture rotted the hay in the fields. Country roads were sometimes impassable, where sparse gravel gave way to soft loam and clay.

Every task that Jimmie undertook required twice as much energy and time to complete. He could scarcely remember what it felt like to tread on solid ground as he carried five-gallon buckets of water to the pig sheds. The animals in the lot didn't gain weight as they should have, and Dona could see her husband wasting away himself with the added drudgery. His shoulders were noticeably bony through his thin cotton shirts, and his spindly legs began to appear more bowed as the wet weeks wore on.

As times got tougher, signing up for government programs became the only avenue open to survival for many farmers. Success no longer depended solely upon the weather and their own efforts. More and more of Jimmie's time was spent on trips to the ASCS office in Madison to make the required reports to the agency or to sign necessary papers for assistance of one kind or another. This predicament was entirely against his nature--this dependence upon the government.

If farmers in North America had a good yield one year, another grain-producing nation, such as Argentina, might have a bumper crop that would fulfill the needs of the world marketplace. Sometimes there was a surplus in some commodities and storage became a problem in the United States. Jimmie and his kind may have worked themselves right out of a job with their increased productivity.

At the same time, tumultuous years were ahead for the Martins' personal lives. Dona didn't attend the services when Mother Bowen passed away in the fall. She knew it would be a hardship on Jimmie to ask him to take time off, and she didn't want to go without him. The girls would all go. They could represent the family.

Grace was buried beside Harvey and an infant daughter in the Junction Cemetery. June and his wife came down from Pierre, S. D., for the occasion. They stopped for a visit at Barb and Don's house in Shenandoah and at Norman's place in Ottawa, Iowa, before leaving the next day. It was the first time June, now called Harvey, had been in the area for over twenty years. The girls each thought him quieter, more reserved, than they remembered--but still darkly handsome. It was a timorous reunion but still an uncertain first step in getting reacquainted. Harvey's wife was friendly, polite, and assertive. She appeared to have a supportive, grounding personality that complemented her husband's nature. His daughters agreed that it gave them a feeling of comfort to see their father settled into a peaceful relationship.

That sad event was followed soon after with the death of Jimmie Martin, Sr. He'd lived in Cedar Springs, Iowa, for many years. Jimmie's mother's health began to fail after the death of her ex-husband. She was hospitalized with suspicions of heart trouble, but no determination could be made as to the cause of her suffering, so she returned home. Though Nora managed a perky pose for their benefit, Jimmie and Dona suspected that she was still unwell and urged her to come to their place for a while. Nora refused, wishing to be in her own home and in her old routine. The two called on her frequently and she recovered slowly, although she continued to fatigue easily.

"Would it be all right if Vikki stayed with you for a couple of weeks?" Coralea asked her mother.

"Well, of course. We'd love to have her!" Dona immediately replied. It had been years since their oldest granddaughter had spent much time with them. Since the grandkids had all gotten into school, they had interests and activities of their own and weren't as excited as they once were about spending a weekend with their grandparents.

"We're going out to Washington for a few days. Vikki doesn't want to miss her work at the Vogue, so we decided she could remain at home if she could stay with you," Coralea explained. She had expected the idea to get an eager response from Dona, and she wasn't disappointed.

"We can do all kinds of fun things together!" Dona assured her daughter. Except for a similar trip of the Simpsons' several years earlier, there had never been an occasion for any of the grandchildren to spend that much time at "Granny" and "PaPa"'s, as they were known to them. Coralea could see her mother's wheels turning, making plans to entertain seventeen-year-old Vikki. The girl had her own car and would be making daily trips to Madison to work, but Coralea knew her daughter always enjoyed the time she spent at the farm, so she had no qualms in leaving her behind.

When Vikki breezed into the back porch with a stack of clothes flung over her arm, Dona met her in the kitchen and quipped, "You must be planning on staying awhile."

"I hope so, if you'll have me," Vikki replied, leaning against the door frame to catch her breath.

"Promise you'll behave?" Dona asked as she pursed her lips and lifted her eyebrows--this from a woman who'd never found fault with any of her grandchildren. If they did anything that caused her distress, it was because they "were teething" when they were tiny, or "probably had a tummyache" when they were older. She definitely had a grandparent's perspective.

"Sherry's room will be coolest," Dona suggested, as she waved toward the stairs. Clerow was excited by the guest in the house. His claws clicked on the linoleum as he scurried around Vikki's feet. The little black dog had belonged to her family for a while. The Simpsons had been unable to house-train the puppy, so they asked the Martins if they would take him, assuming he would be kept outdoors like the rest of the dogs. However, it wasn't long before Dona had made him into a house pet and had even trained him to stay out of the front room.

After several trips out to her old Chevy, which could almost be considered a classic by now, Vikki got her clothing, stereo, and a big bag of toiletries up the stairs. She settled down comfortably in the airy room. There was more space here than in her bedroom at home.

"How do you like working at The Vogue?" Dona asked her granddaughter when the two met again in the kitchen.

"Okay. I like it better than working at the Dog and Suds, but I have to get dressed up. They want us to look nice since we sell clothing." Vikki had worked at the fast-food restaurant until her parents decided the late-night hours weren't a good idea.

"Do you make more at The Vogue?" Dona wondered.

Vikki sat back in her chair and folded her arms emphatically.

"Yes and no. I make more, but sometimes I end up owing them at the end of the month!" She ran her fingers through her auburn hair in a cooling gesture. Like Sherry, she'd started life as a blonde, but her hair color had darkened with time and now reached her shoulders in a soft mass. Dona's natural curl had not survived the generations to Vikki.

"Don't you get a discount?" Dona asked.

"Uh-huh. Twenty percent. That's part of the problem. I'm always seeing something I like that's such a bargain I can't pass it up!" the girl lamented.

Her grandmother laughed.

"Well, at least you're getting some nice clothes," she remarked.

"I just wish I could afford them!" Vikki retorted.

That evening at supper, Jimmie and Dona caught up on all that was going on with their granddaughter. She planned on entering college in the fall, in Madison where she could live at home. She wasn't sure what she wanted to do—she would just take general courses at first. She didn't have a steady boyfriend at the time.

Jimmie suggested that the three of them go to a show some evening.

"Would it be accurate to say we haven't gone to a movie in years?" Dona asked after expressing her surprise at his offer.

"I guess it would. You two find something you'd like to see and we'll go," Jimmie declared. He was obviously eager to show Vikki a good time while she was with them.

"Have you had any visits from Little Willie lately?" Vikki asked as she sat enjoying the meal Dona had prepared.

A mischievous grin spread across Jimmie's face when he heard this question. He gave Dona an expectant glance. Maybe now would be a good time to tell Vikki. He wouldn't want her to be afraid of sleeping upstairs.

"No, not lately. Not for years. I guess he's moved on to haunt some other old house," Dona assured her.

"It was you, wasn't it, PaPa?" Vikki challenged.

"It might have been," he reluctantly allowed. He hated to give in and admit his part in tricking her, but he could see that Dona would never confess her role in the playful charade.

"Stacey really believed it was a ghost!" Vikki declared.

"You didn't?" her grandmother asked.

"Well . . ." Vikki began.

"You sure came down those stairs in a hurry!" Dona reminded her. Vikki had asked some friends down for a slumber party on her sixteenth birthday. Dona primed the girls with 'Little Willie' tales before they went upstairs for the evening. She was in the kitchen cleaning up. The four girls were in Sherry's room giggling and carrying on, as teenagers will. When they heard something hit the other side of the bedroom door with a loud "whack," they all went tumbling down the back stairway into the kitchen where Dona was putting away the supper dishes.

She acted as if she had no idea what they were talking about when they began to describe the startling sound they'd heard. She pointed out that there was no way she could have made it down the front stairway and back to the kitchen before they'd rushed down the stairs. She would certainly not suggest the possibility that another flesh and blood person could have come in the front door--and that he could then have quickly returned to his evening chores!

"Don't ever tell Stacey. Okay?" Vikki asked. "She really thinks it was a ghost!" They both agreed to that, knowing it would be unlikely they'd run into the girl again, since she had married and left the area.

During her growing up years, Vikki had shared many happy times in the old house with her grandparents. It wasn't just a house to her--it was a special place. Vikki knew her grandmother had sought to make it so for each of her grandchildren.

Vikki spent much of her time exploring the place again. She could see Granny's fanciful touch everywhere she looked. As a child, her favorite place had been the toy room, of course. Still unchanged after all those years, it drew her still, even though she was far past playing with the cherished objects her grandmother had saved from her own three girls. There were the doll dishes that had made tea parties with Granny a special part of her childhood. And the wooden cradle that had been Jimmie's grandmother's was still filled with dolls with painted-on hair and eyes that opened and shut.

Vikki knew that the smaller bedroom next to Sherry's, where she was now staying, had once been her mother's room. Now it was the "Oriental" room. She guessed her grandmother had purchased the delicately painted folding screen at an auction. The cot-style bed was low and covered with an ornate spread that also had the look of the Orient. A few Japanese dishes sat on a small table, along with porcelain figures of Geishas.

On the other side of the room, however, were relics from Germany--several pipes with long, curving stems and ceramic bowls--one with the likeness of a man's stern countenance carved in ivory. There were pocket watches, and knives of all sizes, including an oily bayonet. A long, gently curving sword encased in a black sheath hung on the wall above the low display table.

On its own little table nearby sat the music box. It was the only object in the house Vikki had been forbidden to touch when she was a child. She remembered the sound of the soft, tinkling music when her grandmother had played it for her. She picked up the wooden chest and held it reverently on her lap. It had four tunes, the names of which she could see now, faintly inscribed in beautiful, flowing handwriting. She moved a tiny lever over to the position of her favorite, "Tales from the Vienna Woods." When she rotated the metal key on the bottom of the box the bronze cylinder began to move slowly, setting bristles of metal to prick the metal fingers of the keyboard. The tones were so sweet and delicate! She wondered how old the pretty instrument was and what kind of home it had come from. What kind of people had listened to this music and what elaborate journey had it made to get to this place? The simple, wooden box that held the beautiful music maker was no larger than a lunch pail, but Vikki could see why it was one of her grandmother's prized possessions.

In an effort to keep Vikki entertained and to show off her granddaughter, no doubt, Dona invited Nora and her friends out for an afternoon of card playing. The ladies arrived in Ruby's big brown Mercury. She usually picked everyone up when Dona wasn't along.

Besides Nora and Ruby, the two Wilmas made six in the group, so they settled on "Skip-Bo" for their afternoon amusement. Dona had introduced the card game to her grandchildren during earlier visits. Vikki had enjoyed the game but was surprised that the older ladies took to it as they did, since it was basically a child's game. The women were generous in their attention to Vikki, and she easily took on the role of special guest that Dona had intended.

The group of ladies joked with each other and teased her as they would their own family. She was surprised at how swiftly the time flew by. She hadn't known what to expect when Granny came up with the idea, but she definitely enjoyed the day. She knew her grandmother truly appreciated the friends who were her guests.

Ruby, tall and slender, was the most reserved of the group. Aloof in manner, she was yet cordial and warm-hearted. Grandma Martin was solicitous, as always, showering Vikki with compliments of all sorts. It had been but a short time since Wilma Cameron had lost her own precious daughter in the horrible accident on the tracks. Somehow, she had managed to accept the tragedy and to go on as she had always been--pert, particular, and with a droll sense of humor that endeared her to others.

The second Wilma--big Wilma in Dona's mind, as she was about a foot taller than her diminutive friend--was a farm wife who lived on past the Penney Eighty. Her older children had gone to school with Dona's three girls. Wilma Andrews was a talker who kept everyone up on the news of the community. Vikki took to the neighborly woman immediately, though she couldn't possibly have foreseen the event that would one day cause Wilma to become not only her grandmother's, but her own personal friend.

Vikki was impressed by the duration of these women's friendships. They'd known each other well for a long time, yet their attitudes were as fresh and enthusiastic as those of her own peers. Their concern for each other was real enough to touch.

Vikki's visit was soon concluded. Dona was pleased that her granddaughter appreciated the home she herself held so dear. A place of permanence, she knew, could have a grounding influence on maturing children. She was happy to share her love of the house she had so carefully restored.

Dona was satisfied to be an observer as her grandchildren emerged from adolescence into young adulthood. Absent the enormous responsibility she felt in raising her own children, she was able to reflect on the stages of their growth and to appreciate the unique talents and personalities of each one. Vikki was oldest and the first to benefit from the doting attention of her grandmother, but they all, in their own way and time, enjoyed the company and counsel of their elder, either as a repository for their adolescent woes or simply to get away from their siblings. They confided in Dona things they might not discuss with their parents, such as news of their current boyfriend or girlfriend, or lack thereof.

Sometimes one of them would bring a friend along to share the farm experience. Once in awhile Kelly planned a trip to the river for the kind of fishing he'd done as a child. On these occasions the boys spent time at the house with Jimmie and Dona, sharing fish and tales of fish. Stewart came up from Shenandoah on his motorcycle to look for good places to go hunting, or just to walk in the woods.

Although her contributions to the farm operation were modest, Dona performed certain services that were key to the enterprise. One was in keeping farm records and figuring income taxes. Another of her duties was recording and keeping track of the cattle that were born, bought or sold by the farm. She was happy to perform this task for two reasons--she would know where they stood as far as investment and outcome were concerned and, besides that, she enjoyed keeping tabs on their stock of beefy Black Angus cattle. She and Jimmie referred to the animals as "black gold," better then oil, even, for a struggling farmer.

It had taken Jimmie many years to build his herd to its present size of a hundred brood cows. He no longer knew his animals by name, but now each sported a yellow tag clipped onto an ear. The number registered on the tag allowed Dona to record significant events in the animal's history, such as calf production dates, inoculations, or problems of any sort.

As his holdings increased, Jimmie had to rent pasture for his herd a distance from the home place. Sometimes he kept his cattle at a farm near Culver City, just a few miles east, but most of the time he had to go farther to find available grassland. Consequently, the large herd was generally pastured near Fairfield, about an hour's drive distant. This worried Dona, even though Mr. Rivers' fences were good and there was a large pond on the place. Many things could happen that might need more immediate attention than could be given at that distance. Besides, she was concerned that Jimmie spent so much of his time on the road.

Sometimes Dona accompanied her husband on the trips to the pasture. There was a nice restaurant in the nearby town, so they made an outing of it when they went to check on the livestock. Often they went in the big flatbed truck, hauling hay to supplement the waning supply of pasture grasses during a dry period. Most of the time was travel time. When they arrived at their destination, Jimmie counted the cows and looked them over for signs of disease or injury. Then sometimes he would walk the fences, checking for loose or broken barbed wire or weakened posts.

When calving season approached, Jimmie hauled the cows back to the homeplace if they were ones he suspected might have a problem dropping their calves. For the most part, the animals were left to the control of nature and delivered their spring babies out in the open. Dona loved to see the lumps of furry black that appeared at this time of year, startlingly dark against the bright new grass. They would lie in the warming sun, sleeping contentedly as the mother cow grazed nearby. Then, after a few weeks, she would see little bunches of calves resting in a group while a single nurse cow hovered close by. The thought of a babysitter cow amused Dona.

Around September the calves were sorted out and brought back to the home place for weaning. The ruckus then was earsplitting. The calves bawled like the babies they were, and the cows in the area ran up and down the fence in a terrible state of agitation. Dona often managed to be away from home at that time.

His Angus herd was Jimmie's pride and joy, especially the young calves he chose to raise for breeding stock. They were given names and registered according to the specifications of the American Angus Association. When those animals were sold, it was a joyous occasion at the farm for Dona got to make a sizable entry into the asset column of her ledger.

If Jimmie had a bull he especially prized, he would have the vet take a semen collection before he sold the animal. This would be sent to the Hawkeye Breeder's Association in Iowa where it would be kept for future use. The firm used a cryogenic technique that allowed bulls to sire calves far beyond their natural life span.

Clerow, the little black dog that resembled a shaggy mop, was with the Martins just long enough to win their hearts. No one in the family would have imagined the attachment they formed so quickly to the playful little pooch. He was the center of attention when visitors came to the house and the subject of much of their conversation as well.

The dog often went with Jimmie in the truck and one day rode along when he went to deliver a bull to a farm down by Barrow, some five miles away. When it was time to go, Jimmie couldn't locate the dog. He called and called for him and drove up and down the road looking, to no avail. He waited and watched until he finally decided he must go on home without him.

That evening Dona went back with him to search once more. They stopped at farmhouses and asked for help, leaving their name and number for a phone call they hoped would come. When no word was received, they ran an ad in the St. Joseph newspaper, thinking someone might have seen their pet and could at least tell them where to look for him. For weeks, they still expected him to come back, ever hopeful that he'd just gotten lost and would eventually find his way home. They never learned of his fate--lost, dead, or stolen. They vowed to remind each other never to get so attached to a pet again.

Dona's days of retirement proved to be short. In less than two years she was summoned back to the light company to fill in at the power station. The dispatcher there had become medically disabled, and the company was desperate for someone who could take her place immediately.

As far as Dona was concerned, the call couldn't have come at a better time. Financial worries were compounding daily, it seemed, with no let-up in sight. She was aware of the farm crisis and would gladly share her concerns with her husband, but Jimmie continued on in his stubbornly optimistic way, expecting a windfall of some sort to be right around the corner. They could use the income her work would provide, and she was ready to immerse herself in a consuming task that would take her mind off the impending possibility of losing the farm. Her husband would never voice that contingency, but she knew their financial position too well to ignore it.

The assignment turned out to be quite different from her work in the main office. The power plant, located a few blocks north of the Second Street site, had been the main electrical facility for the city until a larger sub-station was built east of town. Now the old warehouse was mainly used for routing the activities of the linemen who operated in the Madison area.

Dona's job consisted of manning radio communications between the trucks and the station, relaying orders and information between the foreman in the office and the crew in their trucks. She had a good speaking voice and quickly mastered the unique requirements of the position. The public rarely came into the building, so her time was spent almost entirely with the men whose activities she coordinated. Many of the fellows were young enough to be her sons and she was at ease exchanging stories and experiences with them. They treated her as a lady while at the same time including her in ribald jokes and teasing that made the days go swiftly. The work she did allowed her to sit at her desk nearly all day, so the job was easy on her physically and she usually arrived home with energy left over.

One of the perks of her position, besides the general camaraderie of her work mates, was playing poker with the guys during the lunch hour. They'd often go next door for a sandwich at the Watering Hole, a local bar, and then spend some time playing penny-ante poker. She had never done that at the main office! The job that began as a fill-in position continued for nearly three years before someone at the main office agreed to move to the warehouse facility. Dona would miss the guys, some of whom had also become good friends, but she was ready to "re retire."

Nora passed away in 1978. Dona was certain it was the darkest day of her husband's life. Jimmie found her lying on the floor in her back porch, as if she had just been going to let the cat in for the evening. Her bed had not been slept in, indicating she had probably lain where she was over the night--not a comforting thought to her son.

Dona waited for Jimmie to come to the house with the news that Nora was all right. His morning routine had become: going to his mother's to check on her, stopping on the way home to get the newspaper from the box beside the lane, then returning to the house for breakfast with Dona. On this morning he tarried in the yard, petting the cats that he often nudged out of the way with the hard toe of his boot and checking the rain gauge mounted on the picket fence.

Telling Dona would be difficult--to say it aloud would make it real.

She felt the heartache that slowed his steps as he entered the porch. His eyes reluctantly met her expectant look--anxiety laced with hope and resignation. There was no need for words between them. She embraced him and they cried together, frustration surrendering to solace in a torrent of tears.

For Dona, the most heart-wrenching aspect of Nora's death concerned Jimmie's sister, Lizabeth. She came from Texas accompanied by her new husband, Jess Swanson. A widower, he had a family, so now Beth had stepchildren, and grandchildren, as well. They would never get to meet their new grandmother--never get to know the spry little lady that had become so dear to Dona and her family. Dona thought what a blessing it was when families lived close together. Nora had been living within sight of the place of her birth--had lived nearly all of her seventy-nine years within a five-mile radius of that very house!

Nora was buried from the church she'd supported for all of that time. For many years she had baked and served the pies and cakes that offered fellowship to grieving families. *What a precious thing, to have that kind of connection to a time and place*, Dona thought. She wished that Beth could feel that, too. But maybe her home in Texas had become Beth's spiritual center, as emotionally binding as Bedford had become for Dona.

Nora was laid to rest beside Jed and Sadie Alice (Merry) Torrance, her parents, in the Anderson Cemetery.

Jimmie wanted his sister to take any and all things she wanted from her mother's house. All she packed up to carry back to Texas was old sheet music and personal items of Nora's, plus some jewelry that had been passed down in the family. He was happy to keep the walnut dresser and the hand-made wooden high chair that had been his grandmother's.

Dismantling Nora's life would be a painful process, so Jimmie and Dona asked the girls to come and help clean out the house that Nora had rented beside the school. Each was encouraged to take what she wished to keep for herself, and everything else would be sorted. There was not enough for an auction, so anything not worth keeping or storing would be relegated to the dump. Not much ended up there, as the decision to throw away anything of Nora's was too emotionally shattering to make. The quonset hut on the home place became the repository for boxes of dishes and pots and pans, and suitcases filled with old photographs not even Jimmie could identify. Merry's piano and Nora's kitchen table were saved, too. No one could use them, nor could they part with them.

Dona picked up Nora's diary from the end of the kitchen cabinet. She sat on the back step with it in her hand. She opened it slowly, wondering if she should--a diary was such a personal thing. But if she didn't read it, whoever would?

The pages of the small book, no bigger than her outstretched hand, were divided into the days of the week, with only a few lines available for each. Nora's handwriting appeared jerky and uneven, probably the result of the stiffness that comes with age and arthritis. Her notes were simple. She had recorded who visited her, whom she had gone somewhere with, or whom she had gone over to see. Some entries told of important events in the town--a Lord's Acre Supper, somebody getting home from the hospital, someone's grandson graduating.

Dona thought about how uncomplicated Nora's life had become. The woman had obviously been contented in her plain surroundings, doing the ordinary things one does simply to exist. In recording the persons and events that were important to her, Nora left a testimonial to the value of friendship

A Hundred Miles to the City

and community. Dona considered this as she continued reading through the pages, right up to the entry on the day of Nora's death. As she read, she began to feel truly blessed by the friendship she ultimately shared with Jimmie's mother.

TWENTY-SEVEN

The wind. Not the typical winds of March, but a steady, unyielding force that drove everything not securely attached to go flying off into the careening air like so much chaff before the storm. The winter's yard clutter, swept up against the picket fence, vibrated like a child's paper and comb toy, making not music but a low moan that seemed to lament its predicament. There had been times when Dona thought she heard the house sing, with gentle breezes teasing a loosened screen, perhaps. But this day the movement was palpable, as if the whole house quivered. The air, though moving with unprecedented speed, was thick with the detritus of the previous season. For two years now the drought had held and even the winter's ice and snow had not yielded enough moisture to bind the particles of soil together that now swirled along at the whimsy of the gale. Sometimes Dona wondered why Jimmie was going ahead with soil preparation. A decent crop was nearly unthinkable at this stage. But he and Dale were down on the bottom, tilling the dry fields just as if it were a normal spring.

Dona had just finished putting away the groceries she'd bought for the family dinner she planned for Easter. She heard Jimmie come slamming in the door. He was at her elbow before she could turn around.

"There's a fire!" he exclaimed urgently. "You have to get out of the house!"

Startled, she stared at him in disbelief, panicked by the look on his face.

"Shall I call the fire department?" she asked as she rushed toward the phone.

"Okay, try . . . but there's nothing they can do!" he stated, as he went toward the bedroom and began pulling out his grandmother's walnut dresser.

By that time, Dale had made it to the house and was urging them to get out. The propane tank was in line with the fire approaching swiftly from the south!

"What do you want us to save?" Jimmie asked Dona.

"The TV, I guess," she blurted. She had already gathered up the manuscript she and Amabelle had worked on. She grabbed the ham she'd bought for Sunday's dinner and ran out the back door as smoke and flames entered the south side of the house. She tossed them down the hill and ran back toward the building. Jimmie and Dale were out with the TV, and she stared in alarm as flames shot into the kitchen.

Jimmie looked at her in resignation as he said, "I can go back one more time . . . what do you want?"

She couldn't think!

"No! Don't go back. Nothing. Let it go!" she cried.

He ran to the front of the house and into the front door. By now she could see flames through the bedroom windows. Now they were in the living room! Smoke poured from the top of the house and lines of fire crept like hungry red serpents along the eaves and around corners and crevices. Paint covering the wood curled and writhed before disappearing in swirls of intense heat.

She didn't want anything else. *Just come back!* She stared at the door as it became enveloped in thick, gray smoke. At last he appeared, with something in his arms! Dale ran up and led him, choking and sputtering, away from the inferno. Dona recognized his burden to be the seed picture that had hung in the front hall. *Thank goodness he went no farther!*

The next thing she knew, the fire truck was pulling into the lane and someone was urging her to get into the car and sit down. Dale had driven her car off the hill and away from the conflagration that now rose into the sky in a tremendous arc of red and yellow. The roar of the wind was amplified by the devouring blaze as it advanced northward, bursting through the tinder-dry boards of the frame structure.

Suddenly, a horrible scream pierced the air, causing everyone to wonder in horror if someone were caught in the hellish blaze! It was the propane tank, ruptured by the intense heat.

Dona sank, trembling, onto the front seat of the car. The consuming body of the fire was now a funnel of flames shooting north toward the park like a gigantic blowtorch. She couldn't bear to see it, but she couldn't look away. Her mind couldn't grasp what was happening. She glanced at the figures in the park rushing from hot spot to hot spot, beating out eruptions of flame as burning cinders ignited brittle grass. She looked again for Jimmie, not trusting her vision of him emerging from the smoke engulfed doorway. He came over to the car and climbed in beside her, temporarily out of the battle--physically at least. Tears of dismay glistened in his eyes and she burst into sobs of her own, weeping uncontrollably on his shoulder. She wondered if anyone could possibly survive such an ordeal alone!

Finally, she gathered herself together and offered her husband a teary acknowledgement. "It's all right, Jimmie. You're still here."

He gave her a tender squeeze and said, "You're still here." That knowledge was the most important thing in the world to both of them and they each knew it.

Flaming bits of roofing sailed northward on the relentless wind, torching the dry tops of trees in the park. Fire trucks from three communities were now engaged in putting out these lesser blazes so the damage could be contained. One soaring ember flew a quarter-mile in toward Bedford and ignited an old barn, but was quickly chased down and doused by an alert volunteer.

Dona began to notice people around--lots of people, some she knew, many she didn't. *Folks who've followed the fire trucks*, she thought. A group was passing around styrofoam cups of coffee. She took one when they came her way, nodding her gratitude when words would not come.

Cars moved slowly by on the dirt road that curved by the lane--the curious but polite, she guessed. She hoped it was possible for those spectators to separate their suffering from the mesmerizing spectacle before them. Joe and Kathleen arrived and slid into the back seat to speak with her.

"How did it start?" Joe asked when the initial courtesies of concern and compassion had been expressed.

Start? Dona hadn't been aware of it starting, it was just there, immediate and overwhelming! It had to have begun somewhere--she couldn't think where. It came from the south. Jimmie and Dale had seen it before she could smell it in the house.

"The burn barrel is around back, but we haven't burned anything in it for weeks," Dona told him. "We were waiting for the spring rains before chancing a blaze there. Besides, I'd have seen a fire there when I drove up with the groceries."

"Maybe it was a spark from the tractor," Joe guessed.

"No. They were both down on the bottom in the field," Dona returned. "Maybe Jimmie will know." She could see her husband headed their way.

When questioned, Jimmie couldn't come up with an answer either.

"It looked like the edge of the ensilage pit was on fire! Then, almost instantly, flames shot up the bank to the shed. By the time I could get to the house, the smokehouse was on fire and flames were spreading on the ground!" he told them.

"I've heard of spontaneous combustion in ensilage before, but wouldn't that happen in the summer when it's hot?" Kathleen wondered.

"We did dump ashes from the fireplace out there, but that's been months ago, and I was sure they were out. Dona cleaned out the fireplace after Christmas and I took out the ashes. There was snow on the ground then."

Jimmie's expression was of disbelief, but Dona could see a troubled frown settle on his brow as he gave the possibility some consideration. *Can it be possible that hot cinders drifted down into the compacted mixture and smoldered there for weeks, during the dead of winter?* It had been dry. Hot ashes that might have remained wouldn't have been hampered by rain.

Dona stared at the still-flaming spectacle on the hill. From her position, parked east of the lane, she could see the void where the back of the house had been. Only the front still stood, the flames beginning to abate. Where earlier she couldn't make herself look away, now she couldn't stand to see the vast nothingness where so much of her life had existed, real and tangible. She imagined the fire starting in the washroom, advancing into the bathroom, burning through her closet of clothes, into the porch and past the freezer. She had to stop thinking like that! It hurt too much to think of specifics. It was like dying a little bit at a time, with a thousand tiny wounds. She would rather have one marauding blow and have it over! It was all lost. Everything. That's the only way she could stand it--all together.

Coralea was with them now. She was struck by how small her mother appeared in the big car. She had always marveled at how youthful her mother looked. Now she saw the years showing on Dona's face. She climbed into the back seat as Joe and Kathleen prepared to leave. She asked if there was anything she could do to help, and knew how empty and meaningless those words must seem.

Dusk approached and the wind began to die down. The flames receded to the black heap that capped the hill where the house had stood. Charred spears were all that remained of the cedar trees near the structure.

Amabelle drove up beside Dona's car. She had coffee and sandwiches to offer. Dona was glad for the coffee but couldn't seem to swallow any of the sandwich. She was so tired! She wished she could lie down and shut her eyes and close it all out.

"I have the book," she thought to tell Amabelle.

"Oh, Dona. You mustn't worry about that," Amabelle assured her.

"We all did so much work on it . . . I'm just glad it was handy to pick up," Dona said. The manuscript she and Amabelle had compiled represented the contributions of many community members, some of whom were no longer living, whose memories could not again be recorded. The historical collection was meant to be a tribute to the town's one-hundred-year anniversary, which would occur in 1987.

Darkness had nearly enveloped the scene when Barbara and Don arrived. In her practical way, Barbara insisted that her folks go home with them and they would stop on the way to buy some necessary things--toothbrushes, underwear and such. Jimmie told them he wouldn't need any underwear, for his personal items were in the dresser he'd pulled out of the fire. Don had to kid him about looking out only for himself, since Grandpa Schmit's dresser, with Dona's things, had not been saved. Neither Dona nor Jimmie realized how very destitute they were until they thought of all the items they were going to need, and very soon. They were homeless!

The rains began during the night. By the time the Martins made it back to the farm the next morning, not a wisp of smoke nor glowing ember remained in the mangled specter that had been their home. And the rain continued, all morning, in a steady drizzle the likes of which had not occurred for at least two years. *Why couldn't it have come one day sooner?* Dona couldn't help but lament, even though she had come to believe that whenever rain did come, it was generally a blessing.

Over the top of the hill, where the house had weathered the elements for so many years, the gray expanse had the look of an ocean sky--limitless and vacant, but weighty and oppressive. Dona had the same feeling she'd had as a child when she had faced the ocean once, in Oregon; as if she might be swallowed up by the void that overwhelmed her senses. She found it hard now to reconcile in her mind that this was, indeed, the location of her beloved home and that it was truly gone. How she longed to go back! *Just one day. Such a short step in time and space, but so far from here!*

She wanted to get closer, to see if there were anything left, anywhere; something she could at least recognize--some small piece of her past she might clutch in her hand. Retrieve. Retain. Revive. She couldn't even build it back in her mind. It was as if the house and everything in it had never existed!

Barbara and Don had accompanied them to the farm. The four made their way up the steep lane that made a circle on the east side of the hill. *Such a small mound of debris for all that has been my whole life!* Dona thought in despair. The ground that had been so hard and cracked yesterday was now soft and slick with a layer of slimy, gray ash.

As the cautious group approached the blackened area, they became aware of the true contours of the destruction. The heap they had expected above ground was sunken into what had been the basement, with but a narrow rim of charred wood crusting the perimeter of the mangled, misshapen remains of all that had once been a comfortable home. The freezer that was in the back porch had tumbled down into the abysmal crater. It was black and dented, but appeared still closed.

"Do you think maybe our papers have survived the fire?" Dona asked her husband, remembering they'd kept their important documents tucked into the depths of the icy storage box against just such a catastrophe.

Jimmie began to climb down into the hole. When he moved the masses around, he discovered some areas were still hot and decided not to venture too far into the debris. He could get to the freezer but couldn't get it opened, so he called for Don to go down to the machine shed and bring up a crowbar.

With some leverage, Jimmie was able to pry open the misshapen box and did, indeed, find the papers, wrapped in their plastic sacks, apparently unharmed.

By noon the rain had let up and Barb and Don had gone on, after getting assurances that her folks would return to Shenandoah that evening. The Martins were to make their home with the Wagners for as long as they needed.

Dona wanted to stay while Jimmie did his chores. She made her way to the side of the yard, an incongruent scene with one-fourth of a picket fence and a gate to nowhere firmly in place. She sat down on the old wagon seat, still in the spot it had occupied for years beneath the tall evergreen tree. Her gaze wandered down the hill to the machine shed. The pickup truck was backed into the shed with its precious load of seed corn--sacks of hope Jimmie had sought to shelter, believing it would rain, believing they had a future. She could see him now working in the lot, carrying feed to his animals. As she looked in his direction, she could almost imagine things were the same as yesterday morning. From here the farm looked the same, except today the dust was gone, and she could see a hint of green as she glanced across the edge of the park.

After awhile, she made her way to the back of the property, where the smokehouse had been. The fire had traveled through quickly, leaving some things partially burned. She found a rake that was blackened, but whole, and picked it up. She would use it to poke around with. She would search along the edge of the site. Maybe she would find something

She had been asked by several well-wishers whether they had insurance. They didn't. They hadn't been able to afford that luxury for years. It didn't matter, anyhow. No amount of insurance could bring back what she had lost. She thought of the family pictures. If only those could have been saved. But, they had been stored in the closet tucked beneath the front stairway. Thank heavens she hadn't thought of them then! Jimmie would have been under there trying to get them out. He would be under there now, in the middle of that pit.

She looked across to the center of the nightmarish remains. A tangle of wires and pipes jutted up at odd angles, as if trying to climb out of the soggy mess. Her eyes fell on something metal, something that had a shape with meaning. She gasped as she realized what it was. *The music box!* Atop a heap of debris, it was almost as if it had been deliberately placed there. No box, soot and ashes all around, the shape of the bronze cylinder was obvious to her amazed sight. It was a small miracle! She found herself crying. She didn't know if she were crying for what she had lost or crying for what she still had. That the house she dearly loved was utterly gone tore at her heart. Yet here she was, home still.

Some time later that day, Dona sat in her car, waiting for Jimmie to get his work completed. Norbert Johnson had come to help Jimmie with his chores. She could see the two men in the tool shed, talking. Similar in stature but stockier than Jimmie, Norb had sandy hair and penetrating eyes that gripped their target. Like Jimmie, he wore loose jeans that were faded and soft from seasons of continual laundering. She decided to walk over and send a "hello" out to Amabelle by way of her husband.

"Norb has a proposition for us," Jimmie told Dona as she approached.

"I have my instructions," Norbert began. "I'm not to return home without you."

"They want us to stay with them for a while . . ." Jimmie stated hesitantly. Dona sensed that her husband was uneasy at the invitation. It would be hard for him to accept help.

"Barb expects us back there, Norb." The last thing her daughter had said when she left this morning was "We're having Easter at our house. You guys brought the ham. We'll get everything else." Beyond that, they truly didn't know where their next meal was coming from. With the bad years they'd had lately, they had been unable to pay off much on the farm, and just getting an operating loan this spring had been difficult. That was when they had something. How could they expect the lenders to extend themselves further now?

"You'd be closer to your work," Norbert reminded Jimmie.

"Why don't we wait until Monday, and if Amabelle is still having such pangs of generosity, we'll see you then?" Dona suggested. That satisfied Norbert, and he left with the assurance that they'd be expected when that time arrived.

When Jimmie gave Dona a "Well, what do you know?" kind of look, she just said, "The good Lord taketh away, and the good Lord giveth." She had long ago stopped looking for incidents to prove her father wrong, but remembering Sam's distrust of all beings Catholic, she was happy now to verify the injustice of his attitude. Norbert was a newcomer to the community and surely had no reason to feel he was in Jimmie's debt.

"You know, it smells like spring today!" she observed as they made their way to the car.

Being without a home was a new kind of challenge for Dona and Jimmie. They had learned to live with loss in many ways, but this particular set of circumstances truly tested their resolve. They did locate with the Johnsons, who made them welcome and as comfortable as they were able to be. The Johnson children were in school full time, so there was plenty of room in the large house in which Nora had been born and had grown up.

The outpouring of support that came from the community was equally generous. All sorts of contributions arrived--clothes, bedding, cash--sometimes in person, often anonymously. Jimmie remembered Nora's items they had stored away in the quonset hut. What unknown force had guided them to save what they had--kitchen tools, pots and pans, everyday items all homes have to have but they hadn't needed at the time?

They would have to find some way to reestablish their lives on the farm. There was simply no money to rebuild the house. They considered moving the old house from the top of the hill in Bedford, where Jimmie and Nora had lived when Dona and he first met. It had been empty for several years now and was in poor shape, but it was a possibility. When they looked into the cost of having it moved, they learned that it wasn't a reasonable alternative, so they had to reconsider.

Junior Wilson, who ran the grocery store in town, asked to meet with them one evening. He brought an envelope he presented to the couple: the collection members of the community had amassed to help out their neighbors. Jimmie and Dona were completely taken aback by such support from people whom they knew to be less than wealthy themselves. The depressed farm economy had exacted a price from most in the area. There were no names, all cash contributions. The Martins didn't know whom to thank, even. *How do you thank those who give you something as precious as hope?* Dona wondered. She found it hard to mourn all that she had lost, when her heart was telling her there was so much more.

An obvious and reasonable solution to their need for a dwelling would be to place a trailer on the property. A mobile home would be a quick fix that would allow them to get back to their farm. They found a nice used one in Glenwood and soon, with the donated funds, had it set up in the park at the bottom of the hill. At first it was hard for Dona to be there, looking up at the scarred hilltop that had once held everything dear to her.

Setting up housekeeping in the modest unit was like starting over for the couple. It wasn't long before they had everything they needed for a comfortable existence in the limited area. Dona had to admit that the compact nature of the dwelling was extremely convenient, with the washer and dryer tucked into the hallway just steps from bedroom and bath. Clearly, not much housekeeping would be required in the abbreviated space.

The major discomfort they encountered was the heat in the summer months, as the structure was in the flat part of the park, away from the breezes they'd enjoyed at the top of the hill. Jimmie constructed a makeshift porch out of lumber scavenged from the old barn. It was large and gave them room to sit out in the evenings and also a place for him to shed some of his muddy clothing before entering the front room.

To Dona, the most astonishing aspect of trailer living was the feeling of being in the middle of nature itself. When it rained, the drops seemed to pelt her head--so insistent were they on the tin roof above. This proximity to the out-of-doors wasn't entirely a bad thing. Previously, she had hardly noticed the animals that skittered around, especially the squirrels. Now she could see them outside the kitchen window, leaping from branch to branch and chasing each other playfully, like little kittens. She had never been so aware of the changes in the weather and the progression of the seasons. The smell of the earth was close, and somehow comforting, to Dona.

To call Jimmie to supper she need only go to the door and holler, as he was likely to be just a few steps away in the machine shed--or just a bit farther, in the lot. He made it to the house much more often than he once had; she supposed because it was so accessible. She appreciated that, as she never stopped worrying about his safety.

Dona transplanted flowers from Bid's place, and one of the girls brought a flowering crab tree for a Mother's Day gift. Jimmie came home from a sale with a couple of wooden wagon wheels that he propped up at the side of their new yard. Some old-fashioned roses soon grew between them, transplanted from Ruby's house in town.

Wearing other people's clothing brought a revelation to Dona. She'd worn hand-me-downs much of her life. She had resented them then, seldom having anything that really fit. Now, somehow, the feeling was different. The articles she wore most often had come from Nora's friend, Ruby Masters, and all had to be rehemmed, as Ruby was a tall lady. Other than that, they fit pretty well, but what touched Dona was that she felt honored to wear them. *Funny how age and circumstance can change your perspective.*

A Hundred Miles to the City

Now that Nora was gone, Dona spent a lot of time with the older lady. Ruby's health was failing, and she needed frequent rides to see her doctor in Whitesville. After a scare with a heart flare-up, a pacemaker was placed in her chest. For a while following her surgery, she hired a local woman to stay with her to do housework and cook her meals. Ruby was pleasant to be with, refusing to be compromised by her present frailties. Dona's family began including her in their gatherings. She had grown up in the community, so she had many tales to tell about the town and its earlier inhabitants.

After they had enjoyed the carefree days of high school together, Ruby's and Nora's life paths had quickly diverged--Nora's to marry Jimmie, Sr., and Ruby's to join the local Red Cross and wait for Lloyd to return from the Great War. Now she still had her white Red Cross apron and cap, along with file cards listing the number of bandages she had rolled from white goods gleaned from every available source. Another set of cards recorded the number of sweaters she had knitted, plus the dates completed and the amount reimbursed for yarn for the project.

Many of the articles in Ruby's home were mementos of cities she and Lloyd had lived in or places they had visited. She evidently enjoyed the life she led, even though she and her husband remained childless. Ruby happily relived many of the experiences of her years away from Bedford as she shared her keepsakes with her younger friend. In the twenties, she had worn the fashionable garb of the flappers and had her hair marcelled for the photo she now kept on display. Dona enjoyed learning more about the era that held such fascination for her.

Ruby liked to crochet and her specialty was doll clothes, so she dressed the dolls Dona bought at an auction. She crocheted house slippers for everyone of her acquaintance and made beautiful afghans--some of which she sold, many she gave away. She helped Coralea crochet her first afghan, the only project of that sort that turned out respectably since Retha first introduced the girls to her hobby many years earlier. Dona remembered how the girls had taught the boys at Star of the West School the art during one long winter of indoor recesses. *That may have contributed to their difficulties at that school*, she thought ruefully.

Because of her pacemaker, Ruby was not to drive, but she often brought her Mercury out to have coffee with Dona. If the two went on from there, Ruby insisted that Dona drive her car. On many days Ruby came out just to spend the afternoon. She was alone since both Lloyd and Nora passed away. Dona appreciated this tie to her late mother-in-law's past, as well as the opportunity to share the perspective of one who had led an interesting life.

Dona knew that Ruby's friendship filled a void in her after she'd lost Nora and her own mother had fallen into senility.

Eventually Ruby made the decision to enter a nursing home, choosing to go to Shady Lawn in Shenandoah, where Retha now lived. She had a private room and took her own furniture, which made the move an easier transition than it had been for Dona's mother. Dona visited them both often, always glad to spend time with Ruby while she could still enjoy visitors, unlike her mother, who was now unable to communicate. Seeing her mother in such an uncomfortable, dependent state was very difficult for Dona and the rest of her family, as there was nothing they could do to ease her suffering.

Probably the most fortuitous decision Dona made that summer was in going to work as a census taker. Amabelle had been employed for the first round of listing residences for the count. Now they were hiring people to distribute forms to the rural areas. Dona would need to take a test at the employment office in order to qualify, then go to St. Joseph for a few days of training.

They had several weeks' worth of work, during which Dona and Amabelle covered most of the area around Easton and Glenwood. It was a wonderful time of year to be out of doors and kept Dona from feeling confined by the small size of her home.

Even though many of the roads were familiar to Dona, it soon became apparent why the census leaders were so definite in their instructions. Most small roads in the county had no name, nor numerical designation. Good maps were supplied and it was necessary to keep them handy for constant reference. The forms she was to hand out were pre-addressed and each location received either a long or a short form. Most of the people were friendly and eager to participate in the infrequent exercise. There were some, however, who would rather not tell the government anything, though she assured them the information was confidential.

"I'm amazed at how many living quarters appear to be empty," Dona remarked to Amabelle. They met with the supervisor each day to discuss any problems that had arisen, so they had occasion to commiserate concerning obstacles they had encountered.

"Uh-huh. And not because they aren't livable," Amabelle agreed. "I guess we knew people were leaving the farm, but I didn't realize how many are already gone."

"There're some places where a square mile has no inhabitants at all!" Dona lamented. She appreciated the opportunity to revisit the area she had known well in her youth.

"I ran into a fellow today who used to live next door to my folks, over by Easton," Dona told her friend.

"Did he know you?" Amabelle asked.

"He still called me Donie Ethel! How I always hated being called that--still do, so don't get any ideas!" She was happy with "Dona", even as a child, because Retha had told her the name meant "lady" in Spanish.

"Isn't it sad to see places so run down?" Amabelle asked. "Farms that were thriving homesteads such a short time ago now have windows broken, doors falling off. Some roads are completely abandoned now!"

"Out by Star of the West, where the girls went to school, half the farmhouses are empty. Some houses are gone completely, like the school," Dona commiserated. She wasn't sure how her daughters might feel about that. It had been a sweet-sad experience for them.

The two ladies were competent workers and were asked back when the next round of canvassing took place the following year. This time the enumerators were to personally interview those who had failed to return their census questionnaires. In some instances this procedure required a good deal of tact, but the two were generally successful in securing the information required for a completed form.

Dona considered the work perhaps the most satisfying she had ever done. She was glad their assignments had been mostly rural. She'd felt comfortable in the areas she had been sent. Being rural women, neither lady was intimidated by the ever-present farm dogs, whose enthusiasm could overwhelm a timid person. Dona figured the experience had been a successful endeavor and one that she wouldn't mind doing again, until she realized that, by the next decade, she would probably be too old to go traipsing around the countryside!

The farm economy continued its downward plunge on into the eighties, with farm foreclosures a common occurrence in the Midwest. Jimmie was forced to sell the most productive of his bottomland just to stay afloat. If not for the courage of his daughter and son-in-law to put their own farm in jeopardy to make a deal with the bank, he would have lost his whole operation.

Mainly, soaring interest rates were to blame for the bind many farmers faced. They were badly over-extended. The banks had been eager to lend on bigger, newer equipment. Dona remembered the fuss she'd made a few years back when Jimmie announced that he'd bought an $80,000 combine. She was very angry when he reminded her that he didn't tell her how to run the household and she needn't think she knew how to run a farm! There had been bitter words exchanged, and regretted. He was right. She knew nothing about running a farm. But, so much money! That large an outlay was beyond her grasp! It was seemingly the way of the future, though; you expanded your farming operation or you would be pushed out.

The couple's misfortunes were compounded by a series of incidents concerning Jimmie's cattle. The first occurred in the winter when he was pasturing his livestock at the Rivers' place near Fairfield. Jimmie came up short when he made his customary head count. He recounted and searched the perimeter of the field for an indication that the missing animals might just be out. No breaches in the fence were discovered, so he feared the heavy animals might have been on the frozen surface of the big pond when it gave way. He had no other explanation for the loss. When he inquired around the area, no one reported seeing any cows out.

Years later, when the pond went dry during a rainless period, no bones were found in the muddy residue left in the bottom of the catch basin. A cattle rustler had been active in the northwestern counties of the state during that period, so Jimmie eventually concluded that some of his cattle had made their way to market without his assistance.

As interest rates climbed higher and higher, more and more farmers were unable to pay off even the debt service on their loans. Jimmie was one of these. The bank he had dealt with for years began pressuring him to sell his cattle before they were ready, and while the market was at a low point. Jimmie deeply resented having his farming practices dictated by the bank. He sought relief from every legitimate lender in the area, but to no avail.

Finally, in desperation, he decided to go for a loan to Kansas City. He wouldn't tell Dona specifically where he intended to get it, but she knew it was probably from the mob and wouldn't come without substantial risk. She feared for her husband's safety, and for her own, if anything went wrong. They quarreled and once again existed in a very strained relationship until the cattle were sold and the usury money repaid. Dona didn't believe Jimmie saved any money by pursuing that particular course of action, but she knew it was important to him to do it his way, for whatever that was worth.

Dale began working for the highway department, so Jimmie once again needed to hire a new man. The young fellow came from Madison each day. He was newly married, with three young stepdaughters. Roy was strong and willing, and the two worked well together. Roy's religion prevented him from working on Saturday, which suited Jimmie, as that was sale day, anyway. It was heart-breaking for Jimmie to attend some of the sales, which were often the result of a foreclosure action, but he wished to help make a good crowd to support the unfortunate one who had not been able to make it.

Roy and his wife were soon blessed with a little girl. She was just a toddler when the accident happened. Roy was coming to work, crossing the tracks five miles north of Bedford, just before the junction that led south on the schoolhouse road. The weather was clear and the crossing flat, with no visual impediments for miles. His car was hit by a freight train. In less than a year the tracks would be picked up . . . all that was brought by the railroad, good or bad, would be gone forever.

TWENTY-EIGHT

J., Sherry's oldest, was in high school now and played in a local rock band. His specialty was the guitar, and he wrote some of his own music. His group, "Zap," was to play in Rulo, Nebraska, so Sherry and Dave invited the family to go over on Dona's birthday to see him perform. The club was situated on the bank of the Missouri River. Jimmie and Dona had been there before for catfish dinners. Going there to hear their grandson play would be a very special occasion for them.

The place was old and dimly lit, definitely not an up-scale establishment but evidently popular, as the tables were all occupied by nine o'clock. The evening was to be a treat for Jimmie and Dona, so they weren't to pay for supper nor to buy any rounds of drinks. Earlier in their marriage, Jimmie had insisted on picking up the tab when they went out with any of the family. That had changed in the last few years, and Dona knew her husband was uneasy in the role of guest, even though most families went through that transformation as the younger generation became established in their careers.

Barb's family had to cancel their plans for the event so they could deliver Shelley's cowboy hat to her, up in Iowa. The Shenandoah band was to perform in a jamboree, and Shelley had neglected to take along that part of her costume. Another girl needed white gloves to replace a pair she'd lost, so the Wagners were on a mission. The school band usually placed high in the stiff competition, and they needed to present a well-appointed regiment to vie for the coveted trophy.

"Are you sure he's your son?" Dona asked Dave, as she sat near the band and struggled to be heard above the amplified music.

Dave grinned. "Sometimes I have my doubts," he declared, winking at Sherry. "Check out the hair. I'd say there might be a question." J.'s long ponytail was in contrast to his father's already thinning hair, shaped in a short crew cut.

Sherry noticed Jimmie's trim haircut. He was graying around the temples--distinguished looking, she thought. Dona had stopped coloring her hair and gray strands appeared in hers, as well. Sherry liked it better that way. The lighter streaks accented the curls that circled Dona's face in a soft halo. Her mother was aging but still attractive at sixty-one.

Coralea and Cliff had come from Madison to join the group. They were alone now. Vikki had graduated from college, married, and lived in Nebraska City. Kelly was in college and shared a room in the Phi Sig fraternity house.

"J.'s really changed since I last saw him!" Coralea commented to her sister. "I can hardly believe that's him, either." She thought of J. as quiet and shy, but on stage he overcame his inhibitions, moving with animated gestures as he stroked his guitar. He sang the lead in several pieces and was often the center of attention in the group.

Dressed in leather adorned with studs, J. definitely got into his music. Many of the songs the band played were loud and unfamiliar to the group, but they occasionally played a mellow tune that everyone enjoyed. The dynamic quality of the bright strobe lighting overwhelmed those sitting close to the performers.

"It wasn't that long ago that his little arms wouldn't reach to the bottom of the cookie jar," Dona said wistfully. "The big brown jug sat on the floor in the kitchen, but the treats were still out of reach for poor little J."

"I'm sure you saw to it that he got his share!" Sherry remarked to her mother.

"I bet it's been ten years since we've been here," Dona commented as she smiled her appreciation.

"At least," Jimmie agreed. A few years earlier, making the hour-long trip to the roadhouse was a special outing for them, but they could no longer justify the expense of such a night. Knowing how difficult the farming situation had become, Sherry was pleased to see her parents enjoy themselves.

Smoke was becoming a problem, in spite of the smoke-eaters that hummed overhead, and Dona did her part to contribute to the heavy atmosphere. No one else in the group smoked, so Dona was self-conscious when she lit up, but the habit afforded her some extra relaxation.

"What does J. plan to do after he graduates this spring?" Cliff asked.

"He's going to Missouri Western in St. Joe, he says. He wants to take music courses," Sherry replied. "Dave's not too happy about that," she added, glancing at her husband.

"Well, I don't have anything against his music," Dave assured them. "I just think he ought to consider something he could make a living at."

"It's what he wants to do!" Sherry insisted.

"I don't see why he can't do something that makes him happy and that he can also support himself with, and a family someday," Dave returned.

"This music business is pretty expensive," Valerie, J.'s sister, contributed. She knew her brother had probably spent every cent he'd ever made on the equipment the band hauled from place to place.

"Sometimes what makes us happy isn't what's good for us," Coralea commented.

Dona wondered if she were still talking about J. and his music or hinting about her lighting up another cigarette. But dropping gentle hints was not her daughter's forte. She usually came right out with her opinions. Dona knew her family would like her to quit the harmful habit, and she'd tried, but then she would gain a few pounds and decide that smoking wasn't all that bad, compared to being obese. Besides, it really did help her relax. Like right now. She thoroughly enjoyed the companionship of her family, but the loud music and flashing lights were somewhat unnerving.

"It would be a shame to waste that talent, though," Dona contributed. "The only one in my family who had a knack for music was Hank, and he certainly couldn't pursue his interest in it." She wondered if her brother ever played the harmonica any more.

"Oh, I'm glad he has the ability, and the interest," Dave allowed. "I always wished I could play something myself."

"Lots of kids don't know what they want to do when they start college-- most probably change their minds at least once," Cliff offered.

Tami, the youngest at Dona's birthday celebration, was currently taking piano lessons. "I know I didn't inherit much musical talent!" she emphatically stated. She felt she had the desire but not the natural ability to make her musical pursuits easy enough to be pleasurable.

The party stayed until the first set was completed so they could chat with J. He brought his whole group over to the table to meet his grandparents. Jimmie and Dona were obviously pleased with the evening's entertainment and enthusiastically expressed those feelings to the youngsters. Like J., the other members of the band were subdued off stage. Only their extreme outfits set them apart from the crowd.

Shortly after that the party broke up, as Sherry's family had a lengthy trip home ahead of them. Dona assured them that the evening had certainly been the most unique and memorable way she had celebrated her birthday!

After a time, Dona adjusted to life in the small mobile home, and even grew fond of the simple existence thrust upon her. She spent little time on housekeeping chores. No longer working outside the home, she had ample time to enjoy preparing meals. She'd feared her family and friends would be uncomfortable in the close quarters of the new place, but on holidays the girls and their families piled into the limited space, seeming not to mind the cheek-to-jowl circumstances of such togetherness.

She was more relaxed at these cozy encounters than many she'd hosted before the fire. She guessed maybe she had the philosophy of a true fatalist-- whatever occurs is meant to be. It was hard to accept at the time of the tragedy, and her heart still ached when she allowed herself to dwell on all they had lost. She often reached for something useful, some small item she had not needed for a while. Then she'd remember. She didn't have it anymore!

They had hung the seed picture in a prominent place in the back bedroom, alongside the wicker rocker gleaned from Nora's things. Jimmie's great-grandmother, Cecilia Hawk, had constructed the elegant arrangement some time in the late 1800s. The ornate frame fit on a shallow wooden box lined with folds of creamy satin. The design, in the shape of a wreath, featured flowers of many sizes fashioned from scores of seeds meticulously glued into place. Dona couldn't imagine how the woman had found so many different kinds of seeds, and how she had thought to arrange them so artfully! She had seen no other work like it, in books or in museums. She was glad Jimmie had managed to save the special keepsake.

Dona still mourned the loss of the walnut cradle that had been in the toy room, holding Jenny and new Jenny, dolls of Coralea's, and Sherry's two "Tuckys." Those things were precious to her, not the fancy pieces she'd bought at antique auctions. They could be replaced. Not that she would ever want to. On the day of the fire she quickly realized that "things" weren't that important.

On days after, when she went back to poke among the ruins and look for something to cling to, she had shed tears because there was nothing. She kept the remains of the music box, though she was certain it could never be restored. She had all but the wooden handle of the ash scoop she'd used in the fireplace. The bully banks that had marched down the front stairway were ashes heaped upon melted mounds of copper, the residue of her collection of coins for the grandkids. Of all the glassware in the big house, the only piece she recognized now was a ceramic ashtray Stewart had made for her in an art class. That she kept and used. Though it was discolored and grainy, it still bore the initials he'd scratched into the base.

One day when she had time on her hands, she sat down with a spiral notebook and made a list of all that had perished in their home. She started at the north end, going through each room and listing every item on every table, curio shelf or windowsill. She wasn't sure why she did this. If they'd had insurance, it would have been a helpful accounting of their domestic assets. Maybe she recorded the items to get them off her mind, as people make notes so they won't have to remember things. Anyhow, it seemed to work that way. She had preserved them, after a fashion, so they no longer haunted her memory.

Losses of a more personal nature soon befell Dona and the remaining Schmit family. Her brother died a pitiable death of lung cancer in the Veteran's Hospital in Des Moines. Then, just six weeks later, his wife Beulah was gone, too. Dona was saddened, but angry, also, because the woman had seemingly willed herself to die, wasting away to eighty pounds by refusing to eat. *Didn't she know life must go on, no matter how much the entire world changes around you?*

Within a year of their passing, Dona's oldest sister, Earlene, died of kidney failure linked to diabetes. Her husband came back to Missouri for a visit, mainly to see his aged aunts who still lived in Edgerton, Iowa. Little else that he recognized was left in the town where he grew up. Emmett finished his solo trip that fall and passed away at home in Oregon, dying of cancer before Christmas. Nineteen eighty and eighty-one were very sad years for all in Dona's family.

The passing of her mother was the hardest for Dona, even though Retha was bedridden and lost in senility for a long time before her death at eighty-seven years of age. Putting Retha in a nursing home had been heart wrenching for Dona. It was a family decision but ultimately left to her to accomplish. Retha had been hospitalized two times for dizziness and disorientation in the preceding months. Also, she had injured herself in the dark one night by sticking her hand into an oscillating fan. In addition to these physical lapses, Retha had signed a check for work by a band of repairmen that amounted to ten times what the job was worth. Dona was still employed at that time and unable to monitor her mother closely at home.

The decision had not been easy for Dona to make. She owed her mother so much and wanted to do what was best for her. Retha didn't want to be in a care facility and walked off down the road a couple of times, intending to go home. Sadly, Retha's mind began to slip. She lost track of who people were and remembered only events that happened long ago. Her personality changed with the dementia, and she sometimes swore like a sailor, using words her daughter was surprised she knew. Dona and the girls visited her often, just to sit and hold her hand. They remembered the kind and generous soul that was once such a bulwark in their lives. Carrie and Miriam came, too, though not as often, since they lived farther away and their families still needed them at home. Grant had passed away in Albany in 1962.

The Martins' first grandchild to marry, Vikki, chose a small, private wedding in Nebraska, where she went to live after college graduation. When Kelly married a year later, he and Sandy, his high school sweetheart, were united in the bride's church in Madison. It was a simple ceremony for which PaPa purchased a new suit, light blue in color, which Dona thought made him look youthful and quite spiffy.

The young couple moved into a trailer court in Madison, and Kelly continued study toward his college degree while Sandy worked at a drive-in banking facility. Kelly worked in construction in the summer but needed employment throughout the year. Jimmie hadn't hired anyone after Roy's death. He needed an extra hand on the farm but hadn't found anyone whose assistance was worth the wages he must pay. Hiring his grandson might be just the solution for Jimmie. He would be flexible and energetic and had a genuine interest in the farm.

Not long after her children were gone from home, Coralea became separated from her husband. Her folks weren't completely surprised by the move, since she had been attending many events alone for some time. She didn't seem to be concerned or particularly saddened by her circumstances--it was as if she were finished with that part of her life and ready to begin another. Coralea moved out of their family home and into a small rental trailer in the same park as her son. As far as Dona knew, her daughter hadn't confided in anyone the particulars of the estrangement, so she couldn't guess whether or not it was likely to be a permanent arrangement.

Dona found Kelly to be easy to please but hard to fill up at lunchtime. He was definitely still a growing boy, and she wondered if she and Jimmie weren't spending more on him at the grocery store than they were paying him in wages. He always praised her cooking, especially her pies, which were now her specialty. It was almost like cooking for a family again. Of medium stature and slender, Kelly had his mother's hair and eyes, but Dona's dimples, she was certain.

PaPa obviously enjoyed having his grandson around, and Dona wondered if Jimmie might be hoping to influence him to go into farming someday. She wasn't sure how she felt about that. Kelly usually roared up on his motorcycle about mid-morning. He enjoyed working on the farm but was not an early riser, and Jimmie had told him that he didn't care which twelve hours he put in each day. Dona thought Kelly's young wife must be an understanding person.

By the time of Kelly's graduation, the couple had concluded that they should find employment that would capitalize on his degree in business administration. They would head west to settle in Rock Springs, Wyoming, where he would manage a new lumberyard.

On a snowy February day, they loaded their belongings into a stock trailer and set out, with one Doberman in the truck with him and the other in Sandy's little car with her. Jimmie and Dona went to Madison to help them load up and to help Coralea clean the trailer so she could move in. She had bought their place and would move from her tiny home up the hill. It was difficult for each of them to see the youngsters drive off in the falling snow with such a long trip ahead of them, and not a soul they knew to greet them at the end of their journey.

Visiting Ruby at Shady Lawn was one of the most satisfying elements of Dona's existence. The older lady was eager for company and interested in news of the community she'd long been a part of. Talking with Dona was her connection to the rest of the world, and she never lost her desire to hear of current events. Her natural curiosity kept her mentally alert, and Dona enjoyed the lively discussions the two shared. Ruby was determined to live as fully as she could, regardless of her circumstances.

Unfortunately, her body failed to do its part, and she became more and more dependent on her walker, finally able to ambulate only in her room, just for a few steps. Her heart faltered, but her spirit continued to thrive. It was a lesson Dona was privileged to learn as she spent precious time with her failing friend.

Ruby's final days came early in 1982. She was confined to her bed, weak and unable to rise for a few days before she passed away peacefully. Her loss devastated Dona, who'd been her close companion in her final weeks. The affection that had formed between them gave Dona a feeling of kinship she would carry for the rest of her life.

Sometimes Dona's cares got the better of her. She'd long been aware of the adage, "the world loves an optimist, but hates a pessimist." She believed in looking on the bright side, and she had always tried to live that belief, but it was getting very hard to do. She felt strangely out of sync some mornings--she didn't care if she did anything at all on those days.

She was ashamed of these feelings, knowing she should be supportive of her husband, who was working as hard as ever--as determined as he'd ever been to make the farm a success. Jimmie never allowed room for adversity or impossibility to enter his thinking. He just went on, fueled with energy born of a positive conviction she herself must lack. She often found herself dwelling

A Hundred Miles to the City

on the edge of despair. There were so many losses, too many to accept. Many of those she cared for were gone. She began to see her days wide and empty before her.

One afternoon, her attention was commanded by a passage she came across while scanning through a farm journal. It was a bit by "anonymous," describing what it means to be a farmer. The words that caught her observation were: "He is so far from a telephone and so close to God." She thought about that for a while. Her husband was not a religious man; but, still, that phrase did describe Jimmie. He had faith. His only need was to see the seed he planted thrust its shoot up through the black soil. He knew his crops would grow, the rains would come, the next year would be good, even if this year was not. Nor last year, nor the year before that. He had the fortitude required to farm. She envied him that.

Not long after that, Jimmie and Dona were invited to Nebraska City to attend the christening of their first great-grandchild. Vikki had joined the Catholic Church when she married, and now her baby daughter would enter the faith as well.

The church was not large, but beautifully adorned, with stained glass windows that glowed in the sunlight. A short service was offered by the elderly priest in attendance. His remarks were warm and personal, as he had served the parish for many years. He had given the couple their marriage instructions a few years earlier. Dona was surprised that the rites so closely resembled services in the Christian Church. It was a moving and life-affirming ceremony they all shared as one family.

Gradually, the melancholy that had settled upon her began to leave Dona. Perhaps it was the sense of life's going forward that took some of the sting from the pain she felt. There was a new little one with her future ahead of her, a future possible only because of those who had gone before. Witnessing a beginning was the tonic that soothed the depression to which she had nearly succumbed. Her spirits were lifted with the prayers offered up on that simple occasion.

When Ruby's estate was settled, Dona learned that she had been named sole inheritor. Ruby had made Dona her guardian when she entered the nursing home. She would have been in control of Ruby's financial affairs had she become incapacitated, which mercifully never happened. Also, Ruby had deeded over her house in Bedford to Dona and Jimmie. She wanted to insure that they had a place to go if they ever lost the farm. Dona figured it could be sold to help pay Ruby's expenses, if needed.

The assets Ruby left in the bank were more than enough to settle her affairs, so Dona invested the rest in CDs. She kept the house as it was for the remainder of that year, going to visit it occasionally to touch things that had been Ruby's. She took a few items for her own, mainly Ruby's clothing. At Christmas, instead of buying gifts for the girls, she invited them to Ruby's house and let them choose something they liked.

The next spring, Don and Jimmie shingled the house, and Dona and the girls painted the outside. Then she had an auction to sell the household goods she didn't want to keep. She and the girls were clerks for the sale, so the auctioneer's percentage was the only expense incurred.

She considered moving into town--it would be more comfortable for them. They'd have a dependable water source, for once, but she couldn't ask Jimmie to leave the farm. So she put the house on the market.

When bids failed to materialize at the price she'd set, Dona refused to compromise and decided to keep the property. There were several vacant houses in Bedford, so the market wasn't too good at the time. She'd wait. She kept Ruby's car, also. Jimmie figured they could use a back-up vehicle, and Dona felt the car was more a part of Ruby than the house was.

The Martins realized that, with the help of Ruby's funds, they could replace the house that had burned. In her belongings were a few ancient documents that represented stock in certain companies, including mining interests out West. Dona was excited by the possibility of hidden wealth in those unlikely resources. Also, Lloyd had amassed a collection of old and rare coins that she would have appraised. While her common sense told her they probably weren't worth much, she still entertained the prospect of finding a treasure in Ruby's generous gift.

Once she'd conceived the new house in her mind, Dona turned her energies to making that dream a reality. She consulted house plan books, then called contractors and asked for bids on a specific design. Both she and Jimmie were shocked at the estimates quoted by the carpenters. It had been several years since anyone in the family had built, and the price of the materials, as well as labor, had increased dramatically.

But that setback didn't deter her for long. Any time she could pull Jimmie away from the farm for a few hours, the two headed for St. Joseph to explore other possibilities. They considered a modular home. They would get more for their used trailer if they traded with a mobile home dealer.

They toured many show homes of that type in the area. Some were too fancy, some too small. It was August before they had found a design they both liked at a price they could almost afford. The best course of action would be to put a basement under the unit so they'd have double the space and a better place for the utilities. With some dirt work done on the hill, they could have a double garage in the basement, a luxury they'd both appreciate.

Dona could hardly believe her eyes when the earthmovers began to cut down the hill. There was already a crater where the basement had been, so Jimmie and Dona decided to have the area leveled to that depth. The new dwelling would be placed in front of the earlier location. The yard would be less precipitous, and the house's elevation would still be considerably above the park.

The men working the blades had been on the job for just a few hours when they announced they were going to another site for a more pressing project. This bit of news sent Dona into a minor rage. She knew the work must stay on schedule if they were going to get into their new home that year.

"Why don't you do it?" she asked her husband. Jimmie did have a D4 Caterpillar on the place. He and Dave had bought it in a joint venture so they could dig, or dredge out, ponds on their respective farms.

"You know I don't have time right now," he reminded her. He wished he could, but his crops and his chores were a full-time job already, meaning dawn to dusk. And he had no hired help now.

"Then show me how to drive the Caterpillar, and I'll do it!" she stated defiantly. He knew better than to laugh. She was serious.

"I don't know if you could do it," he began cautiously. "It's not the same as driving a tractor. Those levers are hard to maneuver. You're probably not tall enough to reach the clutch."

"I've seen small guys operate them!" Dona insisted. "Let me try it, at least." He could see she was determined. He'd learned that much about her in thirty years.

Operating the big machine was a challenge for her. The noise was the worst part--that, and the bone-rattling vibration of the powerful engine. However, she persisted. She was soon at work clearing the brush already pushed aside and leveling off the area where the house had been. She wanted to keep the limestone wall that had supported the old house, so she carefully worked around a portion of that. The rest of the foundation she shoved aside, hoping to use it in the future, perhaps in a rock garden.

Jimmie laughed aloud at he sight of his wife riding majestically atop the beastly machine, her gray hairs glittering in the sunlight! He went to the house to fetch a camera. He was not one to take pictures, but this was a sight that must be recorded!

In a week the men were back on the job, and Dona relinquished her role as a construction worker. She figured she'd saved them a little time and herself and Jimmie several hundred dollars but knew the real work was still there for the experts to accomplish. Before long they had the basement excavated and ready for the concrete men to come in and set up their forms. That crew was ready to work and efficient, accomplishing their part of the task in just a few days. Now Jimmie and Dona would wait for the house to arrive.

That spectacle was both interesting and unnerving to Dona. She couldn't picture the massive structures that were moved in on trailers ever becoming the attractive dwelling they had chosen. The pieces were aligned with the back of the foundation, then jacked up and rolled onto the supporting concrete walls.

The outside of the house was pre-finished, even the roofing, except for the ridge row. However, the inside would need to be completed. Carpet was to be laid after the connections were in place. The hitch came after the two pieces were set up. The furnace man had to wait on the electrician, who was waiting on the plumber, who was held up by . . . *God knows who*, Dona fumed! She was eager to get into the new place.

Late in the fall, everything was finally completed, inspected and accepted so they could move in. When the workers had been paid, the Martins had spent nearly as much on the place as a frame house would have cost. Nevertheless, it was an exciting time for the couple. This would be the first time either Jimmie or Dona had lived in a new house.

On the Saturday morning of the move, all the family came to help the couple carry their things up the hill. The furniture they'd saved from Ruby's was brought out from town to help fill the huge living area.

One feature of the new place Dona had insisted upon was the fireplace. It wasn't brick, but a pre-fabricated unit and Dona didn't know if she'd have the courage to start a fire in it. Anyhow, it was attractive and she'd once again have a mantel to decorate.

Spring found Dona working in the yard, planting grass seed and setting out plants in her new flower garden. Soon the grass came up, lush and green. She could once again look from her front window and admire the park north of the house, absent now the trailer with its accompanying shed.

An added perk of the new place was that she could look from her window above the kitchen sink and see across the circle driveway, far across the bottomland to a line of trees marking the course of the Platte River. She'd be able to watch from the house as Jimmie worked in the field or tended his stock in the nearby lot. At night, she could see lights farther to the south,

A Hundred Miles to the City

where a tiny town and several farms were lit up, twinkling like clusters of earthbound stars.

A few days before the move up the hill, railroad men working from the north came through town, pounding free and levering up the steel rails that no longer served any purpose. Dona could see them coming for weeks ahead, as they slowly progressed along the abandoned line that extended south from Junction.

Sounds of their efforts rang out across the flat bottomland. "The Anvil Chorus." The words slipped into Dona's mind and she thought of the delicate music box that played the sweet melody. She wondered how the haunting tones could be produced by steel ringing on steel. She watched the men work from her front room window. It was unsettling, the ease at which they were dismantling the very essence of the thing, once so powerful and magnificent, that had shaped the lives of so many. Her reaction surprised her, although the sheer noise and presence of the trains had never failed to stir her emotions.

Beginning with the day, so long ago now, that her sister had boarded the passenger train in Summerville and slipped out of her life, Dona's existence had been touched by the mighty machines. She thought of Union Station in Kansas City, closed now for several years. How it had bustled with activity during the war years, when the railroad had been her own lifeline as she boarded the "Bug" for the frequent trip home to Bedford!

Soon the town would have existed for one hundred years. The mighty railroad, that had changed the destiny of the entire countryside, had lasted less than a century! How transient that made her feel. By the time of the town's centennial celebration, the reason for its being would be gone--so quickly, so completely, so finally!

As she watched and listened, the memories she summoned were bittersweet. So much of the life of the community had been brought and served by the railroad. She remembered sleeping in the old house, feeling the bed shake as scores of coal cars rumbled along the track, rattling windowpanes as they passed through the night. The train had been a part of the place, an element of the scenery she loved so much. *But it also brought death and destruction,* she remembered darkly.

The men worked just a block or two away, their noises mixing strangely with the sounds of the farm. Dona thought of the coolies and their chatter as they toiled in a land foreign and forbidding. *No, that would have been on the West Coast.* She would have to re-read *East of Eden*. John Steinbeck had written the moving account of the Chinese immigrants and their role in the grueling task of forging through the western mountains. The public library in Madison might have a copy she could borrow.

Perhaps it was the Irish who had labored to lay this particular section of iron rail. They would have come out of cities in the East, leaving the world of woe they'd found after staking their dreams in the promise of the new country.

Now these men, of many races, were undoing the mighty task accomplished by those first struggling crews. Such an upheaval! She imagined the course of the track bed, a corridor of encroaching vegetation rapidly reclaiming the route once swept by steam and cinders. There were only two junctions on the southward avenue where Jimmie had to cross over the tracks to access his fields. Now these would be safe passages, at least.

When the men had gone, nothing was left but the elevated berm, a ribbon of earth between furrows formed by the displacement of soil for the incredible project. A gravelly topping spilled from the height, with a few rotting ties left behind for anyone who might put them to use. Jimmie took his lowboy trailer down and hoisted up several he'd save for some future purpose. He already had stacks of lumber scattered over the farm that he'd assigned the same hopeful fate.

A Christmas to remember. Dona had always loved the special holiday. She associated it with family gatherings and general good will. She had no inkling that this one would be any different, though she'd already modified her usual holiday plans.

Christmas Day at the farm had been a given. Practically every year since she and Jimmie married, the girls and their families had gathered to celebrate the holiday with them. This year she expected no guests on December 25. Both Sherry's and Barb's families were having the holiday at their own homes, then coming to the farm the following Sunday. Dona realized her grandchildren would want to spend time with the families of their girl or boy friends. Vikki and her new baby girl would spend the day with her in-laws, and she wouldn't come to Madison until the weekend. Kelly and his new wife, home for the holidays, would be at her parents' home for Christmas dinner, so Coralea would spend the day alone.

It was probably working out for the best, for the day was very cold, with six inches of snow already on the ground and a possibility of more at any time. Jimmie hauled a load of hay over to Fairfield while Dona stayed home and prepared a simple holiday meal for just the two of them. She was in the kitchen keeping dinner warm when she saw Kelly drive up with Coralea. She went to meet them at the door.

"I didn't think you were coming today . . ." she began.

"It just seemed like the thing to do," her daughter announced as she stepped into the warm interior. The day that started out clear and bright had become cloudy and the possible snow seemed more probable by the minute.

"Why didn't you bring Sandy?" Dona asked her grandson.

"I left her out at her folks'. She wanted to spend more time with her sisters--they don't get to see each other very often. She assured me that she wouldn't miss me!" he replied. "Where's PaPa?" he asked, thinking he'd go out and lend his grandfather a hand.

"He went over to Mr. Rivers' to feed the cows. He should be home anytime," Dona told her guests.

"What smells so good?" Coralea asked.

"I fixed some baked tenderloin. There's plenty . . . and pie, too," she added, winking at her grandson.

"Oof! I don't think I could eat even that right now!" he declared. "We had a big dinner out at the Hawkins'."

After they'd visited for a while, it became evident that Dona was anxious about Jimmie.

"How long has he been gone?" Kelly asked. He knew it took almost an hour to get over to the pasture, on a good day.

"He left around ten-thirty this morning. He said he would be back by one o'clock," Dona said. It was after two by the time they'd arrived at the farm, so Kelly and Coralea were concerned, also. When Jimmie hadn't appeared by two-thirty, they decided to go look for him.

"He may have had trouble with the truck," Dona suggested. "He took the old orange flatbed and it's not too reliable." If he had had a breakdown, he must be very cold by now, she feared, though she didn't voice that specific worry.

"Or he might be stuck," Kelly put in. "It's not far to Mr. Rivers' house, but he might not even be home, if PaPa needs help. We had better go while it's still light."

"We'll take my car, it's heavier. And I want to drive," Dona told them. "I know the road pretty well." Neither of them doubted that she'd make the best time, also.

There wasn't much conversation in the car as they sped along. The snow had been on the ground for several days, so the highways were clean for the most part. However, the day had turned overcast, with clouds lowering, seeming to bring the gray sky down over them as they progressed. The last few miles of the journey were over winding, hilly roads, and to top that off, snow began to fall in ever-increasing density. By the time they reached the lane to the pasture, visibility was drastically curtailed by the gathering storm.

From here on the path was flat and narrow, lined on each side by barbed-wire fencing, which aided Dona in determining the location of the road. The maintainer hadn't made it to this out-lying roadway, and the snow appeared to be six to eight inches deep, at least. That assessment was possible only because of the tracks made by Jimmie's truck some time earlier. They appeared to be in the middle of the path and gave Dona a guide to follow. Still, the car occasionally fishtailed, with snow building up beneath the chassis as it skimmed the surface of the deepening snow.

A sudden pull to the right and an over-correction sent the car to the side of the road, angled against the piled snow, but still on the roadway. Coralea and Kelly got out of the car and pushed, easing the wheels back toward the middle of the course. After a few tries at rocking the car back and forth in the packed snow, Dona finally maneuvered the machine to a front-forward position. She decided to relinquish the wheel to her grandson, in hopes that he would have more success then she had had. The chances of their coming to Jimmie's rescue were becoming remote. However, not one of them was willing to put that thought into words.

The snow was letting up when they finally brought the car to the gate of the enclosure. Several yards beyond the fence, atop a slight rise, sat the old orange truck. It was parked facing them, the hydraulic bed elevated at a steep angle and the door of the cab open wide. The motor idled unevenly, the only sound discernible as the three approached the gate and opened it. Strangely, there were no cattle in sight, and no sound of their presence, although there should be around a hundred in the pasture. Two large bales of hay had tumbled from the truck onto the scuffed area where the cattle would feed. Dona entertained desperate thoughts as she stared at the abandoned truck.

The color drained from her face as she considered the scene before her. What if Jimmie had been overcome with fumes as he'd tried to keep warm in the archaic vehicle? What if he'd had to adjust a part of the dumping apparatus and been caught in the powerful hydraulic machine? She couldn't step any closer, fearing what she might find.

Kelly went on, saying he would check it out and see if he could locate PaPa. He slowly approached the cab and reached in to turn off the ignition. He circled the area and returned to tell the women he had found nothing to indicate what might have happened. No cows were in sight down the other side of the hill, either. They were each relieved to learn that the eerie tableau was not the site of a tragic accident.

"He must have gone to holler up the cows and couldn't find them," Kelly guessed aloud. "I'm going to see if I can locate him." He waved his hand toward the east, where the pasture extended over a hill.

"Jimmie usually checks out the pond to make sure the cattle can get water," Dona told him, as she once again imagined a scene too horrible to dwell upon.

Coralea started toward her son, but he motioned for her to go back, saying "It's quite a distance to the end of the pasture. You stay here with Granny." She wondered if he wanted to shield her from the disturbing possibility that had entered his thoughts, also.

The two women watched as he moved swiftly over the hill and out of sight.

After the engine's arrhythmic labors were halted, a smothering silence descended on the winter scene. The swiftly waning daylight reflected off the snow, giving the sensation of light coming from the ground, rather than the sky. A mass of gray clouds appeared ready to tumble onto the earth, an ominous sign to Dona as she struggled to regain her confidence.

"He does this kind of work every day," she assured her daughter. "He's dressed for the cold."

"The cows probably got out and he's rounding them up," Coralea continued the hopeful dialogue. "Kelly can help him."

Time dragged on, with less and less verbal interchange in the car. It seemed like hours but must have been only twenty or thirty minutes since Kelly had gone. Darkness would soon be upon them.

"I'm going to look over the hill," Coralea stated, as she got ready to leave the car.

"Better take the flashlight," Dona said as she reached beneath the seat to retrieve the aluminum shaft. She checked it out before handing it to Coralea. She felt it wasn't much for her to hang onto where she was going. It was unreasonable, she knew, but Dona dreaded to see her daughter go over that hill, too.

Her anxiety deepened with each minute that passed as she sat in the car alone, waiting. The grayness of the sky touched the top of the snow and snuffed out the last remaining glimmer of day. Her breathing labored as the oppressive atmosphere weighed heavily on her senses. She found she couldn't do any more waiting--she must do something physical! She walked to the top of the rise, hope and hesitation confusing her steps as she made her way through the snow.

She gained the high ground, where she could see her daughter ascending the hill beyond the pond.

Coralea knew it would be dark soon and wondered how much farther she dared go into the unfamiliar territory. Surely she'd find them soon. *How much farther can the pasture extend?*

As she stepped over the crest of the hill, she could barely make out the fence row that marked the boundary farther down the slope. She saw a figure. No! Two figures! Her knees softened as she gasped and strained to prove her vision correct. Two people were moving toward her!

Instinctively, she knew her mother was behind her. She turned and threw her arms in the air in a wide arc to signal her discovery. "There's two!" she shouted across the narrow valley that separated them. She ran down the hill to meet the men as they approached, slowly and unsteadily.

"Where did you find him?" she eagerly asked her son.

"He was wandering around in the middle of the cattle. He seemed to be in a daze," he replied. It was obvious that Jimmie was weak--Kelly supported him as they moved purposefully along.

Dona hurried to meet them. She appeared nearly as drained and exhausted as Jimmie. They made it back to the car just as the last light of day faded away.

Kelly took the wheel and maneuvered the car back onto the roadway and into the path they had plowed earlier. The trip out was easier, partly because of the beaten trail, partly because their worst fears had not materialized.

Jimmie didn't say much on the trip home, except "I'm all right," and, when they gently pulled off his boots, "It doesn't hurt. I can't feel anything."

His sweat-dampened socks were pulled off to expose toes that were white and stiff. He was unable to move them when asked, which caused them each to worry about frostbite. Dona massaged one cold foot while Coralea worked on the other one. Drowsy in the warm car, Jimmie wanted to sleep, but they kept him awake, fearing he might pass out and suffer more damage to his already-stressed system.

"The cows were out in another pasture and he was trying to get them in," Kelly offered by way of explanation for the ordeal. "When I finally saw PaPa, he just looked at me strangely and kept saying, 'Kelly? Kelly?' like he wondered what I was doing there."

Jimmie later told his family he thought he had become disoriented after being out in the cold for so long. He hadn't felt chilled, he just didn't seem to be getting anywhere. He refused to see a doctor for his feet, saying they would either get better or they wouldn't.

A Hundred Miles to the City

Soon some of his toes turned black and stayed that way for several months. They were painful to him for years afterward, but he didn't lose any. He figured he had survived in pretty good shape, as did his thankful family. It seemed to Dona that, once again, her pleas to the fates had triumphed over the mindless brutality of the elements

TWENTY-NINE

With the passing of the railroad, certain developments brought a gradual shift in the tempo of life in Bedford. The once thriving, nearly living and breathing, trains had been dead to the community for many years, hesitating for a while on the tracks only if there was an emergency. Otherwise, the town couldn't even be considered a whistle-stop for the big engines, whose business lay farther down the line. Once the tracks were gone, a substantial piece of real estate was open and accessible to a good road that served several farm communities.

An elevator was built by MFA on the property. The wide roadway that once caught mailbags thrown from slowing trains now supported the fat tires of chemical spray conveyors. Semis loaded with grain pulled in and out in season. Pickups driven by farmers and agricultural workers stirred the dust ground from cinders by ghost trains of the past. In Jimmie's mind, it was as if an overlay could be peeled back to reveal the past hidden beneath the progressive frenzy of the present. Not that he minded. The drying fans of the new facility were a bit noisy but only added a soothing hum to the sounds he'd become used to--the constant racket that consumed the community of creatures in his charge. He knew if he didn't hear it, he'd be deafened by the silence.

Just a few yards away from this enterprise, Carl Flint had opened a gas station/garage and built a new house where Eva could cultivate the flowers she loved, and everyone could enjoy them. A block up the street, the old produce house was now a hobby shop where a former Glenwood girl taught ceramics classes and sold her greenware. A new post office had been built across the street next to the general store, on the lot that had once been an outdoor theater. Catty-corner from that, the old bank building, which had housed the post office, was torn down and replaced with a metal barn that served as the garage for the Horton-Bedford fire truck. Claude Davis worked his magic in the tin shed east of that. Jimmie could always take small motors in to Claude and know he'd have the machine ready to go, promptly and economically.

Albert had finally quit the service station business and sold out to a fellow from Roseville who liked to pump gas but wasn't a mechanic, so that part of the enterprise suffered. However, there was a new garage in town to fill that need. A new building had been erected next to the little house where Dona's folks had lived with the girls.

The brick school had been added onto a couple of times--the first time when the districts were consolidated, then later for a kindergarten class. The new parts were of steel, not brick, but colored to match the original structure. The school's windows were replaced with smaller, more efficient ones, and a new sign above the front doorway declared the modern name, South Johnson, and was adorned with figures of playing children.

Dona and Jimmie had no reason to be at the facility, except for once each year when the Bedford Alumni celebrated there with a basket dinner. Jimmie especially enjoyed those affairs and took his turn at hosting the event. At first Dona just tolerated the evenings, being the one left out when the former classmates were into serious reminiscing. As the years went by, however, she came to enjoy the company of Jimmie's peers nearly as much as he.

Several young families had moved into the community during the past decade. In most of these households, the parents worked away from home-- many at the industries in Madison that drew their work force from the rural population. The majority of pupils in the elementary school were now bused over from Horton or in from the surrounding countryside.

Students were no longer allowed to walk over the culvert into town to Junior's store for lunch. Cafeteria food was delivered by van from the high school at Horton. A crossing guard was hired to direct safe passage across busy Highway H in the morning and after school. New playground equipment stood beside the old, and a quarter-mile cinder track looped around the former softball diamond in back of the school. A chain-link fence was added to keep playground balls out of the ditch and the road. Only the core of the building and the gymnasium still existed in the form Jimmie had known.

The principal of the school was an acquaintance, so Dona offered to share a bit of local color with the students. The color was orange, as in monarch butterflies. Dona had long been amazed at the phenomenon Jimmie had discovered several years earlier. The migration of certain butterflies evidently took place in the corridor occupied by Bedford, for each year the delicate flyers found perches in the cedar trees at the Martin farm. They were first spotted hanging from branches in the tall trees behind the old house. Then, after the house burned, they shifted their overnight roosting to the trees by the lane, close to the machine shed.

When she and Jimmie lived in the trailer, Dona had often witnessed the annual arrival, early in September, of thousands of these traveling creatures. The first wave would come in before dusk, and arrivals would continue on into the night. By morning several trees were covered with orange and black wings, folded and resting, ready to begin anew the journey that daylight inspired.

Dona found their exodus a sight to behold! The movement of the fluttering horde seemed orchestrated by an unseen force that lifted them skyward, as one body. This she invited the students out to see. It was a spectacular event, and for a few years she predicted the occurrence by the increase of butterflies in the area. Then she sent word to the teachers. When the students came, they were quiet and respectful. Dona wasn't sure they were truly in awe, or whether it was just very early in the morning for them.

The teachers at the school sought to promote their students' writing skills by encouraging them to choose pen pals in the community. They would write personal letters a few times during the year. One third-grader picked Dona, who was pleased to correspond with her new little friend. In answer to the girl's questions, Dona related tales of her own childhood and told stories about how things were done "in the olden days." She was amazed at how quickly she had changed roles from interviewer to interviewee in the scenario.

One quiet afternoon Dona looked out to see Stewart drive up the lane. She was working the Sunday crossword puzzle at the table just inside the patio door.

He's got a girl with him, she noticed. *That would be Donna Kay. And, yes, there's her child, too; "B" something*--she couldn't remember. She hurried to greet them. Stewart nearly had to duck to get through the doorway. Already he was the tallest in the family, and he was still growing! Beside Stewart, the girl appeared diminutive. Her cinnamon eyes matched the color of her softly styled hair. This was a first for Dona's grandson, bringing a girl to meet them.

"Granny, this is Donna Kay," Stewart announced. He'd obviously practiced this in his head and was determined to do it right. "And Brandy." The child's dark hair was curly. *Charmingly like Stewart's,* Dona thought. *It's funny how the boy in the family is often the one to inherit the curls. He probably curses them like I always did.* Except, as the years went by she had grown to appreciate the convenience of her natural hairstyle.

"I'm glad to meet you both," Dona replied in her soft, deep voice. "And how old are you, Brandy?" she asked the little girl.

A Hundred Miles to the City

"Four and a half," Brandy announced proudly. She spoke up boldly. Dona knew right away that the child was accustomed to being around adults.

"PaPa's out working on the pump," Dona announced as they settled onto the straight chairs by the little table. "Can you stay awhile, or should I go out and ring the bell for him?" Sounding the iron dinner bell was their signal that he should come to the house right away.

"Oh, no! Don't do that. We'll go find him if he's not in before we go," Stewart assured her. "What's this?" He picked up a large photograph that lay on the table.

"Take a good look," Dona encouraged.

"Oh, it's the farm!" he exclaimed. "It looks different. How'd you get it?"

"A fellow came by. I guess he flies over and takes aerial photographs, then peddles them to the landowners. You know PaPa--the ultimate soft touch."

Donna Kay said, with a sly smile at her friend, "No, that's Stewart!"

They all laughed at that. Dona felt that her grandson was about the easiest person she'd ever known to get along with. Even when he was very young, she never needed to entertain him. When the whole gang of grandchildren were around--eight of them--he was quiet, but get him alone and he became relaxed and talkative.

"It doesn't look right, somehow," Stewart observed as he again scanned the photograph.

"The place looks neater from above, doesn't it?" Dona asked. "You don't see the horse weeds along the fence rows nor the old machinery parked under the trees."

"Except for that row of cars." Stewart pointed to a line of six or seven automobiles a distance in back of the house. "I'm to blame for a couple of those, and so is Dad." Don had parked Corvairs there to get parts to restore the one he was preparing for a show car, a '66 convertible. When anyone in the family's car quit running, it was pulled into place, consigned to the farm's automobile graveyard.

Brandy had been sitting patiently on her chair, playing with the little figures she'd brought along. Dona was sorry there were no toys in the house. There was no toy room any more to take her to. Nor had there been any room in the little trailer for toys to entertain children.

"Do you suppose she'd like to play with a deck of cards?" Dona asked. It was all she could think of.

Brandy reached over and tugged at her mother's sleeve. She pointed to the cabinet behind Dona where a rack of poker chips could be seen and gave her mother a pleading look.

"Of course you can play with these," Dona said as she brought them down and set them on the table. "They're as good a toy as I've got!"

Soon the child was busy rearranging and stacking the colorful disks. The little group sat chatting for a while.

"Where did you two meet?" Dona asked.

"Stewart works with my brother at the Wagonwheel," Donna Kay answered, referring to a restaurant in Shenandoah, where they all lived.

"Actually, Shelley is dating Donna Kay's brother," Stewart added, referring to his younger sibling. "We decided to keep it all in the family."

Eventually, Brandy drifted over to the glass door to watch the kittens playfully springing at each other on the back step.

"I'll go down and see if I can give PaPa a hand," Stewart offered.

"Brandy and I will go out and play with the kittens, if that's all right," Donna Kay suggested.

"You don't need a kitten, do you?" Dona thought to ask.

"Oh, no. I don't think so," Donna Kay began. "We have an old cat . . ."

"Ginger!" Brandy piped up.

"She's been very patient with Brandy. She might not want to share her territory," her mother added as they stepped outside.

Dona wished Jimmie spent more time in the house. It seemed to her that he always missed the company who'd come to see them both. But she knew he didn't choose to work on the pump on Sunday afternoon. The animals had to have water. The Martins' well had never gone dry, even in the drought years, but keeping the pumps working was a constant concern for Jimmie.

The well and pump that supplied water for the house were no more dependable than the system that served the livestock. Besides the fact that the motor sometimes wouldn't work, the quality of the water was becoming increasingly suspect. The water available to the Martins was what they referred to as hard water--full of minerals and difficult to work into a soapy lather. The inside of the teakettle Dona kept on the stove was thickly crusted with residue, making her wonder whether the water was even fit to drink. The new house was wonderful, but the problems with the water supply were worse than ever. Luckily, Eldon's place was on city water, so Jimmie hauled water from there when necessary. Though a costly alternative, a tank on the forklift of the tractor was frequently put into service. No rural line had been run out to the Martin place, so they'd continue to make-do with the existing mechanism.

Later in the fall, Jimmie moved the combine down to Bid's place. Dona drove behind him in Ruby's car, lights flashing. He knew she'd have to control herself to go that slowly, but she'd do anything, cheerfully, to promote the cause of safety on the farm. When in her car, Dona covered ground as quickly as the law would allow--no, quicker, usually. She'd never gotten a speeding ticket. Jimmie figured the patrolmen just couldn't believe an innocent looking little woman would be going that fast! If the couple ever needed to get somewhere in a hurry he always let her drive, as they were sure to be stopped if he were at the wheel.

The combine hunkered along over the narrow dirt road. In places, trees encroached upon the bladed surface to meet overhead, lower branches scraping against the machine as it lumbered on. Turning onto the gravel to head south, Jimmie noticed the color in the timber on the Penney Eighty. He knew Dona was back there now, extolling the beauty of the season. She never failed to appreciate the dramatic transformation that swept over the countryside each fall.

Nothing left at the Looker place across the road but the big red barn. It was something of a landmark, especially since Dona had painted the side of it--not red paint, but black, in big letters that declared, "Jerry Wallace played here!" The couple had gone to a fair to see the popular singer perform and had gotten his autograph. Dona found out later that his grandparents had lived on the Looker place for a short time, and he had spent a summer with them. So she took it from there. No one ever came along to dispute her claim.

There wasn't much traffic on the road any more. Most of the old homesteads were abandoned, or completely gone. But there were two fairly new houses farther along the way, where young couples had chosen to raise their families. They farmed some, but they also drove off to work each day.

A small cemetery was situated on a portion of the Penney Eighty, on the right as Jimmie passed. It was known as the Stingley cemetery, and most of the gravestones bore that name. Hiram Stingley's monument was the largest marker. He had probably been what Jimmie would characterize as "a big feeler." There had been no interments in the small plot since 1948, and evidently no perpetual care provisions were made, either. Dona sometimes burned off the area--to give the prairie grasses a chance to grow, she said.

They would soon turn into Bid's place and no one had passed them. Only a couple more deserted farms on to the south before the gravel road took a jog to meet Route J. Not much down at Barrow to cause commerce on the road. The farmers hereabouts had banded together to keep out a big hog operation and were successful in their efforts. But keeping the onerous corporation out of the area hadn't prevented the conglomeration from taking over the market.

Jimmie was one of the few remaining swine operators who kept free-range livestock. His hogs were outside, except for the short time of farrowing.

Since both the Armour and Swift packing plants in St. Joseph had shut down a few years earlier, Jimmie and other small farmers found it increasingly difficult to market their livestock. The stockyards only operated on certain days and most buyers preferred to purchase in large numbers. Jimmie had once been able to count on his pigs for a reliable cash crop, but that was no longer the case. More and more, big cooperatives controlled the marketplace.

There was a nip in the air the next morning as Jimmie drove his pick-up down to park beside the old barn. Weathered boards still clung tenaciously to the massive structure. *How many years has it been since Bid last brought his cow in to milk, or threw down hay to her from the loft? Bid was old as long as I knew him. That's probably the way folks think of me now!* he mused.

The house's skeleton sat a few yards away, inhabited now by raccoons--true opportunists if he'd ever seen any. The pump he remembered seeing beside the back step was now missing, the booty of another kind of opportunist, he supposed.

The combine shuddered to life and he set off to do another day's work. He no longer had the expensive machine he had paid so dearly for, but an older, somewhat battered model that he could usually count on to do the job. He followed the rutted path he had worn over the hill toward the river. It had been several weeks since the field turned rusty orange with the first temperature plunge of the fall, and now the vines cringed, withered and brown.

The next field over, part of the Anderson place, was even more secluded than this. It was land-locked, accessible only through Bid's place, never having had a road to it unless you'd count the narrow swale Dona was certain was the old wagon trail. It was to this place Jimmie and his wife came to look for morel mushrooms each spring. They never failed to find a mess or two, nestled in the undergrowth where the woods extended nearly to the river's edge.

When down here, he felt as one with the elements. It was so peaceful! He often saw deer and reported to Dona whenever he did. She was still protective of the graceful, delicate animals, even though they had begun to be pests, and hazardous, as well. She would run off any deer hunters who showed up on the place--unless they were her grandsons, of course.

Jimmie gazed across the river to the expanse of fertile fields just recently harvested. His own short stewardship of productive and convenient farm ground came to his mind. He had been forced to sell off his bottomland to satisfy his lenders. Now other farmers dreamed the dream that had once been Jimmie's--to coax that good, black earth into peak production. In truth, his reality never had matched the vision he'd created. There was certain to be a part of the acreage too wet to plant or to harvest--too much gumbo, with clods that clung together like clay and baked to a spectacular hardness under too much sun. He guessed he was happy to let others amuse themselves with that particular fantasy.

Most of his hillside soil was easier to work, though it took greater effort to reach. It hadn't really made that much difference--having less land. He had all that he could do now and was contented doing what he wanted, where he wanted, when he wanted. *Not too many men are that lucky,* he told himself.

In spite of the troubles he had, Jimmie knew the satisfaction of having no regrets for the decisions of his life. He had long realized that no one ever really owned the land. They were just allowed to care for it for a while. And he did care for it! He shared a oneness with the land, as if his body were a part of it. In a way, he felt as permanent as the earth he worked upon.

From Dona's perspective, Jimmie was shielded by a blessed stoicism she could never attain. He'd suffered personal losses, as she had, but he was somehow able to accept these very intimate tragedies in a way she could not. He was often called upon to serve at the funeral of a deceased community member, and he never failed to answer the summons, regardless of the work that had to wait. Frequently, the fallen one was a previous soldier, one whose name appeared on the service board now on display in the town's meeting room. Jimmie had been deferred from duty in World War II because of his position as head of a household. Perhaps he now sought, in a small way, to repay the debt he owed those soldiers--a final tribute to the sacrifices they'd made long ago. Men from the American Legion in Atchison or Horton performed the twenty-one gun salute to honor their departed comrade.

Many of Dona's former friends were now gone from the area. Following Junior's death, Caroline Black returned to her native Milwaukee. Dona's good friend and bridge partner, Gail, died slowly and painfully of emphysema. Her suffering was difficult for Dona to witness and made her realize, with no small amount of guilt, that she should get serious about quitting her cigarette habit.

When Amabelle was stricken with breast cancer, Dona thought surely such a good person would overcome the dreaded disease. Her friend had been the picture of health, and, in Dona's mind at least, much too young to die. She hadn't seen her children marry nor experienced the unique joys that grandchildren bring to a family. Tragically, the advance of the disease was swift and immutable, and she was gone in less than a year. Amabelle's death touched Dona very deeply. The two had shared many memories--uncovering and writing the town's history, working on the area's census, and recovering from the disaster that was the Martins' fire. Dona had developed a sincere admiration, even love, for the generous and genuine woman who had become her friend.

Perhaps these reminders of her own mortality prevented Dona from accompanying Jimmie to the many memorial events to which he was beckoned.

Ruby's house remained empty for several years. Dona couldn't bring herself to sell her friend's place for the pittance she was offered. She kept the place presentable, mowing the yard frequently and tending the old-fashioned roses that bloomed profusely each spring.

It was in the spring of the year that Vikki and the little girls came to the place. There had been trouble in the marriage for some time. The girl had been patient and forgiving--her husband was a veteran of the Viet Nam War and had problems she could not comprehend. Besides Sarah, whose christening the Martins had attended, there was now six-month-old Hannah. Dona was sad to see her granddaughter in this unfortunate position but knew that a home in turmoil was a burden no child should have to share.

The children's father had gone to Minnesota to join some of his family, so Vikki was now a single mother, a situation Dona knew intimately. Remembering how much she had relied on her family, she determined to help her granddaughter in any way she could.

Vikki had her teaching degree, though she hadn't gone into the profession after having a disappointing student teaching experience. But now, were she an instructor, she could spend her summers at home with her children. She sought a position in the area and was accepted at the Washington School near Atchison, just seven miles from Bedford. She'd need to go to summer school in Madison to pick up some courses to qualify for secondary education. She would be teaching English, so she could go to her aunt for advice, if needed, since Sherry now taught that subject in Carroll.

The Ruby house, as Dona called it, would be the perfect place for Vikki and her girls. Only a few improvements must be made before she could move in. Bedford had no laundromat, so Jimmie installed a washer and dryer in the back porch and put in a new water heater. Vikki brought some furniture from Nebraska, and she and her mother found used appliances at auctions to finish out the necessities.

Before the little girls were there long, Jimmie and Dona had hung a swing for Hannah in the backyard. It was made from a fiberglass spring-horse and hung just above the ground, so she would not hurt herself should she fall. PaPa strung a rope swing up in the pin oak tree for Sarah, her big-girl swing. The shapely tree towered over the backyard. Dona found a picture of Ruby standing beside the same tree the day she and Lloyd planted it, the sapling not much taller than Ruby herself. Later, Dona came across a receipt for the tree, purchased in 1957 for $15. It was in Ruby's recipe box, along with her Red Cross records.

Vikki found a babysitter for the girls in Atchison, a young mother with children in school. She took the girls there as she went to work and picked them up after her day's duties were completed. When she went back to the school for evening activities, Granny and PaPa cared for the kids. When Joe and Kathleen came over to play cards, the girls were just another part of the entertainment. If Dona and Jimmie needed to go somewhere while the children were in their care, they took them along.

This worked out very well for a while. The little house was well insulated and quite cozy for them. If any good had come from her move, Vikki felt it was in having her family close by. Here, her folks were both near, in Madison, and Granny and PaPa were eager to fly to her rescue if needed.

On a very cold day, mid-winter, Vikki's car slid into a ditch on the way to school. Neither she nor the girls were hurt, so she hurried the children on to the nearest house. No one was at home so they went on in to use the phone, as Vikki felt the owners would understand their intrusion necessary. She called PaPa to come for them, and he took them on to Atchison. Vikki left a note to explain the emergency and also called later to apologize to the homeowners, who assured her that she had made the right decision. The accident inspired Dona to suggest she care for the girls herself. They would be comfortable at the farm--they spent a lot of time there already. She wanted to try it.

After Christmas, Sarah and Hannah began going to Granny and PaPa's each day. The wooden high chair that had been Nora's was rescued from the shed. Joe Vetters fashioned a wooden spindle on his lathe to replace a missing one. More toys migrated out to the Martin house. The arrangement suited Dona. She took advantage of the excuse to stay in the house when the weather was brutal, and having a family again pleased her. She felt truly needed. Her life took on new purpose, and it seemed to her that Jimmie was spending more time in the house, also.

Jimmie had his first experience with diaper duty, and the couple saw Hannah take her very first steps. When the two Wilmas walked out from town to play Skip-bo with Dona, the two little girls were nearby, behind the wet bar, in houses of their own they'd formed with pillows and cushions. They could confiscate anything in the house, and Dona would allow it.

Hour after hour was spent with Granny at their side, singing along with Raffi tapes or watching their favorite nursery rhyme videos. The most special thing they got to do in the house was to climb into the big whirlpool tub together with some bubbles. Tub toys became permanent fixtures in the new house. Sometimes Sarah rode along in the pickup and watched as Jimmie went about doing his chores. In the house, Granny sang to Hannah and told her the stories she'd told to two generations before.

When the weather was nice, Dona tied the red wagon onto her lawn mower and pulled the alternately singing or squabbling duo down the lane and on into the "Enchanted Forest." The little caravan putted along just fast enough to keep the girls satisfied in the wagon and slowly enough for them to observe everything along the way. Dona had them look for fairies among the foliage when they were near the woods, assuring them that they would be certain to see some tiny, winged creatures if they would be very quiet and look very carefully.

The little girls loved to play in water, so Dona sometimes filled the wagon and gave them spoons and plastic containers to make concoctions. They would be busy for hours, pouring water from one cup to another, adding rocks and sticks and a generous amount of seasoning--dirt.

Dona left the girls alone with these pursuits one day while she worked in the kitchen. Before long, they appeared at the back door, with Hannah covered in a layer of mud. Sarah had painted her sister black! The littler girl didn't know whether to laugh or to cry, but Dona detected some apprehension on Sarah's face, who had seen her grandmother assume a hands-on-hips pose at sight of the spectacle. A smile slowly came to Dona's face, then she laughed aloud and told Hannah she looked like a tar baby! Then, of course, she had to tell them that story before she went to get her camera and record the high jinks. Finally, she hosed them both off and hauled them inside for the remainder of the day.

It took Dona awhile to realize she might be having a heart attack. She was alone with the girls. It was Saturday morning and Vikki had gone to the hairdresser in Whitesville. When Dona had offered to watch the girls, she didn't feel well, but having them around would keep her mind off her aches and pains. Now, she wondered if she had made a wise decision. She lay down on the couch. Maybe the pain would pass.

Visions of the children alone filled her imagination, and she knew she should get help. She phoned Vikki, who came from Whitesville as quickly as she dared. By the time she got there, Dona thought she would be all right. Then, suddenly, the dull pain was back, tightening her chest and leaving her breathless. Vikki called her mother in Madison.

"Granny's sick. I need you to come down right away!"

"What is it?" Coralea asked, concerned.

"I don't know, but please come," Vikki pleaded. Coralea had never heard her daughter so upset. The urgency in her voice told Coralea that she must not hesitate. Before she could get her shoes tied and leave the house, the second phone call came.

"PaPa's here. We're taking Granny to the hospital in St. Joe. Meet us at Horton Junction."

Coralea flew out the door and sped south to meet them at the designated intersection. They weren't there. She didn't know whether she'd missed them or if they weren't there yet. She decided to head toward Bedford. She met them just over the hill, and they waved to her to follow them on to St. Joe.

By the time Coralea found a parking place and entered the hospital, Dona had been admitted into Emergency. Vikki sat beside Jimmie in a little alcove.

"They won't let me in!" Jimmie announced, obviously distraught.

Coralea read the desperation on the faces of the two and dreaded what she might hear. She didn't know whether her mother was alive or . . .

"She's in emergency surgery," Vikki said tearfully. "They're working on her now."

Her mother was in critical condition, but Coralea prayed there was at least a chance she would recover.

"Where are the girls?" she asked her daughter.

"They're with Wilma Andrews," Vikki replied. She was grateful that Dona's friend had been available in this time of crisis. She lived in Bedford now and the girls were familiar with her and so would feel secure. "She'll keep them as long as we need her to."

There wasn't much more to say. The three sat silently for a time, holding hands and occasionally reassuring each other with a pat on the shoulder. When a new sound emanated from the other side of the door, a fresh set of worries added to the anxiety of those nervously waiting.

At last a doctor came out and asked to speak with the husband. Coralea and Vikki stood with Jimmie--they couldn't bear for him to get bad news alone. When the man motioned them to stay, they each dared hope his words might be encouraging.

When Jimmie entered the recovery room and saw his wife lying immobile with plastic tubes attached to her from flashing and beeping machines, he fainted.

They quickly hooked him up to an EKG machine. The doctor warned that he might be having a sympathetic heart attack. They put a heart monitor on him and sent him out to walk around the parking area. The contraption would signal back any irregularities that occurred as he exercised.

It seemed to Jimmie that everything had stopped. Nothing moved. Cars and people changed positions, but he heard none of the customary noises that should accompany those transformations. Everything around him was stark and dull, at the same time--flat, ordinary, without meaning. It confused him! What was he doing out here? He wanted to be in there, with her. If only he could hear the low, comforting tones of her voice once again!

By that time Barbara and Don had arrived at the hospital, anxious to learn the prognosis for Dona's recovery. They were startled when they met Jimmie walking in the parking lot with the harness strapped to his chest.

"How is Mom?" Barb asked, a baffled expression overtaking her features.

"She's in ICU. The next twenty-four hours will tell, the doctor said. She's in very bad shape!" Jimmie went on to clear up the confusion concerning the mission he'd been sent on. Barbara wondered if maybe the doctor tried to alleviate his stress by removing him from the intense situation. Perhaps the doctor feared the hospital atmosphere, added to the trauma of his wife's condition, might lead to disastrous results for Jimmie's own health.

All they could do now was stand near Dona and hold her hand. She was obviously sedated to keep the pain at bay. Jimmie couldn't believe the ghostly figure on the bed was his wife. In the thirty years they had been married, she had been the one constant in his life, the unfaltering ally who gave purpose to his own future.

The first few days were critical. Dona was in and out of consciousness, smiling wanly at her visitors when she was awake, but unable to speak. Her movements were faltering--she could barely lift her arms to help the attendants change her position.

Several days passed before she began to respond to her surroundings. She continued on in the intensive care unit, with visitors limited to the immediate family. The doctor indicated that she would require a long recovery period. Her heart was badly damaged, and there were no surgeries available to repair it. She was lucky to be alive.

Finally, the gray pall began to leave her skin and some of the sparkle crept back into her faded brown eyes. She began asking questions of her husband. *How are you managing? How are the girls taking this? How long until I'll be able to see them?*

While Dona was in the hospital, Jimmie received a call from Lizabeth. Jess, her second husband, had lost his struggle with cancer. Dona encouraged Jimmie to go to Texas--he might forever regret it if he didn't. Jimmie was the only one left now of Beth's family. She would need his presence. He would probably get airsick, but he decided to take medication and make the trip. He was picked up at the airport in Dallas with no glitches in the travel plans, and his sister did appreciate his support.

"We're going to go see Mommy Girl!" Jimmie announced as he picked up Vikki and the girls at the Ruby house. It was a name he had bestowed upon Dona some years earlier.

"Is she home now?" Sarah eagerly asked.

"No. Not yet. But we can all go and see her now in the hospital," Vikki replied. She knew the girls missed Granny terribly and were puzzled about where she had gone.

Hannah was not yet two years old. The hospital was a vast, unfamiliar place to her. Dona was sitting up in an armchair when the little group entered her room. She broke out in a broad smile, in spite of the oxygen feed that still remained at her nostrils. She wished she could pick both girls up, but knew she mustn't move by herself.

Sarah edged over to her chair. She was curious to find out more about this change in Granny. She cautiously leaned against Dona's legs and stared at the strange paraphernalia that seemed to be tying her down.

"Come and give Granny a hug," Dona pleaded as she stretched out her arms to the younger one.

Hannah put her own chubby arms behind her and moved back a step. She wasn't sure this apparition was really Granny! Tears came to Dona's eyes. She was scaring the child! She knew she had been ravaged by the attack, but this was tragic proof of it. *I may never be the same,* she sorrowfully realized. A terrible sadness swept over Dona after she was rejected by the innocent child. She knew her life had changed perceptibly, but this was one disappointment she hadn't anticipated!

Vikki hurried to make excuses for Hannah's hurtful behavior.

"She's just upset by all the things in the room," Vikki offered. "You don't look right to her with all these gadgets around."

"She's mad at me!" Dona stated abjectly. "She thinks I deserted her! Oh, honey, I didn't go because I wanted to." She began crying softly.

Jimmie picked up Hannah and she threw her arms around his neck.

"She'll be home soon, and everything will be fine," he declared, as he fought back tears of his own. He wished he truly believed the words he spoke.

THIRTY

"I don't know if I can do this!"

Jimmie reached over to give Dona's knee a gentle squeeze.

"Sure you can. I'll drive up by the patio door and we'll go right in," he assured her.

"I didn't mean that," she returned glumly. "What I meant was, I don't know if I can handle being an invalid." She wondered how he would handle it. He had always been considerate of her, but she was no longer the "her" he was used to. She'd watched him nurse his animals with tenderness and patience, but she had never known him to have much sympathy for people who were sickly.

"You'll get better, Dona," Jimmie insisted. "You've come through this so far. I know you can do it."

"I can't even go down into the basement! The doctor said 'no stairs,'" she persisted.

"Whatever's down there that you need, I'll bring it up," he retorted. "Besides, this won't last forever. You'll get better."

He was so optimistic. Sometimes she thought it was a perverse quality of his. Other times, she loved him for it. Like now. If she had ever needed a cheerleader, this was the time. She was demoralized by fear. She was afraid to push herself, terrified of the outcome if she failed to recognize her limitations.

"I won't be able to take care of the little girls anymore!" Dona continued fretting.

"Vikki will bring them out to visit anytime you want--you know that," he encouraged. "For a few days, they're all coming out to stay with you while I do the chores. But, remember, you mustn't pick the kids up. Let them wait on you, for a change."

She smiled. She knew she had spoiled them by anticipating their every desire.

A Hundred Miles to the City

Dona was happy to be going home, but uneasy, also. She had a purse full of medicines and a head full of instructions from her physicians, but felt enormously unqualified for her own recuperation. And right now she was overcome with fatigue. She laid her head back against the seat and rested with her eyes closed for the remainder of the trip home.

It was just a few steps to the door, and Jimmie held her arm as she stepped over the threshold into the living room. She would like to sit down at her usual spot beside the small table and have a cigarette, but no chance of that. The doctor had stated, without mincing words, that she'd not likely survive a second heart attack. He also made it very clear that her condition was probably brought on by her smoking habit. During her time in the hospital, she'd had no opportunity to smoke, since she was near an oxygen supply. Maybe she could make it last and finally be successful at breaking the habit. She certainly couldn't ask Jimmie to buy cigarettes for her, not after all this!

"We had better park you in bed for a while," he suggested. He figured the ride home had exhausted her.

"Yes, that's a good idea. I can't tell you how good it is to be home! I feel like I never want to leave this place again!" Her weak smile was sincere and he knew it.

"Your personal chef will be busy in the kitchen while you rest," he announced. He had put a little hand bell on their bookcase headboard. "Just ring this if you need anything. Nurse Martin will be right in!"

In the ensuing days and weeks, Dona spent much of her time on the couch or in bed. Vikki and the girls came out often. Vikki did some cooking, though not much was needed, as Dona's friends brought by casseroles and pies. Joe and Kathleen had a splendid garden—they had shared their produce with Dona and Jimmie for years. Jim Ed had married Kathleen's sister Rose, his high school sweetheart and one of the Wisdom girls who lived in the big house many years ago.

The little girls hovered around Dona, happy with her now that she was home again where she belonged. Generous with comforting hugs, they were happy to run and get things for her. Now that she was immobile, she was even more available to listen to them and to play along with their childish fantasies.

When school started in the fall, Vikki arranged for a young mother who lived in Old Town to care for the girls. Sally Gates still had two little girls of her own at home, near the ages of Sarah and Hannah, so the arrangement worked well. Her husband was a rural mail carrier, so he was there at lunch and supervised Hannah's noon meal. She loved the extra attention, and both she and Sarah were happy with their new playmates.

Eventually, Dona began to take back her kitchen. She felt truly at home there. Jimmie had stocked up on supplies so they would not have to go shopping soon. Her kitchen was compact, with a small table in the center, so few steps were required for her to get an adequate meal on the table.

She opened the door to the basement. It seemed such a long way down that flight of stairs! She wondered if she would ever go down there again. Now that it was off limits, she was drawn to it. There was nothing down there she really needed. The Christmas decorations were stored in a couple of cabinets. And the freezer was there. It might be unhandy at times, but Jimmie could bring up what she needed if she remembered to tell him ahead.

From her vantage point at the top of the stairway, she couldn't see much of the basement--just the back, where Jimmie's desk was positioned in good lighting, so he could read the equipment manuals stored there. They were so numerous now that they overran the desk and were piled on the floor. Next to that was his new "hot house," where he coaxed his most delicate creatures into living.

The old Mercury convertible was pulled into the back of the basement. They should probably get rid of it to make room for the Ruby car. It had turned out to be a godsend. Someone in the family was always borrowing it to meet some emergency. Not long ago Coralea had used it to pull her disabled car home from Columbia. She had gone down to watch Sherry run in a marathon and had hit a deer in the pre-dawn hour.

Though they no longer licensed the convertible, Dona considered it a classic. The South Johnson students used to borrow it to show off the homecoming queen in the school's annual parade. She had suspicions that mice might have taken up residence in it now. They usually managed to get in through the garage doors at the onset of cold weather. That was one reason the area was mostly Jimmie's domain already. She could live without the use of that stairway.

As she convalesced, some of Dona's energy returned, and she began to miss her previous activities, especially driving. When she was confident enough to drive alone, Jimmie parked her car by the back door so she could just step outside for a trip into town to Junior's store, or to Vikki's or one of the Wilmas'. This freedom contributed greatly to her frame of mind, and soon she was able to go with Jimmie on some of his necessary excursions to St. Joseph--or to the new Iowa Beef Packers station by Glenwood, where he took his hogs to be shipped on to market. Both their lives regained a degree of normalcy when Jimmie and Dona could be together for the day-to-day activities necessary in running a farm.

"Where's Mommy Girl?" Jimmie called as he stepped into the doorway of the utility room.

"In here," Dona answered from the back room. She'd started a new library there with a couple of small bookshelves and the desk Bert Ellis had made. She had purchased the little walnut desk at his estate sale, wishing to keep something the old carpenter had constructed.

"I'm going to run a hose from the well over to the stock tank, so you'll have to save some water for here in the house. I'll have to use the pump for a few hours at least," he told her.

"Can't you get the other pump fixed?" she asked.

"It's shot! I've cobbled it together as long as I can. I reckon we'll have to make do until I can get it replaced." He knew that wouldn't be soon, as there were no funds on hand for another expense right now.

"I'll run the sinks full and save a couple of jugs," Dona said as she turned on the tap in the back bathroom. "Do you think the well will last?"

"It's never run dry yet!" he assured her.

"But you weren't using it for the livestock then," she reminded him.

"Well, we'll see," he said as he stepped out to return to the tractor he'd left idling in the drive.

This would be an inconvenience, at best, but Dona knew how strained their finances had become. Bills for her medications were substantial and not likely to get any lower, though she did, already, cut some of her pills in half. That seemed to work well enough.

Dealing with the water situation became a serious hassle for the Martins. More than once, water was pumped from the deep well faster than it could seep in from the underground source that would replenish it. Jimmie hauled water from Eldon's place for the livestock, but at those times the house was temporarily without running water, a critical necessity for running a modern household.

Rural water had been available to the people in Bedford for several years, greatly contributing to the quality of life in the small town. However, farms were served only if the rural line passed by their location. No one else lived down the Martins' road, so no line was brought south from town.

The girls decided an appropriate Christmas gift for their parents would be to have the water line laid the quarter mile from Bedford, so it would be on their folks' property, at least. If the Martins wanted it, it would be available. It would be an extra bill each month, but vastly more convenient than the current situation. Jimmie and Dona were agreeable to that set-up, so their water problems were finally solved.

In the fall, Vikki began seeing a man whose family was from the Atchison area. When they dated, she took the girls out to stay with her grandparents. By now, Sarah was four and Hannah two, old enough not to require the lifting and carrying they had when they were younger. Dona and Jimmie were both happy to again have the sunshine of youthful laughter in their home.

After Christmas, Dona asked Vikki, "Don't you think we could care for the girls again, at least part time?"

"I don't know, Granny. They might wear you out, being here all day long," Vikki hesitated.

"Jimmie could help. He wants to! He spends a lot of time in the house in the winter anyhow. He can do most of his chores after you're finished with school," she insisted.

"Well, let me ask Sally how she feels about this. The girls would love it, I know, but I don't want to make that change unless it'll work out with her," Vikki suggested. She thought it likely that the babysitter would appreciate the extra days of calm at her house.

It was eventually decided that the girls would go to the farm on Tuesdays and Thursdays and stay at the Gates home on alternate days. At first, when the girls were with them Granny and PaPa were both in the house most of the time, or else they would all be off on a group excursion. They had equipped their Mercury with an extra car seat for Hannah, so one wouldn't have to be juggled from place to place. They had begun watching soap operas during lunch--Jimmie no longer felt he must listen to the noon market reports--so a good part of the day was spent relaxing in the house.

PaPa took Hannah with him to Junior's store every day, seeing to it that she picked out some candy and got some for Sarah, too. Often when he was seen in the area, he was packing a little girl around, bundled up snugly with the tiny brown work gloves she had wanted "just like PaPa's." Sarah would rather stay in the house with Granny, coloring or helping fix dinner. She wasn't interested in getting out and getting dirty as her sister did.

For much of the time they were outside, Hannah was in the machine shed with PaPa, fiddling around with nuts and bolts and watching him as he tried to fix some piece of machinery. Soon she had little tools of her own, a tiny hammer and pliers that she carried around with her. In the house, she'd work on the plastic truck she often rode around on, tapping the wheels and the molded engine and frowning thoughtfully. Jimmie was amused at how

A Hundred Miles to the City

she had picked right up on that, for in truth, he often did just that--work on, but not necessarily fix, his equipment.

In her young eyes there was no difference. The object of his labors rarely looked any different to her after he had worked on it for hours. During those exasperating times, he tried to do his cursing inwardly, as he had promised Dona he would, but one day while Hannah was working on her truck he heard a distinct, "Well, Je-sus Kiste!"

Visitors often remarked on how little the girls resembled each other. Sarah's hair was dark, straight, and long--beginning to trail down her back. Hannah's had finally come in blonde and curly, lying in soft ringlets over her head. Both were blue-eyed, but Sarah's eyes were a bright sky blue and Hannah's were a pale cornflower hue.

Dona watched from the house while Hannah, Tippie, and several cats trailed behind Jimmie as he carried buckets of corn from the crib to the farrowing houses. Every now and then he'd stop and turn, obviously to answer a question the child had posed. Dona was amazed at his patience. He brought a tiny white pig out of the shed for Hannah to pet. Then she wanted to hold it, but it soon wriggled away and he had to rush and snatch it back. It was a sight to behold! Hannah wanted the squirming little creature until she had him, then she'd drop him and PaPa would have to chase him down all over again.

One afternoon Hannah spent hours sitting beside the pump housing, watching Jimmie as he struggled to replace a broken fitting. She never wandered far from where he was, down in the pit beside the well.

Later that evening, after Vikki had picked up the girls, Jimmie said to Dona, "Guess what she asked me today?"

"Well, I don't think I can guess. What?" She asked, amused.

" 'Am I a runt?' " And he laughed.

"How in the world did she come up with that?" Dona asked.

"I don't know. She's so full of questions, I only half listen sometimes. She wanted to get down in the pit with me, but the well's there, so I told her she was too little," he replied, puzzled.

"She's probably heard you referring to the pigs in the box in the basement," Dona guessed. "I imagine you told her they had to be helped because they were runts--too little!"

He figured if Hannah was going to remember everything he said, he had better start listening to her a little more closely.

It was a real blow to Dona and Jimmie when Vikki told them of her decision to remarry. It would mean another move, this time to northern

Iowa--even farther from home than she had been in Nebraska, where the girls were born.

Her intended had two boys in his custody part-time, so it would mean blending two families, which was often difficult no matter how good the intentions. Dona invited them for dinner, and she liked the boys. They were certainly nice enough. But she and Jimmie had a hard time accepting the fact that the girls would be leaving.

"Why don't you let the girls live here with us for a while?" Dona suggested to her granddaughter.

"I wouldn't want to do that, Granny," Vikki quickly replied, surprised at the offer.

"Sarah could go to kindergarten here. She knows some of the other kids," her grandmother insisted.

"Granny, I know you mean well. But I can't give up my family!" Vikki anguished.

Dona could see that she was making an unreasonable request, so she backed off a bit.

"Just for a while, until you get settled in Iowa."

"I'm sorry, but we really need to do this right away. We have most of the summer left to get acquainted before the boys go back with their mother." Vikki wasn't going to change her mind. That was obvious.

Vikki and Tom were married in a little church in nearby Culver City, a compromise since they couldn't be married in the church by a priest. Only Tom's brother and his wife were present to stand up for the couple in the simple ceremony.

Soon the new Lister family relocated to Boone, Iowa, where Tom worked for the railroad. He had applied for a transfer to Hudson, Wisconsin, so they might be moving again by fall. To the Martins, this was not good news, as the new family would then be twice as far from Bedford.

When Jimmie went to the bank for an operating loan in the spring, the lender refused his request. Already in arrears to the firm, he had been warned that he needed to look to paying down his debt. As discouraged as he was, Jimmie understood their position. Bankers were not farmers. They couldn't continue to invest in crops that might never be harvested. The banks themselves were in trouble, as well as every facet of the nation's economy that relied on the success of the farmers for their own livelihood. Equipment dealers were especially squeezed, since few farmers had capital to invest in new machinery, no matter how badly it was needed. Businesses in farming communities closed their doors because of the desperate slump in current farm income.

Though he expected it to be an exercise in futility, Jimmie went to other banks to seek the necessary backing for his spring planting. His request was turned down each time. His age was never mentioned as a reason for this denial, but he was conscious of not-too-subtle suggestions that many men his age were retiring. He was certainly not ready for that. He knew he wasn't as strong as he once was, but he could still do more work than many of the young fellows he hired.

After trying without success at nearly every lending institution in the area, Jimmie resigned himself to the fact that he would have to operate with what he had on hand, as best he could. Consequently, in the next few months his farming enterprise became greatly curtailed. That situation allowed him to spend more time with Dona. She had always been a helpmate in his endeavors. Now she needed him to be the strong one, the one she could lean on. He resolved to keep their lives on the farm as normal as possible for as long as possible.

In other years, the spring months were consumed with cultivating, planting and treating his cropland. Now most of Jimmie's activities dealt with the care of his livestock, so he had more time to spend on other pursuits. He became more active on the town board. On election day, he served as an election judge, in Dona's place. He and Dona spent more time on shopping trips to K-Mart or Wal-mart. He would let her off at the door of the store, then go park the car. When they were finished, he would pick her up at the door. Their shopping excursions were time-consuming affairs, as she moved slowly and sometimes had to sit and rest.

Their friends began coming over more often to play cards or just to visit. They socialized with Joe and Kathleen Vetters frequently, often playing bridge until late at night. Jimmie had developed into a skillful player and was as likely as anyone to be the master for the evening.

Dona wondered if she still harbored some resentment toward Kathleen because she had once been Caroline Black's best friend and consistent bridge partner. Dona had felt like an outsider then, but now she knew her place in the community and was grateful for Kathleen's friendship. The petite woman was witty and mischievous and generally fun to be around. Joe's hobby was woodworking, and he presented the Martins with several walnut bowls he'd turned on his lathe. The couple had moved from their earlier farm to one where they raised some cattle and maintained a big garden plot, but Joe no longer tilled any land.

Lizabeth was to remarry, and she and Fred invited Dona and Jimmie to Hawaii for the event. The couple declined, saying the Ameses would have to do the traveling when they met. Once, Dona would have given her eyeteeth to go to Hawaii, but was content now just to see the wedding pictures from the beautiful islands. When Beth brought her new husband to Missouri for an introductory visit, he was liked immediately by both of the Martins.

The couple spent a few pleasant days on the farm and toured the area of Lizabeth's youth, then encouraged Dona and Jimmie to come to Dallas to see their place. When the girls heard of the invitation, they tried to convince their folks to go, but neither wanted to. Jimmie still didn't care to fly, and Dona now felt insecure away from home. The itchy foot she thought she had inherited from Sam was gone for good.

As a result of her grave illness, Dona was acutely aware of the passing of time. It seemed that the days of her life were gaining momentum and speeding past as she sat and convalesced. Already she and Jimmie had seen each of their grandchildren graduate from high school, and now they were all married, except for the youngest, Tami.

J. had married a woman with two children, and they were now expecting a baby of their own. Val married a schoolmate from Carroll and they lived in Madison, where they both attended college. Stewart married Donna Kay, whom he'd brought by the farm; and her brother and Shelley married. That couple moved away to South Missouri, but Stu and Donna Kay settled in Shenandoah. Their older sister, Debbie, married a farmer she met while teaching in Browning, and they bought a farm in the Albany area. Sarah had been the flower girl for Debbie's wedding the past summer.

Kelly divorced, remarried, had a son, and now traveled as an outfitter for a hunting concern out of Seattle. The Martins received postcards he'd penned from such exotic places as China, Mongolia, and Russia. Their grandson seemed to enjoy trekking around the world, but Dona thought she detected a trace of homesickness in his messages.

Dona yearned for her family to get together again, maybe at Christmastime. That was becoming harder as the years went by, with in-laws to consider and the addition of others with their own traditions. She was glad they each found time to come to the farm occasionally, and she and Jimmie now made them the focus of their attention while they were there.

In mid-summer, Granny and PaPa went to Boone to bring Sarah and Hannah back for a visit. Hannah would go to Bible School in Horton, and both girls would spend time in Madison with Grandma Corky. The girls had made friends with other children in Bedford so entertainment was no problem.

On most days, Grandma Corky and Sarah picked up Hannah from Bible School each morning, then met Dona back at Horton Junction in the evening, so she'd be ready for the next day. Hannah enjoyed the crafts she learned at the church, and she and Granny worked together on similar projects in the evenings. It was Hannah's first experience at school without Sarah, and she enjoyed the special recognition that was hers alone.

All the family, including Vikki, down from Wisconsin, went to the program offered at the week's end. It was a charming presentation, and Hannah was coaxed into joining the program. But she must have gotten stage fright, as her mouth never moved during the singing. She was highly praised for her efforts, anyhow.

The Bedford Centennial celebration was held during the girls' stay. It had been one hundred years since the village had been moved from Old Town to the base of the big hill. The train that had spurred that tremendous upheaval in the small community was now a part of the past and existed only in the memories of those present and in the photographs now on display in the community center.

An extensive parade moved from the school grounds, across the culvert, and down the main street of town, turning at the fire station, then at the Methodist Church and continuing on past the former Christian Church. Dona sat with others watching from lawn chairs by the house across the street, once the home of her mother. She wished Retha could be beside her now, alert as she once was and comforting with her mere presence.

Sadly, Dona thought the decision she had helped make for her mother may have been the wrong one. She had been selfish, wishing to prolong her mother's life, to keep her with them longer. Retha ended her years in misery--years in which she knew no one and hadn't even the comfort of memories to sustain her through the aching despair of a slowly declining body. Dona wondered how long it would be until her first thoughts of her mother no longer focused on her image in that hospital bed, lying helplessly in confusion and discomfort. Surely the time would come when recollections of her mother readily returned to the Retha she had once been.

Dona remembered the transformation that had come over her parents when they moved into the Bedford area. Their life together wasn't much easier than it had been, but they seemed to have left many of their personal differences behind when they left Summerville. Dona realized she no longer thought of that town as her own home, but now of Bedford--a displacement of affection so gradual she was unaware of when it happened. Her love for the city was now eclipsed by the strong sense of belonging that tied her to the quiet town.

She recognized also, as she sat enjoying the afternoon, that another great change had taken place in her life. She was no longer a major contributor to the affairs of the community. She'd done her part in planning the event, but it was left to others to execute those plans. Dona had hoped to arrange one part of the day's festivities. She'd written to Jerry Wallace, the popular singer whose name she had emblazoned on the red barn, and asked if he'd come and perform at the event. His wife wrote a nice letter back, indicating that Jerry's schedule was filled and he would not be able to attend. Dona allowed that he probably wasn't often asked to perform for the mere compensation of good will. He likely didn't recall that his grandparents ever lived on the Looker place, nor remember the town at all.

Most people here were younger than she, Dona knew. Many of these youngsters were born since she had come to the community. To them, she was a regular old-timer, just as she once thought of Merry Torrance and Earl Rickman. Perhaps that was one reason for her affinity to the place. Actually, getting up in years wasn't as bad as she'd expected. There were certain advantages. You were automatically granted a degree of respect, and you certainly weren't expected to contribute as much. She was amused to note, also, that she had passed from "miss" to "ma'am" without even realizing it!

It was good that Claude Davis had bought Chloe's house. He'd been caring for it for Ana's sister for several years, mowing the lawn and keeping everything in running order. Maybe he'd move into it. The place had been home to two of the town's matriarchs; first, Mary Lamb, who, in her nineties, spent most of her time in the parlor, listening to her favorite ball teams on the radio. She interjected her personal opinions above the announcer's voice whenever she felt so inclined. Then Chloe Simpson had returned to town and lived in the trim, white house until her death last year.

The dwelling was one of very few in the town that were built on an entire quarter of a block. It sat in the middle of its lot, a level expanse of lawn stretching out on each side. Only a couple of redbud trees broke the even greenness of the yard. Dona had helped move them in from the timber a few years back, an effort by the town board to beautify the area. The sidewalk that led to the house was flanked by brick pillars capped with concrete spheres. The home was still elegant and lent a stately appearance to the street. It was an appropriate domicile for the town's most senior citizen. It would be fitting for Claude to live there--he was not the oldest but probably the most enduring inhabitant of the town. Dona thought he had probably lived in Bedford his

A Hundred Miles to the City

entire life. She would have to change the gender of his station, though. Claude might not take kindly to being known as the town's matriarch!

An impressive program was presented, with speakers extolling the town's progression from its early beginnings. One of the town's younger men had agreed to emcee the event. He now led the assembled group through the pre-arranged program. Jimmie helped coordinate the day's activities, passing in and out of the building and greeting folks as they approached.

As usual for local celebrations, concessions were offered inside the building, along with a chance to buy tickets for the afternoon raffle. The book Dona and Amabelle had compiled for the occasion was also for sale. Dona had dedicated it to Amabelle and Ruby. She hoped the simple publication would help keep alive the memory of those now a part of the town's history.

She thought of Ruby, whose remains lay in the Anderson Cemetery, not far from Nora's--less real than the Ruby she kept alive in her mind. Dona was certain the way of immortality lay not in the opening of the ground to receive the body but in assimilating the essence of the person into the hearts and histories of the people and place. A person's time on earth should be marked by more than just the dates of birth and death. Such a meager testimonial to a life lived!

Dona remembered the records she and Amabelle had researched for their historical booklet. She had wanted to find out more about the town's earlier inhabitants but was limited to the newspaper issues preserved on microfilm at the university in Madison. Other personal information was lost, as those who bore witness to their lives had all passed away. If only more had been written down, preserved! Oral history was interesting, and initially more complete, but doomed to disappear as time went by and memories failed.

How will Bedford's history be written now, with no newspaper? How can future historians look back to this time and learn of the families and circumstances that now exist? There will be no accounting available, none! Dona felt such an omission would be akin to robbing people of their past. Then she thought of Junior's paper, that he religiously mailed out each week to every household in the community. She wondered if he kept copies of the printings and determined to ask him about that sometime.

The single-page paper that Junior composed dealt mostly with retail issues, but he added items of personal interest that made the missive entertaining and informative as well. It occurred to Dona that being an editor or a spokesperson for a group was a powerful position and that those who document events are somewhat able to interpret history to their own specifications. It would be quite a responsibility to attempt to chronicle an era. Much would simply depend upon what you chose to tell and what you chose to leave untold.

Dona had long been interested in genealogy. She'd mapped out her lineage, as well as Jimmie's. But that no longer seemed like enough. She realized that people like her folks, who had come late to the town, wouldn't belong to the archival records of Bedford, simply because of the timing of their residence. She thought that was unacceptable and made up her mind to do some writing that would record, for her family at least, some of the particulars of their lives here and at Summerville.

The day was overcast and matched her mood. Was it not fitting, Dona thought, for the sun to desert them, too, along with the hope they'd each clung to for several years? Surely birds sang and kittens frolicked somewhere this morning, but for Dona the world had turned ominously gray. She wished she could stop the day from advancing, if only for Jimmie's sake. To say it was breaking his heart would be an understatement. His whole being would soon be ripped apart with the savage predation of monster wolves tearing at some defenseless forest creature. Well, maybe she was being a little dramatic. It was hard to imagine her husband completely resigned to such an ignoble end.

"Maple Tree Investments" was stenciled on the doors of the trucks pulling onto the property. Their mass quickly dominated the area beside the machine shed. A full contingent of jeans-clad workers dismounted and began surveying the machinery Jimmie had lined up on the old road that ran through the grove. Their equipment was impressive--four large flatbed trucks and a high-loader. It was obviously well used, probably some earlier inventory the firm had confiscated. *Stolen* was the word that stuck in Dona's mind!

"I'll be civil. These guys had nothing to do with the conditions that caused this situation. They may have been farmers, too," Jimmie stated in response to Dona's advice to stay in the house with her.

"Hah! Farmers wouldn't be doing this!" She didn't care if they *were* good people trying to make a living. It was a hateful thing to do.

Dona has such romantic ideas about farming, Jimmie thought, though, in truth, he knew that her feelings and his own were much the same when it came to their relationship with the land. He went out the door, intending to keep his eye on the interlopers. They would have their manifesto, but he wanted to make sure they checked off each item they removed. He wanted everything accounted for. Every piece of machinery had cost him something, no matter how decrepit it might look to others. He didn't intend to let any of it just disappear.

The tension had been so great building up to this day, it would almost be a relief to Jimmie to have it over. There was no sense in pretending this was an unexpected development. He'd known for some time that this reckoning was coming. He'd never faced it square on, as he must today, but it was an overriding presence in every decision he'd made for a good long time.

It would be hard to say just when the crisis could first be called that. There were so many variables in farming, so many ups and downs with varying degrees of impact on his operation. It would be impossible to single out one occurrence that, taken alone, could have made the difference between survival and liquidation.

There was no doubt in his mind that the seventies had still been good years. The price/cost squeeze had been tight, but there was an upsurge in land values that gave him the equity to make up for it. The value of his acreage increased by fifty percent during the decade. It was obvious that government policies favored larger operations, and all the analysts believed the trend toward larger farms was the way of the future.

That had made sense to Jimmie. Using his land for collateral, he could expand his operation and remain competitive. Lenders were ready to extend credit generously because they, too, expected land values to continue to rise.

The number of small family farms had already begun to decline. Of the six or seven farms that thrived in the Star of the West school district a couple of decades earlier, only one continued to support a family. Jimmie's own holdings included parcels that had been the basis of livelihood for at least four families.

Could he have foreseen, back then, the conditions that would conspire to bring him to this reality? He had been more confident back then, had known he would do whatever was required to be successful. He felt he had done so. Honestly. But, what, then? Not every farmer was losing now.

In the house, Dona wandered from room to room, trying not to just stand at the window peering out. The scene playing out down the hill should be accompanied by some somber music, or at least have thunder rolling in the background. Instead, the sun had broken through and bathed the area in such stark light that it hurt her eyes to watch.

She was on her fourth cigarette of the morning. That was very bad. She had been able to limit herself to that number for the whole day. She felt she just had to have an outlet for her nervous energy.

She wondered who the Maple Tree Investment people really were. Maybe they were part of some big insurance company. Dona had heard of such associations. The First Bank in Shenandoah had sold Jimmie's loan to the corporation, one of many bad loans that threatened the solvency of the lending institution.

Jimmie had been angry when he learned his loan had been turned over to a liquidator. He saw that as the final, incontrovertible action that took the fate of his farm completely out of his control. Up until that time, he could cleave to the hope of securing an additional loan to keep his operation afloat. And he had, right up until that moment, struggled to save the assets he'd been building for the last thirty years. He had gone from bank to bank, hat in hand, to plead for more backing. Dona had been too ill to go with him, which may have been better for Jimmie, as he would rather she didn't have to see him grovel.

Dona wished she could have been more active in her support. She couldn't shake the feeling of being useless and inconsequential, when what her husband needed was a strong partner.

Dona stood in the front doorway, hoping Jimmie would see her and come in to lunch. She'd rather not ring the dinner bell. He would be alarmed, thinking something was wrong. Jimmie was going from one zone of activity to another. He seemed to be having conversations with some of the men. But, then, she knew her husband--he would find some endearing quality about the devil himself! She had to admit that none of the men appeared to be the ogres she at first imagined.

Everything that was not nailed down would be leaving the property today. Literally. Every piece of machinery worth moving, even the little Ford tractor she had used for mowing the lawn. Jimmie had told her he'd try to buy that back somehow. All the livestock. Dona couldn't imagine how they might make a living on the farm now. The only thing remaining would be the land, and it was leveraged to the limit at the bank in Madison. She knew that was the one reality that allowed Jimmie to accept the other losses--he would still have the land. She sensed he hadn't completely abandoned the idea of someone in the family taking over the farm.

She'd seen Jimmie's hopes dashed so many times, it broke her heart that he must undergo the ordeal the day presented. Dona wondered whether her husband was in complete denial of the true situation, knowing he couldn't be, with the current takeover underway around him. Still, it was obvious to her that he hadn't quit. He displayed no down-in-the-mouth attitude that would be expected. Her own fleeting faith was surely being tested. She had no idea how the coming months would play out, but never once had she heard her husband complain, "What will we do now?"

Can he possibly be entertaining the prospect of continuing on the farm? She wondered. Then, *How can we not?* she tearfully lamented.

"What about the livestock?" Dona asked when Jimmie finally made it to the house. There had been no sign yet of stock trucks arriving.

A Hundred Miles to the City

"They were over at Mr. Rivers' this morning, loading the cattle," Jimmie replied. "They say they'll be here to get the pigs before the day is over. I asked them where the equipment would be sold and they said in Madison, most of it, but they didn't know when."

"We can get along without the little Ford tractor," Dona said. "We don't have to mow so much."

"I want to buy back the 'H'," Jimmie stated. "They said they'd let me know when it'll be sold. It probably won't bring much, and I'm used to its quirks."

They spent some time sitting at the table, pretending to read the newspaper, before he announced, "I'm not very hungry, Dona. Maybe you can save it for tonight."

She hadn't much appetite either. She wondered where the men in the trucks had gone to find a meal and decided she really didn't care. She got up and began removing the lunch items from the table. She stopped behind Jimmie's chair and dropped her arms down over his shoulders. She leaned her face toward him and pressed her lips to the top of his head. His soft hair was still fairly thick but beginning to gray throughout. As she embraced him gently she asked, "How are you doing?"

"I'm okay, Dona. We've been through worse and we survived." He spoke in a tone of resignation. Dona was surprised that he considered the fire and the loss of their home to be a greater catastrophe than this. It was for her, she knew.

"I'd better get back down there," he announced. The house seemed to represent a kind of barricade right now, a place where he felt safe and unassailable. He wasn't eager to leave it but knew he needed to look after their interests now as much as ever. He left, hoping to return soon, with this nightmare over at last.

The heavily loaded trucks had been leaving and returning all morning. They would soon have the equipment removed from the property. It was beginning to look bare on the place, although the most useless of the machinery still remained. Nothing Jimmie would ever be able to use again, he reckoned. He was beginning to feel as decrepit as the rusted contraptions he had assigned to his back lot. Maybe he had outlived his usefulness, too. He certainly felt it today.

Had he lacked the courage and commitment necessary to succeed at farming? Had he taken off too many Sunday afternoons? Gone to too many sales? If he were alone, or one of a few struggling now, he might rightly believe he had failed; but so many--fifty percent of small farmers by the end of the century was the current estimate. It couldn't be just his own shortcomings, if that was any consolation.

But Dona didn't blame him. That knowledge made all the difference. She hadn't agreed with all the decisions he had made concerning the farming operation, but generally the two of them had been of one mind in matters of importance. Except for politics and card playing, that is. To live together in harmony was all he could expect in those areas.

He had sought to claim Chapter Twelve bankruptcy as a last resort. Not that he wanted to, but it would have been a solution. He was glad now that it hadn't worked out. Not that being bankrupt was any worse than today's disaster, but that option was bound to leave creditors he knew high and dry. He didn't desire to repay those who had been generous with him with that kind of treatment.

Even the dog, usually at Jimmie's heels, hung back from the activity, as if shunning the upheaval in his familiar surroundings. Tippie watched from halfway up the hill, not in retreat but not in participation either.

There was no doubt in Jimmie's mind that the proceeds realized by this company for the sale of his equipment would be miserably low, only a fraction of the interest he had paid on it through the years. Most of it he had bought already used but in good condition, as most of it remained. But with so many farming operations being sold out, the market was glutted with machinery. It was just one more indication of the interdependence of the farming economy.

Every time your neighbor's land or equipment sold cheaply, yours lost in value also--part of the supply and demand equation that had hurt American farmers when the green revolution allowed other countries more of the world market. That, and poor government policies, in Jimmie's estimation. When farm commodities were used as a political tool, the nation's small farmers paid the price. Not that there weren't some programs that had helped Jimmie's operation. He'd benefited from price supports, and once, from disaster relief. But, on the whole, he often wished that the agriculture department would just butt out and leave him to farm in a truly open and fair marketplace. When he began thinking like that, Jimmie remembered the years of overwhelming surpluses and knew that some sort of organized action would always be necessary.

It would be easy to blame the banks. When the recession had hit in '81, Jimmie was already mired in debt. Interest rates soared to fourteen percent, as land values bottomed out, sending his equity plummeting. In the past, the solution offered by the lending institutions was more debt, handing Jimmie another loan for an anchor when he was already barely afloat. No more such largess was being offered. However, Jimmie had to look no farther than to his own uncle to see what could happen if bankers were too forgiving. And, although Jimmie cursed the banks regularly, he had to admit he couldn't recall anyone twisting his arm, forcing him to sign on to more debt.

He hoped there would be a lull in the procedure, but before the last of the machinery was loaded, Jimmie saw the first of the stock trucks entering between the brick posts. It would be a long afternoon. There were over three hundred pigs on this place, plus the brood hogs he kept at Eldon's. He didn't know what the market was doing. It had been up lately. He figured it was just his contrary nature that hoped it would be otherwise today. If he hadn't so much empathy for the beasts, he wouldn't have put out feed for them yesterday. Corn wasn't bringing much on the market, but still it was cheaper to grow than to purchase at the Co-Op or MFA, which he had had to do fairly consistently since he had lost the bottomland. That crucial development had unalterably influenced his future.

The relative calm of the morning came to an abrupt halt when the first stock truck was backed against the loading chute and the men began herding good-sized pigs toward it. Tippie sprang into action when he heard the commotion in the stock pen. He'd often assaulted the obstinate creatures, but now seemed to consider it a personal affront when strangers were in their midst. He became so agitated and caused so much mayhem Jimmie felt he had better remove his dog so the workers could get their job done. He couldn't see tying up a dog that had never had a collar around his neck, but he would shut him up in a corncrib.

The middle of the three storage sheds was already occupied by chickens. Only a dozen or so hens were left now, but they kept Dona and Jimmie supplied with farm-fresh eggs. He coaxed his dog into the farthest metal crib and fastened the door.

Dona was amazed at the racket going on down in the lot. She had helped Jimmie sort pigs for market but didn't recall that much commotion! Well, she'd complained about pigs enough--their smell, their stupidity, their incursions into her yard. She found it difficult to believe she actually hated to see them go now. But she knew Jimmie was right. They had been the one asset that had permitted them to hang onto the farm this long. She kept the farm records, so that truth was painfully obvious to her.

It seemed that recent events were forcing them into retirement, whether they acknowledged it or not. What could Jimmie do with no animals and no machinery? Rent out his land? They couldn't make enough on that to pay the interest on their remaining debt. They had their home, free and clear, but what would they live on? Others had suggested they sell out completely and move into town, but what would that gain? They still would have nothing to live on. Jimmie might be able to get a job of some sort. He was certainly able-bodied and a good worker. She felt that the current crisis was happening at the worst possible time in their lives. If they were younger, she would not be so helpless and Jimmie probably could have gotten another loan. *Such foolish thinking,* she decided. *Isn't that everyone's wish, to be young and healthy?*

The truth was, if she hadn't been over sixty-five when she had her heart attack, they'd be worse off than they were now. Without Medicare, they couldn't have paid the astronomical medical bills. And, although Social Security didn't provide much, it was better than nothing. Even Sam had finally reconciled his opinion of the program, recognizing that the money you took out of the fund was money you'd contributed during your working years.

Dona lay down for her nap. She knew she should keep that concession she had made to her illness. But the commotion outdoors made that impossible. Maybe when Jimmie was by her side they would both be able to get some rest.

Except for the raucous addition of hollering, thumping, squealing, grunting, and shrieking, the afternoon's routine was the same as the morning's. The same trucks that took one batch of pigs out returned later to be reloaded and sent out again. It was late afternoon when the last piglet was shoved aboard and the rack-gate dropped behind him. Every hog, boar, gilt, shoat, piglet; white, red, black, striped; large, small, swift, ponderous – all porcine animals present were shipped out, protesting loudly of their own accord.

Jimmie had told the men there might be a few pigs out in the timber yet. It was impossible to keep them all in. Some animals just seemed to be hermit-like, avoiding the masses in the cacophony of the feeding trough. They would take to the woods whenever they got the chance.

He didn't, however, tell them about the thirty gilts he had secreted on the old stock truck, parked back on a remote path down by the river. Nor about the nine cows that just happened to be out on another farmer's property. His main problem now was in just how to tell Dona.

She was sitting at the table with a cigarette between her fingers when he entered the house. He knew she had been sneaking smokes but chose not to acknowledge it, thinking his presence offered at least a little deterrence to the habit.

She gave him a baleful look. "I'm glad you didn't help them load the pigs," she said. "I was afraid I might have to shoot you." Her smile helped to ease the tightness he bore in his shoulders. He found himself smiling back.

"It's all right, Dona. I know how you feel. If I thought it would make me feel better, I'd open up a pack myself!"

He decided he might as well come right out and tell her what he'd done. It wouldn't get any easier.

"Why didn't you tell me?" was all she said.

"I knew you wouldn't let me do it," he replied.

"Well, we've certainly been doing our part in supporting the banks all these years!" she stated emphatically.

He breathed a sigh of relief.

"Where's Tippie? They didn't take him, too, did they?" she added.

"Oops!" He turned sheepishly and hurried down the hill toward the corncrib.

THIRTY-ONE

Put, put, put, chug! Put, put, put, chug!

Jimmie was home. She loved that sound. The uneven rhythm of the tractor's powerful engine was a soothing lullaby to Dona's ears. She knew her husband had entered the farm by way of the old lane that connected to the racetrack. Actually, Jimmie hadn't even been gone from the farm, as he now kept his small herd of cattle on the Penney Eighty where there was enough forage for the animals he still owned. The summer had been dry so the grass was sparse, but he supplemented that resource with "nubbins" from the cornfield across the road at the Looker place. The drought had ruined the corn crop on all high ground this summer, so he would probably have to chop that field for ensilage. For now, he carried buckets of the abbreviated ears over to his cows. He called it their dessert.

Jimmie's tractor had finally found its way back to the farm. In early spring that year, Coralea received a call from her mother, entreating her to go to an implement dealer's north of Madison and help Jimmie load the machine onto the back of his stock truck. The day was windy and bitterly cold, so Dona knew she shouldn't go herself and would be of no help to him if she did. But she had worried that he might need someone to hold the brakes on the truck. Coralea was happy to put her mother's mind at ease by performing that small favor.

As it turned out, the business had a loading dock for just such purposes, and all went smoothly. The Farmall H could be considered a classic, but it was as modern as most of the equipment her stepfather now worked with. Coralea knew that many people became attached to a car and could see why Jimmie might want to regain the implement he had spent hours atop nearly every day for the last thirty years. Still, she could see why the dealers were ready for the antiquated workhorse to leave their lot.

A minor roar unfamiliar to Dona could be heard over the sound of the now-idling tractor. She rose from the couch to gaze from the window, wondering who might have driven into the lane. It was a bus! It resembled an old school bus, but was painted a grayish-white and was trimmed in a dark color that had faded to gray on the flat surfaces.

The massive vehicle came to a halt near Jimmie's tractor, and a fellow sprang down from the door and walked toward Jimmie. The man was tall and wiry, with cascading blonde hair.

Why, it looks like J.! Dona thought, somewhat amazed. Her grandson was still growing--must be nearly as tall as Stewart now. And the hair! He must have gotten a perm. It was curly and long, down to his shoulders.

Dona watched as her grandson made awkward stabs at backing the bus into the vacant space beside the quonset hut. *Uh-oh*, she thought. *It's definitely a candidate for the largest piece to come to its final resting place on the farm.* Then she reconsidered. After all, the thing had arrived only ten minutes earlier. Maybe she should give it more time before she assumed it to be another assemblage of suspect hardware parked on the place. With the years, Jimmie had become even more solicitous of the youngsters in the family--no request was ever denied.

J. came up to the house but stayed just long enough to say hello to his grandmother. His friend, a fellow member of Zap, their rock band, had come to pick him up and take him back to St. Joseph.

"He's afraid to turn off his car--it might not start again!" J. explained as he hurried off.

After the boys drove away, Dona looked expectantly at her husband.

"I told him he could leave it here for a while," Jimmie said, grinning, knowing what she was thinking. "They're going to fix it up and use it to haul their band equipment. It needs some work."

"Obviously," Dona smirked. "Did you ask him what he's doing nowadays?" *Something lucrative, besides playing in the band*, she hoped.

"He's working nights at Schullykil; they make batteries in Forest City. Besides that, he's taking some classes at MO West again--technical courses, he said." Jimmie opened the fridge to get a drink of cold water. It was early in the day, but he was dry already.

Soon the Wilmas were at the door. They walked out from town to visit Dona nearly every day. She envied them their good health, though Wilma C occasionally had bouts with minor ailments. Both ladies were over seventy-five, but their vitality still served them well. Marvin Andrews was gone now, so Wilma A lived alone in Bedford in the house that had belonged to her uncle, Bert Ellis. Dona fondly remembered the pretty place that Sam and

Retha moved to when they first came to the Bedford community. It had obviously been cared for by capable and tender hands: those of Bert and Ana before they retired and moved into town.

"Hold the coffee, Dona. What we need now is water!" Wilma A announced as she and her diminutive friend entered the cooled space. The Martins kept a couple of air conditioners running for most of the warm season. Dona thought they kept the air in the house cleaner and gave Jimmie a comfortable oasis to retreat to. At such times as this, the day's heat was stifling.

"I didn't know I was so hot until we walked by the withered, dusty weeds along the road!" Wilma C exclaimed.

"This is the driest summer I can remember," Jimmie commiserated as he prepared to go out and finish his morning chores. "The ground has some huge cracks in it. You could lose your hat if you dropped it!"

The three women decided to spend the rest of the morning inside playing Skip-bo, and then Dona would drive the Wilmas back to town.

There were some things that the Martins could not get at Junior's store in Bedford. One could learn the news of the day there and receive sympathy for bad crops or congratulations for a new grandchild, but some commodities necessitated a trip to a larger town. For Jimmie and Dona, that was usually Whitesville, to the northeast, or Shenandoah, to the southwest. Barbara lived in Shenandoah, and the rural hubs were more or less equi-distant from the farm, so the couple more often went by way of 71 Highway south to Shenandoah.

The Wagners lived in the newer part of town, where shade trees were just beginning to shield the ranch-style houses that lined the avenues. On many streets, enormous maple, oak and sycamore trees spread a leafy canopy over large houses obviously built in an expansive era. The summer greens were now fading from the area's maples, and clusters of color adorned the tips of exposed branches.

"Can you come down Sunday and help us with the car show?" Barbara asked her folks when they stopped for a visit.

"I don't know what kind of help we'd be . . ." Dona began.

"We need someone to help tally points for the contest. Cork said she'd help. You could be inside, here, if you want," Don assured her.

"We'll be at the park most of the day," Barb stated. "We usually have a couple of hours after the judging ends to get the points added so we can hand out the trophies at four o'clock. That can be done here at the house as well as anywhere. You've always been good with figures, Mom," she encouraged. "We'll have supper here when it's over. I have lasagna, and chocolate chip cookies . . ."

That was enough to convince Jimmie that they should come and help. He wasn't busy on the farm right now. He gave his wife a tentative look.

"What time do you want us?" Dona asked, smiling.

Quite often, either Don or Stewart was in charge of the local car show. This time it was Don, but Stewart would help. Classic cars of all types were entered in the competition that would spread out over the city's park, not far from the Wagner home.

The day was warm, but mature trees scattered throughout the park provided shade for spectators and entrants in the event. Don had set up a scorer's table under a large oak tree, where he displayed the trophies he had ordered for the winners. It was an impressive array--the Best of Show award was over two feet tall, with a walnut base supporting a golden cup.

Show cars were lined up beneath the sheltering trees. Participants came well equipped for the day, with lawn chairs, coolers, and a wide range of accessories to accompany their entries. Some of the highly polished autos had restraining ropes surrounding them to keep smudgy fingerprints from spoiling the sheen--or, more importantly, to prevent mishaps with metal jeans studs or other abrasives.

Don's three entries were lined up at the end of the park, north of the swimming pool where Shelley once spent her summer as a lifeguard. Don had begun, years ago, by restoring a red Corvair. Then he added a white one and recently had put the finishing touches on a blue one--all convertibles. His meticulous work on the body of each model paid off, as he had a room full of trophies he had won at shows throughout the area.

Stewart had brought his show car also--a red Chevrolet convertible. He had already won several trophies and was working on gaining points toward the Master's classification.

Barbara and Coralea spent much of the day at the scorer's table, handing out forms to the judges and keeping tabs on their progress. After the deadline for the forms to be in, stacks of paperwork were conveyed to the Wagner home for the next step--compiling the ratings to determine the day's winners. Other Corvair Club members helped in the intense work of tabulating the figures and the group finished up with time to spare.

Dona and Jimmie went to the park to watch Don award trophies to the waiting contestants. It was a lengthy affair but progressed smoothly, with Don adding a bit of levity with off-the-cuff remarks whenever he could. Stewart gave his grandparents a ride back to the Wagner house in his convertible. Dona rode in the back seat and had a fleeting urge to slip up on the cushioned back and ride like a queen in a parade. She decided not to embarrass her grandson.

Later on in the fall, Barbara and Don passed through Bedford on their way to the farm. Don patiently swerved the car to avoid a big dog that was lying in the middle of the road. He gave Barbara a knowing look as he did so.

A little farther on, Barbara exclaimed, "What in the world is that?" She pointed to the sky above the brick posts that marked the entrance to the Martins' property.

Dark particles floated in the air, buoyed by the breeze of the November evening. A fluid rush of punctuation marks peppered the air above, like a typewriter gone mad with interjections. Some of the phantom fragments were hundreds of feet up in the sky, hanging in colloidal suspension.

When they came closer to the strange phenomenon, they saw that the dark particles were actually pale, but shadowed in the bright light of the sun.

"It looks like husks of some kind," Don observed, as they drew closer to the unusual sight. "Someone is harvesting in the area, I would guess."

"I've never seen that before!" Barbara declared.

The two concluded that the season's lack of moisture had probably caused the chaff to be so light that it blew wherever the wind would take it.

As they passed through the portals, Don noticed one of the cast-iron lanterns had toppled from its post and was lying a few feet away, beside the fencerow.

"I'll see if I can put that back before we go," he announced.

"How've you been?" Barbara cheerily asked her mother as she took off her jacket, getting comfortable in the house.

"I'm fine. What are you two up to?" Dona asked this but was certain she already knew. Any time she could no longer handle a certain household chore, and knew that Jimmie would likely never get around to it, she hinted to one of the girls about it. Barbara and her husband seldom came for a purely social call but were always ready to come and help if they had a purpose.

"We want to help you winterize the house, Mom. Where can we start?" Barbara asked.

"Well, these aluminum windows don't fit snugly--the kitchen window's the worst. There's some caulking downstairs in cans on the shelves on the north side--no, south side. I can't seem to get my directions straight in this house. You'd think I'd have lived here long enough to be oriented by now!"

Soon the couple had the cans brought up and were uncoiling ropy strands of caulk saved from the previous winter's use. Barbara could see why her mother couldn't handle the job. She had to climb up on the cabinet, remove the curtain and the whatnots, and maneuver the clay-like substance into position. She knew she wasn't doing the neatest job in the world, but it should keep the cold air out.

Dona passed more caulking up to Barbara. Don had gone out to retrieve the lantern.

"How do you like your contacts by now?" she asked her daughter.

"I'm getting used to them," Barbara answered. "They're the soft kind, so they're not as difficult to wear as the first ones were. I guess if the kids can do it, so can I."

Dona guessed that she would have to get used to them, too, although her daughter didn't look right to her now, without her glasses. She had worn them since she was in grade school.

Barbara hadn't changed her hairstyle in years, which pleased Dona, since she admired the short style. Barbara's dark hair was thick and lay in soft, manicured waves that gave her an unruffled look and required very little upkeep. Unlike Barbara, Dona's other girls must periodically have their hair curled. Dona decided that sometimes life was fair, as the other two had never had to deal with eyeglasses.

"Why don't you stay for supper?" she suggested, as they finished up their project. She began putting things back into place on the ornamental shelves that bracketed the large window.

"We can't. Don has to get ready for his night class," Barbara told her mother.

"He's going to teach more today?" Dona asked with surprise.

"Oh, he enjoys it!" Barbara assured her. "He only has seven or eight night students and they pretty much know what they're doing. They're adults and about all Don has to do is make sure they're using the equipment properly. Some of them have been coming to his classes for years." She smiled, as she acknowledged to herself that it was probably Don's favorite part of his teaching assignment.

The Wagners were soon on their way back to Shenandoah, having accomplished the goal they'd set for the afternoon. Dona knew she would never again be able to keep the house up as she wanted without the frequent help of her family.

Before she came to the dog in the road, Coralea cut her wheels to the right, noting that now the dog was black. For years, the dog that occupied the spot had been of a large, pale-colored breed. Same spot, different dog. By now, though, the animal was a part of the geography of the town, marking the exact center of the roadway and causing northbound cars to veer to the east, southbound cars to the west. The dog never made a move toward abdicating his position, and she'd never heard of a dog being struck there. Coralea wondered if the post was one that had to be won by a canine contender, the way children vie for "king of the hill."

One humorous aspect concerning the dog's position had been mentioned at a family get-together at the Martins'. The dog was situated midway between the Methodist Church and the Church of Christ of Latter Day Saints. Could it be he had a divine purpose in keeping the sects separated? Another conjecture touched upon was that the creature, always a massive dog, guarded the town against any danger that might approach from the south. Or, maybe the animal's reason for being was to keep the orneriness of Bedford from following the road out of town and contaminating the countryside.

Coralea chuckled to herself when she came upon that obvious sign that she was nearly home. She wondered how many times her mother and Jimmie had passed that stubborn sentinel.

The winter had not been easy on her mother. Dona had had bouts of coughing spasms. She seemed to nearly choke before getting the racking upheavals under control. Her voice had always been low in tone, but now it was losing the soft, mellow quality that had made her speaking voice so pleasant. Deeper than before, her speech had become raspy and seemed to require much effort.

Coralea was in the habit of going to her folks' every Sunday for dinner. Dona didn't get out much in the winter and appreciated the company. The two usually worked on a jigsaw puzzle together. Often Dona would have it set up on the card table and sorted by the time Coralea arrived. On one such Sunday, their discussion turned more serious than their usual fare.

Gradually, Dona had fallen back into her smoking habit. She no longer attempted to hide this fact from her family, figuring the deceit probably hurt her more than the nicotine. So when she lit up a cigarette while they were working on the puzzle, Coralea was not surprised but made no effort to conceal her disappointment.

Dona was aware of her daughter's feelings but had enough difficulty reconciling her cravings with what she knew to be the wiser choice. Dona related to her daughter the heart-wrenching moment when Hannah had found her smoking and tearfully wailed, "I don't want you to die!" That stirring scene bothered her still, several months later, but evidently not enough to inspire her to give up the habit.

"You know how we all feel about your smoking!" Coralea reminded her mother.

"When you get to be my age, there's not many pleasures to look forward to," Dona complained.

"You're not that old, and there's lots of things you can do," Coralea insisted.

"That's easy for you to say. You're young and have your life in front of you!" Dona lamented.

"I don't see why you say that, Mom. You can enjoy things just as much as I can. You're either alive or you're not! There isn't any reason why you can't enjoy seeing a movie, or watching television or visiting just as much as anyone else." As she spoke, Coralea saw tears come to her mother's eyes. She wished she could take back what she had said. She would like to change the subject, but Dona continued.

"You've probably noticed that Jimmie manages to be out of the house when it's time for the little girls to say good-bye."

"I guess I never thought about it," Coralea admitted.

"He's afraid he'll cry. He thinks he might never see them again, or that maybe everything will be different when he does," Dona told her daughter.

"They're not that far away!" Coralea hurried to say. "We can go visit them again, like we did last fall when we met at Ledges." The park in Iowa was a convenient meeting place, centrally located since the Lister family had moved to Wisconsin. Vikki had wrapped Hannah in a big box and presented it to Granny for her birthday. Reflecting on the conversation later, Coralea understood her mother had wanted to discuss her feelings of mortality. She had glossed over the subject much too casually. She knew she had been insensitive and vowed to be more empathetic when the opportunity presented itself.

Dona was at first upset by the interchange. She couldn't believe her daughter was so heartless. *Coralea has a very simplistic perception of life. How can she not see the difference that my illness has made? My life is not the same now. When you know you're nearing the end of life, that truth is constantly with you, coloring everything you do!* She didn't want to confront her future, or lack of it, but the realization was always there, and it was becoming more of a burden as her condition deteriorated. She could no longer deny that she hadn't much time left.

Sadly, she realized her condition was as obvious to her daughter as it was to her. Perhaps Coralea refused to acknowledge the seriousness of her illness because she didn't want to accept it. Dona guessed that was the natural defense for a person to make. In a way, she knew her daughter was right. She would have to be a fool to fret away the time she had left. There was much she wanted to do yet.

When Dona overheard Jimmie say to Coralea one day, "All she ever does is sleep," she figured it was time to tell her husband what she intended to do. Granted, she did spend a lot of her time reclining on the sofa, and for much of that time she was only resting. But, for the last several weeks she had also been thinking--organizing her thoughts for her project. It was all-important to her and it was time she got started. Now she would confide in Jimmie and begin writing in earnest.

Since she had had a difficult winter, Dona didn't get out much, nor did she want to take time away from her purpose. At the end of May, though, she gladly set aside her ambition in order to play hostess for a visit from Beth and Fred. It was Beth's fiftieth high school reunion, so she and her husband would spend a few days at the Martins' and they would all attend the annual Bedford Alumni dinner. Dona was happy to dress up and go to the celebration at the school. Many of Beth's classmates made it to the special occasion. Her years of separation from the community seemed to melt away as Beth charmed the group with her friendly manner and soft Texas drawl. Fred, too, fit right in with the small crowd that had come to be Dona's allies, as well.

Besides that enjoyable evening, the group went on a Memorial Day tour of the cemeteries, a tradition Beth usually missed. On most years, Dona faithfully decorated the graves of her family, along with Carrie and Coralea, and she and Jimmie went to the Long Branch Cemetery for the Martins' side of the family.

On this day the group placed jars of peonies on the graves of Nora; her parents, Merry and Jed; and Ruby Masters. Then they went to Horton and decorated the graves of the Torrances--Vincent, Sadie, Herbert and his twin, Hanna. The Torrances had been reunited in death. Dona was exhausted by the end of the day but happy for having observed the demonstration of familial love that tied the living to the departed.

The Community Center was truly the center of activity when the town had its annual celebration. The local board had chosen to name the event "Bedford Fun Days" and succeeded in making sure that commodity was in good supply for gamesters of all ages.

One thing that could always be counted upon was that the day would be hot. Having an August date for the celebration guaranteed that condition. Heat and dust, however, were accepted as minor inconveniences for the exuberant crowd. By now the charms of summer vacation were wearing thin for most of the youngsters of the area. The day would give them one last hurrah before the beginning of a new school year.

Dona approached the day with mixed feelings. She knew the exertion of the extra activities would be tiring, but many of her family planned to participate, and she certainly approached that aspect with anticipation. Since her daughters had moved from the community, they weren't often involved in the activities of the town. Besides them, Vikki and the girls were down from Wisconsin, and Debbie and her family planned to come, as well.

The downtown area was beginning to fill with fun-seekers by the time Coralea delivered Dona's pies to the center and joined Vikki's family for the parade. Wooden benches, formerly church pews, faced the main street. However, much of the crowd chose to gather on the east side to take advantage of the shade provided by the tall brick structures. Only one in the row of buildings was still used for business. Junior Wilson's Kent Feed warehouse occupied the space that was formerly Galen's Garage.

This morning Junior was doing a booming business, though his profits would be consumed by his outlay for candy and gum for the event. He would push a wheelbarrow with his daughter on board, tossing out treats to the expectant youngsters lining the way of the parade.

Many of those gathered had brought comfortable folding chairs, but some merely leaned against the decrepit buildings or sat upon long-abandoned doorsteps. Near the corner, an old single-bottom plow hung menacingly above the sidewalk, part of a sign contrived over the front of Jane Herring's one-time grocery store. The heavy object once advertised a hopeful antiques business, but now only persevered because of its rusty hardware and the disinclination of anyone to disturb it. No one seemed threatened by its precarious position.

The customary parade fare was supplemented this year by Bob McGeorge's restored red convertible, a vintage buggy driven by a couple from Glenwood, and a float upon which several community members modeled clothing from by-gone eras. Sherry was in the latter group, dressed in a delicate blouse and skirt kept from Ruby's things. There was no question about who would don the lacy ensemble, as Sherry was the only one in the family whose tiny waist would fit into the tight skirt. The warm day made the slow ride through town a little less enjoyable than Sherry had anticipated.

The floats in the parade were rustic, quite unlike the Rose Bowl offerings Dona had seen on TV. One flatbed truck supported the entire Walker family--grandparents, aunts, cousins, everyone--descended from an early settler of the community.

The local 4-H Club staged a one-room school on a lowboy pulled by a vintage tractor. The presentation was complete with desks, chalkboard and flag, and peopled by schoolmarm and students outfitted in period costumes. Dona realized that many in the present crowd had not attended such a school, as she and her daughters had.

Phi Mu, a women's social sorority, also rode on a flatbed trailer. The ladies had prepared vignettes of pioneer life, including spinning, butter churning and soap making. Dona recalled her own personal experience with the latter. She and June had "cooked up" a batch of lye soap in an iron kettle when they had lived on the Richey place. She thought perhaps she would have had more success in the endeavor if she had attempted it a little later in her life. At the time, her dreams and ambitions were still centered in the far-away city life she had left behind.

The crowd showed its appreciation for an impromptu cooling-off that startled some of the onlookers. A local fellow had equipped an old riding lawn mower with a wooden shell that resembled a skunk. Now and then the skunk backed up to a section of the audience, raised its tail, and spewed a substantial stream! The initial reactions of surprise and dismay were soon replaced with shouts of approval and a general desire by the rest of the crowd to be sprayed, also. That entry was the hit of the short parade that quickly wound its way to the community center and to its own rapid dispersal.

Jimmie would help with the kids' tractor pull, to take place next on the street by the center. His day's participation had begun much earlier than that, however. He had first hauled in pig panels and set up a small corral in back of the building. The pig-catching competition would take place there later in the day. Jimmie had brought in a dozen piglets for that amusement and would later bring in one of his large breeding sows for an activity that Dona would oversee.

The junior tractor pull was a well-attended event and kept most young families entertained for the rest of the morning. Dona spent her time inside the center, where fans whirred noisily, keeping the place cool. The old church building was now equipped with a full kitchen, installed upon the platform. Ladies of the community were already serving sandwiches and pie and trying to keep up with the demand for iced tea and lemonade.

Dona joined Wilma A, who sat at a card table selling tickets for the day's raffle. Wilma's brother, Jim Ed, and his wife were there, enjoying a respite from the clamor and heat outside.

"When will Bingo begin, Dona?" Rose now asked.

"I don't think they start until around noon, when noise from the tractor pull is over," Dona offered. She didn't have anything to do with the Bingo game, so she wasn't sure. The local sorority ran that concession, and Dona usually played, but she wasn't sure if she could take the heat today. On the other hand, the Bingo tent would offer the only shade to be had in the afternoon.

"I probably won't last long," Rose volunteered. She'd had heart trouble before Dona was stricken. "We'll come back later tonight when the band is here."

"Rex Wallace's supposed to be here, I guess," Jim Ed contributed to the conversation. "I'm not sure what kind of singer a politician might make!"

"Have you heard anything about Wilma C?" Dona asked her friend.

"They've put her in a nursing home," Wilma answered. "I think she'll be able to come home, though, when she recovers from her stroke. Albert goes over to Whitesville to visit her twice every day."

Dona made a mental note to seek Albert out to talk with today. He must be very lonely. *How many years have they been together*, she wondered? She and Jimmie had celebrated their thirtieth anniversary a few years back. She couldn't imagine her life without him!

Barb and Sherry entered and approached their mother.

"Where are the guys?" Dona asked.

"They went out to help Jimmie load the old sow," Barbara replied.

That reminded Dona of her job for the day. Coralea and Vikki had volunteered to take care of it for her.

"You'd better find Coralea and see if she's ready," Dona suggested.

"She and Vikki are out setting up now," Sherry told her mother. "Jimmie's going to put the crate over at the corner of the lot. There's a little tree there that will give the sow some shade."

Dona laughed. "Well, how about the rest of us? Isn't that just like him, to think of his pigs first?"

When they came into town, Coralea and Vikki had brought, besides Dona's pies, some lawn chairs, the card table, a money pouch, two bottles of Palmolive Liquid, and a tablet for keeping track of the weight guesses. For a quarter, participants could try to name the poundage of the pig, and closest to the correct number would win the pot--minus ten percent for the community center. It would be a simple operation.

When Jimmie delivered the sow in her crate, he also brought a cream can of water and a dipper.

"You need to have this contest in a hurry because as soon as the greased pig contests are over I'm hauling her back out to Eldon's place!" He left them with instructions to splash some water onto the caged creature every now and then.

Dona sat with Coralea while Vikki went to enter Hannah into the pig-catching competition.

Barbara's daughter, Debbie, and her husband came strolling up with their new son.

"Do you really have a baby in that thing?" Dona asked. The canopy on the child's stroller was draped with a light cloth to shelter him from the hot rays of the sun.

Debbie grinned demurely, revealing an even row of pretty, white teeth. She had her mother's shy smile, which Dona thought Barbara had gotten from June.

The proud father of the sleeping infant looked over the operation set up to hawk guesstimates from passers-by. He put in his quarter and made a guess. He was a pig farmer, so Dona figured his estimate would give others a clue to a reasonable range of speculation. Debbie made a guess, also, and they all chuckled, as she knew even less about farming than her father, Don.

"I can't believe all the paraphernalia you have for that child!" Dona teased her granddaughter. "When the girls were little, I just grabbed up a diaper and went." *Something to push them around in would have been a real luxury!* The substantial conveyance was hung with diaper bag, bottles of water, baby wipes, toys, purse, camera--even a folding umbrella.

"It's about time for Hannah's age group in the greased pig contest," Coralea announced to the group. "I'll take care of this, Mom, so you can go over and watch with Vikki."

"We've got to see this!" Debbie said with interest. "I remember the cute pictures you had of her from last time." It had been two years since the little girls had been to the Fun Days.

The Palmolive detergent Dona brought to town earlier now served as the grease for the greased pig contest. Jimmie squirted the liquid liberally onto the back of each piglet before letting him go in the corral. The smaller children had already had their turn, and it was time for the five to seven age group when Vikki brought up a chair for Granny to sit and watch.

The afternoon sun was beginning to take a toll on the crowd. Dona observed that most of those remaining were young families with children who were competing in the afternoon's games. If she didn't want to see Hannah scramble after those pigs, she would already be back in her cool living room.

Vikki noticed a fellow videotaping his grandson in the pig contest and wished she'd thought to bring her own camera. She had been faithful in making tapes of the girls' activities since they'd moved away and always shared them with Granny and PaPa.

At her time to compete, Hannah joined the small group of kids, mainly boys, in the small arena. PaPa turned three little pigs into the enclosure; the whistle sounded and the race was on! Pigs and kids darted in all directions--the pigs confused by their attackers, the children equally startled by the spunk of their quarry!

Hannah wasn't as aggressive as she had been two years earlier. She obviously wasn't anxious to get into the mess. When she was younger, she had dived right into the action. Then she had succeeded in dragging a slippery, squirming victim over to the stock tank, where the game's helpers had obligingly tipped the tank over and helped her scoot the struggling squealer into it. She was enormously proud of the white ribbon she had won. This time, however, all the winners were little boys, who had to be hosed off at the end of the competition.

The action progressed to the older groups, where no girls at all chose to participate. The size of the pigs Jimmie provided increased with the size of the contestants, so the high school boys were faced with some weighty animals. Dona worried that the pigs might be harmed, the way they were being leaped upon and thrown around. But Jimmie probably knew how much they could take--doubtless he had done such wrangling himself, many times.

When that excitement came to a close, Dona decided to drive back to the house where it would be blessedly cool, so she invited the rest of her family to go with her. Debbie took the baby--he was awake and not enjoying the heat--and her folks went along to visit. Sherry and Dave headed for home, as it was a long drive back to their farm near Carroll.

Coralea and Vikki stayed with the activities awhile longer. Both little girls competed in the obstacle course that had been constructed in the side yard. It consisted mostly of hay bales, rubber tires, and a water hazard. When that was over, Coralea and her daughter retreated to the Ruby house, a block away.

Vikki and the girls had spent several weeks there each summer. Coralea had helped them strip the walls and hang new wallpaper, and then they painted the woodwork so it was freshly white. Dona wasn't sure how she felt about these changes to the house that had been given to her by her dear friend. But, Vikki had bought it and could make whatever improvements she wished. Dona was just happy to have the little family close for a while.

It was late in the afternoon before Sarah came in, excited about her winnings at the Bingo tent.

"I won a set of dishes!" she exclaimed. "Can you come and help me carry them home?"

"Well, lucky you!" her mom said as she got up to go and help.

They found Hannah happily perched on the "hot seat" at the dunk tank, soaking wet and ready for the next big splash. She would spend another hour there with her friends before she was ready to give it up. The girls were acquainted with several of the area kids, and Fun Days was a special time for all of them.

While they were packing up the dishes, Jimmie came by. He'd taken his stressed-out livestock back to the farm, where he would like to have stayed, also, but there was more to be done here. The place would need to be cleaned up before the evening's entertainment arrived.

"Who do you think won the 'Guess the Weight' contest?" Jimmie asked, grinning.

"Who?" from Vikki.

"Debbie! The pot was only $7, but Debbie won it!" She had been as surprised as anyone and received a lot of teasing about it. "Say, that's quite a set of dishes," Jimmie added.

"I won them," Sarah told PaPa. "They're kind of a funny color, though."

Jimmie didn't say so, but he thought they were just about the ugliest dishes he'd ever seen, dark brown with muddy-yellow trim. He reflected briefly that Dona was usually the one to spend time playing Bingo. Now it was her great-granddaughter!

"Maybe we'll see you tonight if it cools down a little," he called back over his shoulder as he walked on toward his next task.

Art Wallace's band was often called upon to play at small-town events. Their country-western music fit well in the homey, outdoor atmosphere.

Dona and Jimmie sat in lawn chairs amid the modest crowd gathered for the evening's performance. The band played on the back of a flatbed truck pulled across the intersection. Jimmie was surprised Dona still had the energy to come to the show. She had been tired lately and the day's heat had drained even him, accustomed as he was to working outdoors.

Vikki and the girls came to sit with them for a while but stayed only until the raffle drawing was completed. Nearly everyone in the community contributed to it, which made up a good part of the day's proceeds.

"It's been a nice day, hasn't it?" Dona remarked as they sat relaxing in the cool evening air.

"It's been a long one," Jimmie offered. He had to admit he was tired and appreciated sitting and being entertained for a while.

"Do you suppose this celebration will run as long as the Horton Picnic did?" Dona asked wistfully.

"Who knows? We've had seven already. That would be about ninety-some to go, I reckon." He wished he could believe they'd see a few more themselves. The last year had been a struggle for Dona, though with the coming of summer her coughing fits had finally subsided. She increasingly had to lean on the furniture for support. Deep wrinkles were etched on her face, and her make-up didn't mask her gray pallor. But she still had the wonderful smile that never failed to brighten his day. She had been working on a project lately that he hoped she would be able to complete. It was obviously very important to her, and she had already accomplished much more than he thought she could. Jimmie occasionally felt his own vulnerability when he exerted himself on a rigorous task. The shortness of breath he experienced never failed to surprise him. He didn't tell Dona this and chose to ignore it himself, as much as he could.

Dona enjoyed the music. It reminded her of the country tunes Doc Liston played for the exiting of his outdoor theater. Those were bittersweet memories--pleasure mingled with pain and disappointment. Now there was seldom any entertainment offered in the town. The world had become smaller. Now, in no time at all one could reach amusements of all sorts, and television allowed you to experience many without even leaving home.

The city seemed so close now, though she no longer had any desire to go there. If not for Miriam's family still being in Kansas City, she didn't care if she never saw the place again. Dona remembered when the city held such magical allure for her! For a long time she yearned to go back and recapture the excitement of the bustling place. How her perspective had changed!

Miriam had taken Dona with her to the Summerville alumni reunion a year earlier. Dona enjoyed the afternoon in the gymnasium of the now-defunct school. Many people there still remembered her as Donie Ethel, and she missed some she had anticipated seeing again. Her favorite teacher had passed away. Dona remembered that he had given her ego a boost when he had her tutor some older boys on their algebra problems. She would like to have told him she'd gotten her GED, so she was finally a graduate. That would have pleased him. Her former friend, Bea Swanson, didn't attend the event. She had played basketball with Dona on that very court.

The gymnasium was still in use for some affairs. Auctions were held there, as well as family reunions. The kitchen and cafeteria were late additions to the structure, so they were still adequate for a dinner theatre. Plays were offered by the community once or twice each year. Dona and Jimmie had gone to one of those with Carrie and Frank a few years back.

The musicians in Art Wallace's band came from several small towns in the area, but none from Bedford. Dona remembered when Bill Lynch played his steel guitar at the New Dell in Shenandoah. No Lynches left in town now, except the stepmother. Nor McMurtrys, Clines, Blacks, or Torrances. The

Wisdom girls had left but had come back. Kathleen and Rose were both here tonight with their husbands. Dona wondered if any members of the other families would return. She hoped so. She felt tied to the community with an unbreakable bond, even though many present now were strangers to her.

"What's that?" Dona asked Kathleen, indicating the item on her friend's lap. It was simply encased in a neatly folded newspaper, but Dona sensed its value as her friend caressed it.

"It's for you," Kathleen replied as she handed the object over to Dona. "I had it made for you."

Dona carefully opened the package to reveal a plain picture frame that held a photo of a house.

"It's the old house!" Dona exclaimed. In the dim light, the structure's outlines were not clear, but she easily recognized the stately place she had so loved.

"It was taken when my folks lived out there," Kathleen told her. "Does it look as you remember it?"

"Yes, it does! Thank you--this is very thoughtful of you!"

Dona was surprised that thinking of the old place didn't hurt her as it once had. She missed the blazing fires they'd had in the huge fireplace, and her new home lacked the character of that earlier one, with its creaks, groans, and sighs. There had been times she'd felt the old house was trying to talk to her. But, their new home was comfortable and convenient for Dona and Jimmie, and the family often gathered there. The laughter of children and grandchildren insinuated itself into the rooms and lingered to delight her days long after they had all gone home. Dona felt that she and Jimmie had come to a farm already rich in history and had nourished it with lives of love, making it a special place for many following generations.

She was so grateful for her home! When she was young, she never imagined the contentment a person could feel in belonging to one particular place. Maybe she hadn't been in one spot long enough to purchase the privilege she now enjoyed on the farm. Perhaps you had to laugh and cry, maybe even live and die in a place before it was actually yours. Dona wondered if a person's place in a community could only be bought over a period of time. Each time you passed over a sidewalk, a street, or a threshold, you gained interest in the site, gathering equity as you invested the minutes of your life. It was all here, everything she really wanted--here and on the land that was theirs, just a quarter mile away.

"He sounds almost like Jim Reeves," Kathleen observed.

"Not bad for a Republican!" Joe allowed.

Rex Wallace, Art's son, had entertained the group with a couple of Western songs.

"Yes, he does," Dona agreed. "He has a very mellow voice. I could listen to him for a long time." She knew the man was a state representative from the Madison area and was surprised at his talent for performing.

Before leaving for the evening, Jimmie purchased a tape Rex had recorded. Dona could listen to him as often as she liked.

THIRTY-TWO

Time could be your friend, or it could be your enemy. Dona was well aware of that maxim. She never doubted that time might heal all wounds and lighten all sorrows, but she also knew that time passed swiftly when you wanted it to slow, and was likely to run out if you squandered it.

Dona wrote the last chapter of her life. Or, more accurately, she spent the last chapter of her life writing. Jimmie no longer found her "sleeping" on the couch when he dropped by the house, but usually in her chair, steno pad in hand, filling page after page with her small, precise handwriting. She had begun early in the summer, shortly after Beth and Fred left to return to Dallas. She had only to complete her morning routine before she was back in her recliner, pen to paper.

Morning was the best time for Dona. Since Jimmie was doing less farm work, he took time to enjoy a leisurely breakfast. The energy with which he met each day seemed to flow into her as well. There was a spring in his step as he began his daily regimen, regardless of the exacting tasks that lay ahead. By the end of the day, he would be moving slower, and smiling and talking less. Often, twilight would find them each napping in front of the television, both body and spirit in need of replenishment.

Before she allowed herself to begin her chosen task, Dona took care of her own morning chores. She kept her kitchen tidy, dishes cleared away into the dishwasher, countertop bare and gleaming. She removed the clutter from her mind as she organized her surroundings. There was often a load of laundry to do--a batch of Jimmie's jeans and overalls, and maybe the rugs from the utility room floor. They were always full of mud, sweat, and tears--no, manure, mostly of the hog variety--that he knocked off in there several times each day. At least the grime was usually contained in that one small area. Jimmie's bathroom was just across the hall, so the rest of the house was spared the earthy siftings and aromas of the farm.

When she first conceived the project, Dona's goal had been to write something of a historical nature, similar, perhaps, to the tapes she had made of Woodrow Nelson's experiences. She felt she had lived through a period of dramatic changes in lifestyles, in history, in technology. As she attempted to formulate a workable format for her undertaking, she realized that the major sociological changes of her lifetime had already been chronicled by people much more knowledgeable than she, and that her time would be better spent in writing what she knew best--her own life.

Dona hoped she would be able to tell, without being whiny, what it was like to be a child living in the Depression era. She wanted to be honest about her own family's troubles without making unfair assumptions or casting blame. She could barely remember her own grandmother, and she was thirteen years old when Grandma Kate died. She wanted the little ones of the family to know her more intimately than through a photo in an album or a name on a monument, and to know those she had loved--Mom and Dad, Hank, Grant, Earlene, and many others.

Dona realized she now knew intimately more people dead than alive--a sobering thought! All the more reason to write down her memoirs. They would be a tribute to those in her life, as well as an accurate portrayal of the lives of common people during her span of existence.

Dona was energized by the personal proposal she made for herself. She was eager to begin each day, wishing to record what she remembered of her own past and that of her family. She wrote quickly, as her thoughts developed. She wanted to keep the account in chronological order to make it easy to follow. She sought to make her writing interesting and also to keep it a factual reflection of real occurrences.

Occasionally, Dona attempted to record a part of her life that was difficult to put into words. She was overcome with emotions she had a hard time identifying. Still, she knew honesty must be adhered to if her document were to be accurate and readable.

Whenever one of the girls dropped by, Dona asked her to read over a few pages and give her a critique. Mainly, she wanted help with grammatical problems, but the girls rarely found mistakes. They were impressed by their mother's skill in transposing her memories into interesting reading material. And, because they knew their mother was mainly self-educated, surprised at the small number of technical errors in her writing.

A few weeks after Bedford Fun Days, Dona received a call from Merle Hanna. He'd made an extra tape of the greased pig contest Hannah had participated in and he invited Dona to come out to his home to pick it up.

"Why don't you go with me?" Dona asked Coralea, who happened to be at the Martins' at the time. "They have a new house, and I'm sure they'd like to show it off."

"Where is it? Not far?" Coralea inquired.

"Out near Black Oak. Remember where that is? It's real woodsy out there."

Coralea did remember. Her classroom had gone there for a picnic once, on the grounds of the Black Oak School.

The home they visited was set back off a remote gravel road, nestled in a grove of tall oak trees. The dwelling was of a rustic design that fit well in the pastoral surroundings. On entering the large living room, Dona immediately noticed the unusual flooring, a parquet pattern composed of various hardwoods.

"My! What an attractive floor!" she exclaimed.

"I did it myself," Mr. Hanna told her. "It took me quite awhile to put it together, there are so many small pieces. But it is one of a kind!"

"It reminds me of the floor in the house in town where we once lived. Do you remember it?" she asked her daughter.

"Uh-huh. It's about the only thing I do remember about the place, though, except for the cellar where Grandpa kept the leeches!"

"I'm not surprised you remember that. Dad kept them for bait, but you girls were afraid of them," Dona recalled.

"It's funny that all those times Grandpa went fishing, I don't remember him ever taking us along, except for up in Minnesota," Coralea remarked.

Dona laughed.

"You're probably the reason he went so often! No, really, he did a lot of fishing before any of us came along."

"How did you come to build out here?" Coralea asked of Mr. Hanna. "It's really pretty, but isn't it kind of hard to get to?"

"That's why we like it!" he assured her. He gave them a tour of the place before they had to leave. They both thanked him for the hospitality and for the tape, for which he refused payment. Coralea and her family would later cherish the record of the Fun Days events, not only for the little girl's antics but as a remembrance of Granny and PaPa as they had been in their last months.

"This area is where white settlers first came to the township. Did you know that?" Dona asked her daughter as the two walked to the car. Coralea replied that she did remember reading that somewhere.

"And did you know there's a place in the woods where they say the grass will never grow again?"

"And why is that?" Coralea asked with interest.

"An intruder murdered a local couple who settled there. When the law caught up with him, they found him hiding in back of a woodpile. There was a shootout, and he was killed. They buried him on the spot. They said he was so mean and low that the grass would never grow on his grave!"

"Where do you learn things like that?" Coralea asked.

"Oh, from talking to the old folks, mostly. They're all gone now, except for Millie Baker, and she went to live with her daughter in Kansas City," Dona answered. "I don't suppose anyone knows where the spot is now. It was said to be close to the first school--that was north of the Black Oak School we knew. Even that one is gone now, and the road up to it closed. Things change."

"It's too bad there's not a map of those places. You can't even tell now where Star of the West used to be. It's just a pasture--no trace of the school is left!" Coralea hadn't particularly liked the place, but still she hated to see it just disappear.

"Maybe someday someone will take it upon himself to see that these pieces of history are preserved," Dona suggested, though she knew the pace of modern life didn't allow much time for such pursuits. It was strange, and she couldn't put it into words, but she felt as if she were a part of that past she now discussed with her daughter. Here she was, in Black Oak Grove, Mr. Hanna's chosen home site, in the very area that drew Jimmie's ancestor more than a century earlier! *Was I meant to be here?*

It was well into fall before Dona began typing her manuscript. Vikki had replaced her own typewriter and gave the electric machine she had used to her grandmother. Dona had to adapt to the rapid movement of the Daisy flywheel and the responsive keys. However, she soon adjusted her touch and was able to type rapidly and accurately.

The light was best in the north window, so Dona set up the card table there, where she could look out over the park. She loved the brisk, autumn days and wanted to see the color shift as the days shortened and cooled. She imagined the earth preparing for the long winter of rest ahead.

The year had been a good one on the farm. The dry, cracked ground that resulted from last year's drought had healed with the spring rains, and the year had continued with a succession of favorable climatic conditions.

Dona sensed that Jimmie was more rested than usual at this time of the year. He had little harvesting to accomplish, but the acres he planted were highly productive. His swine operation had nearly rebounded from the setback of '88; there were, again, pigs all over the place. She reminded herself of the "smell of money" thing.

Usually, Dona kept at her project all day long. One October afternoon, she decided to take a break and go over to the Penney Eighty to witness the transformation sweeping across the timber. At this time of the year it was, in her opinion, the most beautiful spot on earth; even the shaded streets of Shenandoah were no match for the unspoiled display nature alone provided. And she admired the timber almost as much in the spring, when dainty redbud blossoms infused the forest with shades of pink and purple. From her home on the hill, she could look across the feedlot then and see the western bluff of Hogback Ridge, vibrantly painted in splotches of violet. It was a feast for the eyes that she was honored to behold.

Dona drove the Ruby car out onto the racetrack, over the abrupt hills and through the gate to the ridge. Trees on both sides of the well-worn path rose to obliterate the outside world. She was enveloped in a cocoon of color and serenaded by the vibrations of woodland insects. The seamless blue sky faded ever so slightly where it touched the treetops.

She had asked Jimmie if they might separate at least a few acres of the Penney Eighty from the rest of their holdings. If they should ever lose the farm, they would still have a piece of the prettiest part. He agreed that it would be a good idea but hadn't followed through with any action. And she knew he never would. To do so would be admitting that the possibility was real, and that outcome was not an option in her husband's mind. "Why plan for the unthinkable?" was the way he saw it.

Dona remembered when she brought Nora and Ruby here, more than a decade in the past, now. They had loved this landscape too, and, she realized, had probably known it better than she did. She had read in an old newspaper that a class from the school on the hill had gone to Eliza Penney's for their class picnic. That was early in the century. And, according to Claude, the town's WWII victory garden had been just over the hill from where she stood.

Dona wondered if there had ever been a house on the place--there was the remnant of a small shed near the garden site. The walnut tree near the crest of the hill looked barely alive, a victim of last year's drought. It had what looked like a fence post imbedded in its trunk, further evidence of human habitation sometime in the past.

Eliza was Hiram Stingley's daughter and probably came by the property through dowry or inheritance. She had worked in the same bank as Uncle Vincent, but was of an earlier generation. Was she a generous lady who lived in town but kept the acreage, or had she actually lived on the place? Dona thought about Mr. Penney. She never knew of him, but he must have been in the picture at some time. Dona wished the trees could talk so she could cross-examine them for answers to her riddles.

The cool weather of autumn had reduced the summer's swarm of insects dramatically, but Dona observed a few monarch butterflies flitting along the tips of tall weeds. She knew there were always a few left behind, some that would not make the long journey to Mexico. Those thousands that would were already gone from the area. She missed their migration this year, but it always occurred within a few days of her September birthday.

She'd looked for articles on the amazing phenomenon and had found a piece in the *National Geographic* magazine. It featured a scientist's study of their flight pattern and ultimate destination. She read that the butterflies spread their wings to gather warmth from the sun before flying from their overnight roost in the trees. Perhaps the delicate voyagers possessed a sort of solar cell that human beings had not yet deciphered. She was astounded to learn that the insects that attempted the incredible course were several generations removed from the ones that had returned northward the previous spring! That was truly a miracle!

Only once had Dona caught sight of the multitude of butterflies as they approached their overnight roosting spot. As she drove along the blacktop beside the school, she saw scores of the captivating creatures hovering above the soybean field where the bottomland stretched away to the Platte River. The moving mass seemed to progress in a southerly direction, meandering as it went.

The insects weren't flying in a swarm, as bees do, nor in a birdlike flock, but rather in loosely knit companionship, with each pair of russet wings separated by a distance of perhaps thirty yards. They weren't keeping to a steady course but dipping now and then to alight on the dark green foliage, obviously taking sustenance of some kind--food or moisture to propel them on to their predetermined destiny. Dona wondered if their amazing odyssey passed through this area because of the lush soybean fields. Or, had they been coming as far back as the days of the bluegrass harvest? The random ballet of leapfrogging fliers seemed to be part of an endless voyage that swept her along as well.

At first, Dona thought she heard thunder. But, with such a cloudless sky? Then she saw them, coming from the northeast, low on the horizon--a group of three jumbo C130s. The drone of the powerful engines permeated the stillness with convulsive force, bringing the rest of the world into Dona's peaceful sanctuary. It was a disturbing intrusion, and yet, somehow beautiful and moving. She despised the machines of war, but still, *where would we be without them*? She had had those same mixed feelings when she worked on the gliders in Kansas City. She was grieved that they were needed but certain that when they were, they had better be there. She guessed it was admiration she now felt for those who had conceived and built the machines and for those who must fly them, if called upon.

There was trouble in the Middle East right now; Iraq had invaded Kuwait, ostensibly because of the oil fields there. So far, the official United States' response had consisted mostly of saber rattling, but she feared drastic steps would soon be deemed necessary by the government. In today's interconnected world, far-away conflicts were no longer remote threats, but real and immediate global concerns.

The huge, steel gray carriers flew so low Dona could almost reach up from her spot on the hill and brush the underbelly of the middle machine. The planes barely skimmed the tops of the trees beyond her before they were gone from sight, on their way back to Rosecrans Airfield in St. Joseph.

The air wing performed such training maneuvers periodically, so she'd seen them many times before. She wondered why they flew so low--to avoid radar detection, or maybe to keep out of the airspace of other aircraft? They left behind a vast stillness, even more soothing than before.

As she headed for home, Dona mused on the name of the familiar roadway. It had always been called the "racetrack," but she couldn't imagine it was ever useful for that purpose. It was hilly and narrow and seemed to get narrower every year. Before Bedford was uprooted and moved over the hill, this had been the only route to town. Now it was rarely maintained and used but little, primarily by Jimmie to reach his outlying parcels of land.

She turned into the old lane beside the machine shed. She'd stop and chat with Jimmie and Dave. They were surely finished by now. Dave had volunteered to help when Jimmie had the vet out to "cut," castrate, the pigs. Sherry and Dave were living in Madison for the present school term. He had retired from his work for the IRS in Cainsville, and she was pursuing her master's degree in education.

The tractor blocked the way on the old roadbed, so she swung the car around to head back the way she came. As she backed around into the grove, turning to see through the rear window, she caught sight of an old elevator in her way. She slammed her foot onto the brake, but it slipped off and pressed firmly onto the accelerator, propelling the car into the air, astride the elevator! The rapid ride startled her and caused a minor commotion as metal scraped on metal.

She barely had time to turn off the motor before Jimmie and Dave were beside her, asking if she were okay.

"What happened?" Jimmie asked anxiously.

"Were you trying to 'shoot the moon'?" Dave quipped.

"I guess my foot slipped," Dona said, as she broke into an embarrassed grin. "It looks like I'm stuck!"

After he stopped laughing, Jimmie got the tractor and pulled his wife off her precarious perch atop the elevator. The antiquated implement had been so long in the same spot that the wheels had sunk several inches into the soil. Dona guessed she had chosen the right machine to pick on, since the impact did little to injure her or to mar the rear of the Ruby car.

"How would you feel about going down to see Val and Gary's new baby?" Coralea asked her mother one day in late October. Sherry's oldest daughter lived in Lee's Summit now, and Chelsea was just a few days old.

"I'd like to go, but Jimmie's in the middle of harvest, so he can't get away right now. This would be a gorgeous day for a drive down along the Missouri River, though!" she replied with enthusiasm.

"Then I'll call and set it up with Val. We won't stay long, and I'm sure they're eager to show off their first child," Coralea said.

The autumn day was everything one could ask of a benevolent Creator, crisp and clear. Falling temperatures had dressed the bluffs in shades of scarlet and gold. Ripening fields of soybeans had turned from deep green to bold yellow, their voluptuous vines spreading a carpet of gold across the countryside.

Close to Halloween, many country estates were decorated with pumpkins, gourds, bales of straw and shocks of corn. These were interspersed with witches, goblins, ghosts--every apparition associated with the season. Before one opulent country home, a graying wagon, with Ma and Pa Scarecrow on board, was pulled by a horse of straw. Parts of human effigies protruded from giant bales, as if hapless bumpkins were rolled up in their own hay. Dona thought the beautifully manicured estates were probably not farms at all but sentimental holdings of aristocrats who had made their money in a more lucrative field.

Their route took the pair close to Kansas City, near enough to see the skyline of the metropolis that had once so enthralled Dona. Now she was happy to view it from afar, separated from the noise and confusion, mainly traffic, that she now associated with the place.

Baby Chelsea, with pretty blue eyes and an abundance of dark hair, favored both the March side and the Hawkins side of the family each was sure. Valerie was friendly but reserved, as always, and happy to see her grandmother feeling well enough to be out enjoying the day.

The visit was brief, as it was meant to be, and the two women were back on the road by mid-afternoon.

Around seven o'clock, Dona and Coralea were on the last part of their journey, approaching Bedford from the west. Shortly after going through Horton, they noticed a thick column of smoke rising from the east.

"Someone's got a fire going," Coralea casually observed.

Dona would rather not think about fires, especially ones burning where this one appeared to be. She said nothing.

After passing over a few more hills, they could see that the conflagration was definitely south of town.

"I'm sure it's down on the bottom somewhere!" Coralea declared. She knew by the look on Dona's face that her mother imagined a fire at their farm again. She wanted to hurry the car along, eager to prove her fears wrong, but apprehensive, also. She wasn't about to say it, but she felt her mother's worst fear might be coming true. Seen from where they were on the flat roadway, the smoke appeared to rise from a spot directly in line with the Martin house on the hill!

"It's the dump, Mom. I'm sure of it," Coralea lied. She knew an emotional assault would be as devastating for her mother as another physical crisis.

"No one ever burns off the dump but me, and surely no one would do it now in the dry season!" Dona worried.

A sick feeling arose in the pit of Coralea's stomach. By the time they reached the Platte River Bridge, she was certain the worst was truly happening!

"Jimmie wouldn't be in from doing his chores yet, would he?" she wondered. At least he wouldn't be in harm's way if the horrible scenario actually played out.

"No, he shouldn't be . . ." Dona weakly interjected.

Not until they reached Bedford and had turned the corner to go south could they make out just where the fire was burning.

"It *is* the dump!" Dona gleefully announced, so happy to learn the innocuous nature of the blaze that she could run down there and kiss whoever started it! She knew she would never completely shed her visceral reaction to the specter of flames.

Jimmie didn't know who'd set fire to the rubbish accumulated in the old river bed; the town had used the convenient spot as a dump for years. With the passage of strict EPA rules, the practice had been discontinued. But somehow trash found its way out there, and this time ignited itself as well.

A Hundred Miles to the City

"Do you know where the folks are?" Sherry asked Coralea by phone one evening.

"No. I haven't seen them since Sunday. Is something wrong?" was her sister's hasty reply.

"Well, I've been trying to get in touch with them this afternoon. I can't get any answer. I called Barb and they weren't there."

"I can't imagine Mom going out on a day like this! It's really cold and windy out there. You know how she says the wind stops up her head. They must've had somewhere they had to go," Coralea volunteered.

After hanging up the phone, Sherry turned to her husband and relayed what little she had learned.

"Jimmie didn't mention having to do anything different today," Dave remarked, noticing the sheen of wetness forming in Sherry's brown eyes. She was worried and he figured he might as well prepare for a trip down to the farm.

The possibility of problems for her folks weighed on Coralea's mind, also. She tried, without success, to reach them by phone. *Where are they? It's way past dark; Jimmie should be in from doing the chores by now. If they aren't at Barb's or Sherry's, where else can they be?*

They arrived at the farm simultaneously, Sherry and Dave pulling around the circle drive in back of the house just as Coralea drove into the lane. A lamp was on in the living room, and Sherry saw her father's form slumped in his chair just inside the patio door. No sign of her mother.

She hurried from the car and slid back the heavy glass. Jimmie stirred in surprise as she stumbled into the room, with Dave and Coralea close on her heels. Dona came in from the bedroom, where she'd obviously been preparing for the night.

"Where were you?" the interlopers asked as one.

Jimmie glanced at Dona with a look of amusement.

"Christmas shopping!" she told them.

"I can't believe you went out on a day like this to go Christmas shopping!" Sherry exclaimed.

"Well, we did," Jimmie affirmed. "What are you all doing here? Is something wrong?"

"No, we were just a little concerned," Dave allowed, admitting to himself that he had probably been as anxious about their welfare as the girls were.

"Well. That explains why Barb called a little bit ago," Dona said. "I should have asked them to come up, and we could've had a party!"

As their unexpected guests prepared to leave, Dona thoughtfully remarked, "I'm sorry if we worried you."

"I guess maybe it's payback time!" Dave suggested. No one was ready to deny that.

Dona didn't mention that the Christmas shopping they had done had nothing to do with buying presents. Mr. Wright, at the print shop, had told her he could get her manuscript copied in time for the holiday if she could get it to him by that date. And she had. She and Jimmie had agreed to forego the usual gifts for the girls and their families so they could use those funds to finance the special keepsake of her memoirs. Her family didn't know she had set this goal or that she had gotten so far along with her writing. What she had accomplished in the past few months had been done in secret. She and Jimmie had enjoyed the intrigue they shared and she could hardly wait for Christmas! *Oops! As Mom would say, "You're just wishing your life away!"*

"I asked Corky to bring up the Christmas stuff," Dona told Jimmie.

"I can see that," he returned, noting the boxes of various sizes stacked on the dining room table. "Good."

"I'm saving your help for hanging the lights," she went on to say. It was barely past Thanksgiving, but she liked to stretch the holiday season out as much as she could.

"You've gotten the tree out already!" he exclaimed as he stepped through the kitchen into the large living area.

"That was the easy part! All I had to do was unfold the branches. I don't think we'll even mess with the light this year." The tree was of aluminum that shimmered in red, blue or green when a beam of light passed through the tinted filter. Dona and Jimmie had always had an evergreen tree in the old house, often one they'd gone to the timber and cut themselves. She loved the pungent smell of a freshly cut tree. It was, to her, an integral part of the season's celebration. But, after the fire, she wished to take no chances and chose to make that small concession to caution.

"Let's just go over the fireplace and the wet bar this year," Dona suggested, as they untangled strands of colored bulbs. "I'll set out some decorations on the tables, and we can put Ruby's lighted wreaths in the front windows. They'll be like welcoming beacons at the front of the house."

"Who all's coming?" Jimmie asked.

"Everyone, nearly," Dona replied. "Kelly and Travis are even coming from Seattle!" Their grandson had recently divorced, so he was now a single father. That saddened her, but she had to allow that frequently things did work out for the best. She knew her own girls were happy to have Jimmie in their lives and equally pleased that he was the grandfather their children now loved.

A Hundred Miles to the City

"The tree is going to look kind of bare this year," Dona observed.

"Maybe we can go ahead and buy some little gifts for the kids," Jimmie suggested. He knew it would be a few years before the children appreciated the touching composition Dona had worked so hard on. He was certain that the girls, and Dona's siblings too, would treasure the intimate record of her past and of their own roles in it.

On Christmas Eve, Jimmie opened the glass door and poked his head in. His face was red and raw. The flaps of his woolen cap were pulled down over his ears and his eyes watered--*stinging from the biting wind*, Dona guessed. She could see that his nose was running. *He probably doesn't even know it--likely, his face is numb!*

"Is there anything you need from the store, Sugar?" Jimmie asked.

"No. I've just fixed vegetable soup. Everyone's bringing for tonight. Aren't you about ready to come in?"

"I'll be in soon. Would you mix up some milk for Tippie and the cats?" He was gone. She noticed that the dog stuck his head out of the doghouse but made no move to follow. *Wise animal--Snowball is probably in there too.* Backed up against the house, the little shelter was often occupied solely by the cats.

Except for her husband's having to be out in the cold, Dona liked this part of the year. The house was a secure refuge where she remained comfortable, sheltered from the rigors of winter. She had spent plenty of her days in drafty old houses, some loved, others not. It occurred to Dona that she and Jimmie had been on this place nearly thirty-four years, though she couldn't imagine where all that time had gone! She couldn't remember living in one spot more than three of four years before then. No wonder she felt so at home on the farm!

Outside, Jimmie couldn't hurry as much as he would like. The stiff wind challenged his every step. Normally he didn't mind the cold. The musky heat exuded by the animals warmed him from within as well as without. Today he had on insulated boots and insulated coveralls--nearly everything he wore was of the insulated variety. The special clothing served well to retain his body warmth, so only his exposed skin was vulnerable. His face was beyond the stinging stage and well into absolute numbness. He feared his nose might snap off if something bumped against it!

By five o'clock, guests had begun to arrive. Vikki and her family, who were staying at the Ruby house for a few days, were the first to enter. Tom's boys brought their Nintendo along for entertainment and soon had it hooked up to the old TV in the back bedroom. Vikki thought her grandmother made quite a picture, sitting in her little recliner with the control pistol in hand, knocking down ducks in the shooting gallery! She was having as much fun as the children were.

Sherry had volunteered to make the chili this year, Barb brought her chocolate chip cookies and other confections, Coralea brought a relish tray from Hy-Vee, and all three persuaded their mother to surrender her kitchen to them for this one night. For dessert, an assortment of pies was brought by an assortment of people, Dona included. She was still the premiere pie-maker in the family, but Sherry could prepare a tasty contender for the honor. No pie from Faye this time. Norm called to say they couldn't make it. The horrible wind and bitter cold made it a nasty night for anyone to be out, but Dona wondered if Norm was afraid he would be called upon to perform. Last Christmas, Vikki had worked up a reindeer skit that simply had to have more actors, so he and Jimmie were coerced into putting on antlers and trotting across the living room/rooftop. Dona thought it a charming enactment but was surprised the men agreed to participate. Well, she'd miss Norm and Faye. They had been coming to Martin gatherings for several years now.

Besides the Bowens, Val's family was also absent. About the time everyone was beginning to worry, Val called to say they had gotten as far as Gary's mom's place, near Platte City, and decided they had better not try to make it up to the farm. It was risky, and with the new baby, foolish as well, to be out in this weather. There was some snow on the ground, but the real dangers were in the low temperature and the fierce wind.

"Do you remember the winter of '61-'62?" Coralea asked.

"We all remember that one!" Dave declared. "The snow was so deep, the snowplow didn't get to our road for days."

"It took us three days to get from Jefferson City to the farm. We spent the first night in Lexington--the bridge was closed. Then, the next day we started on again and got as far as Cameron and had to spend the night there at Barb and Don's. It was usually a six hour trip!" Coralea recalled with animation.

"That was the only time I remember Highway 71 being one-lane, from five mile corner into Madison," Dona interjected. "The snow was piled as high as the car on both sides! Jimmie spent all day blading off the driveway so I could get to work."

"What happens to the animals if you don't feed them?" Sarah asked PaPa. She couldn't imagine a day going by when he wasn't out carrying feed to the sows shut up in their little houses.

"Oh, they hunker down and wait it out. Back then I didn't have many cows, and they had shelter beneath the barn. Deep snow doesn't hurt the livestock too much, unless it happens during calving season," PaPa answered.

"What happens then?" the little girl pressed.

Jimmie gave Vikki an apologetic look as he came up with the truth. "Then you may lose a few." He saw concern written in Sarah's bright blue eyes. "But, that hardly ever happens. You've seen me carry a calf into the basement, haven't you? Sometimes they just need a little help in getting into this world."

"Those were pigs!" Sarah reminded PaPa.

"Not always. But you're right--that's what I usually do bring in. When animals are born in a litter, its much more likely that one's going to be weak. With just one, the mama cow can usually nurse it along, unless the poor creature has bad weather to contend with, too." Jimmie wished he'd had as much success with his makeshift incubator as he led the girls to believe. All too frequently the little animal hadn't made the miraculous recovery he claimed when he told the girls the box was empty because of an upgrade in the condition of his four-legged patient. "The animals are pretty tough! They can take the cold a lot better than we can," he went on to assure her.

Travis, now five, played behind the wet bar in the niche the little girls were happy to share with their cousin. He was a striking child, with dark hair and eyes. Deep dimples creased his face when he smiled.

Kelly no longer traveled with his job. He had purchased a house on a large property in one of Seattle's suburbs and was renovating it for resale. He also planned to develop the rest of the property, to take advantage of the demand for real estate in the area.

"I think you should raise deer or elk here, PaPa," Kelly suggested. "They don't require much care."

"How would I keep them in? I can't keep the cows in--how would I ever keep deer in?" Jimmie laughed.

"You've got a point there!" Kelly agreed. "Actually, the way it's done is, they put up high fences, about twice as high as yours."

"They're wild animals. I don't think they should be penned up at all!" Dona interjected into the conversation.

"There's a good market for their antlers right now," Kelly offered. "In Asian countries the antlers are used to make remedies for all kinds of ailments." They were most sought after for use as an aphrodisiac, but he decided not to mention that.

"That would mean dehorning them," Jimmie reckoned. "I've been involved in dehorning cattle, and I can tell you, it's a very bloody ordeal!"

Kelly couldn't argue with that.

"Guess what they feed them . . . besides pasture grasses, that is," he said.

"What? I wouldn't know the first thing about how to care for elk, or deer, either."

"Turnips! At least in New Zealand." It was obvious to Kelly that PaPa didn't think much of his idea for converting the farm. And he was right, of course. The farm would never be the same if those particular changes were made. He figured there was an opportunity for profit in such a scheme, but realized, also, that the bottom line wasn't the most important consideration.

"I think I'll just keep the animals I've got!" Jimmie announced with finality. He didn't think farming in northwest Missouri was ready for that kind of change. Transformations were occurring now that he wasn't ready for. Many stockmen of the area shipped their calves off to be fed out on lots with thousands of other animals. The hog farmers, too, were shifting to confinement operations--smaller than the big co-ops, but factory-like in basic structure.

Jimmie didn't think it necessary to operate in that fashion. He believed the process could still be carried out by breeding livestock and bringing them to market on the resources of the area. It *should* work. He was convinced of that. If only he could have a few good years strung together!

By six o'clock the house was filling up. J. and Beth had arrived. There were four children now, with Noah the youngest at the gathering, since Debbie and her family didn't come. Shelley's family lived near Buffalo and weren't able to make the trip this time. Brandy, now in junior high, was there with Donna Kay and Stewart. Tami brought her date, a fellow in J.'s band.

Dona loved the way the place came alive as her family gathered. Though not everyone was present, they were all accounted for. She knew where everyone was--knew them to be safe, not "somewhere in France," as her mother once had to settle for. Dona was grateful for that. The older she became, the more she needed to keep track of her family, to know they were okay. Anymore, that was pretty hard to do, as scattered as they were. But for tonight, she was satisfied that all was well.

Dona sat back and watched the celebration, more guest than hostess. This was a treat for her, not having to do any of the work--at least, very little of it. She enjoyed observing the evening's progress. First was the traditional reading of the Christmas story. She insisted on that acknowledgement of the meaning of the season. Barbara read from Nora's Bible as everyone sat quietly, listening. Jimmie had clipped two short branches from a fir tree. They now lay across the hearth, lending their unique aroma to the cozy atmosphere. Christmas lights lit the recesses of the room and added a warm glow to the celebration.

Soon there was the confusion of the gift exchange. The children passed gifts from beneath the tree, packages were opened, thanks expressed, and the torn wrappings gathered into a big box. The used bows found their way to Brandy this year. They usually got stuck on a young lady in the family.

Beth had sent Dona a watch with a card that read, "Since you won't come to Texas, we'll have to send Texas to you." It was a delicate gold wristwatch with the outline of Texas engraved on the face. Dona stretched out her arm to show off her gift. She'd spent most of the evening in her chair but now leaned across the wet bar. A string of lights surrounded the little niche, forming a diffused halo of color around her. Dona's large eyes glistened with emotion. She wished she were able to make the trip to Dallas so she could see Beth and Fred again.

Dona was nervous. It was almost time for her to bring out her books. She had put so much of herself into the demanding opus, she hoped her family would appreciate the gifts. She noticed that Jimmie was fidgety, also. Well, he had certainly made sacrifices, too, so she could get her manuscript completed in time.

Dave and Don left the room, then returned from the spare bedroom with a huge box, beautifully wrapped and obviously very heavy. They sat it down in front of the fireplace.

"It's from all of us," Sherry told her folks.

Dona crossed the room and began carefully pulling the paper away. The gift was a new television set, in an elegant oak console!

"How pretty! We really do need it--you probably were aware of that!" she exclaimed. They had been getting a poor picture with the old one for quite some time. She and Jimmie looked it over carefully.

"You're probably wondering what we got for you . . ." she began, as Jimmie stepped into the bedroom to retrieve the cardboard box that held her manuscript.

"It's my story. I hope you like it," she said, as she handed a thick binder to each daughter. "I have some for the grandkids, but from there on, you'll have to share!"

"I was afraid you'd stopped working on it!" Sherry exclaimed.

"How did you get it finished already?" Coralea wanted to know. "I haven't seen you work on it for months!"

Jimmie grinned. "Remember the night she told you we were Christmas shopping? That's the day we took it to Wright's to be printed."

"I did have to hurry a little at the end to get it ready by Christmas. I'm sure it has some mistakes, but I feel like I've accomplished something, at last."

Many gathered were aware of how useless Dona sometimes felt. She'd been such a vital person, eager to participate in whatever pursuits came her way. It was easier to accept the changes in her health than it was to witness her disappointment at being incapacitated. Consequently, the occasion was especially joyful, for her family knew what it meant to Dona to complete her autobiography. The girls felt the undertaking was truly a blessing, as it had given their mother a sense of accomplishment and obviously buoyed her spirits.

"It's a part of you, Mom. It's the best gift you could ever give us!" Barbara warmly assured her mother.

Before the girls left, Dona asked each to write a bit of her own version of their childhood, so she could add those to her memoirs as well.

After everyone had gone, Dona anxiously asked Jimmie, "Do you really think they'll like it?"

"Of course they will!"

"I don't know if it can stand the scrutiny of all those teachers! We're in the second generation now, you know," Dona worried. Now that Debbie and Vikki were teaching, and Val had a teaching degree also, each daughter had a daughter in the profession.

"They'll like it. How could they not like it? It's mostly about them!" Jimmie reckoned.

Besides her own autobiography, Dona had included extra material featuring her grandchildren. She hadn't gotten that far in her personal life's story, but she wanted them to know they were each important to her. Also, she included copies of her moving description of the devastating fire and a fanciful piece of gothic humor she had written.

The three girls visited later, privately sharing their reactions to their mother's manuscript. They found they had had common experiences when reading the entire story for the first time. Touching phrases caused them each to laugh and to cry. Each claimed she could almost hear the written words spoken in their mother's deep, mellow tones, as her voice was when she had sung them lullabies so long ago.

Both Barb's and Jimmie's predictions had been apropos. The tender accounting of her own personal history touched each girl very deeply. The gift was truly the most generous and thoughtful they could imagine.

Dona's love of history was evident in her writing. Her knowledge of the events of her era and her ability to recount occurrences in a meaningful manner gave her recollections a significance that spread beyond the confines of one person's experience. While she wrote about her own family, the happenings

A Hundred Miles to the City

she chronicled were largely universal occurrences in the lives of all who shared her period of time in the nation's heartland.

The undertaking revealed Dona to be a capable writer. Her narrative was simple and concise, but beautifully recorded. The words flowed smoothly, tying her recollections together in easy-to-read progression. She had arranged her material into sections: first, the beginnings, her own youth; then the war years, the early lives of her children. She had compiled stories from glider pilots who had contributed their experiences to *Winged Victory*, a magazine that featured the motor-less fliers. She included these in the section that dealt with her welding work in the war plant in Kansas City. One section featured anecdotes concerning each of the children of the family. In the last part of her book, Dona retold some of her earlier stories, including the "Good Friday" one about the fire that razed their old home and a lighter, whimsical tale about an allegorical house.

In all, she had amassed eighty-five pages, which she interspersed with a few pictures--one a portrait of her three daughters, one a news photo of her and Jenny Green welding in a storefront window display. Both were taken in Kansas City during the war.

The girls noted with appreciation that Dona had given a touch of sentiment to her work. She had interjected titles of songs appropriate to the era and to the flavor of the accompanying passage. Again, each described hearing the notes being sung by their mother as they read the words she had penned. To them, the document was diary, memory book, historical fiction, and tribute, all rolled into one.

Taking advantage of the good light, Dona and Coralea sat at the card table beside the north window. A map of the Middle East was taped to the wall nearby. The United States was engaged in Desert Storm in Iraq, a military action designed to liberate Kuwait from Saddam Hussein's invading regime. The jigsaw puzzle was nearly completed. Coralea had done most of it while she conversed with her mother, who was still in the kitchen clearing away the remains of their Sunday meal.

"I let Laura read your manuscript, Mom. I'd told her about it--she's interested in history. I hope you don't mind," Coralea said. Laura was a co-worker of hers at Jefferson School in Madison.

"Of course not! I wouldn't expect it to be interesting to her, though, unless she knows our family pretty well," Dona allowed.

"She really liked it! Her folks are from Junction. They lived in the same area as the Bowens," Coralea assured her mother. "She thinks you're a good writer. She suggested you give a copy to the Historical Committee."

"I'd thought about that," Dona admitted. "Do you suppose they'll want it?"

"Yes, I do!" Coralea assured her. "I only have one complaint about your writing, Mom," She further hinted.

Disappointment clouded Dona's face as she asked, "What's that?"

"You quit too soon! There's not nearly enough of it. You stopped at the time of your marriage to PaPa."

"Well, you know all the rest," Dona asserted.

"But we'd rather see it through your eyes," Coralea said with sincerity.

"Someone else will have to write it if there's going to be more," Dona insisted.

"You're just tired now. You can add to it later," her daughter suggested.

"We'll see," Dona replied with finality. "Joe and Kathleen were over to play cards last night. They stayed past midnight!"

"Well, you must be tired, then."

"No, not at all. We had the best time! I've never enjoyed their company more!" Dona enthusiastically exclaimed.

Soon the puzzle was completed. It usually took the pair hours to join the myriad pieces together into a picture, but today the time was shorter. Coralea prepared to leave.

Dona followed her to the door.

As Coralea reached for the handle of her car door, Dona called, "Do you have to go so soon?"

"I'd better, Mom. I have some things I need to get finished before school tomorrow. Thanks for dinner, again!" She drove away as her mother stood in the doorway, waving. Later, when she replayed the scene in her mind, Coralea couldn't remember her mother ever watching her leave before.

The phone call came in the middle of the night on Wednesday.

"Mom's gone," Barbara's voice came brokenly on the line.

Coralea tried to grasp the truth. "She was doing so well . . ."

"I know. I talked to her just yesterday! She said she felt fine. We met Jimmie on the way to the hospital, but it was too late! We've talked him into staying with us tonight. I'm sorry, Cork. I need to call Sherry now. We'll talk tomorrow."

Coralea's thoughts turned immediately to the image of her mother standing in the doorway, asking her to stay. If only she could replay that single moment in time--have that one opportunity back! If she could just hear the soothing voice one more time. Coralea's sad feelings of regret would persist, even though she knew that everyone who'd lost a loved one unexpectedly wished for the chance to say or do the right thing. It was surely a universal desire of the human condition, to say a proper good-bye.

When the three girls met at the farm, they agreed that writing her story was probably what kept their mother going for the last year of her life. When Dona passed away, everything was in order in the Martin house. Except for the clothing they were wearing that day, everything in the house was laundered, folded, and put neatly away. The dishwasher was empty and all the shelves were straightened, as if Dona had planned her exit for that appointed time.

Printed in the United States
125692LV00004B/7/A